A MESSAGE FROM GRANDPA

During that evening at Grace's apartment we tried to make sense of the day. The Abraham-Power identity issue had taken a back seat to the mysterious letter.

"You're certain?" Grace asked. "I mean, it's not a lot to go on. Just a couple sentences."

"Yes. One hundred percent. I saved all of the letters that Grandpa sent when I was overseas. It's exactly the same handwriting."

"What's this about a watch?"

"I'm not sure, but after Grandpa died, I was given his old Nazi Party pocket watch." I gauged Grace's reaction to the "N" word. Her eyes widened slightly, so I continued with a practiced disclaimer. "It was something that he received when he was forced--" I paused for emphasis "--to join. That's all I can think of. And in case you're wondering, he spent the war at a research facility on some island in the Baltic Sea."

"How did he get to the USA?"

"There was a program that brought German scientists to the States so that they could continue working during the Cold War. I think the only people who remember it now are historians."

"Sorry. Grandma watches The History Channel, not me," said Grace. She picked up the letter and silently re-read it. "Is this watch valuable or something? Is it gold or silver?"

"No. It's just shitty pewter. The case is rough because Grandpa scratched off the Nazi eagle. It doesn't even work."

Grace studied the letter. "It is in the watch," she read. "Have you ever taken it apart?"

"Yeah. There's nothing inside except rusty gears and broken springs. I only keep the damn thing because it belonged to Grandpa."

Grace laid the yellow paper on the coffee table. For a couple minutes we silently reclined on the couch and stared at the ceiling. I raised my head when I felt her get up. Grace disappeared into the kitchen and returned with a bottle of Jinro and two glasses. "You didn't actually need to buy an entire case," she said.

"That was the wager," I replied, "and this has been a weird, weird day. If you need help with that, I'm your man."

"You'll note that I have a glass for you," said Grace. "Care to revise your stance on Korean girls and drinking contests?"

"Forfeit," I said. "Pour."

1

For Beebo and that Spanish summer

Yesterday, Walking

Jim Miller

...Vaccinia (smallpox) vaccine is a highly effective immunizing agent that brought about the global eradication of smallpox. The last naturally occurring case of smallpox occurred in Somalia in 1977. In May 1980, the World Health Assembly certified that the world was free of naturally occurring smallpox.

Because of vaccination programs and quarantine regulations, the risk of importation of smallpox into the United States was reduced by the 1960s. **As a result, routine vaccinia vaccination was discontinued in 1971.** In 1976, the recommendation for routine vaccination of health-care workers was also discontinued. In 1982, the only active licensed producer of vaccinia vaccine in the United States discontinued production for general use, and in 1983, distribution to the civilian population was discontinued. For several years all military personnel continued to be routinely vaccinated. However, only selected groups of military personnel are currently vaccinated against smallpox.

Since January 1982, smallpox vaccination has not been required for international travelers, and International Certificates of Vaccination no longer include smallpox vaccination...

Source: "MMWR Recommendations and Reports." *Journal of the Centers for Disease Control and Prevention* 40(RR14) (1991): 1-10.

Prologue

"88-Fat-Fat-88" ISN'T A Nazi Salute...It's A Honolulu Bar On South Beretania

"Captain Cutshaw Now Heads The Polish Department of Wetland Security..."

June
2018

"I think these are about done," I said, as I stirred a toasted mass of grasshoppers that cooked over the fire on a small sheet of tin. At first I thought that Andrew hadn't heard me, staring intently as he was down into the valley at the crumbling brown grid that had been Hendersonville. From this side of Turtlehead Peak we could only view the southern end of the valley, though I had seen the entire Los Vegas metro-cadaver laid out more times than I could count. Like neighboring Hendersonville, it was dry, dusty, and an eternity away from Sin City's glory days. No color, no light, no flash. The relentless Mojave sun was a force that cracked plastic and peeled paint as God sprayed UV bleach on The Strip, after which His desert wind deposited dust like a dog kicking dirt over its shit.

Andrew had heard after all and he moved over to the fire. We had humped sacks of bugs up from the other side of the peak, down where an old BLM reservoir still held enough water to qualify as a tiny oasis for both man and insect. There sure as hell wasn't any grass near our camp, let alone grasshoppers, since it was located under a wind-hollowed sandstone overhang that partially shielded us from unfriendly eyes and the hot sun. We were below the peak summit and only our flanks were open; otherwise, we could fire down slope or pick off rappelling visitors. Andrew had led me here on the night when we escaped from Vegas. Though the moon had risen over Turtlehead Peak by the time we began to climb, and though Andrew had mentioned previously scouting the area, I was still impressed. A long part of the hike had been in the dark, and he only had moonlight and the memory of landforms seen by day. Sure, I could have easily found this place as well, but that wouldn't be a fair comparison. Andrew wasn't a local boy, though to simply say that he wasn't from around here would have been an *extreme* understatement.

I moved the hot tin off of the rocks, scooped some sand over the small flame, and used a twig to scrape the bugs into two generous piles. Andrew sat down opposite me and gingerly picked a grasshopper off the top of his heap. He tossed the fried insect from one hand to the other, blew on it, and crunched it up in his mouth. "Not bad," Andrew stated, as he reached for another. "Hot."

"The coyote grease cooks them as well as the fire."

"How much is left?" asked Andrew.

"This is the last of it."

There were broken coyote bones on the ground from when Andrew and I had smashed out the last bits of marrow. The scattered slivers and small fire pit might have led an observer to also expect spears and atlatls. Andrew, however, carried an M16, whereas I was armed with a quad-barrel pipe musket.

I was older and skinnier than Andrew, but age aside and allowance given for recent hardship, my physical condition wasn't too bad. Like me, Andrew was a thin white man, but in his early forties and roughly a decade my junior. He was about six feet tall and had mostly dark hair that showed a little gray as it grew out from a buzz cut beneath his fatigue cap. The nametag on Andrew's uniform read "CARLSSIN," and his branch tag identified him as belonging to something called "USASE." Andrew wore a subdued patch on his shoulder that, upon casual glance, appeared to be a standard US flag. A closer look, however, revealed that the flag had only five stars that had been arranged in a circle.

Andrew had traded TSA black and phony corporal chevrons for his real uniform's more age-appropriate sergeant major stripes. His dusty woodland-green fatigues were mismatched to the brown Nevada desert, and the cracked leather of his combat boots only had the memory of a shine. Still, Andrew's present attire was more sensible than the all-black and hotter-than-hell TSA uniforms in which we had previously masqueraded.

Unlike Andrew's military cap, my "hat" wasn't really

a hat at all - it was just some heavy brown canvas that I had tied around my head so that caking sweat and skull contours could persuade the material to go along with the illusion. My footwear had once been things other than shoes - if you could call tire tread and canvas straps "shoes" - and they took me back to the almost-domestic time that I had spent sewing and cutting in Old Man Zhang's shoe shop. I wore museum-grade jeans that had been made in some far-off and now almost mythical place like "Thailand" or "Chile", and I had found them in a ULVN market scrounge stall. They were just a pair of ancient imports that had arrived when people still spoke of things like international trade, and now dirt and grime had made my pants more gray than blue. My green shirt was cut from hotel curtain material, and it was torn at the elbows and sun-faded at the shoulders. It had been a handmade present from Rosetta Zhang, back when I had known her as Rosie. Sweet and tough little Rosie...she had kept a smile on her face when I made a Scarlett O'Hara reference, though I knew that she had no idea what I was talking about. In a world where people came and went at the drop of a hat, I was glad to have Rosie's wearable memento.

Andrew's brown eyes took in everything, and I sometimes wondered if they actually closed when he slept. He looked again at the dusty city below and spoke in a near-whisper. "We'll have to move soon. We might have position here, but we still have to eat."

"It's the *drinking* that worries me," I replied. "When they finish searching the springs around Red Rock, they'll hit the old BLM reservoirs." I considered my shrinking pile of grasshoppers. "TSA and their scout scum tend to notice guys filling canteens and beating the grass for bugs."

We couldn't hide forever, nor did we want to. We intended to take our game back into the former Entertainment Capital's black heart, even though the wager was a long shot with a bookie whose unit patches came from nonexistent military outfits. That made me wonder about something.

"So what's all of this like?" I asked.

Andrew looked up. "Whaddya mean? What's *what*

like?"

"I mean, what's this world like for *you?*"

"What's it like?" Andrew repeated. "Same for me as it is for you. Goddamn pile of shit."

"How's it different, though?"

Andrew paused and reached for his M16. "Well, for me," he said, as he examined the rifle, "this worldline is a quantum skew. That means, for example, when I pick up my weapon I notice strange little things, like--" he paused to flip the receiver and touch the forward-assist button "--this. I know The Black Rifle inside and out, but I've never seen this feature before. I guess it's a good idea, since these pieces of garbage will jam on a pinhead. I swear, AKs trump Mattels in *any* universe."

"'Sixteens with bolt assists? That's all?"

Andrew took a breath. "No. It's not just small stuff." He nodded toward the valley. "A skew, a *significantly deviated* skew," Andrew paused in emphasis as he lowered his eyes and shook his head, "means seeing municipal death camps in America. A skew means driving a truck powered by human grease." Andrew looked up. "And a skew means it's 2018, but Las Vegas isn't a glowing crater - y*et.*" He gave me a wry look. "Sorry. I meant to say *Los* Vegas. Spanish here also seems to be kinda odd...but as for the world in general, I'm not sure that it's extremely different. The tech level is about what I would expect. Maybe if things had held together for five or six more years cells might exist, though estimating zero-point regression isn't really my specialty."

"*Cells?* You mean beepers, right?" I asked. "I remember those. First, the cops and drug dealers had them, and then everyone wore them on their belts. When the world went down, they didn't work anymore. The phone lines also went dead around the same time."

"No. I'm talking about little cellular phones. On delayed or stop-collapse worldlines they typically emerge a year or two after beepers."

"I remember cellular phones too," I replied, "but they were huge. The user had to lug around a briefcase power pack."

"Yeah, those were the early models. Then they

become really small. Everybody gets one. You can go into restaurants or stores and everyone is on the phone. Lots of one-sided conversations, all the time. For those worldlines, the entire planet is like an obnoxious call center."

I envisioned a world of self-important assholes walking around as they seemed to carry on conversations with themselves. "Sounds kind of annoying," I said.

"It is. The internet and cell networks are great though, while they last. The governments usually censor things or shut it all down around 2016 or 2017."

"I remember the internet," I said. "It *was* great, but it was a pain-in-the-ass to sign up at the ULVN computer center when I was in college. I was lucky enough to have a computer in my own classroom when I started teaching, though."

Andrew gave a half-smile. "On later worldlines *everyone* has a computer. They become cheap and common. People can surf the 'net on their phones or close their eyes and use implants."

"Implants? Like surgical implants?"

"Yeah. Subdermal neural interfaces."

"Like a transponder? Or a chip tracker?"

"Somewhat. Same general idea, but a helluva lot more range. Global, in fact."

"That's pretty significant," I said, "like some major sci-fi."

Andrew shrugged. "One future giveth and another taketh away," he said. "A hell of a lot of taking has been done here, but this world is still just a skewed variant of a general theme. Given a chance at zero-avoidance, your worldline and my own might even have entered into the same event class." Andrew shook his head. "I guess it's a little late for that, though. Still...it's interesting to see what the fabled Lost Wages actually looked like - even if, to me, it's really an alternate version from your universe. Our realities may not be siblings, but they're definitely cousins."

"Maybe *second* cousins," I mused. "You've mentioned a lot of differences. You also seemed pretty surprised when I told you that 9/11 happened in 1996."

"Well, sure. That's five years sooner than…"
Andrew's voice trailed off. He looked up for a moment,
and then back at me. "I think what you're getting at is
something that people in my line of work call an
'unlocked dimensional algorithm' - but this world, as bad
as it is, still doesn't qualify for that label."

"Unlocked? That doesn't sound very high-tech."

"It's the next step beyond a skew," explained
Andrew. "It means that your C-205 unit has failed to
screen out the freak shows of infinity. Instead of a
layover in somebody else's different-but-recognizable
twist, you get a one-way ticket to the carnie trailer.
You're dead because in 1985 a herd of triceratops
stampeded you. You're dead because you displaced to a
worldline where Earth's atmosphere lacked oxygen, or
maybe your unit performed an inaccurate gravity trace
and the planet is thousands of miles away while your
frozen and exploded ass floats through the space that it
occupied hours before."

I nodded. "Well, that…that sounds like a bad way to
go." I made a hobo knuckle, wiped the tin clean, and
sucked the grease off the back of my finger. "I guess it's
safe to say that you've never been caught in one of
those unlocked-whatevers. But how many skews have
you seen?"

Andrew cocked his head. "Me? This world popped
my cherry."

"What?"

"Hell, yes! I'm making it up as I go, just like you and
the rest of the natives."

It was my turn to be taken aback. "But I thought--"

"You thought that I was an old hand at this?"
Andrew's head dipped and his shoulders sagged as he
sadly laughed. "I've piloted twenty-seven
displacements, but all to past idents within my own
worldline's event class." Andrew noticed my
puzzlement. *"Identicals,"* he explained, "are the
opposites of unlocks. They're easy missions to
worldlines of insignificant variance - realities whose only
differences are random and meaningless things like
some eleven-year-old kid in Tulsa, back in 1980, picking
chocolate instead of vanilla when the ice cream truck

came up his street." Andrew paused and turned his eyes in the direction of Los Vegas. "But it's not *that* strange here," he added. "How else could I have known about you? Or this place? Lake Meade is a hell of a long way from Fort Tampa."

"Yeah," I agreed. "But not much further than an old Philadelphia shipyard or Camp Hero."

Andrew shrugged. "Vegas was a surer bet...so to speak."

"But you could have gone to...*a Vegas*...that was more like your own."

"That would have been easier," agreed Andrew, "though I have to say that *my* world's Vegas is nothing but a glass-rimmed gamma field. Understand that a singularity collapse isn't like reading a road map and picking a detour. When I got the failure warning, I didn't believe it. I thought it was a hardware fuckup or a programming glitch." Andrew let out a bitter chuckle. "For a second, I didn't even know what was happening. Then I had to wrestle with the computer as hard and as fast as I could just to get through to this worldline. Now I know how a dead stick feels to an airplane pilot. Bumpy landings on highways and fields look pretty damn good when compared to flaming wreckage."

"Or charging dinosaurs," I added. "So any landing that you can walk away from is a good landing? Or a good *displacement,* I mean?"

Andrew nodded. "That's how it felt at first, but after a few days here I started to wonder about frying pans and fires. And whether or not I'll walk away remains to be seen. No offense, but your reality isn't exactly a picnic."

"Well, at least *this* world hasn't had a nuclear war."

"True. But it sprayed weaponized smallpox on a generation of unvaccinated kids and now TSA pagan-Nazis are turning people into bio-diesel."

I had no rejoinder, so after a few moments I changed the subject. "How many missions did B-17 pilots have to complete before they could go home?" I asked.

Andrew smiled. "I don't know the answer to your question, but I like the comparison. Unlike me, I think that those men got extremely paranoid when the ends

14

of their tours approached. Maybe I'll paint *Memphis Belle* on the side of my C-205 - that is, if I ever see it again."

"What's a Memphis bell?"

Andrew looked at me. "Are you kidding?" he asked, but I could only shrug. Andrew gave a small sigh. "Well, I guess we've discovered another little difference. Where I come from, the *Memphis Belle* was a B-17 bomber flown by one of the most famous aircrews of the First World War."

"A B-17 in the *First* World War?"

"That's right."

We both opened our mouths to say something, but we just shook our heads. Andrew continued to eat, but after a few moments, he spoke again. "Quantum variance is the engine of multiverse expansion," he said. "It's constantly growing in ways that the human mind can't understand or even observe, so don't expect to find meaning within the process." Andrew ate his last grasshopper and continued. "Forget all of the butterfly and tsunami bullshit, because reality lacks evolutionary purpose. It's just a string theory virus that begs for any stupid excuse to spew out slightly-mutated copies of itself. Watch," he said. "Want to see a new universe created right before your eyes? This is how easy it is. I can pick up a rock," Andrew said, as he pointed at a stone a few feet away, "or I can leave it on the ground. Whatever choice I make will branch the multiverse innumerable times, but what are the actual consequences?" Andrew half-leaned over and stretched out his hand, then stopped, sat up straight again, and left the stone untouched. He looked at me. "None. On this same spot, but in a trillion-trillion different universes, I'm sitting here holding that rock, but in a trillion-trillion other universes, including this one, I'm not. Did my choice change our situation? No. We're still hiding from the TSA in the desert outside of Vegas. Most human decisions don't make a damn bit of difference, either way."

As Andrew spoke, I barely noticed a dot moving around on his head. Figuring that it was just a sand fly or some other insect, I paid no attention. This was my mind's first reaction because things like laser sights had been so far removed, for so very long, from common experience. Like other artifacts from humanity's more technologically advanced past, they were out of sight, out of mind, and then virtually forgotten. My old memories returned, however, when the silent red bug settled on the right side of Andrew's head and a bloody mass of brain, hair, and shattered bone exploded from his left temple.

1

We Kept Praying The Safeword, But God Wouldn't Stop

It's A Thousand Years To Christmas,
~~Mr. Halloway~~
Jack

*December
1988 [2.0]
(1-of-2)*

*If you can't get laid in Vegas, something is...wrong.
The year is 1988. Again.
I'm in Vegas. Again.
And I seriously doubt that I could get laid.*

* * *

Terrie Gilliam got it right when he made *Brasil.*
When the TSA abducted me, my front door came
crashing down and they burst in with their guns drawn.
Zip ties were around my ankles and wrists in a
heartbeat, a black hood was yanked over my head, and I
was dragged out of my home.

I thought about that awful night as I sat at a
Maryland Parkway bus stop. The year was 1988, and the
Transcendental Security Administration didn't yet exist.
The horrors of the future were still undreamt of, and all
around me was life. Bustle, noise, cars. Jerks driving by
and shooting each other the finger. Hot asphalt tar-
stink. Young guys strolling in shiny poplin trousers that
only locals could sport with a dry crotch. Girls
experimenting with scrunchies and berets in their quest
for eighties Big Hair alternatives. A few ULVN Rebels
trying to look as unshorn, as tangled, and as plaid as cool
Seattle kids.

It's too hot in Vegas for strung-out lumberjacks, I
thought. *At least tear your sleeves off. Grunge isn't big
yet, anyway.*

I had outlived this world, but now it was back and
staring me in the face. Or, more precisely, *I* was back.
On The Strip, I knew that tourists were eating, drinking,
fucking, gambling, and wallowing in abundance. I
smelled delicious restaurant food and heard music that
was produced by playback, and not by survivors huddled
around a campfire to strum twine and tap on tin cans. I

reveled in road ragers' passing curses and their exhaust pipe carbon perfume. The excess, ignorance, stupid kids, stupid clothes, and stupid attitudes...were beautiful. Beautiful! The fat Los Vegans were luxuriously overweight. No, *gorgeously* overweight. To me, food seemed to follow people around and beg to be eaten.

One-thousand, nine-hundred, eighty-eight. I can rub my eyes. I can pinch myself. Nobody makes eye contact because I'm an old skinny bus stop derelict clad in filthy black TSA fatigues that look like they came from a SWAT team yard sale. I don't care, though. This world doesn't have to look at *me*. I'm overjoyed to look at *it* - even the meaningless details. The wads of sidewalk gum possess interesting textures. Bus shelter graffiti makes me applaud the writer's proper use of tense. This place, or perhaps I should say that this *time*, is Christmas – all day, every day.

God Bless Us, Every One!

A mother and her two youngsters walked west on Flamingo toward Maryland Parkway. Maybe the boy was four or five, and his sister was six or seven. The girl wore yellow pants that almost matched her blonde hair, and on her brother's tee shirt was a picture of...Cooky Monster! I remembered Cooky Monster. Cooky Monster never actually ate cookies. When he chewed macaroons and chocolate chips, he always smashed them into messy flying crumbs until there was nothing left. He had to, because his throat was just a piece of black felt stitched to the back of his mouth.

Though Cooky Monster couldn't swallow, I certainly could, and it was time to do so. I reached into a plain OD military assault pack, pulled out a bottle of water, and took a long warm drink. Vegas is a dry furnace, winter or summer, future or past, and even a younger man can easily get heat exhaustion, let alone a tired fifty-something who has spent days trudging across parched dirt.

A passing taxi flashed a strip bar sign. A generic naked bimbo reclined under the joint's logo, and I had a delusional vision of a blue-furred and non-swallowing stripper. I blinked and shook the hallucination out of my head.

* * *

On the way back to Vegas I had bought some food and water at a truck stop. A pouch in my pack contained an assortment of strange currencies, and when the bored clerk took my cash without changing expression, I was glad that I had checked Andrew's note cache for appropriate money. Yes, I was sure that the cash was all real, and that it had actually circulated within various multiverse realities...but I was also certain that "North American Sterling" or "Nevada Silver Pesos" wouldn't have had much purchasing power.

I had approached my chronological re-acclimation with caution. I sat beside the highway and watched vehicles pass until, like a Greek trireme that followed a coastline, I forced myself to slowly walk through the desert while I kept the road safely within sight. I told myself that the endless stream of cars, along with my recently experienced view of Lake Meade - once again captive to Hoover Dam's intact concrete - were just some of the wonders to which I would have to adjust my mind. I relaxed somewhat, but not to the point that I approached the asphalt's edge and put out my thumb. Even if a charitably adventurous soul *had* been willing to pick up a dirty old backpacker, I was sure that if I spilled a bizarre tale about how my black uniform was actually that of a future TSA colonel, I would have quickly been put back out on the road. Maybe I could have invented a more believable story...but I knew that no one was going to give me a lift anyway.

* * *

The old Vegas Transit buses didn't run as often as the CAT buses which would replace them in the nineties, and I grew impatient. I couldn't remember how long Grandpa and I used to wait. Did the buses run on the hour back then?

I spotted a nearby construction site. It was a future coffee house, as announced by an "Opening Soon" banner, but it was to be a coffee house with an end-of-

20

days distinction. I felt an eerie fear as I watched men attach studs and raise framing on what appeared to be just another Flamingo Road retail space.

"Are you okay, mister?"

A slightly overweight and middle-aged woman dressed in a tan-shirt-black-slacks service uniform had spoken. I wondered why. A distressed bum was reason enough to walk down the street to the next stop, not stay and express concern.

"Wh-what?" I stuttered.

"Are you okay?" repeated the matronly hair bun and garish red lipstick.

"Yeah, yeah," I said. "Fine." Perhaps I turned to face the woman a little too quickly because her smile wavered and she backed up a step. Her nametag read: *CARIBBEAN CASINO – MARY R. – GILLETTE, WY.*

I turned back toward the construction site. The scene was like watching drywall go up in the New Reich Chancellery, for I knew that the scheme that would one day be discussed therein would be an Agenda 2030 Final Solution update.

Mary R. noted my interest. "It's going to be a coffee shop," she said. "One of those new Starboy places."

"Starbuck," I murmured.

"Pardon?"

"The company's name is Starbuck. From Seattle. That place is going to be the Mission Center Starbuck."

"Oh?" said Mary. "Are you from Seattle?"

"No," I replied. "I lived – er, I mean *live*, down on Hacienda."

Mary's uniform had long sleeves and my TSA fatigue shirt was cuffed at the elbows, so our smallpox vaccination scars were covered. The old blister of lamb's blood on my right tricep was my personal sign of Passover, and it was the same for Mary R., whom I guessed had been born in the 1940s. Yeah, that seemed about right. She looked like a forty-something. My own tine mark, however, was from another universe's Summer of Love.

Maybe You'll Get What
You Want This Time
Around

December
1988 [2.0]
(2-of-2)

No matter how things turned out with my personal mission, I was, barring disease, accidents, and whatnot, going to be in *Las* Vegas on September 11th, 2001. That was roughly thirteen years away and I would have to stick around and wait. There could be no quick and convenient jump to a more preferable time. I was stuck.

"Well, Marty, I'm sure that in 1985 plutonium is available in every corner drug store, but in 1955 it's a little hard to come by!"

The voice came from a classic movie screen inside my head. "No Doc," I muttered, "not plutonium. Dicadmium methyltetraselenide." Like Robert Money's Mephistopheles, it was such a *Mouthful in Manhattan,* and even harder to find than it was to say - except that Grandpa's clues had helped me find that little MacGuffin. That no longer mattered, however, because knowing where to find the 'selenide was now as useful as knowing where to find a gas station when I didn't have a car.

* * *

I peered northward up Maryland Parkway. *Where was the damn bus?* I considered walking south, toward a Maryland traffic light near ULVN where Hunter S. Thomson had famously paused for his end-chapter reflection. *Poor soul*...but at least he had delivered himself while still under the impression that his Breaking Wave was the final high water mark. I remembered what year it was and realized that Duke's unneeded and unwanted seventeen were still to come.

Huh. How about that?

There were four directions, and Thomson's future specter suggested that I go south and take a left on

Hacienda. I had to go back home, seek out my own ghosts, and avoid those that crowded the streets. There were phantoms up Maryland and all along Flamingo, some of ugliness already realized, and others of that yet to come. Four blocks up Maryland, a young nightclub singer named Jinjer Rios was murdered in April of 1987 when I was nineteen years old. When I looked far west down Flamingo, I could almost make out the Koval intersection where a man named Tupack was gunned down in September of 1986, and then died four days later at Desert Sunset Hospital. To the east, a gun battle would erupt in Club 662 in 1990 and then move outside to the Flamingo sidewalk. A woman and two men would die in the street, and I would be twenty-two years old, on the other side of the world, and in love.

But what if none of those things had happened here? Or what if they were to happen at times different from their occurrences in my universe? What if chains of tiny events across eternities of worldlines had never linked up in this particular reality?

What if my string theory doppelgänger had never even been born in this world?

I had noticed other things that were different from the past that I remembered, so for a moment it seemed like my quantum double's non-existence was a distinct possibility. If that were the case, then my purpose for being here would be sadly negated. Still, this town and this time were much, much better than the pit from which I had recently escaped. I had, in fact, exponentially upgraded my reality.

Bilge to First Class, baby.

2

That's A Great Idea. That's Great! But...More Of A Long-Term Thing

From Manzanar To Wounded Knee, We Pledge Allegiance Unto Thee

September 2017

Mindless zombies lash out, but say nothing. Ideologues are different. They take the time to explain their violence.

"All of the meat on your old unscarred ass was stolen from Mother," said the TSA punk as he raised his rifle butt to hit me again. "You've got this coming! Consumer! Fucking useless eater," he growled. I didn't need to see under the guard's mask to know that his teeth were bared in a pit bull snarl. The guard had lost an eye to smallpox, and his impaired depth perception was probably what allowed me to dodge the blow.

Variola pustules could occur in eyes as well as on skin, and when they did, corneas were transformed into masses of unseeing white scar tissue. Most of the guards at DS-21 had smallpox scars, but I seldom encountered partially blind captors. Even in the desert, where white skin tans to a uniform brown, pustule scars remain very deep and obvious. No amount of sun can prevent them from looking like clusters of random pink sears, as if the survivor's entire body had been rolled over a bed of lit cigarettes. The marks that smallpox leaves upon dark complexions are equally cruel, and raised lumps of unpigmented blotches stand out in mottled contrast from undamaged skin.

I forced my way back through several prisoners to put some distance between myself and the angry guard. Fortunately, his need to abuse me took a back seat to the need to keep the line moving. After all, I hadn't committed an infraction. I was just waiting for the port-a-potties when the guard had decided to bash me.

* * *

I think that I may be exhibiting symptoms of…scurvy? The people in my prisoner group are experiencing similar physical issues. Our gums leave blood in the corners of our mouths when we eat, and like others, I have odd purplish blotches on my arms and legs. It's so strange, but when I consider the camp diet, scurvy seems possible. Our MRE rations are opened before they're tossed out, and every item that might contain vitamin C is removed - which seldom leaves much to eat.

I thought that it took months and months to develop scurvy, though. Could I really have such a condition? Maybe. After forty-seven days of eating dried bread and a little preserved meat, expect a visit from Mr. Scurvy. But after wearing the same drawers for an equal amount of time, the Urinary Tract Infection Fairy won't *necessarily* come calling. This realization occurred to me on the morning of September 22nd, 2017, as I was in line to use the port-a-potties at the Southern Nevada Water Authority Detention Site 21, or simply DS-21.

The scent of my body and filthy clothes should have made me gag, but I remembered something that I had read long ago in regard to US soldiers who had served in the Gulf War. They reported that, after about a month of the heat, dirt, and sweat, their olfactory neurons no longer registered constant body odor stench. At DS-21, the stink came from everyone except the guards and the new detainees, the latter of whom still smelled of homemade deodorant, shampoo, and other niceties.

Prisoner attire was determined by circumstance of abduction, and some individuals were still in their pajamas. If things were rushed, and if the list were long and the night short, victims were yanked out of their beds, gagged, bagged, zip-tied, and thrown into a van. If TSA work orders were light, however, people were permitted to dress and put on shoes.

Like the new prisoners' decent smells and cleaner clothes, there were also ways to distinguish the greenhorn guards from the old hands. The jeeps initially tried to comply with TSA regulations by wearing their issued face masks, but after getting a taste of how the Nevada sun overheated black uniforms, the "executioner hoods" were exchanged for simple respiratory masks, as if the guards were about to board the Tokyo subway at the height of flu season.

If I could have stepped out of the situation and dispassionately studied the guards, I would have laughed at their idiocy. The thugs wore black fatigues in the roasting heat and brandished assault rifles around terrified captives. I guessed that over-accouterment was a time-honored tradition among such types, but instead of Gestapo-gray, the TSA wore black ripstop, and instead of K98s, they carried M16s.

DS-21 rules were simple: Sit on the tarps. If you spoke too much or too loudly, expect a rifle butt in your face. If you stepped off of a tarp, expect a bullet. Listen for your number. Don't stand up until four-thirty morning roll. If you had to shit, too bad. Shit call was at eight AM and four PM. If you had to piss, you did so from the tarp edge and onto the surrounding rocks and sand, though this was ill-advised because minimal amounts of water were doled out per day. Like others, I caught and drank as much of my urine as possible. Some stripped, pissed on their clothes, tipped their heads back, and wrung urine into their mouths. Then they draped their damp garments over their shoulders for a little relief from the heat.

* * *

The four gray tarps measured roughly forty feet by forty feet and were tacked down with large metal spikes. Each had a central pole and stabilizing lines that secured an overhead shade. Separate from the rest and at the head of the pit near some old FEMA trailers were a red tarp and a blue tarp. After being herded from one gray tarp to the next, and after observing those ahead being divided into two sets, I knew that soon my group would be taken, one-by-one, into one of the trailers.

The goings-on within the trailers were hardly a mystery. The largest was a dingy cream-colored fifty-footer. It seemed to be a chow hall and break area where the guards took turns in a field kitchen or simply got out of the sun. The second trailer wasn't really a trailer, but rather, a steel rail container where weapons were turned in at shift change and in which prisoner rations were kept. Detainees were individually taken from the front gray tarp and into the third trailer.

Lee Van Kleef had a band of Confederate POWs to play music over his 1860s Gitmo soundtrack, but it appeared that such trifles were over the TSA's budget. The thin metal sheeting of the third trailer, or the "Three Trailer Hot Unit" as the guards called it, muffled nothing, and the first time I heard the sounds, I knew that I would have to quickly devise a mental shield.

So, I decided that I wasn't hearing torture. I WASN'T hearing TSA monsters peeling minds from souls and souls from bodies. I was, *in fact,* hearing excellent porn, because with a touch of imagination, cries of agony can pass for moans of ecstasy. Hats off to Mr. O'Brian. With a bit of a mind flip, I was into a time slip. Or a pornographic perception slip, rather.

The folks inside Three Trailer engaged in some erotically advanced stuff. Even back when I was a young man, I never really got into asphyxia, let alone fingernail plucking and amputation. Maybe these things weren't that popular among the Blue Tarpers, either...sure, the raw necks and missing nails indicated open-mindedness, but such kinkiness must not have been their cup of tea, so they called it off with a single plucking and a single choking. But those dead Red Tarpers...wow! They had been sexually adventurous with two sets of five apiece, empty eye sockets, and spines as twisted as spiral staircases.

Or...perhaps the Red Tarpers had forgotten the safeword.

Five to one baby, one in five...and the Blue Tarpers got out alive. Sometimes they walked from the Hot Unit without assistance, and those who did were always escorted to the blue tarp, where they again sat down and fainted, or just stared into space and trembled like shocked Kiowa Sun Dance survivors. I sometimes imagined that they smiled. Who wouldn't, after having so much fun?

Blue Tarpers used their left hands to rub or squeeze a spot on their right arms. Whispers among my tarp group suggested that microchips were being implanted, though I knew that this was impossible. Microchips were just another extinct piece of hi-tech, and if hardware was indeed being injected, then it was more likely that the bumps in prisoners' arms were just low budget transponders.

A stretcher dumped other prisoners on the red tarp. Instead of sitting, the Red Tarpers *piled.* Sometimes one or two twitched when they were loaded onto the meat wagon...but by then most were still and stiff.

The Blue Tarpers departed DS-21 within seven days of their Hot Unit orgasms, though most left before. A vehicle that had once been an old Clark County school bus, hurriedly slopped in black paint with slivers of yellow peeking through, arrived on Mondays. Unlike the meat wagon, the bus never actually drove into the camp. Instead, Blue Tarpers stood in single file while the guards snapped on ankle chains. Then, weak and stumbling, the Blue Tarpers climbed the earthen ramp, exited the gate, and were prodded into the bus.

I couldn't know for certain what criteria were being used to decide who went to the blue and red tarps, but I could guess. Though hungry and traumatized, the people who boarded the black bus were younger and stronger than me. Most were from generations that might have received smallpox vaccines during military service or work in the health care industry. There were also some much younger people whose faces bore scars, and for them, survival was an especially tenuous proposition. TSA doctrine classified them as traitors because they had cast their lots with unreformed and non-Earth-Mother-worshipping "old unscarreds". Since smallpox didn't always cause sterility, these Blue Tarpers may have been saved by their possibly-viable vesicles and follicles, for such were the people with whom American demographics had limped along since the 1990s. I knew that some of the older ones must have also had children of their own, either claimed long ago by Shakpana or maybe even "serving" with the TSA. Each time I saw a TSA drone I was forced to acknowledge this, for Blackshirts didn't just magically appear out of thin air. TSA thugs once had, and maybe still had, older parents. Maybe the guards were able to protect their mothers and fathers by signing up with the

TSA, or maybe their families were already dead. The former scenario was easier for me to accept than the possibility that the scarheads had sold out their own parents.

There were equal numbers of old men and women sprawled upon the red tarp, so I guessed that the fact that a male can father children well into his seventies wasn't a primary factor within the Big Ugly Picture. Perhaps those who still recalled another world, another time, and freedoms now unknown were excluded from the agenda. Maybe it was even simpler than that, for in a world of limited resources, it seemed the bet was on young slaves rather than old ones. The former boarded black school buses, probably bound for work gangs, while the latter's corpses were hauled away like cordwood.

* * *

The "water detention basins" were created back in the late eighties. At that time, they just seemed like expensive make-work kickbacks on municipal contracts. Purportedly for the collection and management of desert runoff, the basins were deep and wide excavations in empty blocks throughout Los Vegas.

What were they called in other cities? In Tallahassee, what was the official designation for strange fenced-off pits? "Emergency Alligator Holding Areas?" And what about the razor-wired holes in Burlington? "High-Security Maple Syrup Collection Centers?" Yeah, I know, that's stupid...but the point is, evil doesn't require particularly plausible excuses in order to conceal itself. People jealously guard their blindness, and "American Denial Techniques" probably would have been a popular ULVN doctoral program.

- **So, Johnny, what did you study at university?**
- *Me? I earned a PhD in American Denial Techniques.*

Are you fucking kidding me? "Water *Detention* Basins?" But this Freudian slip, like other red flags, went unheeded.

TO WIT:

Red Flag #1 – *The Vegas basins weren't connected to the city's actual flood channels.*

Red Flag #2 – *Flood basins don't require concertina-topped fences because water doesn't escape by climbing over chain link.*

Red Flag #3 – *Actual retention features, such as bentonite seepage barriers, were absent.*

The basins resembled surrender camps that the Corps of Engineers had scooped into Kuwaiti sand during the Gulf War. Like the pits that I had seen on the news before the TV stations permanently signed off, the basins were a few acres wide, ten to fifteen feet deep, and featured sloped sides - thus making it very easy for a small force of captors to control a large group.

The basin at Desert Inn and Rainbow had a vehicle ramp bladed into its northern slope that allowed a weekly porta-potty truck to exchange empties. A guy once tried to hide in one of the toilet tanks. He almost made it, but a guard ran over to the truck before it went up the ramp. The engine stopped, and I heard the *snap-click* of an M16 charging handle, followed by shots into one of the green plastic outhouses. The guards then ordered some detainees to fish the guy out of the soup and dump his corpse on the red tarp.

The shots had ended after the seventh pop. Seven *used* to be a lucky number in Vegas. So had twenty-one, but the TSA designation for this camp had changed that. **DS-21.** Hunching over in the Mojave heat and waiting to either be tortured to death or slave-shipped off to God-knows-where definitely changed the concept of "going bust."

I wish that I could be a kid again. I wish that I could sit on the green shag in Grandpa's living room and watch his big black-and-white Zenith. I wish that I could talk to Julie from **The Electronic Company.** *She would know what to do. She could give me some good advice.*

"Jack."

On day forty-seven I thought that I heard someone whisper my name...or maybe my mind was cracking in time with my sunburned skin. I had sand in my hair, nose, and ears. My graying beard was scraggly and itchy, and my mustache was a crust of dried saliva and MRE crumbs. The rations that I could eat before they were snatched away by younger, stronger, or simply more savage detainees hadn't been enough to keep me from counting my abdominal fiber ridges. If I had been going to a gym, I could have congratulated myself on getting a six-pack...except that my six-pack had broken into a twelve pack, then an eighteen pack, and finally a case.

"JACK."

Detainees were not allowed to stand, so I had to frequently change my sitting position to prevent my legs from going numb. I shifted slightly and slowly extended my legs. I was careful not to kick the back of the person sitting in front of me, though I needn't have worried. He was elsewhere, mentally-speaking, and wouldn't even have noticed a boot-to-the-head. The man still mumbled to his ghostly wife a week after she had stood and walked off of the tarp. The woman was halfway to the port-a-potties when Abe Zapruder busted out his camera, but Jackie wasn't there to scrape up the scattered bits. The man's wife had broken the rules in the morning, and by that afternoon she had been tossed onto the back of a truck similar to the one which made toilet pick-ups.

"JACK SIMMERATH."

I turned. "Why the hell are *you* here?" I asked in a low voice. "You should have left on your own. You could have escaped."

"Nice to see you, too," Grace whispered.

* * *

Asian and Caucasian aging processes are analogous to electrical switches. Westerners are born with gradual dimmers. Hair grays. Skin sags beneath failing eyes. Backs bend and joints stiffen. Years pass, and the lights slowly go down. In the East, however, physical transition differs. It's not a slowly turning dial; instead, it's a light switch, on or off, bright or dark, like something to be abruptly flipped when exiting a room.

Grace's beauty hadn't yet left the building. My friend had never divulged her exact age, but I had always assumed that we were close in years. Maybe if I had been Korean I could have shown greater understanding when things bothered Grace, like when she touched her cheeks and complained about fading texture and elasticity, or when she moaned about her darkening complexion, despite big *ajumma* dealer-brims and sun block. I was unable to relate, however, locked as I was into my own age-slide that manifested every failing at the second it occurred. While my belly softened and expanded, Grace still slipped into the jean size that she had worn back when we were students at ULVN. While my hair grayed and fell out, her own remained black and shiny, with only an occasional white strand as the subject of enormous fuss.

Grace moved closer, and the nearer she got, the more I smelled a home-brewed post-apocalyptic Old Slice facsimile. Like her ageless appearance, Grace's toiletry tastes had remained constant. In this broken-down society, now without corporate-based, gender-programmed, and mass-produced deodorants, Grace still managed to locate a man's grooming product.

"I've been here almost seven weeks," I breathed. "I don't know why you hung around. You should have taken off like we planned."

"I felt like I should wait," Grace replied. "Last night I went back to your house. I knew that you were gone, but I just wanted to check. They were waiting."

Something occurred to me. "Then why are you with *this* bunch? You should be in the back."

Grace didn't reply as she watched a man who had risen to his knees. His pants were down around his thighs and he held his penis in one hand, while in the

other he caught the flow of urine in his upturned palm. The man raised his free hand to his lips, then pulled up his pants and sat down.

I repeated my question. "I don't know," Grace said. "This is just where they put me. You were facing the other way. Maybe you were asleep." She looked from side to side. "So this is where they've been taking people? No wonder the surrounding roads are closed."

"Do you think it would have made any difference if anyone had seen this place?" I whispered.

Grace seemed to sit up a little straighter at my question, almost in subtle indignation. "Yes. If I had known sooner, then I would have left town. And I would have taken you with me."

I sighed at Grace's too-late notion. Regret and debate were meaningless now, but I still felt an urge to remind her that *I* was the one who had been desperate to flee. I remained silent, though I still registered a mental response. *We knew,* I thought. *We all could have guessed that this shit was going on.* But no one had done anything. We had chosen to think that, if we just went about our business, we would be okay. We all had PhDs in ADT. "If I've done nothing wrong, then I've nothing to fear," as the ostrich-head-in-the-sand saying went. It was, however, our very *existences* that were the offense, and *not* what we were, or were not, doing. Extermination criteria are rarely behavior-based, which was why, when people froze like cockroaches on a kitchen wall, or like jackrabbits behind scarcely-concealing bushes, it didn't matter. The bugs were swatted with newspapers, and the hares received .22 caliber bullets...though I surmised that when my time came for Three Trailer's Hot Unit, I would experience something much more exotic than a rolled-up *Los Vegas Review Journal* or a thirty-grain rimfire.

3
Wearing A Mask Of False Bravado

~~Jesus, There Is Only One Woman In The World.~~
~~One Woman, With~~
~~Many Faces.~~
Jack, There Are Many Women In The World.
Many Women, With
One Face.

February 25th, 1993

Sometimes a wall of cellophane separates me from younger college students. Sure, we can chat and study, but a relational disconnect exists between their high school graduations and my military discharge. Off-campus socializing can also be awkward, because a transparent barrier stretches between me and my not-yet drinking-age classmates.

A similar partition exists at the ULVN registrar counter. While others stress about their work-study arrangements, financial aid, and part-time job survival drudgeries, the plastic wrap appears and I just sign on a few dotted lines while Grandpa's estate lawyers, along with Uncle Sugar's token GI Bill gesture, do the rest. Another twelve credits. Another semester in ULVN's Carlson Education Building. Another increment closer to a Nevada teaching license.

The word "estate" can conjure images of hedges, fountains, and butlers, but in the case of my inheritance, it consists of patent royalties. It seems that Grandpa had possessed an eerie knack for predicting the industrial future. I don't have access to all of the monies, because Grandpa left instructions for funds to be divided between myself and another party whom the executors can't disclose. Still, my half of the statement indicates that I'm fairly well off. But so what? For now, I just want my tuition and rent. Some goof-off cash once in a while is also nice.

* * *

I sometimes patronize military dives. There's a familiarity attached to such places that I don't feel in college clubs and casino bars, and the ULVN saran wrap checks itself at the doors of establishments around

Nellis Avenue and Craig Road. Tonight I'm unwinding far from the University District and within walking distance of Nellis Air Force Base. This is a neighborhood of plank-and-stud affairs with neon names like "The Runway," "Green Bat," and "The 99th." Hookers, booze, poker machines, and all manner of sins not yet sufficiently sampled by barracks boys tend to congregate around the base gates. These are places of yellowing lights and torn felt, with more than a few listed on first sergeant "off limits" rosters.

I'm in an air force bar, but, unlike other enlisted haunts, you wouldn't know it from the sign over the door. While other joints bear the names of units and aircraft, I'm drinking in a place that calls itself "Grand Hole," a moniker that might lead one to assume that, elsewhere in Vegas, there are other bars rated as "Average Hole" and "Substandard Hole."

I don't mind the filthiness of Grand Hole. I don't mind the dust on the floors and tables. The cum stains on the bathroom walls speak of good times - though a bloodstain on the plywood floor of the men's room testifies to the fact that Grand Hole and I once shared a less-than-pleasurable moment. Like Hyundai, KIA, and kimchi, my four front crowns came from South Korea. When I last saw my *real* front teeth, they were on the floor of the Grand Hole men's room.

It happened - *when?* Two-and-a-half? Three years ago? The stain is in the second stall, and every time I go into the bathroom I check if it's still visible.

※　※　※

I recognize most of the visiting unit patches on Grand Hole's temporary duty, or TDY, wall. I can look at the other patrons and pick out young airmen, as well as buck, staff, and tech sergeants. I can also ID the senior NCOs, and at the moment I'm observing some old retro-sergeants as they ape around a woman at the bar like traumatically-brain-injured Neanderthals. Instead of animal skins, the men wear faded tees that carry the names of long-retired athletes and characters from old beer ad campaigns. The retros' receding hairlines and crude humor vie for the attention of a placid angel whose quiet dignity still carries enough devilish undertone to keep the bartender busy. It's her water to their oil, and the only places where mixing actually takes place are behind the bar and in the cavemen's fantasies.

"Senior Retro-Sergeant Fashion Analysis" serves very well in estimating the period of service for an enlisted man in civvies. Retro-Sarge has probably upgraded his wardrobe only once, and that was about ten years after basic training. He's worn daily green or blue for years, and once those civilian rags that were present during his high school senior year are swapped out, Retro-Sarge reckons that he's good-to-go until retirement. To carbon-date the man, carbon-date his duds.

Spud McKenzie, circa 1987, appears on a threadbare tee. 1987-10 = a probable sixteen-year master sergeant who enlisted four years after the Paris Peace Accords and during the same year that *Stars Wars* hit theaters. The Schwartz is with him tonight.

The 1986 Danish Bikini Team is also present on the shirt of a likely senior master, who, long before he developed a senior master's gut, enlisted a decade before I did.

Is that...? Yes. That's Max Headspace, or rather, what's left of Matt Brewer's badly faded 1985 techno-visage. ***And. Blue. Nylon. Sumerian. Parachute. Pants.***

Sumerian parachute pants? No. Really...? Yes, definitely Sumerian. Oh, wait. They could *possibly* be Babylonian. Nope, Sumerian. The crotch cuneiform gave it away.

I think that an ancient chief master sergeant has been unearthed.

*　*　*

So there the girl sits, and there the old fools gather.

She's an attractive young woman whose talk empties pockets. It's easy work for the quick-witted and in this girl's case, just perching on a stool with a smile on her face and her thighs squeezed together as tightly as those of a *Little Home on the Prairie* schoolmarm helps Grand Hole turn a profit. Her attention is for men who keep drinking, but should her focus stray, just look as if you're preparing to leave and suddenly she'll think of an engaging topic of conversation. You don't have to give her your credit card number, but you *do* have to buy another beer. You can order something for her too, but chain-of-custody is vital in a world of roofies, so after the bartender mixes the girl's colored-water stage prop he'll place it directly into her hand, but leave your drink on a napkin.

I study Schoolmarm for a few minutes. She's an Asian woman, dressed in blue jeans and a blouse, and she appears to be about my age. Schoolmarm periodically makes eye contact with another girl at the other end of the bar and taps her glass with her little finger. Surely the retro-sergeants see this, but they don't care. They're all nineteen again, back at Osan, and about to get lucky.

The routines are different with the other girls, but just as regular. A white girl over at a booth arches and flips back her long brown hair. No one notices that she always looks across the room while doing so, because when her underwires adjust, the men's conversation pauses. Another girl plays at being a server, though she really isn't. Most of her time is spent lingering in various nooks and answering catcalls with flirtatious responses. Occasionally she even takes a seat with patrons.

"Sweetheart, that's illegal," I think, though I doubt that either the Liquor Board or Heath Department care about what goes on in this dump. Probably the only thing that shows up on anybody's regulatory radar is the single bank of video poker. The machines are ornamented with ashtrays, bottles, and empty glasses like a greasy row of trashy neon Christmas trees, and Gaming Control couldn't care less about a House girl encouraging the drunks.

The ladies check on each other, and in turn, three guys playing cutthroat glance at them as they chalk their cues. The men could pass for moonlighting base cops, except that their hair is out of reg. I know that the trio is on the job because the USAF doesn't allow jugs and the Nellis Marine det hangs out at a different bar. The muscle is doing okay, though. I imagine Patrick Swayzie commending them for innocuously blending with *Roadie*

House customers.

I spot a woman across the bar. She's probably a buck or staff sergeant. She's pale and on TDY because her skin obviously isn't based in southern Nevada's rotisserie. Temporary orders to Vegas aren't a cottage cheese license, but I guess that she didn't get the brief when those shorts went into her duffel. No matter. It's been a week since my last ULVN freshman, and hunger never saw bad bread. Or NORAD thighs.

I got the first look four minutes ago, and it's three minutes and counting from the second. I estimate that I have about thirty seconds to walk over to where she stands. Then I need to smirk, look her in the eye, and say something mildly derogatory. But leave the leg commentary alone. She's being brave tonight, but I still shouldn't risk it. I'll carefully go for the clothes, or better, the way she slightly sways to the music while sipping her drink. Those are fair game. I won't smile. Never smile. Only smirk. When she replies with her own stinging observations, I'll lob responses from behind my mask.

The constant smirk is key. It's my mental erection and my marble phallus of composure. Not quite a smile, not quite a sneer, but something in-between that lets her know that, despite her overall failure, I'm still willing - *maybe* - to put aside my contempt and offer her a chance that I know she doesn't really deserve.

Actually, we *both* know that it's a chance she doesn't really deserve.

I have twenty seconds to ready myself. It's time to be a bastard, because the path into a woman's pants winds through her indignation. Men make a mistake in thinking that the term "erectile dysfunction" applies exclusively to a soft cock. You'd better get it up mentally as well, or you can expect to see a woman's back - but not in the good way.

Fifteen seconds.

Where's my smirk? When I think about it, something inside me can't find the smirk anymore. Performance anxiety, perhaps. Maybe I'm thinking about it too much.

Or am I not thinking about it enough?
Five seconds.
*I can't get It up. My asshole factor has failed me.
My clever shitheadedness...where is it?*
And...zero.

The buzzer sounds.

She turns away, as anticipated, and I'm utterly crushed. Of course I'm crushed. Aren't I crushed? *I'm so very, very sensitive,* I chuckle to myself while coughing on a swig of beer. I tell myself that I shouldn't be laughing. This is a serious condition. I have Erectile Attitude Dysfunction.
"That's the spirit. She wasn't your type anyway."
*Who's this? Why, it's the Schoolmarm.
Curious.*
"Are you kidding?" I calmly reply, though I'm privately taken aback by the entire non-event already having been observed and evaluated. "She was *exactly* my type. That pasty cellulite screamed 'No Strings Attached'. Wherever she's TDY from, it's far from here. Soon she'll return to God-only-knows-where and her regular squeeze...or a squadron sweetheart role."
Schoolmarm pulls up a chair. "Heyford," she states.
"What?"
"RAF Upper Heyford. Joint British-American base. All of these guys are in town for Blue Flag."
I take a drink and lean back in my chair. "Well, I guess that explains the skin."
Schoolmarm's a cuteness overload. I like the way her ears stick out. I see pixie-tips, though her hair is down. She has small and honest eyes with single lids. Also cute. I hate it when Asian girls get that goddamned eyelid surgery. Even the name of the procedure sounds fucked-up. **Blepharoplasty.** What the hell *is* that? The term makes me think of a blue-faced and auto-asphyxiated Ramses II hanging by a belt in a Bangkok hotel closet.
Schoolmarm's smile is the same fake expression that she's been distributing all night, and I understand why the old men are addicted to it. Those crooked teeth are

so white that they probably glow in the dark. Her cute little eyes get even smaller and cuter when her smile pushes up her cheeks.

Would it be possible for her to dress more... *conservatively?* Especially in a place like this? The bar's A/C doesn't exactly keep the desert at bay, but Schoolmarm still looks cool and dry in her blouse. I haven't seen teal satin since middle school, and she looks good enough in it to make me wonder why. Satin is made for clichés: "Tight enough to show that she's a woman, but loose enough to show that she's a lady." Satin is unforgiving, but it fits both the aforementioned bill and her trim, but not overly thin, body. I don't doubt that Schoolmarm's a woman, though I might be disappointed to learn that she's a lady.

Maybe I should retract my "conservative" observation, because Schoolmarm only appears so from a distance. Now that she's sitting at my table, the satin show puffs at the open top buttons and I'm treated to the tantalizing freebie that the old NCOs were getting. I'm not seeing much, really - my estimation is "A" cups with "B" foam wishful thinking - and certainly far less than the no-bra freejug pummeling that my eyes receive while walking The Strip. Yet, I'm getting turned on. She's good. I'll give her that. I'm only shown what I'm supposed to see, and at the moment I'm obviously expected to look down her shirt.

She crosses her legs. Out of habit, I'm pleased to note that her toes point in my direction, though this feeling is dispelled by the realization that I'm dealing with a professional who is accustomed to playing off of a man's reactions even before he has time to react. When Schoolmarm's jeans pull up slightly on her ankles, it's safe to assume that she notes the fact that I like the little frills on the tops of her cuffed socks. In those flats she stands about five-five, but seems taller. But why socks and shoes? Most of the women here, even the Housies, are wearing shorts and sandals.

Schoolmarm has makeup on her right temple. It looks like she's trying to hide a spot of dark pigment that's about the size of a quarter. In any other situation I'd judge the mark to be an age spot, though that clearly can't be the case. It's the only thing I've seen so far that isn't on Schoolmarm's set list.

Uh-oh. Here comes one of the bouncers. It looks like he's got a fire under his ass. Relax, pal. I didn't come up to her. She approached me. Besides, what the fuck is the problem? I'm drinking and minding my own business, aren't I?

He doesn't even see me. At first.

"Can I walk you out, darlin'?" he asks. Something tells me that Schoolmarm's safety has been a bit more on this guy's mind than that of the other Housies.

She offers a friendly smile. *Only.* "In a minute," she answers. "I just finished."

"Can I get you something?" The guy ought to be on his knees and panting. Maybe he is. *He already knows everything that she ever drinks, I think. But he still asked. Awww. That's sweet. Next, he'll check under her mattress for peas.*

She smiles at him, and then at me. Either smitten and smothering muscles...or a stranger.

Choose.

I can tell that she wants to be kind, but I can also tell that this has been going on long enough to have become an annoyance. "A cooler," she says through her tightening smile. "Peach."

It is done.

"Sorry darlin', let me get that cap," he says. *Well, at least it's real, I observe. Her first all night, I'll bet.*

He lingers like a steward awaiting the first sip, and she knows that he won't leave until dismissed. "Thanks, Ted. I'm just going to sit for a minute. I'll let you know when I'm ready."

More panting, more pawing, but the leash isn't in hand, so it's not yet time for a walk. Back to the pool tables. Slowly. With backward glances at me.

Shoo-shoo.

Schoolmarm lets out a giggle when I ask if I should watch my back when I leave. She raises her bottle, but before putting it to her lips, she remarks: "Just once, I'd like to hear the word 'crush.' Or 'infatuation.'"

"Why not?" I ask. "Those seem like appropriate terms. *Darlin'.*"

She answers with her mouth but her eyes tell me to go fuck myself. "Yeah," she says, "but if he's a white guy like Ted, the only thing I ever hear is 'yellow fever.'"

I wince.

"Heard that one before, have we?"

"Once or twice," I reply. I sense that she's taking mental notes. I look to verify that the bouncer is back at the pool table. Though he's gone, his spoor is still very strong. *Why so much Old Slice?* I wonder. *Was that the only thing cheap enough to bathe in?*

Something falls out of Schoolmarm's bag. "Is that a textbook?" I ask.

"Yes," she says, as she leans over to pick it up. "Sometimes I study after my slam."

The volume is 100-series Ed Psych. Uncle Sugar's Patent Office, by way of assorted corporations, bought me the same edition last semester before they started to appear with obnoxious "USED" stickers. I'm about to ask Schoolmarm where she attends, but I'm interrupted. One of the retros has noticed us and is approaching in a drunken amble. *Get rid of him fast,* I think. *Ted the White Knight's first wave of manly scent was bad enough.*

"Hey Gracie! Where'd you go?" asks the old NCO. His .19 blood alcohol tongue makes a "Grayshee" sound. Ears prick up at the pool tables and my nose shuts down. *Jesus!* I think. *Him too? Did* everyone *here wallow in Eau de Rank?* I see Schoolmarm's instant and merciless smirk go up. *Nice hard-on...for a girl,* I observe.

She turns to address Spud McKenzie and his hairy bellybutton. Maybe the retro rubbed Old Slice over his body *after* he put on the shirt...or maybe the shirt carries a long-term accumulation of stud aroma.

"Hi again, Mike. Is Alice taking care of you guys?"

"Yeah, but we miss you."

Schoolmarm nods in my direction. "Mike, have you met my boyfriend, Carl?

The master sergeant doesn't even look at me. "Humph," he snorts, then turns and stumbles back to the bar.

"That was easy," she says.

"Uh, '*Carl*'?"

"Sorry. First thing that popped into my head."

"'Gracie', is it?"

"Grace." She looks directly at me and pronounces her name with scalpel-edged enunciation.

"You seem pretty attached to your stage name," I say. *Sensitive spot, huh?*

"That's everyone's assumption," Grace replies. She studies me for a moment. When Grace speaks again, her tone is more relaxed. "I thought that you were a local with that dated little goatee. But you're ex-military, aren't you?

I nod and add: "The two aren't mutually exclusive." *What's wrong with my goatee?*

"Are you enjoying your follicular freedom?"

I shrug. "I've been out for a while."

She makes an exaggerated effort to look behind me. "Ponytail already grown and cut. Oh, don't be surprised. I'm not psychic. All of you guys do it after getting discharged."

"Are you done entertaining the AARP?" I ask.

"I'd better be, though I can still feel some of them looking over here." She sips and rolls her eyes. "Alice can work a little harder, because I'm finished for the night." Grace nods toward the girl who has taken her place at the bar.

"That shouldn't be too tough. There isn't even a stage in this place."

"Of course not. I do have *some* standards."

"Standards?" I fumble in an awkward moment. "I didn't mean--"

"I know," she interrupts, "but we obviously don't make as much as dancers. We get fair cuts, though."

"Oh?"

"Mmm. In some ways, it's even easier than dancing."

"How?"

"Well, I'm essentially a mannequin. We all are," Grace explains, as she gestures at the other girls. "Men dress us up instead of stripping us down."

"You seem to be wearing the same clothes that you had on when I came in."

"Memories, Captain Literal. You can do better than

47

that."

My expression is a cross between skepticism and confusion. "Men dress you in memories," I say, perhaps more than a bit dubiously.

Flirty Girl is in our vicinity, but I ignore her and wave over another beer from one of the real servers. "I, uh...something has gone over my head," I say.

"Certainly not *her* game," observes Grace. She watches Flirty Girl for a moment before addressing my puzzlement. "Take those men at the bar. They all served Asian tours when they were young. It always comes up before the night's over."

"So?"

"So, they're getting old and numb. Only two of them were still in the air force, and I think one said that he was going to retire later this year."

I scratch my head and take a drink. "I'm still not getting it."

"None of them saw *me*. That guy who walked over finally remembered that my name is Grace, and not Yong-in or Joo-hee or whatever. Some nights, when I'm here 'til close, I hear maybe ten or twelve different names, all from old men who think that I'm their private Madame Toussaud's."

Huh, I think. *I guess that makes sense.* I look over to where Alice alternately beguiles and fends off the ancient tees. "I see that Alice is--"

"--Asian?" interrupts Grace.

I nod. "But the others aren't."

"No. That's because the customers aren't all the same, either. Three o'clock *mud shark.*" Grace grins as she emphasizes the slur, but I don't respond to her racist bait. Instead, I look in the direction of the Breathtaking Rack Station and note that its clientele has shifted to an African-American demographic. Grace motions with her eyes at the House girl in the booth, whom I reason by this time has rubbed raw patches under her tits with unique combinations of spinal yoga and overly-cinched Roland's of Los Vegas.

"So? What do you see?" asks Grace.

I do indeed notice something. I've already sensed that Grace's co-worker is a local, but her skin is even whiter than that of the TDY girl. Not an easy feat in Nevada.

"What - what's wrong with her? Is she a Goth? Is she sick or something?"

"No," explains Grace. "That look is part of her job, along with a phony Brit accent. She's a drama student, and really good, too. Sometimes she puts on a Dutch routine if Camp New Amsterdam is in town."

"So - the old white guys like Asian girls and the black guys like dying white actresses...?" I rub my eyes and shake my head. "Help me here."

I receive a superior look from Schoolmarm Grace. "I don't know this for a fact, but I'm guessing that all of those guys are recently back from England, Iceland, and other places in northern Europe. You know, places where black men experience--"

"--what white men experience in Asia?" I say, completing her thought.

"Exactly."

"That's an ugly generalization, don't you think? I know you've been teasing me with your little racist jabs," I pause, "but isn't that approaching the real thing?"

She just shrugs and smiles. "Maybe. *Definitely.* But it works around base. The owner is a shrewd guy. He doesn't have to groom teenage boob jobs at Silverado High, and I don't have to work a third job."

The Triumph of Commerce, I muse. Well, at least no women are being degraded in the *usual* Vegas sense. I look at Schoolmarm Grace. She's an actress using her ethnicity in a role. They all are. A job like hers requires an ability to quickly perform behavioral analysis, and I know that she mentally completed my assessment within minutes of sitting down. Now something else is happening.

"Okay Mr. Former Hero, how about our mud shark?" she asks.

"I can do without the knot tags," I respond in a low voice. "You can drop that one, too."

Grace obviously enjoys the ease with which she can make me squirm, so she takes another little dig. "Any SPGs in your past?" she asks.

"Yes, yes. I get your point, and no, I've never been to Singapore. You, however," I say in an attempt to shift the conversation out of epithet mode, "look like a *Han* girl."

Grace pauses and her eyes widen in surprise. Then she laughs a genuine on-the-house laugh. "That's the safest and most diplomatic way I've ever heard a white boy say that he doesn't know if I'm Chinese or Korean."

"Hanguk saram," I blurt out.

Grace responds with a disappointed sigh. "Most of the guys who gravitate toward my end of the bar, or rather, *these,"* she says, as she pulls her eyelids back until they are fine lines with lashes, "try to get me juicy with garbled nonsense. But I admit that I've picked up some language at this job from returned GIs...though mostly just coarse junk."

"Adoptee?"

"No. My dad just insisted that we were *Americans."* She shrugs. "Whatever."

"I'd say he was right. Not many *Korean* girls would say something like that."

For the first time, I sense that she is off balance. There is a pause. "And how would you know?" she asks, mouthing the question from a wary sidelong look. I don't answer. Instead, I see a false opportunity and force an idiotically rakish grin that only makes Grace sigh again. "You should have stayed with the Han thing," she says. "I get so sick of guys trying to impress me with broken bits and pieces." Grace pauses to flash her eyes in a way that lets me know that I am about to be spectacularly pile-driven. "But maybe you actually *are* fluent." She smiles, again in a genuine and non-commercial expression, but so tinged with dark satisfaction that I flinch. "Go on. Let me hear you. And I promise to take you home and show you why those antique prostates over at the bar are oozing in their pants."

Shit. A two-point reversal and a mental bitch-slap for good measure. But I can still throw a random Hail Mary.

"Sallong-gae."

Pause. Her eyes widen again. She seems to freeze

for a moment while deciding whether to scream for Musclehead Ted or simply laugh at my weirdness.

The latter. A disaster is averted...but I push my luck. *"Jook-in-dah."*

Her laughter dies. And did she just *tsk-tsk* me? I think she did. Her smile fades to half-strength. "Sooo solly," she says in a cold and mocking accent. "It look like you be spend-uh night with you hand-uh. Or you go Pallump."

Well, so much for that.

"My hand *in* Pahrump is more like it," I grumble. Who cares? I've already hit the iceberg.

My despair boosts her smile to a sadistic seventy-five percent. Unexpected, but noticeable. So far I'm zero for two, and here comes the third pitch.

"A loom salon," I say. "In Pallump."

Hmmm. Ninety-five percent. But no home run. Horseshoes, hand grenades, and a fatal glance at her watch. Grace reaches for her bag and gets up. "Well, Carl, it's been nice talking to you. And you even bought yourself another beer. I'm flattered."

"My name's Jack," I say, though Grace is already gone...along with the chance that she knew I didn't really deserve.

No. We both knew.

F
Too Late To Beg You
Or Cancel
It

Visions Of Swastikas In My Head,
(King Alfred) Plans
For Everyone!

September
2017
(1-of-3)

For a while it had looked like we might pull through. Things started to come back, and Vegas again became a destination city, post-apocalypse style. Sometimes I saw overweight people. Hoover turbines re-illuminated the Vegas nights. Nevada's silver pesos traded for Utah's coal marks. McKarran's rocketlites were an increasingly popular travel option. We had hotels and diversions again. At first, the shows in a few reopened casinos were small and mainly-local affairs, but this changed as more people ventured through the desert with bio-diesel cars, alcohol bikes, and even plain old bicycle convoys. These travelers wanted entertainment, so re-enter gambling, live music, and hokey magicians.

Welcome home, sequined costumes, giant headdresses, boot-leather breasts, and sixties choreography! Nice to see you again, tumblers, gymnasts, and leotard women twirling thirty feet in the air on hair extensions!

It was this latter group who were to cause complications for the personnel at DS-21. Maybe they weren't strictly gymnasts and acrobats. Perhaps part of their act had included Houdini-style escapes, because somebody had possessed the presence of mind to slip a key or small blade into his or her mouth before the TSA pulled down their black hoods. When the gymnasts were thrown onto their tarp, they passed the implement quickly and undetectably among themselves as they cut out sections of canvas.

There really wasn't time to wait for a better escape opportunity, because human frailty simply would not grant it. After just one or two days in the camp, dehydration and exhaustion took too great of a toll, and

I think that the entertainers sensed this. An old military axiom stated: "Professionals are predictable. It's the amateurs that you have to watch out for." In this case, a cadre of highly trained and coordinated performers was about to go up against an amateurish assemblage of programmed killers.

Camp guards who carried M16s were old hands because the jeeps received black powder weapons that vaguely resembled the nineteenth century's quad-barreled Imperial Lancaster rifle. Somewhere in the Vegas Valley a shop cut lengths of roughly ten gauge pipe, fastened them in bundles of four, capped the ends, and wired strikers near touch holes. Then these monstrosities were fitted to Cochise stocks and painted black. The shooter had four individual blasts of twelve thirty-caliber balls per barrel, or one massive shoulder-slamming salvo. The weapon had short range and low power in comparison to modern smokeless pieces, but that was irrelevant. It was a classic sawed-off shotgun, quadrupled, and able to hang, draw and quarter a human body without horse assistance.

For ten to fifteen minutes every evening the incoming guards and those they relieved exchanged weapons at the rail container, and spotty perimeter coverage was left to latter-day musketeers. The freshly-abducted performers saw this opportunity immediately, and though it didn't present good odds, it was the best that Fate could offer.

* * *

Brad Pit needed human fat to make the creamiest and richest soap, and in the role of Dyler Turden he showed Edward Nortin how to quickly and safely vault a fat dumpster's barb-topped fence by tossing a protective mat over its wires. The concertina that ringed DS-21 was worse than simple barbs, so the acrobats folded their strips of tarp into double and triple thicknesses. They rose in unison and manipulated the long strips like Chinese placard teams flipping mosaic boards. The entertainers danced in a criss-cross pattern toward the slope as they whipped and folded the material in a gymnastic routine that might just save their lives. The acrobats' bare feet glided over sharp rocks and hot sand in a supremely disciplined and silent ballet, and for some long seconds the guards who stood in line to check their M16s didn't know what was happening.

Two perimeter guards noticed, however. Apparently one of them had never actually practiced firing his quad-barrel, because he didn't seem to expect what happened when he pulled the trigger. The man shouldered his weapon and shot through the chain links, but without bracing for heavy recoil. The fence shuddered and swayed and the guard was knocked to the ground. An immense boom announced that much was amiss, and a newly-ruptured mesh of blasted wire beckoned to the camp prisoners.

My tarp group had attained seniority among the damned, for we were next in line for Three Trailer. We all knew that the end was close, so that was why my group, the ones who were the weakest and most exhausted, were able to find strength. While others froze in denial or attempted to negotiate divine bargains, those who stared death in the face took action.

"Come on, Jack," urged Grace. She struggled to her knees and managed to stand, but her legs buckled and she fell. Others had similar problems, but they desperately wanted to attend the birthday party.

Yay! Fun for all boys and girls! Come on, Jack! We're invited!

The entertainment was far better than a lame clown on a tiny bicycle. There were acrobats! They formed cheerleading jump bases and propelled each other into the air, and in time to cannon salutes! No expense had been spared. The acrobats were so good that they seemed to be suspended on magic tarp carpets...! But, since I was one of the older kids, I decided not to tell the youngsters that it was all done with wires. Maybe razor wires.

Grace regained her feet but hit the tarp again when I expended what energy I had left to throw a crab block across her legs. In my feeble state it was the best that I could do to quickly knock her over. She was stunned and confused, and my mind couldn't formulate a quick explanation, so I just rolled over and used my body weight to pin her down.

Sounds made by other guests had prompted my actions. Behind us I heard partygoers warming up for a rendition of *Happy Birthday to You*, but to be honest, their voices were, well, *terrible*. Off key. No sense of time. I was a polite guest and would never express this view aloud, but...it just sounded like they were bellowing obscenities. There was the sound of instruments too, but not your typical party-favor noisemakers. There weren't any horns or whistles, but there were many clicks as charging handles were pulled, followed by palm slaps against release buttons as bolts chambered bullets. The party's rented popcorn cart was suddenly very loud. In fact, it drowned out the singers.

Strange accompaniment, I thought, though it seemed to fit the bad singing. This was still a terrific celebration, regardless of the grating cacophony and the popping kernel barrage. I appreciated the outdoor venue because it allowed Grace and me to relax on our picnic blanket and observe the fun and games. We hadn't joined the sack race, but maybe we *should* have because none of the participants made it to the finish line. "Heck, we could have beaten those guys," I said to Grace with a smile. All of the racers had stopped hopping and skipping. They just writhed on the ground in laughter, and some were so out of breath that they didn't move at all.

Now that the sack race was over, the kids over by the *piñata,* or rather, *piñatas,* were at the center of activity. Those *must* be piñatas hanging on the fence, right? I guessed that when my focus had been on the sack race, the acrobats had wrapped up their performance so as to make way for piñatas. Yes, of course. That was it. But I had missed the festivities, and now candy, toys, confetti, and ribbons were spilled on the ground beneath empty papier-mâché husks.

The kid who batted those piñatas had been a bit overzealous, because the lower halves of some were on the ground while the rest were still suspended in snarls of concertina and tattered tarp. Maybe the kid had used one of those signal cannons instead of a stick. Yep, there he goes. He just blasted one of the piñatas again, even though it's clearly empty. Another wet chunk of red papier-mâché just fell to the ground.

Fun is fun, but there *is* such a thing as excess. I'd guess that he's the spoiled birthday boy. All of this effort and expense was put forward, only to have him fixate upon piñata dissection. He's going to become an embarrassment to his overly-indulgent parents in a moment. Let's just hope that the scolding takes place far from the guest's ears. For form's sake.

"God-*fucking*-damn it!" screamed a TSA officer.

Apparently not.

* * *

The man walked with authority and I didn't need to see his insignia to know that he wasn't just a flunky guard. First he was on the perimeter slope, then he slid through the fence's blast-holes, and then he climbed back up the slope. His head jerked back and forth as he struggled to accurately determine how many pieces were produced by how many wholes. The man looked at the pieces, wrote on a clipboard, looked back at the pieces, and scratched out what he had written. He was accompanied by two guards. Their M16s were at the ready and their dustless black uniforms indicated that their days were spent days indoors with their master.

"Fuck! *Fuck!*" the officer roared at the two quota-ruining perimeter drones. "There isn't even enough left for half soap credit!" The fence guards cowered as the enraged officer kicked a human head through the torn fence. The head rolled down the slope and stopped near the same shredded tarp where it had recently possessed a body. I couldn't hear the next words because the yelling stopped. The officer composed himself, said something to his personal guards, and walked back to the trailers.

One bodyguard trained his rifle on the two perimeter men, while the other let his own weapon go to sling. The latter stepped forward, yanked the empty quad-barrels away from the TSA peons, and barked a command. For a moment the two disarmed men looked at each other and then again at the guard, who repeated the order. The perimeter men began to remove their uniforms, and when the garments were off, the bodyguard gathered the weapons, clothes, and boots and carried the armload in the same direction in which the angry officer had walked. The other guard then fired bursts into both perimeter men. Their naked bodies dropped, one face-first, and the other in a half-spin.

A full metal jacket 401(k) seemed to constitute the TSA's early retirement program.

* * *

I can recognize the look of a scared thug who knows that he's in some serious shit. Even though the camp guards wear masks, I can see their fearful eyes. Ugly little brains go into overdrive and dry skull gears grind as TSA drones focus upon preserving their own asses.

I know the routine by now. The old black school bus comes first. It parks at the top of the slope and waits for the living. A couple hours later the meat wagon shows up to haul away the dead. Both the bus and meat wagon loads are monitored, and I've observed clipboards and body counts for both. Therein lies the problem for the Trash-In-Black. Half of today's bus passengers are on the red tarp...and some, quite literally. From my group's gray tarp, I can see all the way through a dead man's empty chest, directly to where the root of his esophagus once was.

If I were a guard, I would blame the TSA schedulers for this mess. I mean, if an entire acrobat troupe is scheduled for abduction in a single night, that's just asking for trouble. Any neophyte student of genocide knows that it's preferable to keep people captive with strangers. Hell, even the Triangular Trade slavers mixed victims from different tribes and tongues.

* * *

No one could talk now, or even whisper. Grace and I huddled close and squeezed each other's hands. I kept my head low, but I could still look ahead. That was when I noticed the scared thugs. Their eyes were a little wider and darted a little faster. The naked corpses of their former cohorts were displayed atop the red mat's pile of pieces as reminders of how fortunes within TSA ranks could quickly fall.

There were voices behind me:

"Detainee 022573. Plant gang."

"Check," replied another voice.

"022574. Plant gang."

"Check."

"Wait."

"What?"

"Scratch that one."

"Scratch?"

"Yeah. Headcount for the old dairy is full. She's too damn old, anyway. Use her for next week's soaper list."

"We're done, then?"

"No. One more."

"Alright. How about that one?"

There was a pause. Something was being decided.

"No. Still needs to be younger."

"For what?"

"A kippy-jo."

"*What?* Why the fuck are *we* tasked with that bullshit? No good ass ever comes through here, 'cept for them show people, and now they're all dead. All we got left are unscarreds. A catcher detail should just go out again!"

"Keep it down and help me find something that might pass for pussy up on Fremont."

Another pause. Eyes moved over my tarp group's bowed heads like hot spotlights.

"I see one."

Footsteps crunched toward Grace and me. Even in my exhaustion, I had to suppress an urge to attack one of the punks when he knelt, grabbed Grace's hair, and pulled her head up. I think that Grace must have sensed this, because she gave my hand a warning squeeze.

"What kinda chink are you, bitch?" snarled the guard.

"Korean," said Grace, almost in a whisper.

"*Kereen?* What the fuck does that mean? You tryin'

to get fancy with me?" The black-gloved hand tightened its grip on Grace's hair and yanked again.

Before Grace could answer, the other guard spoke. "Same as 'Jap' or 'Chinaman'," he muttered.

"How old are you?"

Grace's response was smooth and natural. "Thirty-five".

The guard released her hair and stood up. "This is the last one, right?"

"Yeah."

"Thirty-five, my fucking ass. She's just an old unscarred."

There was a scared tone, almost of warning, in the reply. "She could be thirty-five. She *could* be. Look, a task is a task."

"Lemme see that," said the other guard, as he snatched the clipboard out of his companion's hand. "What about those in the back?"

"All spoken for. I double-checked. Gimme that list. You can't read worth shit."

There was silence, then an angry response. "Fuck you, uppity. Just 'cuz you know your letters good, you think Earth Mother watches over you."

I detected a smug and superior silence.

"Fine. That's just fuckin' great," continued the illiterate one. "Alright. Put her down."

* * *

Grace didn't go through the Hot Unit. None of them did. Not on that day. When the black bus came, the guards just went down the line and snapped on ankle chains. Grace and I held hands for as long as we could until they pulled us apart, and then it was the standard march up and out of the camp. Grace tried to look back at me as she walked, but she had to turn to keep from falling and being trampled.

After they took her I stopped caring about how much time I had left.

Shut Your Eyes, ~~Marion~~ *Jack!*
Don't Look At It, No
Matter What
Happens!

September
2017
(2-of-3)

My life's end arrives a couple days after the birthday party.

    *   *   *

At last I understand how **Hope**® is the greatest villain and the monster that facilitates the worst of evils. **Hope**® holds me over a Mayan *chacmool* as priests split my sternum. **Hope**® places me beneath the cold electric lights of Dr. Mengele's vivisection table. **Hope**® gleefully brandishes Comrade Deuch's bone saws and branding irons as it runs through the halls of a former Phnom Penh high school.

Folks, what we saw, but refused to believe, was that we were already dead. But **Hope**® told us that if we chose to comply, obey, and cower, there was yet a chance that we could make it out alive.

False choice.

Hope® *isn't* the thing with feathers – it's the thing with quills. When people are already condemned, the only thing left to decide is how to die. This is a real man's *minor* consideration since he's already resolved the big issue; namely, whether or not he can escape death.

Nope. Not possible.

On to the next item of business.

Captain Real Man knows that his ship is doomed to mutiny and murder, so he cuts the lifeboats and blows out the hull. Real Men purge themselves of **Hope**®. They face up to the fact that they're already corpses and refuse to quietly go under.

Not me, though. A long time ago someone called

me a "coward with a weak mind". I can't remember who, exactly, but...someone. No matter. She was right. A Real Man would have taken at least one smear of SS shit with him as he was flushed down the *Reichtoilette.* A Real Man would have done it before they shaved his head and stole his shoes. He would have struck when they came to his house, or he could have been pre-emptive. A one-for-one, two-for-one, or even five-for-one trade would have stopped the bullshit in its tracks. Even at its height, the entire *Wehrmacht* didn't number over Six Million. When Pol Pot's *Santebal* kicked down the door, Mr. Real Man wouldn't have cared about cutlery versus AKs. He wouldn't have concerned himself with the futility of knives in a gunfight. Mr. Real Man would have understood that he couldn't save himself. Sorry. He couldn't save his own wife and children, either. But he might have saved someone *else's* family... because he had abandoned **Hope®**.

Not here, though. Los Vegas was as mired in **Hope®** as Phnom Penh and the Warsaw ghetto. In this crippled post-plague TSA pit, it was everywhere. **Hope®** had preceded Hell, but then stuck around to help it limp along on a crutch of phony options.

Again, I was a coward with a weak mind. I had held on to **Hope®** as my group shuffled from tarp to tarp and got closer and closer to Trailer Three's Hot Unit. I had peered through cattle car slats as frozen rails vibrated across Eastern Europe. I had marched down the banks of the Tonle Sap on my way to a classroom ankle chain, while my national myth assured me with every step that this wasn't happening to *me*...because things like this simply didn't happen in my **Wonderfully Exceptional America®**.

I was strapped into something that was like an un-upholstered dentist's chair. A water bucket, long-handled brush, and floor drain meant that what was going to happen would require cleanup. The cavalry wasn't coming, even in my delusions. No Harry Tuttle for me.

I was going to die, and in great pain. I didn't even know why. Because of a neo-pagan fantasy? Because of some mutated descendant of Al Gorey's old Climate Change Scam-O-Rama? There had been sharp pebbles on the ground outside. I should have opened a vein in the night while the guards dozed.

No. I *should* have attacked a guard. My tired old ass wouldn't have done any damage, but it would have been a more dignified death. Now all I could do was provide a fantasy porn soundtrack for the poor bastards outside as I experienced a bureaucratic procedure that would put an official stamp on my demise. I felt what that girl in *The Stillness of the Lambs* had felt when she looked at the walls of the well and saw the broken nails of those who had gone before, except here the nails and bits of flesh were just debris that had swirled on top of the floor screen like hair that clogs a shower drain.

It rubs the lotion on its Hope®.

There were splatter stains on the ceiling and a stainless steel tray held implements that further reminded me of a dentist's office...except that the tools were large, sharp, and obviously without any application beyond simply ripping out teeth. Or eyes. Or tongues.

PUT YOUR HOPE® IN THE FUCKING BASKET!

I remembered my little Ruger 10/22. Now it was in some looter's possession as, according to Grace, my home had been ransacked. *I **Hope®** the next guy has the nuts to blow one of your filthy black-masked faces off,* I thought.

Grace. She had rattled off to God-knows-where in an old painted-over school bus. When I thought of her I remembered the crucified thief's plea to Jesus:

Remember me when you get to heaven...or wherever they took you.

Coward. Weak mind. *Me.* I should have gone down swinging when the TSA showed up at my house, instead of allowing myself to be captured, zip-tied, and thrown into a van.

For a moment there was a chorus in Three Trailer. I heard the ethereal voices of three million Filipinos, of unknown numbers of extinct Native Americans and African slaves, and of Chinese, Irish and every other group that had been used or simply exterminated by a thing that was once called The United States Federal Government, but now was known as the TSA. Ghostly groups of Hiroshiman, Baghdadi, and Branch Davidian children looked at me and sadly shook their heads.

"Why didn't you fight?" they all asked.

"Why didn't *you?*" I shot back.

"*We* did."

* * *

The warm-up act consisted of two men who didn't speak or look at me. They wore white surgical gloves and black masks.

I felt a stabbing pain in my right arm. I cried out and tried to lurch forward. Something entered and exited, but left a knot in the wound. A cold and hard seed had been shot into me on a snap of compressed air. I felt a warm rivulet flow down to my elbow and drip from the underside of my forearm.

I heard a door open as the TSA thugs wheeled the injector tank into my view. The men snapped to attention, but with bowed heads. One dropped the injection gun onto the metal tray with a clang.

"At ease. I'll take it from here. You. Stay," came the commands. "You. Out." I heard one man obediently march to the exit and shut the door behind him.

The voice was like that of Eli Wallack, but as an old man. It was Tuco Benedicto Pacífico Juan María Ramírez, come back to dub the lost soundtrack of a restored spaghetti western. You could tell that it was still the same person and the same character...but somehow things were different. The tone was familiar, but older. It was definitely not the voice of another low-level worker bee. It was that of the angry officer who had kicked someone's head through the perimeter fence.

When the officer moved into view I saw that he was a white man of average height and build with a gray and thinning buzz haircut. He wore a mask, but the parts of his visage that weren't hidden indicated that he could have been from the "old unscarred" generation. I saw, however, red and purple blotches on his forehead and neck. His epaulets bore colonel's eagles, but like the other uniforms at DS-21, his shirt lacked a nametag. "Give me that," the colonel ordered, as he turned to the subordinate and thrust out his hand.

They had a picture of me, but when the colonel snatched it away from the underling it didn't appear as though he really needed it to make a positive ID. I didn't actually see the picture, but I easily guessed what it was by the way the officer grabbed my chin and jerked my head from side to side. When the colonel was done he put the picture in his pocket.

The underling spoke in a nervous near-whisper. "Sir, I must respectfully convey Colonel Norres' directive regarding the record material. He wishes that it be returned to his archive."

The colonel's response was quick and harsh. "Adherent Erikson, you serve me well, and I expect that you will continue to do so. Therefore, you will inform Colonel Norres, pathetic former-LVPD drone that he is, that I chose to retain the 'record material.' And Erikson, should you speak again of this matter, I will collect one of your fingers." In the following silence I wondered if Erikson had fucked up before and was already without some digits.

Liquid poured behind me. "Drink," came the flat command as a large cup of clean and cool water was pressed to my lips.

"Drink." Another command, another cup, and then one more after that. "Good," said the colonel to his subordinate. "Do it."

And so it ends, I thought. *At least it'll be quick. I guess I'll never know what the water was for.*

"Atropine, Colonel?" asked the adherent in a still-nervous voice.

"Mmmm. Yes. Thigh. A Pretty Lady...and a Wet One, I think, but no more. Make it believable. In fact," continued the colonel, *"I'll do it."*

The man took two gray cylinders, both slightly larger than ball point pens, out of his pocket and brought them

66

down on my leg with sharp force. I remembered
atropine, or "Pretty Lady," from my military days, but I
didn't know what a "Wet One" was. Spring-loaded
needles shot into my flesh and dispensed potent drugs
that, in another time, had offered protection from
chemical nerve agents as well as quick jimson weed
highs for delinquents.

Before I went under I saw the left cuff of the
colonel's black sleeve pull up slightly to reveal
something on his wrist that looked very different from
his 'pox scars.

It was the edge of a purple birthmark.

* * *

*ULVN's Moyer Student Union is kind of empty today.
It's a good place to study.*

"May I sit?" I ask.

"Sure," she says, as she motions at an empty chair.

"Do you remember me?"

*"Give me a second." She takes off her glasses and
taps her chin. "Carl. Hello again."*

*I sit and put my book bag under the table. "Well,
that was the name that you gave me."*

*She lays her pen beside her glasses. "Your name is
Jack. Dr. Crank called on you enough times, didn't he?"*

*"I'm afraid that I don't know your name," I reply.
"Your real name, I mean."*

"Yes, you do."
"Yes, you do."
"Yes, you do."

"'Grace' is your real name?"

She just smiles.

*"Okay. Fine," I continue. "'Grace'. Not Gracie.
Never, ever, Gracie."*

"Good. I'm glad that you remembered."

*"I think that we're at the same practicum school
during this semester."*

She nods. *"My classroom at Manch Elementary is four doors down from yours...Jack Simmerath."*

I start to speak, but Grace holds up her hand. *"I told you the night we met that I wasn't psychic. Your name was on Dr. Meckley's list when I went in for my district assignment."*

"Ah." I suddenly feel very self-conscious. Am I fidgeting? Oh God, I am. Stop. Don't do that. C'mon Grace. Say something.

"Do you know what the problem is with the student union?" she asks.

Oh good. No more uncomfortable silence. *"What?"*

"All the ripped-up piñatas."

I look up and see that the student union ceiling is a forest-like canopy of concertina wire from which many broken corpses hang. Their empty ribcages, missing limbs, and frozen looks of terror slowly turn and twist overhead.

I try to scream, but I can't.

The walls of the student union melt, as does Grace's face. Like a hot crayon, her visage flows, shrinks, and disappears, as if she had dared to look into the Ark of the Covenant while collaborating with Nazis.

We'll All Start At The Clark County Blood Donation Center And End At The Roswell Sperm Bank

September 2017 (3-of-3)

The air is cooler and floodlights have replaced the sun. I hear the muffled drone of the camp's single generator. Bugs crawl on my head. Bugs take off and land on my face. I'm sunburned and feverish pain is in my skin. I've been dumped on the death pile, but I'm still breathing and puking. Knotted cramps twist my scrawny old gut like the relentless birth contractions of a womb that I don't have. My stomach isn't unloading sparse survival rations. I'm well beyond that. It's the dry heaves, except that they're not dry, as TSA drugs force gastric secretions in the absence of food stimuli. It's just acid followed by more acid. My extra-water ration belly has apparently been deflated by a "Wet One", because atropine has the opposite effect.

My dilated pupils won't completely focus, but I still recognize a woman lying beside me. Her name is Laura, and she used to be a pharmacist. She's pretty, in her forties, and has long brown hair. Laura's figure indicates reasons to keep fit and attractive. We once had a whisper conversation in which Laura explained that she had been born in France and had caught the tail-end of an Alsace smallpox vaccination program. We're positioned in a way that makes us look like lovers and we gaze into each other's eyes. I still can't see very well, but I don't have to in order to realize that I'm not actually gazing into Laura's eyes, but rather, into the empty black sockets where her eyes used to be.

You never get used to shit like this. Even when you're about to die yourself, **you never get used to shit**

like this. *I don't care about how much horror you've witnessed in your life. You just can't grow completely numb. "Desensitized", as I think film critics and Pentagon officials used to describe it.*

I don't understand why I'm still alive.

I'd be inclined to think that the Fabulous Transcendental Security Administration in Fabulous Los Vegas has Fabulously Fucked Up, except for one nagging detail: the constant sting in my arm. Why chip and hydrate someone who's destined for the meatwagon?

It doesn't have to make sense, I tell myself. *Remember, this is the government. Besides, given my condition, it's a stretch to assume that I'll be alive for much longer.*

I don't dare close my eyes, or the puking will resume. Being conscious, I'm aware of just how ill I am, though I can't stir. It's like drug-induced sleep paralysis - that instant when an alien hand-job is about to milk you dry, but you can't move or cry out. In this moment I'm thankful for UFO abduction tales, because I can choose to believe that I'm not facing the corpse of a lovely woman and a productive human being who experienced a TSA eye scoop prior to being murdered. Instead...I *choose* to believe that I'm looking at a little Gray who has enormous dark areas where human eyes would be. He's here to comfort me and to tell me not to worry, because this isn't the end. Aliens are about to deploy from the Mother Ship and intervene. On his home world the price for abductee-harvested human semen is comparable to the price of bear bile in China, so naturally, in the name of interstellar commerce, this mess will be sorted.

I'm old, but I can still cum, I hear myself pleading. *So please save me. Save us all.*

Alright, he telepathically answers. *Just so long as you can assure me that this has nothing to do with* **Hope®**.

Nothing whatsoever, I reply, as another searing jet of acid surges out of my raw throat. Or maybe he just jerked me off into an interstellar specimen cup.

* * *

The generator's drone stops. That's what awakens me. I can't see anything. Crusted Lilliputians have tied my lashes together and my sight is secured under a lock of hardened mucous. Still, I can tell that the Nevada sun, and not a floodlight, is on the other side of my eyelids.

I'm breathing - sort of. Am I breathing? Something slowly comes in, shallow and small, then slowly goes out, shallow and small. My stomach is still. I'm not in pain. I feel relaxed, like I'm on a soft recliner.

Death!

It's not such a big deal, after all!
I'm flying! I'm leaving my body, right?
No. I was just slung onto the meat wagon.
Oh. Well, no problem.
I don't feel anything.

Everything is fine.

5

Her Petals And Men Beside Arch Stanton

Saddle Up Your Octopus
And Ride For
The Khan

July
1994

Grace and I had been classmates in the ULVN elementary education program for only a few semesters, but we had reached friendship's thick-hided milestones in record time; that is, we could hurl racial epithets and sexist slams back and forth, tell each other to fuck off, and then go catch a movie, get a cup of coffee, or cram for exams. Today we food shopped, and durian fruit was the topic of our coarse banter.

"Oh God," I said, as we walked by a frozen fruit case. My fingers lovingly passed over some frost-glazed packages of yellow pulp. "I love this stuff," I remarked, with a *can-I-please-please-please* expression. "Even this frozen crap is good. Hmmm? It won't stink up your apartment."

Yes, it would. Merely the empty package would fill Grace's home with the unique aroma of an old meat cooler packed with sweetly putrefied cottage cheese. I didn't care about the smell, though. I considered durian to be delicious, like creamy vanilla custard. In fact, it was my favorite fruit.

"'Oh God' is right," said my friend. "Your fingers are going to smell just from touching that plastic. Why do you think that I would let you in with that? Just because I'm Asian? It doesn't even come from Korea."

"Oh, *puh-leez*," I responded. "Don't give me your 'Stereotypes-In-Round-Eye-Land' routine. Some Koreans *do* like it. And for your information, there are two tiny durian orchards on Jeju Island."

There was a slight pause, so I knew that I had scored with my zinger. "Fuck you, you crazy *migukin nom,*" was the best Grace could do, as she attempted to compensate by exaggeratedly getting in my face like a rapper throwing down onstage. Our faces were close enough that I could have kissed her, right there in the frozen section, in front of all the mostly-Filipino Seafood

City shoppers. I tried to look pissed and tough, but I couldn't contain my grin.

"Is that it?" I asked, while gesticulating in a way that was more reminiscent of a stroke-injured Thom Jones than Eminim. *"Bad American?* Look around - this ain't no *Hanguk,* baby! We in Vegas! Is that all you got? Hell, girl," I continued, "we lucky this place carry *any* Korean stuff - cuz' in case you ain't notice, we in a Pinoy joint!" My awkward arm and hand flailings were more akin to palsy than hip-hop moves, and my faux-Ebonic verb conjugations would have gotten me killed outside on Maryland Parkway. The only other people in the aisle, however, were two stockers, and they were more concerned with checking freezer tags than watching my nonsense.

"Yes, you are definitely nuts," declared Grace. Then the same expression that I had seen on the night when we met, that same night when she slammed me and walked out of a rattrap air force bar, appeared on her face.

Uh-oh.

"Yes, you're right. You're quite right," she said. "In fact, I shouldn't refer to you as a psycho *migukin.* Up at Greenland Market, maybe, but not here. You know what I mean?" Grace flashed a razorblade smile. "Milieu and cultural appropriateness, as we've discussed in class all semester." Grace turned to the elder of the two Seafood City employees. "Excuse me," she said. The man looked up from a bundle of frozen lemon grass, but only shook his head.

"He doesn't speak English," interjected the other stocker, who might have been a high school junior or senior. "Is there something that I can help you with?"

"Yeah," said Grace. "What do you call *that,"* at which she jerked her thumb in my direction, "in Tagalog?"

"Uh, I, uh..." the boy stammered. "I thought you might be looking for some kind of fish or fruit or something."

"No, no," said Grace. "In Tagalog. What?"

There was a pause before the boy spoke. "I know a little Bisaya, but my Tagalog isn't very good. I can ask another employee to help you with your question about the gentleman." The boy's earnestness made Grace giggle.

The older man had observed, and he didn't have to understand English to formulate his own answer. He muttered something under his breath that made the boy cough and look uncomfortable.

"What did he say?" asked Grace.

"N-nothing," stammered the kid. He glanced at his feet, and then at the frozen case. "I, um, I need to go and check about…" We never knew what the boy had to go and check about because he hurried away.

The old man looked up. *"Baliw,"* he repeated with an almost-scowl. Then he turned his attention back to the lemongrass.

"Ah," said Grace, in an overly-sweet voice. She grabbed my arm and rubbed up against me. "C'mon, Mister Baliw," she purred, "we still need some *gochujang* and an octopus."

* * *

Grace's place wasn't far, or perhaps I should say that Grace's *grandmother's* place wasn't far. We left the store and carried our purchases to the intersection of Maryland and Flamingo. Five minutes after taking a right we found ourselves at the entrance to Viva Vegas Towers. Behind a gate and guardhouse stood two Y-structure ten-floor complexes that had been built in the seventies - a time when, by southern Nevada standards, the property had been considered a high rise.

"That kid called you a 'gentleman'," Grace snickered as we entered the lobby.

"I don't think he used the term 'lady' in reference to *you,"* was my rejoinder. It earned me a dirty look.

Viva Vegas Towers was more of a metaphysical parallel to McKarran International than a senior living complex. The lobby, halls, and elevators were concourses to boarding gate apartments, in which travelers awaited their seating row announcements. Some received final calls before their rental agreements expired, whereas others' flights had been delayed for multiple leases. No matter. All planes eventually took off.

The gates at McKarran had glass walls that allowed travelers to watch aircraft, while Viva Vegas Towers balconies permitted residents to look at The Strip and wonder if their boarding passes would take the form of heart attacks, cancer, Alzheimer's or something more exotic. Also like McKarran's concourses, with their shops, bars, and souvenir kiosks, the Viva Vegas Towers lobby housed its own amenities, though these were definitely geared to the senior set. There was an in-house doctor's office and a tiny pharmacy. An overpriced convenience store featured arthritic-adapted hand baskets that bent shoppers carried through aisles too narrow for grocery carts. Wafting dye fumes signaled the presence of a salon where senior women stuck their heads inside Drying Cones of Noise and read tattered celebrity magazines. Presiding over it all, in a scene like old photos of the ~~Titanic's~~ *Olympic's* Grand Staircase, hung large lobby chandeliers that were spun in dusty cotton candy spiderwebs and draped with seventies imitation crystals that had yellowed with age like geriatric toenails.

Grace and I carried our bags past the desk. The man there merely nodded and forced a bored semi-smile as his eyes returned to a paper spread out over his crossed legs. It had been the same outside when we passed the gate guard.

"You're obviously not old enough to rent here. How come no one says anything?" I asked, as we walked past windows that looked into a deserted exercise room. The machines inside represented the best rheumatoid range-of-motion technology that the Carter era could have offered, but they were as dusty as the lobby's lighting fixtures. The exercise room's sunken hot tub had been set when the floor was poured, and though it still contained sporadic jet-driven bubbles, Vegas' hard water had left years of rough crusts and scratchy rings that looked as comfortable as broken coral.

"They know Grandma and me. Usually I'm with her," answered Grace. "Younger family members are allowed on the lease."

As we waited for the elevator, it occurred to me that

the lobby area was a proto-attempt at Summerlin's retirement atmosphere, but on a smaller scale. Here matters were condensed on a single level, and accessible by front doors and elevators rather than golf carts and community centers.

We rode up, stepped out on the fourth floor, and walked down the hall to apartment 416. Grace set her bags down and unlocked the door.

"Why don't you have a car?" I asked.

"I sold my car after my divorce. I miss that Civic."

"Are you going to get another one?"

"Well, I'll need something after graduation, but I'm not sure what I'll get. There's a Mercedes outside that belongs to Grandma. She wants me to use it, but I never do. What about you?" Grace pushed the door open and gestured for me to come inside.

"I don't know," I said, as I took off my shoes. "I think I'll just keep riding the bus for a while."

"Have you had many cars?" Grace asked, as she took our bags into the kitchen.

"I had a few pieces of junk when I was in high school," I answered in the direction of Grace's voice. *It's kind of funny*, I thought to myself. *When I was a kid, I worked more than one lousy job to get wheels, but now that Grandpa's lawyers can grant any car lot wish, I just keep on boarding the CAT.*

I wandered through the living room and toward the balcony. The apartment was on the north-eastern wing, so I could look far down Flamingo in both directions or take in a nice view of The Strip.

Old Slice. Somewhere in this place. *Everywhere* in this place. Maybe not in overpowering quantities, but in the air. Hanging around with Grace had attuned me to it - sometimes up close, sometimes from afar, and I could smell it at a distance like Petrus Romanus Pryce could smell young boys ulcerating to be men.

I heard the pad of feet behind me. "This place is great at night. The lights are beautiful," said Grace.

"Yeah," I agreed. "This is definitely the better side. It beats looking out over the ULVN campus."

"I don't mind the campus so much." Grace smiled. "Grandma likes to come out here and smoke when she thinks I'm asleep."

"Where is she now?"

Grace checked her watch. "Now? I'd guess that she's at my great aunt's place in Makiki. Wait, is that right? I can never remember Honolulu time." Grace counted ahead five hours, but still seemed unsure. "Yeah, they're probably sitting on the floor around an old red-lacquered wooden table, silly-drunk, eating fried beef and garlic." A look of affection crossed Grace's face.

"So you've got the place to yourself?"

"Yes. It's just me and the lonely Mercedes until next Wednesday. Grandma is more progressive than mom and dad - except for the cigarette thing. She still thinks that she's a girl in Pusan when it comes to smoking." Grace rolled her eyes but the affectionate expression remained. "Grandma will check the miles on the car when she comes home and chew me out for not driving it."

"Hell, let's take a ride sometime," I said. "Just to suit your grandma."

"Fine. Grandma is hoping that I'll take a road trip before the semester starts." Grace shrugged and changed the subject. "C'mon. Talk and cook."

I followed Grace through the dining room and into the kitchen. "I see that you have a regular table," I remarked.

"And chairs, too. Aren't they *great?* We usually keep five-foot kimchi pots all over the apartment." Grace's sarcasm made me realize that I had simply blurted out my observation.

"Touché," I sighed. "Okay, you're gonna hammer me for this too, but I don't really notice any--" I paused to emphasize my politically correct sensibility *"--ethnic kitchen aromas,* either. Just Old Slice, and I imagine it covers up a lot."

"You're a Vegas bumpkin," said Grace. "I'll tell you one more time: That's a perfume that Grandma brought back from her last trip, and she likes it, I'll have you know. We both do."

"Perhaps you'll forgive my plebeian error in mistaking an exotic scent for one more provincial," I replied with a silly flourish.

"Only due to your request's delicate nature," replied Grace in mock magnanimity, "and it so happens that you and I are about to break a house rule on such matters." Grace gestured at the bounty of spices and sauce from our earlier purchase. "That's why I'm guessing that Grandma is having a great time tonight, since she's not surrounded by cranky old Caucasians who bitch whenever they smell something besides meat and potatoes."

"You really are quite the rebel," I said with a smile. "You're cooking Korean food and *not* driving the car. Next, you'll be smoking on the balcony and inviting white boys in." I raised my hand to my mouth in exaggerated shock.

"Scandalous," was Grace's flat response. "Grandma probably wouldn't get too wound up about having you around, to be honest. She might put on for appearances, but only because she thinks that's what she's supposed to do."

"Not too traditional in that department, either?" I asked.

Grace tried to swallow a laugh but let out an embarrassing snort. "Sorry," she said, as she raised a hand to half-hide her grin. "You, ah, could say that, I suppose." Grace gestured for me to come closer and she spoke in a hushed gossiping-clothesline tone. "In fact, Grandma has a vintage saltine of her own." Grace wore a joking *can-you-believe-it* expression.

"Ha! That's great. She thinks you don't know?"

Grace nodded. "Yeah. It's so cute. I caught a glimpse of him once when I was leaving late." She paused and looked up from a cutting board. "Hey! Why am I doing this? This should be *your* job." Grace grabbed my hand and placed a kitchen knife in my palm. Then she pointed at the counter. "Peppers, celery, carrots. Get to work."

"Okay."

"And wash your hands."

"Okay," I repeated, as I put the knife down and reached for a bottle of liquid soap over the sink.

"Do you like it raw?" asked Grace, as she took the

limp octopus out of a plastic bag.

"It's okay raw," I answered, as I dried my hands and began to cut vegetables. "But I think that octopus has more flavor and better texture if it's boiled for a couple minutes."

"Ah. Me, too. You're the only non-Korean guy I know who can stand this much spice, let alone count *nakji bokkeum* as his favorite food," said Grace, as she mixed a series of very generous red dollops into the sauce.

"That might not be true," I said.

"No?"

"No. I'll bet that if you asked those old sergeants at the bar, there would be one or two who like Seoul octopus."

"Sergeants?" repeated Grace. She stopped stirring and looked confused.

"Yeah. Those old guys from Nellis."

Grace made a puzzled face. "What old guys? What are you talking about?"

I let out an exasperated sigh. "At the bar. You know? That place where you *work?*"

"Uh, you *know* where I work, genius," replied Grace. "We can see it from the balcony. Bookstar, on South Maryland." Her voice had an *okay-I'll-play-along* tone. "We walked right by it."

"Your second job."

"Yeaaah," said Grace. "My *second* job. My second job in a bar. I'm a bartender. Look at me mixing drinks. Amazing. Or maybe I'm a bouncer." She put on a tough face and flexed her biceps.

I brushed off Grace's theatrics. "I figured that your grandma wouldn't approve, but I've wondered what your alibi was. 'Hey, Grandma, I've got midnight extension classes at Nellis. But I don't need to use the car. Ted, Ted, the Smitten Musclehead is coming to pick me up.'"

Grace was no longer baffled, or bewildered, or even mildly amused. She just looked at me. "When you come up with a punch line for this, let me know," she said.

Fine, I thought. *She doesn't want to talk about it. Or maybe she thinks that her grandma has the place bugged or something.*

"I'll take those veggies now, weirdo."

I looked at the cutting board. I wasn't even close to being done, so I began to hurriedly chop.

"Wait! What are you *doing?*"

"I'm cutting up stuff! You said you wanted me to do this."

"Long diagonal cuts! Not like that," Grace said, as she took the knife out of my hand. "Haven't you ever...?" she began to ask, then closed her eyes and shook her head. Grace placed the knife on the cutting board and began to push me out of the kitchen. "Go," she said. "I'll bring it out when it's done."

"But, I can--"

"Go."

* * *

"I think I'm going to sweat all night," said Grace, as she patted a napkin against damp wisps of hair that clung to her forehead. Grace blinked on a few pepper tears, dried her eyes, and twisted her hair back into a bun that was held in place with crossed chop sticks. "Do you want the rest of mine?" she asked.

"Don't tempt me," I groaned, as I placed my hands on my full belly and slouched back in a patio chair. "For a Korean girl who's never actually been to Korea, you're one hell of a Korean chef," I said. "Thank you. That was wonderful."

Cars turned on their headlights as we watched the Flamingo traffic pass. After a few moments Grace stood, collected the plates, and took them inside. She returned with a small green bottle and two shot glasses.

"Jinro!" I exclaimed. "Nice touch!"

Can't have nakji without soju," Grace declared, as she twisted off the cap and filled both glasses. "*Gan-bei,*" we toasted.

"Care to have a drinking contest?" Grace devilishly asked.

"No way," was my instant reply.

"Ah. You really *have* been to Korea," Grace said with a grin.

"Oh yes. And one of the first things I learned was not to have drinking contests with Korean girls."

"Smart man, smart man," said Grace. "But we might as well finish this, because I can't leave a half-empty bottle in Grandma's stash." She looked at me and clicked her tongue. "Come *on*," Grace urged. "You're not even twenty-seven yet. Don't act like a stodgy old man. We can go up to Greenland Market and get a replacement before Grandma gets back."

* * *

At midnight there were three empty soju bottles and two limp humans on the living room floor. "I thought you said you didn't want – you didn't want – *hic* – to have a drinking contest," said Grace. She hiccupped again and giggled.

"This was no contest," I murmured. Then I sat up, swayed a moment, and propped myself against a sofa cushion. "I'm not wasted. I just have a heavy buzz."

Grace rolled onto her side. "And your stomach?"

"Fine. Don't worry. I'm not gonna puke on your grandma's carpet."

Grace collapsed onto her back again. "Damn right you're not."

"I don't feel too back. I mean, I don't feel too bad." It was my turn to giggle. "Hey. Hey," I said. "I wanna ask you something."

"What?" Grace sat up and leaned against the front of the sofa.

"How come, how come...?" I stopped in the middle of my question. I had forgotten what I was going to ask.

"How - *hic* - how come you're so fucked up? Because we raided Grandma's soju," laughed Grace.

"N-no," I said. "How come you're not dating?"

There was a pause. "Who says I'm not?" asked Grace, not quite in a huff.

"C'mon," I slurred. "Y-you're not seein' nobody."

"*Not seeing nobody?*" echoed Grace. "Are you - *hic* - sure that you're going to be a teacher? Why stop at a double negative? Let's go for a triple, shall we? *I ain't not seeing nobody.* How's that? And wasn't my 'ain't' nice?"

I ignored her diversion. "You could date, if you wanted to."

83

"So could you."

"But I'm...but I'm..." Once again I temporarily forgot what I wanted to say. "But I'm not. Well, not s-seriously."

"How profound," was Grace's response.

Before our conversational brilliance could resume, my fingers touched something that had fallen between the couch cushions. "How many channels do you get?" I asked, as I looked at the remote control. Grace just shrugged.

"Do you have...do you have...?"

"Do Grandma and I have cable?"

"Yeah."

"Yes, we do," Grace said, as she took the remote out of my hand. "I don't watch the TV much, but Grandma - *hic* - always watches some old movie channel and PBS." Grace hit the power button and a large entertainment center screen lit up.

"What are you in the mood for?" she asked.

"H-how about some music? Videos or something?"

"Okay," said Grace, as she pointed the remote in the screen's direction and pressed a button. Nothing happened. She frowned and looked at the remote, then held it up and pressed another button. Again, nothing. "Grandma," murmured Grace, "why do you keep doing that?" She made another half-hearted and unsuccessful attempt to change the channel, then dropped the remote on the couch. "S-sorry," Grace hiccupped. "Grandma has locked this program. I hope you like PBS." Grace slowly and carefully rose to her feet. "I gotta get some water. Do you want some water?" Without waiting for my reply, Grace listed toward the kitchen.

I heard the icemaker on the refrigerator turn on, followed by the clinks of ice cubes and the sound of pouring water. Grace came back with two glasses. "Stay hydrated," she said, as she handed me some ice water. "That way your hangover won't be so bad." Grace didn't have to tell me. I had learned that boozing principle years before.

The soju had brought some pleasant nostalgia, but when the cold water hit my tongue, I realized that I was thirsty for liquid that didn't remind me of watered-down vodka. We emptied our glasses in one go, then looked at each other and swirled our ice. "More," Grace said, as she took my glass and returned to the kitchen.

I glanced around the living room while I waited. "Did this place come furnished?" I asked.

Grace returned and handed me my refill. "No. We got this stuff--" Grace paused to swallow a hiccup "--at one of those sell-off places. Grandma picked it up when they cleared the old Aladdin."

"W-what's with that piece of linoleum?" I asked, as I motioned at a corner of the living room.

Grace leaned back on the couch and looked straight ahead. "Still dizzy," she mumbled. "What did you say?"

"What's up with the lino spread over the carpet?"

"Not lino," said Grace. "Wood veneer. Grandma likes it there. She says it reminds her of Korea, but it reminds *me* of Grandma."

"Oh," I said. "I have a thing for green shag, myself. That was my grandpa's flooring of choice." I paused for a moment's memory of Julie, *The Electronic Company*, and Grandpa's big Zenith TV. "But that's something I remember about Korea, too. Wooden floors with heating pipes underneath." I leaned forward to place my empty glass on a coaster. My motor skills were soju-soaked and I missed, but I got it right the second time. I leaned over again to wipe the coffee table with my shirt tail.

"Don't worry," smiled Grace. "Just no vomit on the carpet." A tiny hiccup escaped. Grace smiled and put her hand over her mouth.

"Your grandma locked the porn channel?" I asked.

Grace closed her eyes as she spoke in sodden sarcasm. "Yeah. Grandma likes Spicy TV."

I watched the muted screen for a few moments. "Well...I didn't know that guy had a show on PBS."

"What guy?" Grace still didn't bother to open her eyes.

"Oh, what the hell is his name?" I muttered, as my brain backfired in a skull-puddle of rice liquor. Then it came to me. "Ned. Ned Power. He makes pornos," I declared.

The TV program appeared to be an utterly wholesome DIY woodworking show. *I guess Power is broadening his horizons,* I thought, as I watched a bearded and graying forty-something fellow with glasses and a midsection-tight plaid shirt cut boards on a rip saw. An aspect of the wood was apparently very important to Power's presentation, because he silently pointed out something as he held up a section of a woodworking project. Suddenly, he was audible:

...and remember, before starting, that you must verify the moisture content of your pine stock to avoid warping. And, of course, always wear appropriate safety equipment and follow manufacturer guidelines...

There was soft drunken laughter beside me. I turned and saw that Grace had picked up the remote and unmuted Power. She was thoroughly entertained by his woodworking advice, and a few hiccups followed Grace's giggles. "I can understand why Norm Abraham works in porn," she said. "Talk like that always gets me *sooo - hic - hot.*"

"Who's Norm Abraham?"

Grace pointed at the TV screen. "Norm Abraham, host of the *New Yankee Woodshoppe.* If Grandma were here, she'd be watching this."

I wanted to say something, but I didn't feel like talking over Ned Power's vital wood-moisture-content advice. I reached over and hit the mute button. "No," I asserted. "That man is Ned Power, porn star." Adamance improved my drunken enunciation.

"Whatever," replied Grace.

"Goddammit! Seriously."

"Mumph." Grace curled up on the couch. "Do you jerk off to him?"

"No. To his co-stars," I indignantly said to the balled-up kitten. *Cute, sweet, and harmless - like a hand grenade sewn inside a rag doll.* "Oh, who am I kidding?" I grinned. "His hairy belly is amazing." I laughed while noting the way that Grace could turn me on a dime. *Sexy. Cute. Smart. Why wasn't she dating?*

"Grandma was going to get tickets to the *Antique*

Traveling Roadshow at Railhead Station but it conflicted with her trip. Abraham is going to have his own stage day."

"When?"

"Not sure. But the *Roadshow* is going on now."

"So is HotCon."

Grace opened her eyes. "Really? Where?"

"At Xanadu. Gee, I've never seen you so interested in porn."

"I think that we're on the same page, Mister Pretend X-K."

"Case of soju? For your grandma, of course."

"Deal."

6

And Real-Life Situations
Lose Their
Thrill

~~They~~ *I* Want To Know
Your Secret But
You Are Not
Telling

July
1994
(1-of-7)

When I met Grace in the Viva Vegas Towers lobby she tossed me a set of keys. "I think you remember where it's parked. I feel like being chauffeured."

*   *   *

Mirrors adjusted. Seats adjusted. Belts. Check, check, check. Hot car, hot girl, and...me.

Incongruity on four wheels.

"Of course, if you meet Grandma, none of this ever happened," Grace cautioned.

"None of what?"

"This," said Grace. "I'm under strict orders not to let anyone else drive."

"Nice time to tell me," I said, as I pulled out and took a right on Flamingo. "I really hope that's not for insurance reasons." If such were the case, then I would immediately stop and let Miss Daisy take the wheel of her grandma's panzer.

"No," Grace assured me. "Grandma's coverage is ironclad and comprehensive."

"Is she gonna dust for prints or something? You already said that she checks the odometer." When I only received a *maybe-so-maybe-no* smile, I decided to just trust that the license, registration, and insurance were in the glove box. I made a mental note to reset the seat when we got back, since Grandma would certainly notice Grace's nine-inch growth spurt.

It was fun to drive the Mercedes, though my presence behind the wheel was a case of automotive pearls before swine. The car was powerful, with an automatic transmission, lots of blue leather, and an A/C that scoffed at the Vegas summer. That was my best summation, since otherwise I really didn't know a damn thing about German luxury cars. If it wasn't an old Datsun or beat-up Toyota truck with a greasy and well-worn *Chillton's* behind the seat, then it was as familiar to me as a moon rock.

I took a right on Maryland and another at Tropicana. "One day we're going to put on our caps and gowns and walk down the middle of that place," Grace commented as we passed the Mack and Thomas Center.

"It's coming," I replied. "I hope that they clean up the dirt and cow crap beforehand."

"When does the National Rodeo start?"

"I don't know. When we see crowds of lost cowboys and horse trailers, I suppose."

"And when we see Rangler butts."

"Why, Miss Kwon! I do declare, you have a cowboy fetish!"

"Not necessarily that specific," laughed Grace. "By the way, you don't happen to have any Ranglers, do you?"

"Of course," I replied. "But I keep them locked up in the barn, otherwise my horse wears them around the apartment."

Grace giggled and rolled her eyes. "Okay, enough," she said. "I was going to follow up with a question about your equine endowment, but I'll let that go."

"Thanks," I said, as I made an exaggeratedly sad face and glanced downward at my crotch. Grace just shook her head.

After we crossed the intersection at Paradise, Grace pointed at McKarran's taxiing aircraft. "Does that remind you of the old days?" she jokingly asked.

"*The old days?* It was only a few years ago," I said. "And no, not really. I'm pretty sure that there aren't any weapon troops at commercial airports."

"But just the jets and stuff, I mean."

I took a quick left look through McKarran's boundary fence. "Nope. But," I continued, "don't take this in the wrong way, okay? I know that we kid around a lot, but... don't get pissed off."

"What? *What?* Out with it."

"Okay. I just--I just want to say that being with *you*

is what reminds me of the old days. *Good* old days," I quickly added.

Grace was silent for a moment. "I'm not offended by that," she said in a quiet voice. "Maybe I should be...but I'm not."

* * *

We bypassed the Cowardly Lion's shopping walk and went directly from MGM parking to the Flamingo footbridge. As we approached the Tropicana Hotel, Grace quizzed me on the events of the previous day, when we had paid a visit to the Railhead Station conference center.

"Okay, what did we see?" was her overly-general query.

I grimaced. "I don't know about you, but what *I* saw was a geek mob living out *Homes Improvement* fantasies via a porn star who made a fortune with his *Filthy Debutante* series."

"No," corrected Grace. "We haven't established that yet. What we saw was a man who injured himself while promoting woodworking tools."

"What, that scratch on his hand? That was hardly an injury."

"But it'll be enough to settle this," said Grace, in smug reference to our soju wager. "We both saw it, didn't we?"

"Yeah."

"There you go."

* * *

For me, *The Norm Abraham Sanding and Table Saw Spectacular* had been a sedative. I was the single burned-out light bulb on a bright marquee of hard core narrow-focus enthusiasts. When Abraham said something about a tiny detail of a saw blade, the entire house erupted in laughter. When he mentioned a minor feature concerning a table saw's motor, a stunned and amazed hush fell over the audience. The whole thing was a strange religion in which it was impossible for me to believe, because I didn't even understand. Or care.

That is, except for the final segment, the *pièce de résistance,* the somethin'-somethin' that seemed like it could be a telltale Venn intersection between the very

92

disparate worlds of a PBS host and the director, producer, and star of such "masterworks" as *Bus Station Buttfuck Babes, Volume IX.*

"I'm really excited about the applications of this next item," said Abraham. He was dressed in the same wholesome red plaid shirt, jeans, and shop boots that he wore on television, and his already prominent New England abdomen seemed additionally fortified by Nevada's western frontier buffets. "Once you've adjusted the new Dack and Blecker Sandro-Glove to your personal size," continued Abraham as he fastened a Velcro cuff, "you're ready to experience an entirely new dimension in personalized wood surfacing!" Abraham held up his hand to reveal a single glove that might have been an industrialized version of Mike J.'s rhinestoned trademark, except that it ran well up Abraham's forearm like a gauntlet wired to a pocket calculator. I looked around the audience. Everyone was on the edges of their seats. Grace even seemed mildly interested.

"Just take the Sandro-Power control," said Abraham, as he unclipped the small control box from his belt, "and start at a conservative setting. Then gradually match the unit's performance to the task." Even though we were seated some rows from the stage, Grace and I heard the glove's black wetsuit-like material make a buzzing sound.

Several items sat on a stage table. There was a small red stool, an orange picture frame, and a weathered and flaking half-scale wooden angel. Abraham put on a face shield and lightly caressed the legs of the red stool. Wherever the fingers of the Sandro-glove touched, they left bare wood. The house let out an awed gasp.

The empty frame was next. "And for multiple layers of paint or other heavy stripping challenges, simply increase the setting," Abraham said. The glove's buzzing tone changed pitch as he went on to leave the wooden frame as naked as the stool.

"Now, we can see that this statue includes some fine carving, especially around the face and wings," continued Abraham, as he gestured at the wooden angel. "The Dack and Blecker Sandro-Glove is quite capable of removing old varnish and oil without damaging delicate features." Abraham studied the statue for a few moments, smiled, adjusted the control, and effortlessly smoothed away every inch of the angel's old finish. As promised, no details, or at least any details that I could observe from my seat, had been sanded off.

Scattered orgasmic sounds came from the otherwise rapt attendees. They stood, first one, then two, and then whole rows of dorfs clapped in solemn reverence. For them, it would have been the perfect sweaty-sheet cigarette, but in the midst of giving a triumphant salute, Abraham threw his left hand back and accidentally caught the tip of the angel's wing. The Kaw-Liga seraph crashed to the stage and Abraham sustained a scratch on the back of his wrist. A member of the PBS camera crew stepped forward to provide a bandage.

Grace and I stood to half-heartedly applaud, because otherwise we would have been like two people who remained seated in the bleachers during the *Star Spangled Banner.* When Abraham nicked himself, however, the entire audience went still, like an anxious crowd holding its breath while a steel water tank is opened to find out if Houdini has drowned. In that awkward moment our perfunctory clapping echoed in the silence as Grace and I failed to react to the onstage situation as quickly as the rest. My face flushed and I jerked my hands down.

"He's okay! He's fine," announced the cameraman, as he put a band-aide wrapper in his pocket and knelt to pick up the angel. Abraham smiled and raised both his bandaged and Sandro-clad hands. Jubilant relief washed over the crowd.

I turned to Grace as she began to clap, but then she stopped and looked at me. Grace rolled her eyes and lowered her hands.

"Yes," I agreed. "Let's get the hell out of here."

A Boot Stomping On A Human Face
Every Monday, Thursday,
And Friday. Also
On Sunday *(By*
Appointment
Only)

July
1994
(2-of-7)

Instead of entering the Tropicana Casino, Grace and I took another footbridge over The Strip to Xanadu. Xanadu was a giant A-frame whose open interior was mimicked by Luxor, its much younger faux-Egyptian neighbor. Xanadu's twenty-four-floor east and west wings faced The Strip and I15 in sloped banks like a giant pup tent, while its end silhouette matched Luxor's pyramid. Xanadu had been constructed in the mid-seventies, when property developers had apparently believed that a Los Vegas casino could bear the name of an ancient Mongol capital if a sufficiency of vines spilled over its balconies. Years later, in an attempt to strengthen Xanadu's vaguely Asiatic theme, some large and highly stylized bronze tigers and *maybe* Chinese dragons were placed in the atrium and casino...but these merely caused Xanadu to appear as if Captain Steubing had married a P.F. Chang's to a *Six Million Dollar Man* episode.

As we walked through the valet port and were embraced by Xanadu's air conditioning system, Grace turned to me. "Did you ever hear that story about what they were originally going to build here?"

I shook my head. "I may have grown up in Vegas, but there's a lot of stuff that I don't know about this town."

"There was a gaming company that wanted to build a castle."

"A *castle?*"

"Yeah. Some kind of fairy-tale place. It was going to be called 'Excalibur', I think."

"How did you learn that?" I asked.

"The Marjory Barrack Museum on campus has a gaming exhibit with sketches and models and stuff. You should check it out sometime."

I was glad that the castle idea had failed because I had a sentimental history with Xanadu. I knew this place, though Xanadu itself had never really known what it was. Therefore, by default, it ended up as a reflection of plastic seventies fashion, mashed potato architecture, and a demoralized nation that had defaulted off the gold standard and lost its first major military conflict. Xanadu was forever wedged in a decade between divine sixties LSD and dehumanizing eighties crack. As an awkward middle child of Vegas history, it had inherited neither firstborn Rat Pack glories nor updated scenes of volcanoes, pirate ships, and desert Space Needles. Xandu was constructed on seventies dreams of a better future, but whether or not the eighties had *actually* heralded a "Morning in America" was irrelevant at 3850 Los Vegas Boulevard, because there it was always a long night of Vietnam denial, the Iranian Hostage Crisis, and short-shorts roller disco.

Nevertheless, I liked Xanadu. Grandpa had taken me there many times. There used to be a nightclub in the atrium during the Disco Era, and as a junior high kid I had watched the excitement from walkway overlooks. After Yvonne Ellison and the Gib Brothers faded the discotheque was temporarily succeeded by a hastily-conceived and rather generic Circus-Circus Adventuredome rip-off. Now Xanadu's tired interior had resigned itself to mimicking the Sammy's Town atrium with an abundance of real and fake trees, sculpted concrete rock formations, recorded animal sounds, and water features that pumped and re-pumped chlorinated Mercury Site strontium-90.

Grace and I navigated the random and psychologically delaying visual field that was the casino carpet. Random colors, shapes, and no real discernible theme was in itself the theme of every casino floor, as were blacked-out ceilings and featureless walls. These were the mental shackles of random reward systems. Flashes, chirps, bells. Dingdingding. Dingdingding.

Look at the machines. Look at the tables. There aren't any clocks here. The carpet is just messy quicksand. Sit down. Play some blackjack. Or some slots. Time has stopped. Relax. You're a winner. You have a right to feel special. And you will.

Promise.

What bullshit. What a mind fuck. Casinos were solipsistic vortexes, in that players could not be certain that homes, families, or even lives existed in the outside world. Was there *really* an outside world at all? It was hard to tell, amid the rush of cards and chips. Some people fought the addiction, whereas others embraced a codex. Like most locals, however, Grace and I were immune to both. This was a requirement of Vegas Valley residence, otherwise you weren't really a local, or at least you wouldn't be for long.

I spotted the line before Grace did. It had to have been the HotCon line, I reasoned. The attire, accouterments, and conduct indicated that it couldn't have been anything else. There were people in casual street clothes, but other attendee appearances were thematically appropriate for a convention that celebrated professional sexuality. Lots of latex. Lots of leather. Lots of skin. HotCon was the tide that lifted all vessels...and the waiting crowd knew that the collective floating of their individual boats was close at hand.

Abandon all hope, ye closed-minded who enter here...but hold onto your butt plugs, trust chains, and Vinny D'Onofrio grain-silo-water-tank-flesh-suspension rings.

* * *

Something that I always felt was overlooked about trust chains was the fact that they required goodwill from *everyone,* and not just from one's partner, or partners, as in the case of multiple-strand links. Stainless steel was okay...if you were destitute and without taste. Most chains were 14K, though this could have posed an awful invitation to criminals, as well as imbuing the term "snatch-and-grab" with horrific new connotations. This wasn't an original thought on my part, however, since many of the chains had rather obvious magnetic safety clasps.

As we got closer to the line, I noticed that this particular form of mutual adornment had grown in popularity. Of course, at Folsom Street there would have been no problem with people standing around and openly displaying their Prince Albert Pluses and deep VCH connections like genital tin cans on strings...but this was a Nevada casino, and the most that was permitted, at least until the main attraction opened and inhibitions could be cast aside, were chains that draped downward from almost-nonexistent skirts or Daisie Duke cameltoes, then back up into bulging black leather flies and spandex banana hammocks.

A few autograph seekers had pens and posters that depicted their favorite adult performers. A woman behind us carried a bag that held a dildo, and I assumed that it had some kind of sentimental value, since it seemed rather unremarkable. Every few minutes the woman took it out and rubbed it between the two inflatable life rafts that hung from her breastbone. She waited for security to walk past before pulling this routine, and the way the woman tittered reminded me of a note-passing grade schooler.

All-in-all, the good times appeared to have started in the waiting area. This was a church social. Robin's-egg-sweater ladies prepared ice cream beyond the atrium ropes while the deacons honed their fellowship deliveries. They weren't ready for the flock. Not just yet. Xanadu had never upgraded to an actual convention space, and prepping the make-do central interior took some time. This genuine celebration of phony cling-clang sex in a fake rim-ram jungle would wonderfully and essentially reflect Los Vegas.

The atrium entrance was usually unregulated. On non-event days anyone could wander through and enjoy the sights, but now the passage from the casino to Xanadu's hollow core was blocked by a particular breed of enforcer. From a distance, they could pass for police. That was the idea. SiteSec's whites and Wackyhut's turkey bacon blues were deliberately avoided, though closer inspection revealed corporate badge numbers that were on file with Xanadu security and not the LVPD.

The line behind the ropes was long, but not all of the security personnel manned the barrier. Four Pinky Floyd Pork Inflatables were outside the ropes. They moved up and down the line and looked for those who didn't seem to fit. As we lined up behind the rest, Grace snickered.

"What?" I asked.

"Did you ever watch *Sesamie Street?*"

"Sometimes. It was on before *The Electronic Company.*"

"Do you know the *One of These Things* song?"

I paused. "Oh yeah," I said. "I think Ernie sang it." I began to recite the tune. *"One of these things doesn't belong here, one of these things is not like the others —"*

"Shhh! Stop," said Grace as she grabbed me and buried her face in my chest. I felt warm bursts of breath through my shirt as Grace muffled her laughter. She raised her head and looked at me with both a grin and glaring eyes, then nodded at an interaction that one of the House cops was having with someone a few yards down the line. We only heard one side of the conversation:

Hello folks. Xanadu Security. I noticed that you have your children with you today, and I just wanted to make you aware that this is the line for HotCon. No, no. Well, it's a...convention of leading figures in the adult entertainment industry. Ahem. Yes. No. The buffet line is at the other end of the gaming floor. Perhaps you're thinking of Sammy's Town. Yes. In that establishment the buffet is indeed located near the atrium. No. The other end of the gaming floor. Yes. Of course, I'll be happy to escort you.

"Wow," I said, after the family passed by. "I wonder what kind of 'buffet' those parents thought this line was for? That guy obviously isn't a real cop."

"Yeah, I'd say that this is his part-time thing," said Grace. "The rent must come from a second customer service job."

"Unlike him," I said, as I again lowered my voice and

looked over Grace's shoulder. "I'm guessing that a private security job was his 'B Plan' after he got kicked off of the police force or discharged from spec-ops." Grace started to turn around, but I grabbed her shoulder. "Slowly," I whispered.

This House cop was unlike the other. He was buff and bald. His tight sleeves contained sixty-five pound curl swelling. He walked up and down the line – no, *paced* up and down the line, looking, looking, looking. On his belt he wore a frustratingly tethered stick and an unfairly holstered .40. The turkey bacon liked to caress both captives, until he realized that someone might be watching, and then he hastily lowered his hands. But the longing fingers slowly crept up again to feel the pistol's polymer frame and the metal nub of the magazine's floorplate that was small and firm like an engorged clitoris. The turkey bacon's other hand slowly stroked the smooth length of a black billy club that ached to smash the skull of a nothing civilian.

The pleasure and release in feeling a cranial collapse...the orgasmic penetration of broken bone through skin...red ejaculate pulsing out a cherry creampie...it was so hard to resist.

But...not here. Not now. At least, not all the way, no matter how good it might feel. Another time. Another place. **Soon.**

- *Well, maybe just a* **little.**
- **But what about the casino cameras?!**
- *Don't worry. They're watching the tables.*
- **We can't! All of these people will see!**
- *Shhh...we're just doing our duty...it'll be justified...it's* always *justified...c'mon...*
- **Maybe...maybe just a little taste...oh yesss...**

The First Annual ~~Montgomery Burns~~ *L.T. Horluchl* Award For Outstanding Achievement In The Field Of Law Enforcement Excellence

July 1994 (3-of-7)

"Thank you, miss," said Sergeant Ron Norres of the Los Vegas Police Department. "This is a preliminary report, so I'd like to re-verify your name, address, and telephone number. You may be contacted for further statements or testimony."

I placed a hand on Grace's arm, but she shrugged it off and shot me an *I'm okay* look. "Sure," she said. "Grace Kwon, Apartment 420, Viva Vegas Towers 10611 East Flamingo, 89119. 702-252-1973."

"Mine, too?" I asked.

"After Miss Kwon has finished. Occupation?"

"Student," answered Grace.

"Okay," said Sergeant Norres. "And you were in line for the, ah...*convention event?*"

Grace nodded.

"Convention event," I repeated to myself. *C'mon sarge. Don't be such a violence-loving and sex-hating robot. You can say it. It's okay. HotCon.*

"Show me where you were," directed Norres in a flat voice, and Grace silently pointed at a spot near Xanadu's atrium entrance. Several yellow tape barriers enclosed the area and white-gloved PD personnel daubed Q-tips at red pools on the floor. Others took photos and used tape measures to record distances between a short string of bullet holes in Xanadu's wall. When I eavesdropped on nearby interviews I heard minor detail variations, but everyone related similar stories.

"Tell me what you saw," said Norres.

Grace took a deep breath, and it was then that I saw through her tough façade. Her eyes were clear and she seemed composed, but when Grace inhaled she shuddered in small gasps like a child that is on the last leg of a nine-round temper tantrum. Hesitatingly, I again placed a very light hand on her arm, and again it was instantly pushed away.

"Uh, well," began Grace, "it happened really fast. Everything was fine, you know, it seemed like people were having a good time. Then that guy –"

"Do you mean Security Officer Drabbus?"

"Is that his name?" asked Grace. Sergeant Norres nodded. "Okay, yeah, he was walking around, and the couple over in that part of the line," Grace motioned ahead, "were just having a moment, nothing really hardcore or anything, just kissing."

"Continue."

"Ummm, what were the names of the man and woman?" asked Grace.

"That information isn't important," replied Sergeant Norres in a curt tone. "Continue."

Grace paused and looked up, then took another shaky breath. "Okay, he - *Drabbus* - yelled something at the couple, maybe 'get a room' or something–"

"So you can't remember exactly how the civilians verbally assaulted Security Officer Drabbus?"

Wait a goddamn minute, I thought. *What did he just say?*

"They didn't say anything, I don't think. They were just kissing," said Grace.

"Is that all?"

"Well...well, yes, but that Drabbus guy didn't even give them time to stop. He just grabbed their TC–"

"TC?" Sergeant Norres glanced up from his report form.

"Trust chain," clarified Grace. "One of those chains that lovers use to connect their--"

"I'm aware of what it is," Norres interrupted. "Then what?"

"He tore it out! Of both of them! He--" Grace clapped a hand over her eyes as she tried to block out the terrible scene.

This time Grace didn't push me away. She reached out and I took her in my arms. I didn't say anything, and in mere seconds Grace's composure returned. I sensed how something that had melted in a difficult moment cooled down and re-hardened, but not so hard that I didn't receive a small and grateful look when Grace let go.

Norres waited.

"So," continued Grace, now in an almost clinically detached tone, "the man and woman just fell down and curled up. The woman started to scream, but the man...he just froze. He didn't make any sounds, and I think part of his dic--uh, *penis,* was still on the chain." Grace looked over at the crime scene. "Someone picked it up already."

"Got it," nodded Norres. "Go on."

"Then Drabbus started hitting them with his stick. First he beat the man, and I thought that the guy might be dead or in shock, maybe. The man and woman were both on the ground. The man was bleeding so much, it was like blood was just running out of his pants. The woman, too, she was bleeding, but not like the guy. Then one of the other guards shot Drabbus in the - leg, I think?" Grace looked at me and I nodded. She turned back to Norres. "Yeah. Drabbus was down, but still trying to get his own gun out when the other guards jumped on him."

"So initially, Security Officer Drabbus used his stick to defend himself, but then the civilian attack became so violent that he was forced to draw his sidearm?

Grace looked at the cop.

I looked at the cop.

Pause.

"You know, I think I'll let you take a moment to think about that," said Sergeant Norres, "and while you do, hand over your driver's licenses so that I can get your home addresses." The cop's smile and tone were very slow and very cold. When I answered, I also spoke very slowly, and very, very carefully.

"Sir, we rode the bus. I'm carrying ID, but it's only my school ID. My ULVN Rebellion Card." Softer, softer still, like a man pulling a bomb out of a bear trap. "With your permission, I can reach into my pocket and get it out, although I don't think it shows my address. Sir."

Don't call it. Pleasepleaseplease don't call it...

"You know, when civilians get frisked, a lot can go wrong. Really, really wrong." Norres paused for effect. "So if I have to search you for suspected drugs or weapons, I'm not going to discover that you actually *are* in possession of a state-issued ID, am I?"

We were in a crowd. The security room eyes-in-the-sky were upon us. There were other cops nearby, and some of them *might* have had enough semi-humanity to step in if Norres totally lost it. There were TV cameras, too. Everything would be on the Rodney King record, and Norres knew it. So I just *breathed* my answers.

"No, sir."

Norres stared at me. "Well, then I suppose we'll do the best we can." He raised his report form and pen, but never took his eyes off of me. "And I guess I don't have to tell you that lying to law enforcement is a felony." Norres' eyes bored into me like drills. "You know, a trip to the detention center can get bumpy. You may beat the rap, but you won't beat the ride."

Something shifted inside of me. In that moment I knew that Norres wasn't really a man, but merely a uniform trying to cover up for another uniform. Ultimately, it would do whatever it wanted to do, so my next bluff came a little easier. What would happen, would happen.

"Name and address."

"Jack Coolidge. 2830 Decatur, Cross Apartments, number fifty-eight."

"Zip."

"89104."

"Phone?"

"702-854-6250."

The uniform looked at Grace, then at me, then back at Grace. "You know, I didn't quite get your address, Miss *Kim.*" The uniform raised its clipboard. "Give it to me again."

There was softness from Grace as well. "My name is Grace *Kwon,* officer," she said before repeating her information. When she was finished, the uniform gave a satisfied nod and turned to me. "Now you. Again."

I'm Jack. My mother's family name was Coolidge. My mother and father died crossing the intersection of Sahara and Decatur when they were twenty-eight and thirty. Twenty-eight plus thirty equals fifty-eight, which reversed is eighty-five, and that was how old Grandpa was when he died. I'll never forget the zip code of that intersection. Sin City 702. Grandpa died at age eighty-five when my Air Force Specialty Code was 46250.

"Alright," said the uniform. "I'm guessing that you two have thought about that other matter, and that you'll both do the right thing." The uniform looked slowly at Grace, then at me, and added: "Most of the officers here know Jerry Drabbus from when he was on the force. If you keep that in mind, there won't be a need for interviews down in County."

Good luck in finding us, I thought, as the uniform swaggered away to continue its intimidation campaign.

For An Acquaintance Who
Seldom Forces ~~Himself~~
Herself, But Is
Difficult To
Be Rid
Of

July
1994
(4-of-7)

- *You can cry in front of me. You don't have to cover your face.*
- I'm not crying.
- *Not now...but you were when we got back to the parking garage.*
- Please drop this.
- *But you're my friend.*
- And you're mine. Listen, I appreciate the concern, but let it go.
- *Alright. Alright!*
- I didn't mean it like that. Sorry.
- *Don't be. That was fucking awful. What's wrong with people?*
- Everything.
- *Sure you're okay?*
- What did I just tell you?! Alright, tell me: Are *you* okay?
- *Well, yeah. I mean, that was pretty fucked up, but I'm okay.*
- Then this is all that you need to remember: If you're okay, then I'm okay. Automatically.
- *Automatically?*
- Yes.
- *Why is that?*
- Because I'm stronger than you.
- *Oh.*

I started the car and turned on the air conditioner. "You're smarter, too," I added.
"How?"

"By giving that pork rind a phony apartment number…though maybe you should have given a fake complex, too, but no matter. That was still good thinking."

"I'd say you're flattering me, because the fake address was *your* schtick, and I liked the way that you could repeat all of that nonsense without a mistake." Grace seemed sincere, but then I realized that not only was she tougher and smarter, but she was also a far better actor.

"Oh, right," I said, as I solemnly nodded with a face as serious as an amateur such as myself could manage. "It wasn't a fake address." I turned and winked. Grace gave me a confused look, but I understood. It was key to stay in character all of the time. You never knew who might be watching.

All bases covered.

Better. Stronger. Faster.

Bionic Grace.

* * *

"What is that guy putting out?" Grace asked, as she watched a man swiftly tucking papers under windshield wipers.

"Fliers. Probably porn," I guessed.

Grace looked at me until I got out of the car.

The guy's clothes were dirty, his hair was long and stringy, and his face was a sun-dried apple. The sole on one of his cheap shoes was about to fall off. He carried a dirty cloth sack that might have once been a laundry bag, and inside were wads of fliers wrapped in rubber bands. He had to work fast, since cam-alerted security was probably already coming to shoo him away, and then he would be back in the hot Strip sun handing out hooker cards to passing tourists.

"Hey. Whatcha got?" I called out as I locked and closed the Mercedes' door.

The man's head jerked up. He saw that I wasn't

MGM security, but he still skipped the Mercedes and flipped wipers on a neighboring Olds.

"Fliers," he said. "Take one?"

"Sure. What're they for?"

"No idea. Just paid to shuffle." The man frisbeed a paper my way and disappeared behind the next row of vehicles.

He's just Transporting *lots and lots of little Li-Hui Lin slips all over Vegas,* I thought, *and refusing to look at the contents of his bag because he thinks it makes him more of a pro than Jason Staytham.*

A one-shoed survivor getting by on fantasy.

Hang in there, Bo Jangles.

Grace unlocked the door and I got back into the car. The vehicle's interior could not keep out an eruption of car alarms that now echoed through the parking garage. I laid the paper on the center console and buckled in. Grace picked it up as I piloted the Mercedes in a downward spiral to street level.

"It looks like we didn't have to go to Xanadu," she said.

"Why's that?"

"Because, according to this, Ned Power has been banned from the property pending...pending..." Grace looked at the flier to quote it directly. *"Pending investigation of the incident,"* she read.

"Incident?"

"Yeah. It doesn't say what 'the incident' was, but here's a hammy of Power shrugging and grinning. Any idea?"

"No," I answered. "I'm afraid I'm not current on the local porn scandals."

"Hmmm...it looks like he's throwing a swastika," observed Grace.

"What?"

"A swastika. He's making the sign."

"Since when is Ned Power a *racist?*"

Grace shrugged. "I'd say he's a better pornographer than Nazi. His swastika is backward."

I gave the picture a quick glance and saw that Grace was correct. Power's thumbs and index fingers were hooked together in an ineptly reversed crooked cross.

"What a dumb ass," I muttered.

"Maybe he's a Buddhist," quipped Grace.

"Doubtful," I snorted.

Grace continued to study the picture. "I suppose that Abraham and Power really do look alike."

"So what's the point of that flier? Just to tell people that he won't be at HotCon?"

"It says that he's got a competing show at the Adult Ultrastore."

"Which one?" I asked.

"*The* Adult Ultrastore," Grace said, as she pointed westward.

Really? I thought. *No more time to process what just happened?* Hmmm. Well, I guessed that none of the HotCon mess had directly involved *us.* I was shocked, but I felt okay. Plus, I had a new Grace Rule that I could use to determine how she felt. But still...I was unsure. I didn't go back to the eastbound lane at the Koval light. Instead, I pulled out from the MGM to the edge of Tropicana. I could only take a right and proceed to The Strip, but I put on the turn signal anyway. I figured that it was the easiest way to ask her if she was certain without *actually* asking.

"If you're okay, then you know how I am," Grace repeated as she looked straight ahead.

Roger that.

Next stop: The Adult Ultrastore.

~~Saving Private Ryan~~
Clamping
Airman
Gomco

July
1994
(5-of-7)

Cross The Strip. Pass the Rio and the hulk of Pink E's. Pass Budget Weeklies, Wendy's, and Wild Bill's. But if you pass the New Orleans, you've gone too far. If you cross Wynn, you'll have to turn around. If you go under the tracks, then you haven't paid attention.

The Adult Ultrastore. Safety and hygiene were never issues there. Security staff monitored both the store and the parking lot, while horny germ freaks were comforted by Lysol fumes in the bathrooms and Byotrol vapors in the booths. The Adult Ultrastore was West Tropicana's landmark equivalent to West Sahara's Statue of Liberty. A *perpetual* HotCon in two-story blue-and-purple Mission-style, the Ultrastore was open all day, every day, to satisfy everyone's consenting adult needs – even on Christmas. *Especially* on Christmas.

Social stigmas regarding massive sex shops dissolved at the Adult Ultrastore like sugar in wormwood, for it was as respected in the Vegas community as a sacred prostitute in ancient Rome. This again made me wonder what Ned Power had been up to at Xanadu with his little "incident." It couldn't have been *that* bad, I reasoned, or else the Ultrastore would have also banned him. Ishtar could be as much of a prude as Inanna, especially when they were both in town for the same convention.

Grace and I weren't on a date, of course, but the situation still made me reflect upon how I hadn't paid a ritual visit to the Adult Ultrastore in a long while. Everyone who came of age in the Vegas Valley had their first Ultrastore date. It was a special moment when couples, young and old, knew that it was time. For the jeeps, it meant sifting through professional cheese and Shatner spasms in search of clips and electrodes and other youthful paraphernalia, while for the aging hormonal drop-off crowd the Ultrastore was a heroic measure ER of poppers, cock rings, and nine-Inch rubber resuscitation.

The Adult Ultrastore had nothing to offer for those whose sexual thrills derived from the depraved and dangerous, because its inventory was as safe as its disinfected surfaces and patrolled premises. Everything was screened and checked. No hidden snuff in coded packaging, no Franklins in the amateur section. Records on file, custodians listed, and 18+ at the time of filming. Big names, big companies, safe sex, and even safer sales.

The Ultrastore should have a wedding chapel, I thought. *That would be cool.* I felt mildly nostalgic. I wanted to ask Grace when she had last ventured out this way, but as I turned off Tropicana I thought better of it.

* * *

"It looks like a county fairground," I observed.

"Ummm, *yeaaah,*" agreed Grace Lumbergh. "It'll be *greaaat.* Big tents and sawdust and hotdogs."

"And not even as bad double entendres," I added as I found a spot for the Mercedes. As we left the car I took note of the people in the growing crowd. They didn't seem very...*exotic.* By comparison, Xanadu's bunch made the Ultrastore folks look like the rings of a thousand-year-old Mundane Tree. Singles, couples, polys, and swappers. Gay, straight and everyone in-between. Some ULVNers, some geriatrics. But no latex. Very little leather. No *exceptionally* exotic surgeries.

Is this a Kiwanus fundraiser? I wondered. *Are kids going to start showing their prize-winning steers? Did these people show up for NASSCAR?* It seemed like Grace and I had a greater chance of meeting Danika Patrik than Tera Patrik.

The Ultrastore event incorporated a funnel strategy. The main stage and tent complex were surrounded by cones, tape, and SiteSec slugs. To get inside the event, one had to enter via the Ultrastore's front entrance, be digested through the merchandise, and shat out the back.

"Whoa, whoa," said Grace, as we approached the

admission table. "Twenty-five bucks? Just to walk around a parking lot?"

"But we'll get to rub elbows with the stars," I joked. "Plus, we can pick up some cherishable keepsakes."

Grace looked dubious.

"And a case of what your grandma likes costs more that twenty-five bucks. At least here in the States."

At that, Grace continued toward the Ultrastore's entrance. "Let's do this," she said.

We bought the Beast's hand stamp, stepped inside, and discovered that the line diverged into separate areas of interest. One path went straight ahead to the booths and shows, though a red-lit sign informed potential peepers and Cleanex Kings that there weren't any vacancies. A staircase led to the second floor's tees, herbals, magazines, and mood wear. The Left Hand Path went to bathrooms, offices, and stock. Grace and I took a right to movies and toys.

We waltzed among other shoppers, simulated genitalia, walls of whips, clit vacuums, penis pumps, and racks of flicks. Grace was leading me to the large glass dildo case when someone cut in on our dance. Well, it was more of a *something,* rather than a *someone.* It was a weird déjà vu in two parts. The first manifested itself as an illusory sensation, while the second appeared in the form of a Robert Blayke avatar.

First, the sensation.

I felt as if I were looking backward through a pair of binoculars. For a moment Grace seemed far away and at the end of a blurry mental tunnel. The woman in the mirror was closer than she appeared, however, and Grace slowly grew nearer and returned to focus. Though perhaps it wasn't Grace. But it was someone who, from behind, looked like Grace. Was it Grace? I couldn't be sure. The woman stood with her back to me as she contemplated the glass case's penile goods. The case itself seemed to have changed. No longer was it the massive wall cache of cocks, but a rather humble little offering with only a dozen or so dildos. The wall display also seemed to have transformed into a kind of –

vending machine? Yeah, that was what it resembled. No longer was it a special place that required the key of an Ultrastore employee like a diamond case in a jewelry store. It was now similar to a machine that sold cold drinks. All one had to do was feed a few thousand ~~won~~ through the slot, but instead of a can of soda, a nice new rubber penis would be dispensed.

I no longer stood in a pornographic supermarket. Rather, I was in a long hallway with many doors that were numbered 1,2,3,F,5,6,7,8,9,10, and they didn't go all the way down to the floor. Instead, they sat over raised thresholds that might have been as high as eight inches. The noises behind the doors were obviously those of people fucking, but I couldn't understand the words that were mixed with cries of passion. It might have been because they were muffled, or it might have been because they weren't screamed in English.

Hmmm.

Now, about that Robert Blayke matter...

He walked down the hall toward me. The scene wasn't *Beretta 92F*. It was full-on David Linch. It was *Lost Freeway*. He was the Mystery Man, in all of his red lipstick and heavy pancake majesty. And me? Apparently, I was Will Pullman.

The Mystery Man's creepy eyes looked through me. The expected *Lost Freeway* party scene dialogue came out of our mouths:

- *We've met before, haven't we?*
- I don't think so. Where was it you think we met?
- *In Film Hotel, at Bucheon Station. Don't you remember?*
- No, no, I don't. Are you sure?
- *Of course. As a matter of fact, I'm there right now.*
- What do you mean, you're where, right now?
- *In room 416. Film Hotel.*
- That's fucking crazy, man.

- Call me. Dial the number. Country code eighty-
two. Go ahead.
- I told you I was here.
- How did you do that?
- Ask me.
- How did you get inside the Film Hotel?
- You invited me. It is not my custom to go
where I'm not wanted.
- Who are you?
- Give me back my phone.
- It's been a pleasure talking to you.

I returned his phone, and the Mystery Man faded into the shadows at the far end of the hall. As he disappeared, other things reappeared. I found myself back at the Ultrastore. At some point I must have walked over to the dildo case, because I was now beside Grace. I turned and looked at her. Yes, that person was definitely Grace and that was definitely the Ultrastore's glorious dildo collection. I glanced around, but I only saw the Ultrastore's inventory and the other shoppers. I looked at Grace again.

"*Jesus! Give me a break, will you?!*"

"What?"

"I'm a straight woman, okay? I like dicks. OKAY? Get over it."

"Wha-what do you mean?" I stuttered.

"I mean, stop staring. You've been giving me weird looks."

I took a breath and looked around again. No hallways, no doors, and no Robert Blayke. "I'm sorry," I said. "I feel kind of strange. I think that I just had a waking dream or something. I didn't mean to stare."

Grace studied me for a few seconds. When she spoke her tone indicated belief. "Sorry. I didn't mean to snap. Are you alright?" She smiled a little smile. "Well, I *did* mean to snap...but I'm sorry that I misunderstood."

I shook my head. "Yeah, I'm okay. It was just... *strange.* I don't know what just happened." I took some more deep breaths. "And to clarify, I don't have a problem with your dildo admiration. The opposite, actually. I'd sooner smash a stained-glass window than insult a connoisseur such as yourself."

"Careful, Dreaded Pirate Roberts," warned Grace.

"No, really," I said. "Look at the quality here, the detail in concept and skill in execution. Masterworks."

Grace grinned. "I think realism owes to the fact that this part of the case holds life casts. These aren't Michelangelos, I'm afraid." Grace pointed to where each synthetic phallus bore the name and nude picture of its corresponding porn star. These particular dildos were anatomical-study grade, whereas lower shelves only contained discounted and oddly-colored latex cylinders with small clit-teasing protuberances attached near their bases.

"Yeah, I know what you mean," said a voice behind us. "But Lovellyx still does a great job with their repros. I liked working with those guys. They were very professional."

Grace and I turned to see a forty-something, yet very boyish face with a not-quite-pug, not-quite-button nose and a rakish shock of golden hair parted on the side. The man's short sleeved-shirt was red rayon that smoothly draped over his pecs and well-muscled arms. A naked Geoff Striker usually smiled or had a Zoolandish "Blue Steel" thing going on in his movie posters, but here he stood, fully clothed and gazing into the dildo case with a rather somber expression. He was sharing his thoughts with two strangers, rather than fucking them on camera, and his silent stare told me that he was looking at something a lot further away than the simulated-penis inventory.

One-Mississippi. Two-Mississippi. Three-Mississippi...

"Nice to meet you, Mr. Striker," I said, as I put out my hand.

The porn star's presence returned with a blink. He took my outstretched palm and smiled.

"Call me Caspar," he said. "And you are?"

"I'm Jack, and this is my friend, Grace."

"Hi," said Grace.

"Here for Power?" asked Striker.

"Yeah," said Grace. "We went to HotCon, but something happened that closed the show. Power wasn't there, anyway."

Striker grimaced. "Neo-Nazi or not, I think that it'll be a long time before he's allowed back at Xanadu."

What the hell happened at Xanadu? I wondered again.

"Would you like an autograph?" asked Striker.

"Yeah, sure," I said. "Er, I don't have –"

"That's okay," said Striker. "I can get something from the clerk." He returned a few moments later with two signed glossies of a naked, gigantically hung, and considerably younger man. The pictures were as casually proffered as salt at mealtime, but the act of taking a signed genitalia-centered shot from the subject himself seemed kind of surreal to me. Not so for Grace, however. She thanked Striker and smiled as she checked out his picture. Then she held the shot up to the dildo case for comparison.

"Pretty true-to-life," she observed.

"Yeah, like I said, the Lovellyx team does great work," agreed Striker. "But sometimes I wonder if my cast would look better with a foreskin." Striker pointed to another enormous cock behind the glass. "Take Lonny Randsome, for instance. He looks terrific uncut." Striker sighed, ran his fingers over the case like someone mourning over a coffin, and leaned close enough to fog the glass. Grace lowered the picture as an uncertain look crept across her face.

Striker sighed again. "I've lost more than just my snoodle," he lamented. "I had some dreams once. I wanted to be a nurse."

Grace gave me an uneasy glance. I shrugged slightly, and her eyes returned to Striker. She put on a weak smile, though she needn't have, because the porn star wasn't seeing us anymore.

I suddenly couldn't see Striker or Grace anymore, either.

I heard *another* Grace sing a tune that lent new meaning to the act of "going down the *White Rabbit* hole":

One dildo makes you larger,
And one dildo leaves you small.
And the one the Ultrastore sells you,
Doesn't get you off at all.

Was there hallucinogenic gas it the ventilation system? This was a perfectly reasonable question, since I seemed to be having another Adult Ultrastore Reality Break.

The products within the dildo case turned into rows and rows of enormous corndogs that revolved under convenience store heat lamps. I was in a hallway...but not like before. It had standard yankee-doodle GSA doors. The floor was covered in GSA tile. I spotted a *Gauntlette* video arcade game inside a barracks dayroom.

Oh shit. The Mystery Man approached again.

JACK NEEDS REALITY, BADLY!
JACK NEEDS REALITY, BADLY!
JACK NEEDS REALITY, BADLY!

Hey. That's wasn't Robert Blayke. That was...Clarence. The angel.

"I'm not sure why *you're* here," I said. "I've never wished not to have been born." *Awww.* Clarence was such a cute little guy. He was a perfectly indispensable and utterly polite angelic butler. I loved Clarence's WWII-era RAF uniform, but he seemed rather old to be an Angel Second Class.

"Yes, I'm quite baffled myself. Have you had an inclination to jump from a bridge lately?"

"No."

"Well then, I'm off." Clarence snapped to attention and gave me an open-handed English salute.

"Please don't do that," I said. "I'm enlisted, like you."

"Right," Clarence replied, as he marched down the hall.

"And no goose-stepping, either!"

*   *   *

I'm going to my barracks room and turning in. If I'm
late to day shift, Master Sergeant Jones will have a shit
fit. Now, where's my door?

Ah. This is it. **Except it looks like I'm already here
with Carl.** Well...maybe this isn't my room. No, no. This
is definitely *my room. So why are Cornfaggot and Jack-
Off here? I don't know, but I'll play along. I have to, or
else someone will guess my secret. I always know
exactly what to say, and just how to act.

"Why're you homos up in this pig?" I ask. "NCO club
all full?"

"Hey Peterson," says Jack. Carl nods, then asks:
"What's up Peterson? You need something?"

"I need a hot pussy hole." Heh. Perfect answer,
perfect lie.

"I mean, is there a reason why you're in my room?"
asks Carl.

"Your room?" I shoot back. "Cornfaggot, you have
cum in your brain. This is my room, and I'm crashing."
Still in uniform, I jump up onto my bunk. Then I take off
my boots and let them hit the floor, followed by my shirt.

**Excuse me? Over here, gentlemen. On the bunk.
EXCUSE ME!
I SAID: "FOLLOWED BY MY SHIRT." HELLLOOO?
THAT MEANS I EXPECT TO SEE LITTLE SPARKLES IN
YOUR EYES, BOYS.**

**Jack...?
Carl...?**

Breeder bastards.

They only glance over. Carl puts his hand on his
forehead, closes his eyes for a second, and goes back to
talking. So I have to interrupt. Goddammit, I WILL be
acknowledged! I've never been this buff and beautiful.
Or maybe this short and obnoxious. Heh. But those guys
brought my magnificence upon themselves.

"You fags can hang out for now, but you'd better be

gone when I wake up."

Jack and Carl's conversation pauses again and I hear Jack say in a low voice: "My roomie's still on TDY. Take his bunk if you want."

"Did you hear me? No butt-fuckin' in my room!"

That'll get their attention.

"Yeah, Peterson," Jack sighs. "We hear you."
I turn over and f-a-a-art. Nice and loud and long. I hear footsteps and the sound of the window sliding open. Then more footsteps, and the *plop* of Jack's smooth little ass sitting down.

Okay. If I need more attention, you can bet that I'll let you know. I guess that you guys can continue with your silly conversation:

- *Okay, where were we?*
- Getting cut.
- *Oh yeah. It's just to prevent infections and stuff.*
- **Nah. See, that's just how they sell that part of Agenda 2030. You want me to show you in the book?**
- *No, man...you don't have to do that. I believe you. But are you absolutely sure that Intel Is for you? I mean, maybe Dreadful was right! Maybe you should remain a weapons troop. I can see how you stress and study and all that, but this stuff just seems retarded. Who the fuck needs to learn that shit? It's creepy and weird. C'mon. It's just making you crazy, dude. Can't you see that?*
- **Not real? Okay, lemme ask you something. What's the easiest thing to get into: a chick's pants, or her shoes?**
- *Shoes. Does your textbook have a* Pulp Fictitious *chapter?*
- **I'm serious.**
- *So am I. No girl can refuse a foot job, just like no dude can refuse a blow job.*
- **Why is that, do you think?**
- *I dunno. Because it feels good, I guess.*

- Yes-and-no. It feels good, yes, but it's not as simple as that. We've been learning about surgical psy-ops that use something called "proximal neural stimulus."
- *Sorry. Never heard of it. Sounds like you're training for the Hospital Squadron instead of Intel.*
- The reason you can turn a girl on with a foot job is because her sex drive and the sensory network for her lower limbs share a property boundary in her brain, and like all neighbors, they tend to stick their noses over the fence. If the feet are having a party, then the pussy wants to come over.
- *Dude...I don't think it's quite that simple.*
- Oh really? How about a little CIA bedtime story to make my point.
- *Sure, secret agent man. You're so full of shit.*
- Trust me? This is something we learned in class. It's gonna freak you out.
- *No, motherfucker! What are you* doing?
- C'mon dude. Just take off your boot!
- *Oh, alright, for Chrissakes. Now what?*
- Gimme your stinky-ass foot. Okaaay...there and there...do you feel that?
- *All I feel is some moron with a gay foot fetish pinching my fee...SHIT! AH! FUCK! WHAT THE FUCK?!*
- Ha-ha! Told you!
- *What the fuck did you just do to me?!*
- Ha ha! That's what – ha ha! That's what I meant!
- *That wasn't an orgasm, dickhead! My sack just got sucked up into my asshole! Get the fuck out of my way. I gotta stand up and walk around for a minute.*
- Ha! You okay?
- *Yeah. Fuck you. What the hell did you do to me?*
- Cremaster reflex on overload, dude! Like when the doc smacks your knee with a rubber hammer. Nerve endings in the feet can bullshit your body's thermostat into thinking that it's too cold for your sperm to survive, so your cremaster yanks your nuts up into your pelvis! Ha ha ha!
- *Yeah. Hilarious. What good is that? Why the*

fuck would I try to do that to a woman? Last time I checked, girls didn't have nutsacks.
- No, but they do have proto-muscles that could have developed into cremasters. That's like asking why guys have nipples.
- *So what's the point, then?*
- The point is, when you force a reflex in a gender where it doesn't naturally occur, the brain doesn't know what to do. It mistakes the sensation for something more familiar.
- *An orgasm.*
- Yeah.
- *Carl, why...why do you know this? It's like that crazy shit in your textbooks. I know I keep saying this, but what the hell does this have to do with military intelligence?*
- Intel and the CIA use it. See, men and women are way different when it comes to pain and psychological vulnerability. If you're interrogating a man, shit is pretty basic. Get out the electrical cord and the waterboard. For a man, it just gets worse the longer it goes on, but that's not how it is with female prisoners. A woman can take more pain than a man, and the longer it goes on, the more her tolerance kicks in.
- *But I don't see how cumming would be a bad thing. I wouldn't shake in fear If someone threatened me with a blowjob.*
- That's because you're thinking like a guy. If POW camps had glory holes, no dude would ever want to leave. But imagine you're a girl from some Middle Eastern sandbox. Chances are, your dad and uncles pinned you down when you were nine and took a pair of shears to your clit, so maybe you've never even *had* an orgasm. Bad as that was, now you're in some CIA black ops prison and a bunch of white guys are forcing your body to experience very intimate and intense sensations, over and over again--
- *Jesus-Fucking-Christ, Carl. Just stop. Please. I–I don't like this conversation. I still don't like the shit you're learning about, either. I mean, I gotta*

be honest. We've been friends for a while, and I think you're a cool guy...but this shit...it can change a person, you know? Reading about it all the time, thinking about it all the time. I thought Intel was about intercepting messages and studying spy satellite photos and stuff.
- It mostly is.
- *Yeah. Mostly.*
- Dude, I'm not looking to get out and join the CIA. I anticipate twenty years of desk work, pilot debriefs, and teaching classes about the latest Soviet air defense systems. That's it. No more humping bombs in freezing rain or scrubbing Vulcan barrels or shit like that. I wanna hang up my fatigues, put on some blues, and stay indoors until retirement.
- *That sounds a hell of a lot more normal.*
- Yeah, man. And if I pick up a few pointers on how to get girls off along the way, what's so bad about that?
- *Hmmm. Well, when you put it that way...nothing, I guess.*
- Damn straight. I'll teach you that orgasm thing, too. We'll be the toast of the squadron skanks! Plus, there's another foot trick that I wanna let you in on.
- *Let's get something straight: You're not gonna do any more weird shit to my feet that makes my balls freak out.*
- Ha-ha! No, dude. That's not what I meant. We're learning dirty fighting shit, too. Last week I learned a cool way to break a guy's foot.
- More *foot stuff? Seems like a lot of twisted-ass podiatry.*
- Very funny, smartass. I'm trying to tell you about a smooth way to take somebody out!
- *By stepping on feet? Big deal. I figured that out in first grade. Are you gonna teach me how to scratch and pull hair, too?*
- I'm serious, fuckstick! I wanna teach you! This isn't like just stomping on somebody's toes.
- *Alright, alright. Sometime, but not tonight. We*

can do more of your superspy stuff tomorrow.

- Roger that. The orgasm-foot thing, too. It's awesome. Seriously.
- *Yeah, okay. I believe you...maybe it's a tested principle, and you demonstrated it very effectively. What did you call it, again?*
- Proximal neural stimulus.
- *Hmmm. Okay.*
- Well...it's only "okay" in the case of the ladies, Jackster.
- *No shit. I think my balls are still halfway up my butt.*
- No, I mean there's more to it than that. Proximal neural stimulus is the reason why the U.S. government wants to keep the baby circumcision thing going in the States.
- *Whoa, whoa. Cutting the skin off little boys' dicks turns them on? What the fuck are you talking about?*
- No, dipshit. Circumcision re-wires male's brains so that they can be more easily manipulated. It speeds up internal transitions from violence to docility, and vice-versa. *Voilà!* A population of men designed for military recruitment.
- *Bullshit. If that were true, then the entire male contingent of the Israeli Defense Force would be a chaotic clusterfuck. And the American military, too!*
- Come on, Jack. Think about it. When does a *bris* take place?
- *What's a bris?*
- It's when a Jew gets cuts cut.
- *Oh. How the hell should I know? I'm not Jewish.*
- On the eighth day. The *eighth* day! There's a neuro-developmental reason why the Jews wait for a few days, man! Stateside docs freak out if a kid's not cut ASAP because that's when a baby is most susceptible to a *permanent* proximal stimulus imprint. American males have half of their reasoning toolboxes emptied at birth because a boy's sexual center and his decision-making abilities go hand-in-hand. To us,

everything looks like a nail *because* part of our hammers got sliced off.
- *Bullshit, bullshit, bullshit! I'm circumcised, and so are you. We're not robots or confused drones.*
- No? We're wearing U.S. military uniforms, aren't we?

Jesus, will those two douchelings ever shut up? Just deal with it, Jack! I happen to prefer cut cocks...but not that you'll ever know.

"Zip it, fags!" I order. "I've gotta get some sleep before day shift!"

"OW!" I yell. Someone just hit me across the face!

"Alright, you two pussies are about to get your asses kicked!" I growl, as I rise from my bunk.

Shit! I just got hit again!

Who the fuck is hitting me?

And why am I standing outside of a gigantic porn shop?!

Sid Worley And The Baby Shower Curtain Child Support Judgment

July 1994 (6-of-7)

"Hey-hey-HEY!" I yell, as I back up and raise my hands in a defensive posture. "Grace, what the fuck are you doing?"

"Jack?"

"Uh, YEAH. Knock it off! What's the matter with you?" My tone is a mixture of anger and confusion.

"What's the matter with YOU? I had to drag you outside before we got kicked out. OR arrested. You kept calling yourself and somebody named Carl 'faggots'. You were yelling and farting." Grace grimaces and sticks out her tongue.

"I don't remember doing that," I reply, now in even greater confusion. "We were just standing by the dildo case. Alright. Then we met Geoff Striker. Okay," I continue, as I tick off memory factoids on my fingers. "He gave us some pictures," I say, as Grace holds up two nude glossies to verify that I am correct thus far. "Then he starts to act a little strange—"

"And then YOU start to act A LOT strange."

I rub my cheek. "Ouch," I say, as I shoot her an upset look. "And now I'm standing outside getting slapped by my best friend." *How red is my face?* I wonder, as I walk over to a car. I bend over and check myself in one of the side view mirrors. Yeah, my cheek is pretty in pink, but when I straighten up my face is met by Grace's soft fingertips. "I-I'm sorry," she says, as she lightly rubs my skin. "I had to do it, but I'm still sorry."

I gently take Grace's hand and lower it. "I'm alright," I grouse. My genuine upset is quickly replaced by a childish pout, but as I look at her, I can't even pretend to sulk.

Turned on a dime, once again.

"Best friend?" she asks. *Soft-eyes-soft-voice-soft touch.*

"Yeah," I answer.

Grace's fingers again try to smooth the harsh color out of my cheek. This time I don't stop her.

"It's okay," I say.

"Are *you* okay?"

"Yeah."

"I really am sorry."

"Let's forget it. I've had a concussion from a bomb rack smacking me on the head. I *probably* got a concussion when two assholes slammed my skull into a barracks locker. I broke my nose on the *outside* of a windshield, and I've had my front teeth knocked out by a toilet. I can take an open palm once or twice." I send a little frown Grace's way. "Maybe even three times."

"I thought your front teeth were real."

"Nah. These are crowns."

"Really?" Grace tries to pull my lip up and check my dentition as if I'm a horse.

"Hey-hey-HEY!" I exclaim again, as I back up and out of her reach.

"The military did nice work."

"Military? No. These are courtesy of Doctor Ha, Bucheon Back Alley Dental Genius. My flight chief was pissed because I didn't go to the base dental office, but those losers sucked serious ass. They probably would have pulled my remaining teeth and given me wooden dentures."

Grace laughs.

I try to say more, but I can't. I want to remember more, but I...can't. Somebody helped me find a Korean dentist. Someone took me to see Dr. Ha. But...I can't remember who...

"Jack! Look at me! Stop it! STOP IT!"

"Wh-what?"

"You just started to flip out again!"

Grace's upset makes me incredulous. "I'm fine!" I exclaim. "What are you talking about?"

Grace doesn't say anything. She just looks at me rather skeptically and folds her arms.

"C'mon! Okay, do we need to do this again? Fine.

You just asked about my teeth. I told you that I got them fixed by a Korean dentist. Then I said someone took me to see Dr. Ha, but I couldn't remember who. That's it. I'm okay. I'm okay!"

Grace continues to stand with her arms folded, though she does look slightly less doubtful. Then she does something that I don't expect. She double-taps me.

When you get double-tapped with a gun, it sucks. When you get double-tapped with a hug, it's great. Instead of two fast bullets, you get two fast squeezes. When the first squeeze ends and you think the hug is over, the next squeeze gets you by surprise. When Grace double-taps me I put my face against her hair, and it feels so good that I hardly notice how my nose gets assaulted by Old Slice. *Maybe she even puts it in her shampoo*, I think.

"What was that?" I ask.

"Hug insurance," she explains. "So you *stay* okay." Grace gives me a quick stroke of the cheek and a stern little smile. "C'mon," she adds. "I didn't pay to slap you around a parking lot."

* * *

Two clerks shove past us with paramedic urgency. "They're going over to the dildos," says Grace, as she motions for me to follow. When we arrive at the wall case, we see despair.

"I shouldn't have quit school," moans Geoff Striker, as he faces his reflection and its background of penises. His face leaves a long streak on the glass as he falls forward against the dildo case and slides down to his knees.

"Oh Jesus," whispers Grace. "This is *still* going on? I just sorted out one crazy *migukin*." She lifts one eyebrow and gives me a glance. "And now here's another."

The clerks and someone who could pass for a bouncer are concerned; after all, Striker's work has contributed to their livelihood. "Sir, Mr. Striker, sir," says one of the clerks in a low tone as he kneels by the aging X-K. "Sir, why don't you take a moment in the office? Just have a breather in the back, you know, something to drink, and relax for a minute." The clerks and the bouncer notice that a small group of curious shoppers has congregated in the area, and they don't like it. They look around with angry eyes and silent *get-the-fuck-out-of-here* waves, but when the clerks speak, their tones are gentle. "Please, sir. It's okay," says an Ultrastore employee, as he and another staff member take Striker's arms and help the shimmering red rayon and blonde hair back to its feet.

The bouncer takes an aggressive step forward while another bouncer comes down the aisle. Their hard expressions tell me that they're going to bulldoze a path through the onlookers. So I clap. Loudly. I don't need to glance at Grace to know that I'm getting her standard *WTF?* look, but then I hear her clap, too. Then everybody starts to clap.

The bouncers stop, and their expressions soften. The clerks find that Striker is able to stand on his own. He looks around the group. A little smile appears on his face. When rayon gets wet it changes hue, and a few grateful tears have left dark burgundy spots on Striker's red shirt.

* * *

"Clark Gable collapses at Mann's Chinese," I said, as we made our way toward the back exit.

"That guy had a few regrets, huh?"

"Definitely. The Adult Entertainment Guild apparently doesn't cover therapy."

Grace pinched my arm. "But at least Striker was present the entire time," she said. *"Psychologically, I mean."* She gritted her teeth and gently headbutted my arm.

"Yeah, yeah, I know what you mean," I grumbled. Then I changed the subject. "Maybe I'll leave a photo here," I said, as I slipped one of Striker's glossies from between Grace's fingers. "An Ultrastore Easter egg."

"No, I'll keep both of them," objected Grace, as she retrieved the picture. "These are great," she added, in an amused and completely non-erotic tone.

"I wouldn't hang that picture where your grandma can see it," I said.

"I actually got it *for* Grandma."

We stopped in the aisle and laughed. "Nice one," I said.

"Thanks. You know, maybe we shouldn't go outside. Not just yet."

"Not done looking?" I asked.

"I'm done, but you're not. C'mon. No wonder you've been cracking up. I've kept you on the *Last Train to Cocksville* all day."

"Insufferable dork," I chuckled

"Time for a detour." Grace put her feet on an empty lower shelf and climbed up. Her eyes scanned around the store. "You know, this place *also* caters to your tastes." She stepped down and motioned toward another wall case. When I didn't move, Grace grabbed my arm and pulled. "Oh, for Chrissakes, Jack. Come on. Let's have a look at the vaginas. You *need* to check out the vaginas. You can say it with me. VAH-JYE-NAHZ. I swear, sometimes you're as bad as those fake prisses in class."

"Fake prisses?" I echoed, as I found myself being marched toward the Ultrastore's gynosynthetic offerings.

"Yeah, you know," said Grace, "the dancers and hookers who pay ULVN tuition by doing what they do, then give convent poses on campus."

That's kind of an odd thing for you to say, I thought. *Your work environment is hardly family-friendly. But I'm not touching your comment. Not even with a ten-foot dildo.*

I disentangled myself from Grace's tractor beam but kept walking. "There are also guys on campus working that routine," I said. "But I know exactly what you mean. Do you remember Marie in Tests and Measures?"

"Marie?"

"Brown hair, pretty, petite. Front row in the Hendrix Auditorium. Aced the midterm."

"Okay, yeah. She's in Literacy Programs this semester."

"I was drinking at the TI about a month ago and I went outside for the pirate battle. When I went back to the bar, I saw her at the front desk with some guy in an

129

expensive suit who looked like he was her grandfather."

"Maybe he was," said Grace with a grin.

"Oh yes. I'm *sure.*"

We stopped in front of a glass wall much like the one that we had just left. "Well, here we are," announced Grace. "The cunt case. Ta-da!"

"Classy. I've never heard you use the 'C' word before."

"Don't lecture. *You* were the one yelling 'fag'". Grace grabbed my arm again. "Okay," she said, as if addressing one of her elementary practicum classes, "let's say that one together, shall we? Ready? *CUNT.* C-U-N-T. CUNT."

I just shook my head and looked inside the case.

"No?" giggled Grace. "Well, keep working on it. I thought you were a little looser than that, but you're positively repressed...when you're not acting like a belligerent homophobe, that is."

"I'm *not* a homophobe," I said. "It was like...I was in a dream and looking at myself through the eyes of a guy I knew overseas. Weird. I haven't thought about Peterson in years," I muttered.

We peered into the boys'-toys case. The level of detail previously seen on the B.O.B. side of the house was absent, and some of the display items were rather baffling. "Grace, what is *that*?" I asked, as I pointed at an object that looked like a large cush ball with an attached latex cuff. "Seriously – I really don't know what a man is supposed to do with that. Is my penis supposed to go in the opening? But then why is the sleeve *underneath?* And what's with all those rubbery strings?"

My friend shrugged. "I don't know. *You're* the one with a dick. Be creative."

"Creativity is an obvious requirement for this product," I observed. I studied the strange item from another angle, but again nothing made sense. "Grace, does any part of your body even remotely resemble... *that?*" I asked. Grace laughed.

"What?"

"The broader implications."

"What do you mean?"

"I mean," answered Grace, "the idea of feminine mystique. You wouldn't see it by comparing sex toys."

"Maybe it's as simple as orientation," I suggested. "I personally don't get it, but there might be some men at the dildo case who know what's going on here...maybe some women, too."

"Sure, but the straight women's stuff is as basic as it gets. As for this, uh, *merchandise,*" Grace continued, as she motioned at the glass case, "I'm as lost as you. In fact, some of it is just hilarious." She pointed at another cush ball-thing, except this one had a small cord that led to a battery case. "Oooh. It's *electric,*" Grace laughed.

"Maybe an overwhelming imagination might not be enough after all," I said. "How much can the male mind deny? I don't think that sensation potential exists here." I paused to think of an example. "When I was a kid my grandpa gave me a big refrigerator box. I used crayons and tape to convert it into a spaceship. Guys have great imaginations, but they need *something* to work with. See, these are better," I said, as I motioned at a row of pelvic reproductions. Like the true-to-life penises, the products to which I referred had the names and pictures of associated adult actresses. "I don't know how real these might feel, but at least I understand what they *are.*"

"Yeah, *suuure* you don't know how real they feel," teased Grace, as I studied Jemma Janison's latex lips.

"What's the plural of 'clitoris'?" I asked.

Grace paused. "Clitorises," she said. "Or is it 'clitorii'? I'm not sure."

"Oh, and you dare to criticize me for *my* vocabulary deficits," I said with fake incredulity. "You're supposed to become a teacher, too."

Grace rolled her eyes. "I really doubt that we'll get many questions about the plural form of 'clitoris' from elementary students," she said. "Did you ever see *Cashiers?*"

"Classic."

"If you remember, half of the dialogue in that movie consisted of the main character bitching about blowjobs and snowballs, while at the same time bragging about the ease with which a guy can get off." Grace looked at me.

Expectantly.

"Ummm, you got me," I confessed. "I guess that's all true, too."

Grace turned back to the case and laughed, but not a mean laugh or a *GOTCHA!* laugh. Then she took a step toward me and delivered another playful headbutt to my arm. Grace looked up and smiled, but again, not with smugness or condescension.

"A Glasgow Kiss from Seoul," I observed. "You'd better be careful. Forehead scars close doors."

"From Asheville," Grace corrected, "and with perfect skin and all the opportunity it affords." She paused for an exaggerated hair-flip-head-shake combo. "And a Vegas boy from...?"

"East Hacienda."

"Lost East Hacienda boys," she said. "Or maybe just boys in general...with minds as confused as their sex toys." Grace nodded at the cush-things. "What?" she asked. "What's that grin about?"

"Your comment about sex toys. It makes me remember something kinda funny. Well, kinda disgusting, really."

"Waiting." Grace put her hands on her hips.

"It's pretty nasty."

"Waaaiting."

"Okay. It was back when I was enlisted. After I got to my permanent base all of the shower bay curtains were taken out of the barracks bathrooms."

"Latrines. You have to say 'latrines.' That's what they call them on *M.A.S.H.E.D.,*" Grace teased. "Latrines. LAH-TREENZ."

I ignored her and continued. "The first sergeant ordered them to be removed."

"Ah. Completely appropriate. Conservation of precious military shower curtains."

"No. It was because everyone soaped them up and jerked off with the plastic, vinyl, or whatever-it-was."

"Mmm. Innovative."

"And then everyone showed up for sick call with the same drip."

At that, Grace ran out of wisecracks. She wrinkled

up her nose and stuck out her tongue. "Yeww! Gross-gross-GROSS!"

"Just imagine a big infected condom that got passed around an entire squadron," I added. "That's basically what we're talking about."

Grace had closed her eyes in revulsion, but when she opened them again, her wit had returned. "So if I ever see a bunch of baby shower curtains crawling around your apartment, you won't need to explain anything."

We were interrupted by a voice on the store intercom. I recognized it as the same one that had tried to console Geoff Striker, except now it was in **Big PR Event Mode** - *Boats-On-The-Water! Bikinis-On-The-Beach!* I half-expected an *Additional Offer Of Ginsu Steak Knives If I Acted Now,* but instead, all shoppers were informed of the impending *Big-Event-Outside! Event-Outside! Outside!*

"I guess it's starting up," I observed. "Are we done here?"

"DefInItely."

~~Las~~ *Los* Vegas, ~~Ray~~ *Jack,* Isn't Really A City;
It's More Like A Celebration
Of Everything
Evil

July
1994
(7-of-7)

Grace and I showed our hand stamps and were squeezed through the Ultrastore's back door sphincter. We were outside the store, but inside the tape.

"I guess that something like this wouldn't be complete without *them,*" I noted, as we passed a row of three inflatable waving men. The air tube had disconnected from one man's base and he was crumpled on the ground, though he still looked up with a painted-on smile while his umbilical flailed.

"Ugh," said Grace. "Sun. Too much sun." She shielded her face by holding Geoff Striker's dick pics over her head.

"Let's get under a tent," I suggested. Grace nodded and we moved past a series of life-sized cardboard cutouts that advertised the latest adult videos. Most seemed to be sex parodies of mainstream films, as in the case of an actress whose flight suit was half-removed by a fondling alien in *Independence Play,* and another which showed a muttonchop-wearing stud with adamantium claw-penises emerging between his knuckles.

"Gee. *SeXXX-Men,*" scoffed Grace. "That's so inspired.

"Do you want to get a beer or something?" I asked.

Grace shook her head. "Not here. But we could stop at the Monte Carlo Basement later, if you want."

"Yeah. I guess I'm not in a pisswater frame of mind either."

Event parking had been granted to a news van that had a KSHO logo splashed across its side and a big Seussian uplink dish on a telescoping roof support. A Malibu Reporter Ken spoke to someone inside the van

134

and walked off into the crowd. After a few moments a ruggedly handsome face peered out from behind the van's open rear doors. "Dale!" the man called, as he surveyed the area. "Dale!" He cursed, shook his head, and ducked back inside.

Activities took place around a podium stage, over which a banner announced: *Ned Power - The Living Due.* On the platform I spotted yet another cardboard video advertisement that featured Ned Power in a cheap Confederate soldier costume. His long gray hair was pulled back into a ponytail and he wore glasses that looked suspiciously like they could double as woodshop safety goggles. Smaller pictures of naked and compromisingly-posed young women surrounded the central Power image. The placard read: *Filthy Debutantes, Volume 194: New Orleans - The Filthy South.*

"I'm going over to the stage," Grace said.

"Okay. I'll join you shortly. I want a wiener-dog balloon hat." Before I could locate an inflatable headgear booth, however, someone spoke to me. I turned around, saw no one, and wondered if I was having another mental episode.

"Excuse me," the voice repeated. "Here. Down here." I looked in the voice's direction and discovered that Richard Gear's head, circa *North American Union Gigolo,* had been placed atop Wee Hombre's body.

"Don't be embarrassed," he said, with a charming smile that only *An Officer or a Gentleman* could manage. "I seem to have misplaced the help. I was wondering if I could get a hand with some equipment."

"Uh, yeah, of course," I answered. "News crew, right?"

"Right. Only take a sec," he said, as we walked to the KSHO van. "Name's Jason."

"Jack."

The interior of the van looked like one of those spy vehicles in the movies - you know, the kind where men in black wear big headsets as they hunch over consoles and eavesdrop with super technology. Someone had customized one of the consoles with Gratuitous Dead dancing bears, and I figured that this probably wouldn't have been allowed in a creepy government surveillance van.

"I just need you to lift these cannon plugs," said Jason, as he pointed at a heavy conduit mass near the floor, "while I pull my fib-op rack loose."

I lifted several awkward bundles of shielded connections while Jason freed a device that might have been a 1950s child's polio frame, except that it was matte black and featured several quick-release pin attach points. When Jason nodded I lowered the mass to the van's floor and stepped out. He brought the rack to the edge of the doorway, slid backward onto the ground, and put it on. The apparatus looked like an empty backpack frame with handlebars.

"Thanks," Jason said.

"What's that?"

"It's an adaptive device. "I've been using Lyne Stabs on assignments for almost five years. This is actually my third set. Know anything about journalism or field production?"

"Nothing," I said. "How does it work?"

"Well, it's really a scaled-down version of a steadi-cam," Jason explained. "These," he said, as he touched two vertical tubes that were slightly thicker than the rest of the device, "are internal gyros, and this," Jason added, as he tapped a jack near one of the handgrips, "is my fib-op point. Like so." In less than five seconds Jason's practiced hands had attached a digital camera to a crossbar between the handgrips and two external batteries to the attach points below his hips. A slight shudder passed through the frame as the gyros came to life. To further demonstrate, Jason did a quick Chubbie Checker while the frame compensated for the twisting motion via joints around his midriff and hips.

"That's cool," I said.

"More than that, it enables me to capture perspective from both my natural angle," Jason said, as he tipped the camera's view screen to let me see that it was filming from below, "or that of a taller person." Jason pulled a small vertical knob on one side of the frame and it telescoped upward like a tiny periscope. Now the camera screen portrayed me from my own eye level. "Not bad, eh?" asked Jason. "Maybe someday they'll invent a camera with view stabilization, but until then, I'll use this contraption." Jason scanned the crowd for a few seconds. "Let's go find my talking head and cover this thing." He shut the van doors and started to walk, or maybe gyro-glide, toward the crowd.

"Your talking head?"

"I shouldn't use that term," Jason admitted, "but after watching them come and go, you know, the pretty people out in front...ah, well. I need to watch what I say." He smiled. "There he is. 'Interfacing', as I think it's called. HEY! Dale!" Jason waved at the Ken doll that I had seen earlier. The man saw us and excused himself from a conversation.

I spoke as Dale approached. "Did you guys cover that mess at Xanadu?"

"No, another crew was assigned. It sounded like just another cop or security shooting, if you ask me. *Official Cover-Up at Eleven.*" Jason noticed my sigh. "I'm right, aren't I? If you do this job long enough, cynicism and reality become one. You wouldn't believe some of the tapes that I've seen, as well as the tapes that I've seen *disappear.*"

The Ken doll had stopped to chat up some surgically-bolstered mams. "Your colleague's waylaid again," I observed.

Jason smiled. "He's not as bad as some. He's actually pretty good."

"How many times have you covered this?"

"Fourth time."

"Oh really? Power has been doing it for that long?"

"No, the stars change. Last year it was Joey Silver. This thing gets bigger each year," explained Jason. "It's become something in its own right, and less like an off-Strip HotCon. For me, though, the best part of working this side of town is eating on the channel's tab over at The New Orleans Oyster Bar." Jason looked up, grinned, and nodded for me to follow as he went to retrieve the on-screen talent.

Dale expressed concern as we approached. "Do I look okay? Do I look okay?" he fretted.

"Never better," said Jason. "Really good. No shine,

no pores. Did you just have a touch up?

"No! How can I do this without make-up?" Dale looked like he might stamp his feet.

"A pro like you? Hell, let's knock this out!" rallied Coach Jason. "One take! We don't need anyone else!"

"Really...d-do you think...?"

"In three, and two, and —"

Hi, I'm Dale Cantrell, and I'm here at the Adult Ultrastore for an event that traditionally adds to the fun of HotCon. I'm told that another KSHO team reported on a violent incident earlier, in which some intoxicated attendees allegedly attacked Xanadu security staff, and HotCon has been temporarily shut down. However, for fans of the adult entertainment industry and visitors to our fair city, the fun is still happening out on West Tropicana!

"Okay, cut there," said Jason. "We'll get some of Power's podium speech and insert it. Now let's grab some faces." Dale nodded and began to recite rehearsed lines in the directions of the nearest attendees:

Hi, are you from Los Vegas? Are you having fun? That's great. [Next] That's great. [Next] That's great. [Next] Hi, are you affiliated with the adult entertainment industry? Oh. That's just the name you perform under. I see. Yes, yes, I get it. Ha ha. Ahem. Those are a few of the films that you've starred in? Great. Well, thanks for taking the time to speak with us, and I hope that you have a great time. I'm sure you will.

"Tough job, huh?" asked Jason. "Sometimes I can't believe that I get paid for this." He looked up at Dale. "I think that's enough. We'll update when Power gets here." At that, Dale turned and wandered away. "I need to make a mental note of where he gets off to," said Jason. He turned to me. "Want to learn how to uplink to a Five-Six Class high orbiter?" he asked.

"Sure."

"Oh shit!" Jason snapped his fingers. "Cancel that."

Jason looked around. "No Dale. No producer. Nobody." He shook his head, then looked at me. "Never mind the satellite. Would you help me with this stab? I need a hand to take it off."

Back at the van Jason reversed the procedure that I had seen earlier. Fib-op in, camera off, batteries out. "Okay, if you could just steady it when I unbuckle," he said. "Thanks. They don't allow pictures or equipment in the store."

"Hey, no problem. This was interesting. Are you - uh - going to do some shopping?"

"Yeah, before this crowd cleans them out."

"I was in there earlier. Believe me, they have an ample stock of dildos and movies."

Jason laughed. "No, not that stuff. Ever since the Feds started to lean on Whole Paycheck and Wild Goats, I've been buying my naturopathy supplies at porn shop 'energy and performance' supplement counters." Jason chuckled. "Most of the herbs that I need have no 'energy and performance' applications that I'm aware of, but I can still find them here. It's amazing how an apple a day, plus a few million in porn-bribes, can keep the FDA SWAT teams away."

* * *

"I was beginning to think that you were upstairs making a movie," said Grace.

"I met the KSHO crew," I said, as I pointed at the van. "Maybe we should give up our teaching ambitions and major in journalism."

"*Pfffft,*" responded Grace. "I'll probably see you on a movie poster next week. I thought the announcer said that it was showtime. How much longer will we have to wait?"

"Not sure. I'm getting impatient, too."

Milky Derma-Grace wanted to stay out of the sun, so we remained under the tents and watched the people. The crowd still seemed average and bland, but now that I was able to observe them in greater detail, I supposed that some could have worked in adult entertainment. It wasn't easy to pick them out though, given ubiquitous Vegas aesthetics. For example, a woman who stood by the stage had heavily processed hair, sculpted calves, pectoral cantaloupes, and future basal cell carcinoma. She could have been featured on the parking lot's cardboard promotionals, or she could have also been a Vegas-assimilated business executive. The same went for a guy over by the cones who talked to one of the SiteSec turkey bacons. He obviously had a gym membership, a decent stylist, and sun damage equal to that of the woman. His trouser-pouch looked like a potential money-maker, but he could have also been a hung *maître d'* or an insurance salesman.

I then spotted someone who made me realize that I understood nothing about the requirements of porn physiology, for walking through the crowd with an H_2O_2 babe on each arm was The Porcupine. Here was one of Ned Power's fellow legends, and the sort of man who could hold his own with the likes of Long John and Peter South. The Porcupine appeared to be taking a break from shooting late-night-penis-growth-snake-oil infomercials, though he did seem to be endorsing a new product, and his wing girls handed out fliers.

"Oh my God, that's Don Laramie," said Grace. "I thought he was dead."

"He did actually die some time ago," I said, "but his back hair is still alive, so it re-animated the body and assumed Laramie's identity. Don't stare at the corpse too long, or the hair will know that you're on to its game."

"He's selling something," Grace laughed. "C'mon."

As we got closer, *I* was the one who struggled not to stare, because with each step I again appreciated how wrong I'd been in my understanding of porn appearance standards. I had mostly noted traits outside of the pants, while here was an aging and overweight *Planet of the Hirsute Apes* extra who had proven that, even though a cigar was sometimes just a cigar, a ten-inch pole could never be mistaken for anything less than a career. Or...maybe there really wasn't a "Don Laramie" at all. Maybe there were just people who had been selected for the task of providing life support for the celebrity cock, and after one host died, the organ was attached to a new body for veneration by future generations.

It certainly wouldn't have been an original scam, because giant penises, like left-handed Höfner 500/1 bass guitars, were easily grafted onto impostors.

I paused in front of the writhing clutch of scaly autograph seekers that surrounded Laramie. "Do we really want to slither into this?" I asked.

Grace looked at the group. "Well, on second thought..." Her voice trailed off in mild disdain. "Do *you* want to?"

"Oh, what the hell. Someday I might pass The Porcupine's autograph on to my grandkids. Want one?"

"Yeah, what a rare treasure," was Grace's sarcastic response. "Geoff Striker and Don Laramie, all in one day, and all before the main event. What more could a girl ask for?"

When I got closer I noticed that there was so much glistening hair product on Laramie's neck and shoulders that it ran, mixed with sweat, in thin rivulets down to his moobs. *Vegas must be hotter than LA,* I thought. I saw small wads of sweat-damp body hair matting under Laramie's tight red tee, which read:

¡PIE DEL MAIZ DEL HOMBRE!

The bimbettes did their part to increase awareness of Laramie's latest product. Unlike Laramie, who *gave* autographs, his escorts *received* autographs. They had their own pens, and allowed members of the crowd to sign their breasts, bellies, and buttocks. Occasionally someone would try to cop a feel, but the bimbettes teasingly shook their fingers and lightly slapped offenders' hands. The bimbettes had hiked their short skirts and lifted their shirts so many times that the elastic was stretched out and the garments resembled shapeless potato sacks. Like the perspiration and hair grease that trickled down Laramie's chest, the simulated blondes experienced their own streaking issues as sweat and water-soluble ink ran down their thighs and midriffs like mascara tears.

*- Care for an informational schedule? Left boob?
  Sure.*
*- Care for an informational schedule? Right cheek?
  Okay – but don't be nauuughty!*
- Care for an informational schedule? Hey! Outer
  thigh!

And then it was my turn.
"Care for an informational sched--"
"Yeah, sure. Two!" I yelled.
"And would you like to sign my--"
"No," I interrupted again, "I just want Don's
autograph." The bimbette quickly handed two fliers
back to Laramie and he signed them on her back as fast
as he could. I realized that the women were more than
eye candy and cheap thrills. They also provided a
deliberate buffer between The Porcupine and his public.
Laramie laid down a rock-n-roll scrawl, handed the fliers
back to the bimbette, and she passed them to me.
"Is that what you're selling?" I asked, as I delayed
the line for a few more seconds. I pointed at Laramie
and gestured across my own chest. "What does that
mean in English?" I had to yell, though we were
practically face-to-face.
Since I hadn't requested more autographs or
permission to draw circles around her nipples, the girl
paused. "What?" she shouted.
"What does his shirt say?" I called back.
"Pie del maíz del hombre means 'magnum love
energy of the stallion'. Could I interest you in--"
"Thanks," I said, as I faded backward into the throng
without waiting to hear the sales pitch.

* * *

"Why didn't you write on her tits?" smirked Grace.
"For the same reason I stopped wearing diapers and
scribbling on walls," I said, as I handed her an
autographed brochure. "Hey. This is bullshit!" I
exclaimed, as I read the paper.
"Is yours the same as mine?" asked Grace.
"Yeah." I looked back at The Porcupine's queue.

"What a dickhead. He wants people to buy his garbage, but he can't even bother to give them a real signature."

"Who is *Stan Van Gundie?*" asked Grace, as she turned over her flier.

"And why is Laramie on a pocket sports calendar?" I added. *"The Heats?* We're not in goddamn Florida. And what's with the three-piece? Don Laramie didn't become famous because of his exquisite taste in menswear. Fuckin' jerk. I hope that he doesn't sell any of his stupid 'horse love potion' or whatever-the-hell it is," I groused, as I walked toward a trashcan.

"Wait," said Grace. "Don't throw it away."

"Why not?"

"Maybe it means something. Maybe that's his real name, you know? I mean, how could 'Don Laramie' be anything but a porn name?"

Grace had a point. "But he should have written the name that he's known by," I replied, as I again moved to toss the flier. "I don't know who 'Stan Van Gundie' is."

"Give it to me," said Grace.

I shrugged and handed over the flier. "What are you going to do with that?"

Grace just grinned. "What's *your* porn name?"

"What do you mean? I don't have a 'porn name.'"

"Sure you do. It's the name of your first pet, followed by the name of your first street or neighborhood."

"So you're saying that he--" I paused as I pointed in Laramie's direction "--had a pet named 'Don'? I think that Laramie, or Van Gundie, or whomever he is, comes from New York, not Wyoming."

"C'mon," Grace said, as she handed back my flier. "Play along. I'll write my porn name on this one," she said, as she produced a pen, "and you write your porn name on that one. Then we'll trade and open them together."

I had to think for a moment before I borrowed Grace's pen. "Okay," I said.

"Okay," she smiled. "One, two, three."

We both laughed. "Was it a dog or a cat?" Grace asked.

"It was a cat," I said, "but he acted like a dog

sometimes. He was a calico with black spots, so I guess that's why we called him 'Pepper.'"

"Pepper Hacienda," laughed Grace.

"And Chère Anguk," I chuckled. "I actually know where Anguk is. Been there lots of times. It's pretty close to Insa-Dong and Jonggno." I paused as something occurred to me. "Didn't you say that you'd never been to Seoul, or even Korea?"

"Well, I guess that I've *technically* been there," replied Grace. "But we left when I was three. Anguk was my very first neighborhood."

"Oh. So your parents were into Sonny and Chère? Or just Chère?"

"No, no," explained Grace. "I actually named my dog 'Chair.'"

"Uh, *Chair?*"

"Yeah. My mom says that when I was little and still learning English, I liked the way 'chair' sounded as a word. I just liked to say it, so that's how Chère got his name."

"A male dog named 'Chère'?"

Grace rolled her eyes and smiled. "Yeah. He was a little white dog. He was my best friend."

I had a vision of a little girl, so far from home and in a place where the people looked strange and gibbered in a weird tongue, with only her family and Chère the Dog. I also saw a little me playing with Pepper the Cat while Grandpa smiled and looked on. These distant flashes of childhood innocence quickly disappeared, however, because Grace and I now stood among people who had waited in line for the autograph of a man whose only claim to fame was that he had been born with mammoth genitalia. We had paid to attend an event that featured yet another man whose primary talent was filming young women who probably lived to regret the things that he paid them to do. Behind us was a giant store that was crammed with plastic penises and rubber vaginas, and it stood in a city built upon dice, cards, foolish risk, and painful loss. There sure as hell hadn't been any calico cats or little white dogs in our lives for a long time.

Grace reached out for the Chère flier, which she

folded up with the one that bore the name of my cat. She placed them in my back pocket and smiled when I suggested that we leave. At that moment, however, a vehicle pulled into the lot.

Max had arrived, and the Wild Rumpus was about to start.

The limo reminded me of a hearse. It was old, black, and had expired McKarran lot decals on its windshield. The limo's key-scratched doors were touched-up with slightly-mismatched spray paint. The driver got out, opened the rear passenger door, and alligator cowboy boots swung out onto a "red carpet" that was actually a series of taped-together hall mats.

Imagine a piece of paper placed over a magnet. Sprinkle iron filings on the paper and they cluster near the magnet. This was the crowd around Don Laramie. Now place a more powerful magnet under the paper. The iron filings leave the first magnet and gather around the second. The more powerful magnet paused on the red rubber mats to await his introduction.

The event was MCeed by a fellow who projected a serious porn veteran aura. He wore a sweat-soaked white dress shirt that was open to his pasty navel, and his combover caused his head to look like a sparsely-thatched Quonset hut with jowls. He didn't put out his cigarette when he took the stage, and the first sound that blasted out over the crowd was that of smoke blowing into the microphone:

Good afternoon, ladies and gents! It's good to see you all here today. I'm Bill Krenick, as some of you might remember from my pioneering work in Berlin and Mexico City. It's great to be here at the Ultrastore, and it's an honor to welcome the Father of Porn Pro-Am, The Master Talent Scout, and The Living Due that so many babes have paid to break into The Biz! Let's give a big round of applause for Ned Power!

When Power ran up to the podium, I noticed that his hair was slightly mashed up on one side like that of a

145

child after an afternoon nap. Power's clothes had sitting wrinkles, especially the black slacks that stretched tightly over the tops of his gator-hide boots. As Power shook Krenick's hand and took the mic, I saw that his red tee proclaimed: **MAN CORN FOOT.**

Thank you, thank you. Thanks, Bill. Heh-heh. And thanks to the Ultrastore for this great welcome! My upcoming feature is going to be my hottest, and like the sign says, waaay down south! I've been tying up some loose ends in New Orleans all week, and it's great to be back in Vegas! Some may say that Sin City leaves you feeling like you've been fucked, while The Big Easy leaves you feeling like you've been seduced...but I wanna tell ya, sometimes you NEED to get fucked! Yee-haw! Viva Los Vegas!

Hoots, cheers, applause, and women flashing their boobs. Marti-Gras comes to West Trop.

From our vantage point, Ned Power looked like Norm Abraham, except for his attire. But there was no way, I realized. *No.* This man could *not* be the same fellow who hosted the wholesome plaid-shirt-maple-syrup-family-woodshop hour. Not possible.

"I definitely see how they could be brothers," admitted Grace. "Even twins. But let's settle this."

"I think it's already settled," I said. "Do you want to take Rainbow up to Greenland? It looks like I owe your grandma a case of soju."

"Don't you even want to check and see if he has a scratch?"

"No. If he's been in New Orleans all week, then..." I paused as I watched Power, then shaded my eyes and squinted to get a better look at what he was doing.

"Then – *what?*" asked Grace. She turned around to face the stage. "What is it?"

I smiled as I watched Power open a small box at the podium and remove something that looked...familiar. As he spoke, I turned to Grace. "You know, maybe I was a little hasty in conceding defeat. Let's get a better look." Grace responded with a curious expression and followed me through the crowd. On stage, Power continued:

...and why did I try it out on the ladies in this upcoming Filthy Deb *installment? Because this little baby lives up to the Lovellyx name! It's everything you would expect from a subsidiary of Dack and Blecker! Allow me to introduce you to the future of pleasure innovation, the Lovellyx Digits of Desire Glove!*

I stopped. "We've seen this before," I declared.

"Uh...yeah," agreed Grace.

"Okay, now he's going to show us the little control box," I predicted.

"And now we're going to see the sanding surfaces — no, wait, that's different. He's got jell pads," Grace observed.

"Now he's pretending to use it on his assistant," I added.

"Why is he only pretending?"

"Because county statutes don't allow sexual contact on outdoor stages from nine-to-five."

*   *   *

I turned on the Mercedes' air conditioner. "Ahhh," said Grace, as she held her face near the vent. "Why are we waiting?"

"I just want a minute until the idiots leave. I don't mind sitting out the first wave."

Grace turned and nodded in mock solemnity. "I knew that I was right to trust you with this car. You're very cautious."

"Do you want to drive?"

"Nah," declared Grace, as she stuck her face back in front of the vent.

I rested my hands on the wheel and watched the exit procession honk and curse its way out to Tropicana. "Okay," I began, "here's my verdict."

"Let's hear it."

"I know that you're right. Abraham and Power aren't the same guy. I was ready to believe that I'd won our bet. I was so sure. But I guess you're right."

Grace leaned back in her seat. "Your reasoning?"

"Power didn't have a scratch. I can't argue with that. The man is either a comic book mutant with a

147

healing factor, or else he's a separate person. As much as I'd prefer to live in an alternate superhero universe, I still gotta accept the latter."

"Yeah," agreed Grace. "Besides, Hubert Jackman is *infinitely* sexier than Ned Power. But what about the other things? Power and Abraham are almost identical and they have the same voice. Plus, those goofy electric gloves are practically the same product."

"Well...I think that they must be twins. And they both have deals with Dack and Blecker."

There was a tap on the window. "What the hell?" I asked. I was instantly annoyed because I had specifically chosen a parking spot that wouldn't block anyone's exit, but some whiny prick still wanted me to move the Mercedes. I cracked the window. "What do you want?" I bellowed.

"Jesus, Jack," Grace whispered. "He probably just needs to get by."

The man stepped back and I saw the words **MAN CORN FOOT** on his red tee. Grace and I exchanged shocked looks. "Relax, kid," said Ned Power. "I just want to talk."

"Go on," whispered Grace. "It looks like we're gonna meet another porn star."

I rolled down the window. "Uh, hello," I said.

"Jack Simmerath?"

"That's right."

"Here." Power held out an envelope. "This is for you."

The exchange happened so fast that I didn't really know what to make of it. "How do you know who I am?"

Power didn't answer. "Here," he insisted.

I looked at Grace, who only shrugged. I reached out the window and took the letter. It was a little smudged, but otherwise unremarkable. I turned it over and saw that my name, along with the number *1994, was* written on the outside. There wasn't an address.

What the hell?

I was confused, but Power wasn't. "Okay, open it," he said.

"What?"

"That's your name on the outside, isn't it? Open it."

I ripped the end off of the envelope and removed a piece of paper.

"Read it out loud," said Power. "I'm supposed to hear you read it."

I gingerly unfolded a page of old yellow GSA tablet stock and discovered a message written in pencil. The writing was clear and sharp and the paper wasn't faded, but it felt strangely stiff and almost brittle, as if it might disintegrate in my hands like flakes of pressed rice flour.

"Just read the damn thing!" Power huffed.

"Alright," I said. *"Think, Jacky! It is in the watch and behind the eight. PS - Please excuse the delivery man. One does the best one can, especially in the Disco Era."*

I had no idea what it meant. I looked up and saw Power walking away. I jumped out of the car and followed him. "Wait," I called out. "What is this?"

Power stopped and whirled around. "Look, I don't fucking know you. I don't give a shit about you. If your girlfriend wants to shoot a scene, my agent is my P.O.C. But if I ever hear from you again for any other reason, I'll have you busted for stalking. Are we clear? Tell the old man that I've held up my end of the deal and we're quits."

"Deal? What deal?"

"I'm serious, kid," warned Power as he gave me a stiff-arm and resumed walking. "Get the fuck away from me."

I stopped and watched as Power was re-engulfed in autograph seekers and boob flashers. Then I returned to the car.

"I'm still gonna buy a case of Jinro," I said to Grace as I buckled in, "but I just saw something that might interest you."

"Oh? What?"

"When I took the letter out of his hand, I noticed that the reason why Power doesn't have a fresh scratch is because he has an old scar."

* * *

During that evening at Grace's apartment we tried to make sense of the day. The Abraham-Power identity issue had taken a back seat to the mysterious letter.

"You're certain?" Grace asked. "I mean, it's not a lot to go on. Just a couple sentences."

"Yes. One hundred percent. I saved all of the letters that Grandpa sent when I was overseas. It's exactly the same handwriting."

"What's this about a watch?"

"I'm not sure, but after Grandpa died, I was given his old Nazi Party pocket watch." I gauged Grace's reaction to the "N" word. Her eyes widened slightly, so I continued with a practiced disclaimer. "It was something that he received when he was forced--" I paused for emphasis "--to join. That's all I can think of. And in case you're wondering, he spent the war at a research facility on some island in the Baltic Sea."

"How did he get to the USA?"

"There was a program that brought German scientists to the States so that they could continue working during the Cold War. I think the only people who remember it now are historians."

"Sorry. Grandma watches The History Channel, not me," said Grace. She picked up the letter and silently re-read it. "Is this watch valuable or something? Is it gold or silver?"

"No. It's just shitty pewter. The case is rough because Grandpa scratched off the Nazi eagle. It doesn't even work."

Grace studied the letter. *"It is in the watch,"* she read. "Have you ever taken it apart?"

"Yeah. There's nothing inside except rusty gears and broken springs. I only keep the damn thing because it belonged to Grandpa."

Grace laid the yellow paper on the coffee table. For a couple minutes we silently reclined on the couch and stared at the ceiling. I raised my head when I felt her get up. Grace disappeared into the kitchen and returned with a bottle of Jinro and two glasses.

"You didn't actually need to buy an entire *case,"* she said.

"That was the wager," I replied, "and this has been a weird, weird day. If you need help with that, I'm your man."

"You'll note that I have a glass for you," said Grace. "Care to revise your stance on Korean girls and drinking contests?"

"Forfeit," I said. "Pour."

777

That's A Very Serious Comic, Man

~~Donald~~ *Jack* Heard
A Mermaid
Sing

Summer
1976

"Okay, Jacky," Grandpa whispered. "You have him."

My aim was good and the .22's sights were easy to use. The blade at the muzzle fit into the notch halfway down the barrel and created a pretend line that reached out to where a skinny gray jackrabbit sat.

"How come he doesn't move?" I whispered. "Why doesn't he try to run away?"

"The hare thinks that, if he sits very still, you cannot see him," answered Grandpa. Sometimes Grandpa called jackrabbits "hairs".

Why was the jackrabbit so stupid? I could see him just fine. He was sitting on the other side of a little bush. I could even see his big buggy eyes. I pulled the trigger and the gun bumped against my shoulder while the jackrabbit did a somersault. Then I did exactly what Grandpa had taught me to do. I pushed a button in front of the trigger guard and dropped the rifle's little magazine into my hand. Then I pulled the bolt back and a bullet flipped out onto the ground. Without letting the bolt handle go, I turned the gun over, stuck my finger into the hole where the magazine went, and pushed another little button inside the gun. I took my hand off of the bolt handle and it stayed open. I clicked the safety on and gave the gun and magazine to Grandpa. I could tell from Grandpa's smile that he was happy because I was so careful.

"Now let us go get him," said Grandpa.

"Okay," I said. "But first I want to find the bullet." I went down to my hands and knees and felt around in a dry clump of grass.

It was easier for me to clean jackrabbits when the head and skin were already off. Grandpa began the cleaning job and let me finish. Without faces, the rabbits just seemed like red meat sacks that we opened up and emptied.

154

"Be careful with this part," Grandpa said, as he stood behind me and showed me where to cut. We slowly pulled a purple tube from between the rabbit's legs. "That is his poop," Grandpa explained. "Try not to cut it open."

I knew that I did things that my classmates didn't do. I wanted to tell other kids about my grown-up fun - the hunting, shooting, hiking, camping, and the nighttime stars that I saw when Grandpa and I were far from Los Vegas. But instead, I talked to my classmates about dodge ball, TV shows, and comic books.

* * *

I cut my finger in the summertime when Rowe Elementary School was on vacation, so I didn't have to sit at a desk with a big bandage on my finger and explain to my teacher and the other kids that I had forgotten Grandpa's knife instructions to always "cut away" from myself. My right index finger had a cut that ran from the tip to the first joint. I had cried a lot, and on that day we stopped everything and just left a headless meat-sack rabbit hanging on a juniper branch. Grandpa tore off a piece of his shirt and tied it around the cut, and when we got back to his big green car he pulled me close and squeezed my finger with one hand and drove with the other. I think the maid must have cleaned my blood off of the car seat, but there were still some spots on the green floor carpet that never came out.

We weren't even back on the road to Los Vegas when the Army Men pulled up. Their cars were big like Grandpa's car, but they were black. The Army Men never wore green Army Men clothes. They wore ties and their clothes were always black. Their guns were black, too, and they never carried their guns on their hips like the cowboys on TV. The Army Men carried their guns on belts under their arms, and I couldn't see their guns when they put on their black jackets.

Gravel crunched when Grandpa stopped the car, and the Army Men's cars made the same sound. The Army Men ran up to the window of Grandpa's car and when they saw my blood they grabbed their guns and pulled Grandpa out. One of them began to talk into a radio that looked like a big black brick with a shiny antenna sticking out of one end. I was scared, but I didn't cry any more. When Grandpa was pulled away my finger started to bleed again, so I squeezed it myself.

The Army Men ran around and pointed their guns up and down the road, but there wasn't anyone there. Two Army Men pushed Grandpa onto the hood of the car and felt under his torn shirt. Then Grandpa's face got really red and he started to yell. He pushed the Army Men back, got up, and pointed at me. Then the Army Men all looked at me. They stopped running around and yelling and they put their guns away. Grandpa was still yelling, though. His face was even redder and he waved his hands.

One of the Army Men carefully unwrapped the piece of Grandpa's shirt and took some bandages out of a white box. He wiped something on my finger that was orange and smelled funny, and when he sewed the cut I didn't feel anything. Then the Army Man put a bandage on my finger and patted my head.

It Changes, Because
~~You~~ *Grandpa*
Looked
At It

Fall
1976
(1-of-3)

When Grandpa and I come here he just sits at a picnic table and watches the water, but I like to look through the chain-link fence on the edge of the cliff and watch the boats. Some of them have sails and some have motors. Sometimes I see people water skiing.

I guess that this is a place to have barbecues and stuff, but Grandpa and I never have barbecues here. There are metal tables and shades, and there's room for lots of people, but other cars just drive by. Everybody goes down the road and under the cliff to where the boats are parked. I mean "moored". Grandpa says you don't park boats. Grandpa says one day we can go out on a boat, but we never have. He always turns here and stops.

Sometimes I think that we're the only people who come here, except for the park rangers. They get out of their trucks and say hello to Grandpa, then they look in the trashcans and leave. The first time I looked in the trashcans there was only a little garbage in the bottom. I put a soda bottle in one of the cans when we were here before, and it's still there. Nobody puts new garbage on top of it.

I guess there *are* other people who visit this place, but they never come to the parking lot. They always park their black cars down the road. Grandpa says that the Army Men watch us with binoculars.

It's hot and dry so we always bring sodas and snacks. There's a town along the way called Overton, and it has a little gas station that sells soda and ice cream and stuff. It seems like we're far from home, but Grandpa says that our house is only about fifty miles away. That still seems far to me, because I know that the little green

157

number signs by the road are a mile apart, and a mile is sort of a long way.

I always bring something to play with. After I finish my soda and snack I usually bounce my ball on the concrete, but today I stop. Grandpa has put a pencil and a piece of paper on one of the picnic tables. "Leave your ball for a moment, Jacky," he says. "I want to play a different kind of game."

"A different kind of game?"

"Yes. A drawing game." Grandpa pats the bench and waits for me to sit. He puts the blank paper and pencil in front of me. "Draw something. Not a car or a house. Draw something different. Draw something that we can see in Los Vegas, and I will try to guess what it is."

I think for a moment. Then I pick up the pencil and try to draw a happy fat man sitting in a big chair with grapes in his hair and a cup in his hand.

Grandpa turns the picture upside down, to the side, and then straight. He smiles. "Bacchus! *Gott des Weines und Heiterkeit!* I think that you like the Fountain Show at Caesar's."

I grin and nod. I don't know all of what Grandpa just said, but I heard him say the right place. "I like it when the statues come to life."

"Okay," says Grandpa. "My turn."

I watch as Grandpa draws something, but I don't know what it is. Mountains, maybe? "Is this something to see in Los Vegas too, Grandpa?"

Grandpa pauses. "Ah...no. I am sorry Jacky. For my picture, I will draw something that is not in the city." It seems like Grandpa has changed the rules of this game too fast, but I don't say anything. When he's done, he slides the picture over to me.

I look at the paper. Grandpa can draw really good, but his picture is kind of funny. A big airplane is *under* the mountains, instead of *over* them. Maybe Grandpa is making a joke. "Come on Grandpa," I say. "How come the mountains are on top of the airplane?"

Grandpa smiles in the way he always smiles when he's teasing me. "Oh, yes, yes," he says. "That is not right at all." Grandpa takes the paper back, then draws a bunch of lines like water between the plane and the mountains.

"Aw, *Grandpaaa*...now the airplane is under the mountains *and* in the sea." Grandpa isn't playing a game. He's just teasing me.

Uh-oh. Maybe he's *not* teasing me. Now Grandpa looks like he looks when he's about to tell me something *cool*. If he winks, then I'll know for sure.

Grandpa winks. Then he gets up from the table and takes the picture with him. "Are you coming?" he asks.

I swing my legs out from under the table and stand up. *What's Grandpa doing?*

Grandpa walks over to the place where I like to stand and watch the boats. He kneels down and puts the paper against the fence. "Ah," he says.

I look at the paper, then I look at the mountains on the other side of the lake. I smile. "You did a good job, Grandpa."

"And the lake?"

"Uh-huh. That's how the lake looks, too."

"But we cannot see the airplane."

"I think it's supposed to be a *boat,* Grandpa."

Grandpa's big eyebrows scrunch up and he takes the picture off of the fence. "No, Jacky. I did not try to draw that boat. It just happens to be directly above the airplane. There is a big bomber airplane in the lake. It crashed there many years ago."

I screw up my face and cock my head. Grandpa is fooling around again. Isn't he? Maybe Grandpa isn't fooling around. *There's an airplane in the lake? Neat!* I watch Grandpa's face. No, he's not being funny. He's telling the truth. *A crashed bomber!* Now I look through the fence at the spot where the boat sits. "What happened, Grandpa? How did it crash?"

I don't understand what Grandpa says – *"all-tee-meeter air-or"* – or something. He looks at me. "It was an accident, Jacky. The plane flew too low over the water and crashed."

"Are there dead men in the plane?"

Grandpa seems surprised. "No. Absolutely not. We, er, *they,* all lived."

"What about bombs? And machine guns?"

"No."

"Oh." *How can a bomber not have bombs and machine guns?*

"There are much more exciting things on that plane," says Grandpa.

"What? What? Like *gold?*"

Grandpa gives me a funny look. *"Gold?* It is an aircraft, Jacky, not a sunken pirate ship."

"Can we get on a boat, Grandpa? Can we go on the lake and see the plane?" I look at the people swimming around their boat. "Is that what they're doing? Are they looking at the airplane?"

"I am afraid not," says Grandpa. "It is far too deep. Only divers can see the airplane. Those people have no idea what is beneath them."

"Okay! We can dive, right? The water isn't too dirty, is it? We're going to go scuba diving!" I smile and raise my arms, but only for a second.

"No."

"No? But...but how come? How can we see the plane?"

"We cannot."

"Why not?"

"Because it is a secret."

"A *secret?*"

"Yes," says Grandpa. "A secret that I want you to always remember. Can you do that?"

Your Little Feet
Working The
Machine

Fall
1976
(2-of-3)

When I got off the school bus I saw that a big black car had followed. It didn't bother me as much as it used to, but I still didn't like it.

"Jacky," Grandpa called from the garage, "is that you?"

"I'm home," I said, as I walked out to where Grandpa worked.

"How was school?" Grandpa was bent over his microscope. He always seemed to be bent over something - funny machines, piles of papers, and long, long math problems.

"It's okay. Fourth grade is kinda the same as third grade."

Grandpa squinted. "Ah," he said at something he saw in the microscope.

"Grandpa?"

"Mmm?"

"Can you ask the Army Men to stop following the school bus?"

Grandpa sat up. He looked at me, rubbed his eyes, and put on his glasses. "Now Jacky, I think that we have talked about this already. Captain Dreggs' job is to make sure that you get home safely."

"Sometimes my friends tease me. The black car is always there when I come home. Why do the Army Men live next to us?"

"Well, it is about my work," Grandpa said. He patted his microscope. "My work is important. They just want to make sure that we are okay."

That was that Grandpa always said. *Everybody* wanted to make sure that we were *okay.* Sometimes Grandpa had to leave for days, and when he did, there were always people who made sure that I was okay. The Army Men were like babysitters - sort of - except when

161

they took off their jackets and I could see their black guns.

They were nice to me, I guess. They let me watch any television program that I wanted, so I watched *The Electronic Company.* The Army Men never cooked. The maid and the cook always went home on days when the Army Men came over. The Army Men called restaurants for deliveries. They also talked to somebody named "Control." The Army Men always said: "Control, Sergeant Such-And-Such, authenticate such-and-such, the time is now such-and-such, clean stand, all clear," or "Hello, Verrazano Pizza? One large and one small pepperoni to 699 East Hacienda."

I liked pizza, but I got kind of scared when the Army Men asked me what I wanted to eat. On weekdays I got up for school and had cereal, but at night I couldn't think of anything to say, so I always stammered, "P-pizza."

The Army Men liked to stay in the kitchen, play cards, and call that Control guy. I just wanted to go into the living room and watch TV. When pizza came I opened the big flat box on the floor, right there on Grandpa's green carpet, and pretended that I was sharing slices with Julie from *The Electronic Company.* It was sort of like an imaginary tea party, but with cheese and pepperoni.

Operation Junior
Garden Splicer

Fall
1976
(3-of-3)

"Sometimes it is good to walk, *ja?*" Grandpa stretched his arms and took a deep breath as we followed the sidewalk north from where Hacienda crossed Maryland. I smiled at Grandpa and nodded.

Grandpa wore one of his short-sleeved yellow striped shirts with suspenders, and we both had hats. Grandpa's hat was brown and sort of like a cowboy hat, but not as big. There was a little feather in his hat that had shiny green and blue colors. My old baseball cap was brown like Grandpa's hat.

When we crossed Tropicana I turned to the left, looked far down the street, and saw Paradise Elementary School. Grandpa told me that Paradise and Ward Elementaries were closer to our house than Rowe Elementary, but the Army Men didn't want me to go to those schools. Grandpa said that, before I started first grade at Rowe, the Army Men weren't going to let me go to school at all, but he told them that he didn't want a teacher to come our house and for me to live in a box. I don't think that they were *really* going to put me inside a box, but I still wouldn't have been able to meet my friends at Rowe.

Sometimes the Army Men waited at my school to pick me up, but if I wanted to ride the bus, they would just follow in one of their big black cars. But not too close. I asked Grandpa to tell them not to follow so closely because the other kids teased me.

* * *

I saw a lot of ULVN college kids as Grandpa and I walked up Maryland. Grandpa always called them "kids," but to me they looked like grown-ups. Lots of the college boys had long hair and whiskers. The college girls liked to wear shirts with little jewels glued to them and shorts that were made out of old jeans. They sat

163

under the big umbrellas in front of Moose MacGillicuddy's and drank beer and played guitars.

Grandpa and I walked past the turn for my school on Rochelle Avenue and went to the Flamingo intersection. After we crossed the street Grandpa said that he wanted to rest for a minute, so we sat down in the shade at a bus stop. The bus had just gone by and there wasn't anybody else there.

I looked back across Flamingo. Three Army Men hurried to cross, but when they did, they stopped by the big traffic light pole. I guessed that Grandpa had told Captain Dreggs not to let his Army Men get too close. The Army Men looked kind of dumb because they weren't doing anything. The people who walked by gave them funny looks because the Army Men just stood around the light pole in black clothes. Everybody else was wearing shorts and tee shirts like me, or at least short-sleeved shirts like Grandpa. The dumb Army Men wore hot clothes and sunglasses, but they didn't have hats. *They always get bad sunburns,* I thought.

I asked Grandpa how far away the Army Men had to stay, but he didn't say anything. He looked kind of like he was dreaming, or maybe like he did when he stared at the water when we drove out to the lake. I didn't think that he heard me, but I didn't ask him again because I wanted to know what he was staring at. I didn't see much when I tried to look where Grandpa was looking, except for some tall apartment buildings. There was a big sign by the buildings that said: "Viva Vegas Towers."

Viva Vegas Towers was a new place, and when I was in third grade I saw men building it every day when I rode the school bus. I liked to watch the men and look at the big machines, but now I was in fourth grade and Viva Vegas Towers was finished and kind of boring.

"Did you say something, Jacky?" Grandpa closed his eyes and shook his head like he was waking up.

"How far away do the Army Men have to be, Grandpa?"

Grandpa looked down the street. "Well, I asked Dreggs for more distance than *that,*" he said, "but those men are too paranoid to listen." Grandpa sighed and squeezed my hand. "Just try to ignore them," he said, as we got up and started to walk again.

I didn't know that we were going to walk so far. Were we going to the Boulevard Mall? I hoped so, because there were some toy stores and bookstores with comics there. I also liked to walk around the Boulevard Mall because it was so big.

We didn't go to the Mall though, because Grandpa stopped at a new store along the way with a big sign that said: "WE 'R' TOYS." I didn't know exactly what the sign meant, but I knew that it had to be something good because I saw the word "toys".

"Is this a new store, Grandpa?" I asked. Grandpa nodded.

"I think that we can find what we are looking for here."

"What are we looking for?"

"We are going to build a model, Jacky."

"Together?" I asked. Grandpa nodded again.

I was excited. Sometimes the other boys in my class brought their model cars and airplanes to school for Miss Brooks' "Good Morning, Classmates" time. I wanted to make models, too. "Are we going to build a race car? Or a ship? What are we going to build?"

Grandpa looked at me and smiled as we went into the store. "A B-29," he said.

"Bee-Twenty-Nine, Bee-Twenty-Nine," I repeated. "What is it, Grandpa? Is it a fancy car? Is it a racer motorcycle?"

Grandpa kept smiling. "You shall see."

* * *

We called it our secret airplane, and it was as big as the table in the dining room. The wings were wider than I could reach when I stretched my arms out. Grandpa and I built it during fourth-grade Friday nights. We ordered pizza and soda from Verrazano and steak and tea from Stringles, and Grandpa told the Army Men not to bother us in the garage, because that was where we had our super-special-top-secret model-and-movie nights. Grandpa even bought a new little TV and a big heavy black machine called a "Beta" that played movies.

We went to a special store to pick out movie-tapes every Friday.

Friday nights were the BEST. I got to pick one movie, and Grandpa got to pick one movie. That was the only rule Grandpa had for model-and-movie night. Well, I guess that there was the rule about the Army Men, too. Grandpa wasn't joking, because one time the Army Men came over from next door, and Grandpa got really mad. He yelled in German at the Army Men while I waited in the garage. Then I heard him yell at Captain Dreggs. When Grandpa got mad at Captain Dreggs he always called him "Air Dreggs" or maybe "Hair Dreggs." I don't know why Grandpa called him that because Captain Dreggs' hair was really short.

On our first model-and-movie night Grandpa told me why it was a secret. He told me as we opened the big model airplane box on a table that we had made from two sawhorses and a big sheet of plywood. "This is the kind of airplane that is in the lake," said Grandpa. "I want you to learn about it."

The model was really neat, and as we built it I could see that the real airplane must also have been very big because the plastic men that went inside the model were tiny.

Grandpa said we could hang the airplane in our house when it was done. "But how can we do that if it's a secret?" I asked.

"I think that there will not be a problem," said Grandpa. "We do not have to tell anyone else that it is the kind of bomber that is in the lake." Grandpa gave me his special Grandpa wink. "Remember our secret. Always remember our secret."

I Don't Mind The
Sun Sometimes

Spring
1977
(1-of-2)

I liked to ride in Grandpa's big green car. When I
could read the shiny name on its sides, I learned that it
was called a "Buick Roadmaster." The reason I liked the
car was because it was roomy and I could put my books
and lunchbox next to me on the big seat. I also liked the
Roadmaster because when we went somewhere in it,
Grandpa was the only other person in the car. That was
another rule: When we were in the Buick Roadmaster,
Grandpa drove, and not the Army Men. No Army Men
were allowed. It was just Grandpa and me. For other
trips around town, though, we rode in a big black car
with black windows and an Army Man driver, or, if
Grandpa was mad at the Army Men, sometimes we rode
the bus. When we did that, two of the Army Men
walked with us to the bus stop. When the Army Men
followed too closely, Grandpa would turn around, say
something in German, and stare at the Army Men. They
would back up after that. Grandpa and I always got on
the bus first, found our seats, and then the Army Men
got on and sat a few seats behind us.

I liked Grandpa's big green car the best, but I also
had fun on the bus with Grandpa because we could talk
and look at things. Sometimes I forgot that the Army
Men were on the bus, except when someone tried to
talk to Grandpa and the Army Men got out of their seats
to interrupt the person.

Once two drunk men with dirty clothes said
something to Grandpa and wouldn't stop bothering him.
The Army Men moved up and sat in the seats behind the
drunk men. The Army Men reached up and touched the
backs of the men's necks, and I heard little popping
sounds like chicken wings being pulled apart at dinner.
The drunk men looked like they were sleeping with their
eyes open, and the Army Men reached between the bus
seats, grabbed the drunk men's sleeves, and kept them

from falling on the floor of the bus. Grandpa saw this happen too, and he covered my eyes until we got off at the next stop. When we left the bus the other people were still talking and looking out the windows. Nobody noticed that the drunk men were sitting so still. I tried to ask Grandpa what had happened, but he just smiled and pulled me close while the Army Men waited to follow us onto the next bus.

* * *

I always knew when we were going to take a ride in Grandpa's car because he wore his hat that looked like the one he wore in the picture on his nightstand. Grandpa said that the picture next to his bed was taken near a place where he worked when he was young. The place had a funny name that made me giggle because it was hard for me to say - it sounded like "pee-on-the-moon, duh" or "pee-na-moon-da". Grandpa smiled when I tried to say it.

I thought that Grandpa looked tall and handsome in the picture. He wore a long white coat like the kind a doctor wears, and Grandpa was only a little taller than an older man who stood beside him. The older man looked kind of like Grandpa. He wore a suit and a little hat, and he had glasses and a curly mustache. The man seemed very happy, and he had one hand on Grandpa's shoulder. Grandpa said that this was the only picture he had of my great-grandpa. Grandpa always kept part of the picture covered. He put strips of black tape along the left edge of the glass in the frame, so I never saw my great-grandfather's right arm and shoulder. Once Grandpa and I were sitting on the bed and while he told me a story about his father, I tried to pull the tape off so that I could see what was under it. Grandpa stopped me and said that I must never do that.

Grandpa had another picture that he kept in a special cardboard envelope. I didn't know why he was so careful with it, because it didn't seem like a very good picture. It was one of those pictures that people take when they hold the camera in front of their faces and smile because there's nobody else to take the picture, except there *was* another person. Grandpa looked like he was tickling her or something, and he had one arm around the lady to keep her next to him. The lady didn't want to have her picture taken because she had one hand over her face. I could still see her mouth though, and it looked like she was laughing. She had black hair and skin that was whiter than Grandpa's skin. Grandpa was young in this picture too, but maybe a little older than in the other picture. He had a big grin and his hair was all messed up. He looked silly and happy.

Every time I asked Grandpa who the lady was, he just smiled. It was a funny smile, kind of like he was thinking about something, but he never answered, except for one time when I asked him if the lady was my grandma. He nodded. I asked him if she had died, but he said no. I *think* he said that she hadn't been born yet...or something weird like that. I didn't understand, and I tried to ask Grandpa more questions, but he just put his special picture back in the cardboard envelope and didn't talk about it anymore. I decided not to ask any more questions about the picture, because too many questions made Grandpa look sad.

* * *

The letter from Miss Brooks was sealed, but I opened it on the school bus. Most of the other kids on the bus opened their letters, too. When I saw the "B" that I got in Social Studies, I felt so bad. I went home and gave the letter to Grandpa. He looked at the open flap and raised an eyebrow, but he didn't say anything.

As Grandpa read my grades I just stood there and looked at my shoes. Then at the ceiling. Then at the kitchen table. Then my dumb eyes felt kind of itchy or something. *Stupid eyes.* I wiped them on the back of my hand. Grandpa smiled and kissed the top of my head, but I still knew that the only way, until my next report card, for me to keep track of Mon-El's adventures would be to ask my friends if I could read their comics.

Most of my friends liked Batman and Superman and guys like that. There were only two boys who read about Mon-El, and only when he happened to be having an adventure with Superman. That thought made me feel a little better. Yeah, one of my friends would probably let me read their comics, and, except for my social studies grade, I had all "A"s. Grandpa seemed happy with me, anyway.

I sighed as I unpacked my lunch and changed out of my school clothes. I wanted to tell Julie about my day at school, but *The Electronic Company* wasn't on yet. Grandpa came into the living room as I sat in my favorite spot in front of the TV.

"Jacky, you did not have to change into your play clothes. We are going out again."

I turned to see that Grandpa held his dark glasses and wore his brown hat.

"Where are we going, Grandpa?"

"I thought you said that the boys in your class got comic books from White Cross Pharmacy."

My heart jumped. *White Cross!*

"We cannot get three comics because you didn't get all "A"s, but perhaps we can get two. Your other grades were quite good." Grandpa had a little smile.

I was still happy. I thought that I had wrecked our whole deal. I turned off the TV. I would talk to Julie tomorrow.

Grandpa watched me press the Zenith's power button. "Jacky, would you like to watch something else? You will be in fifth grade next year. I am rather surprised that you still watch *Sesamie Street.*"

"I was just waiting for *Sesamie Street* to be over, Grandpa. I wanted to see *The Electronic Company.*"

"*The Electronic Company*...you watch that program a great deal. Is it your favorite?"

"Yes. Grandpa?"

"Mmm?"

"How come the Army Men don't know our secret?"

Grandpa shook his head. "They do not *need* to know our secret."

"But they're soldiers. Don't they know soldier things? Don't they know soldier secrets?"

Grandpa laughed. "No. Only generals and people like me know such things. *Herr* Dreggs is a captain, and his men are sergeants."

"Oh," I said. "Is a captain more than a sergeant?"

"*More?*"

"Uh-huh. Is a captain the boss of a sergeant?"
Grandpa nodded.

"Is a general more than a captain?"
Grandpa nodded again. "Much more."

I looked at Grandpa. "Are you a general, too? You said that only generals and people like you know secrets."

"No," said Grandpa. "I am not a general." He paused and smiled. "It is difficult to explain, Jacky. I was a scientist, then I was a prisoner of war, then I was a research asset, and finally I became a Black Project leader. Now I sometimes wonder if I am again a prisoner." Grandpa sighed and his smile went away.

"But you told me that you were a doctor."

"Well, I am, but not the kind who helps sick people. Sometimes doctors do other things."

"You're a scientist, too? What do you do?"

Grandpa paused. "Well...I am the kind of scientist who discovers the things that your teacher talks about in science class. I am the kind of scientist whom the American military wants to keep safe. Now I think I need to be the kind of scientist who teaches a young boy things that he will not learn by watching television."

I wanted to ask more questions, but Grandpa just shook his head. "Not now. Do you want to go out or not?"

* * *

I thought that the seats in Grandpa's big green car smelled funny when they got hot. I rolled the windows down, but that didn't help much. Even though I didn't know as much about cars as some of the other boys at my school, I did know that Grandpa's car was kind of...old. It could go fast, though. There were big fins on the back of the car that reminded me of a fish, and the shiny parts on the front looked like a grinning robot with headlight eyes. When I got into Grandpa's car I had to pull hard to open the heavy door. The radio had silver knobs and the steering wheel was really big. The seats of Grandpa's car weren't like the seats in the Army Men's cars or the seats on the bus. They were wide like the bleachers in my school's recreation room.

Grandpa's old pocket watch hung on a chain from

the rear view mirror. I took it in my hand and looked at it, then I held it to my ear and heard it tick. There had been a picture on the watch, but Grandpa had scraped off most of it. When I looked closely, though, I saw that it might have been a bird, sort of like the eagle on a dollar, but it was black. This bird wasn't holding a bunch of arrows and branches. Instead, it had been standing on something, but I couldn't figure out what that part of the picture had been because it was all gone. Grandpa had scraped that part really hard.

I watched Grandpa as he stood by the front door and talked to one of the Army Men. When Grandpa finally got into the car he smiled at me, but I could tell that he was mad. As we drove further down the street, I thought that maybe the Army Men weren't going to follow, but one of their big black cars pulled out behind us. It was sort of like when the Army Men followed the school bus. They tried not to get too close, but I saw them anyway.

*　*　*

White Cross Pharmacy was about half-way between the fancy hotels on The Strip and the big robot cowboy that waved on Fremont Street. When we got there I almost ran inside, but instead I waited at the front door.

The older kids at Rowe Elementary would say that I've "fucked up", but I can't talk like that around Grandpa. I was mad at Miss Brooks. The "B" on my report card was going to stop me from finding out if Mon-El had won his fight with Mordrew the Merciless. My report card earned me parts one and two of Mon-El's adventure, but not part three.

"I didn't have time to make my Paiute village diorama look good," I said, "because it took a long time to learn about atoms for the static electricity experiment."

"You know, Jacky, your social studies grade is also important."

"I know, but I like science more." I think Grandpa liked it when I said that.

Grandpa took one of the comics off of the rack. "They do not finish the story at the end? When I was a boy in Ulm, whole stories were in one book." Grandpa

172

turned the pages, and I could tell that he was thinking. He was about to ask me something.

Get ready...

"What are the parts of an atom, my boy?"

Here we go. A new comic book deal, maybe?

"Electron, proton, neutron." *Yay! I remembered!*

"Well, I suppose that is where it starts," said Grandpa. I wasn't sure what he meant, but Grandpa's smile told me that I had given a good answer. He wasn't finished, though. "What do the parts do?"

This question was harder. "They're like...like the big bulletin board that Miss Brooks made of the solar system. The proton and neutron are sort of where the sun is, and the electron makes a circle around them." I remembered words under a picture in my science book. *"Diagram of a Hydrogen Atom,"* I said.

Grandpa's smile got bigger. "I suppose that deuterium was chosen to illustrate a neutron," he said, sort of to himself. Like before, I wasn't sure what Grandpa meant. "Why does the atom have the same number of protons and electrons?" he asked.

I was so close. I could almost feel the pages of the third comic book. I had to think hard. "To stay... balanced. Like two kids on a teeter-totter who weigh the same, I guess. That's how come you get shocked, like when we rubbed the socks on balloons in class. The electrons get mixed up. Some atoms have too many, and some don't have enough. They want to get balanced again. Electricity is the electrons trying to get back to where they belong. It's kinda like they're mad, and they'll sting you when they're getting straightened out."

"And what about neutrons? What do they do?"

"Well...not very much. They just kind of sit there. Um, the proton and neutron are together in the necklace."

"Nucleus," said Grandpa. "I think that is an adequate fourth grade response. Good answers, Jacky." Grandpa mussed my hair.

That was it? No third Mon-El?

"Well, I think that it is time to go," said Grandpa. "Do you have two comics?"

"Yes," I said, as I looked at the floor.

"Okay," said Grandpa, as he took part three of Mon-El's adventure off of the rack.

"How come...?" I began.

"This is *my* comic," said Grandpa. "A deal is a deal, Jacky. But maybe I will let you read it sometime."

* * *

We didn't go back home. Instead, Grandpa turned the opposite way on The Strip and I wondered if we would pass the big robot cowboy. I liked to go up The Strip, because I could look at all of the big signs and hotels. I liked to look at the tourists because their clothes were different and a lot of them wore big silly hats and carried cameras.

Sometimes Grandpa and I walked on The Strip, too, and when we did that, I knew that Grandpa was looking for someone. When he found them, he would smile and say *"Guten Tag"*, and someone wearing a big hat and carrying a camera would talk to Grandpa in German. When they finished talking, Grandpa always seemed sad. Today Grandpa wasn't looking for anyone, though. He smiled at me as we left The Strip, then he looked in the rear view mirror and frowned as he drove onto the freeway.

"Are we going to the place where you work, Grandpa?" I asked.

Grandpa didn't answer me right away. He was still watching the cars behind us. *"Drecksau,"* he said, in a mad voice. I turned my head and saw the Army Men's black car. "Just a moment, Jacky," said Grandpa.

Our car slowed down and the black car got closer. Though we had just gotten onto the freeway, Grandpa started to turn onto an exit. I didn't need to look behind us to know that the black car was also turning. Grandpa kept looking at two other cars as well, both slightly behind us and in the right lane. At the last moment, Grandpa reached over and pulled the tab on my seatbelt so tight that I could barely breathe, then he hit the gas and yanked the wheel. I sank backward into the green bench seat as the engine in the Roadmaster roared. We crossed the white dotted line and went back into the outer lane, well ahead of the two cars that Grandpa had been watching, but they honked at us anyway. I loosened the belt enough to look over the seat again. The black car was gone and Grandpa laughed.

Like the older boys at Rowe Elementary School would say, Grandpa was fucking cool.

Grandpa smiled at me and when I smiled back he rubbed my hair into a mess. I didn't fix it. I just kept smiling. We were leaving town now, and we passed signs that had pictures of ladies in jewels and feathers that said: "Come Back Soon!"

I remembered the question that I had asked earlier. "Are you going to work, Grandpa?" I repeated. I had never seen the place where Grandpa worked.

"To work? No, not today, Jacky," said Grandpa. We are just out for a drive. It is nice to drive sometimes. Do you think so?"

I nodded and rolled my window down a little. The roller handle was kind of hard to crank, just like the heavy car doors were a little hard to open. I didn't roll the window down too far though, because I didn't want the wind to flip the pages of my comic books. I gave Grandpa a *Can I?* look as I half-reached for the White Cross bag. He nodded, so I started to read.

"That comic book does not have jokes," said Grandpa. "When I was a boy in Germany, we called them 'funny books,' and they had cartoon stories to make us laugh."

I looked up from the comic. "These are hero stories," I said.

"Ah," replied Grandpa. "Do you like this Super-Man?"

"I like Superman," I said, "but this story is about Mon-El."

"I know about monel," said Grandpa. "It is a fine marine-steel alloy."

"*Mon*-El. It isn't steel or Superman. Mon-El is another hero."

"A hero, but not like Super-Man?"

"No. Well, sort of. He can do everything that

Superman can do, and he's even a little stronger, too. But lead makes him sick. And he's a scientist."

"A scientist! Then I am glad that I bought that comic. I like scientists."

"Me too," I said.

Fucking-Super-Cool.

A.K.A. Second Chances
At The "Top Secret"
Bonnie Claire
Airstrip

Summer
1977
(2-of-2)

"We are here, Jacky."

Grandpa laughed when I sat up. "The seat gave you a funny face," he said. I looked in the rear view mirror and saw lines across my cheek.

"Where are we?" I asked.

"Lathrop Wells," said Grandpa. There was a gas station, a few houses, and a big building with a sign that said: *The Shady Mustang Ranch*. "Have we ever been here before?" asked Grandpa.

"I don't think so," I said, as I rubbed my face. I wanted the seat marks to go away.

"We are close to Death Valley," said Grandpa. "It is on the other side of those mountains."

"Are we in California?" I asked. "Miss Brooks said that Death Valley is in California."

"Miss Brooks should look at a map," said Grandpa, "because some of the monument area is in Nevada, too."

"It's really hot here," I said. "Can we get something to drink?" By "something to drink" I meant a soda.

"We need to do something else first."

"What?"

"I will show you," said Grandpa. We got out and went to the back of the car. I thought that Grandpa was going open the trunk, but he didn't. Instead, he took out his little pocket knife, got down on his knees, and began to feel under the bumper and behind the license plate. "There," he said, as he stuck the blade behind the plate and scraped off something. Grandpa looked at the tiny thing in his hand and gave it to me.

It was maybe half an inch long and it looked like a roll of copper wire inside a glass seed. "Neat," I said.

"What is it?"

"This," said Grandpa, "is a radio. It tells the Army Men where we are. The Army Men put them in our clothes and in our shoes, too."

"They do?"

Grandpa nodded. "But they are easy to find. I took them out of the clothes and shoes that we are wearing today. This was the only one on the car. One day Army Men and police will put them inside people, too."

"Why put them *inside* people?"

Grandpa stood up, folded the knife, and dropped it into his pocket. "Because when you are grown, they will be faster and easier than tattoos." Grandpa got a funny look on his face and he stared at the mountains around Death Valley. "I must prepare you," he said in a strange voice.

Grandpa blinked and shook his head. When he spoke, he sounded like Grandpa again. "Let us have some fun, Jacky. I know exactly what to do with that little radio."

* * *

Across from the Lathrop Wells store and the funny ranch that really wasn't a ranch was a small rest area. It had some bathrooms, tables, and benches. Grandpa parked his car behind the store, but we could still look across the highway and watch the rest area. There wasn't much going on over there. A big truck started up and left, and a few minutes after that a family with some little kids stopped to use the toilets.

I took a drink of my Nevada Lime Cola and thanked Grandpa. Grandpa just smiled and took a drink of his own soda. I kind of wanted to read some more of my comic book, but I also wanted to watch the rest area.

"Do you think they'll be much longer?" I asked.

"No," said Grandpa. "Their kind are like dogs, always sniffing, always trying to get back on the scent. They will probably --" Grandpa stopped and I turned to see that two black cars had parked at the rest area.

Eight Army Men ran to one of the toilets. One of them knocked once, waited, knocked twice, waited, and then kicked the toilet door open.

"They followed that little radio into the toilet, just

like you said they would, Grandpa!" I laughed and almost spilled my cola.

"Ja. Not so bright, those men."

We watched as the Army Men came out of the toilet and stood around. One of them spoke into a brick radio for a few minutes. Then they got back into their cars and left.

"Are you ready to go home?" asked Grandpa. I smiled and nodded.

* * *

It was nighttime as Grandpa drove home. First I saw the glow of the lights and then I saw the tops of the hotels. We were still far away and on the dark highway, so I asked Grandpa if he would turn on the light inside the car so that I could read, but Grandpa said he wouldn't be able to drive. Then I tried to read by the little light inside the glove box, but Grandpa told me to close the glove box because it was still too bright. So I just sat and watched the road.

"Grandpa, will the Army Men be waiting for us when we get home?"

"Yes."

"Will they be mad at us?"

"Ha!" laughed Grandpa. "I certainly hope so."

I watched the city lights get brighter. "Aren't you afraid of them?"

"No, my boy. I am too important to them, and you do not need to be afraid, either. For now."

This was one of those times when Grandpa said things that I didn't really understand, but they still made me a little scared. "When will I be afraid of them?" I asked.

Grandpa kept his eyes on the road. "In about forty years," he said. Then Grandpa reached over and grabbed my arm. Sometimes he did that when he was driving and he wanted to pull me over for a hug, but not this time. He just kept feeling my arm like he was looking for something but not finding it. Grandpa took his eyes off of the road for a moment to look at me. In the dashboard light his face looked worried.

Grandpa pulled the car off the highway and turned on the light. "What's the matter, Grandpa?" I asked, but

179

Grandpa didn't say anything. He pulled up my tee shirt sleeve and ran his fingers over the skin of my arm.

"Zeigen Sie mir Ihren Arm! Show me your arm!" said Grandpa. He stopped for a second like he remembered something, then he reached over and began touching my right arm in the same way that he had touched my left. He didn't do it for very long, though, so I guessed that he found what he was looking for.

Grandpa let me go, fell back on his seat, and took off his hat. He covered his face with it for a few seconds and took deep breaths, then he looked at me. I pulled up my right tee shirt sleeve and turned my head to see whatever it was that Grandpa had found, but all I saw was my arm. It looked the same as it always did.

Grandpa grabbed my left arm again, but this time in the hug way. He pulled me close and tight, then he let go and sighed. Grandpa turned off the light, put the car back into gear, and we continued down the road.

* * *

I'm on my way back to Los Vegas and I'm staring at the dashboard light of Grandpa's Buick Roadmaster. It makes a rectangle in the dark, but I can't see the speedometer or gas gauge. It's just a dim outline.

That's odd. Am I in the back seat? And if I am, how can I see the dashboard, especially as it appears now, just sort of hovering over me, like...light peeking through a coffin's lid seal.

I realize that Grandpa and his Roadmaster are many years in the past, but still and always driving back into town as I clutch my precious comics and fall asleep. To hell with this stupid TSA post-apocalyptic shit-world. I had a Grandpa once, and he was fucking cool. That's all that matters.

Damn it. I don't care if I'm now an old man myself. I still miss Grandpa.

I'm not dead, after all. Why can't we just get this over with? The TSA doltamatics even managed to screw up my death. Idiots. I'm just riding along in the back of the meat wagon. Someone has taken the time to box me up. More light enters through small holes that also let air pass over my body. Yes, I'm still alive, but I wouldn't say that Terrie Gilliam's Commando Heating Engineer has rescued me.

Wait. This isn't exactly the standard meat wagon treatment, either. Is this the diesel truck to heaven? Or hell?

Can I move? Arms...no. Legs...no. Neck...yes. I raise my head slightly and look down at my body. The movement seems easy. I feel, well, stronger. In fact, I don't feel particularly close to death. I'm not up to wrestling bulls, of course, but something has certainly improved, physiologically-speaking.

There's a tube in my mouth. Needles are taped to my arms. I suspect that I've eaten quite a few meals through my veins. I seem to be strapped down, but not as if I'm a prisoner. It's more like I've been secured, rather than restrained. The hard surfaces of the box are dulled by a soft pad. Hmmm. I don't feel a catheter, so I must be diapered.

A cool feeling tells me that the IV dinner bell just rang. It spreads out from the needles and moves throughout my body.

Ahhh.

Whatever those spikes are pumping feels good. Maybe this is the truck to heaven after all.

Back to Dreamland.

And With The Right Kind
Of Eyes You Can
Almost *See* The
High-Water
Mark

Summer
1977

There's a white mark on the rocks around Lake Meade. It's a long line that people call a "bathtub ring", and it shows where the water used to be. I stand behind the fence on the cliff and look at the mark below. I like to pretend that the water is low enough to see the airplane.

Grandpa calls to me from a table. "What is in your pockets, Jacky? Show me."

My pockets? I dunno. I go to the picnic table and turn my pockets inside out. A broken and chewed pencil stub falls out, along with a nickel, a penny, and a piece of bubble gum. I bend over, pick up my things, and put them on the table.

Grandpa looks at the gum and smiles. "Interesting. I carried similar items when I was your age. Tell me about these things."

I sit down. "Uh, okay. This is a pencil I borrowed from the boy who sits in front of me at school, and--"

"I already know what these things are, Jacky," Grandpa says, before I can tell him about the gum. "Please tell me what they are *for*. What can you do with them?"

"I can write with this pencil," I answer, "but it needs to be sharpened. And I can buy some more gum in a machine with this," I continue, as I point at the penny. "I want to save the nickel, though."

"And this?" asks Grandpa, as he points at the gum.

"We can share it," I offer. "Do you want to split it?" Grandpa smiles and nods, so I take the wrapper off, pull the gum into two pieces, and give one to Grandpa. We both smack and chew with silly noises. Grandpa blows a bubble first, but when it pops it gets stuck in his beard. I laugh as I watch him pick the sticky pink gum off of his whiskers.

Grandpa takes the gum out of his mouth and puts it in the wrapper. "Jacky, I want to imagine something. I want to pretend."

"Pretend what?"

"Let us pretend that we do not have a car. Let us pretend that we are here alone, and we only have our clothes and the things in our pockets."

"How will we get home?"

"That is part of this pretend game," says Grandpa. "How *will* we get home?"

I think for a moment. "We could wait here. We don't have to do anything."

Grandpa tips his head. "Why do you say that, Jacky?"

"Because if we sit here long enough, the Army Men will come and take us home."

Grandpa looks surprised, but I don't know why. "What's the matter, Grandpa?"

"Not that, Jacky. In this game, that is what we *do not* want to happen." Grandpa takes a breath and clears his throat. "I did not explain well. This will help you understand." Grandpa gets up. "Come with me," he says, as he walks toward the cliff's edge. When we get to the fence, Grandpa takes his car keys out of his pocket and throws them over the cliff.

"Grandpa!" I exclaim. I go to the fence and lean against the chain link as I struggle to see where the keys have fallen. I doesn't matter, though, because they're gone. "Grandpa, why - why did you do that?" Grandpa doesn't answer as I follow him back to the table.

I'm starting to feel a little afraid. "You said that this was just a pretend game," I say. *What are we going to do? Maybe we really will have to walk down the road and ask the Army Men for help. Or maybe we'll see the park rangers.* Then I think of something. Grandpa is just teasing again. I get it. Those weren't *really* the car keys. "Okaaay, Grandpa," I say, with a little-bit-afraid smile. "Now it's time for you to empty *your* pockets."

Grandpa looks at me, but he still doesn't say anything. He stands up to empty his pockets. The only thing that he puts on the table is his wallet.

A-ha. I know where to look. I reach for the wallet, and Grandpa still doesn't say anything. I pick it up and open it. There's some money, Grandpa's driver's license, and another thing that looks like a driver's license, but it says *"US DIA."* That's all.

I really don't like this game.

What are we gonna do?

I remember the little radios that the Army Men like to put in our car and in our clothes. I get up and start walking to the car.

"Where are you going, Jacky?"

"I want to check something." Grandpa gets up and follows me.

I get on my hands and knees and feel behind the license plate, in the spot where I saw Grandpa scrape off the little radio when we went to Lathrop Wells. I touch something and pull it off of the plate. It's a car key.

You Have To Understand, Most Of These People Are Not Ready To Be Unplugged

Fall
1977
(1-of-2)

This is the best camping trip that Grandpa has ever taken me on. I like the nights here. It's almost as cool as the air conditioning in our house, and I like the stars. We skipped our Friday model-and-movie to visit this place, and now it's Saturday night.

I had so much fun today. Grandpa and I shot at empty tin cans with Grandpa's .22 and then we cooked some hotdogs. I also did some exploring. There's a spring not far away, and it has a thing that looks like a little metal swimming pool and a water pipe that comes out of the ground. Grandpa told me how springs work. It's like...when different kinds of earth get in a big sandwich and some kinds of earth are softer and squishier than others, and the weight of the harder and heavier pieces of the sandwich push the water out of the soft parts...or something like that.

This is a good place for Grandpa to camp, because it is kind of close to the road and he doesn't have to walk very far. Sometimes Grandpa gets tired and has to rest.

* * *

On Sunday morning Grandpa shook me in my sleeping bag. "Jacky, wake up. I need to show you something."

"Mmmm, it's still dark outside, Grandpa. Can't we sleep a little longer before we go home?"

"We are not going home yet, Jacky," said Grandpa. "I will start a fire, and I want you to get up now."

I moaned a little but did as Grandpa said. *How come we had to get up so early?* I unzipped my sleeping bag and dressed. I went outside, but Grandpa hadn't built a fire yet. It was chilly, so I folded my arms and pulled my sweatshirt tight around my shoulders.

"Over here, Jacky," said Grandpa. He was standing away from the tent and between some trees.

"I thought we were going to have breakfast," I said, but Grandpa didn't hear me. He was looking at his old watch. The morning was so quiet that I could hear it tick.

The sun started to come up. Grandpa turned and held his watch up into the light. "Northwest," he said. He pointed at something, but I couldn't see what. Grandpa got on his knees next to me. He held his arm close to my head and pointed at the sky again. This time I saw some blinking lights.

"It - it's just an airplane, Grandpa." I wanted to eat and sit by a warm fire.

"Watch the chemical spray trail," said Grandpa. "The view of particulate diffusion is perfect from this altitude."

"What?"

"The smoke. I want you to look at the airplane smoke," said Grandpa, as he stood back up.

I watched the airplane, but I didn't see what was so special about it. It only left a long white line in the sky, but I kept watching as the sky got brighter. Then something funny happened. A little rainbow spread out from the white smoke line, like a long pretty peacock feather.

"Grandpa, look!" I said. Now I was the one who pointed at the sky. The sun was up and I could see Grandpa's face, but when I looked at him he seemed kind of mad. "Grandpa? Do you...do you see it?"

Grandpa still looked mad when he turned to me, but then he smiled. I didn't think his smile was real, though. I think he only smiled because he didn't want me to think that he was mad at me. "Yes," he said. "There are many colors."

"Do you like it?" I asked. Grandpa didn't say anything.

The colors slowly disappeared and there was just a red line in the sky. I couldn't see the airplane anymore.

"Where did the rainbow go?" I asked.

"It is still there," said Grandpa, "but now the sunlight is coming from a different angle."

"Why is it red? I thought airplane smoke was white."

"In a few minutes it will look like regular smoke, but it will not disappear," said Grandpa. "It will still be in the sky even after we have finished eating breakfast."

* * *

"What will Hair Dreggs and the other Army Men do when we get home?" I asked.

"*Herr* Dreggs and the rest will whine and do nothing," laughed Grandpa, as he turned the pickup truck's steering wheel to miss a big rock in the mountain road. "We can rent a vehicle if we so choose." Grandpa smiled. "Do not worry about Herr Dreggs. What I want you to do now is tell me our special secrets."

"Okay."

"Well?"

"The airplane in the water. That's Number One. Never talk about the airplane."

"Good. And what are our new secrets?"

I didn't answer. Instead, I needed to ask a question of my own. "Grandpa?"

"Yes?"

"Why are the airplane lines a secret?" It seemed kind of funny to call them a secret, because everybody could see them.

"I suppose that they are not really a *secret*," said Grandpa, "but there are some things that you should not discuss with other people."

"Why not?"

"Because other people do not know what we know, so they cannot understand. When people cannot understand, they can become…angry. So, for now, we will not talk about the dragon tails."

"Okay. How come you call them 'dragon tails'? Because they turn red? Like the fire of a dragon or something?"

"No," said Grandpa. "Long ago, when plague--"

"What's that?"

"It is when everyone becomes sick and many people die."

"Oh."

"When there was a plague, people did not know about germs. Some thought that God was angry, while others believed that dragons left sickness in the sky. There were also people who believed that Shakpana had come."

"What's a Shakpana?"

"In parts of Africa, 'Shakpana' was the name of the smallpox god. Smallpox is a sickness that killed many people. But you," continued Grandpa, as he took one hand off of the steering wheel and pulled up the sleeve on his other arm, "have one of *these.*" Grandpa pointed at a little round mark on the back of his arm. "You also have a mark like this. It means you will not get sick from smallpox."

I had seen the mark on my arm in the mirror when I got out of the bathtub, but I never paid any attention to it. "Is Shakpana real?" I asked.

"Well, the people in Africa certainly thought so."

I didn't say anything until we were out of the mountains. I looked out the window at the desert while I thought about what Grandpa had said, and then I asked another question. "Grandpa, that airplane smoke - I mean, *dragon tail* - is it going to make people sick, too?"

Grandpa reached across the seat and rubbed my head. "You are thinking now, my bright boy. But no, *these* dragon tails will not make people sick. Not yet. For many years, there will not be any dragon tails. But after you grow up, they will come again."

"Then people will be sick? With the smallpox?"

"Yes."

"But the spots on our arms...don't other people have them, too?"

"At this time, *everyone* has a smallpox vaccination scar. When you grow up, though, people will not get smallpox shots."

"Why not?"

"Because doctors will say that people do not need them."

"But won't they get sick?" I asked.

Grandpa nodded.

* * *

Grandpa drove our big green car home after we

returned the pickup. He talked to me again about our secrets. "I still want you to tell me all of them," he said.

"The bomber plane in the water. Like the one we're making in the garage."

"Yes. What else?"

"Dragon tails. Never talk about them, but watch the sky. When they come again, I'll go to our camping place. If I have to walk, I'll use your map and backpack."

Grandpa smiled. "Very good. And why go to the camping place?"

"Because there's a lot of food and medicine there. The spring is there, too."

"Where is the food?"

I remembered a big mound of dirt that Grandpa had shown me. It hadn't been very far from our tent. "It's inside that lump," I answered. "I'm supposed to dig until I find it."

Vinegar And
Brown
Paper

It's time for recess...but not for me. For Grandpa. When Grandpa gets time off from work, we sort of go on little vacations together. He likes to call these times his "recess", and he always laughs when he says that. It's...kind of a dumb joke, and Grandpa says it a lot. I always smile when Grandpa tells dumb jokes. When Grandpa says them, they're not dumb.

We leave our house, but we don't leave Los Vegas. Grandpa told me that he doesn't have to be back at work until Monday, the same as when I have to go back to school. We're in our big green car.

Grandpa points at something as we get close to The Strip. "Can you read that new sign, Jacky?"

"Exan...Exanaduh?" *That's a funny word. It starts with an "X".*

"*Zzzanadoo,*" says Grandpa.

"Xanadu," I repeat.

"Correct. In English, when a word starts with the letter 'x', it sounds like a 'z'."

"Oh. What is it?"

"It is a new hotel," smiles Grandpa. "You will have your own room."

"My own room? But where will you stay?"

"I will be next door. There is a bathroom between our rooms, so if you need something, you can knock."

I don't need to look behind us to know that a black car is following. "What about the Army Men?"

"Captain Dreggs and his team will be on the same floor."

"How come we aren't going to Sammy's Town?" I ask. I like the little forest in Sammy's Town. It has waterfalls and trees and robot animals. There's a big roaring bear and a howling wolf. They're my favorites.

"We can go there next time. I want to see this new

hotel during my recess." Grandpa smiles at me, and I smile back.

We pull up to the front of the new hotel and Grandpa gives his keys to a *valet*. Heh. I know how to say *that* word. It has a "t", but you have to say "val-aaay". Kind of like the way Fonzy says "Aaay!"

The new hotel isn't like anything that I've ever seen on *Happier Days,* though. It kind of looks like the big white ship on *The Lover Boat,* except there are lots of plants all over it. *Vines,* says Grandpa.

"One moment, please," Grandpa says to the valet. "I forgot our bags." The valet is wearing a white shirt with little golden stripes on the sleeves. His nametag says: *XANADU – NICK R. – HELENA, MT.* He smiles and hands the keys back to Grandpa, and we get out of the Roadmaster. I can't get out as fast as Grandpa because I always have to push the heavy car door open with my feet.

The doors of Xanadu are big and made of glass. They open by themselves when we get close, but they don't make the *Star Track* "shhhk-shhhk" sound.

I hope that Xanadu has a pool and an arcade.

Can I order pepperoni pizza in my room?

Or in my big plastic TSA coffin?

* * *

The coffin lid opens in the twenty-first century and I wake up.

"Easy, easy," says the TSA fuckhead. He's an average unscarred white Joe, late thirties or maybe early forties, with buzzed hair and brown eyes that seem significantly brighter than the usual Transcendental Security Administration zombie-glaze.

"Introductions," he says, as he pulls the lid completely off. I confirm that I've been riding around in a big black plastic box. The lid is thin and light, and I hear it clatter to the side. There's a lot of space in this box, and yes, I'm sure that it's some kind of coffin liner or

sarcophagus. I seem to be the only tenant, though this container looks like it could sleep a family of four.

"Name's Carlssin. Andrew Carlssin, USASE, actually... though that doesn't mean a damn thing here. For now, and for about the past year," he says, as he motions at double white chevrons on his rolled-up black sleeves, "I'm just some nobody corporal from a TSA regional motor pool. An industrial hearse driver," he bitterly adds.

I wonder at the emotion in the man's words. What is this? A TSA slug with a conscience? Or perhaps even a soul? I've never seen this man before...or have I? Maybe...yeah. He might be a guy that I glimpsed several times from the tarps at DS-21. He's the meat wagon driver. Charming. However different he may be from his black-clad fellows, Corporal Carlssin evidently isn't tight enough with Jiminy Kricket to abandon his post as a genocide-victim transporter.

"And I know your name already, Jack Simmerath. I've been waiting for you in this hell. I've been waiting for what feels like an eternity. Pleasure to meet you, finally." Carlssin instinctively holds out his hand, then sheepishly lowers it. "Sorry," he says, as he takes the straps off of my ankles and wrists. Before I can lift my hand, he raises it and shakes it. "How are your eyes? Can you focus on me?" He looks up at what seems to be a high metal ceiling. "Can you see those supports?"

Han Soloe was blind when the Princess busted him out of karbonite, but my eyes aren't quite that bad. At first I nod, but after a moment I shake my head. I realize that, while I can see things nearby, distance viewing is a problem. Despite my age, I've never needed glasses, but now...it's hard to focus. Carlssin is close and I can see him fairly well, but beyond a few feet, things seem to be outlined in fuzz. Even so, the blurred but stationary overhead view indicates that I'm out of the sun. I guess that I'm looking at the interior roof supports of a truck fleet bay.

"No? Well, give it a little more time, Jack. You've been under an auto-pen sledgehammer." It's kind of disconcerting to hear this stranger speak my name, though my identity is no mystery. I figure that, when

192

TSA goes out abducting, they have shopping lists of names, but I don't know why a low-level truck driver would have that information.

When Carlssin takes the tube out of my mouth I try to ask what's happening, but I sound like I've smoked cigars and gargled gravel. "No voice? It'll come back," he says. "Those auto-pens loosen up everything, including the larynx. And your guts, too." Carlssin's look answers my earlier catheter musings. "You'll have to make allowances if you're not the type of guy who gets his diapers changed on the first date, because you're too important to risk an infection. Not when I'm this close. If it matters, you've got the cleanest ass in Vegas." Carlssin gently takes me by the wrist and raises my arm. I'm wearing a black TSA fatigue shirt that's cuffed above my elbows. "Same with the tubes," continues Carlssin. "I've kept these tracks immaculate."

Needle marks preceding those that currently feed me confirm that Carlssin has nursed me for some time. He's set the coffin up as a micro-ambulance. Drip bags are attached to the plastic sides, and there's an array of loose vials, some of them empty, in the bottom. A label reads "Salagen-Pilocarpine", while others are of adrenaline and saline. Near my feet is a small pile of empty drip bags marked "Field, Multi-Sched, MKIII".

"I almost shot those two low-grades who tossed you onto the flatbed," says Carlssin. "I would have, if they had broken your neck or cracked your skull. You see, Jack, without you, I'm fucked, and I probably would have stuck my 'sixteen in my mouth and blown the back of my head out if you had bitten the big one." Carlssin raises a jug of water and pours a cup. "Let's see if you can swallow. I'm out of jelly for your mouth swab." He reaches down into the coffin and helps me sit up. I notice that some pieces of foam padding stick to the perspiration on my clothes.

I slowly raise my hands to take the cup, and Carlssin is careful to support the slack IV tubes when I move my arms. "Alright? Can you sit up on your own?" he asks. When I nod he slowly takes his arm out from behind me. "Slowly. Just a little on your tongue at first," he says. "I've been checking your gums to see if there was enough C in those Multis to save your teeth. I finally got your mouth healed up, but this is still going to burn."

I take a breath, then a tiny, choking sip, then another breath. Despite the Vaselyne or whatever he's been using on my mouth, my throat tissues are dry, and the first tiny dribble of water feels like acid. I'm not as strong as I thought, because now I keenly feel the effort of merely sitting up and drinking. I pause before taking another sip and look at my clothes.

"About the getup," explains Carlssin. "You're now FC Smith, or Jones, or whatever name you prefer. I left your shirt tag blank, and the ID line on your new TSA Justice and Prosperity Card doesn't have a name on it, either. I use a fake name, so you may hear other TSA personnel call me 'Rudy' or 'Corporal Fentz'. Your papers," Carlssin continues, "state that you're part of the TSA East Valley Transport Brigade. You're rated as 'Follower Candidate', which means that you're not a slave or a soaper, but your grade is beneath Private, or "Follower", as they're called. Basically it just means that some higher-up picked you out as having a use beyond filling up a fuel tank or working in the rendering plants." Carlssin pauses to check my cup. "It's an easy role. The young punks won't acknowledge you, and if an officer or NCO questions you, just say that you're an old unscarred who loves Mother, show your card, and tell them that you're serving in Transport. You don't need to understand everything right now, but do you understand what I just said?"

I nod.

"Good," says Carlssin. He pauses again, as if deciding how to say a complicated thing in a simple way. "Jack," he says, "you have to trust me, because we can help each other. I'm sure you think that I'm part of this TSA bullshit, but I'm not. I'm just playing a part, too."

8

Sleep In It, Bathe In It, TRY TO TAKE IT OFF AND YOU'LL DIE IN IT!

I Need A Drink
And A Quick
Decision

January
1986

I once wore an American military uniform, then decades later I found myself in an American death camp with another American in an American uniform who pointed an American assault rifle at me and ordered me to get my old American ass in line to take an American shit in an American porta-potty.

AmericanAmericanAmerican.

Gegrüßet ~~Nichts~~ Amerika, voll der ~~Nichts~~ Amerika, ~~Nichts~~ Amerika ist mit dir.

Wir werden gefickt...

Clean drunks have more in common with filthy prisoners than the former care to admit, and back in '86, there were lots of clean, well-lighted places in Los Vegas. This would not be the case in 2017, however.

Yay.

It wasn't a wheel of fortune. It wasn't cyclic or generational, no matter what the professors and social engineers said. It's wasn't that complicated. It was merely a matter of putting on a uniform - **any** *uniform - and taking off your soul.*

Being an American is *in-ci-dent-al,* ~~Clarice~~ *Jack...*

Sometimes people put on uniforms because they believed false flag-based recruiting campaigns, and sometimes they put on uniforms because they weren't sure what was supposed to happen next in the patterns of their desperately random lives. I was among the latter.

* * *

Eight months after my high school graduation some
NASA O-rings failed and the whole country gasped,
except for me, a young man who stood rooted in a boot-
and-buzzcut orchard, thanks to an air force sergeant
whose pie in the sky had been a bit higher than that of a
Vegas marine recruiter. Unlike *Challenger*'s downward-
spiraling crew module, I felt like my life was on the
upswing. It was the Wild Blue Yonder for me. Neither
NASA nor the local corps recruiter had been concerned
about losing bodies, however, for both knew that
Mommy America would always abandon an ample
supply of swaddled quota-fillers on their doorsteps.
Semper Fi? Hardly. *Semper Occultus* and *Semper Idem,*
Gunny...and one small step for another man on a
Kubrick set.

Four months after basic training I found myself in
South Korea, assigned to the Pyeongtaek Air Base 2502nd
Fighter Squadron as a weapons load crew member, or
"load toad." Bombs and bullets, flares and missiles.
Rain or shine, sleet or snow...like the Postal Service.

* * *

I didn't know if my parents were proud of my
enlistment decision. I couldn't ask my mother and
father what to do with my life, though they were still in
Vegas and quite easy to find. My parents were where
they had been since the early seventies: between
Margaret June Theron, 1896-1963, and Sergeant Joseph
T. Atkisson, 1920-1944.

I was such a little guy at the funeral. I didn't really
understand what had happened. I was scared, but I
didn't understand why. I don't think that I really
understood what death was or what it meant. I was
angry, too. It felt like my parents were fine, but that
they just didn't want to see me anymore.

I told Grandpa over and over that I wanted to go
back to my own house, that I hated his house and that I
didn't want to live with him. I felt like he knew where
my parents were, but that he wouldn't let them come
get me and take me home. Grandpa came to my bed at
night and held me very tightly and rocked me, even

when I kicked and cried and screamed. The Army Men followed him when he carried me around the block in my pajamas until I got so tired from crying that I fell asleep in his arms.

* * *

The broad-chested, thick-wristed, and silver-templed man who had stood hard, tall, and stoic at my parents' funeral wasn't the man who saw me off when I left for Texas. Instead, the Teutonic hero had been replaced by an old man in suspenders and a cloth cap. Grandpa seemed to be shorter, and his clothes were now loose and baggy.

I'm proud of you," Grandpa had said during that day at the Military Entrance Processing Station on Sahara Avenue. I was about to go into a room with a bunch of other high school graduates, strip down, and spread my cheeks so that an air force technician could walk down the row with a flashlight and insure that all assholes were straight, fistulae-free, and fit for hetero-duty. Then I would pull up my pants, raise my right hand, and mumble a few words in unison with a bunch of other guys who'd never actually read the Constitution either.

I didn't understand why Grandpa had said that he was proud of me for joining the American military, because by this time I had figured out a few things about Grandpa. For him, military service had meant being forced into an association with something he abhorred. How many other people could say that their Grandpa was an ex-Nazi? Well, many people could...but I wasn't in Germany. I was in Nevada. For Grandpa, Nazism was like a birds-and-bees talk that he didn't quite know how to approach. He kept putting it off and putting it off, until finally I was old enough to deduce the way of the world on my own.

Things went quickly after the combined asshole-inspection-and-Constitution-mumble. We were hustled out to say our goodbyes, pick up our duffels, and get on a Texas-bound bus, where Air Force Basic Training awaited at San Antonio's Lackland Air Force Base. I think Grandpa really *was* proud of me, but I hadn't done anything except sign my name and raise my hand. Yet, Grandpa was still proud of me. I didn't understand why, but it felt good, anyway.

He shook my hand and hugged me, and then we shook again. His grip wasn't very strong. I should have paid more attention to that. "Your father and mother would have been proud, too," he said.

Well, maybe, I thought, *but I barely knew them. You've been both my father and mother.*

"Remember, Jacky, that I have retained Edward Burnstein in case anything happens. He is the best lawyer in the Valley. Do not worry about me, Jacky. Just focus on taking care of yourself."

In case anything happens, I repeated to myself.

"Call collect when you get there," Grandpa said. He had spent most of his adult life talking to chests full of ribbons and writing in bizarre acronyms, and yet his concept of the military experience seemed rather naïve. When the bus arrived in San Antonio, I wouldn't be shown to my room and asked when I wanted my wake-up call. From the moment I got there, someone would be in my face, 24/7. There wouldn't be time or opportunity to do much except for what somebody yelled at me to do.

"I'll call as soon as I can," I said.

"Take care. And remember, every time --"

"--every time we make a new choice, everything changes," I said, finishing Grandpa's sentence. I smiled. This was his motto and his mantra, and the reason why nothing ever got him down. It was like the universe changed depending upon what shirt Grandpa chose to wear each morning.

"That is right," he said. He paused and looked at me with *I-wish-you-weren't-so-young* eyes. "I hope you understand."

"I do," I said, as picked up my duffel.

I really didn't.

* * *

Two weeks later, while standing in formation beneath the barracks overhang of the 3708th Basic Military Training Squadron, I learned that the *Challenger* space shuttle disaster had occurred. My training instructor had announced the news and, despite his

199

previous ironically contradictory yelps about "military bearing", he seemed visibly shaken.

I hoped that the big plastic Mickie Mouse buttons on my plain green fatigue ass flaps were fastened because I didn't want to get chewed out when I marched into the chow hall for morning tray-slop. I wanted to carefully and slowly reach behind and feel my butt pockets, but I didn't dare. There was always some eagle-eyed maggot ready to jump in your shit for moving at attention.

Big green Mickie Mouse ass-buttons were my biggest concern on the morning of January 28th, 1986. Challenger *had exploded over Cape Canaveral? Whatever. That was in Florida, right? Seven astronauts had met their ends?* Well, I supposed that it was a tragedy for their families, but it meant very little to *me* as I stood in the Texas predawn, slick-sleeves rigid at my sides, with my eyes fixed on the neck of a New Yorker named Gagnot. The guy's name was a ragging jackpot for instructors: *"Gag-Not?! That ain't right! Your ugly ass is gaggin' the hell outta me!"* Behind me I felt the glare of a surly and skinny Philadelphian called Perlingi who had become known as "Petra-lunga", or "Petrified Lung", when his pre-BMT two-pack habit found him out on San Antonio's cactus marches.

Gag-Not and Petrified Lung weren't like me, and neither had their option sets been like mine. Gag had flunked out of college, and Lung, at age twenty-six, was a relatively older guy who had just gotten bored with his McJob and McGirlfriend. I don't know how Gag or Lung had made their enlistment decisions, but I guessed that Gag had probably gone to a recruiter upon receipt of an expulsion letter, whereas Lung was likely smoking in bed, looking with dull eyes at a sleeping woman, and wondering if he'd like fries with that.

* * *

Before Basic training actually began, we were herded off the commercial Trailways bus and onto a Lackland AFB Ford Bluebird. We were then driven across San Antonio and through the base gates, and it was during that brief trip that I took notice of the other guys that were to be in my boot camp flight. Most were young, skinny, and rather nondescript kids for whom shaved heads and conformist greens wouldn't subtract much in terms of youthfully silly attempts at uniqueness. Most, but not all. Some of the soon-to-be airmen basics weren't boys out of high school, and they had obviously swung a hammer or two. There were scars and tattoos and hard-as-hell looks beneath scalps that had arrived in Texas in both pre-shaven and supershag states. I made a few mental notes concerning these fellows, because once we had taken our turns in the shearing shed and donned our monkey suits, the warning signs would be gone.

One such fellow sat in the row ahead of me. I would later learn that his name was Jaeger, and he was a textbook mesomorph. Jaeger was a bald white guy. He wore a light-gray baja pullover, but the hood and sleeves were missing. Jaeger was dirty, and in the wrinkles where his bull neck met his shoulders there were thin black mud lines of mixed dust and sweat that rubbed off onto the baja's ragged edges. Jaeger's left hand rested on his lap. His fingers were rough and cracked, and even with the relaxed bend in his arm, Jaeger's bicep resembled an enormous knot of hempen rope. He looked straight ahead with a jutting chin and jaw muscles that bulged his cheeks with each clench. Jaeger was of only average height, but just one of his wrists was as thick as both of mine. He had the kind of skull that made a forensic reconstructionist's racial-ID job extremely easy, for if there were English who could trace their lines to the Conqueror, then Jaeger proved that some Europeans also knew their way back to the Neander Valley.

Richard Gear, in the role of Officer Candidate Mayonnaise, tried to cover his tattoo with a bandage. Enlistee Jaeger, however, had taken a different approach. Straddling the muscle of his arm was a big, dry, and flaking scab where maybe as much as three square inches of dermis had been flayed, or perhaps burned. The removal hadn't been as thorough as it should have been, however, because there were still bits of ink around the edge of the half-healed wound.

Out of the corner of my eye I silently re-connected

the remaining dots. Since the Nordic Sun Wheel was circular, and since Jaeger didn't seem like the kind of guy who would tat-up with the *yungdrungs* of North Vegas' Thai Temple, that kind of narrowed things down.

*   *   *

By week five of boot camp, Jaeger's scab has been replaced with a large pink patch of tissue, though I can barely see it in the light of our "Lackland Laser" flashlights. Our flight stands outside on the squadron's massive concrete drill pad. It's about two in the morning, and we've been rousted and marched out in fire-drill style. We only had time to put on our flip-flops, grab our flashlights and green bunk blankets, and head down the stairs. We fell in on the drill pad and Sergeant Tsheulin called us to attention, Y-fronts and all.

Tsheulin is fucking *torqued.* All of the airmen basics are in their underwear, but he's not. The man wears starch-plated service blues and a round-brimmed training instructor hat. Tsheulin stands like an irate statue as he waits for two assistant TIs whom I see silhouetted by the barracks overhang lights. Tsheulin's backups approach at double time.

We're all busted, though I'm not sure for what. All I know is that I was asleep, and then Tsheulin kicked an aluminum garbage can down the bunk aisles and barked for us to hit the drill pad. I suspect that somebody is about to get recycled.

The backup TIs put us on our faces and start calling push-up cadence. "So some of you airmen like to do push-ups when you're supposed to be in your bunks?" Tsheulin yells. "Alright. I can help you with that." The metal taps of the sergeant's patent-leather low quarters click in the darkness as he walks through rows of young men pressing themselves up off of the warm Texas concrete.

As we pass the sixty-count my arms begin to feel like wet noodles dipped in burning gasoline. I don't dare stop though, even when the seventy-count approaches. I struggle to keep pushing myself up and fake it with half push-ups. I just need to keep moving and keep showing that my mind is doing its best to comply while my body falters.

Somebody pukes and metal taps are drawn to the sound like buzzards to a death rattle. Tsheulin roars the weak link to his feet and puts him at attention. I've never understood why some guys vomit when physically pushed. It's never happened to me. When I go too far, it's my muscles that malfunction, not my stomach.

My arms finally refuse my brain's commands. I struggle for breath and I can't raise my chest. I can't feel my triceps or pectorals and I find myself doing a walrus' side-to-side pinniped motion. There are more puking sounds, along with more shoe taps and harsh hounding.

I glance around. The seals, sea lions, and Billy Shears walruses are giving it their best shots, but most, like me, have been clubbed by the TIs. But there are also a few guys who are still pumping out push-ups, and in the flashlights' collective yellow glow I see an airman with a large pink scar on his bicep who can take as much as Tsheulin can dish out. Jaeger spots me as well.

"C'mon, Simmerath," he calls out over the din. "Don't let these floonic tunics break you!"

Inside, Jaeger is laughing at Tsheulin because he knows that, in any other situation, he could pluck out the TI's lungs, wrap them in a pretty ribbon, and hand them back. *So keep up your cadence, Tsheulin,* I think. *Get your jollies, you silly little fuck in your state pig hat and your patent leather Cinderella slippers.*

Tsheulin doesn't wait for Jaeger and the other exceptional specimens to fall. Instead, he stops the cadence and puts the flight back at attention, though it isn't easy for most of us to get up. A couple guys stumble. There's a vomit puddle ahead of me. I make a mental note to step over it when my formation element marches by.

Tsheulin is flanked by the backup TIs as he orders the flight leader and two other individuals out of formation: "Airman Lumpkins! Airman Johnson! Airman Sheeda!" The specified individuals, despite their exhaustion, double-time it to the front. "Sir, Airman Lumpkins/Johnson/Sheeda reports as ordered, sir!"

Tsheulin ignores them and addresses the flight: "I provided this opportunity for additional PT because Airmen Johnson and Sheeda decided to do push-ups in the bay showers!" Tsheulin turns to face the three. "Johnson, Sheeda, you are now recycled to the junior flight for remedial training. Lumpkins, for your failure as flight leader to insure that these two were in their bunks, you are also recycled. Pack your duffels and get out of my bays. Report to Sergeant Falson's flight, ASAP!"

* * *

One week later the flight stood in formation, at ease, but with our training manuals in hand. I heard someone stutter. No - someone was having problems *reading*. After a sigh and a few moments of silence the frustrated stuttering began again.

There was a tap on my shoulder. I looked up from my manual and slowly turned around. Jaeger stood behind me. I felt a nervous jolt while Jaeger held out his training manual and pointed at a page.

I looked at the words. *"Tactical Air Command,"* I whispered.

* * *

On that night I discovered that my bunking assignment had been changed, though not by Tsheulin's authorization. It had instead occurred when Jaeger put the new flight leader against a wall and informed him that I would be trading places with one of Jaeger's soon-to-be former bay neighbors. It was pretty tough to get to sleep during that first night in my new bunk, especially after Jaeger told me why I had changed beds:

"You're gonna help me read, Simmerath."

9

But It Was There All Along, Metastasizing Beneath The Stars And Stripes

It's Raining ~~Men~~ *Tongues And Pens!* Hallelujah!

A Tuesday In 1987

"Alright, you mu-u-u-therfuckers," Carl Wheat drawled, "get out there and load them gawd-damn jets and do a mu-u-u-ther fuckin' FOD walk." He thrust his hips forward to simulate a potbelly, craned his neck, and marched around the barracks dayroom in a display that might have been a John Kleese rip-off. Other airmen seated opposite the pool table on green GSA office seats began to laugh.

"You think that's funny? That's yer ass! That's YER ASS!" The Minister of Silly Walks became satirically threatening as Carl turned and marched toward me. "Airman Simmerath, just what the hell's so gawd-damn funny?"

"Nothing, uh, *Master Sergeant Jones,"* I replied with a half-straight face as I clicked my heels and gave a Nazi salute. "We'll get right to it."

"Good," replied Carl. "And shine them mu-u-u-therfuckers, too," he said, as he grinned and ground his heel into the toe of my freshly-buffed boot.

"Augh! You fuckstick!" I shoved Carl over to where the others were seated. He sprawled across their laps and they pushed him onto the dayroom floor. Carl propped himself up on his elbow while we all laughed.

Airman First Class Carl Wheat had arrived at Pyeongtaek in March of 1986, three months before me. Thin and of medium height, with brown hair and eyes that matched our green monkey suits, his sense of humor and intelligence had made him quite popular. Carl's wit and knack for imitation made Mauldin-esque shit avalanches more bearable, and A1C Wheat provided a barracks parody every time some fat-ass master sergeant laid down the law.

Carl had been born with a large purple wine stain that started on his left forearm, extended down past his sleeve, and ended on the back of his hand. The birthmark took a somewhat penile shape, as duly noted in idiotic jokes around our weapons flight. Having heard it all before, however, Carl had developed a routine of his own, in which his birthmark was referred to as "The Corndog." I thought that this was a much more accurate descriptor of the purple silhouette, since, if it were to be regarded as a cock, the depiction would have had a rather bizarre "stick" protruding from the head, like an inflamed organ being agonizingly swabbed for clap. Carl handled the purple mark's social aspects in much the same way that Steve Martyn had dealt with his enormous nose in the film *Roxannie.* Just when I thought that I had heard every possible joke about eating corndogs, sucking corndogs, and stroking corndogs, Carl always came up with something new. Carl's unit nickname was officially conferred on the day when our flight was in formation and Master Sergeant Jones had referred to A1C Wheat as "Airman Corndog." Though the weapons flight was at attention, there were more than a few snickers.

I was drawn to Carl's optimism and appetite for life, especially in the Hermit Kingdom's southern compartment, where *waygukin* stuck out like sore thumbs. Self-confinement to Pyeongtaek Air Base, or simply "P-Tek", and its strangely isolated Americana was an easy psychological retreat for many airmen, but not for Carl.

"You know why crackers in Korea are like dogs? Because they can spot each other in a crowd from a mile away," Carl once joked after our pale hides had been denied entry to a Koreans-only Itaewon restaurant.

"You mean corndogs," had been my reply.

Carl had been off-base more than most remote-tour airmen, and he had seen every Korean palace and historical site within and around Seoul. He also took language classes and on more than one occasion had challenged the locals' low expectations by seeking directions in mangled *Hangungmal.* Though a testament to his outgoing attitude, Carl was, however, just making tourist noises. This was illustrated one day in Seoul's Namdaemun Market when he asked a woman at a market stall for the price of a pair of gloves. She seemed shocked, but then gave a lengthy response in Korean, to which Carl could only repeat his original question.

Suddenly reassured that the Big Nose was merely parroting something that he had read in a language text, the woman gave a superior smile and indicated the price by holding up the corresponding number of fingers.

Do Your Stuff While
The Empire
Falls

A Wednesday In 1987

Sometimes newbie-jeep bartenders like to keep cheat sheets behind the bar. Quick reference cards with liquor names and mix ratios can be very helpful. What goes into a *Slow Screw Against The Wall?* How do you make a *Screaming Orgasm?* For answers, just glance at a ring-binder mix card.

If you're conducting an F-16 bomb rack check, you can also just take a glance under the bar and re-check the release programming sequence. Oh, wait. There's no bar, because you're out on the flightline of an air base, and not inside a nightclub. No matter. You're still using a set of plastic-sleeved cards on metal binding rings, and the instructions for completing an electronic bomb-release function check are essentially written in the format of a drink-mixing flowchart. If you can make a drink, then you can also stumble through a fighter jet's weapon ops-check.

Airman Rob Hardesty is in the cockpit and I'm under a wing. Dave Kitts, our staff sergeant load crew chief, is filling out the aircraft maintenance forms. Hardesty is pretending to be a pilot delivering a load of death. The ground power unit makes massive noise in the aircraft shelter so we're communicating via the aircraft crew chief's headsets. There's a wad of wires and cannon plugs hooked up to a bomb rack within one of the underwing pylons, and these connect to a large metal box that features an assortment of switches.

Since neither of us are trained pilots, Hardesty and I are just following a step-by-step set of procedures called a "technical order". Technical orders are printed instructions for particular aircraft maintenance tasks, or any type of air force task, for that matter. Once a young airman goes to technical school and learns how to follow a T.O., he or she is ready to do anything. Even though I'm a weapons troop, I can just as easily march into the chow hall kitchen and follow instructions for making fifty gallons of gravy. Using written orders isn't like learning how to ride a bicycle. It's more akin to riding a pre-schooler's trike. You just pick it up and follow the directions. A chimp could use a T.O.

The aircraft's onboard computer thinks that the metal test box is a bomb, so we're checking to see if the aircraft follows Hardesty's cockpit bomb-release instructions. If it doesn't, I'll get an error message on the test box screen. This particular plane, though, looks like it's ready for action:

> - *Okay Jackster, selecting up a single release, inboard station. Pickle button.*
> - Got it. Single release, station one.
> - *Roger. Selecting up a TER triple release.*
> - No pulse. Got nothin'.
> - *Hold on. I haven't hit the pickle yet. Alright.*
> - Got it. Salvo good.
> - *Roger. Selecting up safe salvo. Pickle.*
> - Got it. Full dump, open arming solenoid.
> - *Roger that, Jackster. Ops check good. Let's pack up and get the hell out of here.*
> - Roger. PACAF ORI '87 en route.

Hardesty and I are still jeeps, but in a week's time this won't be the case. The US Pacific Air Force Command is about to hit Pyeongtaek Air Base with a giant no-sleep and mega-stress Operational Readiness Inspection. The career fate of some general will be determined by the ORI's rating outcome. If all goes well, he'll pin on an extra star. If it goes to shit, he'll retire early. The weapon crews, as well as avionics, aircraft crew chiefs, and every other kind of flightline worker are going from aircraft-to-aircraft and making sure that everything is in tip-top condition.

Number Of Incarcerated Citizens Per Caplta, Number Of Adults Who Believe Angels Are Real, And Defense Spending

GODDAMNED '87 PACAF ORI

All of the bomb loaders had been to the base shooting range to get certified on M12 pump shotguns. They weren't very good weapons, in my opinion. I would have preferred to carry one of the exercise-modified M16s that the SPs used. Those rifles, so as to prevent an actual live-fire during upcoming exercise scenarios, had red metal plugs in their muzzles. The plugs fired laser pulses that allowed the base cops and security forces to simulate gunfights with phony Nork attackers.

Kitts, Hardesty, and I were armament troops, not combat controllers or SPs, but we had been told to expect some fake gunfights anyway. Kitts didn't seem to care much, and had instructed Hardesty and me, in case of airfield penetration, to simply close the massive aircraft shelter doors and wait things out. That sounded good, since most of my "engagement and perimeter defense" training had focused upon how to use my shotgun to destroy or disable matériel in order to prevent its capture. It was pretty basic. Shoot convoy tires and blast radiators. Take fuse cans behind the shelter and slug them.

Precious little was said about using shotguns to prevent *our own* capture. I guess The System considered the bombs to be more important than us, probably because we could be more easily replaced. It was simple to train someone to read a T.O., lock bombs under jet wings, and cram tail sections with flares and chaff. The System could always find guys to bust their asses arming jets. While fuel tanker drivers, mechanics and aircraft crew chiefs filled and fixed the planes, guys like me set fuses, clipped arming wires, and attached gun pods. It was physically demanding work, though not too challenging brain-wise, and the higher-ups had obviously determined that there wasn't a need to train us in using our shotguns to do much more than wreck equipment.

I was trained in a job that completely lacked civilian application. I mean, what could I do? Go back to Vegas and apply for an armament crew slot at McKarran International?

Wait…wait. I guess that is what I did…eventually.

Sort of.

* * *

The red barrel plugs on our shotguns weren't like the plugs on the SPs' M16s. So as to more realistically simulate 12 gauge ballistics, the M12 lasers had range limiters. My load crew was pinned down inside an open aircraft shelter and our fake shotguns couldn't reach our likewise-fake attackers' position behind a concrete barrier that protected an adjacent shelter's power unit.

The jet was gone. That was the important thing in the eyes of The System. The F-16 had taken with it a full complement of simulated weapons, and the only ground personnel left at this shelter were the aircraft crew chief and us, the weapons load crew. The aircraft crew chief, however, was out of the game. He sat in his little chief shack at the rear of the shelter with a red electronic tag attached to his uniform. The crew chief had been "shot" while sweeping up a pool of hydraulic fluid with speedy-dry. Now he awaited pickup and transport to the base morgue processing area, where he would sit out the rest of the exercise as a lost asset. Dave, Hardesty and I had to press against the shelter wall. If we took more than two steps we would be hit and our laser tags would also turn from green to red.

"Didn't I tell you two to close the doors if there was enemy activity in this tree?" Dave hissed. He was torqued, and with good cause. There was no reason for us to be taken out like this. Once the plane had taxied, we should have gotten on the electric shelter engine switches and shut the giant doors. Yet, in those few minutes between the last of the engine blast and actuation of the door controls, a group of aggressors had entered the tree. The crew chief's "death" wasn't his fault though, because Dave was the one with the brick radio. Dave was probably as angry with himself as he was with Hardesty and me. If we also got killed, not only would things seem creepy and weird, but Jones would rip our asses after the exercise for dying when we should have been safely behind four feet of concrete and steel.

I looked at Hardesty. "Jones is gonna put us on Vulcan-barrel detail...*forever,*" I moaned. Hardesty said nothing and Dave glared at me.

The phony North Koreans couldn't sit still for much longer because base defense troops would soon enter the tree; until then, however, they would cause as much havoc and simulated death as possible. At any moment the enemy would leave their cover, enter our shelter with their fake AKs, and turn all of our electronic uniform cards from green to red.

"Fuck," I muttered, this time not caring if Dave or Hardesty heard. "We're definitely gonna be stuck in Release Shop."

"Release Shop? *Is that where you load-toads go for gettin' killed in dumb-ass ways?"*

We jumped at hearing the voice behind us. The person who had crept into the shelter looked like a real soldier. Unlike us, he had a chest rig and a vest. He wore Nomex gloves and carried an actual, albeit red-plugged, assault rifle. The guy was on the leading edge of a force that was about to push the enemy out of the tree. Behind him, far in the rear of the shelter where the smaller jet engine-start doors were also still open, two more similarly-attired figures rappelled down over the high concrete blast shield. When their boots silently touched the floor, they disconnected their lines, took their weapons off sling, and began to creep forward. I thought that they looked like super-ninjas from martial arts movies. They certainly made us look...well, lame. There we were, just some guys in BDUs with shotguns, and stuck against the wall. We even had aircraft form pencils sticking out over the tops of our chest pockets, for shit's sake. We were bomb nerds.

"I'll be damned," continued the man. "Simmerath, you were smart enough to teach me how to read, but you can't think your way out of this bullshit?" When the guy smiled, I remembered all of those nights in the Lackland bunk bay. At first I had been scared of getting the absolute and utter shit kicked out of me by an ex-neo-Nazi, but then I relaxed as I learned that there were some clear advantages to being the private tutor of the most hardcore guy in the flight. Nobody fucked with me, because it was understood that, by fucking with me, you were really fucking with Jaeger. I was, clearly, Jaeger's basic training bitch. If we had been in prison, he would have pounded the hell out of my ass...but at Lackland, anal sex was not what I had been selected to provide. Instead, I had spent my nights reading the BMT Manual to Jaeger, over and over, until he learned what he needed to learn in order to graduate from basic training. I regarded the manual as a very dry bedtime story book for a guy who had burnt swastikas out of his skin. Whether I actually *taught* Jaeger to read was debatable, though I came to enjoy whispering information by the light of a flashlight, almost to the point where I could call Jaeger a friend.

Well...*not really.*

Dave and Hardesty watched as I shook Jaeger's massive gloved hand. Then one of the other men spoke: "Jag, it looks like the field starts in a couple paces." He motioned at the imaginary line of fake death across the shelter floor.

Jaeger looked over his shoulder. "HSH?"

"Yeah," came the answer. "Same as last tree."

Jaeger snorted in contempt. "They still think we can't hit 'em. I got this one."

Jaeger took a breath, braced himself, and rolled across the concrete. When he got to his feet near the far wall, he squeezed off a series of laser ticks in the other shelter's direction. His tag remained green. Jaeger held to cover, moved across the engine blast area, and up again to the opposite wall. He nodded to his cohorts and they returned to their lines at the shelter's rear.

"How'd you do that?" I asked.

"I figured out at Bullis that these play-toys can bounce like a real steel-core '109," said Jaeger. "A four-foot gap at sixty yards?" Jaeger spat on the shelter's floor. "Not too tough."

"Ricochets," I said.

Jaeger nodded. "Into a concrete kill box. You gotta wonder if *real* Norks are that fuckin' stupid." He went to join his companions. "You take care, Simmerath," Jaeger called back. "Don't let your ass get caught like this again."

~~Foreign Object Damage~~
~~[Fabrication Outage~~
~~Code 118]~~
Friend Of Dorothy
[Fabulous Outage
Code 118]

Index-Index-Index
1987

The night that followed the two-week PACAF Operational Readiness Inspection found Carl and me off-duty and drinking. Neither of us knew if the base had passed the inspection, and at that moment we didn't care. Thanks to Jaeger and Co., we had survived the ORI.

Our short hair was matted and greasy, our black boots were brown with dirt, and faint white lines of dried sweat ringed the armpits of our fatigues. Our salty skin smelled as if it had fermented like local kimchi in rubber-and-charcoal chemical suits. When I looked at Carl's face I saw where his gas mask seal had left a dark and greasy ring of flightline dirt in the stubble of his jaw line. I knew that I looked the same, but I wasn't concerned. I was in a military bar that was full of men and women who were equally smelly and dirty. Open ranks inspection, with all of its polishing, ironing, and shaving would wait until Monday.

"God, this shit tastes so good," I said between chugs of beer. It was just some kind of pisswater that the Pyeongtaek NCO Club served in oceanfuls after base exercises - Bud, Kass, or some other weak dreg - but I didn't care. It was icy and alcoholic, and that was all that mattered to the young livers who were allowed in the NCO club until P-Tek's new airman's club was constructed.

Carl smiled. "I hear ya," he said, as he raised his own glass. "Anything is better than MRE beef noodle packets and Orange Capree Sun. Besides, I'm gonna *need* a case of beer shits to get right again." While loading fighters, dodging fake gunfights, and hiding in aircraft shelters,

Carl and I had eaten a fortnight's worth of fifteen-year-shelf-life military meals. MREs were designed to keep airmen and soldiers alive, not maintain their bowel regularity. The phrase "shitting a brick" had been around long before the advent of MREs, or even old-style C-Rations, but it remained very applicable.

I nodded and emptied my glass with a hasty gulp that spilled beer on my already-stained BDUs. Carl smiled through his own swallows as his eyes wandered above the rim of his glass. He lowered his beer. "You know," he said with a smirk, "beer might not be all that those guys will need to get right again." He nodded at a table where some of our Strategic Air Command counterparts enjoyed the company of local working girls.

I looked over at the table and smiled. "Oh, I'm sure that they have lots of penicillin in Louisiana." The SAC men were Second Bomb Wingers out of Barksdale AFB in Shreveport, and I knew the women at their table...as did most other Pyeongtaek airmen. One was a Filipina named Nipa Johnson. Nipa was about twenty-five years old, barely stood over five feet, and was notorious for cruising the base club when her husband, the supply squadron section chief, was elsewhere on temporary duty.

The others were Korean. One was a local girl who called herself "Mary," and she had long black hair that went down to the small of her back. Mary was dressed rather plainly in jeans and a blouse, but on her feet were a pair of leather platforms that were worthy of Paul Stanlee. The third girl was called "Harry." I never knew why. Her hair was not as long as Mary's, and it made me think of a fairy tale maiden who had spun straw into peroxide gold. She wore a blue tee with glitter studs on the back, and stretched over her foam-insert chest, in white block letters, was the bewildering Konglish proclamation:

MAN CORN FOOT

Harry had introduced me to Stanlee Kubrick's *Full Metallic Jacket* when I arrived at P-Tek. Well, I should more accurately state that, after the guys observed me spending my blitzed "green bean" night with Harry, the *entire unit* introduced me to a line from Mr. Kubrick's film. Even though Saigon had been renamed and was in another country many miles away, I still endured about two months' worth of "love you long time" jeers.

Nipa, Mary, and Harry swarmed around the fresh Louisiana meat. Unlike the three-man teams needed to load one of Pyeongtaek's F-16s, B-52 armament crews were composed of five members. The Barksdale men and two other SAC temporary forward crews were at Pyeongtaek to function as five simulated replacement crews for PACAF troops who had "perished" in exercise scenarios. Their mission was to determine how long it took to become proficient in loading F-16s, should a "real world emergency" require their quick deployment. Back at Barksdale there was a temporary five-member Pyeongtaek crew that had dealt with the extreme pressure of trying to function, on ultra-short notice, as B-52 loaders. All weapon troops who participated in such exchange-deployments were the best of the best, to be sure, but to me it just looked like frenzied insanity.

The Barksdale staff sergeant, senior airman, and three A1Cs weren't quite sure what to do with the Pyeongtaek women who draped over them like curtains. "Those BUFF boys are a little shy," I said, in the tone of a local sexual pitfall veteran. I cast my eyes around the NCO club. There were girls everywhere, and all of them knew the base exercise schedule as well as any Nork spy. The bar was packed with stressed-out GIs who needed to blow off steam, and the time was right for girls to make money.

Carl watched the bomber table for a few seconds. "I'm up for poker. You?" he asked.

I nodded. "The shopette is on extended hours. We could get a case of something decent to drink."

*　*　*

"No, I gotta go," I said to Peterson at four-thirty on Saturday morning. I was less drunk than just dog-tired. The other poker players had already left Carl's room. "I wanna crash."

"Dude, c'mon! Look at her! She's hot! Just take her friend, okay? Okay?" Airman Peterson jerked his thumb toward the doorway of Carl's barracks room. "Just look, okay? Just take a look."

"Man, relax," mumbled Carl, as he rolled over on his bunk. Carl's intoxication level didn't register the poker chip stuck to his dirty cheek. "The Jackster's not into it."

"Shut up, Cornfaggot. I'd ask you, but you're such a puss." Peterson gave me a pleading look. "C'mon Simmy. We can tag 'em both. Just look. They're gonna leave if you don't come."

Peterson was a dick, and the only reason he was there was because the poker game had wrapped up just as he was coming down the hall. Peterson had stuck his head in the doorway and accused Carl, myself, and the others of being "a bunch of queers who oughtta be chasin' snatch instead of playin' cards." Peterson was probably all of 5'6", but built like a brick shithouse, and when he wasn't pumping iron at the base gym, he was running sexual cons on Korean and American girls. "Look, they come to the barracks, right? They come to the club, right? I know what they want," was Peterson's refrain to any who might question his perpetual fuck-scams. Actually, there were a number of Korean women whose presence at Pyeongtaek had nothing to do with "what they wanted," but rather, their employment, for the airbase required many locals in order to operate. There were area women who worked in the chow hall, the BX, and Rec Center...but in Peterson's fantasy world, all of them were seeking sex; specifically, sex with him. He made sure that we were all well informed of this.

I groaned, went to the door, and glanced back at Peterson. He nodded and breathed in heavy anticipation. I sighed and took a look.

They were Americans, and I had seen them before. Two white females. No distinguishing marks. I noted that, unlike most of the AGS airmen, the young enlisted women had taken the time to clean up before going out. Both were from the Services Squadron and they worked at the base gym - which made me wonder if that was how Peterson knew them. Though the women stood at the end of the hall, I saw that they were squeezed into anaconda tops and jeans that had been unrolled over their cankles like denim condoms. The girls' barracks-

brassy was up, instead of in Bon Jovie ultra-tease. It really wouldn't have mattered much to me, however, if they had stood in G-strings. The skank factor was too high, and I was just too exhausted. Besides, two weeks earlier I had seen one of them puke between the cars in the NCO club parking lot while her friend squatted for a piss, thus leaving me with a rather dismal impression. They were Caucasian versions of Nipa Johnson's club lieutenants, and I still grimaced when I remembered how my Harry encounter had entertained the squadron.

I didn't need this.

"Whoo," I breathed in feigned amazement. I grinned and turned to Peterson as he silently mouthed the word *YES!* and pumped his fists in the air.

"Where did you line up those two?" I asked, in an intense near-whisper. *I know where,* I thought. *At the gym's weight room towel counter.*

"C'mon, c'mon," said Peterson as he tried to hustle me out the door.

"Alright, I just gotta get my money." I stepped toward the card-and-chip-strewn bed, then paused. "Go! Go!" I said, as I gestured at the door. "Don't let them leave! I'll be right there."

Peterson gave me a wide-eyed grin and spastic nod, then disappeared down the barracks hallway...after which I closed and locked the door behind his stupid ass.

"I'm taking your roomie's bunk," I muttered in the direction of Carl's drooling mouth and glassy eyes. Out in the hall, Peterson beat on the door and angrily demanded that Carl and I go fuck ourselves as well as each other.

Before I flipped off the light I noticed that Carl now had chips stuck in his hair as well as on his face. I climbed over my friend and collapsed onto the empty top bunk. "I guess those girls managed to escape," I muttered. "Why does it always seem like Peterson tries too hard?"

The Reason For
The Memories
You Buried
In The
Dust

I Say Again: Index-Index-Index
1987

"No, man," said Carl. "Don't put your leg at that angle, because you'll fuck up your *own* foot." He shifted his position to demonstrate. "Like this. Use the other guy's leg and heel like levers. That way, when you strike, you'll have enough force to pull apart the tendons in *his* foot." Carl did a reverse half-step, but he didn't completely back into me. He raised his foot slightly along my shin and stopped. "Okay, don't move," instructed Carl. "Just pretend that we were walking together, and you're in the middle of taking a step." I froze, and Carl did a half-pivot that brought his raised foot into contact with my leg. As he slid his boot downward, his heel moved along my shin like it was on a guide rail. He stopped when his foot made contact with my own. "Feel that?" he asked. "I'm barely putting any weight down."

I winced. "Yeah. That would hurt like a bitch if you really slammed hard."

"That's the idea," replied Carl. "We can practice later. I gotta go to CBPO and get my grade for this midterm."

* * *

When Carl and I came back on shift, our load crew chiefs were in Jones' office getting the jet info for the night's loads. I waited in the flight break room with Carl. He wasn't happy.

"What's wrong with a 'C'?" I asked.

Carl looked at his returned midterm paper, then at me. "My grade average just took a nose dive. I'm trying to cross-train, remember? I need 'A's to look like I'm a good candidate for Intel."

221

Before I could reply, a grating voice, like the rim of a flat tire grinding against asphalt, came from the direction of Jones' office. "Corndog, what the fuck are you moanin' about?" demanded Staff Sergeant Dreyful as he entered the break room. "'C' is passin', ain't it?"

Carl's load crew chief was a gorilla skeleton stuffed into a man skin. Dreyful had a purplish complexion that made his cheeks look like they had been burned, and his hair was a bristly black scrub brush. Adolescent acne scars wandered below his jaw line, over his throat, and around the back of his thick neck. Dreyful wore his XXL field jacket tightly buttoned and zipped even when the flight shack's break room was warm. His eyes were small, dark, and only softened on his sixth or seventh Black Satin shot. Dreyful, or "Sergeant Dreadful," as he was known among the airmen, could converse as well as any other walking chunk of slate. Dreyful did not give orders; instead, he growled vague clues that kept his troops desperately guessing as to desired courses of action. Carl was a member of the Dreadful Weapons Crew.

Dreyful made me grateful to be on Dave Kitts' load crew. Dave would jump in my shit when I needed it, but not like Dreyful. Dreyful was known for getting twisted and beating up his crew members...though that had been almost a year earlier. "Dreadful" hadn't been picking on Carl or his other subordinate in *particular*. It was just something that had happened in an odd drunken moment outside of the NCO club.

"I, uh, was only hoping that I had done a little better," Carl quietly replied. He sat up at the break room table, folded the midterm, and buttoned it into his fatigue breast pocket.

"You still tryin' for that cross-trainin' shit?" asked Dreyful. Despite the coarse query, I knew that the sergeant wasn't using his belligerent, "I'm-gonna-kick-your-ass" tone. This was simply as close to civility as he could get.

"Yes," replied Carl, again in a quiet voice.

"Hell," said Dreyful, "you're a weapons troop, not some Intel Squadron puke!"

Carl just looked at the tabletop and was silent. At this, I remembered a scene from *Full Metallic Jacket,* in which drill sergeant R. Lee Ermie, who had been calling out his training platoon's individual job assignments, told future military journalist Matthew Modeen: *"Jesus H. Christ, Joker! You're a killer, not a writer!"*

Dreyful was suddenly thirsty. "Where the fuck is the Mountain Douche?" he groused, while using a soft drink's coarse nickname. Dreyful went behind the break room's snack bar and threw open the refrigerator door. "Goddammit, I want some Douche," he muttered, as he leaned over and poked around the fridge shelves. "Damn Coke," he continued. "Damn Coke, another Coke, another Coke," he mumbled. "Ah," Dreyful finally said, as he stood up with a green-and-yellow can in his hand. "Last one." Dreyful took some quarters out of his pocket and slammed them through the slot in the snack bar's pay box.

"Dreyful!" came a call from the flight chief's office, but Carl's crew chief continued to gulp the soda.

"DREYFUL!"

"What? What the fuck?" spluttered Dreyful, as he put the now-empty can on the bar and left the room.

As Dreyful exited, I was reminded of that night in basic training when Airman Basic Jaeger was out on the concrete drill pad, pumping out push-ups, while Sergeant Tsheulin, a much smaller and weaker man, ran his mouth. If Tsheulin had tried that shit in any other place or time without his pretty uniform and "authority", Jaeger would have disarticulated the TI's spine. It seemed like the situation between Jones and Dreyful was exactly the same.

Carl got up, went to the counter, and picked up the empty soda can. He placed it on the floor, crunched it into a small disk with his boot heel, and dropped it into the empties box.

"What time is your crew loading out?" I asked.

"Uhh, at three, I think," answered Carl in a distracted tone. "Crew showtime at three, so we'll pick up our tools and wait for the weapons convoy around two. You guys?"

"No flightline for us today," I answered. "Our paperwork is up for the quarter. We're in Load Barn all week," I answered, while referring to the Pyeongtaek Air Base weapons-hangar facility that was used to train and re-train bomb loaders.

"Oh. Our crew's not due 'til next month," replied Carl, as he looked in the refrigerator.

I returned to our earlier topic of conversation. "You'll still pass the class, right?"

Carl took a soda from the refrigerator and dropped some quarters through the pay slot. "Yeah, I can still get a 'B' if I do well on the final, but that's not the point."

"What's wrong with a 'B'? You can't be perfect all of the time."

Carl put down the soda and leaned on the counter with both hands. "No, but I need to give it my best shot." He straightened up and looked at me. "It's really competitive in there, Jack. Some are Army, some are State Department, and some are just dependents."

"Ground-pounding geniuses aside," I joked, "working in the embassy doesn't automatically make them Einsteins. Neither does watching AFN soaps in base housing all day."

"No," replied Carl, "but look at this." He walked across the break room to his gear locker. Carl opened the door, took out some books, and sat down at a table. "Somebody sitting at a passport desk or filing visas has time to read this stuff. Somebody sitting on their ass in base housing has time, too." Carl shook his head and spoke in a tone of self-reproach. "And me? I get fucked up after the exercise and take a test with a hangover."

"How many spots are open?" I asked, as I took a seat across from Carl.

"Five. Two enlisted, one officer, and two civilian,

and that's counting the bases in Japan, too. But," Carl continued, "the enlisted slots are also civilian eligible at Command discretion."

"Is that what they said at Personnel?" I asked.

"Yeah. Sergeant Allen said that I'd have a better chance if I took these classes. He said it would look good in my records."

I examined the books. "So lemme see. What is this stuff?"

Carl opened a text. "It's all over the board. Some of it comes from *Jane's,* some comes from *Strategic Review,* and then some of it..." Carl paused and made a baffled face. "Some of it, I have no idea why we're reading it. I mean, I can see the point in learning about politics, weapons systems and enemy philosophies, but stuff like this," Carl held up a book, "is not at all what I expected."

"What? Is it classified shit or something?"

"No," said Carl, as he slid the volume across the table. "Check it out."

The book was *Scientific Ecology,* by Jon P. Holdrin. Graphs and mathematical equations appeared every few pages. "This doesn't look too, uh, *military,*" I observed.

"It's not," replied Carl. "It's just some whacko going on and on about how great it would be to murder four-fifths of the world's population."

"Whaaat?" I gave Carl an *I'm-calling-bullshit* look.

"I'm serious!" Carl exclaimed. "This guy, too," he said, as he held up another text by someone named Kass Sunstein. "These guys are out to kill everybody! They wanna turn the entire world into Khmer Rouge Cambodia!"

I slid Holdrin's bullshit back across the table. "So what do they want to do? Start World War Three? Nuke us all? That should do the trick." I still felt like there was a sick joke coming.

"No, no, not like that," replied Carl. "They wanna be slick. Sneaky. Kill most of the people without starting a war that totally fucks up the planet. Then the people who are left can have everything." Carl opened *Scientific Ecology* to a bookmarked page. "He says here that it would be a good idea to put poison in baby shots. Not enough to kill the baby, but just enough to sterilize the kid so that he or she can't grow up and have more babies. He wants the UN to sterilize poor Third World women with shots, too."

"That's fucked up," I said. Maybe it wasn't a joke after all.

"And check this out," continued Carl. "This Sunstein guy wants to put *more* fluoride in the water."

"What's so bad about that? It's good for teeth."

"That's what I thought, too," said Carl, "but this guy says fluoride kinda jacks up kids' brains when they're at a certain age. But not real bad. Not like retarded or anything. They just don't become as bright as they might have been. He says it later causes...wait, where was that?" Carl paused as he flipped a few pages. "Oh yeah, here it is," he said, as he traced some words with his index finger. "Sunstein says fluoride also builds up in people's bones and causes cancer. Then here," Carl pointed to another part of the page, "he says the government should put uranium hexafluoride in the drinking water by passing it off as sodium fluoride."

"Uranium hexa-hexa...what did you say?" I asked.

"Uranium hexafluoride," said Carl. "Radioactive poison."

"Wait. You're really telling me that these guys *want* that?"

"SwearToFuckingGodSwearToFuckingGod," repeated Carl, as he ran his words together. "And this dude--" Carl held up Holdrin's book "--wants to put aerosolized germs on jets and spray them over cities!"

"You're so full of shit," I said. I held out my hand. "Gimme that." I skimmed a few highlighted paragraphs, then looked up at Carl. He was right.

"See? I told you."

I was confused. How did any of this crazy crap

relate to Carl's desire to change his military specialty? What did shooting up little boys and girls with weird vaccines have to do with analyzing spy satellite photos or briefing combat pilots about enemy air defense networks?

I must have made a freaked-out face because Carl laughed. "There's more," he continued. "They want to put X-ray machines at road checkpoints and at airports."

"Airports already have them," I said. "That's how they check suitcases for bombs and stuff." I had no comment on the X-ray-road-checkpoint idea. That just sounded like some more outlandish nonsense.

"No," explained Carl. "Not for your suitcase. For *you*. And without that little lead apron that the doc puts over your nuts, either."

"Lemme guess: another way to sterilize everybody. Or cause cancer." My incredulousness was turning into skeptical dismissal. Carl seemed to sense this, so he returned to his original point.

"I'm just saying that I don't see why I have to study this insane shit to cross-train into Intel." Carl closed the texts.

I remembered Carl's earlier remarks. "You said that State Department people were in your class?"

"Yeah. Feds and embassy staff from Seoul and Tokyo. Bunch of different guys, and most of them aren't trying to cross-train."

"I don't see any reason for them to waste their time with that garbage, either. But there's a **Brightside, Mister.**"

"Oh? What's that?"

"We can use those books to start a barbecue when the class is over."

There was a pause and Carl shrugged. "I dunno," he said. "Maybe I'll keep them. Just for shits and grins."

Appliance Throwers Of America (ATA) And The Local ~~Salty~~ *Umami* Nation

Post-Post-ORI
1987

I went to the electronics department at the BX. "Special order," I said, as I produced a receipt and handed it to the attendant.

"Ah, just one moment," the lady replied. She knelt, opened some sliding doors under the register, and I heard bags rustle. "Here it is." The attendant stood, placed my item on the counter, and re-checked the stub. "And I see that you've paid. Thank you, Airman Simmerath."

When I got back to the barracks I stole one of my roomie's Kafri beers and went to the dayroom. The barracks VHS player had something on the tape slot that looked like dried pizza sauce, but this didn't interfere with the machine's function. The dayroom was empty, so I grabbed one of the green vinyl couches and slid it over in front of the TV. I took off my boots, put my feet up on a coffee table, and opened the beer. I took off my fatigue shirt, draped it over the back of the couch, and relaxed in my *fuck-you-I'm-off-duty* green tee.

The tape hadn't actually started, but the TV's flicker drew a hyper-sexualized moth into the dayroom. "Dude! What's up, Simmster? What kind of action you got?" If Peterson was still pissed about my sabotage of his post-exercise stereoscrew, it didn't show.

Peterson vaulted over the couch and crashed down onto the other end. He wore a sweat-damp muscle shirt that he had trimmed into thin fraying strips that clung to his shoulders. I could estimate the hour by the degree to which Peterson was pumped up. He was like a metronome in his gym regularity, and if the veins over Peterson's pecs and biceps appeared to be near-bursting, then his daily reps were completed and the time was at least six o'clock.

"One of the jeeps in my shop brought this over from the States." I grinned as I lied.

"Who is it? Amber Linn? Or Tracey Lord?" asked Peterson. His eyes were glued to the TV screen, though it only showed an FBI warning. "I'll bet it's Ginger Linn."

My grin just widened. I sat up slightly to sip my Kafri, then I settled back into a slouch and let out a contented sigh. "You can borrow this when I'm done if you...*need* to." My earnest tone masked my mockery.

"Shit, I don't do that," said Peterson in a slight huff. He managed to tear his eyes from the screen to look at me. "I get all the snatch I want."

I didn't respond. *And I'm King of the Mountain, King of the Mountain,* I thought. If I snickered a bit too loudly, I needn't have worried, because Peterson was utterly transfixed. When the show started, however, we didn't hear a funky porn soundtrack. No *Boom-Chicka-Wow-Wow.* Instead, Reeta Morano bellowed:

HEY YOU GUYYYS!

A light bulb appeared on the screen, surrounded by shifting psychedelic colors and patterns. A group of PBS actors, dated by their afros, polyester, and studded denim began to sing a theme from my Vegas childhood, a KVLX tune that now filled a barracks dayroom on another continent:

We gotta turn it on,
We gotta bring you the power,
We gotta light up the dark of night like the brightest day in a whole new way!
We gotta turn it on,
We gotta bring you the power,
It's comin' down the line strong as it can be through the courtesy
Of the Electronic Company!
The Electronic Company!
The Electronic Company!

Peterson just sort of...looked at me. It was as if he were trying to say something, but then he appeared confused and unable to speak. He made a few unsure and perplexed sounds. Words continued to fail him as he slowly got up and walked out of the dayroom.

I was still holding my sides when Carl came in. I had to take a second to catch my breath and compose myself before I could address his curious *what-the-fuck* look.

"You just missed it," I said, as I pointed at the TV. "Peterson was all hyped-up for a stroker." I relapsed into one final exhausted giggle and pulled myself back up onto the couch.

At Peterson's name, Carl's chest puffed out. He fell to his knees in a dramatic height loss, but his horizontal presentation increased tremendously. Carl's arms bent slightly and his shoulders raised. His lips pursed and his brow lowered. "Pussy?" he said, as he waddled around on his knees. "Pussy?" Carl repeated, as he checked under the pool table and dayroom chairs. He sniffed and snorted like a pig rooting for truffles.

"Yup," I said. "But nothing here. Sorry." This was one of Carl's classic imitations, but it still made me smile.

Carl looked at the TV screen and got up. Morgan Freedman was in the midst of an *Easy Reader* sketch.

"Hey," said Carl, as he took the seat vacated by Peterson, "I forgot that he was on *The Electronic Company.*"

"Yeah. Hell of a long way from *Glorious,* huh?"

"Yeah," answered Carl. "That was a good movie. Is this AFN?"

"Nah," I answered, as I threw my now-empty beer can across the room and into a tall metal trashcan. "It's a tape. I ordered it at the BX."

Carl made a face and asked the question that Peterson would have asked if his tongue had functioned. "Um, *why* did you order *this?*"

Although it was a straightforward question, I still needed a few moments to respond. I began to think that I might not be able to articulate an answer, but then, as I watched the TV, I realized that I didn't have to. "Because of her," I said, as I pointed at a group of Short Circus kids who played instruments and sang *The Vowel Song*.

"Who?" asked Carl. "The girl with the guitar? What about her?"

"No," I responded. "The girl with the tambourine."

"You special-ordered an old *Electronic Company* tape because of the girl with the tambourine. Gee, that explains everything." I hadn't told Carl that I was acting at the behest of *Voyces In Me Hedd,* but by his tone, I might have.

"No," I said. "Well, I mean, yes. Didn't you have a TV show that you loved when you were a kid?"

"Sure."

"What was it?"

"I dunno." Carl reflected a moment. "Okay, I liked Bugs Bunnie."

"Have you ever rented cartoons since you came to the ROK?"

Carl paused again. "Yeah," he said. "I guess I have." Something seemed to click in Carl's head, and he looked at the TV. "Do you feel homesick sometimes?"

"Yeah. Sometimes. When I'm not working. Or getting wasted."

Carl watched the tape for a few moments. "I was a *Sesamie Street* guy," he said. "Who's this kid, again?"

"Julie," I answered. "Well, that was just the name she used when she was on *The Electronic Company*."

"Is she Chinese?" asked Carl.

"No," I answered. "Filipina, I think."

The Vowel Song was over, and now Bill Kosby greeted cast members in a guest slot.

Carl looked thoughtful. "You know, it's kind of funny. The little things that comfort people, I mean."

I continued to watch the TV. It was good to see Julie again, so many years later, and when I was so far from home. She looked the same as she did the last time that I saw her. Same plaid dress with a broad belt, same black buckle shoes, same long black hair down to her waist. Same songs, same dancing, same happiness.

I felt like I wasn't wearing Uncle Sugar's monkey suit. I wasn't in a barracks dayroom in South Korea. Instead, I wore the striped shirt that Mom gave me as a going-away present before she went to heaven, and I sat on Grandpa's green shag and watched his big Zenith TV.

231

When the Army Men came to Grandpa's house, it was lonely and scary, but Julie was my friend during those times. The Army Men let me do pretty much anything I wanted, but they were always there and watching me. They always smiled when they spoke to me, but even as a little kid I knew that there was something under their smiles, just like I knew that pistols were always under their black jackets.

I told Julie about all of my fears and hopes. Julie knew that when Grandpa had to go away for work, I was afraid that he wouldn't return. She knew that sometimes I worried that Mom and Dad would be mad at me in heaven if I forgot what they looked like. Julie knew that, while I was a little scared of the Army Men, I was no longer afraid of a third-grader who kept taking my stuff at school. He had pushed me down more than once by the time the teacher came over, but I had kept getting up. I was proud to tell Julie that he didn't mess with me anymore.

"Sounds like you kept Lil' Jules well updated."

Carl's voice shook me. "What?" I said.

"I gather that things were kind of lonely at your gramps' place," observed Carl.

"I - I didn't know that I was talking," I stammered.

"S'alright, dude. Kind of interesting, actually. What's all the stuff about 'Army Men'?"

"Long, long story." Though my embarrassment quickly faded, I still didn't feel like going into it.

"Okay. But I want to ask you something," said Carl. "What kind of neighborhood did you grow up in?"

"Ummm...middle class, I guess. Quiet." I wasn't entirely sure what Carl meant, and his look told me that I hadn't answered the question.

"Color-wise," he clarified.

"Oh. Baked with double-bleached flour," I replied. "It's not like that now, but it was when when I was a little kid."

"That might explain something," said Carl. "What about your elementary school?"

"Same."

I recognized Carl's *Theory-In-Progress* face. "That could be why some little Filipina girl on TV became your imaginary crush," he postulated.

I thought it was peculiar for Carl to make that leap, and I wasn't sure if I agreed. "I don't know if I was operating on that level yet," I said. "But," I added, "why does any little guy get a crush on any little girl? You know - neighbors, classmates, or whatever."

"For the same reason adults catch each other's eyes," replied Carl. He turned back to the television. "Someone different. Someone interesting or new." Carl's theoretical psychologist face was replaced with that of a jester. "Or maybe it was just the beginning of a serious infect--"

I didn't wait for Carl to finish. Instead, I smashed my fist into his arm. He should have seen it coming, just as I had seen him set up for some lame "yellow fever" ragging. Carl clutched his arm and slumped over. His laughs alternated between moans.

I shook my head and turned back to the TV. "I should pop you again for having to work with your crew *freak,*" I said.

Carl righted himself. His laughter boiled down to a grateful look. "You know I'm just kidding," he said. "And thanks. Really. I owe you. This semester was busy."

I sighed and smiled. "It's cool. I can deal with Dreadful. How did the Korean intro go, anyway?"

Carl rubbed his arm. "Okay. It was actually kind of fun. You know who most of the students were? Korean dudes from the States who wanted to start learning the language. They all had boners for the teacher."

"Babe *sun-sing-neem?*"

"Oh yeah," affirmed Carl. "Teacher-Babe-O-Rama. Some chick from Siheung. I gather she's working two jobs: one out here, and one at a private English joint in Bucheon."

"Any prospects?" I asked.

"Well...let me get back to you," said Carl with a mischievous look.

"Well, good luck with that," I said. "When are you back on the regular schedule?"

Carl smirked and cocked his head. "You mean, when can you return to Sergeant Kitts' crew?"

"Well, yeah. That would be nice," I confessed.

"My finals are on Thursday. I'll see you at the shop on Friday. By the way, when does Dreadful sew on tech sergeant?"

"I don't know. Next month, I think. Hell, why ask me? He's *your* crew chief."

"Man, it's gonna be so nice to go to a different crew," said Carl.

"And it's gonna suck for the whole flight when Dreadful becomes a go-between for Jones and the loaders," I asserted.

"Yeah, but it will still be an improvement for *me.*"

Our conversation was interrupted by my growling stomach. "We'd better hit the chow hall. Beer isn't gonna cut it."

Carl nodded and subconsciously put a hand on his stomach. "I don't have my watch. Was Mister Sundial pumped up?"

"Yeah," I said. "But that was probably half an hour ago." I put on my shirt and boots. "Let's get going."

* * *

"What, have you decided to become a vegetarian?" asked Carl.

"No," I said, as I poked through the vegetables on my plate, "but I took a look at the brats, or whatever those things are, and decided to pass." I pointed my fork at Carl's dinner selection. "You don't seem to have a problem with eating chunks of weird gray dick."

"Not me," replied Carl, as he attacked the item in question's *maybe* food-grade casing. "You should try dog before you leave the ROK," he suggested. "Or octopus. I'm telling you, a night of soju and *nakji* is where it's at, if you don't mind a chaff-n-flare asshole the next day."

"No thanks." I had heard this before, but on nights when Carl and I went off-base for food, I stuck with barbecued beef wrapped in lettuce leaves, while he opted for the internal-acid-burn menu. Neither *bo-shin-tahn* dog stew, nor red pepper-soaked cephalopod, held much appeal for me.

"You'll change your tune someday," Carl said. "Some kimchi-girl will shake up your world."

Unlikely, I thought.

Somewhere in the back of the chow hall kitchen there was a pile of GSA vegetable cans that were empty for the first time since I was about eight years old. I was happy to shovel in the Carter Administration's corn and carrots with a few slices of bread while my friend gnawed on Mr. Reagan's rubbery sausage-like enigma.

"Complete proteins," smacked Carl. "And iron. What if you pass out in the middle of a bomb load?" he teased, in the voice of a Gerber Baby.

"I don't think I'll become anemic any time soon," I scoffed. "One night without a gut full of mystery meat won't kill me."

"Speaking of which," said Carl, "what's on the agenda?"

"Not much," I answered, as I ripped off a piece of bread crust with my teeth. "I need to get a new uniform ready for tomorrow. Jammer piston bled all over me today." I turned slightly in my chair to show where a bomb lift-truck's red hydraulic oil had darkened the pantlegs of my fatigues. "Maybe I'll shine my boots and listen to the radio."

"Breathtaking," said Carl.

"You?"

My friend sighed. "I gotta do the same. There's a Shirt in this latest class, and sometimes I think that he's checking out my 35-10. I don't need some fat old office fuck from CBPO or Supply bitching to AGS."

"Come to my room for a boot party," I said.

"Alright. But why radio? Why not a flick or AFN?"

I smiled. "Nostalgia. I'm going home tonight. Well, maybe not back to Vegas, but over to the Empire of Nye."

*　*　*

"Dude, this shit is fucking cool!" exclaimed Carl. "I hope he talks more about that time travel stuff."

"I figured that you'd get into it," I said, as I rubbed a wet cotton ball over the leather of my already-gleaming boot. "They talk about all kinds of crazy things on this show," I added. "UFOs, ghosts, conspiracies... you name it. This show got me through lots of nights when I was working at Greener Valley Grocery."

"What's that? Some hippy food co-op?"

"Nah. It's just a chain of convenience stores around the Vegas Valley. They hire high schoolers."

"Gotcha," said Carl. "I worked at an Ekson station during my junior and senior years. Intercom radio gets you through the graves, but my manager wouldn't let us listen to anything but some sucky FM soft-rock station. All fucking night long," Carl rolled his eyes as he applied heel dressing.

"My manager was pretty casual," I said. "If we got our work done, he didn't care what we listened to."

Carl looked like he was about to say something, but then a confused expression appeared on his face and he turned toward the radio. "Hey," he said, "we already heard this."

From the Hawaiian Islands to the Virgin Islands, or wherever you may be, good evening ladies and gentlemen. My name is Bart Snell, and I'll be escorting you into the dawn's light...

"Did some dummy at AFN screw up the tape?" asked Carl, while the program's opening theme music repeated.

"No," I explained. "They split the play for this show on Mondays and Wednesdays. The shows are a few days old when they get them from the States. We're about to hear the first hour of Wednesday's show."

"Why only the first hour?"

"So they can cram in Lush Rimbaugh and Karrison Geillor and crap like that. AFN tries to play as much different stuff as possible."

"That's stupid," said Carl.

"Those are the geniuses of AFN for you...but at least we get *something* here in the ROK," I replied.

Bart Snell's canned radio voice continued: "On tonight's show, I'll be taking calls on the wild card line for Whitey Streeter about his latest book: *Abduction: The Galactic Sacrament*."

"Awww," groaned Carl. "I wanna hear more about that Jonathan Titor guy. Who the hell is Whitley Streiber?"

"Witney Streeter," I corrected. "He's this UFO dude. He writes books about aliens and stuff. He's been coming on this show for years."

"So when will they finish that show about time travelers?"

"They won't. Like I said, they only play the first hour of Snell's shows."

"But that makes no sense."

I nodded. I was done shining my boots, as was Carl. "You wanna use my iron?" I asked.

"Uh, yeah, sure. My uniform's still in my room." Carl left, but returned after only a few seconds. He was laughing. "Dude, you left that *Electronic Company* tape in the dayroom!"

"Uh, yeah, I guess so," I answered. "What's up?"

Carl gestured for me to follow. "C'mon, you've gotta see this." As I walked down the hall I heard raucous laughter and a familiar tune.

Curious spectators converged on the dayroom and guys jostled in the doorway to observe an impromptu can-can line. The couch, chairs, and pool table were pushed against the wall and a fellow stood by on the VHS player's *REWIND* button while others waited in their skivvies, shoulder-to-shoulder, to kick up their heels. A bottle of Jacques Daniels #7 quickly made its way down the line in confirmation of the group's inebriation.

"*HEY YOU GUYS!*" roared the squadron's finest, as they began to bounce and flip their imaginary skirts. At this, I noticed that the line's anchor was Peterson.

10

Old Goose Moon
Gallows

A Story From The
Man In
Red

December
1988
(1-of-4)

I remember a cold Korean winter's day when an odd expression spread from person-to-person. It was a few ounces of solemn and serious water that poured from one face into the next.

* * *

My crew was in the middle of an AIM-9 missile rail swap on an F-16's outboard pylon. I was grateful to be a loader instead of an SP because weapon crews performed most of their duties within the relative protection of concrete aircraft shelters, whereas the security guards had to contend with freezing wind at airfield checkpoints. We were about halfway through the rail swap when Master Sergeant Jones pulled up to the front of the shelter in a green expediter van. *Why is Jones on the flightline?* I wondered. *He hardly ever leaves the flight shack.*

I noticed that Jones wore a strange expression. When Dave went over to see what the master sergeant wanted, an odd look also appeared on my crew chief's face. Then they both glanced over at me.

Shit. What have I done now?

Jones turned and gestured at someone in the back of the van. The back door opened and Airman Peterson jumped out. He walked into the aircraft shelter with Dave and, before Peterson yanked his parka hood over his head, I saw that he too had a peculiar countenance. I looked at Rob, who only shrugged.

"Pete's gonna take your place," Dave said. "You need to go see El Tee."

"Lieutenant Hall? Dave, what's going on?"

My crew chief didn't look directly at me. "Squadron got a Stateside Red Cross message for you this morning. Jones will take you to the Orderly Room."

Peterson didn't look me in the eye, either. He just

took a torque wrench out of my hand, squeezed my arm, and joined Rob under the F-16's wing.

That was weird, I thought.

As I walked to the van I realized that there was only one kind of Red Cross message that would require me to report to the Section Officer.

Oh no.

Oh my God.

Jones might have allowed me to ride in the front of the van, but I entered through the back door and took a seat on one of the rear crew benches. That way I was able to hide my face.

Merry Christmas.

Old Jawbone On The Almshouse Wall

When I tried to book a ride on the Pyeongtaek-to-Incheon shuttle I was told that it was full, but Jones made a call to the MWR NCOIC and pulled a few strings on my behalf. Jones told me that I had to wear my dress blues during the flight, but I think that was just some bullshit that he made up. Carl and a couple other guys in the barracks said that it wasn't necessary, and on my flight to the ROK I was sure that I had seen other service members wearing civvies while in transit. If Jones hadn't ordered me to check in with him before leaving base, I might have tried to slip off to Incheon International in jeans and sneakers.

As a weapons troop, I practically lived in my green fatigues. Getting my blues ready was a hassle because they had hung, untouched, in my barracks closet since I was an E-1. I had lost my Basic Training and Marksman ribbons, so I borrowed some from Carl. There wasn't time to get my blues pressed at the base laundry, either, so I used an iron and a damp towel on the night before my flight.

I didn't cry as much as I thought I would. I felt like a dentist had given me a full-body Novocayne injection. From a numb and detached perspective I watched myself say things, do things, get on a shuttle, then on a plane, and finally wait at McKarran's Carousel "D" for a humble duffel that could have easily been a carry-on.

Since I had come from the Korean winter, Vegas' desert climate punched me in the face when I emerged from the gate. My dress shirt got wet almost instantly, so I took off my uniform jacket as I waited with Korean folks that I had seen on the plane and a few other yankee doodles in army green and another in air force blue. *Are they here to bury someone too?* I wondered.

* * *

I drifted outside of my body again. I watched myself watch the tourists as they lined up at McKarran's taxi ranks. Then I watched myself get on the Vegas Transit bus and ride out to Boulder Highway for 1/50th the price of a cab. I watched myself get off at Nevada Palace, debate for a moment about whether or not to walk north to Sammy's Town, then shrug and get a room at the older and cheaper hotel. Nevada Palace was unfamiliar. I had no memories there. It was what I needed.

After I checked in I traded my hot and miserable blues for shorts and a tee. I had traveled for about two days with only snatches of sleep among clouds in cabin windows. I had also refused all of the in-flight fare, though I vaguely remembered a bag of chips at LAX.

Oily hash browns, gray eggs, and toast that had been buttered with a brush awaited at Nevada Palace's run-down diner. A cup of penny-pinching re-brew sat on my booth's blue-green formica table. The crack where the tabletop met the chrome side trim was full of black grime that had been deposited by years of hurried table-wiping.

I placed my order and went to the restroom. Though I wasn't dining with Mia Braveheart at *Pulp Fictitious'* Slim Jack Rabbit's, the plate was nevertheless waiting upon my return. Don't you just love that? When your food comes while you're powdering your nose?

Don't you just love that?

Don't you just love it when you fly back to the States to bury your Grandpa and discover that his heavy-duty lawyers have handled every fucking thing?

Well, I didn't. If I had been given some responsibility or merely something to do, maybe it would have been easier to cope. When your food comes to the table while you're powdering your nose, the next thing to do is eat. Eating requires effort. Effort provides distraction. When a law firm completely settles your Grandpa's

243

affairs, however, all that you can do is stand around and watch.

Because In This Life, You're On Your Own

The funeral director was a tall and sallow creeper in a threadbare charcoal ghoulsuit who seemed to have come straight from the set of *Phantasmic.* He bent down and struggled to release the casket winch, but it wouldn't budge. He glanced up, sheepishly offered a waxy embalmed smile, and gave a couple more futile ratchet yanks. Nothing. Finally, in a fluster, the director stood up and kicked the winch. That did the trick. The catch over-released, and Grandpa's descent was set to a shrill cable squeal. We had to sing the final hymn at the tops of our lungs to keep from being drowned out:

Erstaunliche Gracie, wie süß der Klang, für alte Zeiten werden nicht vergessen, wegschauen, wegschauen...

My voice died in mid-verse, though the other mouths kept moving. I scooped up some dust, kissed the back of my hand, and sprinkled the fistful down into Grandpa's grave.

...wegschauen, wegschauen...

Speak for yourselves, I thought. I stood, turned my back on the strangely blue Confederados, and left the cemetery.

That Little Souvenir Of The Terrible Year

December 1988 (4-of-4)

Go back to the hotel. Take a drink and a nap, then wake up scared, several times, and not know where you are...at first.
  You're back in Vegas.
  You're at Nevada Palace.
  Grandpa is gone.

* * *

I was awakened by a knock.

Edward Burnstein, the main man himself, stood in the doorway of my low-budget Nevada Palace hotel room. He wasn't *completely* bald. He wasn't particularly big or tall. He was a white man in his late fifties with an unyielding gaze and a dark suit that had been measured *thrice* and cut once. His smile was the kind that lawyers reserve for well-heeled clients; friendly, but professional and focused.

Burnstein held out his hand to give me something. I was a little groggy and didn't react, so he reached over, took my left hand, and placed Grandpa's old Nazi Party watch in my palm. Then he shook my right hand. The power in Burnstein's grip made me notice the way his perfectly tailored sleeves could not conceal the movement of muscles beneath. Burnstein was an older man, but he seemed to be in better shape than a lot of the young guys back at Pyeongtaek. Something about Burnstein's manner made me feel like I faced a base commander. No...it was like I stood before a senator. Or a prime minister.

"A personal delivery in exchange for an opportunity to become president of the Russian Federation seemed like a very reasonable bargain," said the lawyer. "I dislike disco dancing, however."

I Only Wanted It From *You...*
You Told Me You Used
To Be A Pirate

January
1989

"Dude, *come on!* We'll be late to formation!" Carl stands outside of my barracks room with his hair tight, his monkey suit pressed, and his boots glittering. I'm dressed and ready to go too, but it's hard to turn away from the window.

I just need a sec. Just a sec. We won't be late.

Okay, ready. Let's go. I'll turn around. Don't make me talk too much, or my voice might crack. I'll be alright by the time we get to the flight shack.

We're walking out of the barracks. I'll hang behind the ol' Corndog.

"Dude," says Carl, "maybe you should have taken more leave or something."

Maybe.

We show our security badges to the flightline gate SP and walk to the flight shack. Carl looks at me. "What are you doing tonight?"
"I dunno. The same thing as any other weeknight, I guess. My crew's not on standby."
"Wanna go into Seoul?"
I look at my friend. "It's only Tuesday. And I'm definitely not in the mood."
"I don't mean for *that.* I've got something else going on."
"What?"
"I'll surprise you."

* * *

After two weeks I had the Tuesday and Thursday train route memorized. Carl and I didn't take the fastest route, but there were fewer transfers. "We can swing back and hit Gekko's afterward," Carl remarked as the multilingual Korean, Japanese, and English station signs went by. "We'll just look like a couple buzzed GIs returning to base."

We got off the train at Anguk Station. "Remember, these are just kids whose parents can't shell out like those of the Gangnam brats," said Carl, as we climbed the station steps up to the street. "They're cool, and it's fun. They *want* to be here, and they won't give you any garbage. You won't believe how driven these guys are. I mean, could you imagine kids in the States doing this?"

I remembered getting out of high school classes and going straight to after-school jobs. I had cash, Grandpa seemed pleased, and I still got my school assignments done. "Well, maybe it's not so weird," I replied.

"Everybody's about our age," said Carl, "except for those two guys who just finished their army stints. Do you remember them? They're a little older. They might bring college work."

"*College work*?" You're the college boy, not me," I said. "What the hell can *I* do for them?"

"Don't worry about it. Just read their papers and fix the stuff that sounds weird. Sometimes their college work is like *Weathered Heights* meets the Jimmy Hendricks Experience. I don't know where their books come from." We both laughed, though I didn't tell Carl that my knowledge of Emilie Brontë had never extended beyond Cate Bush and Pat Benattar.

"Here we go," Carl said, as he motioned at a tiny grocery sandwiched between another tiny grocery and an even smaller restaurant. "I think they've made more space in the back since last time. They might have chairs this week."

I had been to the grocery a couple times with Carl, just to observe, and I had gotten used to sitting on crates. Still, a chair would be nice, though I wouldn't use it much. Tonight I would teach, or maybe just lead the class, and that meant staying on my feet for the next hour-and-a-half...that is, if I were to emulate Carl's style.

"Oops. Hold on a sec, Jackster." Carl stopped outside the door and unrolled his shirt sleeve over the corndog.

"Oh yeah," I said, as I remembered something. "There was a woman on the train who got up and moved to another seat. Did you see her?"

"Yeah." Carl pulled the last inch of his sleeve over his birthmark. "Koreans think I've got wayguk leprosy or something. I don't really care. I just have to remember to cover up before class."

We went inside and a middle-aged Korean man at the register gave us a nod and ushered us into the back. We walked past cases of soju, refrigerated shelves of pickled radish, a dozen kinds of vinegars, and frozen packages of sea creatures that I couldn't identify. We stopped in a storeroom that had a small barred window. The man pointed at a folding table and chairs and said something to Carl, to which Carl gave an extended reply that contained my name in mid-sentence. The proprietor looked at me, nodded, and went back to the front.

Carl's Korean is getting better, I thought.

Carl gave me a pat on the back and picked up a dog-eared English workbook with sticky notes poking out from various pages. "Just do half a page, or if you think it's going well, go ahead and do a whole page," he said.

"What if they have questions?"

"Then answer them," smiled Carl, as he gave me another reassuring pat. "You can handle it. Draw pictures, quack like a duck, whatever, until they get it."

Carl was a natural teacher. He drew cartoons. He used phonetic spelling on a whiteboard that was propped up over a case of Korean ramien. Carl wrote out definitions. He read to them. They read to him. He talked about news and current events. More questions. More definitions. More pronunciation practice. It was fun to watch Carl's English classes, but I wondered if I could do what he did...and what he did, entertaining as it may have been, was highly illegal. American servicemen who taught English classes were targets for Korean Immigration, and it was not unheard of for GIs to be arrested if they got caught walking around Seoul with ESL materials but no E-2 teacher's visa.

This gig was fairly safe, however. The store owner

had set it up twice a week, and it was secure. Carl could be had for pennies compared to what it would have cost to bring in an actual certified ESL teacher, and he seemed to satisfy both the students and the storekeeper. "It's easy," Carl had said. "Just talk a lot, ask questions, write on the board, and have fun. Then you get something in trade." That "something" usually had alcohol in it.

The students sat around the table, some in casual dress, and some in clothes that told me they had attended university classes or come from their workplaces. My heart went out to the latter group. Though occupationally a universe apart, as a young GI I sympathized with kids who couldn't simply go home after putting in their academic hours, but rather, were then expected to go to work or attend private classes. I had spent many afternoons and evenings behind the registers of Vegas' Greener Valley Groceries.

"Amusement," Carl said, "is what keeps them here. That, and your respect. Most of them are leery of foreigners, so shock them with kindness and politeness. For Chrissake," he continued, "you spend your days handling high explosives. This should be cake." Carl retreated to the back of the room and took a seat on a plum wine crate.

I wrote the students' names and seating positions as the table filled up. *Mi-sun. Ho-chul. Sun-hye.* There weren't a lot of students, but I still stumbled over some names. One of the young ladies showed considerable patience, however:

"Sun. Like in sky. S-U-N. Like boy. Son. S-O-N. Hye. Hay...HAAAY. Sun-hye. Now you say."

Other students tried to make it easy for me, and introduced themselves with western pseudonyms. Some of these names, however, were taken from past eras, e.g., Percival, Solomon, and Artemus. There were also more contemporary names, however, such as "Matt" and "George".

Carl had to help me a couple times during that first night because I was never Captain Grammar in high school. This was no big deal, really, as the students had already been through all of that stuff. The "class" was just a matter of going through the book, having conversation, and proof reading. One of the ex-army guys needed help with an essay. Easy. One of the girls wanted to polish a cover letter. No problem. Most of the students' work was within my scope of assistance, and at the end of the night there were smiles, a brave handshake or two, and lots of quick bows. After the last student left I wrote a few sticky notes and placed them in the book.

"See? No problem," Carl said, as he walked toward the front of the room.

"Think they'll let me come back?"

"I think so, but I gotta check with the owner, just to make sure."

"They're really nice," I said.

Carl chuckled. "You expected...what?"

"I dunno. I guess...it's just that we take a lot of shit on the street, you know? Spitting and ape sounds and stuff."

Carl was quiet for a moment, then said: "Yeah, but that's mostly just the people around P-Tek."

"Yeah, maybe." I closed the textbook and stood up. "I'm beat. I feel like I just combat turned three jets, back to back."

"Yeah, it'll drain you," Carl replied. "You don't realize how much until the class is over."

"Jones put our crew on days for at least the next two months," I said. "I can keep doing this until we go back to swings."

"Just keep it to yourself, especially around Jones," Carl said. "I like the trade part of this gig, and I think you need the distraction...but remember that this is all totally uncool, both with P-Tek and the Korean government."

* * *

Carl and I consumed our barter items in the barracks dayroom on the Saturday that followed my first nearly-solo English class. "This isn't bad," I remarked, as I held up my half-empty plum wine bottle. "I don't mind that it's so sweet."

The dayroom television was behind Carl. As he prepared to offer his own opinion, the jerking thrusts of some porn stud and the squeals of some Whomever-Lynn played out in the background. Peterson sat in front of the TV with another guy from our flight named Arteaga. They sucked Coronas and commented on the entertainment.

"Can you believe it? She's been in loads of vids," said Peterson.

"Yeah. Her pussy is still nice," observed Arteaga.

"Yeah. Not all meat-flappy."

"Yeah."

Carl watched Peterson and Arteaga for a few moments. "Those dorks will yank their cocks raw tonight," he said with a knowing smirk.

I blew a raspberry. "I doubt if Peterson even waits to get back to his room."

Peterson noticed that we were watching and called out across the dayroom: "Hey Corndog, is this what you guys sneak off to do on Tuesdays and Thursdays?

"Yeah, there's a demand for purple fisting nowadays," Carl retorted over his shoulder. "You interested?" Peterson didn't reply.

"Ahem," said Carl, as he contemplated his wine bottle. "This stuff is a little too sugary for my taste. And it will really twist you."

"That reminds me of something that my crew chief told me."

"Sergeant Kitts? What did he say?"

"He told me that the hangover from this stuff is even worse than with Stateside ripple. The Kimsters put formaldehyde in it, same as in their beer."

"I've heard that too," Carl replied. "Good old embalming fluid."

"Yeah. Not a lot, but some. Dave says you can keep Korean booze for a long time before it skunks. If this class thing keeps up..." I paused and grimaced at my slip, while Carl put a finger to his lips and glanced over at Peterson and Arteaga. Not to worry. They were now high-fiving over the money shot.

"Er, sorry," I said in a buzzed whisper. "Maybe the store guy will trade soju instead."

"Yeah, maybe. I don't know if there's formaldehyde in soju." Carl put down his bottle. "That's kinda like something my crew chief told me about Korean booze, too. Korean booze *and* Korean women."

"Dreadful? This ought to be a *great* insight," I sarcastically responded.

Carl paused to look over at Peterson and Arteaga. "They'll have hangovers tomorrow from that American beer, but we'll still have headaches from this plum stuff on Monday."

"Corona is Mexican."

"Whatever. My point is, Korean booze and Korean women are similar."

"What, Korean women also contain formaldehyde?" I quipped.

"I mean," said Carl in a small voice, "they both leave you with long hangovers."

The Only Thing That Burns In Hell
Is The Part Of You That
Won't Let Go
Of Your
Life

*March
1989
(1-of-3)*

I have to remember that Harry's name isn't Harry anymore. It's Debbie. That's different now, along with her Rumpelstiltskin straw-hair that's black again.

Perhaps Debbie could have picked a teacher who didn't know that her *other* hair has always been its natural color, though that's behind us. She's a shop girl and a student now, just living on her own in the city. The other students don't suspect anything. I feel like I owe her this, me and all of the other foreign shits whose money was never really enough to buy what it purchased.

I don't know what the catalyst was for her new life. All that I had noticed was that Nipa Johnson had a new NCO club lieutenant, and soon afterward "Debbie" turned up in the grocery storeroom with different hair, nice clothes, and a smile.

I had been pretty shocked by the flashback that I experienced. For a second I was again underneath Harry, whose bouncing and moaning served as my memory's soundtrack for that Pyeongtaek newbie night. Harry's bleached straw had flipped and whipped as I hoped that the little boa constrictor of a condom that she had pinched and pulled down over my cock didn't either come off inside her or pull a Lorena Bobbitt on my member. *Augh.* That condom had been green like those sold in the little Anguk grocery in *kanji*-marked packages that contrasted against the Korean labels on other merchandise.

Debbie has been in the "meeting" - sometimes I don't even call it a "class" - for about two months, and her earnestness is one of the reasons why I decided to find a way to keep teaching, even when Jones stuck my weapons crew on frigid-ass swing shift.

Debbie is wearing a long and demure dark skirt, and she crosses her legs like a lady crosses them. Her blouse is white and as buttoned-up as it can get. *Huh. None of the students have a clue,* I think. Whatever Debbie tells the others in their conversations seems to satisfy. She should have either been an actor or a spy. If her cover gets blown, it will be my fault, not hers.

Debbie takes a breath and focuses as she gets ready to conquer one of her pronunciation issues. It's the old "L" and "R" thing.

We can do this together. "Okay," I say, as I write the word "TREE" on the board. For good measure, I also draw a quick and crude Christmas-tree like shape. "Do you know this word?"

"Yes, I know," says Debbie. The others also nod. "Please read it."

Debbie does so. No problem.

"Good," I continue. I write the word "REALLY" and ask Debbie to also read it. It comes out as "leelee." I point back to the word "TREE" and ask her to read it again, which she does, and it sounds fine. I then tack on an "-LY", and the word becomes "TREELY". I smile. "Can you read this?"

Debbie gives me a curious look. The word is nonsense, of course, but she reads it.

"Good!" I exclaim. I then I rub out the "T", so that only "REELY" remains. "Can you read this, please?"

Debbie pronounces the word perfectly. "I knew you could do it," I say. I point to the word "REALLY", and this time, from the entire group, I hear the perfect "R."

* * *

I was certifiably nuts by the time March arrived because I was still doing something really bizarre, at least by the metrics of most young GIs. On Tuesdays and Thursdays I left base hours before swing shift started so that I could catch the train to Seoul and spend some time in the back of the little grocery.

This new arrangement wasn't convenient for the group, either. If they didn't have to work at that time, most were in school. Therefore, the "English class" became a matter of me waiting to see if anyone could make it. Usually one or two *did* manage to come, so I just proofread papers or explained things that they had written in school lecture notes. The situation was quite different from addressing the larger group, but it allowed more insight on individual student progress.

At first I was embarrassed to admit that I had never read many of the English books that the students brought in, but I soon got over it as I learned that I could still assist in their assignments. It was at this time that a young woman named Kim Mirye started coming to the meetings.

"My friend said you were here," was how she introduced herself.

* * *

When I was a kid I saw a horror film by Jon Carpenter, the title of which now escapes me, but it was about people in the future who sent messages backward in time via dreams in an attempt to warn people about an evil presence in their midst. The movie kept showing these weird dream sequences of an Antichrist figure coming out of a church. I guess that I didn't really understand the plot, but I remember that the dream parts were strange and disturbing.

I let my thoughts wander when I took the train into Seoul. I wondered what the young man whom I was would have done if a senior citizen version of himself had invaded his daydreams to deliver a warning?

- *Get off now. Cross the platform and catch the next train back to P-Tek.*
- What the fuck? Am I asleep?
- *Listen to me. Get off this train. Don't go into Seoul again. Forget the whole English class thing.*
- Why?
- *Just spend your time boozing and hanging out with the other GIs. Do what everyone else does. Take college classes on base. Anything. Just stop what you're doing.*
- **WHY?**

* * *

Debbie smiles a real smile that extends to her eyes and softens them. I've only seen her fake smile before, the smile she used in the NCO club when approaching potential customers. The fake smile was like stagehands lowering a new background for the next act, not like the genuine expression Debbie has when she shows me the marks she received on a paper that we had worked on together. Maybe we were also working on her new identity.

Debbie's paper dealt with automobile design costs - ergonomic preferences or something - and I didn't *really* understand the topic. I had just tried to make it flow smoothly, and apparently that had been enough. I quickly picked up on that point when I helped the students. From the industrial-level spoiled-food composting study that one of the ex-ROK army guys was working on, to one of Debbie's car-related papers, I could help with composition and translation, but not content. That was over my head.

"Ilar--*Debbie,* you write many things about cars," I said one day when she came to the back room. Debbie was dressed in an LG-green work uniform, rather than her usual ultraconservative hybrid Amish-Seoulite getup.

"Yes. I study for car company, also accountant."

"Car company?

"Hyundai. Car company. I will accountant."

"Oh," I said. "You will *be* an accountant."

Debbie smiled. "Yes. I will *be* an accountant. *Gohm.* My dream."

* * *

I didn't care about collecting my barter-booze anymore. After the third time that I left empty-handed, the shopkeeper stopped me on the way out. He held out some bottles, but I raised my hand. *"Ahnee-yo, kahn-sahm-needa,"* I said.

The shopkeeper gave me a curious look. *What? "No, thank-you." That's correct, isn't it?* I wondered. The man continued to hold out the bottles - soju, when I actually looked at them. "Carl-Uh," he said.

"Oh, sorry," I murmured. *"Mee-on hahm-needah."* This time I guessed that I got it right. *"Kihn-jahn-ay-oh,"* the man replied, as he returned to the counter.

* * *

I thought of my future. Maybe I would travel.
Maybe I would go to school. I was quite sure that I
wouldn't re-up. What would I do? I kind of wanted to
go back to Vegas, though location wasn't important.
Grandpa was dead and no one waited, anywhere, for me
to finish my enlistment.

But maybe Grandpa was only *mostly* dead and, as
Miraculous Max reminded us, there's a big difference
between *mostly* dead and *all* dead. "Mostly dead"
means hitting MUTE and watching television out of the
corner of your eye. You can *almost* figure out what's
happening on the screen, but not quite. You can't hear
it, and you can only sort-of see it. So it was with
Grandpa. Sometimes as I walked though Seoul's streets
I looked twice at faces. Sometimes as the trains went
through the stations I did double takes as commuters
flashed by. Sometimes I sensed a shadow sitting in the
back of the grocery storeroom, but when I turned and
looked the chair was empty. I then understood that the
odds of being "mostly" dead were the same as being "a
little bit" pregnant.

I Am Jack's Shambling
Regret-O-Matic

March
1989
(2-of-3)

I think that Debbie is fond of me, and in a way unfamiliar to her. Debbie keeps me apprised of her personal progress as she gets closer to her dream job. It takes a lot to survive as Debbie is surviving. Her strategy reminds me of Nevada's reforming call girls, raw and ropy Northtown hookers, and the Rooster Ranch's Roster of Questionable Choices. All ladies have a chance at mainstream re-integration. It can be done. Resourceful and clever Korean girls, according to P-Tek veterans, overcame the strictures of sterile Confucian society as skillfully as their Christendom sisters covered up mysterious CV gaps. The job - *the real job* - was the hard part, and it required a variety of Independent Woman performance that supported neither Seoul's olive oil vendors nor its hymen-restoration clinics.

* * *

There are two twenty-something young women at the class table, and they seem to know each other outside of this environment. Army George, as I call him, is in attendance and he hides his erection under his book and desperately tries to think of a reason to call me over. Debbie is also here and she waits for me to finish reading her latest paper on why vehicle armrest positions need to be determined by averaging physical traits of specific customer populations. I'm not sure how accounting figures in the topic. It seems more like an R&D thing.

"Jack *sun-sing-neem?*"

I lower the paper and walk over to George. *I'll just give him this. He doesn't have to invent anything. My crotch shot is another bonus.*

"Yes, George?"

"Is it--" he holds out a paper but keeps a text book on his lap "--okay?"

I smile, have a look at the sheet, and hand the paper back like it's a shutter going down in a peep show booth. "I think it's mostly okay," I say, as I make a few light pencil marks under some words. "Perhaps you could check these spellings?"

George smiles, nods, and checks out my ass as I return to my seat on a wine crate. I pick up Debbie's paper, and as I'm about to learn about the ulna-and-radius length differences between Korean arms in the southern and north-eastern provinces, the stockroom door opens.

"My teacher said. It is wrong," Kim Mirye states, as she takes a seat. In her hand is a report that I've seen before.

"Hello, Miss Kim."

"Ahn-nyuhng-hah-say-oh." The greeting is so fast that it sounds like she says: "Yawn-say-oh." It's also less formal than the Korean greeting used by the other students.

It's the end of the eighties, and Miss Kim isn't afraid of a Cleopatra. The sides and back are almost always up in a clip or scrunchie, leaving loose side strands to frame her face under the fringe. While most of the young women in the class tend toward skirts, Kim Mirye prefers slacks and jackets. She has several looks for Tuesdays and Thursdays, and there are always white cuffs on her ankles.

And never plain.
With some kind of frill.
Just so.

Miss Kim doesn't shave her legs. There's almost no need, except for one long black one that I've seen over the top of the lace. I like to sneak peeks when Miss Kim sits and her pant cuffs go up. For some reason this turns me on, albeit coarsely inured as I am, from a very young age, to near-hardcore everywhere, from the blowing leaflets on Vegas streets to billboards that advertise the latest "Gentlemen's Club."

I once handed Miss Kim a pen and accidentally touched the tip of her index finger. I had to take a cue from Army George, and for the next few minutes my lap was the best place for a notebook.

"My teacher said. It is wrong," Miss Kim repeats.

I put down Debbie's paper. "Oh? What's wrong?" *TensesVerbsGerundsContinuingVerbsConjunctionsAgree ments*...all of the shit that comes naturally to me runs together in a mucky mental mess when I try to explain it. But Miss Kim knows it. She works in a virtual English mechanics garage. Miss Kim is a *hagwon,* or private school, language teacher during the morning and a college student in the evening. She's already forgotten more about English grammar than I've ever known...yet I'm giving out something, essentially for free, to folks like Debbie and Army George, when perhaps by Miss Kim's reckoning they should pay private academy fees.

One disgruntled anonymous call to ROK Immigration, or even Pyeongtaek, would leave me screwed.

Miss Kim speaks fine English, though conversing with her requires effort and thought on my part. Carl told me that he had learned, during the course of his Korean language studies, that the *Han* people had been divided for so long that their languages had diverged. Yes, they still understood each other, but the Norks spoke from a 1950s lingual reference, whereas the Southerners used a tongue that had kept pace with the world. So it is with Miss Kim and her form of English. It's always correct and without Konglish mutation, but it's sometimes so disconnected from familiar parlance that I have to pause. *I have no idea why she's here,* I think. She *should be teaching these guys, not me.*

"Subjunctive mood is unsuitable," Miss Kim says, as she touches the tip of her pen to a particular paragraph. "My professor has stated."

I don't know what she's talking about, but maybe I can get an idea if I take a look. "May I read it?" I ask. *Ah. I remember this paper. It's about plans for a riverfront-themed walkway.*

Miss Kim is working toward a degree in urban planning, so topics in this area dominate her written work. Maybe she's aiming to apply for a government position, though I dare not inquire. Civil service must be a huge step up from the cram school scene.

...so as to provide a pedestrian route through one of the most congested areas of the city, the proposed stream restoration will also introduce a natural aesthetic to the otherwise heavy mood of the urban center. I dream that the research continues...

I stop reading. Even if I don't know what "subjunctive mood" is, I do recognize that sentences beginning with "I dream" are out of place in a paper that deals with city development.

"I think that this part, that these words," I say, as I point out the odd-sounding sentence, "should be changed."

"Ewa professor also said. Why? I want to know."

I take a breath. I can only be honest. "I don't know, exactly. I'm sorry, Miss Kim. I just know that it seems strange to say 'I dream' in a paper like this. 'Dream' is a word for the heart," I say, as I place my hand over my chest, "and not for building cities."

Miss Kim nods and takes the paper. She says nothing, but I can feel her accusing eyes.

Fraud.

A fool who doesn't even know the rules of his own language.

Fraud!

Go back to your airbase and get drunk with the other waygukin.

* * *

I don't think that it's fraudulent to want to improve, or to give, or just do something decent. Maybe fraudulence can even be a first step toward something better...yet the world still takes pleasure in pointing fingers.

- Alright! I fucking get it! I GET IT! I'm a fraud!
- Yes. You suck.

- *Okay. So I'll try to improve myself.*
- Don't. That will just make you a fraud AND a hypocrite.
- *Okay, so what do you want from me?*
- Nothing. Stay the same. It's fun to put you down.

*   *   *

My crew had weekend duty. I tried to work, but I was distracted. Not good. When handling explosives, focus is advised.

"Jack!"

Maybe I was having an imaginary argument with Kim Mirye.

"HEY! AIRMAN FUCKSTICK! *JACK!* RAISE THE GODDAMN BOMB!"

I lifted up my head. Dave yelled over the noise of the bomb-lift's engine and jerked his thumb upward. Hardesty also waited on the other side of the bomb and the underwing pylon. His hand was on a bomb-locking ratchet that wouldn't rotate until I operated the lift's hydraulic arms.

Wake up, dude, I told myself as I operated the control. *Get Little Miss Subjunctive Mood out of your head.*

Deep In Your Eyes
You're One
Hundred
Years
Old

March
1989
(3-of-3)

Then there comes a night when I have this dream. I'm a kid again, and I'm sitting on green seventies-shag in Grandpa's living room. I'm wearing the short sleeved shirt with red stripes that my mother gave to me before she died, and an amalgam housekeeper-sitter figure, the same kind of character with whom Steve Martyn's child-self conversed in the opening scene of *Parenting,* is in the dream's background.

Grandpa's big black-and-white Zenith television is on, and I'm watching *The Electronic Company. When is Julie gonna be on?* I wonder. *Goddamn it, I'm fucking sick of waiting.* I didn't use such coarse language when I was a boy, but this is a dream, mind you.

Young Morgan Freedman appears on the screen. I don't know what he's talking about - numbers or the alphabet or something - and he's wearing a turtleneck sweater that sure-as-hell wasn't issued at Shawshank. He's having a conversation with Bert and Ernie.

"Okay, now this is just getting stupid," my dream-boy self flatly states. "Fucking Bert and Ernie weren't on *The Electronic Company.*"

Morgan Freedman stops in mid-exchange with Bert and looks at me through the TV screen. "Young man, you have a foul mouth. Julie doesn't like boys with foul mouths."

"Yeah," says Ernie, in his smart-ass orange-headed way.

"Yeah," agrees Bert.

He's probably Evil Bert.

I sit up and gasp. I blink, shake my head, and swing

my legs off my bunk and onto the cold tile. My roomie is out. I can't remember his duty schedule, so I don't know if he's at work or the NCO club. I hardly ever see the guy, anyway.

I put on some sweats and leave my room. I walk down the hall and into the bathroom. I run some water into one of the sinks and splash my face. A minute passes while I stare at a mirror. Then two minutes. I raise my hands and touch my wet skin. I feel my lips, nose, and eyes. I place my palms on my temples and my eyes narrow as I pull back.

Fraud.

But maybe fraud really *isn't* fraud if you don't actually deceive yourself. Maybe in such cases it's simply entertainment, and the casinos back home could showcase "*Lance Jesuit and His Sexy Assistants, The Solomon's Keys: Shows at 2 PM, 5 PM, & First Kings 10:1.*"

Conjure a spirit for me. One with lacy cuffs, please.

I pull my eyelids back again.

Maybe it would be easier if I were a Korean man.

The barracks floors are eerily quiet. I usually hear music from somebody's stereo, overloaded gear packs scraping against walls, and boots thumping past my door in time with moans and squeaking fuck-rhythms of cheap GSA metal bunks.

A breath in, a sigh out. I lower my hands and my gibbous moon-face returns to its Westernized *moai* form.

We only met a couple months ago.
This is really happening?

Seriously?

Oh my God.

Here we go.

Er, perhaps a moment of contemplation is in order before I nuke Fort Sumpter.

Maybe?

Oh, what the hell.

HUZZAH FOR DIXIE! HUZZAH FOR ADMIRAL LEE AND THE TURTLE SHIPS!

Huzzah for all Lost Causes...

To her, I probably look like a bleached baboon.
I have brown hair.
I have a European nasal bridge that could double as an ironclad's battering ram.
I have green Western eyes that are the same color as little Japanese snare-condoms, and as without epicanthic folds as my circumcised American cock is without a foreskin.

Hmmm. That might not be the best comparison, because when I look closely, like an infant fascinated by a mirror, and when I pull, stretch, and investigate my face in the harsh light of the barracks shitter, I can *almost* imagine the trace of an almond eye peeking out from the generations behind me, though its remnant is far less obvious than my dick's ring-around-the-rosy scar.

11
And One Of Them Was Me

What Are The
Finger Lakes?

April
1989
(1-of-2)

I need to consider my post-military existence. I'm getting the standard reenlistment pitch from CBPO and Squadron, but they might as well keep their "consider the benefits" and "the potential to cross-train" crap to themselves, because the military isn't for me.

The military isn't for me. But...the military is what enables me to remain in Korea.

The military isn't for me.

That's still true - isn't it? I was certain that it was...until recently.

The military is what enables me to remain in Korea.

The military is what enables me to remain near her.

Men have reenlisted for worse reasons.

Let's just keep options open and see what happens.

Maybe - probably - *nothing* will happen, and I'll get dumped back in the 702 at the end of this GI nonsense. Okay. Fine. I'm willing to work at Greener Valley Grocery with high school kids again if I have to, or at whatever other job I can find, until I get on my feet.

Though...I really *won't* have to. The information from Grandpa's lawyers concerning my inheritance is a comfort in moments when I feel adrift. I guess that I'll be able to go to university when I get back home, or do pretty much anything else that I want to do, according to Ed Burnstein, Mega-Attorney-At-Law.

I hope that his "Russian President" thing works out.

The Way We Were
Choosing Lessons
In The Seoul
Kitchen

*April
1989
(2-of-2)*

I try to steady a cheap dry-erase board, but Miss Kim's eyes make me nervous. Her face is like make-up over ice...except that she doesn't need, or use, any kind of foundation. No blush. Nothing. With skin like that, why bother? There is, however, some lip gloss. Unlike other girls with single lids, Miss Kim is not afraid to apply shadow above her creases in a gentle upward fade between her lashlines and brows. I find this especially noticeable because I've seen many K-girls whose eye application simply disappears under single folds.

This back room is never the same from week-to-week because the floor layout changes when the stock truck is unloaded. Tonight I couldn't find a clear place to put the dry-erase board, so I half-write and half-balance it on top of some boxes.

We actually learn here. I feel like my stay on the Korean Peninsula will have a purpose beyond commemorating an old Imperialist vs. Communist grudge match. I wonder if I could become a real teacher back in the States someday? What would that be like? It's never a thought that I considered before Carl got me involved in this crazy little "covert ESL" operation - but why not?

Why not?

Well...maybe because teaching can be a pain in the ass, particularly when one of the students knows more than the teacher.

Oh shit. She's raising her hand.

"Yes, Miss Kim?"

"Mister Jack, I would like to examine this gerund form. Should I revise it?"

What? What is she asking me? Maybe if I look at

her paper I'll understand.

I lower the dry erase board and approach the table. Army George monitors my crotch with each step, but Debbie and the rest are intent upon their work.

I nervously smile. "May I read the sentence?"

Miss Kim's finger underscores the passage in question. "Here," she says. *Running and walking on the proposed Cheonggye-cheon will be welcome activities for The People,* it reads.

"I can understand what you've written," I say. "I think that it's okay."

"This form is correct?" Miss Kim asks. "Not *'to* run and *to* walk'?"

I look at the paper again. I don't know the exact grammar rules for making this call, so I fall back upon the native speaker trick of re-reading and identifying which version "clicks" in my head. "Yes. I would not change, or *revise,* this sentence."

Miss Kim looks up from her seat. I scan her face for an emotion or expression, but find neither.

"The gerund form is conventional," she states - or is she asking?

"Uh, yeah. The Garand is, uh, conventional." *What do old M-1 rifles have to do with this?*

* * *

Another meeting concludes in the back of the Anguk grocery, and Debbie is happy. I've helped her re-write a paragraph concerning factory liaison work between Canada and South Korea. Army George is working on a paper that makes a rough-draft case for improved food-recycling laws. One of George's friends wants assistance in writing about the popularity of a certain landmark fountain in Seoul were gay men meet. This latter paper interests me, since the official line among Korean society maintains that homosexuality does not exist within the ROK. Naturally, I assume that the fountain paper is not a university assignment or work project.

I note that most of the other students give George's friend suspicious glances. There isn't much that I can do about that, but I can empathize, at least as much as a straight guy can, because I'm caught up in a military

270

commitment that doesn't tolerate anything other than straight action. I do note, however, that Miss Kim does not join with the rest when it comes to sending semi-dirty looks toward Army George and his pal.

Huh. Maybe she's open in more areas than just the application of eye makeup, I muse. *I don't think she's ever gonna cut me any slack in the English department, though.*

Oops, she's raising her hand. Here we go.

"Mister Jack?"

"Yes? How can I help?"

"The subjunctive mood. Is it correct?"

Subjunctive mood. Subjunctive mood? Awww, man. Not this shit again.

I stifle a sigh and offer a smile instead. As always, I walk over to the table and read Miss Kim's paper because her knowledge of my mother tongue's mechanics exceeds my own. She knows the drill, too. Miss Kim turns the paper and points at a sentence.

"*If Gyeongii government were to match Seoul proper expend, if the leaders were to receive authority, would the aggregate stone for Han protect erosion?*" I read aloud.

Miss Kim looks up at me. Tonight her loose hair rests in a soft black cascade down to the collar of her blouse. When she slightly raises her head a few strands pull forward over her shoulders, but she brushes them back behind her ears.

I read the sentence again. Then again. Something isn't right. I may not know what "subjunctive mood" is, but I know that the sentence sounds odd.

"One moment, please," I say, as I walk back to where my notebook rests near the dry erase board. I sit on a large bag of rice and write something, actually *two* somethings, and then return to the table. Instead of hovering, I pull up a chair on the other side.

"Do you know this saying?" I ask, as I point at the first item.

Miss Kim reads and nods. "I know this. Maybe it is... *cliché?*"

"Yeah. Probably. 'Give a man a fish and you feed him for a day. Teach a man to fish and you feed him for a lifetime.' Except I'm giving a fish to a woman."

"I do not understand. My question is not about food."

"I know. I'll-I'll try to explain. Please read this second sentence."

"If the Gyeongii government were to match the Seoul proper expenditures, and if the leaders were to receive authorization, would concrete prevent the Han riverbanks from eroding?" Miss Kim looks up. "This is the correct form?"

"I think so."

Miss Kim contemplates what I've written. "English articles are difficult for Korean people, but I understand," she says. "'The.' Here," she points at a spot in the sentence, "and here."

"Yes."

"Explain more, please."

I lower my eyes. When I speak, my tone is one of embarrassment. "I can't. I just don't know the grammar rules you're asking about. I only know what sounds right and what doesn't."

Her inscrutable marble face looks at me from across the table. "You are giving me a fish," she says, "but you cannot teach me to fish."

"In this case, yes," I confess. It's hard to return her gaze, but when I do, I see that she is turning to the back page of her notebook. "Please, Mist--uh, *Jack,"* Miss Kim says, "read this." She pushes the notebook toward me.

If the Gyeongii government were to match the Seoul proper expenditures, and if our leaders were to receive authorization, would concrete barriers prevent the Han's banks from eroding?

I look up from the notebook and something amazing happens. A half-smile flashes across Aphrodite's face without shattering the Florentine. "My truth question - ah, *true* question - was not about subjunctive mood," she says.

Everybody Watch, Everybody Wave

May 1989 (1-of-2)

Harry is still Debbie, and has been for how long? Over four months? Sometimes the end justifies the means. Sometimes the end also justifies the fraud, but that still doesn't make the charade any easier.

Let's be clear about something: *I'm* the fraud here, not Debbie. With the exception of Kim Mirye, I'm pulling it off with the students. In fact, now that my weapons crew is back on day shift, the storeroom has more people than it can comfortably accommodate - and these aren't all just Carl's Monday and Wednesday carryovers. Some people come to see me.

Me. Wow. A not-quite-twenty kid, pretending to be a teacher in the back of a little store...and yet, they keep coming! The shop owner loves it, too. I saw one of the students slip him a few thousand ~~won,~~ so now I have a general idea of what he gets out of this, and it sure as hell offsets the cost of an occasional bottle of booze.

I'm a sucker as well as a fraud, because I don't care if the shopkeeper gets over on me. I show up for reasons other than getting sloshed on bartered hootch. I'm not really even drinking that much anymore. Things are going well.

Things can also quickly change.

Give My Respects To Grace And Virtue, Give My Regards To Seoul And Bromance

May 1989 (2-of-2)

"But I thought that everyone had left," I weakly protested. "I was just picking up papers and sweeping. That's the only reason why I was still there."

"Dude, I'm not jumping on you - I mean, sometimes shit happens. I realize that." Carl stuck his fork into a piece of brown chow hall meatloaf and put it in his mouth. He grimaced and swallowed hard. "Turdburger," Carl grumbled, as he put down his fork. "So what did Mr. Park say?"

"What did he say? I don't know. I can't speak Korean like you."

"Well, what did he *do?*"

I put my fork down as well. The meatloaf really did taste like rehydrated dung. I cleared my throat. "Well, he didn't see anything on Tuesday. There wasn't anything to see, so he didn't do anything."

"And on Thursday?" asked Carl.

"He didn't make much cash, that's for sure. The only ones who showed up were Debbie and Army George." At the mention of Army George, Carl half-smiled and said, "I think George will always show up. The class is on the way to Banpo Fountain." We both smiled.

Carl leaned back. "I'll get something to eat from the Roach Coach this afternoon," he said. "Alright, one more time. Tuesday."

I pushed my plate away and put my hands on the table. "I was cleaning up and wondering which train I was gonna have to take over the river. I was about done and ready to leave when I heard the door creak. I turned around and Debbie was there."

"You and Debbie are turning out to have some kind of weird co-fate," said Carl. "Go on."

"You know, I thought that she had forgotten me. After the first time that I saw her in class, she seemed blank that way."

"I guess that I would have thought the same," commented Carl. "Who knows how many times she's been in the barracks? Hell, I think she's responsible for half of the bent-up bunks. How can the girls on base keep track?"

I ruefully smiled at Carl's remark and thought of my own Harry experience, but I imagined it going on and on in a multiple-partner, geometrically-repeating, and fractally-fucking prostitution spiral.

"The other girl kinda kept me off-balance, too," I said. "Even before all of this happened."

"You've mentioned that before. What's up with her?"

"She's only there on Tuesdays and Thursdays. She teaches English in a *hagwon* herself. Can you believe that? Her name is Mirye. Kim Mirye."

Carl was silent, so I continued.

"I try not to let her get to me, and I usually do okay. She makes me nervous because she's smarter than me when it comes to English, but some of the stuff that she writes is so...*out there.*"

"But that's the case with everybody," replied Carl. "They rarely speak or write English in daily life, so when they do it's correct, but real bizarro."

"Yeah, I know, but..." my voice trailed off.

Carl scrutinized me for a moment. "Dr. Corndog hereby diagnoses a severe case of yellow fever."

I huffed. "You have got, *got* to be fucking kidding."

"Dude, we're not talking about some club hooker, and that's why I think it might be terminal."

"Alright, just let me finish the damn story." I looked at my watch.

"Okay, okay. Just kidding," Carl said, but I knew from his tone that he hadn't been.

"So I'm standing there," I continued, "all wound up from being around this Mirye chick, and thinking that if I had been like Peterson I would just stay in the room and

275

blow a quickie into a tissue. But Debbie comes in again after everyone has left, and she has this look, you know, like she can read every man and nobody can hide anything from her. And it was so quick. She was sucking me off behind some of the boxes, and I'm about to shoot, but then I hear the door open again, and Mirye comes in."

"What did she do?"

"Nothing! She didn't do or say anything! She just did an about-face and left."

"And you?"

"I didn't do anything either, but my dick shriveled down like a pepperoni stick. Debbie was like: 'Hey, where did it go?' Anyway, Debbie went out first but I waited for a few minutes. Then Park gave me your stuff and I left."

Carl looked at his watch. "And on Thursday?"

"Mirye wasn't there," I said. "And Debbie acted like nothing had happened."

* * *

It was the Tuesday after Mirye had walked in on Debbie and me. I was early for class, so I went next door to a little restaurant and had some *bipimbap*. As I sat on the floor and ate at a low table, I noticed that more than once a couple of the Korean patrons turned around to look at me. Were they shaking their heads slightly? And muttering?

I hadn't seen Mr. Park yet...but, judging from the atmosphere in the restaurant, I could only guess at how things would go with him. I got up from the table and paid. Then I took my shoes off of a wall rack where they had sat amid a selection of sneakers with their backs mashed down from being worn like slippers. I put my shoes on and walked out. On the brick sidewalk between the storefronts and the street's edge were several café tables and chairs and a waitress went in and out to serve patrons who had chosen to take in the spring evening. To me, it still felt too cold to sit outside for dinner, but there were two young Korean families who had pushed their tables together so that they could eat and talk while their toddlers played. They took no notice of me. *They must not be from around here,* I thought. *They're not hip to the Dirty Foreigner Grocery Store Scandal.*

"Will you enter the shop?" someone asked. I turned and saw Kim Mirye sitting at one of the sidewalk tables. I couldn't make out her expression because she still seemed to be as devoid of emotion as she had been when she walked in on Debbie and me. Mirye stood up. "Can you speak?" she asked.

"I can speak." I wasn't embarrassed to stand in front of her. *Self-righteous thing,* I thought. "I'm here for the class, the same as always."

"*The same as always,*" Mirye repeated. There was no derision. It was just flat restatement, as if she had echoed my words to better interpret them. "No, not the same as always," she said. I noticed that Mirye was without her book bag. "No class."

"What do you mean?" I asked, though I had already guessed.

"Do not enter the shop. The man in the shop will tell the police."

I was a taken aback. "The police?"

"Yes. The English class now is ended. The English class now is finished."

Okay. Well, that was that. "Why did you talk?" I asked. "You could have just stopped coming. I don't understand why you did that."

After a few seconds Mirye spoke: "I did not say what you and the other one did."

"*The other one.*" *Oh please,* I thought. *I wasn't embarrassed when I saw you, and now I think that I'm actually feeling a little contemptuous. There you stand, a golf ball of tight little repressively-wound rubber bands, probably a virgin,* of course *a virgin, and telling me that you didn't take it upon yourself to close me down for doing what* you'd *be doing if you could venture beyond scared clicks at a Seoul Eros channel.*

Lame.

Have fun writing urban development proposals, à la The King James Version.

I heard Mirye's footsteps behind me when I began to

277

walk back to the station. When I stopped, she stopped.

I turned around. "What? What do you want?" I demanded.

Mirye froze and seemed a little frightened. "I-I do not know," she stammered.

Fine. I continued walking.

"Wait," she said.

But I didn't wait, and Mirye didn't follow me.

Receive Of Her Plagues?!
Hell, Back Up
The Truck!

June
1989
(1-of-2)

Hardesty has the drip and is at sick call, while five other weapon troops already carry tetracycline bottles in their BDU pockets. The Hospital Squadron has notified El Tee, who has, in turn, bitched out the first sergeant. Now shit continues to roll downhill onto Jones. Our flight chief, however, is an E-7, just like the first sergeant, so Jones doesn't bother to dial back his mouth when taking the shirt's calls. Senior NCOs aren't supposed to bicker in front of lower grades, so the weapons flight airmen are listening through Jones' office door while he sends attitude over the phone:

- *I briefed them knuckleheads last week. I told 'em all, and I told the swing shift and graveyard expediters to pass the message on. Yeah. In the daily log.*
[Jones swears under his breath.]
- *They know. I told my load crew chiefs to make sure their guys knew about free rubbers at sick call. I fuckin' did, goddammit!*
[Jones raps his knuckles on the desk.]
- *Oh, is that right?*
[Pause]
- *I sewed on four days before you, Fowler. You might wanna check your WAPS points too, mutherfucker. That little blue clit over your stripes don't count for much.*
[Pause]
- *Well, you can cry to El Tee, 'cuz me an' the Colonel go all the way back to The Nhut. So you go right ahead, mutherfucker.*
[Pause]
- *Yeah. I gotta get the frags down, so wrap this up. Say what you gotta say.*

[Pause]
- *There's always gonna be dosed hookers on base,*
  Fowler. You know that. Me an' you was airmen
  once.
  [Long pause]
- *What?! I thought there was a sick girl goin' 'round*
  or somethin'.
  [*Longer* pause...]
- *Fuckin' weirdos. Where the hell are recruiters*
  gettin' these kids nowadays? Yeah...alright.
  Take the damn shower curtains out. Freaks.
  [We hear Jones slam down the phone.]

We jump away from the door, and when Jones
storms out of the office, all he sees are diligent airmen
sorting aircraft pins, updating T.O.s, and engaging in
other worthy activities. Jones shakes his head and puts
his hands on his hips as he surveys the break room.

"Freaks," he repeats. Then, in a louder voice: "Ain't
none of you dumb asses know what a pussy is for? I
want all of you to get the fuck out of my break room and
get on the line. I wanna see you FOD walk every
goddamn shelter tree in this mutherfuckin' squadron!
And when you're done, I'm sendin' you dipshits over to
Release Shop, and you can scrub guns-n-breeches until
you're too tired to fuck shower curtains." Jones starts to
turn away, but then pauses. He looks back at us, and
when he speaks, his voice is lower and full of
exasperation. "Christ, fellas. Just get a woman once in a
while. What the hell is wrong with you all?"

To *Say* What You Won't,
To *Do* What
You Can't

June
1989
(2-of-2)

I can remember that whole stupid shower curtain thing because it happened on the day that you called me. Actually, you called the AGS Orderly Room, which connected you to barracks CQ, who, in turn, took down the message and tacked it onto my room door. When I read the note, I was surprised to learn that the class wanted to take me out for a good-bye dinner.

When we all met, it felt kind of awkward when you wanted to be seated near me. At the end of the evening we were the last ones to leave the building, and it was then that you called me back to the restaurant stairwell and kissed me. I was a very confused boy when I took the train back to base.

We Must Add "Detective" To Your List Of Accomplishments

*July
1989
(1-of-2)*

I wasn't sure what your kiss had meant...but after a week it seemed reasonable to assume that you had kissed me goodbye. I guess you thought that a so-long smack was the appropriate Western farewell...though I also hoped that someday you would learn that, in the West, we generally didn't French others adieu.

A month later I go into the flight shack and Jones has a note for me. "Got a little something on the side, Simmy?" he says, with what seems to be a stupid attempt at a knowing wink. "At least *you're* talkin' to *girls*. The rest of them jeep blockheads keep fuckin' furniture."

Whatever, Jones, I think. *Since when are shower curtains regarded as furniture?* "Something on the side?" I repeat.

"Your *ajumma* called the shirt."

"Ajumma" means "married middle-aged woman". Jones thinks that he's being funny, but I still don't know what he's talking about.

Behind me, the long-tour flight wits start their 2 Alive Krew *Love You Long Time* crap, but it goes over the heads of the young airmen who played high school football when my Harry-Green-Bean hilarity was all the rage.

Carl is already at the shack and waiting with his crew. I can't help but give him a worried glance. He's a camo cuke, and his eyes advise me to also stay cool. Though some time has passed, I'm still a little scared that someone has caught wind of the illegal teaching gig and called *La Migre*. The Korean rags love it when *migukin* get busted - even nobodies like me.

Great. I'm about to make the papers. Another SOFA-violation footnote, followed by an Article 15...*if*

I'm lucky.

It's also possible that a frilly-cuff-Cleopatra has decided to show me what's what. I never called her after the stairwell kiss. How could I? I have no idea how to reach her. *I wonder if you've noted, Miss Kim, that the ball is now completely in your court?*

"Well are you gonna take the mutherfuckin' paper?" asks Jones. He looks at the other NCOs with a playground bully's "what a dumb ass" expression.

I read the slip. It's actually from El Tee's desk. His secretary took it down, but I don't point this out to Master Sergeant Doltamatic. Really, there's nothing at all on the message that would lead anyone to think that it was liaison evidence. It's kind of odd, but not juicy.

They got my grade wrong. I sewed on senior airman almost two weeks ago, but the note is for Airman First Class Simmerath. There's a number with a time and place, as though this concerned something prearranged, but no name. My first impulse is to hand the message back and ask if there's another Simmerath in the squadron, but I know that there isn't. The slip reads:

> **If a man were to ask for aid,**
> **If corn were to wish for help,**
> **Would it receive a foot?**

WTF? It's strange. It's a way of using weird verse to remind me that something hangs over my head, and that I'm an easy guy to find. Naturally. In this country, no Mr. Round Eye can hide from a woman who knows how to mock him with an English verb form. I'm a puppy getting his big white nose jammed in grammatic shit.

She doesn't think that I'm housebroken.

It's a common failing among barbarians.

Colors Your Eyes With
What's Not
There

July
1989
(2-of-2)

On our first date we ate cooked beetle larvae from one of the street cart vendors on Gwanghamun. I didn't like them because they had a bitter taste. Then we walked around on the grass in front of City Hall. I told you that I had thought you didn't like me, and you smiled and said that you were testing me. I trusted you enough to confess that I felt weird about the whole Debbie thing. You told me that she hadn't been fooling anyone and that the entire class had known that she was a hooker. You also told me that she probably wouldn't be able to get the job she wanted. That made me feel terrible, especially since I thought that Debbie had been succeeding in her new life.

Some of the people stared at us, so you moved a few feet away. You told me that we weren't fooling anyone around City Hall, either.

I Felt The Blood
Go To My
Feet

September
1989

    We took a taxi to Namsan Tower on a fall afternoon. I always thought of the Space Needle when I looked up at the tower, though now those memories make me think of Vegas' Stratosphere Tower.

    We had dinner in the revolving restaurant. It wasn't very good - sirloin with bacon wrap - and it tasted kind of old. The meal isn't what I remember most, though, because I still see your face against one of the observation windows as we looked out over Seoul's endless lights. You turned to me and said the lights were "like embers."

    "Embers." I was surprised to hear you use that English word. When I looked out the window I saw what you meant. You smiled with one cheek still against the glass when you caught me staring.

The Killer You Thought
Was Your
Friend

December
1990

- Hey Carl.
- *Hey Jackster. What's up?*
- Nothing. Your roomie out?
- *Yeah. At the NCO club or something.*
- You didn't go?
- *Nah. It's comics night in room 416. C'mon in.*
- Hey, cool! Where did you buy those?
- *The Stars & Stripes newsstand has them now. Wanna check 'em out?*
- Thanks. I see that you're a Marvel man.
- *Roger that. Jack of Hearts. Always my fave.*
- This doesn't look too bad. What's his deal?
- *He kinda bounces around. He's been in the Avengers, but he's had his own storylines, too. He's gone up against some heavies. Iron Man, Hulk...dudes like that.*
- Is he a bad guy?
- *No. He just gets confused sometimes.*
- What are his powers?
- *He's a half-human, half-alien hybrid. He was exposed to a fluid that gave his body the ability to generate energy.*
- That's quite a costume. So...he dresses up like a playing card...?
- *Fuck you, Jackster! His costume kicks major ass. No gay comments. I'm warning you.*
- I'm just kidding. So that's it? He's a half-human power generator?
- *Yes...I mean, no. He can direct energy at his enemies, and he can use his energy to fly. He's pretty tough and strong, too. I like him because his character has problems, you know? That's why I turned off to the DC universe. Everybody there is like Superman and is invincible. The stories don't really go too far.*

- So what problems does this guy have? If he's tough enough to fight the Hulk, he must be doing something right.
- *Well...he's not that great of a fighter. I mean, he's okay...but his energy power is what makes him such a badass. Sometimes he's not really into the superhero thing, either. If it were up to him, Jack of Hearts would prefer to just hang out and write poetry.*
- Poetry?
- *Yeah. He's not really one of Marvel's most action-inclined characters.*
- So he's a lazy and confused poet who is powerful enough to go at the Hulk when he feels like it?
- *Yeah. Cool, huh?*
- Actually...yes. That reminds me of my favorite comic character in the DC universe. He's got stuff going on that screws him up. I get pissed because DC writers don't use him as much as they could.
- *Who is he?*
- Mon-El. Ever heard of him?
- *Nah. Is he yet another Kryptonian or something? That's boring, man.*
- No. He's a Daxamite.
- *What's that?*
- They're like Kryptonians. They have all of Superman's powers, and Mon-El is even a little stronger than Superman.
- *Borrring...*
- No, it's not! Daxamites have huge problems. Their society is all fucked up. They're like a bunch of super-powered racists, and they don't leave their planet. Sometimes they kill people who visit their planet, too. Mon-El isn't like that, though. He's a good guy.
- *Humpf. That definitely doesn't sound very Kryptonian. Sounds more like super-powered Norks.*
- Plus, Daxamites aren't invulnerable. Plain old lead kills them.
- *Lead? Not Kryptonite?*
- No. Mon-El has almost died lots of times, but he's

done things that are as cool as anything Superman has done. DC has killed off other Daxamites, so you know that it might happen to him, too.
- *That definitely doesn't sound like a DC character.*
- Right. Mon-El's personality is a little like Jack of Hearts, because he doesn't really want to be a superhero, either. He's a scientist who'd rather explore the galaxy with his girlfriend.
- *Who's his girlfriend?*
- Ummm...wait a sec. Shadow Lass, I think. Wait...so are you saying Jack of Hearts also has a *girl*friend?
- *No, I don't think -- awww, you fuckstick! C'mere!*
- Ow! Shit! Ha-ha! Oh fuck, I think you bruised my arm.
- *You deserved it. Respect the Jack!*
- Heh. Gotcha. Ouch. Hey, I wanna ask you something.
- *Non-Jack related?*
- Yeah.
- *Shoot.*
- You ever date a K-girl?
- *What kinda question is that? Who hasn't dated a K-girl?*
- No, that's not what I mean. I mean...you know.
- *Ohhh...we're talking about a different kind of "dating" here, aren't we? The "maybe there's a chaplain in my future" kind of dating, right? Who is she?*
- Mirye. From the class. And I'm nowhere near Chaplainland, by the way. I don't even know what you mean.
Carl?
Hey...are you okay?
Carl? *Carl?*
- *What?! Yeah man, I'm fuckin' fine. Sorry. I, umm, I thought you said that she didn't like you.*
- I thought she didn't. I can't understand her sometimes. She kept in touch after the class crashed. Sometimes she calls the barracks and we talk.
- *Talk? What the hell could you two possibly have to talk about?*

- I dunno. Just...stuff. We usually don't stay on the phone for too long. Maybe we're gonna start spending more time together or something. She says she wants to show me places around Seoul. You ever do that? Just spend time with a local girl? Carl?
Carl?
HEY! DUMB ASS!
Are you even listening to what I'm saying? Or am I just talking to myself?
- *Yeah man, I'm listening! Relax your shit. And the answer is yes. Well, maybe. Hell, you've known me almost as long as I've been in the ROK. You know all of the girls that I've been with.*
- I don't mean "been with." I don't know all of your girls, either. Just forget it, dickhead.

Bow Before Hecate
Man Of Fortune,
Man Of Shame

February 25th, 1990

I can't remember what we had been doing on that day, but I recall seeing you off at the station and crossing the platform to catch my own train back to base. You were really bitchy and I wondered if you were on your period. "Really bitchy" isn't a fair thing to say, though. Your way was just to snap at me once in a while, then lapse into a kind of semi-silent treatment.

I was just about to go down the subway steps when an old Korean man held out his hand and stopped me. He must have been psychic.

"Joe, Joe - you sad? You sad? I tell you Korea woman way," he began, as he looked up at me in his baggy pants and baggier jacket. His face seemed kind and straightforward, and since he didn't hold out his hand at passing Big Noses, I guessed that he probably wasn't one of the little homeless islands who slept on cardboard in the middle of the subway while Seoul commuters flowed by.

"Woman is meat, Joe," the old man said with an earnest look. "Much fire, no enough time, and woman is burn and no soft." He paused to release my sleeve and hold his hand up to his mouth. He screwed up his face and gritted his part-gold and part-black-stained teeth to bite off a piece of imaginary steak. "Joe, woman need little fire, much time, and woman is delicious. Delicious, delicious. No bali-bali, Joe!" I began to snicker, but I suppressed the urge out of respect for the old man. He tapped his finger to his temple and looked at me with even greater sincerity. I nodded and kept a straight face as the baggy pants continued up the subway stairs like a reversed Slinky.

I Opened Up To Page
Thirty-Two, It Was
The Poem And
A Picture
Of You!

April
1990

We were going to spend the day at Gyeongbuk
Palace, so I met you in Seoul. You wore a blue dress with
small yellow print flowers and you carried a cute little
bag. We had lunch at an artsy cafe on Insa-dong - the
one where they filmed that TV drama - and there were
pictures of actors plastered all over the walls. Then we
walked to the palace gates.

I remember the rows of status stone markers that
faced the ruler's seat. I remember the ornate roofs. I
remember the cherry trees.

You told me that the trees were more recent
additions, and that they had been planted by Japanese
occupiers during the Colonial Period, sort of as a way to
"mark" the taking and subjugation of Korea. I asked you
why the Korean people didn't rip out the cherry trees
once the Japanese had been kicked out, and you told me
that, even though they signified something horrible, the
trees themselves were still beautiful, so the people
decided to keep them. You explained it like you were
telling the story of a woman who had been raped and
made pregnant, but, rather than hating the child and
killing it, the woman decided that the child was still
precious in and of itself.

We visited the palace in the spring, and in my mind I
can see you in your blue dress, smiling and standing on
tiptoes, as you pick a single cherry blossom.

My Heart Is Thrown To
The Pebbles And
Sweet Dreams
Of Boatmen
Dancing

June
1990

I followed your instructions and took the train to Bucheon, then I boarded the #15 bus to Siheung. You were waiting for me in front of the huge Kolon Mart. I'm glad that you knew where to find me, because I would never have been able to find you.

We had a picnic on one of the round-top granite mountains on the outskirts of Siheung. The hike was fun, and I enjoyed seeing the Korean families having a nice day out. When we got to the top we could see almost all the way to Incheon.

The ~~North~~ *South* Koreans Just Ordered Another Shipment Of Safety Wire From 18th Chicken Supply

September 1990

You shouldn't have invited me to observe Chuseok with your family if you were only going to chicken out and change your mind. Disinvitations suck.

There's A Crack In The Mirror And A Bloodstain On The Bed

October 1990

Before Mirye and I worked out a way to talk on the phone, our parlance was through pseudonymous notes. I asked her not to call the Orderly Room anymore, so the chief scribe in our communications became barracks CQ.

I got home on a weekday to discover a message on my door. It appeared to be directions to a place in Bucheon. There was a number on the note, which I tried to call. I even got one of the Korean CQ guys to translate the recording that I kept getting, only to be told that there was no such number.

On that weekend I still did my best to follow the directions, but I blew it. I got the continent wrong. I got the decade wrong. Maybe it's unwise to hang around outside a lunch counter, though you're really trying to stay out of the white kids' way. You don't want trouble, but it's obvious that you're there to meet a white girl. Don't do this in Mobile.

Wait. I could be in Memphis. Or Jackson.

Maybe it's 1950. Or 1960. It's hard to say.

Okay, so I'm not *really* at a "**WHITES ONLY**" lunch counter. I'm actually on the sidewalk outside the Bucheon Station Lotteburger. It's 1990. People spit on the ground when they see me. By now I know the standard range of *Hangungmal* curses, some of which precede the spitting. I try not to make eye contact, but I have to, especially since I need to be conscious of where the young men are and what they're doing.

"I sent you a letter," she says when she arrives.

"CQ gave me a *note*," I state. "I tried to call, but the telephone number didn't work."

She just looks at me. *Of course it didn't, silly rabbit.*

Now the people around us look at Mirye. An old

woman with war-era rickets stops her bowlegged shuffle and stares. I've disappeared from the local radar like a bum sleeping under a pile of trash. Mirye, however, attracts attention as a beautiful race traitor. More people stare.

She's wearing a jacket that I haven't memorized. She's trimmed her hair recently. I want to take her all in, to stop and look and have something more than just what I've subsisted on since our last meeting, but I can't. We'd better go.

She knows this, too. More eyes continue to condemn us, even in the few moments that we've stood here. We walk, quickly but not too quickly, together but not together.

*　*　*

I can't remember what number was stamped onto the tab of the cheap plastic keychain. But the room's number, as everyone knows, was 416. Not 420. *That was the wrong room.* I can't remember what we said on our way to the hotel, or what we said in the elevator or in the hall.

But...I can remember how I felt when I realized that we were *going* to a hotel.

Sometimes I remember other things, too, especially in the dreams that I've had since that day. I am Richard and she is Elise. The love hotels of Bucheon Station are ridiculously over-the-top. Gigantic beds, lotions, porn-o-vision TVs. In-room karaoke machines. Mirrors everywhere. The only way that you could miss seeing yourself in action would be if you closed your eyes. Or were blindfolded. With duct tape.

On the way to the room there was a glass case, right there in the middle of the hall, full of dildos of all shapes, sizes, and colors. Maybe it was a vending machine or something. Mirye seemed kind of shocked to see it, and she gaped as we passed. Hell, I was shocked myself. Mackinac Island's Grand Hotel had a reputation that one would assume precluded such vulgarity.

That first time didn't go so well. It's easy to put on a good performance when nothing's at stake. In such cases you can be as dirty and depraved as you want, for free or hire, with a woman or women for hours while you're young, strong, and confident. Swollen-blood-balloon ego trips can last for hours of sweating, screaming, and doing outrageous things that you can't believe you're actually doing. Since it doesn't matter, since you know that you haven't yet found the one that you have to - *need to* - impress, the licking, flicking, pounding, and pulling goes on and on. It's merely practice. You're just getting ready for that instance when it will actually count. Until then, life is a casting call for preparatory masturbation with bit players' bodies.

Had I anticipated that this would again be the case? Did I have an expectation that our encounter would carry more meaning than that of a used condom on a hotel room floor? Part of me had known that the moment was approaching, yet I was still seized by a kind of fear that accompanied back-seat firsties and teen bedroom maneuvers. I was scared and soft. Then scared and hard. Then just scared. And shaking. Scared, despite more worthless run-throughs than I could count and more D-list co-stars than I could recall.

I sensed that this performance wasn't going to be just another rehearsal.

For me.

Opening night would have been difficult even if I *hadn't* been terrified, because amid the Empire waists, Rachmaninoff themes, and bad turn-of-the-century suits, someone slipped, mentioned The Scottish Play, and left a damn'd spot on the sheets at curtain call.

In This Necrologue
Of Love

November
1990

I got off the train at Chungmoro Station. We'd never had a rendezvous there before, and I didn't know the place very well. It wasn't the biggest station in Seoul, but it had a distinctive theme. The ceilings and walls were done up to resemble a cave, or maybe a mine.

I was really out of place. There weren't many waygukin about, like there were at other stations. The Seoulites gave me the standard suspicious or curious looks as they passed. I began to wonder if I had understood you correctly. Was this where we had agreed to meet? For me, Korean place names were sometimes tough to keep straight.

I felt a touch on my shoulder. You stood behind me. I wanted to put my arms around you and whirl you up off your feet, but I didn't. Such public displays tended to piss off the Korean public, and besides, you held two cups of coffee. You smiled, but I think that my smile was probably bigger.

* * *

I wondered if it was love. I wasn't sure. I'd never been in love. Love was just a vague idea or expression, like some weird painting that had to be explained before I could understand what the artist wanted to say. To me, love wasn't a blind man describing an elephant. It was a deaf man signing a symphony.

I wasn't so ignorant or confused that I couldn't separate love from the pleasure of the sex that we had. In those moments, things were plainly physical. I could raise up and look at where our bellies met. If I raised up a little more, I could see myself entering you. Neither of us really cared about trimming down there...my wad of short-n-curlies mixed it up with your sheaf of long-n-straights every time I thrust inside. You were very wet, and on each outstroke, long black hairs clung to the clear latex stretched over the shaft of my cock. You bucked under me, and I was always amazed and excited by your strength. *Every time your legs wrapped around me, the backs of your heels pressed into my spine so hard that I thought you were going to break me in half. I loved it when we fucked like that, but I was also hesitant. I think that I sometimes paused because I was somehow afraid.*

I couldn't fall in love at my age, could I? Was it even possible?

Ridiculous!

No. *Love was only for mature, measured, and deliberate people, and that wasn't me. Young people felt infatuation, not love. Maybe young guys - and old guys, too - weren't really expected to feel* anything. *They just liked to fuck and employ the "L" word when necessary. Right?*
One thing was certain: I needed to keep my feelings to myself, especially in the barracks and at work. Jesus-fucking-Christ. If I had opened my mouth and talked about how I felt about you, I would have been constantly jacked-with. How did I know that? Because I'd seen it before. In that odd stage between a young waygukin's realization that he's done looking, and that moment when he - somehow - got the green light from a Korean woman's family, the razzing was merciless. In a way, the ordeals on the Western side of the equation could be as challenging as the hurdles on the Eastern side. Well, maybe I could have confided in Carl. By that time, he knew that I'd punch him if he made any of his lame "yellow fever" comments.

* * *

I had one hand between your ass and the mattress to steady your hips as I entered you, while my other arm was under your neck. I cradled your head as I nuzzled your cheek and breathed into your hair. It was an odd mix. At the waist, we were just a couple of rutting animals slamming into each other, but up above it felt like I couldn't be tender enough, touch your face and cheeks enough, kiss you enough, or really comprehend the softness of your skin. When we kissed, it wasn't so much the way I kissed you, but the way you kissed me. It wasn't the hard, brutal probe that forced its way down my throat so far that it practically impacted my brainstem. It wasn't the harsh lip-smashing of some overheated squadron skank or the additional-cost "open-wide-and-say-ahh" professional examination of NCO club ladies. Sometimes when you and I were in bed, our lips merely brushed, but it was absolutely electric.

New and unfamiliar things were happening inside me. I was thinking strange thoughts. Sometimes when I was at work, freezing my goddamned ass off as I loaded bombs, I wondered if you had dressed warmly before going to work. And were you eating enough? All you ever had for breakfast was rice and soup. It was what you said you liked. Why didn't you eat more? Your other meals, at least to me, also seemed too small. How could you stay healthy when you ate so little?

Actually, your diet was pretty Korean-standard, but my concerns exemplified the direction of my thoughts. When I threaded arming wire through a fuse, I found myself hoping that you were having a good day at your private English academy. I hoped that the kids weren't being brats, and that the other Korean staff members were kind to you. Your job, your class, your co-workers...all none of my business. I knew that. I wished that those things could somehow become my business, though.

When I wanted to call you at your home, I got help from a Korean girl who worked at the base recreation center. I enlisted her help for a fee. It went like this, remember? "Hello? Yes, I'm a co-worker from Mirye's hagwon. Please, may I speak to her? Thank you." I would then slip my co-conspirator some cash as she handed me the phone. There was a pause on my end of the line for a minute or two as you basically talked to yourself in Korean for the benefit of your mother and other family members, then retreated to a place where you could whisper to me in English. I really hated the annoying games that we had to play on the phone. Those were second only to the games that we had to play to actually meet.

However, I loved to play Trivial Pursuit: Kim Mirye

Edition. *It became very important for me to get the answers right. It definitely wasn't "trivial". I wanted to know and memorize all of the answers. What were the names of the people in your family? How old was your mother? How old were your brothers and sisters? Where did you go to school? When were you happiest? When were you saddest? What made you happy? What algorithm could I use to determine your lunar calendar birthday?*

Those questions came from the basic edition. I was going to keep at it, though, because I wanted to add expansion decks and advanced modules.

* * *

You were originally from South Jeolla's Yeongam County. When your family moved north to Bucheon, your Gyeonggi classmates teased you until you shed the southern dialect. Your dad was dead, and you had some half-brothers and sisters. Your family had lived on a farm, and you had been hungry when you were young.

A starving period had left a dark spot on your right temple.

Your mother's first husband had been a fisherman, but he disappeared. You had worked at one other job before the English academy, and it had been with a shipping company. You were finally able to laugh when telling the story of how you had been fired for accidentally sending a freight container to Bangkok instead of Pusan.

Your mother was overweight and ill. Your dad had been an alcoholic. Sometimes your little nieces got on your nerves. Your dream was to one day design clothes. Your half-brothers were protective of you.

You were afraid to introduce me to your family.

What Yer Askin'...Got A Powerful Price

March 1991

I won't bore you with a description of the ring - after all, you saw it every time that I begged for your hand. Each time I pulled it out you probably thought: "He's reaching into his pocket again, time to think fast."

Even if you weren't impressed by the ring, the clerk at the BX jewelry counter had been. She was also astonished by the speed with which a lowly airman had made the layaway payments. There was no way in hell that I would have been able to buy that ring on senior airman pay. I sewed a lot of stripes, patches and buttons. I went through three cheap BX irons. I bought detergent at both the commissary and the BX. I hated washing everyone's damned crusty underwear and hand-tacking all those stripes. I got a lot of business, though, and all I did was put up a few signs in the dayrooms:

Jack's Barracks Laundry and Sewing Service

I eventually reached my goal and shut down my operation, though for a couple weeks afterward I had to turn away guys who still came to my door with armloads of underwear and greasy BDUs. Carl used to give me hell about not getting a signature loan from the base bank or even a civvy job on base. I never mentioned it, but he was wrong in assuming, except for the latter, that I hadn't already done so.

나는 당신이 필요합니다
나는 당신을 필요로하지 않습니다
나는 당신이 필요합니다
나는 당신을 필요로하지 않습니다

May
1991

It would have been a nice date, if you had said "yes", or "maybe", or...anything. But you changed the subject and pretended not to hear me. Maybe a stalling tactic was better than a flat-out "no".

This particular time was when we went to Changdeokgung. I had heard it called the "Flower Palace" by people on base, though I don't know if I ever heard a Korean person refer to it by that name. Changdeok was more romantic than Gyeongbuk. It had lots of pools, paths, and flower beds.

Do you remember that tree? It was a pine, I think. As a sapling, it had been bent parallel to the ground, then upward, then again parallel, and so on, until the trunk resembled a zig-zag set of stairs. When I looked at the tree, it seemed like nature was trying to tell me something. Yeah, I guess that I was really reaching for meaning - in anything - so in the moment that I saw the tree I took it for a sign to keep trying and to not surrender. I mean, the tree had been bent over, but it righted itself every time, until the branches and needles, despite the seriously distorted trunk, reached skyward. Maybe this was a sign. I wanted it to be. I didn't want to let my feelings get bent over. I wanted to keep reaching skyward.

I should have used the pine tree as an example when I implored you to think about us and consider a viable future. Did you want me to reenlist and stay in Korea? **Done.** I would have pulled a career's worth of overseas remote tours to be with you. Or what about an American community with a majority Asian population? **Also done.** I would have gone down to CBPO and requested orders to Hickam in Honolulu, or even one of the SoCal bases. Anything.

Yeah, maybe I should have used the tree as an example, but I was a desert boy, and all I could articulate was a lame metaphor that involved century plants. You see, Grandpa once told me that, when the century plant matured and developed its beautiful central seed stalk, it meant that the plant's life was ending. This seemed like a sad thing, so I asked Grandpa if, when the stalk began to emerge, the plant's life could be saved by cutting it off. No stalk, no death, right? That was my childish reasoning. Grandpa told me that it didn't matter whether or not the stalk was removed because the plant still knew that its life was over. Grandpa said it was better to let the plant be beautiful before it died, rather than destroy its nicest part without changing anything.

I just wanted you to understand that, even though we were young, our lives were nevertheless finite...so why throw away something beautiful when the world would still take its course? Life was going to continue, so why not have love along with it?

I didn't reach you. My comparison wasn't effective because I got the plants confused. You see, I mistakenly assumed that we were both century plants. Sure, I was...but you were a Gyeongbokgung cherry tree. The desert stalk that was my life could emerge only once, but you had the power to blossom many times.

A Game In The House
That I Grew
Up In

The Vegas TDY didn't hold the same kind of novelty for me that it did for the other guys. After the morning when Jones had announced which crews would be sent to Nellis Air Force Base for Blue Flag, most of the young airmen started thinking about whores and blackjack, whereas I pondered what kind of flowers I would place on Grandpa's grave.

I had some curious conversations before and during the deployment. During the slow-ass, stop-at-Kadena, stop-at-Hickam, in-flight refueled, wander-around-over-the-fucking-Pacific C-130 flight, guys in the unit asked me questions and said things that indicated their belief in my ability to show everyone the best spots in Vegas:

- *So, you're a hometown boy, right Jackster?*
- Yeah.
- *What's the Nellis NCO club like?*
- Dunno. Never set foot on the base.
- *Whaddya mean? You're from Vegas!*
- Dude, I was eighteen when I enlisted. P-Tek is my
  first permanent station.
- *Oh yeah. Right. Ummm, so what's* Leopards *like?
  Or* Olympus Gardens? *I'll bet they've got some hot
  girls there, huh?*
- How the hell would *I* know? I've never been to a
  strip club in Vegas. I told you: I was just out of high
  school when I left.
- *Oh. Oh yeah. I forgot.*

* * *

When the Nellis exercise started, my load crew was one of the lucky ones that got selected to be range observers. I mean, we were *kind of* lucky. Maybe about sixty percent lucky, for while this detail relieved us of our usual war-game rush of loading bombs, it also meant that we would observe and count dummy drops deep in the sweltering Nevada desert.

It was an okay duty. We just sat at a mountain observation point, watched for puffs of dirt far below, and called in strikes to Range Control. It wasn't stressful, just hot and boring. Our perch looked like it could have been somewhere in the Sahara Desert because we were way-the-hell out in the 51st Sector of the Nellis Bombing Range. Every day, a silent and expressionless Nellis Security Police captain got us past the range checkpoints and drove us to the top of a mountain called "Liberty Peak".

We ate our lunches and drank lots of water as we sat beneath green canvas sun tarps. For the next twelve hours, Dave, Hardesty, and I watched the desert floor with GSA binoculars and took tally of how many bombs struck a parched salt flat called "Groom Lake."

Groom Lake wasn't much to look at. Before it had been given a target designation, Groom Lake appeared to have had a dirt airstrip, around which still stood a few dilapidated buildings. I won a bet with Hardesty over whether or not a bomb would hit the old shacks. The weapons were only concrete-filled dummy units, but when they struck the ground the amount of dust they kicked up was still impressive. After each wave we compared notes and Dave got on the radio to call in the drop count. Then we watched the sun go down and waited for the range truck's headlights.

* * *

Our TDY digs weren't bad. P-Tek essentially took over the top floor of a Ho-Jo on Tropicana and Industrial. We only got a couple days off during the entire TDY, but that didn't matter. The airmen were young and full of stamina, and as for the fellows who had never been to Vegas, the mere prospects of gambling and fucking in Sin City were sufficient to fuel quite a few sleep-deprived adventures. I wasn't particularly interested in ogling whores and shysters in places that I had already seen a million times, so I got a lot of rest. I used my breakfast *per diem* in the downstairs restaurant, and each day when I met Dave and Hardesty out in front of the hotel to catch the Nellis shuttle, their eyes had enormous bags and their bodies stank of metabolized alcohol, cigarette smoke, and God-only-knows what else.

That was essentially my TDY routine until the last night before the squadron had to palletize its shit and head back to South Korea. All of my explanations as to why I didn't know what the Nellis club was like or where to find the best strippers in Vegas were again forgotten because the weapons flight airmen had decided to conclude Blue Flag with a blowout in some bar that *I* had allegedly recommended:

- Jackster, guess where we're going tonight!
- *Ummm...where?*
- Grand Hole! That place you said was the best joint for getting wasted and laid!
- *What? I don't know of any place called - wait, what was it again?*
- GRAND HOLE, DUDE! C'mon! That place you told us about!

After several more of my fellow airmen thanked me for letting them in the "local angle," I just decided to go with it:

"Grand Hole."

Sure. Whatever.

Er, I mean...you're gonna LOVE it! The hottest skanks! The cheapest beer! The perfect place to see Blue Flag out with a bang! You'll be able to tell those losers back at P-Tek about the great time that you had in Los Vegas!

~~Incirlik~~ *Nellis,* Sing! *BIRA,*
BIRA, ON THE WALL,
WHO'S THE MOST
FUCKED-UP
OF US
ALL?

June
1991
(2-of-3)

"Grand Hole", indeed. What a goddamned dump. Seriously! Why the hell would anybody think that *I* had suggested it? It was just a low-budget bar near the main Nellis gate. Some of the weapons airmen gave me knowing looks, as if I had let them in on a cool secret, but what did they expect? A gigantic orgy in the back room? Whiskey shots and blowjobs in the john? What?

No, guys, I thought. *This place stinks. Really. It doesn't even have a stripper stage.*

P-Tekkers weren't the only PACAF troops at Grand Hole. There were units from Hickam and Osan, too. Grand Hole, regardless of how badly it sucked, was full.

I needed to relieve myself and the line at the bar looked like it required patience. "Gotta piss," I said to Carl.

"Copy. Wanna beer?"

"Sure."

The shitter was packed. It only had two urinals and three stalls, and every guy in line had a haircut like mine. I tried not to wonder if the urine level on the floor would rise above the thickness of my soles.

Ahhh. My turn came at last. My relief was such that I didn't pay much attention to the voice behind me.

"You don't listen too good, do you?!"

A Johnny Tyler *Tombstones*-type sounded drunk and torqued. There was gonna be a fight.

Whatever. None of my business.

"Hey, shithead! I'm talkin' to *you!*"

I got hit from behind. Someone drove the heel of their hand into my shoulder blade and I was knocked forward, directly into the urinal, and I smacked my head on the wall. There was a big scuffle-commotion among the other guys, but I was clearly the target of someone's rage. Accumulated piss-dribble got all over me when I fell back and onto the floor. The guy who had been lame enough to take that cheap shot while I had my dick in my hand was also lame enough to kick me when I was down. I tried to scramble back up, but staggered, tumbled, and knocked open one of the stall doors. "Wait a fucking minute!" I yelled. "You've got the wrong guy!"

The asshole didn't seem to hear. "I told you to leave Joo-hee alone!" he roared, as he pulled his foot back for a boot-to-my-head that knocked my mouth into the commode's hard porcelain. I had a vision of little white cocktail onions in a tumbler of red grenadine and yellow whiskey sour...but the onions were really just my four front teeth sitting on the floor in a puddle of blood and piss.

Seven Bones To
Trump Boot
Leather

June
1991
(3-of-3)

I had a pill bottle. I can't remember what generic name the label bore, but when I showed it to the guys, they all took one look and said: "Vicotin."

I was so woozy on the flight back to P-Tek. The drugs that I got from the Nellis clinic really knocked me out. Still, while I lay behind a bunch of palletized weapon tool boxes in the C-130's belly, I had some semi-lucid moments, in which I worried about what you would do when you saw me. You would probably be shocked but try to hide it. Hell, I would have been shocked if you had returned from a trip without your front teeth. Maybe my sad shape would even reinforce your reluctance to go Stateside - I mean, I was fine when I left Korea, but when I returned, I was beat-up.

Hardesty and Kitts had offered to help me pack, but I told them it wasn't necessary because I intended to wait until after takeoff before hitting the pills. When I medicated it was like I was a space traveler in cryogenic suspension. The flight out of Korea in that Hercules aero-snail had been awful, but it seemed like the return trip was a snap.

I can't remember who shook me awake when we landed. I was still mildly dazed and Kitts told me to skip download and debrief, as per El Tee. So, while the crews unloaded their tools, I went through the line and out the other side of P-Tek's return processing building. You were waiting on the other side of a chain link fence, along with a number of your countrywomen and an equal number of my own.

I dropped my duffel and tried to cover my mouth with my hand, though you instantly pulled it away. You didn't seem as shocked as I had imagined you would be. Instead, you seemed...energized. I was nauseous and dead tired, but as soon as I had dropped my bag in the barracks, you put me in a taxi to Bucheon. You knew exactly where to go, and from the back seat you called out directions to the driver.

We stopped in a Bucheon back alley. You paid the driver and helped me out of the taxi and into a dentist's chair in a tiny cramped basement. The old man there seemed reluctant to work on me, but you exploded in his face with a flurry of sharp and fast Korean words that made him cower. He asked you to ask me if I was on any drugs before he prepared his needle, so I produced the vicotin bottle.

When I woke up, the daylight that had entered though the small basement windows was replaced by night-street neon. You sat on a stool in front of the dentist's chair with a hard look on your face. The old man seemed very tired and there two younger white-aproned assistants also in the room. They swept up red wads of gauze and took a big rubber bib off of my chest. Most of my lower face was numb, and what wasn't numb felt like soft rubber. I had to raise my hand to my jaw for assurance that I still possessed a mouth, and instead of a bloody and broken gap, I felt the smooth edges of four new front teeth.

My Heart Under
The Jeju
Runway

July
1991

My mouth was fine long before we took our Jeju Island trip. For me, arranging things had been fairly straightforward. I applied for leave, got Carl to pull a weekend standby with Kitts' crew, and bought the tickets. Well, you actually bought the air tickets and booked a hotel with my money, because it was easier that way. I just stayed in the background and let people assume that you were traveling with your family or Korean friends. Everything else for you was difficult and complicated. You had to concoct a phony weekend trip with some girlfriends who would cover for you.

The hotel room was tiny, but the view was magnificent. It was like looking out over the sea from a windowed closet. The restaurants in Seogwipo City had just about anything we wanted, but I was happy with bibimbap.

My memories of hiking around Mt. Sambang are mostly scenes of you laughing as we climb along a stone creek bed. The shrines and caves live in my mind as images of you standing in front of that huge underground Buddha.

The clean wind on Mt. Halla was so different from the air in Seoul, especially when we took the taxi up to that touristy green tea plantation where the almost-misty breeze never stopped. We drank tea, sat on mats, and looked out over endless rows of perfectly-groomed trees. I can close my eyes and see you smile at me with a small cup in your hands.

One Of These Days, You'll Come Out Of Your Haze

September 1991

I wanted to bring up the matter of marriage when we again went hiking on Siheung's granite mountain, but I didn't. I just enjoyed the day and the chance to be with you. Plus, I thought that we were making huge progress because you said that I could meet your mother. It may not have been an invitation to Chuseok...but that was okay. I was going to meet your mother!

Except...I didn't get to meet your mother. Instead, we just went to your sister's home and had dinner with her family...which was nice, I guess.

Shall Be Found, Forever
Sloughing
Sycorax

November
1991

I used to get such a kick out of being stopped at the doors of nakji restaurants. The host would speak to you in Korean and caution you to look after me, the foreigner, because we were about to enter a nakji establishment and the spicy dishes therein might melt me like the Wicked Witch. Then you would assure the host that we were there at my request.

The final time that this happened wasn't as memorable as it had once been. It was the same for the food...and maybe for the company, too.

I Hoarsely Cry
- Why?

December
1991

You met me in Bucheon a couple times. I met you in Seoul a couple times. We had noodles at an Insa-dong restaurant on Christmas Day.

메리 크리스마스

Kerguelen
Cabbage
Kimchi

January
1992

I got drunk with Carl to celebrate the New Year. Yay.

새해 복 많이 받으세요

12

Winding Up, Winding Down, In Tears I Go

Hey, ~~Max~~ *Jack,* A Guy Gets On The ~~MTA~~ *SMS* Here In ~~L.A.~~ *Seoul* And ~~Dies~~ *Cries.* Think Anybody Will Notice?

February 25ᵗʰ, 1992

A couple hours ago Mirye and I had sex in a love hotel near Bucheon Station...for the last time. I don't know why we did it. I don't know what it was like, either. Maybe it was good. Maybe it wasn't. It doesn't matter.

She's about to go up those stairs. She'll get on the bus from Bucheon to Siheung. I'll stay here and wait for the train.

I don't see the Korean people going to Seoul. I don't hear the kids talking and laughing. I don't see the newspaper kiosks and snack displays. I don't sense the constant stares and occasional "look mom, a foreigner" finger-pointing.

Mirye isn't standing especially close, so the old people aren't spitting at us. I won't have to deal with racist bullshit at our backwater rendezvous spots anymore, and she won't have to worry about the repercussions of being seen in public with a Big Nose. The familial deceptions will no longer be necessary, either.

Gee, everything's going to be just fine, isn't it?

This quaint intercultural experiment draws to a close and some Chinese hymenoplasty tourists will get bumped to the back of a Seoul clinic line. Mirye can go on to find a viable Korean guy, but during late-night hen sessions she can whisper scandalous tales about the foreigner she fucked when she was young:

He looked like a bleached baboon.
He had brown hair.
He had a European nasal bridge that could have

318

doubled as a Geobukseon battering ram.

He had green Western eyes that were the same color as little Wae-in condoms, and as without epicanthic folds as his circumcised Migukin cock was without a foreskin.

I'm thinking again of the pine tree at the Flower Palace. I've tried to be that tree. I've *desperately* wanted to be that tree. I was broken when Mirye thought better of inviting me to Chuseok, when I was denied the chance to meet her mother, and when I received delayed responses to my proposals, or none at all. I'm not able to right myself anymore. Not after today. No more bending or breaking for *this* cloven pine. I may as well imprison Ariel within my golden growth ring and shove the diamond up my ass.

I was so proud of the ring and what I wanted it to represent, but such sentiment is like a saccharine teenybopper song. Now, each time that I look at it, I feel increasingly embarrassed. Not *quite* ashamed, but almost. The ring is just a symbol of something that I can't have.

I didn't bother to pull that pathetic scrap of trash out of my pocket today, though I did have it with me, just in case a miracle occurred and a single word from Mirye transformed it back into the lovely thing that I had originally seen in the BX jewelry case. Miracles rarely happen. I realized this when, over lunch, Mirye looked away when I re-posed my question. I've discovered that if you do it more than once, the "popping" element disappears. Thereafter, the question is merely "posed" and "re-posed," but never again "popped."

I thought that we had a mission statement.
She thought that we had a shelf life.

What a waste of time.

Nevertheless, she was "The One." I don't know why. I can't provide a reason. Academically, logically, and culturally, she was a terrible selection for me, and vice-versa. People don't make these choices for themselves,

319

however. Some other force or entity does that, and, more often than not, He/She/It gets everything way, way wrong. So, to all of the fortunate ones out there who land "The One": Fuck you.

FUCK YOU!

Mirye is about to leave and I feel like I can't even draw a breath. I do, though, but she puts her finger on my lips.

"I have to go," she says.

I know. Maybe I even understand. But I'm still dying inside. *Don't do this.* Please *don't do this.*

I'm never going to see you again, am I?

I just want you to know something.

Please let me tell you something.

No. She puts her finger on my lips again and shushes me. "I have to go," she repeats.

* * *

I didn't make it back to the barracks before I cracked. I found a seat on the train and hunched over with my face in my hands. I tried to be quiet, but the Korean commuters still witnessed plenty Barbarian Theater. Everyone stared when I raised my head to check the passing stations. A few sneered.

Fuck this goddamned country.
Fuck these goddamned people.
Korea for the Koreans, Koreans, Koreans, I say.

There was also a lot of staring when I got off the train at Pyeongtaek, except it was from the other Big Nose GIs at the station. I saw understanding in some of the young men's eyes:

- I've been there, too. You'll get over her.

The lady roundies seemed less sympathetic:

- A K-girl ripped out your heart? Suck it up, traitor.

I didn't catch a taxi back to base immediately after I got off the train. Instead, I lingered for a few moments on the platform and took some deep breaths. I wiped my eyes one more time and was about to leave when I heard the rails hum. I paused, walked over to the edge of the platform, and looked up the line. In the light of the oncoming train I held a brief internal debate, then decided to toss the ring, rather than myself, onto the track.

In A Little While I'll Be Gone

March 1992 (1-of-2)

This is my final exercise at P-Tek.

Hell, this is the final exercise of my **enlistment.**

* * *

Carl steps into the power unit lights at the aircraft shelter's entrance. It's still cold here in the ROK, but Carl isn't wearing a parka because his chem suit keeps him warm. There aren't any attack simulations taking place, so, like everyone else, Carl's gas mask is in its web belt pouch. The SP looks at the picture on Carl's line badge, then at his face, and nods him past the barrier ropes.

There are five aircraft shelters in this flightline tree, and Carl's crew is next door. It's hour fourteen of this exercise shift, and Dave and Rob are getting some shut-eye in the small crew chief shack at the rear of the shelter. There's no jet here, and there won't be until after tonight's sorties. By then, however, my crew will have been relieved. We're just passing time, and it's my turn to keep an eye out for Jones and the AMU officers.

"Jesus Christ, Jack. You look dead," says Carl.

"Fuck you, too," I mumble from my seat on a shelter ventilation pipe.

"Do you guys have any MAU-12 pins?"

"Dunno. Maybe. Have a look." I reach into my chem gear jacket and pull out a set of keys. Carl takes the keys and opens my crew's big roll-away weapons tool box. He rummages around until he finds a handful of long pins attached to red *Remove Before Flight* streamers.

"Are you guys getting off at 2200?" Carl asks, as he returns the keys

I blink. "What?"

"When is swap-out for this shelter?"

"Couple hours."

"Same in our shelter. Wanna get some chow later?"

"Chow?"

"Yeah," says Carl. "You know? Grub? *Food?* Chow hall is on twenty-four-hour exercise schedule, or are you gonna hang out and glue your asshole shut with some more flightline MREs?"

I nod. "Sure. Meet you at the flight shack." Then I add: "You're starting to sound like Jones."

Carl gives me a funny look. "Shack's locked up, dude. We're in the middle of an exercise, remember?"

I shake my head and snort. "Yeah. Sorry." I push myself up from my seat on the pipe. "End of the shift. Tired. Yeah, I'll meet you in the dayroom after I dump this chem gear."

"You'll need to drink some serious Hyte after they call Index," says Carl. "You're gonna be alright. You're almost out of here, remember? You'll tell Uncle Sugar to go fuck himself a in a couple weeks."

"Double-digit midget," I murmur.

"That's right. You're so short that you're walkin' under doors! And soon you'll be a free man and looking up some of your old Sin City tuna. All of this shit will just be a bad dream." Carl pauses, and I know that he's not referring to the drudgeries of military life. "You're gonna be alright, man! Seriously. And nothing helps you forget a woman better than another woman, especially if the first one's on the other side of the world."

I stare across the empty shelter as I speak. "You'll be done too, sort of. No more humping bombs."

"Fuckin' 'A'," says Carl. "I was starting to think that I'd never make the cut."

"You've earned it...though it's still kinda hard for me to picture you as an Intel spook."

Carl smiles. *"Spook?* I think that's just the CIA."

"I'm not so sure. Some of that crap you've studied is unbelievable."

Carl shrugs and changes the subject. "Do you know what you should do? As soon as you get back, you should hock that damned ring and get a couple desk whores. "

Carl's suggestion makes me nauseous and I turn away.

"You - you still have the ring, right?"

I look at the wall. "It's not like that. She never took it."

"So where is it?"

I don't say anything. I don't want to go there, but Carl does.

"Jack? Dude, where?"

"I tossed it down onto the tracks at P-Station. I stood there and watched the wheels smash it like a penny."

"You are absolutely fucking kidding me."

"No."

A few moments pass before Carl speaks. "Look on the **Brightside, Mister.** At least your discharge is going through."

I frown. "Why the fuck shouldn't it? I've been a good little monkey."

"Word has it," replies Carl, "that some guys are getting involuntarily extended. They're gonna start that 'stop-loss' policy pretty soon. Maybe next month."

"Why?"

"Iraq."

"*Iraq...?* Wait. I thought the fun and games were canceled when that Hussein dude pulled out of Kuwait last year."

"Nah. Shit's back on. The squadron's probably gonna deploy to Turkey."

"Why? *For what?* The Iraqis fucking *left Kuwait!* And what does any of that bullshit have to do with the USA, anyway?"

"You sound surprised, Jackster."

"What do you mean?"

Carl seems amused. "Haven't you heard the rumor mill?"

"I don't know what you're talking about."

Carl glances around the shelter. Kitts and Hardesty are still asleep, and the SP is far out of earshot. "Oil and bucks, man. It's all about oil and bucks. Washington will invent a bullshit reason for war, no matter what Hussein does. You shouldn't need a soon-to-be Intel jeep to tell you that a composite black ops wing at Incirlik has already been making civvy runs."

I'm silent for a moment. *"Civilian* targets? In Iraq?"

Carl glances around again and nods. "Yeah, for almost a year. There's another war coming, Jackster. Actually, it's already started."

I frown. "That can't be true."

"Why not? Do you need to hear about it in morning formation before you'll believe it?"

"But-but we...we don't bomb women and children."

"Since when?" asks Carl. "Besides, bombs aren't the only weapons that can be dropped from planes."

"So what else are we talking about?"

Carl doesn't answer. He just turns around and leaves the aircraft shelter.

Forever's Gonna
Start Tonight

March
1992
(2-of-2)

On the Friday before my flight the guys commandeered some tables in the NCO club for a shop get-together. I had sewn on buck sergeant, so at last I was an actual NCO in the NCO club, and not an airman waiting for my own club to be built.

I was half-buzzed when Carl and Hardesty whipped out some duct tape. Before I could move, my arms were securely wrapped to my chair. Then guys started dumping ketchup, mustard, and mayonnaise on my head. Beer soon followed.

It was a weapons troop tradition. Stupid? Probably. Messy? Absolutely. And the club manager was *pissed*. The entire weapons flight laughed its ass off. Somebody got me a couple towels after they cut my hands free, but not before the camera flashes stopped. There were a lot of handshakes while the latest crop of jeeps, E-1s fresh from the States, got busy mopping.

I returned to my barracks room. After I had showered and turned in, there was a knock. I rose, opened the door, and found a falling-down-wasted Carl. We shook hands and he tried to tell me something, but his speech was so slurred that all I could do was prop him up, put on some sweats, and walk him back to his own quarters. Carl's roomie assured me that he would turn my friend on his side and listen through the night.

I borrowed a pen and a slip of paper, upon which someone had already written: 남자 옥수수 밭. Unlike Carl, I couldn't read Korean, so I didn't know what the message said. I turned the paper over and, on the other side, wrote a little "hail and farewell" note to my buddy. Then, as Carl lay passed out, I buttoned the paper inside the breast pocket of his fatigues and returned to my room.

I had been packed and ready to go for days. And no, I wasn't going to wear my damned service blues on the flight back to Vegas. I was out. I was *done.* The CBPO pukes had given me my DD-214 and told me that an honorable discharge would be sent to my stateside address. I had responded by saying that there *was* no stateside address, but that I would contact Randolph AFB when I had a place to send the certificate. I didn't really care, anyway. The 214 was all I would need for employers and college applications. There was a week's worth of rest booked for me at Sammy's Town, followed by another week at Xanadu. It was more than enough time to consider my next move, and more than enough time for Ed Burnstein and Crew to get the inheritance teat lubed-up and ready to express.

I caught the MWR shuttle to Incheon International the next morning, but I didn't look out the bus window as Korea passed by. The sky was clear when my plane took off, but I didn't look outside the cabin either, until after I had boarded my connection at LAX. After touching down at McKarran, I picked up a rental car, visited a twenty-four hour IHOP on Flamingo, and continued down to Boulder Highway. I checked in at Sammy's Town, showered, changed, and, in a state of *severe* jet-lag, looked out my hotel window at a large shadow looming northeast of Vegas.

Sunrise Mountain. Clark County, Nevada. About four-thirty AM.

* * *

This Sammy's Town suite is much better than that shitty Nevada Palace single where I stayed when I returned to bury Grandpa. Well, in *most* respects it's better. After a few drinks, both at the big rotating atrium bar downstairs and back here on the bed, I can appreciate the newer appointments and greater attention to housekeeping, but...the walls seem thinner. Much, much thinner.

I keep drinking. I'm about a quarter of the way through this bottle of José, but it doesn't help me ignore the sounds coming though the walls. I can't tell if the other guests are partying or having loud sex or exactly what they're doing. But I can hear them. I can hear *all* of the people in this hotel. Mere tequila can't keep them out of my head. They're probably talking about the last time that I saw her, though it's none of their damn business. Gossiping shits.

Or...maybe I'm hearing *her* voice in another room as she tells someone about the last time that we were together. She's laughing all the way through that story - you know, the one about the lovesick American boob whom she once dated. What *was* his name, anyway?

Still...she remembers?

Really?

Let's listen. Yes, that's her, in some other room, or maybe in *all* of the other rooms. It doesn't matter how far her laughter has to go to reach me. I can't drink enough or clap my hands over my ears tightly enough. These hotel walls are just sunsets and dirty sheets, and there will never be silence behind any of them.

I should stop counting walls, just as I should also stop counting the days between this moment and the last one that we shared.

Sure. I can do that. Time to move on.

Bullshit.

Seasons will accumulate, but it won't matter. The future holds years as thin as rice paper panels, and none will distance me from the last time that I saw her. She will always be in the next room, and I'll always hear her voice through yesterday's walls.

This bottle of José is nearly half-empty...like me.

I haven't slept in almost seventy-two hours.

Time to pass out.

12+1

I'll Be Dead Long Before February 2̶5̶ᵗʰ, 1̶9̶7̶3̶ 12ᵗʰ, 2092

Now It Should Be Incandescently Clear That No One Who Has Any Concern For The Integrity And Life Of America Today Can Ignore The Present War. *Except Jack.*

Grace stared at me like she didn't understand. "That's either the saddest or the most childish thing that I've ever heard you say." She bit her lip through a smile, reached over to pinch my arm, and assumed the tone of a little green master of The Schwartz. "Don't pout. Pouting turns to baggage, and baggage turns to damage. Much pouting in you I sense, young Jackwalker."

"Of course you do," I said. "Maybe women don't see guys like me as being especially...*fit,*" I paused, "but it almost happened once." I looked up at the sky for a moment. "That's what I like to believe, anyway."

Our lives, going forward and looking back, had little common reference. I knew this because Grace tended to disclose snippets of her past via hackneyed "twenty-something divorcée who hasn't finished college" laments. Shared career goals aside, our relationship forecasts also diverged. I knew with certainty that Grace would find what she was looking for, whereas my romantic future held as much promise as a ghost masturbating in a rear view mirror.

I wasn't embarrassed anymore by the memory of coming on to Grace in a military bar, though the idea of *me* trying to pick *her* up was now enveloped in an air of absurdity. It made me appreciate what I perceived as the unspoken terms of our present association; namely, friendship's glass ceiling kept my shortcomings safely irrelevant, Grace continued to brandish a jeweler's monocle, and, while one diamond searched for another, we both pretended that I wasn't a chipped rhinestone.

12+1

I'll Be Dead Long Before February 25~~th~~, ~~1973~~ 12^(*th*), 2092

Now It Should Be Incandescently Clear
That No One Who Has Any Concern
For The Integrity And Life
Of America Today Can
Ignore The Present
War. *Except*
Jack.

Grace stared at me like she didn't understand. "That's either the saddest or the most childish thing that I've ever heard you say." She bit her lip through a smile, reached over to pinch my arm, and assumed the tone of a little green master of The Schwartz. "Don't pout. Pouting turns to baggage, and baggage turns to damage. Much pouting in you I sense, young Jackwalker."

"Of course you do," I said. "Maybe women don't see guys like me as being especially...*fit,*" I paused, "but it almost happened once." I looked up at the sky for a moment. "That's what I like to believe, anyway."

Our lives, going forward and looking back, had little common reference. I knew this because Grace tended to disclose snippets of her past via hackneyed "twenty-something divorcée who hasn't finished college" laments. Shared career goals aside, our relationship forecasts also diverged. I knew with certainty that Grace would find what she was looking for, whereas my romantic future held as much promise as a ghost masturbating in a rear view mirror.

I wasn't embarrassed anymore by the memory of coming on to Grace in a military bar, though the idea of *me* trying to pick *her* up was now enveloped in an air of absurdity. It made me appreciate what I perceived as the unspoken terms of our present association; namely, friendship's glass ceiling kept my shortcomings safely irrelevant, Grace continued to brandish a jeweler's monocle, and, while one diamond searched for another, we both pretended that I wasn't a chipped rhinestone.

"It's not that I don't believe in love," I said, between sips of coffee. "I *am* saying, however, that it may not exist for me...here."

I was taken aback by Grace's expression because something in it told me that, while I certainly wasn't a diamond, neither was I a mere rhinestone. Grace and I would never be candidates for the cover of a trashy romance novel, but I wasn't merely in the Friend Zone, or even the Best *Guy* Friend Zone. I sensed that had entered into the Best Friend Zone, and, as such, I probably could have told Grace that I was encopretic, and she would have offered to buy me some adult briefs. You could tell a best friend things that lovers couldn't handle, and as long as certain lines weren't crossed, a man like me could have no better friend than a woman like Grace.

"So you're saying that you can't find love here, in Vegas, because you keep shitting your pants?"

I froze like I had been dipped in liquid nitrogen, but after a moment I broke my tongue loose. "What?"

Grace leaned over again with a bigger smile and a harder pinch. "Yeah, I'd say that we're best friends. Must be. Any other girl would be freaked out when you talk while you're thinking."

I sighed and closed my eyes for a moment.

"You don't really wear diapers, do you?"

She couldn't be serious, so I wasn't either. "Yeah. In fact, I need to be changed. Can you help me out?"

Grace looked away and held up her hand. "Okay, best friends or not, we need to change the subject."

Except we *didn't* actually change the subject. We just sat there for some long minutes. I looked at Grace out of the corner of my eye, then grinned and looked away when she noticed. When I glanced back at her, I caught her giving me a sidelong. This happened several times until we burst out laughing. A few of the other patrons turned to look at us.

"Freak," declared Grace.

"You, as well."

Grace returned to the original topic. "I don't buy

your 'no love here' thing. I mean, no matter where you go in the world, be it Seoul or Vegas, you're still the same person, aren't you?"

"No," I said, as I put my empty cup on the table. "As Ms. Bush said: 'Outside gets inside.' It has to. We become slightly different people every time we wake up and get out of bed."

"I think that she was actually referring to nuclear fallout," asserted Grace, "but no matter, because it still doesn't make sense. How can you sit there and tell me that some mess from your past keeps following you, but in the next breath say that you're constantly changing? If that's true, then why not take out the garbage? The poor old demons whom you keep dragging around might not even remember who you are."

For a few moments I sat in a Sioux teepee and tried to explain to Chief Grace that a Bluecoated memory from Yeongam would pursue no matter where I went, but the Chief kept telling me to chill out because a certain bitter young sergeant didn't exist anymore, and in his place there was only a ULVN student called Dances With...well, certainly not *Wolves,* but some kind of new name that reflected personal transformation. "Hallucinates With Spaniels," perhaps.

"You're...right," I admitted. "You're right. There's something wrong with me." I didn't intend to sound like a pity-party RSVP. My tone was that of an empiric observation, but Grace still frowned.

"Stop that. Right now," she said. "Everybody has to grow a new heart at some point, except most people learn to move on as *teens.*" She put on a baffled look and threw up her hands.

My response was quick. *"Bull. Shit.* The world is full of 'First Love' and 'The One That Got Away' stories. I spot 51/49 hearts every time I walk down the street. They're not just nostalgic tales to amuse old friends. I see middle-aged people who look and act like some crap that happened to them in high school is still on their psychological front pages."

"Is that also what's holding you back?" Grace asked. "Wait...you don't need to answer that." She paused for a moment, and when Grace next spoke there was kindness in her voice. "There are no guarantees, Jack. Love is like opening a new business. Location, location, location. And you're home now. You're not in somebody else's country. You're not floundering in another culture. Aren't you lonely? Don't you want someone?"

"Someone?" I echoed, as I exaggeratedly looked to my left and right.

"Yeah. When was the last time?"

I blew a raspberry. "Last week. Some film student."

"You know damn-good-and-well that's not what I mean," said Grace. "I don't care when you last put your penis on auto-pilot." She tried to take a drink from her empty cup, then in slight frustration put it on the table.

"Ah," I said.

"So?"

"Years."

"I thought so." Grace lowered her gaze and was quiet for a moment.

I reasoned that Grace wouldn't understand unless the situation were placed in a different context. I was sure that if I really pressed about her own efforts, I might receive a litany of episodes and anecdotes that illustrated Grace's earnestness. I laughed at myself and the naiveté that I had shown during those times when I thought that Grace hadn't been dating, especially on that idiotic night when we had gotten drunk at her grandma's apartment and I had asked why. The truth was, Grace *had* been...but not in the easy way like me, a Mr. Sleazoid who seldom even remembered women's names. What I had failed to understand was that ninety percent of a woman's vetting process takes place before words are even exchanged, let alone the initiation of a dating period. Grace had likely conducted lots of little good-faith auditions, but nobody had yet made her team.

Fine. I knew how to put a different spin on things. A bit drastic, perhaps, but it would make the point. "Why not you and me?" I asked. Blunt. Plain. Uncomfortable.

Silence. Grace looked away and didn't reply. She wasn't actually considering the possibility. No, that scenario had been evaluated and discarded a couple years earlier in a rattrap military bar. Grace was trying to think of a merciful way to say that it was impossible.

You don't understand why I'm not working on something long-term? I thought. *Really, Grace? Okay, then why don't you consider* me *in that role?* **Ah-haa!** *Cat got your tongue? Or perhaps your tactful declination?*

I didn't enjoy watching my friend squirm. I just wanted her to understand why my life was as lame as that of Billy Cristal's character in *When Harry Meets Sally.* I looked at Grace and saw an angel on her right shoulder and a devil on her left.

"What she's looking for," said a pitchfork-wielding Barbra Strysand.

"And what she'll settle for," said a little winged Geoff Bridges.

"Not you," they stated in unison.

"Alright," said Grace.

"Wait - what?!"

"I said: 'Alright'."

Hold on. This isn't the anticipated outcome of the exercise!

Strysand and Bridges looked confused and vanished.

"Change your mind already?" asked Grace. She wasn't smiling, grinning, fidgeting, or doing anything else that might suggest that she was putting me on.

I. Didn't. Believe. That. This. Was. A. Possibility.

I'm not against it. It's just that I've grown accustomed to...certain ways of thinking.

This kind of scares me. Probably because I care about you.

Definitely *because I care about you.*

Turned on a dime. No, in this instance I'd say upside-down. I've lost count of how many times you've done this to me.

I felt like I maintained my outward composure. "I'm not sure that I actually meant--"

"No?" Grace interrupted. "I thought that I heard

you clearly."

Composure, huh? Then why is my heart racing? I'm still in my twenties. I can't have a heart attack, can I?

"Jack, I'll be honest," continued Grace. "I've thought about it. You're nice looking. You have direction. You have some quirks, but your heart is kind and I can talk to you about anything."

I slowly sucked in a burning breath. I had thought that Grace's standards were set much higher.

"What?" Grace demanded. "I'm not allowed to get lonely, too? You'll have to excuse me if I don't troll around the Film Studies Department," she said, in a way that made her words sting. "And I've had a taste of domesticity, if you'll recall. It was good, when it worked. I want it again. Going from a ring, a man and a home to a city bus and Grandma's apartment on the other side of the country doesn't exactly represent a step forward in my life's progression." Grace shook her head, but not in condemnation or frustration. It was more like confusion. "I don't understand you, Jack. When we first met, I took you for a hypocrite. I mean, sometimes you seemed almost...*virginal.* You acted like a church lady when I mentioned how some of the girls in our classes were students and substitute teachers by day, then dancers and call girls by night. That time when we went to the Ultrastore was pretty weird too, but not because you acted like such a head case - it was because you didn't even know what half of the merchandise was. Yet you've told me things about your time in the military that make all of that seem tame. I've been hanging out with you long enough to see a pattern: Every semester, without fail, you date several people for a few months and then simply forget them after finals. It's like you're on a schedule or something."

I was kind of surprised by Grace's observations, especially since I thought that I had cleverly layered my social interactions. But even with no overlaps, Grace had eventually intuited the big picture. I was kind of...*relieved?* The *All-Seeing-Eye-Of-Grace* was upon me, but I was still accepted - though at this moment I was also being critiqued. I wondered if she did the same thing. Of *course* she did. Women were pros at "need-to-know-basis" social routines.

"Why not make a memory that lasts longer than a semester?" asked Grace

Again: I. DIDN'T. BELIEVE. THAT. THIS. WAS. A. POSSIBILITY.

"I can see inside you, Jack. I know what you're doing. Every minute that we sit here, your mind becomes more and more confused." Grace seemed to make a drastic decision. She grabbed the arms of her patio chair and prepared to stand. "Don't be so...*fucked up,* Jack. I won't let you. I know you. I'm too close to you. Don't back away from this. Please, no mental circuses. Just this once."

I gave a weak smile. She was right. I was melting down in all of the "what ifs". I wanted to speak, but I knew that anything I said would only confirm Grace's assertions.

"And if you act differently afterward," continued Grace, as she took out her car keys and rose to her feet, "if you brush me off or get bizarre or stupid, I swear, I'll run over you with Grandma's Mercedes." Grace motioned across the parking lot.

"What are you doing?" I feebly asked.

"I'm going to pull the car up, and when I do, I don't want to see you sitting there fumbling around. Just turn off your brain and get in."

I Won't Fake It Like
The Other Girls
That You Used
To Know

September
1994
(2-of-2)

"Where are we going?" I asked. Grace looked away from the road and gave me a wink. When she pulled into Xanadu's parking garage, my question was answered.

As we got out of the car, I tried to speak. "I remember the last time we were here...that awful thing..."

"Shhh," said Grace. "Think back. I know that you like this place. You liked it as a boy. You told me so. Besides, Grandma is home right now, and I'm really not much for your roachy shoebox." Then she added: "You're loaded. I don't know why you insist upon renting in that Hacienda dump complex."

I swallowed hard as we crossed the footbridge over to the hotel and rode an external inclinator down to the main entrance. My vision seemed foggy and my mind was distracted, but I was vaguely aware of a moment by one of the hotel's front desks. I saw Grace talk to someone and produce a credit card. Then she took me by the hand and I found myself in an elevator, and then in a dark hotel room with one large bed.

When I opened the curtains I discovered that the window looked out over the atrium. In my haze, I hadn't even noticed what floor we were on. I looked all the way across the hollow hotel, over the tops of phony trees, simulated concrete land features, and groups of hotel guests. Rows of room windows on the eastern side of Xanadu's interior space indicated that we were on about the tenth floor.

My thoughts raced. Why was I freaking out? I was about to go to bed with a beautiful woman. I should have been eager. I should have been excited. The head of my cock should have been red, swollen, and screaming to be let out. I should have felt a hot wave through my skin, and I should have grabbed Grace and shoved my tongue down her throat the instant we stepped into this room.

Well...*no.* That wouldn't have fit this situation, and especially not this *woman,* very well. It was Step #1 in my *Liberal Arts Freshman-From-Boise-Or-Wherever-The-Fuck-She's-From* Sexual Flowchart.

I fidgeted by the window and was half-afraid to turn around and face Grace. *What now? Ah, yes...let's take a look at some of these free touristy show magazines on the table. I wonder if there's a Bible in this room. Do they still put Bibles in hotel rooms? That looks like Xanadu stationary. And a pen. Does it write? Yes, it does. Let's draw a happy face. Terrific. Let's look out the window again. Not much going on out there. Is it kind of stuffy in here? Sort of. Let's look for the A/C thermostat--*

I bumped into her when I turned around. Without taking her gaze off of me, Grace reached up and jerked the curtains closed. Her shoes were by the door, and she had silently approached in stocking-feet. Grace didn't put her arms around me, though. Even as she pressed against me, she only looked up. One of her legs forced its way between mine. She shifted her thighs and hips up and down against my jeans like we were two kids having a desperate dry hump in a school library.

"You're off balance," she whispered, as she rubbed her leg a little higher. As if to prove the point, Grace finally did raise her arms, though not to put them around me. Instead, she placed both palms on my chest and shoved me down onto the bed. Grace could have fallen on me, but she caught herself and slowly brought her body down against mine. I felt the tips of her hard nipples though her bra and tee, the soft press of her breasts and stomach, and the movements of her lower body as her legs again spread against mine. Our lips brushed for a moment but didn't meet in a kiss, and I tasted a sweet but faint mix of chocolate and coffee on her breath. Her arms and shoulders were firm and strong as she both steadied herself and pinned me to

338

the bed, and I wondered if Grace could feel my heart beat in the same way that I sensed her own hot pulse.

Her hips slowed and stopped. Our cheeks pressed together as Grace let herself rest atop me. She moved her arms in a wide and slow circle over the bedspread as if she were a face-down snow angel. She took my face in her hands and we could have had an amazing kiss, but then Grace spoke in a loud and rough tone that jarred me out of the moment.

"What are you? A bloodhound?" She raised up and rolled off.

The room's ceiling stared down at me. "What?"

"Why are you sniffing me like that?"

"Like what?"

"I told you: I don't wear Old Slice."

"Okay. Let's call it 'Dokto Breath.'"

Grace sighed. "Is this your...*special*...way of telling me that my hair smells like cigarettes?"

I sat up. *"Cigarettes?* When did you start smoking?"

Grace looked at me in the darkness for a long moment. "Okay," she said. "I get it. I see where this is going. I knew that this would happen." She slid across the bed and reached for a small clutch that sat next to the Mercedes keys and the room's card folder. Grace switched on a lamp, took out a small silver square, and I heard a popping sound as she used her thumbs to force a tablet through bubble-pack foil. Grace then hopped back on the bed and scooted across. She touched my face again, but this time, it wasn't in a slow and intimate way. Rather, she abruptly reached up and squeezed my cheeks.

"What are you doing?" I asked through pinched fish lips.

"Open your mouth."

"What *is* that?"

"Vaguera. Grandma keeps a couple tabs in the car."

"Your grandma? Why the hell does she have that?"

"I told you. She's got a geriatric saltine."

I pulled my head away from Grace's hand. "What makes you think *I* need it?"

She folded her arms and fixed me in an iron look. "You need it."

"I'm only twenty-seven. Come on."

"Yeah, your *body* is twenty-seven, but your *mind* is ninety-seven. You know, sixty-eight percent of all impotence is psychological."

I was taken aback. "How do you know that? Are you suddenly a doctor? And why do you think I'm impotent?"

"I don't," Grace answered. "In fact, all of the awkward, *after*-morning-after moments that I've seen you have with campus girls tell me you're not." Grace gave a small and smug *you-haven't-been-fooling-anyone* smile and continued. "But I still refuse to take a chance on your scrambled brain short-circuiting your otherwise functional dick. Now, open your mouth. Good. Now close your mouth. Swallow. Let me see under your tongue." I suddenly had fish lips again as Grace tried to peer into my mouth. It wasn't necessary. The tablet was small and had gone down easily, just like the condition it remedied.

I pulled away again. "You could have at least offered me a glass of water," I grumbled. "What is this, an institution?

"Interesting idea," answered Grace. "Maybe."

"I hope that was real Vaguera," I said. "I hope you didn't just slip me some BZ or something."

"No," smiled Grace. "Not necessary. You own 'psycho' already."

Well, at least I feel less nervous, I thought. *But now what?*

Grace seemed to think the same thing. She looked to the side and flopped back onto one of the pillows while I stretched out beside her. I closed my eyes, but opened them again when I remembered the TV.

"Don't-you-dare," hissed Grace, as I started to reach for the remote.

"I think the sexy-sexerton just left the room," I muttered, as I got off the bed and went back to the window.

I opened the curtains and looked out. It occurred to me that, when I was a kid, Grandpa and I had always stayed on Xanadu's higher floors. I looked across the faux-jungle, but this time I raised my eyes to the upper levels on the other side where external halls allowed guests to exit their rooms and gaze downward over railing and through plexiglas. I remembered when it had been such a thrill to people-watch from high above, even though the safety barriers had eliminated any real possibility of falling.

As an adult, I realized that Grandpa had liked Xanadu for trysting purposes. Of course! Ha. It was perfect. We had hung out together at the restaurants, arcade, and pool during the day, and at night I was close by, but in another room when company called. Now it was my turn to continue the generational sexual experiences of Simmerath men at Xanadu...except that I wasn't having much of a sexual experience.

Hey.
Hmmm.
Ouch! Houston, we have problematic auto-inflation in an elbow-macaroni position!

I adjusted myself with a sense of urgency. I didn't take the time to unfasten my pants. Instead, I sucked in my stomach, jammed my hand down past my waistband, and found the head of my cock with my fingertips. I tugged it upward, where it was free to comfortably rise in a safe vertical position against my stomach. I unbuckled my belt and opened the top button of my jeans as I felt the sensitive tip scrape the elastic band of my underwear and touch the rough denim outside.

Nice.
Maybe the Vaguera had been a good idea, after all.

Brain-penis dysfunction wasn't going to occur, thanks to my dear friend and her anti-neurosis chemical insurance policy. No deductible. Copulation guaranteed. Things might be dull and drab on Grace's side of the room, but sexy-sexerton was definitely making a pharmaceutically-assisted comeback over by the window.

What should I do? Just turn around?
Ta-Da!
Heeere's Johnny!
Boinggg!
No.
But...Jesus Christ! I've got a fabulous hard-on!

And, speaking of Jesus...I wondered again if the room contained a Bible. *Do people read the Bible when they come to hotels? Well, maybe. Maybe they read Revelations when they get depressed from losing at the tables. Maybe that's why there's stationary and a pen in each room, so that people can write their gambling-loss suicide notes. Where is the stationary that I saw earlier? Was there something written on it already? I dunno. It's kind of warm in here. Maybe I should ask Grace to turn on the A/C. Where is the thermostat--?*
This time when I turned around and bumped into Grace, her arms instantly wrapped around me. I tasted the chocolate and coffee again, but sweeter and stronger in the wetness of her lips and tongue.
Grace suddenly pulled away. "Jack, say why we're here," she half-whispered. "Say it. Be in this moment. Say what we're going to do."
"Be close," I murmured, as I moved forward and lowered my lips to taste the soft skin of her neck. "Touch," I breathed.
Grace slowly lowered her hand to my partially-open jeans. She stroked the stiff shape there, its length still confined within cloth except for the naked pink head that pressed up toward my belly. I started to put my arms around her, but Grace raised her hands and pushed me back. She then unbuttoned my shirt and lightly raked her nails across my chest. "You'll have to do better than that," Grace said in a low and hot growl. She placed her index finger between her lips, sucked for a moment, and gave me an evil smile as she slowly lowered her hand. I couldn't look away from Grace's dark eyes, even when she tugged my fly open and put her hand inside my underwear. I gasped when I felt her smooth warm fingertip trace moisture from the base of my cock to the very tip. Grace's finger lingered for a

moment to follow the delicate edge between the shaft and head. *"That was a touch. We're going to do a lot more,"* she breathed.

Grace was a hot power surge and a sensual EMP attack that Vaguera warnings failed to mention:

"If you experience an erection lasting for more than four hours, seek medical attention."

Nah. Try again.

"If you experience an erection lasting for more than four hours, seek methamphetamine and additional sex partners."

No. Still not quite right.

"If you experience an erection lasting for more than four hours, treat the old man whom you'll one day become to a hot jerk-off memory."

That's it.

Things wouldn't be weird or stupid afterward. Grace had said so. I think maybe she'd even promised.
She *had* promised. Hadn't she?
Right?
Right?
My best friend. Hell, my *only* friend. I once heard someone say: "A fuck buddy isn't a real friend. You can't have sex with your *real* female friends."

The hell you can't!

Your *real* female friends are the only ones with whom you *should* have sex. This was an example of me correctly reading the situation. Grace wasn't here to *make love.*

No shit, Sherlock. Brilliant deduction.

What had tipped me off? The pills? The scratches

on my chest? The fact that she had charged a room and yanked my pants down?

Oh well. Even a guy like me could accurately interpret a woman's intentions once in a while...just so long as that same woman attached her clues to my thick skull with a rivet gun. Maybe I was just a broken clock, and this happened to be one of those two times in a day when I actually displayed the right time. However, in this instant I wasn't feeling broken. Far from it. In fact, I had arrived at the "remember your discrete condom" moment.

If there's anything more idiotic than a round, condom-shaped wear pattern on a wallet, I can't think of what it is. Before condoms were sold in pinch-packs I was aware of the doltamatic aura that enveloped an obvious wallet condom. Even before my days of foreign hookers, barracks skanks, and college freshmen, I appreciated the value of simply taking a moment to carefully roll the package and place it in a wallet corner or even a coin pocket where it wouldn't be detected. In high school, when I thought that carrying a condom imbued me with sexual magic, I knew that latex talismans had to be concealed.

After a while though, I learned that carrying a wallet condom, no matter how well hidden, was a bad idea. Sometimes people snoop in your wallet. Sometimes the packaging leaks, and when gooey lube starts to drip out onto the counter while you're paying for movie tickets, things get awkward.

Heh. So when I produced a condom, James Bonde-style, from deep within the watch pocket of my Levis, there was an unexpected reaction from Grace:

- *Whoa, whoa. What are you doing?*
- Protection. You know.
- *No.*
- No?
- *No.*
- Why? I might have something. You never know.
- *Doubtful. No, impossible.*
- How can you afford to say that?
- *I can afford to say that because I have complete*

*confidence in your sexual OCD. I'd bet that you've
NEVER been to bed without a condom. Ever.
Knowing you as I do, I'm certain that you'd insist
upon wearing a condom with a sterile virgin.*
- Well, I...I don't see anything wrong with being
careful.
- *Me neither. That's why I've found protection to be
mandatory...except with you, you silly dork.
Gimme that. Into the trash, okay? Leave it there,
Jack. Unlike some of your ULVN dalliances, I'm all
grown up. I make big girl choices. I don't depend
on men to look out for me or my body. If I say
there's nothing you need to worry about, believe
me. So, do you trust me?*
- Why not? We've come this far. You've kidnapped
and drugged me. You may as well look out for *me*
and *my* body.
- *Don't dodge the question. Do you trust me?*
- Yes.

I reached down and pulled the bottom of Grace's tee
shirt out of her jeans while she ran her fingers inside the
waistband of my shorts and tried to pull them down.
My underwear came to an abrupt stop. "Oops," she said
a bit sheepishly. My hard cock had leveled into a
horizontal position and had forced its way through the
front opening of my hiked-up underwear. For a moment
Grace tried to pull the elastic forward so the head could
slip back, but it was like watching someone try to pull an
already-assembled model ship through the narrow
mouth of a glass bottle. "Here," I said, as I grabbed the
edges of the opening and pulled forward. I hunched
over, thrust my ass out, and my dick was freed. I
stepped out of my crumpled jeans and underwear and
lowered my arms to shrug off my open shirt.
When Grace pulled off her tee she tangled her long
black hair over her face and added to the delicious
wickedness of her half-hidden eyes. I slipped Grace's
bra off the sides of her smooth shoulders, cupped her
breasts for a slow moment, and lightly brushed my
fingertips over her small brown nipples. I lowered my
hands and felt Grace's muscles tighten as I stroked down

her sides, to the top of her jeans, then back and forth where denim and skin met in a smooth transition. I turned my knuckles over and felt their rough contrast on Grace's taut belly, and then I brought my hands up to her neck, again only touching her with the backs of my fingers. I felt myself coming dangerously close to *making love,* rather than *fucking*...not good, especially after I had patted myself on the back for recognizing expectations.

I slowly lowered my lips to hers. It wasn't a long kiss. I was breathing too hard and my heart was pounding. I was pleased to sense that it was the same for Grace. As I returned my fingertips to her breasts' gentle rises, Grace gasped and I felt her tremble, but then her hand shot up, went around my neck, and pulled my lips back to hers.

Grace's hands moved over me with increased speed and force. Her kisses grew more direct and deep, and though she only ran her hands over my back and shoulders, sometimes lightly scratching, sometimes squeezing, she was pushing her belly harder and harder against my cock. My right hand was in her hair, while my left temporarily resisted a powerful urge to slip from the small of Grace's back to a much lower position.

Get it together, Jack, I thought. *A woman doesn't cram Phyzer's Hopeful Diamond down your throat on Epic Foreplay Night. But you'd also better keep in mind that* Zero-To-Sixty In Under Six Seconds *only works in car commercials.*

She's getting more...dare I say it? Frantic.
Rough, even.
Perhaps this situation does indeed call for Epic Foreplay, but in a Zero-To-Sixty format.
I heard a voice from my past:

"If the feet are having a party, then the pussy wants to come over."

Sage conditionality...though at this point the pussy was about to bust down the door.

She should like what's coming, given her current

mood. Thank you, Intelligence Community dungeon masters.

* * *

Your opponent isn't carrying a knife or improvised shank. You've verified that already, so don't worry about a bunch of sticks in the side when you close. Rotate your hips to her side, like you're getting throw leverage, otherwise you're going to get your nuts smashed on her knee. Don't leave the strong side open, either. Head low, to the side if you can, or you'll get your head split. You shouldn't have an erection while doing this, but never mind. Do the best you can.

Don't run double fists up her front. Instead, clap your hands and forearms together like you're praying. That way, nobody gets scratched or bruised, but it still seems dangerous and exciting while allowing you to immobilize her arms at the shoulder joints. But don't actually lock them. Just keep them pinned and close. Besides, one hand needs to be free to unzip her jeans.

Pause. Assess her response.

- Is she into it?
- **Affirmative. Way into it.**
- Press on.

Where's the bed? Directly behind her? Perfect. Now it's time to use that leverage we talked about. Release her arms, turn her hip up and off of yours, and back she goes. Her feet will bounce up from the edge of the bed if you've done it right. Guard your balls against the bouncing feet, grab the legs of her jeans at the hems, and pull. Hard. Re-assess her response.

- Is she still into it?
- **Roger.**

Fine. Drop her jeans on the floor and proceed with your regularly scheduled programming.

* * *

Grace is on her back, eyes wide, mouth open, with a scarlet blotch spreading across her chest and neck.
Wow. That's what I call a flush.

Note To Self: *If I'm ever in this situation again, remember how Grace likes to get things started.*

"That was...*hot,* Jack," Grace panted, as she raised her head slightly. "Very - *huff* - very unexpected, especially from *you--*" she paused for another breath "--but if you ever do it again, I'll rip your dick off."

Note To Self: ***Disregard previous Note To Self.***

"Shut up," I snarled, as I reached down and grabbed Grace's ankles. I don't think that I'd ever seen her look so surprised, and maybe for a second Grace even tried to kick at me, but then I felt her legs relax.

I was instantly on my knees by the bed. *It's time for a neighborhood foot party. Time to downshift - but not too much. No light caressing, no nibbles - well, maybe a few nibbles - and remember that we're going for those home-run neural proximals. But don't get caught up in visualizing reflexology charts, because a woman's sexual self is more than just a pair of feet. Make it look like a bona fide foot rub. Don't just concentrate on those two small spots on her outer foot and a tiny bit of ganglia under her middle toe. C'mon. She mustn't suspect anything more than an honest massage, because if she busts you, it'll be as embarrassing as audibly counting half-thrusts during tantric doggystyle.*

Well, maybe a few light caresses are okay, but just for the sake of subterfuge. So, here we go!

* * *

- *Ummm...*
- *Er...*
- *Hmmm.*
- **That's curious.**
- *Women usually try to fake those. God knows we've run a gamut of sexual thespians.*
- **But...we've never seen a woman attempt to *hide* one.**
- *Hiding it appears to be as futile as faking it.*
- Ugh. Well, this is aw-w-w-kward.
- *Maybe this is what it's like for a woman when a*

guy blows his wad too soon.
- She just sniffed. Or was that a sniffle? Yes, that was definitely a sniffle. Now she's covering her face. Now she's shaking.
- *Oh. My. God. She's the crying kind.*
- OhMyGodOhMyGodOHMYFUCKINGGOD...
- WhatShoulWeDoWhatShouldWeDoWHAT SHOULDWEDO?!
- *Okay. Deep breath. Think. Fucking think, damn it!*
- Alright. Alright. We know what to do.

I jump up. Stupid cock. It's still a Vaguera tent pole, but swaying around from the base when I move too fast. Kinda painful. No matter.

I pull up the blankets and begin to wrap Grace's naked body. She tries to fight me off, which isn't too hard, since I have to keep my erect and waving penis well away from her swats and kicks. I don't give up, however, and soon she is bundled up. I pull off the bedspread and cover my own nakedness.

Grace looks like a big Baby Jesus in a tightly-wrapped Xanadu swaddling cloth. Her hair is a black tangle and her eyes are red from tears, but at least she's stopped crying. Grace gives me a *WTF?* look. That's good. She doesn't seem so fragile anymore. I want to see the tough Grace again, but we're not quite there yet. So, first I cradle her, and then I squeeze her. I try to think of something to say, but I come up with nothing. I get the hair out of her face and wipe her eyes. Then I squeeze her some more. I still can't think of anything to say.

"Get me out of this straightjacket, idiot."

I quickly unroll the makeshift blanket-cocoon.

"Gimme a minute, huh?"

I leave Grace sitting on the side of the bed and facing the curtained window. I go into the bathroom. Instead of having a military-style romp with the shower curtain, I sit on the edge of the tub, read the labels on little shampoo bottles, and wonder how long my fake hard-on will last.

* * *

After a few minutes Grace calls me out of the bathroom. "Get back in here," she orders.

I leave the bathroom. Grace is standing naked with her hands on her hips. "I'm not sure what you just did to me," she says, "but that was one of the hardest and weirdest orgasms that I've ever had. I wanted to get my money's worth out of that Vaguera, but now I can't decide if I want to chop off your balls and use them for earrings, or if you've turned me into a first-hit junkie." Grace glares at me and jerks her thumb toward the bed. "Well, we're gonna find out."

As I obediently approach the bed, I realize that Grace won't be able to use my balls for earrings because I dare to respond in a way that indicates my testicles are far too large for practical use as jewelry.

"The first hit is always free," I say.

Her Hooks
And Her
Grace

- I can't believe that we still come to this place.
- *Why? Did you think that our lives would be completely transformed after we had our first years of teaching under our belts?*
- Well...maybe I had some assumptions, yeah. But... The Anchor-on-Crown? Still? When will we finally get to shed the college scene?
- *Well, give it time.*
- I have. All I've learned from that is, given enough time, life tends to sour.
- *Jesus, Grace! This is supposed to be a celebration, remember? And us for "souring", that's when you throw out the entire batch and start over - which is what you've done. None of your angry divorce talk tonight. New city, new career, new life. Copy?*
- *Copy?* For all of *your* talk about new beginnings, your lexicon is certainly full of past-life leftovers. I'm sorry, though. You're right. Cheers! Hooray for us!
- *Cheers! We made it. We really did. And we both got picked up for next year, too.*
- So what are your closing arguments regarding Addelier Elementary?
- *Mmmm...that's a tough summary. It was all I could do to keep my head above water this first year. How about three pros and three cons?*
- Okay. Cons first.
- *Number one: the idiotic DARE cops!*
- Ha ha! I agree! What pissed you off the most?
- *Well, my Monday mornings were totally shot to hell. Almost no instructional time! This idiot got up in front of my kids in his fucking black Gestapo uniform - which in itself seemed weird, because I thought that the standard LVPD outfits were khaki -*

anyway, he yelled and gestured and spluttered about the "evils" of marijuana and told the kids that they had to write special tattle-tale notes on their parents if they had drugs or if the kids thought that their parents were doing something wrong... my God. It was like he wanted to turn my class into a bunch of little informants. It was just sickening.

- Amen, Jack. Nothing to add. Next?
- *Next? Ummm...oh yeah. The special education teacher drove me crazy. I had a class of twenty-seven kids, and one-third of them were classed as SPED! I know my kids, and I can tell you that it was a stretch to ID all of those children as needing IEPs. Their work was as good as that of the rest of the class and they got along fine with their peers. Yet I lost nine kids for half a day, every day. The make-up work and "mainstream-adaptive" nonsense made me tear my hair out.*
- Well, you know why it's like that, don't you?
- *No. Why?*
- Because each one of those kids in the SPED catchment was worth three times as much to the district in terms of federal dollars. If a kid gets caught in the special education trap, regardless of actual ability, there's no way he or she can escape.
- *Some of my fellow teachers said that, too.*
- And lastly?
- *Admin.*
- Ah yes. Admin. "The Ones who wield the paperwork nit-combs."
- *Ha! No shit. That's good. They were always sending back my lunch requests and roll forms for the smallest nonsense.*
- Yes. I went through all of that, too. Okay, now the good parts.
- *The good parts are easy. Brittany, Max, and Kiana.*
- Kids, right?
- *Yeah. I'm sure that you had your favorites too, and for the same reasons: sweet, kind, helpful, and hard workers.*
- I had Ellen, Mai, and Rambo.
- *Uh, "Rambo"?*

352

- Yeah. There's a big Cambodian immigrant community up near Bridger Elementary. "Rambo" is actually a common name for Khmer boys, but in their culture, it doesn't refer to a 'roid-head running through a jungle with a machine gun.

You Can Concern Yourself
With Bigger
Things

Grace and I drove out to the Lake Meade Overton Lookout. The lookout area was as deserted as it had been when I was a kid, and if I had gone over to one of the trashcans with a flashlight, I wouldn't have been surprised to find one of the soda bottles that I had placed there in my childhood.

Silly sex. That's what it was, and it had been great. I fucked Grace on the hood of the Mercedes, in the moonlight, and under my own steam - no Vaguera required. It was so much fun. Just....*silly*...and fun. Grace laid back on the hood and rested her calves on my shoulders while I stood in front of the bumper. We stayed in that position until I pulled out, squirted the hood and Grace's belly, and let out a bizarre howl that sounded like a coyote on helium. Grace laughed.

I flopped down beside Grace, just as she stuck her hand in a big wad. She shook her head and gave me a wet slap across the chest. "Nice shooting, Wild Bill," Grace chided. "I'm sure that's just *terrific* for the paint. Why am I even here if you just wanted to have sex with the car?"

* * *

The desert night was silent, except for the small and distant voices of an all-night boating party far below. Grace and I dozed in each other's arms until the sun began to creep over the Nevada mountains. Then we sluggishly began to stir and reach for our clothes.

I glanced skyward as I picked up my shirt. Some jets had passed in the night and the sky was criss-crossed with lines. Grace hadn't seen me look up, but she caught my shocked expression.

"What? *What?!* Snake? Did you just see a snake?" Grace climbed back onto the hood and leaned over to survey the ground.

"A snake? No."
"What is it, then?"
"I don't know for certain. Can I ask you something?"
"What?"
"Look up at those jet trails."
"What about them?"
"What color are they?"
"Color?"
"Yeah. Just tell me how they look to you."
Grace studied the sky for a moment. "Maybe... maybe *pinkish*. I'm not sure. It's kind of hard to tell until the sun comes all the way up. Why are you so freaked?"
"I'm not. I just..."
"You just *what?*"
I shrugged. "I don't know. Forget it."

*　*　*

Grace wanted to drive back into Vegas, which was kind of odd. She usually insisted that *I* take the wheel.

- *Jack, I need to tell you something.*
- What?
- *I...I've been talking to my parents.*
- Okay. What's going on with them?
- *They want me to move back to Asheville.*
- What?
- *I said: They want me to move back to Asheville.*
- Why? Vegas is where your job is. Your grandma is here, too. Aren't you the only family that she has out here?
- *No, no. I have an older cousin who's married and lives in Vegas. But that's not the point.*
- You mean...you're actually considering it?
- *They're my family, Jack. Jack?*
- I'm listening. I don't understand. You can't be serious.
- *I know it's hard for you, Jack. I know. I can't question them, though. In my culture, that's how it is.*
- But you once told me your dad insisted that your family was an *American* family. How can they

dictate to you like this?

- *Maybe we're Americans only until the Korean part kicks in.*
- Well, I'm *all* American, and I want you to stay. I want you to stay *here,* and I want you to stay with *me.* Or, you know what? I'll compromise. I'll give up the *here* part, if I can keep the *you* part. Maybe I'd even like the Carolinas. Who knows?
- *Jack...*
- I can get a teaching license in the Asheville district. Sure! Is that in North Carolina or South Carolina?
- *Jack...I don't think that you understand. There are some things in my culture that are done in certain ways. My divorce wasn't one of them, but now things could be...different for me. For my family's reputation.*
- What do you mean?
- *I mean...they want me to meet a Korean guy.*

14

- The plane is ten miles out, Mr. Vice President. Do the orders still stand?

- Of course the orders still stand! Have you heard anything to the contrary?!

Fucking moron.

Chankiri Trees In The
Sky With Diamond
Chemtrails

05/MAR/97

Hi

I've been thinking about you lately, and I hope that I have the right address. I don't mean for this letter to be an awkward intrusion, but if there's some way for you to give word that you're okay, it would mean a lot to me. My number and e-mail are still the same, so if phone and internet services ever come back, please don't hesitate to contact me. I'm still at the same mailing address on Lone Mountain, too. You don't have to give me any details about your life, and I won't ask. I only want to know that you're okay.

I think that the last time I sent an actual paper letter was when I wrote to my grandpa from Korea. I figured that I'd better send a letter to you soon, because I've heard rumors that the Postal Service might cut back or even close down.

I guess we're going to war again. I thought that the first Gulf War was the end of that nonsense. I understand why people want to retaliate for the World Trade Center, but I'm not too sure that I see the wisdom in going to war when things are getting worse and worse Stateside. There's a pediatric plague going on, yet our fearless leaders are about to invade a country on the other side of the world? Morons.

Also, I thought that the hijackers were all Saudis, right? I don't understand why the USA is going to attack Iraq (AGAIN) because of something that a bunch of Saudis did. I'm glad that I'm not on active duty anymore, because I'd hate to get abandoned in the Middle East if the USA fell apart and couldn't bring me home.

Do you still get TV or radio news where you are? It's getting harder and harder to find out what's going on here. The TV is dead, but I can still tune into a few radio stations.

Things in Vegas are getting pretty crazy. There was

a huge fire in the Mandalay Bay and The Strip is practically a ghost town.

Some of my kids are gone. I assume that you've been through that, as well. I pray that your family hasn't experienced a loss. People are saying that it's some kind of smallpox. I've spoken to senior citizens who agree that it looks like smallpox, but it isn't like any kind of smallpox that they can remember. It strikes so fast. The kids that I've lost started the day fine, but by the afternoon some were gone. The blisters raise up over their skin in minutes, even before the EMTs get to my classroom. I don't know what your situation is like on the east coast, but here they tell us that there isn't any vaccine stockpiled because everybody thought that smallpox had been wiped out.

I don't know what the city and district officials are thinking, and most of all, I don't understand these parents! If I were them, I'd put my kids into a car and head for the hills. The radio stations keep saying that everything is fine, and that the outbreaks are just "isolated events", but that's bullshit. Kids are dropping everywhere. Everybody can see it, but they just act like robots or sheep or something. I can't even talk to people about what's going on, because they either deny it and change the subject or just turn away. Even Principal Kuhntlass at Addelier did that to me! I tried to ask that evil bitch what was going on, but she just told me that I "needed to get on the right side of history and stop asking questions." What does that mean? WHAT DOES THAT MEAN?!

I'm not sure how much longer this situation is going to continue for me. CCSD has been laying off teachers in droves, so I guess that I'll stay in Vegas until they let me go. I'm not sure what I'll do after that. I don't think that anyone is sure of anything nowadays.

God bless you and keep you, Grace, wherever you are. I hope we meet again someday.

Jack

Not Quite A
Year Since
She Went
Away

March
1997

I don't even live in this neighborhood anymore, yet here I am, sitting at a bus stop on Russell Road, and watching the McKarran jets take off. There aren't many, though. It's more like I'm just *waiting* for the jets to take off. The airport used to be such a hub.

The valley classrooms are now emptying, hopefully in part because terrified parents of surviving little ones are *finally* keeping them home from school or desperately trying to get them out of Los Vegas. Ambulances have stopped running in this part of town, but I can still hear them wail from afar. Poorer folk can't afford the bribes, and there are fewer places to take the sick kids, anyway. The children's hospital at Desert Sunrise has turned away patients for a couple weeks. Last Thursday I heard that some desperate parents went in and shot up the Student Services Clinic at ULVN, but I don't know if anyone was killed because local radio news doesn't get much play. I'm actually kind of surprised to have heard about the clinic incident since most services at ULVN are shut down.

The perfect-hair-telepromptoids who sat behind news desks and announced the latest hotel shows and celebrity Strip sightings are gone. My TV just makes white noise. Somebody from Governor Gwynn's staff is on every radio station repeating the same crap about how we all need to stay calm. The Feds, or, more precisely, Nellis Public Affairs Officer Major Eden Sheldon and Staff Sergeant Scarlett Martes do the intros and outros for canned FEMA clips. It's tough to keep abreast of local matters, and except for late-night radio, it's almost impossible to get info about the rest of the country. I scout around the after-dark AM dial to hear skips from California and Arizona, but it's all pretty much the same: recordings from state governors, followed by terse martial instructions from local military bases.

I'm shamefully selfish. I'm a grown man, sitting at a bus stop, and crying in public...though that's very common now. It's the *reason* why I'm crying that marks me as a disgrace. I'm not crying because it really looks like the world is coming down. I'm not crying because there will be many young faces missing from future family albums.

Grace left almost a year ago.

I'm a selfish man, and I'm crying for a selfish reason.

It's All Relative To The
~~Size Of Your Steeple~~
Trance Of Your
Sheeple

April
1997
(1-of-2)

Historically, the lesser form of smallpox had about a five percent death rate, whereas the more virulent strain took roughly one-third of its victims. Sometime between 1975 and 1997, after the UN had declared smallpox eradicated, the virus likely experienced a covert *Plum-Island-Fifty-Percent-Mortality-Extreme-Makeover,* after which state health departments, backed by cops and National Guard units, started to haul lime and operate bulldozers along highways outside American cities.

* * *

There were two calls that I made from my apartment on Lone Mountain Road early every morning, starting from when the kids began to get sick. Before I put on my backpack and pedaled to work, I picked up the phone and made a call to the CCSD Ed Shed on Flamingo to find out if the district had been shut down. The second call was to Addelier Elementary itself, to ask if the school was open. Ed Shed personnel got nasty with me early on when I started to call (my guess was that hundreds of teachers were doing the same), and sometimes I couldn't get through. Camille at the front desk always picked up at Addelier, however. I was told the same thing, every day, from both sources: Yes, the district was operating, and **yes**, Addelier Elementary School was on its regular schedule.

- *Yes, there's a pandemic raging among the children, and we're right on track. **Yes**, parents, keep sending your children to school. **Yes**, teachers, keep coming to work. Don't ask questions. Just do it. Do it, do it, do it.*
- Okay, okay, okay. **Baa-aa, baa-aa, baa-aa.**

Destroy Another Fetus
Now - We Don't
Like Children
Anyhow

April
1997
(2-of-2)

CCSD classroom roll sheets were legal documents and there were particular ways in which they had to be filled out. When a child went to school, his or her name received an accompanying red diagonal line, top left to bottom right, in a roll sheet date box. In the case of an absence, the box was marked with an additional red diagonal line, top right to bottom left. The number of red "X"s on my roll sheets increased every day.

* * *

Principal Kuhntlass came out to my portable and gave me a district surplus notification on the afternoon before Addelier's track break was to begin. As she handed over the letter, Kuhntlass offered some pat and plastic condolences and assured me that I would soon get picked up again in one of the other CCSD Vegas regions. The speech was obviously one that Kuhntlass had kept on mental file for too long because it didn't reflect the new reality. Maybe the things she said had been true in the past, but either Kuhntlass hadn't picked up a paper or turned on a radio lately, or she just didn't give a damn.

I wasn't shocked to lose my job. It was anticipated, though in light of what was happening, who cared about a teaching position? It was like that old Gerry Seinfield routine in which the comic joked about laundry detergent commercials...except this time it wasn't funny:

If you're wearing a tee-shirt covered in blood, maybe laundry ISN'T your biggest problem...

Yeah, I had lost my job. Big deal. Unemployment

wasn't my biggest problem, just as the USA would have been in much better stead if unemployment had represented *its* biggest problem. Or a war. Or even unemployment *and* a war.

After Kuhntlass had delivered her "you're laid off, pack your things and get out" speech, she started toward the door.

"Just one question before you go, Principal Kuhntlass."

She stopped. "What?"

"Why didn't the district close the schools before it came to this? Especially when they figured out that it was smallpox?"

Kuhntlass exuded contempt. "I've explained that already," she replied, in the coldest voice I had ever heard. "You should have looked around and gotten on the right side of history. Turn in your keys and district badge to Camille when you leave." Kuhntlass slammed the door on her way out.

The classroom was perfectly silent, but I thought that I heard other principals and other superintendents, not just in the Vegas Valley, but everywhere, answering other teachers with the same words that Kuhntlass had used to answer me.

* * *

I was still in the classroom two hours later. I finished packing a few final bits and pieces into a box and paused, sat down behind my former desk, and stared at one of the bulletin boards. I had liked to post the kids' good grades and art and whatnot on the classroom walls, but children disappeared so quickly that I had to decide whether or not to remove papers, either when a student stopped appearing in class, or was taken away by EMTs. I ultimately decided to keep all of the work up, regardless of whether or not the child was present.

There had been a couple of times when I had felt my mind buckle, and *I* wasn't the one bearing the brunt of *real* loss! Being a teacher and losing a student wasn't comparable to what parents went through. Mine was only a sample of other people's sadness. I was just a spectator, or maybe a reporter, and I conducted interviews about situations that I couldn't fully experience. I didn't see the young parents crying in bed at night. I didn't feel the silence and emptiness over breakfast. I was merely Mr. Slmmerath, the second-year fifth grade teacher in portable number three, who crossed out names on roll sheets and tried to keep the remaining scared kids talking and functioning. When parents came to my classroom to clean out desks and cubbies, I dared not ask questions or even try to express how sorry I was. My manner was like that of a silent intern or nurse who takes next of kin to an empty hospital room to remove personal effects.

As I looked around my classroom for the last time, Kuhntlass' words suddenly made terrible sense - but only for a nanosecond, because I simply couldn't accept it. What I had suspected and what I had feared, as well as the "dragon tails" that Grandpa had warned me about long ago, came together in a realization that I desperately **WANTED TO DENY.**

There had to be something else going on. There was some other answer.

I was crazy.

I was just a ridiculous conspiracy theorist.

Yeah. That was better. It wasn't the world. It was me, and I absolutely insisted upon being wrong.

The kids who disappeared from my class weren't absent due to 'pox, because their parents had kept them home to avoid the disease.

So they were okay!

And what's more, there were probably lots of parents who had ignored the official news reports and government reassurances and wisely decided to keep their children home! Right?

Right...?

BS101: INTRO TO AMERICAN DENIAL TECHNIQUES

Three Credits

No Prerequisite

Baa-aa, baa-aa

15

"Once In Every Generation A Plague Shall Fall Among Them." That's What It Says In The Book. Seems Like You Maybe...Went A *Little Too Far* This Time.

JP-8 For A Penny, Barium And Aluminum For Tuppence, Clean Graves For Nothing

August 1997

I don't know if I've received a patent royalty deposit in the last three months because I've been locked out of my credit union account. I had a little cash-stash outside, but it's almost gone. I can't find out when or if financial institutions are going to reopen, but I suspect that if my money isn't in my hand, then it doesn't exist - meaning that, when my pocket cash is gone, I'll be destitute. I can stay in my apartment until the end of next month, but then, barring income from a replacement job...hello streets.

Damn. All of the money that I had saved from my teaching job was in the credit union. Why can't anyone get some news? The only things on the radio are those stupid military announcements and the president's recorded speeches. Yes, we're fucked. I get it. The kids are dying. Everything is falling apart. *Stay-calm-stay-calm-stay-calm.* I FUCKING GET IT...but would somebody PLEASE explain to me why some things - like banks and credit unions, for instance - have to shut down? I mean, the tellers, loan officers, and presidents weren't unvaccinated kids! The generational human resources that were running society are mostly still here. The old vaccinated pre-1971-model humans are still on their feet; therefore, most of our economic infrastructure should still function.

Key word: **"should"**

Whom Necessity
Had Made A
Gambler

September
1997

I stand outside of a Greener Valley Grocery on Lone
Mountain and wonder if I should buy something. My
apartment tap still works, but I need food. There are
canned goods in this convenience store, so maybe I
should get some. Greener Valley Groceries also carry
milk and eggs, which is kind of unexpected because
those things are scarce in larger groceries. The expense
is also greater, and I might not have enough cash.
Maybe I'll only get some canned beans or something.

I stop to read the door postings before I go inside. I
need to find a shitty survival job. I worked at a Greener
Valley Grocery before I enlisted. Maybe I should ask
about hours at *this* store.

"S'cuse me pal," someone says. "There's nobody in
the back. I need to use the front door."

I turn and see a guy who wears an orange
Andersonville Dairy uniform. He's white, about five-ten,
maybe a couple of years older than me, and lucky
enough to still have a job. He pushes a milk crate dolly
and I'm blocking his way. "Sorry," I mutter, as I step
aside and hold the door. A couple minutes later he re-
emerges with an empty dolly.

"Still looking?" he asks.

"Yeah," I reply, as I go back to perusing the ads.

"Those are mostly for security guards."

"I'd be a guard." I expect the Andersonville man to
leave, but out of the corner of my eye I can see that he's
looking me over. *I'm not really in the mood for a gay
milkman right now,* I think. Then he asks a question that
assures me he's not looking for a date: "Can you handle
a 12 gauge?"

I look at the guy again. This time I notice that he has
a nasty butterflied split on his left cheek. Around the
split is a fading bruise that has turned from blue to a
reddish-orange color that almost matches his dairy

uniform.

"Yeah. I certed on the M12 in the military."

"M12?" he repeats. "I've heard of an M16, but not an M12."

"That was just the designation for old slam-fire Winchesters."

He nods. "A vet. Good. That means you don't have a problem getting up in the morning."

"Mornings aren't a problem. Empty days are."

He pauses. "All we have are double barrels. Is that alright?"

I shrug. "Mister, I'm not sure what we're talking about, but I can use a break-action too, if that's what you're asking."

"What did you do before?"

"I was a teacher over at Addelier." I gesture in the school's direction.

The man squints and cocks his head. "Is your name Sim - er, Sem--"

"Simmerath. Jack Simmerath. I had a fifth grade classroom before I got surplussed."

"My daughter Sandi went there. Miss Jordan's class. I've kept my kid locked up at home for about six months. No way in hell I'm letting her out until I'm sure the 'pox has passed." He sets the dolly upright and extends his hand. "Name's Mark Tipton."

I shake the milkman's hand. "What can I do for you, Mark?"

"Will you take minimum wage?"

"And count myself lucky."

"Good. I'll talk to my boss this afternoon. If you want a job, be here at four-thirty tomorrow morning with a pair of gloves. I'll bring the shotgun."

As I watch Tipton load his dolly and drive away, I wonder why I'll need a *shotgun* to work for a *dairy*.

Crawl While
The City
Sleeps

Andersonville dairy trucks were loaded by two-person teams. One individual drove a forklift onto the product rotation warehouse floor and used a hanging remote-stop switch to open a large cooling unit. Once the hydraulic doors on the cold locker were fully open, the forklift was used to move crate pallets. Each truck held three pallet loads, and between forklift trips the second person took dairy crates off of pallets and loaded them into the truck. Mark drove the forklift, and I loaded crates.

* * *

Mark and I took a delivery break. Before we got some coffee from the cafeteria, however, Mark gave me a tour of an unfamiliar dairy building. As we entered a large warehouse I noticed two diesel engines on thick concrete pads and five ten-foot-high metal mixing bowls. That's what they looked like to me, anyway.

"This is the pasteurization shed," Mark said. "How's your nose?"

I stopped. "What?"

Mark turned around and grinned. "How's your nose?"

"Er, fine, I guess. How's *yours?*"

Mark laughed. "I guess that it's been shut down long enough to air this place out. So you can't smell that?"

I sniffed. "What?"

"Back when the plant was up and running, the processing crews wore breathing masks in this area."

"Why? I thought you said that this was where the milk was pasteurized."

"It was. The smell was unbelievable. It was like wading through a sour phlegm swamp."

I grimaced. "I don't understand. It was just milk,

right?"

Mark rapped his knuckles on one of the huge bowls. "Well, yes and no. Big dairy processing plants have other concerns."

"Like cheese or something? I've heard that cheese-making smells bad...but I've never seen 'Andersonville Cheese' for sale."

"No, they didn't make cheese here. It was just that..." Mark paused and motioned for me to follow as he grabbed a chain and released a sliding metal ladder. I looked up and saw that it connected to a series of catwalks.

"The guys who worked here had tethers," said Mark, as he pointed at metal rails that ran parallel to the ladder and catwalks. "But I trust that you'll be careful."

I followed Mark up the ladder, across a catwalk, and onto an observation platform. It had a control panel that featured dials and stop switches. Below us and on the other side of the bowls were four stationary sealed tanks that were connected to twelve-inch double-valve pipes.

"Those are emergency antibody detection shunts," said Mark, as he pointed at the tanks. "Each one can completely divert a batch from the production chain before contamination spreads."

"What do you mean by 'contamination'?"

"Cattle diseases. Remember, this place stopped being an actual 'dairy' back on the 1940s. Andersonville is a processing center."

"But what kind of diseases?"

"Well..." Mark paused and scratched his head. "I guess bovine tuberculosis is the big one, because that's transmissible to humans. There's also brucellosis, and that's pretty bad, too."

"Brucellosis?"

"Yeah," said Mark. "Really nasty stuff. Symptoms like malaria, except it's bacterial. It also destroys men's balls."

"Bullshit."

"No, it's true," said Mark. "That's why this place had to be able to take an entire batch out of the chain."

"Didn't anybody check the milk before it got here?"

"Yeah, but dairy cattle can be latent carriers, and sometimes diseases can't be detected at feedlots." Mark scowled. "I kinda think that's just lobbyists talking through FDA and USDA puppets, though. The processing crews have to, or *had* to, do antibody sampling at every step. If there was a positive test, then whole batch got dumped."

I snorted. "Really? So they just flushed few thousand gallons of disease onto the ground?"

"No. The shunt tanks isolated everything while a particular production step was bypassed and disinfected. Then the company had to pay for disposal. But to be honest, it didn't happen that much, at least with the big diseases."

"And by 'much', you mean...?"

"Maybe once a year."

"And aside from 'big diseases', you mean...?"

"Well, cowpox would come through here fairly regularly."

"Cowpox?"

"Yeah - it's sort of like--" Mark paused and his voice lowered "--smallpox, but mostly harmless to people. Like chickenpox, I guess." Mark's eyes were on the floor. He took a breath, lifted his head, and forced his voice back to its usual tone. "Cowpox still had to come out of the chain, but it could be disposed on-site." Mark pointed at a tank on the end of the shunt row. "That one was for cowpox. It's seen more use than all of the other tanks combined."

"So that tank connected to a sewer drain?"

Mark smiled at my naiveté. "No. It piped to an incineration unit that was used for both cowpox and and heavy-dose product--"

"Sorry for so many questions," I interrupted, "but what does 'heavy dose' mean?"

"No problem. 'Heavy dose' is milk that was taken too soon after the cow's hormone injection cycle. You see, all of the commercial lot suppliers had to shoot up their animals with growth hormone in order to maintain production, but if product arrived with too much BGH expressed in the milk, it couldn't be used. And that," Mark said, as he pointed at the giant bowls, "was the purpose of the protein integrators." Knowing that I was about to ask yet another question, Mark continued: "A cow is just an animal, with an animal's limitations. There comes a point where drugs produce diminishing returns in terms of milk production and most of what comes out of the udder is a kind of mucous that separates from the calcium. It's like blood-streaked YK Jelly with flakes of white paint. It doesn't look like milk, and it can't be sold as milk. But, after seventy-two hours of low heat and automated hydraulic stirring, it's ready for the carton. While it's cooking, though, it smells like shit."

"That's...disgusting."

"No kidding. That's why I don't allow my little girl to drink milk. I don't want her to get her period before she loses her baby teeth. My wife, Linda, never let Sandi drink milk, either."

Hmmm, I thought. *"Never let." There's some pain behind that past tense.*

"Pasteurization isn't really to stop germs," Mark continued. "The secondary isolation system is for that. Pasteurization is used to make vats of drug-snot resemble milk. See, that's not what they teach kids." Mark did an embarrassed double-take. "Sorry. I know you used to be a teacher. No offense intended."

"None taken." I surveyed the bowls and tanks for a moment. "There's nothing going on in here."

"There's nothing going on in *any* of the processing sheds."

"So what are we delivering?"

"This past summer's milk. Once it's processed, the product can be held in cryo for months. Those 'expiration dates' on cartons are actually stamped far ahead of time. We're just emptying the cold storage units but not rotating anything in."

"How much more is there?"

Mark paused and looked up as he did some mental calculations. "Well...I'm trying to find another job within the next couple months." We were silent for a moment, then Mark looked at his watch. "Let's get some coffee," he said.

Share Some Greased Tea With Me

I only had to shoot at someone once during my stint with Andersonville, and that was with Grandpa's .22, not the 12 gauge. Mark had shown me how to make "cut shells" from regular double and triple buck loads, but I never felt the need to send homemade .72 caliber glasers through car doors. Instead, when some stupid punks had tried to run the truck off the road, I just hung my 10/22 out the window and laid down a fake rock-n-roll wrist spasm over the roof of their car. I had never bothered to learn how to expertly bumpfire a .22, but it was enough to scare the dipshits. There were a few wild shots behind us, but they didn't follow.

Mark and I were careful, especially in the predawn. In the dingy back lots of convenience stores there were dumpsters, grease traps, and box piles where thugs could hide. Mark told me that he had been jumped during his deliveries, and that was why his face had been so jacked up when we met. Milk thieves! *Lame.* Mark said that when he woke up on the pavement behind a Greener Valley Grocery he still had his wallet and the truck was idling. They had knocked him out and taken a couple crates.

Mark expressed disdain for his attackers' criminal non-genius: "I mean, why not rob me? Or take the entire truck? *You know?* They could have cleaned me out."

I thought for a moment. "Maybe they were new at it. The way things are going, otherwise honest people might not have the experience to pull off things like pros, but they're pushed into it."

"Yeah, I suppose." Mark pulled into a dark predawn lot and made a circular headlight sweep before he stopped the truck. "Anything?" he asked.

I shook my head. "Clear."

We got out of the truck and approached the store's back door. Mark rapped on the metal and pressed his work ID against a small window. I heard a bolt and key on the other side, and then a flood of light hit the back sidewalk as the door opened.

"Mornin'," said a young Hispanic man in slacks and a blue dress shirt. He was wearing a red-and-green Greener Valley Grocery stocker's apron that didn't quite cover the grip of his holstered Glock. "Just setting up some shelves when I heard you knock. I hope you weren't waiting too long."

"Good morning," Mark and I said in unison. I looked around the guy's work area. A boxcutter and a pen were on the floor, along with a handbasket full of random shelf items.

"Is Perri here?" asked Mark.

"Yeah, up front. I'll get her."

Semi-autos and minimum wage, I thought. *When everything goes to shit, everyone needs, or becomes, a security guard. I wonder what his* real *job was before the meltdown?*

A tall and attractive blonde girl, about the same age as Mr. Glocker-Stocker, came to the back. She nodded in recognition at Mark and gave an *I'm-tired-as-hell-but-always-friendly* smile. Her name tag read: *PERRI T. - LAS VEGAS - MANAGER.*

"Whatcha got for me today, Mr. Andersonville?"

"Four crates," replied Mark. "Same place?"

"Yeah, same--no, on second thought, you can have the top and middle racks of the walk-in."

"That's more space than this delivery needs," observed Mark.

"The last shipment of canned soda is gone, and I don't know where more is coming from," said Perri T. "The only drinks we sell now are milk and bottled water." Mark headed for the back door as Perri T. sadly shook her head. After a moment she stopped, looked at me, and spoke in a sharp voice. "They're called boobs," she said. "All girls have them. Trust me."

"I, uh, er," I stammered, "I was just reading your name tag and wondering if 'Las Vegas' is misspelled, or if you're from New Mexico."

I got an *it's-really-none-of-your-business* look, but Perri T. put on a fiberglass smile and humored me. "Neither," she said. I'm actually from Winnemucca, and my name tag was wrong when I got it. I just never fixed it." There was a pause. "Andersonville doesn't seem to issue name tags at all," Perri T. noted, as she looked at my stained and ill-fitting orange shirt. "And you are?"

"Jack. My name's Jack S."

Perri T. studied me for a moment, then bemusedly held out her hand. "Nice to meet you, Jack S."

I shook her hand with embarrassed hesitation. "Um, nice to meet you, too, Perri T."

Perri T.'s corvette-face disappeared. Maybe the smile that replaced it wasn't fake, but it was only as real as anything else in Los Vegas.

*   *   *

After we had unloaded the truck and were preparing to leave, Mark commented on my homemade rifle sling. "That's a new use for duct tape," he grinned.

"Yeah, well...I just want to keep this on my back all the time. Frees up my hands to help with the load, too."

"I appreciate your alertness."

"Thanks. These early mornings are tough, though. I wish that I had some coffee at home. I ran out about a week ago."

"Coffee? I think there are still some cans in the cafeteria kitchen. You should take one. Or two."

"Just walk out with it?"

"Sure, before someone else does. Breakfast and lunch stopped a couple months ago when the processing crews got laid off. The rest of us have been taking food home. If you see anything else you want, just grab it. Management is going to lock up the kitchen soon."

"Alright," I answered, as I lifted the dolly into the back of the truck. "You're gonna have to point out the cafeteria. The only places I've ever seen are the office, loading bay, and processing shed."

"Okay. I'll give you the grand kitchen tour."

"Mostly I'd just like some coffee," I said, as I closed the truck's rear door.

As Smooth As A Young Cordwainer's Skin

October 1997 (3-of-3)

I score an unopened can of Pholgers, but the cafeteria detour makes us a little late in returning to the loading docks. There's only one other truck besides ours, but the two guys who drive it aren't going anywhere. A skinny and enraged old Asian man and his .45 are seeing to that.

Crap, I think. *Is this a robbery? Or is this bad acid with a 1911? Dude seems to be a little old to be an acid freak, though. But he most definitely appears to be crazy.*

Of all the stupid times to leave my .22 in the cab...

Shit.

The other crew is face down, hands behind their heads, and very willing to surrender whatever is wanted...but they have no idea what is wanted. There are two open wallets on the ground, but these just seem to make the old man angrier. While he screams and stomps on the wallets, I drop the coffee can, grab Mark's arm, and try to pull him back. Oops. Too late. Mister .45-A-Saurus' vision must be based on movement, because he spins toward us.

"Down!" screams the man as he raises his weapon. Mark and I hit the ground. The guy doesn't have to tell us to put our hands behind our heads as he dashes over. "Sick cow!" he yells. "Sick cow place! Sick milk place!"

"What the hell...?" Mark murmurs. "What is this guy after?" Mark raises his head. "Okay! Okay! Just tell me what you want!"

The man looks at Mark and slightly lowers the .45. "The safe place," he says.

"Payroll," I whisper.

"No!" screams the man, as he delivers a bruising kick

to my ribs.

"Wait a minute," says Mark, in a tone of realization. Then, in a much louder voice: "Sick milk!"

Again, the man seems to rein in his rage, and the gun lowers. "Yes! Sick milk place!"

"I know the sick milk place," replies Mark.

The pistol rises, and the man's voice is a growl. "You obey me! No trick. You obey me, or die!"

Mark slowly gets to his feet. "Yes. I know the sick milk place."

Sick milk? I hope that Mark knows what this guy wants, because I certainly don't. I hear the doors slam on the other crew's truck and its engine roars. The old man doesn't even turn around.

"Okay. Yes. I'll obey you," says Mark.

"Yes," says the man. He looks down at me. "Go together."

Like Mark, I arise in slow motion. We still have our hands over our heads.

"The processing shed?" I whisper.

"No," breathes Mark. "A little veterinary lab." Mark speaks up. "Yes," he says to the old man. "I'll take you."

The old man looks at Mark for a moment and then motions for us to start walking.

* * *

Mark and I were back on the road thirty minutes later.

"Jesus," I remarked, as I ran my hand through my hair and looked out the window.

Mark blew a raspberry and shook his head. "Drama at the dairy," he said.

"*Crazy* drama at the dairy. What the fuck just happened? Some old weirdo goes ape shit and steals disease samples from a vet lab? What the hell is he gonna do with that? Get tuberculosis? Or that other thing that rots your nuts off?"

"Brucellosis."

"Yeah! What the fuck?"

"I don't know," said Mark. "But he didn't actually take the Bruce or TB. He only wanted the cowpox samples."

The Thief That Men Fear

I met Mark at the Greener Valley Grocery before sunup. We filled Perri T.'s cooler and delivered to the other stores. Mark acted...strangely. All of the caution that he usually exercised was absent. No lot checks. No concern about unfamiliar cars. Nothing. He just drove up to loading doors and got out. Mark didn't say anything to the store managers and he didn't have much to say to me, either.

We returned to the dairy after our early run, but Mark didn't pull the truck into the load line. He just turned off at the edge of the employee lot and killed the engine. I looked at Mark, but all he said was: "Lunchtime. We'll load up after." He got out of the truck without closing the door and walked to the cafeteria.

I also got out, went over to the driver's side, and shut the door. The kitchen was mostly empty, so I didn't know what Mark intended to eat. Usually we brought our own low-budget lunches or picked up canned food during deliveries. It wasn't even lunchtime yet. What the hell was Mark doing?

I wasn't sure what to do, so I watched the other delivery trucks load up while I waited for Mark to return.

I suddenly remembered the times when Mark had mentioned his little daughter.

I ran to the cafeteria.

* * *

Andersonville Dairy's commercial kitchen was like chow halls and student unions everywhere, except for the dead man who hung between a dough-riser rack and an overturned cellophane cart. Mark had stood on the cart and kicked it out from under himself. His noose was

380

a Hobart mixer's heavy power cord. A scrawled sheet of paper taped to the front of Mark's shirt explained everything:

THERE IS NO SMALLPOX IN HEAVEN
SANDI AND LINDA SEE YOU SOON

Mark had done his best, but just keeping his child at home apparently hadn't been enough to hold Shakpana at bay. I considered Mark's suicide note for a moment. "He wasn't Catholic," I murmured, as I went to tell a supervisor that either the cops, who probably wouldn't show up, or the contact in Mark's file needed to be reached. *And I guess he wasn't divorced, either,* I thought, as I left the kitchen.

Whale
Syrup

My milkman career ended in the place where it started.

* * *

Interesting synchronicity, or coincidence, or correlation, or...whatever. Perri T. is hanging a "CLOSED" sign on the door of the Greener Valley Grocery as the sun comes up. I start to get back in the truck, but I turn around when hear the door open.

"I knocked on the rear door," I say, "but nobody was there."

"It's just me, and I'm locking up."

"Oh. I didn't know that this place was closing."

"The shelves are bare, but there are still a few things in the back...if you want to have a look."

"Uh, sure," I say, as I step inside. I confirm that the store is empty as Perri T. leads me down an aisle.

"Done, huh?"

"Yup."

"Funny timing. This was the last delivery of my last run."

"What's next for you?"

"No idea. You?"

"Same."

There are some boxes in the storeroom that contain paper plates and plastic knives. A split bag of briquettes lies on the floor. I only see bits and pieces of convenience store junk that I don't need and can't use.

"Anything you want?"

I shake my head. As I take a step backward, she takes a step forward.

"Anything?" she repeats.

* * *

We engage in some perfunctory kissing that lasts for about ten seconds before she breaks away and walks to the front of the store. I hear the *clicks* of the top and bottom door locks. Perri T. returns to the storeroom and opens the deactivated cooler's back stock door. We step inside and the kissing resumes for roughly eight seconds before I lift her shirt and flip the cups of her bra up over her boobs. Each mam is groped for an average of four seconds before I turn Perri T. around. My hands reach around to the snap and zipper on her jeans while she sticks her ass out and grips the empty shelf racks.

I've never been the kind of guy who likes to spit on his dick or especially enjoys having his dick spat upon, but for a standing-rear-mount-quickie it's kind of standard procedure, along with the spreading of ass cheeks and labia and working the spittle up-and-down with the head of your cock until the woman's lips are slick and ready. A slight additional spreading precedes the initial thrust, and with a rush and a push, England and an empty Greener Valley Grocery cooler are ours. There follow a couple minutes of strangers panting together, then a pull out, and bursts of creamy silly string are shot across Perri T.'s ass and lower back.

Then I realize that I'm not wearing a condom.

What the hell is wrong with me?!

I'm gonna pay for this.

16

So You're Telling Me That 41 Was A Teenage SS Infiltrator Who Later Married Aleister Crowley's Daughter? I Guess... That Explains A Few Things About America

In Baltimore,
Jack

December
1997
(1-of-3)

There was a problem in my apartment. The tap had stopped running and the water that I had kept in my bathtub was gone. I had a quart of water in a plastic bottle and a half-jar of tequila. That was all.

There was a problem outside my apartment. My delivery job didn't exist anymore and Vegas grew increasingly dangerous.

There was a problem inside me. When I laid down on the bed I gasped from a sharp pain that shot straight down the center of my cock and under my balls like a hot metal chopstick had been rammed up my urethra. My hands instinctively pressed my crotch and I rocked until the pain faded.

I took a deep breath and slowly relaxed on the bed. This is what happens when you fuck a stranger in the back of a convenience store without a condom. Along with locating a new water supply, I also had to find some antibiotics...or consider hiking out to the mountains, where I knew a large stash of hermetically sealed medicine awaited.

Damn. The ghost of an infectious and long-forgotten barracks shower curtain had finally tracked me down.

* * *

Three bullets came through my apartment wall. The first projectile was a big slow slug - maybe a .45ACP - and it didn't exit the small portable TV that it knocked off of a shelf. I was jolted awake but had the presence of mind to roll out of bed and onto the floor. The other two bullets, not striking anything except drywall, passed all the way through my place.

I stayed on the floor for about five minutes but nothing followed. I hadn't even heard a weapon discharge, though I doubted that anyone was going to the trouble of using a silencer. More likely, the shots had been fired from inside another house or apartment, the walls of which had absorbed most of the report.

It could have been my guts, rather than the TV's shattered glass, lying on the floor.

Why did I even *have* a TV? Because I thought that someday sitcoms would be back on the air? Was the dark and silent device an idol for my unuttered prayers and my hopes that someday things would return to normal? *Was* the world going to come back? *Were* things going to turn around? As I looked at the fractured plastic housing and triangular shards of broken screen, I knew that the dead electronic god had given me an answer. It certainly wasn't the answer that I wanted, but at least the universe wasn't bullshitting me.

Grace was gone. Grandpa had been gone for a long time. I had once thought that at this point I'd be married, grading papers, and attending staff functions, not dodging bullets, suffering from an STD, and solo-boozing in multi-block blackouts. The post-apocalyptic slope looked downright greasy, and I didn't need Vyggo Mortensen and his cinematic son to walk down Lone Mountain Road and give me a wakeup call.

I could have been hit by those slugs. I could be dead on the floor.

It was time to get scarce.

I dressed and went to my closet. I put on my old mo-pack, which contained enough supplies for a three-day walk, even though I knew that I wouldn't actually be traveling that long on my bicycle.

* * *

My bike had a cheap knock-off *ní'ìvì* rack that I used to rest the mo-pack low on my back, yet well above the overinflated rear tire. My 10/22 was stuffed in, muzzle-down. Along with my supplies, I also had Grandpa's pocket watch and his pictures. I would never need to return.

Urban bicycle travel, especially at night, wasn't bad, stealth-wise. I could pedal faster than a man could run, especially since I was motivated by fear, and my silent bike enabled me to hear far ahead. I took evasive detours when I spotted torches and occasional piles of burning tires and wooden pallets.

I almost stayed. I had wavered in the open apartment doorway, handlebars in hand, second-guessing myself. Bullet holes, busted TV, no job, no rent, major violence escalating all over town...yet I still had a moment of doubt.

Get out while you still can, and under cover of darkness, I told myself. *Get to the mountains. You know where. Just do it. Your little infection problem will be solved...if you're tough enough to ride a bike with a raging case of drip.*

You can do a lot of thinking on a bicycle, especially when you need to keep your mind off of the fire ants inside your dick. It was time to take a ride to the darkness at the edge of town. It was time to take a wrong turn and just keep going, and maybe somewhere in the night I'd find a bottle of zythro and a volleyball that bore a bloody hand print.

The Pickin's Have Been Lush And Yet
Before The Evening Is Over
You Might Give
Me The
Brush

December
1997
(2-of-3)

The moon was The Strip's brightest light.

* * *

The pines that had once grown on the eastern "shore" of Lake Bellagio stood dry, dead, and naked over thin sidewalk blankets of fallen yellow needles. I noted that someone had half-chopped, then torn, one of the trees out of its sidewalk slot and placed it across The Strip's northbound lanes. The chain with which this had been accomplished was still around the trunk, and tire marks were visible on the edges of the curb and median. I paused for a moment and tried to figure out what this was about, but came up with nothing.

As I contemplated the blocked lanes I saw someone cross Los Vegas Boulevard near the Flamingo intersection. The shadow stopped to observe me as well, then waved and resumed walking. *This is definitely not like any post-apocalyptic movie that I've ever seen,* I thought. *Maybe that person was here to get water, too.*

Water. It had been so integral to the Vegas fantasy, from Caesar's fountains to The Venetian's canals, and in cavalier blindness Los Vegans had taken it for granted. Sprays, fountains, phony lakes...who the hell were we kidding? But I was a hypocrite, for I had enjoyed the nonsense, too. I had loved the musical fountain show at Bellagio. Mental strains of *Time To Say Goodbye* directed my eyes toward the place where couples used to watch the synchronized water jets. My present circumstance made me grateful for humanity's collective environmental retardation, for I reasoned that some water probably remained in Bellagio's big fake lake.

I heard a shot, but it wasn't like that of an AR or the bark of a .40. It was a distant-sounding and full-power rifle report - 7.62 NATO, maybe?

One round. Turn the bolt, bring it back, push it forward, turn and lock it...ah, there's the sound of a second shot. Waaaait...a third shot? No. The dispute is settled.

I pedaled onto the sidewalk and stopped to look out over Lake Bellagio. The scene was creepy because the water was black and the moon was the only source of illumination. In the daylight, however, I would have seen the "lake" for what it was: a rapidly-evaporating basin of slime that was as dark and menacing as a clogged rain gutter. Trash floated in the brine, and when I looked down from the walkway rail I saw an upside-down pickup truck. The sludge only covered a few inches of the vehicle's roof and roll bar.

It was about a fifteen foot drop down to the water level. I looked at the crashed pickup and saw that when it had plowed through the stone rail it also dislodged a section of concrete. The large rectangular slab reminded me of news clips that had shown sections of the Berlin Wall coming down. I realized that seepage from this damage probably accelerated water loss, but it also provided a sharply descending path via rubble that had collapsed into the hole.

I shifted my pack off of the faux-ní'iví and dismounted. I leaned my bike against the rail, removed my pack, and set it beside the bike. I pulled out four water bottles, my filter pump, and Grandpa's 10/22, which I could no longer carry across my back because the duct tape sling had disintegrated. I cycled the action, set the safety, and slowly descended into the gap. After a couple steps I slid backward on loose gravel and hit my head. I'm not sure how I bumped the .22's safety and pulled the trigger when I went down, but thankfully, the gun was pointed away when it discharged.

"Well, so much for stealth," I muttered.

I gingerly felt my shins and femurs and prayed that I wouldn't discover a joint where one wasn't supposed to be. *Good. No bone shifts, no sharp pains. Ripped pants, though.*

A warm trickle ran down my forehead and cheek. I touched the top of my head and my fingers came away wet. There wasn't much that I could do about a scalp laceration except leave it alone. I had experienced a concussion before, and I knew that my present injury wasn't as serious. I wiped, or probably *smeared,* blood from my eyes and hoped that the wound would soon coagulate.

I got up and collected the bottles and 10/22. I took out the weapon's magazine, cycled the chamber empty, and put the magazine back into the rifle without re-chambering a round. I didn't want to directly touch my injury, so when I got to the water's edge, I filtered two bottles of water and dumped them over my head. My face probably looked like a wet and bloody mess, but that was unimportant.

As I slowly pumped Lake Bellagio's water I reflected on the fact that Brightman and Bocelli hadn't been heard there for years. The Bellagio show had tried to evolve and remain relevant, just as Treasure Island, another Vegas dinosaur, had scrapped the cutlasses and cannons in favor of ratline floozies who flopped their scars and silicone four shows per night. In Bellagio's case, it was decided that the water jets would go, and in their place, underwater track-driven and oversized gondolas "floated" out, upon which ladies who hadn't made the Treasure Island cut danced a strange mermaid-costumed can-can. The girls had to do their kicks from under fake fish tails like a row of Rockette were-trout.

* * *

The West Flamingo Vonn's was boarded up and overturned grocery carts were strewn throughout its dark parking lot. The place looked deserted, so I decided to stop and take a breather. That was when the bullet struck.

A spray of liquid over my shoulder mixed with the bloody smears on my face. I carried my water bottles in a lower compartment, so I assumed that I had been splashed with my own blood and shock explained the absence of pain. My bike tipped and I hit the pavement. I struggled to un-pin my leg from beneath the bike's frame while the pack's awkward position made me flail and cough like an overturned tortoise on a broken respirator.

"Are you going to search his shit?" asked someone. "Looks like he's got a backpack."

"I'm not touching him. And if *you* touch him, you'd better stay the hell away from me."

"You sure? You shot him. First dibs."

"So? I couldn't see that he was bubbled. Christ, he's puking blood. Look at his face."

"Ugh...yeah. Back up, back up."

The two cops retreated a few steps. I continued my strained breathing and writhing while their flashlight beams moved over me.

"Seems pretty old to be a bubbler."

"You kidding? Look at that black pus. I've seen 'em this old before."

"Shouldn't we at least end him?

"Why? He's already on his way out. You wanna waste a round? I don't know where he thought he was going on a bike. Looks like he's half-dead already."

"What, then?"

"Fuck him. Let the sani-trucks pick him up." The cop began to walk away, then paused. "You coming? Or are you gonna stare at his nasty ass all night?"

The one who had lingered turned and joined his partner. I heard voices over radio fuzz, but the sound soon faded and the parking lot was silent again.

The cop had referred to me as being a "bubbler," meaning that he thought I was one of the smallpox-infected people whose skin erupted in black blood-blisters and whose breath shook and gurgled due to respiratory lesions. After the cops left I regained my breath and pulled myself out from under the bike. I was still alive. I wasn't in shock. The pack had taken the round...but what was all over my face? I touched my cheek and looked at my fingers. I saw nothing but a dark moonlit smudge, so I went to my pack for a flashlight. I listened to make sure that the cops were indeed gone before I half-covered the bulb and switched it on. I looked at the mess on my hands and silently thanked my lucky stars for the fall that I had experienced, the bleeding gash that it had caused, and the ink from a shattered pen. "Paddy boy," I whispered. For a man descended from mixed German-and-whatever-else stock, I seemed to have enjoyed an inexplicably large slice of Irish luck.

I examined the pack. On the left shoulder there was a burst of shredded nylon, along with ink and small wet chunks of compressed charcoal. I reached in and withdrew the broken pieces of one of my water pump cartridges and picked out the plastic slivers of pen.

I was shaken, but I had to keep moving. I shifted the ruined compartment's undamaged contents to other sections and hoped that sometime before the night was over the cops would return and see what had actually happened...especially since I had taken the risk of staying an extra minute to arrange the shattered pen and filter pieces to spell: "FUCK PIGS."

I was about to rest the pack on the ni'ivi again, but when I righted the bike I discovered that the gear cassette was damaged and six spokes in the rear wheel had snapped like broken levers against the asphalt and curb edge. I made a fist, swore under my breath, and silently lowered the bike. Then I knelt by my mo-bag, loosened the straps, and took out the 10/22. I was grateful that the pack had rested on its exposed butt when the cops were nearby.

I placed the carbine in a nearby shopping cart and lifted the pack to balance it on the edge of the cart's basket. I turned, backed into the shoulder straps, adjusted the waist belt, and lifted the pack. It wasn't overly heavy, but I knew that, compared to the bike, it would be slow going. I decided to leave the cart because it was noisy and slow. It could have helped save my energy, but I wouldn't have been able to instantly step into a shadow. My footsteps were also much quieter than rattling cart wheels. I picked up the 10/22 and began to walk down the sidewalk in my new bubbler/homeless backpacker disguise.

I moved at a slow pace and rested when I needed to. I really felt the pack's weight by the time I got to the desert's edge off Blue Diamond. I trudged out into the brush, removed the pack, and sat on the ground for several minutes. I realized just how tired I was as I unzipped a compartment and took out an object that resembled an oversized twist-up sunshield for a car dashboard. I tossed the object onto the ground and it came to life, uncoiling, unwinding, and expanding, until it transformed into a micro-bivvy. I slipped a sleeping mat, a reflective emergency blanket, and myself into the tiny shelter.

Carefully! Their Kind
Prefer More *Subtle*
Compounds!

Chemtrail attacks require precision because a gust of wind or a spot of rain can cause a payload to miss its target. Strike agents are therefore aerosolized and blended with ATR-altitude dispersants to ensure that they don't become concentrated in some areas and sparse in others. These components, combined with biochemical binders, create very effective pathogen delivery vectors.

I was immunized, so, for me, smallpox exposure lacked consequence. This was not the case, however, in regard to the terrifyingly bizarre psychotropic effects of the weaponized disease's chemical companions.

* * *

It was about noon when I hiked over a small rise and discovered the object. At a distance, it reminded me of the descriptions that I had read in reports of the Roswell UFO crash: silvery, round, and very strange-looking against the desert background. It was more cylindrical than disc-shaped, however, and much smaller than an aircraft or flying saucer.

As I got closer, the object seemed more like a jet fighter's external outboard fuel tank, except it was too stubby and made of unpainted aluminum. I wondered if a pilot had deliberately jettisoned the drum, or if the release had been accidental. I struggled to read stencils that had partially skidded off against rocks and sand. The container bore a long lot number, a New World Health Organization class five biohazard symbol, and some unfamiliar acronyms.

There was a lengthwise rupture in the drum's metal skin and most of its contents had escaped. White dust was spread over the impact site like someone had reversed a shop-vac and blown cocaine over an area half the size of a football field.

I didn't touch the container, but that didn't matter because I had walked through the chalky whatever-it-was and breathed the surrounding air. When I saw the cute purple kittens crawl out I knew that I had made a serious mistake, especially when they started to meow Sonny and Chère songs.

*   *   *

I saw **Back To The Futures** *when I was a teenager, and I thought that the George MacFly character, as portrayed by Quentin Glover, was great. My subconscious, however, acting many years later and in concert with a freak-o-rama chemtrail substance, must have believed that the MacFly character was ABSOLUTELY GODLIKE.*

*   *   *

I headed out to the southern Nevada mountains in my own interpretation of the Rip Van Winkle tale, except that I wasn't going to sleep the years away. Instead, I had booked a seat on a long-term psych-episode that would log more frequent flier miles than a trip to Jupiter.

Winnie-The-Pooh – Chapter 1

IN WHICH WE ARE INTRODUCED TO WINNIE-THE-POOH AND SOME BEES, AND THE STORIES BEGIN

The Adventures Of Tom Sawyer

CHAPTER I. Y-o-u-u Tom Aunt Polly Decides
Upon her Duty--Tom Practices Music--
The Challenge--A Private Entrance

Yesterday, Walking – Chapter 17

IN WHICH JACK CREATES A SUPPLEMENTARY
PERSONA NAMED FRANÇOIS DILLINGER
KRONAG, *AND THE GENTLE READER*
IS KINDLY ADVISED TO
SKIP AHEAD TO
CHAPTER
18

SERIOUSLY. . . TURN TO PAGE 465.

SERIOUSLY.

~~Legion~~ *KRONAG:* Jesus I know, and Paul I know, but who are *you?*
~~Hamlet~~ *Jack:* I am Mr. Fishmonger.

* * *

My moonlight wasn't ruined when somebody told me that I was the last man on earth. I can't remember who told me, though. Maybe it was someone I met in college.

* * *

I wish that I had a *Heavier Metal* gundark (or whatever that flying animal was), like Kenny and the hot cartoon chick rode. I'd ride the shit out of that thing. Hell, yeah.

* * *

A gundark is an animal with regenerating ears, right? Or is that a Brahma bull?

* * *

I'm healthy now, but when I first arrived at this retreat my goddamned urinary tract tortured me. This meant that my bladder evacuation process was a curious thing, especially at night, when it felt like I strained to chip a hole in the Hoover Dam with a Swiss Army knife. Then I experienced Divine Relief, and now I'm fine. It's terrific to get that kind of assistance, but I have to say that I'm not the best candidate for a solo wilderness adventure. Maybe I was foolish to come here, but it's too late to change places with a young couple who could repopulate the Earth via the old Abel's Wife Strategy.

* * *

God talks to me now. He told me to call Him "Hellion." He wants me to write an unauthorized autobiography. FYI.

* * *

As inheritor of nothingness, I enjoy some additional perks besides breathtaking night skies, the most important of which concerns Divine Access. When the Almighty's switchboard only has my call to handle, it's easy to get through. All of the clean God-is-love souls and their polar opposites are gone, and the conversation now falls to Yours Truly. I'm not the worst, and hardly the best – I'm just the last caller on the line. I think that before the bottom fell out it was easy for The Hellion to just brush off the majority of prayers that He received, sort of like a presidential CYA "plausible deniability" approach. I mean, consider some guy in Denver who prayed for a promotion that could be translated into a Cancun fortnight and a new SUV, while on the other side of the world a captive Srey Pak child also prayed that, even if she couldn't escape from nights of blowing corporate Japanese porcupines and middle-aged American boil-asses, maybe she could just *please* die before her ninth birthday.

How do you think The Hellion prioritized these appeals? That's right. The little one got her first class boarding call, non-stop to heaven, before the year was out, whereas Denver Guy was ignored. No biggie for Denver Guy, though. He just went a little deeper in debt for that smooth ride and then he lied about a week in Kissimmee. He was okay with the snub, because Denver Guy knew that, in a world of ebola, Yodok, Gitmo, and AIDS orphans, The Hellion's inbox was stuffed. Shit, maybe The Hellion never even *heard* Denver Guy's petition, since his entreaties were likely drowned out by all of that silly war, disease, and poverty stuff. God never got the message. It was possible. **Plausible deniability.** Besides, The Hellion helps those who become their own Santas...as the little sex slave realized before she jumped in front of an oncoming truck.

But the plausible deniability angle doesn't really figure in His business now, because mine are the only prayers out there. The freebies are gone, too. If I had been a better person I might have gotten in on some of the comps that The Hellion used to hand out, but instead, I got a task. A chore. I'm supposed to write about my life. I don't know why. Some sort of Beckett-*Molloy* joke, maybe. It's just the job that I was given, and when I'm done, I'm hoping that it will be my turn for assistance...though I'm a little nervous about what that might mean. I can see myself wandering around the Mojave for forty years until I'm granted the reward of once again meeting another human being. Yay. If I reach 146 years of age, my conversational skills might not be that great...which isn't to say that they're much of anything now.

Maybe my reward will be commensurate with the degree of skill with which I execute my unauthorized autobiography. I'm a shitty writer, though. Maybe I should just forget about it and go directly to the Golden-

Calf-Ba'al-Sodom? Nah. I'll give this book thing a shot. It's not like I'm pressed for time.

*   *   *

I don't know when the Minoan civilization became extinct or when the Roman Empire was at last considered "fallen." I can't remember when the Cortez Smallpox + Mineral Extraction Company turned the Incan Empire into South America's biggest strip mine. Do you know why? Because those peoples were long gone when I showed up, and the seasons had turned. Textbooks recorded their snuff reels as distant events, just like the exploits of the grandfathers who swam inside the USS Arizona and the great-great grandfathers who wafted around Gettysburg. Things grew more immediate for me, however, when World Trade Center moms and dads needed controlled-demolition-DNA-matches, after which General Shakpana's multiple marches to the sea necessitated bulldozers and lime trucks. Smallpox beat Mabus, or Nyarlhotep, or Dijal, or whatever-his-name-was to the punch. No rapture. No Armageddon. I guess there really will be a Millennium of Peace, though.

I'm rambling.

Get fucking used to it!

The USA has now assumed its own Incan posture, and the passing days mean what they have always meant to the desert animals. I hear coyotes speak in the distance, and Al-*CIA*-da never figures in their nightly lunar supplications.

My neighbors' late-night yelps serve as a substitute for AM conspiro-supernatural talk shows. I once had a fun habit of staying up late to hear prattle about ghosts, aliens, time travel, shadow people and whatnot...it was all so serious and real-sounding, like an airwave version of *Ripley's*. It was also a comfort and a shield from the monotonies of life to imagine that there was a mystery to human existence, even if that meant something sinister. The important thing was that there was *more* than just a nightstand death clock that burned off minutes until it was time to get up and go to a salt mine.

Vegas radio host Bart Snell talked a lot of horseshit in his day – and a lot of truth. Long-term listeners always knew when Snell laid out the straight skinny because he got nervous on-air, but the guy could yack about ghosts and poltergeists and weird symbols appearing on *Exorcism* stills like he was doing the Jerrie Lewis Telethon. Snell loved to tease out even more nonsense from his loonies by playing their attention-seeking games. Such was the sequence for fringelings from coast-to-coast as waning D+D interest was replaced by wee-hour AM.

But when Snell's twilight was *truly* touched, he freaked out like anyone else. Case in point: those 1988 faxes from a guy claiming to be a "time traveler", and who wanted to warn the nation about 9/11. True, that particular seer might have missed the mark with his nuclear war prediction errors, but late-eighties talk of jets hitting the World Trade Center Towers blew both Snell and Jeannie Dixon out of the water. Maybe the guy really *was* a time traveler.

The final *Bart Snell Show* was broadcast on July 29th, 1997.

*   *   *

There was only static when I listened to the radio. The shortwave feature was broken, as I discovered when there might have actually been broadcasts on those bands. I also tried to find AM stations on night skips, but I couldn't pick up a thing. Albuquerque was apparently gone, as were Salt Lake, Phoenix, and LA. Even the obnoxious 100k+ watt Sonorran Radio Caroline accordions had fallen silent...though there were a couple instances when I thought that I heard Spanish, but I just couldn't be sure. Aural hallucinations are harder to dismiss than the visual variety. I have visuals all the time. Movie stars, historical figures, people from my past...they've all dropped in on my mountain camp. Sometimes I've found them entertaining, sometimes annoying, and sometimes I just ignore them. The radio ghosts are harder to brush off, however. *Did I hear something? Did I? Was that a man's voice? Could that sound be music?* It's stuff like this that will supersize my crazy, and not the patently stupid hallucinations of a brain that increasingly hungers for the sight of another human.

*   *   *

(Below are notes from my thigh pouch notepad. I scribbled these while I did the Tomas Hanks Emerald Mile firecock routine. They concern the "unauthorized autobiography" that The Hellion wants. – KRONAG)

Okay...I've GOT to get this book started. If I don't, The Hellion won't help me, and I won't just carry on with my current state of being fucked...I'll advance to the next level, and thereby be ultra-fucked. I don't want that. So welcome to my infection blotter:

Day 1 - I'm trying to write, but my fingers have been up my ass all morning, trying to give birth to a grapefruit prostate, kidney infection, piss back-up - the works. This is a hell of a way to begin a book, but it helps take my mind off the pain. It's at moments such as this that I'm glad everyone else it dead. Could you imagine? What if some hikers, hunters, or a forest ranger found me like this? Alone, looking like a Tet Offensive cast-off, wallowing amid the brush with one hand jammed into my nether region while the other holds a pencil and notepad - wait...no, considering the kind of kinksters who populated southern Nevada, I wouldn't be greeted with revulsion - more likely, I'd hear someone exclaim: "Wow, and I thought that I had specific fetishes!"

I left the hut last night and collapsed. The sun's been up for about three hours, and I've been here all night...just me, the stars, and the coyotes. I'm on my own, of course. Well, that's not counting Harry, but she's still in the hut, and certainly of no assistance in my current predicament. At least Tomas Hanks had Johnny Coffee there to untie his urethra. Hell, even Wilson the Volleyball could probably help me. But no. All I have is a juniper burl who yells at me in Konglish.

The coyotes' cacophony stopped about two hours before sunrise. Their yowls helped me get through the night, and I was able to focus on the sound and leave my pain for a while. I managed to do this long enough to catch some sleep, though the cold awakened me later. It's been getting so damn chilly at this elevation, especially at night. Maybe I'll move down to the desert floor, but I just hate to leave the spring. I don't like walking the 1/8th mile as is, and water is hard to come by down below. I'm also scared to walk back into Vegas, because the Nellis side of the city has been remodeled, Hiroshima-Nagasaki style.

I increasingly appreciate the value of mental health and I'm sure that there are many sights in Vegas that are beyond disturbing. I'm doing the Hamlet thing as I hallucinate a forest of fishmonger therapists. I've got water, shelter, piles of provisions, and nothing ugly in the immediate vicinity. I'll stick it out and sit tight...ohhh....shit. I gotta stop here and just be still. Even the act of moving this pencil is killing me.

Day 2 - Forget it. Thirsty. In the dirt.

Day 3 - I'm lying in the brush with my BDUs and underwear still down around my ankles. Hoover Dam protocols are in full effect. There is an anthill hereabouts and I have to kill recon scouts so as to prevent them from returning to HQ and revealing my location. It feels like I'm passing stones while the perpetual grapefruit labor continues. I'm so tired and I have a burning thirst. I have to get up. I'm pretty sure that I'm gonna die if I don't rinse something through my screaming Mono Lake kidneys.

Day 4 – I passed out last night and woke up before sunrise. I'm scared to move, though the pain has lessened. I can move a little now. There's mud under my hip because I pissed in the night. Ugh. The smell is nasty. It's a cross between tomcat spray and a skunk with a yeast infection. I'm gonna try to crawl back to the water jug in my hut. I've got to move because the mess on the ground is attracting more ants.

Day 5 – I'm back in the hut. Harry is lecturing me and telling me that I've got to jerk off at least twice a day. This is key, since I'm 106 years old...but all I have to inspire me are Hallucino-Grandpa's gay porno mags, and I've been using them to start fires. If someone had told me when I was a kid that one day I'd regard masturbation as a chore, I'd have laughed. I suppose that a strict spanking regimen will help with the prostate, but not with the lower back pain or urethritis. H.G. stored some vacuum packs in the hut. I pray that one of them contains antibiotics.

Day 6 – The back pain continues. H.G.'s vac-pacs only held cooking spices.

I had a Clarkian 2001-esque dream last night. I was Dave, looking into the giant prostate obelisk, and it was full of angry little walnuts. I think that the only anatomical structures that have ever been described as being "walnut-sized organs" are enlarged human prostate glands and the brains of horses...but I know for a fact that horse brains are considerably larger than walnuts, so how did this get started?

The obelisk exploded into a nebula that looked like Jesus would have looked if He had lived long enough to experience a prostate-walnut-grapefruit-horse brain.

MC 900 Foot Horse Prostate.

Magnificent!

Yeshua of Nazareth died when He was...what? Thirty? Thirty three? Man...I wish to fucking hell that Longinus would use his spear to drain my problem...I can almost read it now: "And blood and water flowed forth from

His prostate." Maybe the Spear has partially done its work, though. That, and my Right Hand of Destiny. I'll do some more writing later.

[End of blotter – KRONAG]

Where Is The Harm In Talking
Out Loud When I'm
On My Own?

I like to make a kind of soup from Hallucino-Grandpa's MRE stores. It's fairly tasty, and H.G. equipped each ammo can (in which he buried these foodstuffs), with an assortment of spices and dry items. I'm presently experimenting with a tuna noodle entrée, boiled rice, and curry powder. My dish looks a little strange, but the aroma is quite nice. I raise my ladle, but before I can have a taste, I hear a shout:

Hey! KRONAG! Hey!

Oh man...what's the problem? "Yes, I'm here," I call back into one of the hut's two sub-chambers. "What is it?"

"Hey!" A little less shrill this time. I hang the ladle on one of the tripod hooks and sigh.

"Hey! Why you breath like that?" *Uh-oh. The shrillness is returning. I'd better get back there.*

"What is it?" I ask, as I look into the chamber. She's lying next to the sleeping pad and bedroll. She's rolled over onto her face, and all I can see is a rough patch of wood behind her ears and under her mossy black hair.

"No lub. No lub!" she exclaims. I roll her over. Now she can speak. "No love."

"What do you mean?"

"No care."

"Why do you say that?" I ask. "I take care of you. I keep you safe. I talk to you and spend time with you. When I go out I always take you with me."

There's a pause. "No always." Another pause, then: "No sex me." *Oh God. Here we go again.* Before I can think of some excuse, she continues. "You coward with weak mind."

That wasn't necessary, but her English isn't that great. Maybe she doesn't understand the gravity of such an insult. *Oh, bullshit. She knows exactly what she said. Her English is better than mine, when she wants it to be.*

I feel a flash of anger, and I have an urge to blurt out: "Why?

411

Because I haven't worked up enough imagination to cum on a chunk of knotty juniper?" Something like that would really hurt her though, so I keep it to myself.

I look at her again. Am I supposed to blow up in her face? Is that what she wants? Am I not showing enough fire? Or appropriate levels of male-sex-toy-imagination?

Well, things could be worse. I could be stuck out here with a horny anthropomorphic cush-ball.

"Look, I don't think you should say things like that. I try to make you happy. You have a right to say anything you want, of course, but I don't think that you're being fair."

She is sullen for a moment, and her eyes go to the flagstone floor. "Why wrong..." she begins, then stops and thinks for a moment. "Meaning: What wrong with me? Why you outside sleep four day?"

Ohhhh...this could be worse than getting her mad. Much worse. All shrillness is gone, and I hear weepy tones...I gotta think fast. The cogs and gears heat up and I realize that there's an upside to the honesty of grapefruit. I gotta use the correct body language, so I take her in my arms and my hug is returned, which seems odd, since she doesn't have arms. I'll never figure out how she does that.

"It's hard to pee. Can't sex you. I'm sad. You're beautiful."

She considers this for a moment. "Leelee?"

"Mmmm. Hurts a lot."

"I help?" she asks, but that's not a road I want to go down, either. I don't need a bunch of juniper slivers in an already troubled organ.

"No, I just need time."

Harry gets really cuddly. "You no coward, you no weak. No true."

I give her a little kiss. "The food is almost ready."

Harry sniffs. "Good smell."

I'd Make A Deal With God *The Hellion,*
And I'd Get Him To
Swap Our
Places

Oh God, not this shit again.

That was my first thought when my burning lower back roused me.
I didn't want to disturb Harry, but I needed to get out of the hut. I had
fallen asleep in my sweat-soaked BDUs, so I didn't fumble for clothes.

I thought that I had gotten better, but my improvement didn't last.
The relapse distressed me for reasons other than the simple return of
my grapefruit. I wasn't a doctor, but even *I* knew that sometimes when
serious illness seemed to suddenly and dramatically ease, it wasn't
necessarily cause for celebration. Take, for example, the relief-filled
intermission between rupture and sepsis in the case of a burst appendix,
or that cruel period of "recovery" known as anthrax eclipse, during which
an infected person experiences miraculous relief while spores pause for a
day or two before filling the victim's lungs with bloody foam. I prayed
that I wasn't about to discover a nephritic parallel to these conditions.

I kicked over the cooking tripod and empty pot as I staggered out.
I guessed that Harry was really tired, because I didn't hear her wake up.
Some deep charcoal ember holdouts from the dead fire flashed as my
careening boot heel dug through the fire circle. My blurred vision and
kidney stone-like agony made me sway as I paused to ascertain that I
hadn't kicked a spark onto something flammable. My body weight then
shoved against the door and I fell out into the cold night.

A small burr pressed into the palm of my left hand as I crawled
forward, but I hardly noticed. I couldn't see the moon above the tree line,
but the gentle lunar glow that slipped over the tall shadows told me that it
was about four o'clock. I collapsed and rolled onto my back. To my relief,
I discovered that a cold and smooth stone was beneath me. It felt so
good, like a caveman's icepack. The low temperature of the stone was
further decreased by my wet BDUs. I was foolish to have kept the wet
clothing on, but the night was still, and that was probably the reason why
I wasn't perishing from a chill factor that my sweaty garments would
have worsened.

For a few moments the earth seemed to undulate in waves that

413

passed through massive segments like giant shifting thoracic bands. I half-expected the illusion to continue and for the brush, or maybe even the pines, to morph into huge insect legs and antennae...but then the hallucination faded. Perhaps some prank-pulling enzyme realized that my jaded brain was not particularly impressed by visions of giant bugs. It was rather basic, and there was no follow-up attempt to create a Burroughs-esque roach-typewriter-hybrid.

At this point, Delusion and I understood each other, so things were kicked up a notch. In fact, I wouldn't say that the amp was cranked to eleven...it was more like twenty or thirty, because while I flopped and sucked in painful half-breaths like a suffocating fish on ice, the Almighty appeared.

Quite a jump, wouldn't you say?

Acid to Elysium.

Pines stood like a shadowy arboreal pipe organ, though not in a particularly "Mormon Tabernacle" or Lon Cheney-esque style. Stars rotated in overnight observatory exposures that formed constellations of horses, lions, giraffes, and other brightly-painted carousel animals. The sky glowed as wooden creatures on striped poles rose and fell amid calliope music and multicolored twinkles from gin palace mirrors.

*Elephants...circus tents...big red noses...juggling...silken kerchiefs...giant shoes...*and the soundtrack for it all was a song that I had loved in my youth. The tune was the magnum opus of master entertainer Quentin Glover, entitled *Clownly Clown Clown*. It played over and over and I felt a need to sing the spunky ditty:

> *As I walked on the ground*
> *I didn't make a sound*
> *Then, in turning around,*
> *I saw a clown*
> *It gave a frown*
> *It stood up on a mound*
> *And barked like a hound*
> *Clownly-clown-clown...*

I stopped singing. Did I hear something? *What was that?* It hadn't occurred to me that I might not be able to completely do as I pleased in this Earth-*sans*-humans situation. There were still folks hereabouts, and some of them might be very large klttles who could do with a midnight snack of delicious KRONAG.

A twig snapped.

Oh God.

I had survived 9/11, the upheaval of smallpox deaths, and was the last man standing. Now I was about to find my head between cougar jaws. The supreme predator species had receded to a single sick and old specimen who was about to die as his proto-cousins had perished eons earlier. I let out a sigh. A nice sleek mountain lion was moving in with the same maneuver that *smilodon fatalis* had used thousands of years ago for its Neanderthal-on-Ritz.

I remembered watching a nature show in which it was explained that cougars liked to go for quick skull and spine punctures with neck twists. *Well, at least it would be fast.* I was thankful for that. *This moment would have made a great Farther Side cartoon* I thought. "Thanks for the company, Harry," I whispered. "Sorry to leave you like this."

"Really? Going somewhere?"

"Ahhhugh! Who the fuck is there? Who said that?!" I yelled. I looked up and saw a man floating in the middle of...a halo? In paintings, halos are usually just seen around or over the subject's head, but this entity seemed to have a "full-body halo". I didn't know that there was an LA Finesse in heaven.

"I know. It's my Nautilus routine," He said. I couldn't quite make out His features because the halo's powerful backlighting created a dark silhouette like that of someone who stood in front of a brightly-lit window. While I squinted upward from my cool-rock position, I wondered: Had I spoken that observation aloud?

"I love the *Triple C* song, by the way," continued the Being. "I get so sick of that old 'hail, hail, fire and snow' thing. Come on. Do I look like I'm in Starfleet? Do I?"

"I, ah...no, I guess not," I stammered, "but I can't see you very well." The act of communication calmed my heart, and He seemed...friendly?

415

"Oh." The light behind Him dimmed, as if someone had turned down an adjustable light switch. "Better?"

I nodded, and as I looked at the Entity, I realized that He was the genius who had written and recorded *Clownly Clown Clown*. He rapidly shape-shifted through various costumes and character roles that He had articulated during the course of His brilliant career. At one moment, He was a teen who wore a fifties poplin jacket and sported slicked-back hair, and in the next, He was longhaired and wild-eyed, as if searching for a dead girl on a river bank. With another shift He cuddled a rat and wore a stuffy dark suit, and all while floating above the brush in His rheostatic body glow.

It made sense. Other celestial beings, back when there were still humans on Earth to worship them, had multiple aspects. The Crone appeared as the Maiden or the Mother when it suited her. Krishna could manifest a female aspect through Radharani. Andraste interacted with her children as a doe or she-wolf. Even the Christians, despite their protestations that each was separate and distinct, had their Godhead of the Father, Son, and Holy Ghost. Like His divine colleagues, it appeared that this Being could also appear in various forms.

"Very good," the Entity said. "But if you need a moniker that applies to every manifestation, you may use 'Hellion.'"

Did I say that out loud, too? I wondered.

"Now, let's see how clever you are," He said.

"Clever?"

"Yes. You appear to be in a *pickle*." The Hellion's aspect shifted and He was now dressed in a filthy Santa Suit. He reached into a large canvas sack, pulled out several sandwiches, and tossed them on the ground. "We have to stand together against the Black Rubber Gloves," said The Hellion. His eyes shifted suspiciously beneath the smudged white trim of His Santa cap. "I see what they did to you, and I want to...to...help...*ahhh*." He stopped in mid-sentence as a look of building pleasure crossed His face. The Hellion's pelvis began to twist in gyrations that spun Him around within His body halo like a ceramic angel rotating on a Christmas ornament. As He turned I saw powerful gluteal contractions within the grimy Santa trousers and a large cockroach fell out of His trouser leg. It lingered for a moment on the sandwich pile and then clicked off into the darkness.

The Hellion regained his composure. "Like I was saying, I want to help you. But you gotta fight too, you gotta figure out what to do. Like in the song. We gotta be friends."

"Like...*in the song?* What?"

"Triple C. But not so loud. They have electronic listening devices."

"Triple C...? Oh, the *Clownly Clown Clown* song. Do You want me to sing it?"

"Yeah. Hurry, before they send a tornado." There was urgency in The Hellion's voice.

I cleared my throat. "*As I walked on the ground. I didn't make a sound--*"

"No!" screamed The Hellion. "You already sang that part while I made my lunch!" His body stiffened and His fists thrust downward from the sleeves of His Santa jacket.

I skipped ahead: "*...and barked like a hound--*"

"Aughh! Now you're ruining the spirit of Christmas!"

Maybe a cougar would have been a little more rational, I thought. I skipped further ahead: "*...then I showed it something that was round...*"

Evidently that was the line for which He had been waiting. A broad and slightly psychotic smile came to His face, so I continued: "*...died, smiled, and fell on the ground.*"

Oops. Bad move. Complete smile erasure. Okay, rewind. Sing the part He likes:

...I showed it something that was round...[smile]...something that was round...[smile]...something round...[smile]...round...[smile]...

Well, He has an odd hymnal, I thought, as I repeated the same bit for the tenth time. Maybe He wanted me to act like a broken record until sunrise, but I was out of breath and my back burned again. I rolled onto my cool comfort rock and was silent. *Ahhh. Well,* I thought, *I'll just close my eyes if He gets hissy-pissy again...c'est la vie.*

"Ah-ha! Something round!" I heard Him joyfully exclaim. "We'll become great friends!"

What? What the hell was He talking about? I opened my eyes and saw that He was pointing at...my crotch. Or, to be exact, He was happily aiming his index finger at my exposed cock. I guessed that during my miserable wallowings my belt had caught on some brush and my BDU trousers were at mid-thigh.

He wants to befriend my dick?

Whatever.

I looked down. *No wonder I've got an infected grapefruit,* I thought. There was dirt in my pubes and tiny pebbles were sticking to the yucky secretions on my shaft like a crab gluing bits of debris onto its carapace. The sight was both disgusting and exhausting. I flopped my head back in hopelessness. *Something round?* I thought. *Hardly.* At best, my cock was roughly cylindrical – when clean. Now it reminded me of an overripe, caramel-covered banana dipped in dirty peanuts.

"Look," I said. "Just kill me, okay?"

"Kill you? I think...that's...impossible, now, my friend." The voice was the same, but the inflections and stresses were different. The Santa get-up was gone. In its place was a fine copperas suit and a thinly-knotted watermark tie. A balisong in His left hand snapped as if it were clipping off fingers in a dark Manila alley, while the manicured nails of His right hand brought a Hepburn-esque cigarette holder to His lips. Smoke curled downward like a descending gray serpent that made me realize that it had been a long time since I had smelled tobacco. And formaldehyde. And tar-nicotine-benzene.

"I have enjoyed the display, but really, personal decorum is in order, even in the wild." He twitched His little finger and invisible hands pulled up my BDU pants. "Now, let's...see...what's to be done about that awkward drainage matter?" The ghostly hands moved to my lower back and invisibly *penetrated* my flesh. It was psychic surgery, and the real thing, too – not like that scene from *Men on the Moon,* in which Jim Carey/Andie Kauffman goes to a scammer to have tumors removed, but sees the charlatan press pieces of steak against his marks' skin.

Divine fingers curled around the grapefruit and painlessly squeezed it down to size. I visualized the Colorado River, once bled to death by casino fountains and Lake Los Vegas, now restored and roaring into the Gulf of California. "Uh, s-sorry about that," I stuttered, even as I continued to be one with the fire hose that blasted down my pantleg and over the top of my left boot. He just smiled and took a drag.

Holy dialysis was next. The invisible hands traced up my ureters to the scorched kidney pies in my lower back. *Flush, flush, flush.* Blessed Drain-Oh and a celestial toilet plunger pounded the clogs downward into my

418

bladder and then out the end of my caramel-peanut-delight like a true believer's urethral stigmata.

I took a deep breath. Wheeew...I stank like a used barf bag. I had a date with a bar of soap and a nearby spring's cold water. Whatever it was that had exited my body had thoroughly permeated the fibers of my clothing. As the rising sun's first rays revealed my filthy state, I resolved to burn my BDUs.

"Why?"

I looked up at The Hellion. He calmly smoked with His legs crossed in an invisible floating chair. "Pardon?" I said.

"Those are clean garments."

"Clean? They're disgusting..." My voice trailed off as I sniffed something. What *was* that? April freshness? I looked down and saw that I was in a pressed and spotless BDU uniform. There was even a shine on my boots. I touched my chin and felt the smoothness of a clean shave.

"Gosh," I murmured.

"I'm nothing, if not thorough," exhaled The Hellion as smoke snaked from His smile.

"Thank you." My fever was gone, and I knew that my future would be one of drama-free urinations.

"A trifle. You have yourself to thank, really. Just use your mind, and you can improve your lot. You can even access my assistance, if you apply yourself."

"Well, yes," I replied. "I'll go on the assumption that You can pretty much do anything You want, so You can somehow help me, even though I'm the last guy alive." I paused and watched Him closely. He would know if that were true or not...but He remained a poker-faced statue.

"Some would call that faith, but I prefer the term 'confidence.' I like your *confidence* in me," He replied. "But, like any kind of magic, you have to know the triggers on this plane to get what, or where, you want."

"Umm...*triggers?*"

"Or sacrifices, if you prefer."

Well, okay, I thought. *But what could He possibly want from me?* "Like a virgin, or the first harvest bushel or something?" I asked.

The Hellion chuckled. "No." Another long drag, then release. "As I mentioned, the trekkie thing wearies me. It's a present without my name on it, like a Minoan Bull in Saint Paul's. But you correctly intuited my preferences, and look at the result. Do it again." He smiled. "I've shown you many faces. More than you need, actually. You should be happy to learn that I've confidence in you, too." He paused. "Just give Them all what They want. Virgins? No. Bull blood? Wrong. You'll have to...do...better."

Aspect shift. Now He slouched and wore a striped shirt. The slicked and precisely arranged hair had been supplanted by a Stooges bowl. He stuck His chin out to create the effect of a strangely exaggerated underbite. "Don't be such a laaame-o, KRONAG," The Hellion mumbled. "C'mon." He rolled His eyes.

Okay, whatever. "No, I don't want to be a...'lame-o'. I'll try not to let you down."

"Jeez, you'd better not. C'mon." He let out a huff. "You only get one shot, KRONAG, so don't think this is gonna to be some kind of Christmas Past, Present, and Future deal. If you blow it, you can't try the *Clownly* thing again. But you can do it. You're not the biggest lame-o. I gotta go."

Zip! The halo disappeared, along with the Entity that it had contained.

All Quiet on the ~~Western~~ *Floonic* Front.

Hmmm. Well, it looked like I'd get another audience with Him, provided I played my cards right. At that moment I didn't know what He wanted in "sacrifice," but I would figure it out. That seemed to be part of the challenge, though I was sure it wasn't going to be as simple as "sign on the dotted line and I'll get you out of this place and time in exchange for your soul." No, I reasoned that there was a different kind of hitch involved, because something told me that the classic Robert Johnson bargain wasn't exactly His style.

Fantine's Teeth
For Cosette's
Kevlar

- I think you helped me a lot. It was so lucky that you were here.
- Help?
- Absolutely. You knew what He wanted. Everything! Amazing.
- Ahhh. Easy. Quentin Glover top movie star. Top book. Top song.
  I love Quentin Glover when I was little girl. I love Quentin Glover
  when I am woman.
- I know. You had all of the answers. A mind like a steel trap.
- Steel mind? "Hard head?"
- Whoa, no-no-no...your mind is strong. You always remember
  things.
- Ohhh...understand. Always go COEX Big Box Quentin Glover night.
  Friends do not go. Boyfriend not go. He hate Glover. I do not
  care.
- C'mere.
- No...hee hee...

* * *

I once perused some pictures in *Drawn Down the Moon* that showed
Gardnerian pentacle sites. I figured that a five-pointed star, one for
each of The Hellion's aspects, was a good place to start.

Harry packed a lunch that consisted of food bars and a water bottle.
I thought that it was a sweet gesture, though I didn't plan to go far from
the hut. I found a flat little spot with an abundance of round whitish
stones. I also spotted a tuft of soft grass and I placed Harry on it.
When I was sure that she was comfortable, I pulled a roll of twine from
my daypack, along with my pocket knife, and cut a couple straight
branches. I tied the twine to the branches and proceeded to scratch out a
circle. I paused for a moment to remember some of the geometric
constructions that I had taught to children in another life, and soon I had
a decent figure laid out on the ground. Not perfect, but certainly worthy
of any trenchcoated Columbyne newsmaker or devil-worshipping Big
Pharma patsy.

About an hour later I finished placing stones over the lines. When
I paused to take a breath and admire my work, I heard applause. I turned,
smiled at Harry, and took a bow. I went over and sat on the grass next

421

to her. We looked at the sky for a while and shared the water bottle. Then I went back to work and Harry resumed reading a book that she had brought – some obscure thing about a Jesuit priest who had explored portions of the Bundie Ranch in the 1870s, then was decapitated by Senator Harry Reed's Corporate Chinese Sunfarm Danites somewhere around Searchlight. It was old and dry stuff, in my opinion.

With the completion of the pentacle, it was time for me to again open my Abrahamic daypack and pull out sons. The first thing was a beetle sandwich. I was a little nervous about this because I couldn't find any roaches around the camp, so I had decided to substitute big black stinkbugs, the stench of which I was only able to contain with mixed success. The sandwich was in a sealed container of doubtful hermetic integrity, and a strong vinegar-like smell crept out when I accidentally pressed on the lid. The insect substitution was much on my mind, until it occurred to me that black beetles had more in common with roaches than blood did with wine, or wafers with cannibalistic T-bone. That realization put my mind to rest.

Accompanying the sandwich on one pentacle juncture was a sacrifice that I knew I would regret wasting if the conjuration didn't work, because on the ground, alongside the sandwich, I placed a pair of black waterproof gloves that I had deliberately ruined by stabbing and slashing them with a hunting knife. As a final measure, I used a stick to stake them to the ground like a vampire at a crossroads. They were utterly destroyed and completely dead. Hopefully this would appease The Hellion's "Jingle Dell" persona.

Then it was on to the *Faster Sofa* aspect, so I walked to the star's next point and pulled another bundle from my pack. Collecting this set of elements had been somewhat difficult, though the items themselves were fairly straightforward: twigs from a red hawk's nest and a jackrabbit leg that had remained in a snare after the hawk had torn the hare's body away. The capture of a jackrabbit had required me to hike down to a lower elevation and set up a subcamp. I had to wait for several days to make the catch, and this caused me to reflect on the fact that I was fortunate to not have to rely upon hunting for my sustenance.

When I returned to the hut, I completed the task of re-staking the live hare to a small platform of sticks that I had fashioned on the lower branches of a tree, well out of reach of marauding coyotes, where my lonely birdwatching activities had revealed the nest of a Northwestern Red

422

Hawk that seemed to have strayed far south of its typical range. A day later I returned to discover that the bird had indeed accepted my offering, which I hoped that the Sofa Helllon would accept as proof that I had sought out and appeased His totem animal.

Now, when it came to *The Door* Warhol Hellion, I was kind of stumped. Even in the year 1969, golden rotary telephones were rare. I puzzled over this for a while and was about to consider substituting another of The Hellion's aspects for appeasement, but then I pondered the issue of symbolism. Even if I missed the mark, He would know what I had been aiming for, and if I was conscientious in the attempt, all the better. It would again be a case of the old unleavened flesh thing.

To this end, I returned to my pack o' tricks and pulled out two empty soup cans. The cans were connected at their bottoms by a length of string, and wrapped in some yellow US Forest Service tape that I had taken from a ponderosa sapling area. No one would ever be coming back to check on the seedlings' progress, so no harm done. I was confident that He would recognize and appreciate the connection between the soup cans and the golden telephone...but then, as I held the cans, a thought occurred to me: The Warhol Hellion had said that He had been given the phone for the purpose of talking to God, but hadn't actually done so, as He had nothing to say. Did that mean that He had never spoken to Himself? I looked at the string between the two cans, then pulled out my knife and cut it. Satisfied, I placed the two cans with their dangling lengths of string at a point of the star.

Catching the jackrabbit for the hawk had been an effort and a hassle, and I wasn't inclined to go through the same process to find and capture a rat. Thankfully, my camp was free of such vermin, and I really had no idea where to seek out a little furry hanta-vector. Thus, I knew that I would have to be even more inventive when it came to satisfying the *Willerd* Hellion. This required some thought, and the more I considered it, the more I realized that the offering, as in the case of the ruined gloves, would also demand equipment sacrifice.

Now, just because I had been fortunate enough to not have unwanted rodents in the hut, it didn't mean that Hallucino-Grandpa, bless his farsighted heart, hadn't considered such a situation, and I was therefore able to again reach into my pack and pull out one of several spring-type rat traps with which the hut had been provisioned. This one, however, was smashed and quite inoperable - ,just the thing, I had reasoned (while repeatedly bringing down a makeshift rock-hammer), to put a rat-loving deity in a generous mood. I laid down the smashed trap and moved on to the pentacle's final point.

The last offering was the simplest, yet I thought that it would be the one most likely to put me over the top, since I felt that it demonstrated familiarity with one of The Hellion's more *obscure* aspects. It wasn't much...just a single yellow legal pad sheet, upon which I had written:

The Earth is still called an orphanage.
Shall I also be called your disciple?

I weighted down the paper at the final point with a rock, straightened up, surveyed the pentacle, and sighed in satisfaction. I looked over to where Harry sat, still absorbed in her book, and carried my pack over to her patch of grass. She looked up from the book, smiled, and returned to her reading. I touched her shoulder, then leaned over and breathed in the fresh smell of her sweater. I laid back on the grass beside her and in a few minutes the clouds had rocked me to sleep.

The sun was lower when I awakened. The book was closed and Harry had cuddled up to me. It was a wonderful way to come back to the world. I slowly turned my head and looked over at the pentacle. What was supposed to occur? I felt impatient. Had I misinterpreted something? Or worse, was my confidence in the offerings unfounded, and they had been rejected?

Harry was now sitting up and watching the sun fall. When I stirred, she looked over and smiled, then sheepishly told me that she had raided the lunch. I replied that it was alright, and that I hadn't intended to be out this long. She wanted to know when something would happen, but I had no answer. I wondered if I had to be under the influence of a spice pack before The Hellion would appear? Or was I just following up on a chain-and-kerchief encounter with a bit of Marley mustard?

Damn. The project had lifted my spirits, but maybe for nothing.
Damn.

"Let's go," I finally said.

* * *

As I stretched out on my bedroll I couldn't deny that I was comfortable and without pain in my kidneys and bladder. I could get a good night's sleep. He was responsible for that. It was a fact, and proof that I wasn't out of my mind.

But...

Tossing. Turning.

Tossing. Turning.

Enough. Flashlight.

BDUs. Out the door.

Just me in the dark pentacle.

What the hell was I supposed to do?

No *Clownly Clown Clown?* Okay. Fine. I stripped naked, except for H.G.'s half-size too big combat boots. The night was cold, but I ignored it. It was time for a song, taken again from The Hellion's incomparable album.

I began to stomp around the pentacle while the light of the flashlight shone upon my boots and bare skin, all the while singing *These Boots Were Made for Walking* in as best falsetto as I could manage. Before I got a brand new box of matches, I heard a mighty and commanding voice:

BEHOLD, I AM ALPHA AND OMEGA, THE BEGINNING, THE END, AND YOUR DENSITY.

I MEAN, YOUR **DESTINY.**

The body halo was back.

"I accept your offerings," He said.

"So you'll help me?" I eagerly asked.

"No."

No? NO? Then why the fuck had I gone to all that trouble? "But... but, Lord Hellion..."

"Not yet, I should say."

Whew. Okay. But what did He want now?

My mind had been read, because I got an instant answer: "I want you to write something."

"Write something?" I repeated. "You mean, like your Gospel or Holy Word?" I was willing to do whatever was asked, but I needed clarification.

"Not exactly."

Oh wait - this was a test, probably. Ah. Right. I knew what to say: "Okay, I think I've got it. A sci-fi romance, like *A Match Made In Space?*"

"No," replied The Hellion. "You must write a story of epic proportions

425

involving pride and prejudice, and the action must take place on the virgin American prairie. Or in Nazi Germany."

I paused. His command sounded like something for a professional writer. It was definitely above my level.

"But...but Lord Hellion...I'm not sure how to do that."

Why did I say that? Stupid! I had a chance to get a hand from an otherworldly being, and I was standing in the dark, naked and whining. *You'd better adjust your attitude, and in a hurry,* I thought to myself. *If He wants you to write something, then you write something.*

There was a long silence while we looked at each other. I began to feel exposed in the chill. The Hellion seemed to be daydreaming. He took out a black comb and ran it though His oiled hair, then replaced it in the breast pocket of the blue short sleeved cotton shirt that was buttoned up to His chin. An oil stain soaked through his pocket.

I slowly picked up my clothes and put them back on, and all the while keeping one eye on The Hellion. Finally, when I was through dressing and The Hellion remained a thousand mental miles away, I spoke again.

"Lord Hellion?"

"What?" He seemed to shake His head slightly, as if waking. Then He looked down at me.

"Do you still want me to write something?"

"Oh yeah, sure, Daddy-O. Just finish up an unauthorized autobiography and run it on over to me when you're done."

"Uh...what?" How could an autobiography be *unauthorized?*

"Hmmm?"

"An unauthorized autobiography? I...I don't understand what that means."

The Hellion fidgeted and grew impatient. "Well, you know...c'mon...just write it. Recopy it in your own handwriting and turn it in. Then I'll get you outta your fix. Gotta go!" And with that, He disappeared.

Great, I thought. *Another test.* I sighed at the stars. *Fine. Whatever He wants.* I resolved to write my autobiography, and then, when I was finished, I would declare that I had neither cooperated nor given myself permission to do so.

Weird.

* * *

So how does one write an autobiography, authorized or not, without making it sound like a long-term shift change log? You know:

1967 – Born.
1968 – One year old. Said a word or two. Not walking. Soiling self.
1969 – Treated for thrush. Wearing shoes.
1970 – 1997: Passing boar tusks off as dwarf elephant ivory amid grain elevator explosions.

Floor Super KRONAG clocking out...

I've never read biographies. I've never really been much of a bookworm at all, though I used to read Louie L'Amour when I was a kid, along with Sprague DeKamp's almost-sexually explicit and blood-drenched *Konan the Barbarian* adventures. Occasionally I'd pick up some of the stuff by Howard, but he spent too much time talking about glints of light on the claws of some creature instead of inspiring my adolescent gristle with deliciously slow descriptions of glistening sweat on the milky boobs of some princess. Therefore, the original Hyborian chronicler was relegated to my literary second string. Is that how I ought to begin a book? By talking about how I gunned down some rustlers with my Peacemaker and then rolled into a frontier town, found the saloon, and "drank lustily while taking a tavern wench with the passion of a Kushite too long on the Aquilonian plain"? Maybe not, because I didn't only read stuff that had to be smuggled under Hallucino-Grandpa's roof. I liked Twain, and I could enjoy Tom and Huck without violating H.G.'s literary mandates.

Let's see...before beginning each chapter, Twain liked to preface the action therein. Could I do that? Nah. It might have worked for him, but if I revealed, upfront, how Injun Joe used to bang Aunt Polly every Sunday night, the reader would just toss the book aside.

What about Milne? Sure, I know that's going back to my very early days, but who cares? I could begin my autobiography by talking about the stuffed animals that keep me company in the Hundred Hectare Wood. Harry could be my Winnie-*ther*-Mandella—

– KRONAG!
[Oops – hold on...be back in a sec.]

- Yeah, coming!
- *Enter house. You.*
- Why? What's wrong?
- *More firewood. Get.*
- Huh? Oh, right. I'm writing now. I'm trying to get the book started.
- *When finish?*
- What do you mean? The book, or just for today?
- *Today.*
- I dunno. Hour or so.
- *Dinner soon, okay? Okay?*
- Right. I'll get the wood.
- *Why book important?*
- Why? Well, because I want to get out of here, you know, go someplace where there's some people.
- *All die. World finish.*
- I know. But I believe He can...He can help...somehow. Harry? Harry, what's wrong?
- *Nothing. Go out.*
- Are you sure that there's nothing wrong?
- *Yes! Stop ask! Go!*
- Alright, alright.

Remember What The Dormouse Said:
"You Can Check Out Any Time You Like, But You Can Never Leave."

I have to bring in some firewood and help out with dinner, so I can't spend much more time here. I think there's something on Harry's mind already, so I don't want to further agitate her. You know, sometimes she...ah hell, forget it. I know that all couples have their disputes, but sometimes she can really wind me up with just the smallest thing. I don't know how she does it. Maybe I should be flattered, because that's kind of a testament to how thoroughly she knows me, right? Then again, sometimes I think I'd like to see her and Wilson the Volleyball on MVT's *Celebrity Deadmatch*. Shit, that's a lousy thing to say. I'm not serious, of course. Well, hold on. Sometimes she gets highly pissed at me and says she'd like to see me in an Extreme Fighting Cage-Death-Match with Kris McKandless.

Right...where was I? Oh yes, I was trying to think of some way to record my life story. I wish that The Hellion would allow me to *draw* my unauthorized autobiography. Harry could help me, too. She likes to hang her own sketches on the hut wall where we can admire them, but sometimes "guests" turn up and take critical liberties. For example, I was admiring one of Harry's sketches and noticed, tacked near her work, that there was a beautiful charcoal of an ivy-covered gothic cathedral with a vaguely DeLaSoul/DeLaCroix flavor. Such things aren't Harry's style, and I definitely got no bitties in the BK lounge, either. As I puzzled over the charcoal's origin, I heard a voice say: "Do you like it? I drew it from memory...because memory is what I have."

I whirled around and told Dr. Leckter to get the hell out of my hut before I ate his tongue. The sociopathic psychiatrist gave a little smile and left, but he didn't walk out the door – he just walked through a wall.

"Asshole," I muttered. I turned to tear down the charcoal, but it was gone.

* * *

- *How feel?*
- Mmmm. Hi. Oh...uh, okay. Pretty good, actually. What's going on?
- *Nothing. Good book. Read night, finish in morning.*

429

- Oh. I saw you were still reading when I dropped off the first time. I woke up again later and you were out like a light. I built up the fire again before I went back to sleep.
- Mmmm. Not cold last night. Comfortable.
- Good.
- Careful.
- Of what?
- Not too much fire, sleep, burn house.
- What, the hut? Nah. I'm careful. Besides - look...see?
  This thing's mostly hard mud with sticks inside. Not easy to burn.
- Oh. Hey, you want read? This?
- Ummm...nah.
- What mean, "nah?"
- No, I don't really want to read it. The Mormons are long gone, and so are the Jesuits. That old religious stuff was more H.G.'s thing than mine.
- Oh. Miss him?
- Sure. Every day. Say, was that book difficult to read?

-Pshaw. Not at all. I found it to be largely a compilation of historical documents, loosely wound together by threads of author narration and elements of local legend. If anything, I was dubious of some of the references, as they seemed only tenuously - and I hope that's not too much of a pejorative - sourced, depending upon the material in which one places the most confidence, be it the Carson City Record, the Salt Lake Times, or The Jesui--

- Okay, okay...I...I was just curious. But you enjoyed it?
- It okay. Good action. Sure you not want read?
- No thanks. But let me see it, please. H.G. collected some odd stuff. I wonder why he had this?
- Because it also have Korean story. Very old.
- What?
- Korean city in Nevada. First city. Open this page. Here. See? Picture.
- Ummm...

- *Why?*
- Why what?
- *Why say "ummm"?*
- Because this is a map of the Nevada Test Range before it became a test range. And this - right here, see? - is about where the *Se Ti-Cah*, or Nephilim, if you prefer, city was.
- *No. Korean.*
- What are you talking about?
- *Han people come, make city. Enter whole world first. First people.*
- Okaaay...if you mean Asiatic, Bering-Land-Bridge-Folks, I see your point...but this wasn't a Native American city. This was built by people who weren't Native American, Korean, or any other Terran type...at least, not more than half-Terran. In fact, Sarah Winnemucca told the Europeans that her people had joined with other tribes to wipe them out up by Lovelock.
- *Clean them? Not understand.*
- No. Wipe. Wipe out. "Kill." "All."
- *Oh! Understand.*

I'm Never Goin' Back
To Buttholeville

I met Harry after I had psych-adapted dream of the film *The Hills Had Eyes*. I hadn't been in the mountains very long when we encountered each other, and it wasn't as dramatic as when Tomas Hanks met Wilson – you know, the whole "paint you with my blood" approach. No, I think it would be more accurate to say that Harry *found* me.

* * *

The days after I hiked out of Vegas were times of bland Matin cubes and daytime tent dozing. My bottles comprised most of my pack weight, and the load got lighter all the time. If I had been healthy "down there," I would have also fallen back upon the old desert survival strategy of urine drinking, but my infection precluded that. Therefore, I recycled my piss in condensation pits to leave the nastiness in the bottom of the hole.

* * *

The word "attrition" kept entering my mind. For me, this term was most familiar within the context of Civil War discussions, since no history prof was fully qualified unless he or she could mention, at least one hundred times during the course of a sequence, how "the struggle became a *war of attrition* in which the North's superior resources gradually ground down those of the South in a continuing *war of attrition*, though the superior Confederate officer corps was able to postpone the inevitable in the *war of attrition*..."

...*war of attrition*...blah-blah-blah...*war of attrition*...blah-blah-blah...*attritionattritionattrition*...

...*AmerikanerAmerikanerAmerikaner*...

Despite my best efforts to sponge sweat and conserve water, I knew that I was in danger of becoming the Robert E. Lee of dehydration. The Mojave forced me closer to a water bottle Appomattox every day as my body lost moisture with every breath, not to mention precious sweat evaporation.

I wasn't sure what to do, or what I *could* do. I worried that my

432

tongue would swell. I imagined that Ulysses S. Grant would stride up and demand that I write General Order Nine while pulling out my swollen tongue. I envisioned huge beef tongues in the "Discounted BSE Offal Section" of Vonn's meat cases. Would my tongue get that big when dehydration set in? Or was that hypothermia? Or hypoglycemia? *Hypohyperhypo*...I didn't know. I just wanted to survive the trip, and for my tongue to remain its normal size.

I couldn't wimp out and return to Vegas, and believe me, this had become a temptation. *Hey, I thought, maybe things have returned to normal. Maybe people have pulled together and are helping each other.* These thoughts vanished on my second night in the desert when a sonic boom-times-ten jarred me awake. *So that's what a nuke sounds like, I thought.* A nuke's lethal "S" wave, however, would have spanned the distance that I had walked in a second. I remembered this after a moment, and it dawned on me that I wasn't already dead. I unzipped my bivvy, looked back toward the city, and saw a flame-filled mushroom cloud light up the sky. "MOABs," I whispered to a lone joshua tree. *A nuclear floorshow without the force and radiation of the Real McCoy. Nellis is gone.*

I returned to my sleeping mat. As I stared up at where the joshua tree's shadow fell on the bivvy, I knew that, although most of Vegas was probably still standing, I should dismiss thoughts of returning.

Borrowed Time And Another
Man's Memories

Hallucino-Grandpa placed both varsity and junior-varsity destination maps in his kit. Since I was never a targeteer or ranger, I knew which one was intended for me. I thought that the comprehensive and assume-nothing nature of the flunky map showed that H.G. should have been an elementary teacher, because it was designed for user success. There weren't any jargon-laden directions, followed by black-and-white topo hodge-podges of wavy lines and confusing numbers. H.G.'s rudimentary strategies included photos of landforms, correlated to a color atlas, along with further fail-safe features in a step-by-step format:

Does the skyline look like this picture? Yes? Okay, you're HERE. No? Can you see a road? Yes? And do the mountains look like this? Yes? Alright then, you're HERE. Do you see this rock? Good. Walk toward it.

H.G. had somehow foreseen this world, somehow, and that revelation had been translated into the pack that I carried and the safe place to which I traveled. Even before the World Trade Center, Oklahoma City, and all of the other American Reichstags, H.G. had known what to do, because he had been through all of it before. H.G. had probably figured (correctly) that this time it would be harder to don Nazi camouflage and ride out the storm. No, when the darkness returned, H.G. had somehow guessed that survival would mean washing one's hands of everything and hitting the road.

I was sure that, when I finally did arrive at H.G.'s "Camp Scott," I would find myself so thoroughly stocked and provisioned that it would be my own whim, and not ration shortage, that determined my length of stay. H.G. had taken considerable pains to create a high level of independent isolation, from a perfectly-matched desert camo tent and sanity-preserving writing materials, to the "one hundred percent recommended daily allowance of every nutrient known to man" touted by the Matin survival cubes in my pack.

Matin cubes weren't the tastiest survival fare, but they were, by far, the most nutritious and longest-lasting. With a fifty-year shelf life and purchase date-stamps of "25/FEB/73", the cubes offered further insight on H.G.'s intentions. He hadn't been buying survival materials for himself. Christ, in 1973, the man was...what? Sixty-three years old? No, this was a case of him looking after me.

My mo-bag contained a Bureau of Land Management and Federal Aviation Administration joint document, and it showed a variety of highlighted aircraft crash sites which were identified by dates and the governmental authorities that had handled rescue and recovery efforts. Some went way back, with the earliest year being 1924. Annotations identified the types of aircraft, except for "OA" designations. Such sites were marked by red "49AACTS/49ES" overstamps, meaning that the lost craft were classified and flown by either Army Air Corps or later US Air Force units. When I checked the map to see if a site was indicated in Lake Meade, I only saw another obnoxious red overstamp and a series of speculative dots and question marks. My exact destination was also something that the map hadn't originally shown, though a spot had been hand-penned in the northwestern Valley. According to the map, I was headed just a bit south of Mt. Charleston, toward the slightly smaller Mt. Pelosi, and near the Buddy Scott Quintet crash site.

I had once watched a special on public TV about hiking trails in the mountains surrounding the Vegas Valley, and there was a brief piece about the Buddy Scott Quintet crash site. As I recalled, the BSt site was fairly remote, and as much of a mountain hiking challenge as it was the location of an air disaster. On the night of January 16, 1970, The Buddy Scott Quintet was returning to Vegas from the SEATAC Peace Festival. The concert was huge, and had left many exciting memories in thousands of young minds. It was also the last time that the Buddy Scott Quintet would perform. In January, Seattle is a cold-ass Shackleton Six Flags, but that didn't deter the multitudes of socially-conscious pop-music peace activists. The "authorities" treated the SEATAC Peace Festival in the same way that similar gatherings had been brought to heel - that is, "those goddamned libs, fags, niggers, commies, and stupid kids got gas and rubber bullets."

When the Gulf War rolled around decades later, however, the media PR machine was more efficient. This time, images of burning children were replaced with bomb-scope IR video game footage, and the public applauded. To me, the only thing remarkable about Gulf War coverage was the fact that there was any effort at all put forth in concocting a cover story. It's hard to say what the long-term US intentions in the Persian

Gulf might have been, since smallpox had brought an end to the Oil Crusades...and pretty much everything else.

The Buddy Scott Quintet, had its members lived, would have probably protested the Gulf War as well. From what I understood, founders Victor Buddy and William Scott were gentle pacifist souls who dreaded the thought of the American Orphan Factory expanding its operations in Vietnam...so their deaths spared them the knowledge that their music ultimately had no effect on that particular conflict. BS4 did make some damn fine jams before meeting their fate in the Nevada mountains, though. I once owned copies of BS4's debut album *You're Victorious* and its brilliant follow-up, *Beautiful Blooms*.

The BS4 DC-9 hit Mt. Pelosi at about seven-thirty PM. The plane plowed into sheer rimrock and smeared hot aluminum down the mountain like Noah's Ark washing Ararat in burning pitch. There were twenty-two people on board, and ironically, some of them were soldiers on their way back home from Vietnam. During the wreckage recovery, William Scott's lover, the actor Clark Grable, offered a reward for the ring his partner had worn - a silver band with an onyx cross setting - but neither the ring, nor the hand that had worn it, were ever found.

Several Vegas clubs hosted memorial parties. There were extensive pieces in the *Los Vegas Review-Journal* and *Rolling Stoned*. The 1970s conspiracy theorist community had the period equivalent of Bart Snell's show running hot and heavy with talk of a collision with a secret Armitage Field Site Four aircraft, and some even claimed that the government had shot the plane down.

Gee, the Feds would *never* have done a thing like *that*.

Rub-A-Dub-Dub,
Thanks For
The Grub

A large black raven landed about fifty yards ahead. When I got close, it flew down the road, waited for me to approach, and took off again. This carried on for a day. When I pitched my tent that night, I wondered what the raven had been doing.

I wound up a tiny diode lantern and reached into the pack to pull out one of the remaining pens and a piece of minimally ink-splattered paper. In the white LED-light I sketched out the day's perspective: the raven, the old tire tracks, and the non-terminating and horizonless background that simply went up the mountainside. I put the pen down and assayed my effort. "Not many happy little trees here," I said, as I crumpled up the paper, switched off the lantern, and laid down my head.

* * *

The next day found me bored with the raven's game, so I no longer bothered to watch. I did a double take, however, when I noticed that the bird had been replaced by the figure of a man. He stood some distance ahead, perfectly still, arms folded, and legs slightly apart. He wasn't wearing a hat, which I thought was strange.

I stopped and stared at the figure. Then, as I put my hands in a resting grip on the pack's shoulder straps, I murmured: "I wonder if he's going to fly away when I get close." When I got near enough to ID the guy, I wasn't really shocked.

"I just wanted to get out of the Union Plaza for a while," said Randy Flag through his big trademark grin.

I didn't even bother to reply. Instead, I mentally checked off the times that I had hydrated for the day. Yep, I had taken a big slug when I got up, and I hadn't missed an hour since. Check. How was the tongue? Too big? Did I have a mouth erection? Nope. Check again. I wasn't dehydrated and I didn't have heat exhaustion, yet I was haunted by the apparition of Jamey Sheradan, er, sorry – *Randy Flag*. Yes, that's right – boots, face buttons, jean jacket, and mega-mullet.

I sighed. "Shouldn't you be carrying a badge or something? And have a better haircut? And a suit?"

He ignored my questions and walked around me like a circling vulture. "I don't happen upon many minstrels out here," he said through his bared teeth. "How's about some *Mammy* for starters?"

Ha-ha. I get it. Hilarious.

"How's the back? Painful? Tired shoulders? Heavy pack, eh? And how's your dick? Do you really think that you'll make it to your dear Nazi grandfather's little Cub Scout camp before your entire lower body rots away?"

I stopped and turned. "Oh yes," I replied. "Let's see: You're about to offer to 'take away my pain,' but I have to ask on my knees. Right?"

Flag's grin wavered for a second, then the corners of his mouth again tightened and his eyes narrowed with pleasure. "Why...yes. That would demonstrate the proper attitude."

"I have no time for this shit," I replied. "Go back to *The Darkest Tower* or the Miskatonic Coast or wherever."

The Three Cripples In The
Buck And Bell...Or
The Unicorn,
Perhaps?!

Five days after I walked out of Vegas I strode into Camp Scott and returned to my boyhood campground. The place looked like it had when I was a kid. I looked like shit. For one thing, I still had ink all over my face - how was I gonna wash it off? With precious water? No. I had just accepted my Jolson-esque presentation and pressed on.

What kind of time did I make during the journey? Let's see...Camp Scott was about 25-30 miles northwest of Vegas, let's say 28 miles...the trek took about five days...that averaged to roughly five-and-a-half miles per day. I'm okay with that. C'mon, dammit! With a full pack and an infection, I think that's acceptable. And traveling through the Mojave Desert, as well? That's pretty damn good!

GFY.

* * *

I was a little kid the last time I was here. The spot looked the same, but - compared to what? A distant memory? I re-checked the photos of my target destination and found one of the rimrock near the mountain top. *This has to be Mount Pelosi,* I thought, as I held the photo up to compare it with my view of the landform. *That's where the plane hit. I'm in the right spot, but the wreckage is further up.* Maybe I would satisfy my morbid curiosity on some afternoon and hike up there after I had settled in.

Where *was* the hut, shelter, or whatever-it-was? All I saw was a long-abandoned campsite. When I opened the map and checked the section that contained the hut's location, I laughed. It looked like those maps that kids drew and gave to their friends during treasure hunts. *Steps to take. Directions to face. Where to dig.* **Dig?** Oh man...I hoped that I hadn't come all this way just to sleep in a hole. If that turned out to be the case, then I resolved to just live in my tent until I had raised some kind of above-ground shelter. I wasn't, *wasn't* sleeping in a hole.

Several low mounds were at the indicated spot. I dug with my pack trowel until I heard the wrinkle of heavy rot-proof synthetic fiber. My heart began to beat faster, as if I really were a child on the verge of discovering one of his classmate's treas--

- *Kronag!* **KRONAG!**

[Oops - I'll continue my story in a minute]

- I'm here! Jesus! What is it?
- *Time.*
- Time? For...?
- *You time jerk.*
- Okay.
- *You jerk! Not forget!*
- No, I won't forget! Just a second. I'm writing now.
- *Ahhh...for Hellion Buddha. Good.*
- I'll get to it in a minute. I'm just trying to finish this bit about when we met.
- *Mmmm. Remember. Good day, at spring. Beautiful, like Jeju-Do. Remember and heart smile.*
- Yeaaah. Mmm. That was a good day, wasn't it?
- *Yes. Happy day. Brave day.*
- Brave day? Ha! Those guys weren't real.
- *Still...mmm...shoot them, kill them.*
- Mmmm.
- *Mmmm.*
- I'll go now and finish this later.
- *Where?*
- I dunno. Outside somewhere.
- *Not inside?*
- No. I don't want to spooge in the hut.
- *Oh. Understand.*

For The Love
Of TI-11

I lifted the tarp after I finished troweling away the dirt. That damned trowel. I felt like I had cleared a snowy sidewalk with a teaspoon.

The hut's door looked like a big woven-stick basket lid and it was wired on one side to a heavy post frame. There was a neatly arranged little entryway that consisted of three steps.

"Go ahead. I think you'll be pleased."

Who said that? I knew that voice. *Magneeto? Gandolf?*

"Really, the Shire boasts no better."

I turned to see Gandolf appraise the hut. I smiled. "I'm hopeful," I said. "I think that Hallucino-Grandpa put quite a stash inside."

"You'd best see," replied the wizard.

I blinked. Once again, my only company was the mountain. Bylbo's cracked glasses and chipped plates gave way to thoughts of Lord Caernarvon, with the major difference being that I had complete permission to enter...no curses here, baby. If anything, I was Tutankhamun coming home. I gingerly reached out and opened the door.

The sunlight revealed the interior wattle-walls to be framed by more peeled branches, tightly woven like the interior of a reed basket, and a smooth flagstone floor. I removed a flashlight from my pack and cautiously proceeded. Then I froze before traversing the threshold and quickly backed up the steps.

I must have seen it first, because if I had smelled it first I would have had respiratory problems like those which resulted from exposure to tear gas. In the middle of the floor, in a shiny pan that resembled an inverted hubcap, was a slightly-melted white block that looked like a partially rain-dissolved livestock salt lick. Over the years it had slowly flowed over the edges of the pan and onto the floor, leaving stalagmite nubs that would need to be removed before the hut could be made habitable.

I sat down next to my pack and slowly lowered my hand that I had instinctively jerked up to shield my mouth and nose. I remembered the sensation of chem-training from my military days and I half expected a similar sensation to hit me...but it didn't. No tears, no coughing. I had been quick enough.

I was simultaneously pissed and pleased with Hallucino-Grandpa. I was pissed because nowhere on the map or flunky flowchart did it say that there was a little surprise awaiting the finder of the hut, and pleased because I was now certain that I would only have to clear out some chemical residue before moving in, rather than piles of packrat sticks, bones, droppings, and other foul crap. In fact, I was sure that after a few days of pretending that I was Kevin Kostner reclaiming a prairie sod fort, I would have a cozy wilderness pad that was just as its maker had left it.

I Am Red! I Am Not Red! I Am Red!
I Am Not
Red!

I figured that the spring had been maintained because it was near an access road and on USFS land. Perhaps there was still a flow pipe and a stock trough. Like everything else, there were pictures and directions to the spring, and these used the location of the hut as a baseline reference. I dug through my pack, grabbed the flunky map, pictures, and a bar of soap. Then I flipped through polaroids and scanned the landscape. *Tree. Path. First boulder. Second boulder. Just over that little rise.* I stripped off my clothes as soon as I saw the trough.

...Ahhhohmygodthatfeelssogood...

I drank my fill and soaped up in the ten-foot government-green tank. The painful infection that I had endured was briefly forgotten in the water's cold relief.

Mmmm. I leaned back and carefully felt my scalp. It wasn't painful, and my bath had softened the dried scab. I glanced in the direction of my clothing pile. "Damn," I said aloud. "I forgot the water bottles." No matter. I could come back later.

I felt like a king...well, sort of. KRONAG The First. And Last. I propped my elbows up on the sides of the tank, closed my eyes, and smiled. The cool water shrank my feverish dick into a hard little beak that poked up from a nest of brown pubes. I was temporarily content, despite being alone in the world and faced with a solitary future in a giant inverted wilderness basket. Well, maybe I wasn't *that* content...and I *wasn't* really a king...but the water and the clean feeling it brought were regal reliefs. No, no...that wasn't right, either. How about a little perspective shift here? I *was* a king. I was king of the entire goddamned world. No Dowd. No Esquire of Gothos. No Cue. No special powers. Just me. King by default.

KRONAG "Default Setting" the First.

* * *

I realize that this is a book and not a movie, but I'm still going to use a film montage. Here's a clip of me as I cut a long branch, turn it into a shepherd's hook, and use it to fish the white noxo-block out of the hut while I hold a wet cloth over my face. Next, I go through Hallucino-Grandpa's supplies. Cut to a sequence in which I look through the contents of a tool box and happily discover a folding shovel. Here's a close-up of my facial expression as I read labels on MREs, Matins, and other foodstuffs. Now I try on H.G.'s BDUs. The last shot is of me on a sleeping mat near the fire with a drowsy smile on my face. Close with an out-of-focus firelight dissolve.

Then **BAM!** A jolting shot of me sitting up, followed by a sharp gasp as I pull myself out of a nightmare. Dawn comes in around the edges of the door. Droplets of sweat on my brow are a nice touch. Eyes wide, I frantically look around. Recognition appears in my eyes. I sigh as my posture relaxes.

Well, that's how it might have looked if there had been a film crew in the hut when I awoke from my *The Hills Had Eyes* nightmare. It had been sort of like *Jeremiah Johnston* meets *Nightmares on Elm Street*. I really shouldn't call it a nightmare, though. Yeah, it was scary in parts, but I was a hero in the end.

Guilt Is Like A Bag Of Fuckin' Bricks. All You Gotta Do...*Is* *Set It* *Down*.

After I blew the fire back to life and fixed a decent breakfast of crackers and reconstituted scrambled eggs, I got dressed, grabbed a water bottle, and brushed my teeth with some *(Clean! Fresh! Clear! Hallelujah!)* spring water. Then I stared at the flames and considered the previous night's dream. In it, I had decided to explore the Buddy Scott Quintet crash site. I hiked upward thorough a dreamscape forest that was like the repeating cartoon backgrounds that you see in the old quickie thrown-together *Skooby Doo* chase scenes. When I got to the top of Mt. Pelosi (well, not actually on *top* — I was just at the base of the rimrock), I found the smashed-up remains of...a Gawa sandcrawler. I knew this was stupid, but nevertheless, I appreciated the attention to detail that was included in the dream, for the chunks of wreckage were corroded, as if having lain there since 1970. I didn't need Obie-Wan to tell me that the long black scars along the hulk's exterior were "too precise for Sandy People — these blaster marks are the work of imperial storm troopers."

I think that my acknowledgment of the Empire's attack cued my REM sleep-stage-manager to send out a squad of storm troopers. I *should* have said something like: "This crawler was obviously destroyed by a platoon of lingerie-clad Jianna Jun clones," but I wasn't quick enough to think of that, and the next thing I knew, Mount Pelosi had morphed into Endore, and I had to run for my life. I sprinted through a rain forest, past ferns and mossy fallen logs, while an eewok kept popping up in the same bushes, in the same repeating-loop background.

Ow! Fuck! A red blaster beam scorched my elbow. *Good realism, pain-wise*, some dream-critic noted in the back of my REM theater. This was confirmed in the following action, as Jean Shalitt materialized next to the repeating eewok...once, twice, three times, and then he was gone. I guessed the review was finished...no, wait...the eewok suddenly sported a huge afro.

Heyyy...how could I outrun a stormtrooper on a speeder bike? I looked back. Yep, I was definitely staying ahead of the guy, though he still shot red, no, wait, *green* bolts of energy at me. I looked down at my legs, which moved at cartoonish *Masque/Roget Rabbit* speed.

Another bolt of green energy sizzled by. I was sick of this. I smelled singed hair. I reached up and felt a hole in the brim of my cool-ass Sly Stones funkadelic headgear.

Another bolt. I got more pissed.

Another.

"Oh *no*," I indignantly yelled, "you did *not* shoot that green shit at me!" I changed direction and headed for a huge redwood trunk. Just before I smashed into a wall of rust-colored bark, I pulled the ejection handle on my pinstriped trousers and was thrown upward while my lemon-cream cabana ensemble exploded against the tree. The speeder also struck the redwood, though as my parachute gently drifted down, I noted that the bike was mostly intact. In fact, it just smoldered at the foot of the trunk while the trooper slumped over the handlebars.

I touched down in the Mojave *(what about those redwoods?!)* and tried to stand, but I was pulled back down as the desert breeze filled my parachute and dragged me over the ground. I fumbled for the straps, which seemed curiously like the straps on a backpack, while the parachute yanked on my chest as if a cop's bullet had knocked me off of a bicycle. I finally freed myself and reached my feet as the released parachute caught the wind and disappeared into the fuzzy fantasy horizon.

I furiously strode over to the speeder bike and grabbed the trooper by the edge of his armor breastplate. I yanked on the neck joint under the back of his helmet and jerked him off of the wreckage. Then I got on his chest like a boy in a schoolyard dust-up and pulled off his helmet.

"Where you at? Where you at?" I yelled. I threw the helmet aside and looked down. The trooper didn't have a Phett-clone face, however. Instead, it looked somewhat like a Gray, but mouthless, and with big wads of flagellating tentacles on both sides of the creature's cranium. The eel-like Medusine whips prompted me to smash the heel of my right hand – once, then twice – against the spot where I estimated a nasal bridge might exist. The eels went limp and flopped down around the thing's tiny gray Shreck ears. Nictating membranes fell over the being's huge monochrome eyes like thin and translucent foreskins descending over the moist head of a spent and softening Downward Dick.

"Now, that's what I call a close encounter," I declared, as I took a seat on a rock and pulled a cigar from a pocket in my flight suit. Puff, sweet puff. *Mmmm.* "For a second there, I wasn't sure where this was going," I said. I half-expected a response from Harry Konnick Jr. or Geoff Goldblum. "Humpf," I grunted. Then, as I took the cigar out of my mouth, I yelled at the sky: "Whassa matter? Run outta playahs?"

"Yes...but I'd like to keep this just between us. I'd hate to lose my teaching job," someone answered. It was the trooper, who was now on his feet, though the space gorgon that I had KO'ed had been replaced by an anomalous-presentation character actor...no, not Minie-Me, not acromegalic Creeper Dude, not the Red Hair Dollop late night host guy...it was that Craven-to-Carter standby, Mike Berrymann.

"Whoa," I said, as I spat out my cigar. The appearance of this fellow did not bode well. In fact, I knew that in another dimension I mumbled and turned in my sleep.

"Now, hold on a sec," I stammered, as I got up from the rock and took a step back. "You're not always the bad guy. I mean, there was that *Ex-Files* episode in which you protected the Christ Child, remember? Remember?"

Berrymann moved forward. "Yes, of course I remember. That was one of the few times when I didn't find work playing a murderous-cannibal-biker." I thought that I saw a soft look cross Berrymann's face, and I wondered if I could talk my way out of this.

"Your ass ain't talkin' your way out of this," Jules said.

"Mr. Winnfield is correct," Berrymann agreed, as he came closer, and as I retreated. "Your reference to one sympathetic role isn't going to bail you out." Berrymann's white trooper armor had been replaced by dusty combat boots and denim overalls with disturbingly dark stains. And an ax.

"So," breathed Berrymann, "meet the family." The brush stirred behind him and a misshapen child of uncertain gender and dressed in dirty mutant Oshe Koshe B'Goshe gritted some rotten teeth and moved forward on all fours. The child fixed me in a gaze that burned beneath filthy desert-dirt-dreads that fell in greasy turd-like logs over his/her/its eyes. Others came out of the bushes, but instead of doing the one-by-one, shock-shot panaflex routine, I just ran.

"Ohhh...bad form," Loman-Rainman-Hook said from an invisible vantage near that of Jules-Jackson. "Bad form...however will this contest be determined if you don't properly appraise your opponents' horrors? How shall the struggle's glory be derived? Dreadful... unworthy --"

I sprinted away, across the face of Mount Pelosi, before Captain Hook could finish. I heard a cacophony of grunts, screams, and roars behind me, and I knew that this was yet another chase scene. There was a puff of air as something narrowly missed my head. I saw Berrymann's twirling ax sink its blade into a strangely bent and contorted pine tree, which shook and rained dry and dead Lake Bellagio needles as I ran through the gardens of Seoul's Flower Palace.

I somehow knew where I was going. *Tree. Path. First boulder. Second. Just over that little rise and...there was the spring.* But what did I expect? To touch "base" and be safe? If this was the game, the mutants didn't appear to be playing, because they continued at full speed over the rise and directly at me. What the fuck was I gonna do? Why did I come here? I looked around for something to throw, at least...

"No! Not do that, *waygukin*! Need Luger 10/22. NEED!"

"What?" I cried out. The voice was not that of the Samuel-Dustin side editorials. It was feminine, and distantly familiar.

"10/22! You stupid! Luger 10/22! GET!"

Right. Right! What the hell was I doing? I had to get back to the hut. I had to get my hands on my .22, then give these broken-DNA-helix-man-cutouts what for. The mutants were almost on top of me, due to the time that I had spent gawking around the water tank and talking to the mysterious voice. But I discovered that I still had my cartoon legs, and it was the mutants' turn to gape as I ran around them, in a big circle, and back to the hut.

I knew the 10/22 would be loaded and ready to roll when I threw open the hut door and dove for it. Mags of thirty CCI dream-Stingers would be delivered as fast as I could send them. Should I shoot from the hut? No. I had to go outside. I had to find a tree, quick!

Crouch. Breath. Pulsepulsepulse. Breath. Shhh...here they come. Moans-roars-grunts. Getting closer, closer...

I had my *Good-Bad-Ugly*-esque tightened jaw ready as I gripped the 10/22 and prepared to let loose with a bumpfire stream of fire that would show just how fast a semi-auto could deliver simulated full-auto rock-n-roll. I had never really learned how to bumpfire a semi-auto, though. But never mind. This was a dream. Right now, I was determined to imitate the skills that I had seen in cheesy eighties action films. *Just average with firearms? Me? My whole life? Nah. I don't know who you could mean. I'm the latest Wild Bill installment. Am I your huckleberry? Hell, no.* I'm your five-hundred-pound blue-ribbon county fair pumpkin.

I could do it. "Be one with your weapon," and all that stuff. I knew it was going to happen. This was now my sixteen-year-old-boy fantasy zone. I was about to pick up a dream guitar that my waking-self couldn't even tune and blow away a fan-filled stadium. I was about to score the winning basket at the State Dream Playoffs, when my daylight scrub-self hadn't even made the team. I was about to find out what that remote hottie senior's sweater smelled like and wake up the next morning with the sheets curiously glued to my belly. And I was a *muthafuckin'* gunslinger, baby.

I stepped out from behind the tree. This time, I *did* take the time to focus on individual reaction shots from each member of the mutant brood. *That's right, bitchy. Look what I got. Uh-huh. Not so eager for that desert cannibal action now, eh? What's up with that ax? Not enough? Ready to go, Uncle-Brother-Dad Jupiter? How 'bout you, quadruped dread boy – SUCK THIS!*

I let the sound techs take some license with my first shots...just like Monny's Little Bill brain-puree in the final sequence of *Unforgotten,* when the Spencer Carbine blows out THX sound systems. It was the same with my opening salvo. It was *Wichita 1812 Leftoverture* on hallucinogenic steroids: The bolt glided back, the mag fed a round, and Zeus let loose. Six-fingered hands, bent spines and drooling inbred bodies flew. Berrymann rushed me with his ax over his head while an awful scream came out of his mouth. One shot sent the ax head flying with a *ping!* and Berrymann stopped, lowered the bladeless handle, and looked at it in bewilderment. It was a "hard R" feature, so in the next instant, a wax mock-up of Berrymann's head exploded and his decapitated body crumpled to the ground, followed by a smug shot of me looking through my sights.

"That's right," I heard Ash say. "Give 'em some sugar, baby." I glanced to my left and saw the Chainsaw-Handed Great One wink, grin, and nod in approval. I returned an "I'm-the-shit" look, then resumed my dispatching.

* * *

In the end, the 10/22's barrel was so hot that it could fry an egg, and on the ground was a red-Karo-drenched pile of semi-human and semi-disassembled carcasses. Kudos to Greg Cannon and his effects team.

I fucking *won* at the end of the movie. Sure, there might have been

449

a Bob Zombie alternate ending in which I was consumed by Berrymann and Company, and all set to Bob Halford's slick throat starch of *Eating Me Alive*...but that was just for the hardcore fans, back in the *Deleted Scene/Alternate Ending* menu.

For He Knows
Not What
He Has
Done

My vacant eyes stared at the fire pit.

Interesting dream.

The post-game breakdown had gone well...up to a point. I knew where my subconscious Knapster had ripped off most of the scenes and characters. I was ready to dismiss the dream as just a piece of mental wee-hour recreation, and not some Carpentarian "the-Universe-is-desperately-trying-to-warn-me" experience, but I remembered the scene at the spring and the voice that had reminded me of my Ruger.

Waygukin.

Wow. Now there was a word from my past.

It's Bingo, Lady. You Can't Cheat. And If You Could, I'd Know About It.

"Halla better."

I jerked in surprise and almost fell into the tank. I knocked over the water bottles with my foot.

"Hello? Who said that?" I was awake. Not dreaming. Sure of it. Was this another hallucination?

"I say: Mount Halla better. Pretty. Mount Pelosi not pretty." It was a woman's voice, the one that I had heard in my dream, and...somewhere, or *somewhen*, else. It came from the vicinity of a fallen juniper, one of the few species of tree hardy enough to have made its final stand long ago on this rugged slope. I fixed my eyes on the old log and carefully walked toward it.

Mt. Halla? Saaay...I knew where that was. What a piece of trivia to pull up. I almost laughed at the stuff that floated around in my skull soup. "You're from Jeju-Do?"

"Jeju-Do?" the voice echoed. I slowed, then stopped to savor the sound. Hearing it was like the sensation that I had experienced with the first gulp of spring water that I had taken after walking through the desert.

"No?" I breathed.

"No. From near Seoul. Siheung Shitty."

It was my turn to laugh, but I squelched it and coughed.

"Okay?"

"Yes, yes. Fine. Ahem. Siheung City. I've heard of it. Famous for its grapes, I believe." Jesus. More brain trivia. Where the hell was this stuff coming from? I'd never even been to Korea. Or had I? Maybe, long ago, in a confusing dream. I couldn't be sure.

"Yes. True." The voice had a pleased tone.

"I'm KRONAG. I have a camp near the road," I said. "Are you camping, too? Ummm – where *are* you?"

452

There was a pause. "Not camp. Live. Tree bottom." Then, as if remembering her manners: "Harry. My name Harry. Please meet you."

"Pleased to meet you too, Harry. 'Harry.' Is that short for something?"

"Debbie. Small name: 'Harry'."

Okay. "Harry." Whatever. If she didn't want to tell me her real name, then that was her business.

"Say, uh – *Harry* – whereabouts might you be?"

"Say-one-more-time-please." The request was spoken in staccato. "Where are you?"

"Oh. Tree bottom."

Tree bottom? What? Oh – she's built a dugout under the trunk. Good idea. Close to a water supply with heavy shelter. Smart lady.

"I'm outside – can you see me? I'm alone. I'm unarmed." *Idiot! Dammit...now she's gonna think that I am armed and dangerous. Dammit-dammit-dammit.*

Silence.

"Please, we're neighbors. I-I've been to the spring before. I need water, too." *Nothing. Was I feeling the leading edge of depression? Wow, it didn't take much nowadays.* "I just want some company," I continued. Thinking that there wouldn't be a reply, I decided to just fill the bottles and leave, but then I heard Harry's voice.

"Me too."

I felt elation. **"REALLY?** I mean – *ahem* – really?"

"Yes."

Okaaay. Now what? "Could you come out?" I asked. "I can go back to my camp and get some coffee or something...?" *That would be so nice. Some of H.G.'s freeze dried, hard-core-caffeinated-Organic-Fair-Trade-Socially-Responsible-Vaso-Constriction...and a new friend. In the mountain air.*

Please-please-please say yes.

More laughter. Still as sweet, but...puzzling.

"Ma'am? Harry? I don't understand."

"What mean: 'Come out'?"

I thought that I'd been clear, but I explained further. "Come out of your shelter, I mean. Can you come out? I'm standing near the trunk, but I don't see the entrance." *She did a nice job of hiding that feature, I thought. I can't see any evidence to betray a dwelling at all.*

453

"No, no. Tree bottom. Dirt branch – no, wait, wait – root. Root. Look root."

Ah, okay, that's it. I'll go down there and look. Her shelter must be near the upturned mass at the trunk's foot.

No, it's not.

"Umm, excuse me – Harry? I still don't see anything."

"What mean?" Did her voice carry a hint of impatience? Easy, champ, I cautioned myself. Don't alienate the only other person on earth.

"Your shelter – it's so well hidden. I can't see where you are."

"You eye close? Blind? You blind?"

"Blind? No...but I can't see where––"

"BY YOU FACE! LOOK! HERE!"

Oh. Okay. I can see you now.

Nice.

That's. Just. Fucking. Great.

In a tangle of upturned roots, nestled amid fibrous twists and turns, was a round softball-sized burl that had the wind and sand-fashioned features of...

Oh God. How inane.

"Debbie," indeed. What bullshit. More like Jianna Jun, circa her *Sassy Girls* days. Yeah, that's right. Miss Banned-Sexy-Dance-Samsung-Commercial herself.

My mind is gone.

GONE!!

Brittle Shells
And Bloody
Hankies

When I realized what Harry was, I was disappointed. I had wanted a human for company, not a tree tumor. I didn't talk to Harry during subsequent water bottle refillings. She kept talking to me, however. Talking, talking, talking. I then found myself glancing her way and giving grudging responses. After a while I started pouring my water bottles out onto the ground at my camp as an excuse for more frequent spring trips. Finally the day came when I took a small saw to the spring instead of bottles, and on that night I whittled off Harry's rough edges before making a comfy place for her by the fire.

*　*　*

I went for a little walk up the camp road and did some thinking. Then I returned and crept back into the hut. Harry was out doing her own thing. Some of the water bottles were gone, so maybe she was at the spring. I wasn't in the mood for her to order me to masturbate again. I expected that one day I'd discover a spot on the hut wall where she had been scratching my toss-tallies like a prisoner counting days in a cell.

I rummaged through some of Hallucino-Grandpa's reading material and found a yellowed copy of Vonnigut's *Hokus-Pokus*. Great book. I read it when I was in the USAF. I flipped through the pages to some of the parts that I remembered, then I laughed at the mental comparisons that I made between Vonnigut's imagined future and how things had actually turned out. *Humpf.* The nasty little world of *Hokus-Pokus* looked pretty good. I mean, at least it had *people*. I had to **laugh like hell** when I re-read the GRIOT™ episode, because I could relate to being geriatrically fucked in a way that even a fate-odds computer couldn't forecast. I also re-read the part in which the murdered student with the red-haired skull was exhumed, the chapter which related how the narrator fucked the hottie in the canoe (that would have been an interesting maneuver), the description of a urethral-fire he picked up as a kid (I could relate to that), the part where he met his one-nighter progeny (no, I couldn't relate), and the discussion of his physiological response to tuberculosis.

Vonnigut vividly explained how the human body, once infected, was not able to defeat the TB bug outright, so it did what it could to contain and segregate the bacillus via pathogenic ossification. At that stage, the body combats infection through calcium accretion, forming little shields, or shells, around the invading bacterium. As far as desperate "B" plans go, I don't think it's too bad, and occasionally it works for long periods. The tubercules can be bottled up, sometimes for years...though eventually they break out, and then it's good night.

I put the book down and considered a marketing angle that might have worked for dairy companies. When the FDA-backed pharmacological monopolies jacked up the prices of isoniazid and PAS-R drugs to the point that county health offices could no longer afford them, the corporate dairy industry could have boasted about the importance of calcium in TB latency: "Now, with one-hundred percent RDA of tuberculin shell material!" Milk cartons could have shown pictures of both abducted children and tubercular children. Or maybe abducted tubercular children.

The toppled tree near the spring obviously hadn't drunk enough milk. Maybe that connected to Harry's origin. She was a subterranean phytopathogen that had been encased in woody gnarls to prevent her from spreading throughout the entire tree...and yet, the juniper had fallen.

Bacillus shells and the hardened nodes they form are one thing, whereas tree burls are quite another. For example, when a burl's knotty grain is cross-sectioned, sanded, and polished, it becomes exotic and gorgeous, but if this process were performed on a tubercular tissue mass, the result would be unattractive.

And When He Turned Around
And Looked In The
Back Seat,
She Was
Gone!

I haven't participated in a lot of "glory hole" discussions in my life, mainly because glory holes were never more than an occasional diversion for me, as opposed to guys for whom they were a lifestyle - I mean, for that crowd, G.H. action superseded most other forms of sexual release.

A few rifts existed among G.H. proponents, and these mostly centered on positional dynamics. Some fellows were adamant in their stance that heaven was best accessed via camel, whereas others maintained that it was more fun to be on the other side of the needle's eye. That was nice, I supposed...but I had never really possessed any unique insights to share when these discussions got started, a fact made excruciatingly obvious when I committed a gaffe one night among airmen who were patronizing a Seoul suck wall. I guess it was a necessary part of my education, however, and it helped me to fully appreciate *La Ley Supremo* of cock slottery.

"Super #6 - on a nightly basis, when I can!" Laughter all around the table. Assent.

"Yeah, because I'm down here every night of the week!" More laughter. A card is flashed. "One more punch!" Other cards come out for silent review...then dissent.

"#6? Whatever. The wrap-up on #3 is great. I swear, the operator is in my head." A murmur, then a few nods. Counterpoint.

"But beginnings are where it's at. No fluff charge." Was that a disdainful sniff?

"I ain't changin' my slip." *Whooo.* A churl plays at connoisseur.

"Yeah. But like anything else - work together, get the job done."

"I always do." Joviality dead and buried. A pall falls over what I had thought was a gathering of chums who had congregated to mull matters of G.H. importance. It was like that scene from *La Femme Nickita,* in which Annabelle Parillaud is counseled by the senior femme fatale: "Smile when you don't know the answer. It doesn't make you any smarter, but it's nice for others."

The silence around the table grew oppressive, like CIA interrogators pressing an enemy combatant's confession out of a waterboarded witch. I could bear it no longer. I started to speak...and thus showed everyone at the table that I was far out of my element.

"Maybe if you knew who worked #3 and #6...?" I realized that I had made a mistake even before the sentence was finished. My voice became that of a Grand Dragon who suddenly realizes that he's standing at the podium of an NAACP convention. One or two airmen politely excused themselves, whereas the rest abruptly got up and left.

You see, that was the major pull of the glory hole. The mystery, the thrill of it, and the solid wall, traversed only by the interdimensional meatcraft when it ventured through the fellatial wormhole. Or, if sci-fi wasn't your thing, there was also an occult angle, in that G.H.s allowed one to experience clairvoyance via simulated veil-penetrating suck-offs. Glory holes could accommodate photon torpedoes, seminal ectoplasm, and pretty much anything else, depending upon the strength of one's imagination. By suggesting that identities on the other side be revealed...well, that was the bungle of an outsider.

I should have learned a lesson on that day. Maybe I did, but it was so long ago that I forgot and had to re-learn it. Whatever the case, I fucked up twice in my life in regard to the G.H. principle; the first case being the above incident, while the second involved a G.H. that I found in the woods.

It's like looking a gift horse in the mouth. If you find a glory hole that makes you happy, just leave well enough alone. This guideline could probably be extended to general human relations. Think of your partner as a G.H. Does that person make you less miserable or maybe even happy? Yes? Okay, good, that's all. Shut up. Quiet. Shhh. When you start to whine and whinge, just imagine that you're Scoot Evil being "shushed" by your dad. Appreciate what you have.

How is it possible to see, or sense, the energy of a wilderness G.H.? It's not terribly difficult. All you have to do is follow animal tracks, usually those of coyotes and porcupines, because these creatures are also into glory hole action, though I would advise caution when considering use of a porcupine G.H., as quills are sometimes left behind. Also, ascertain that you have not mistaken a woodpecker nest for a tree trunk pleasure pock. These are important safety tips.

I found a wilderness G.H. It happened one day after Harry had shooed me out of the hut for some prostate maintenance. She told me that lunch would be ready when I got back, and when I stepped out, she was kneeling by the fire, boiling rice and octopus for my favorite dish, *nakji bokkeum*.

I smiled as I trudged off into the woods, happy at the thought that my morning would consist of masturbation and Korean cuisine. *Where did she find an octopus in the La Madres?* I wondered. Then I shrugged. She was wonderfully mysterious, and it was best not to ask too many questions (See? See? G.H. principle). Time to think of cumming-for-health. Hmmm. *"Cumming For Health."* Seems like there was once a game show by that name. Or maybe I'm thinking of *Bowling For Columbyne*.

Being a 106-year-old old guy is a drag in many, no, *most* respects, with one exception being the mental Fantasy Library. Extreme senior citizenship brings with it a vast mental fantasy compilation that is comprised of basic memory material, as well as *could-have, might-have,* and *what-if* sexual fictions. As a teenager, the Fantasy Library was merely a stack of "I wonder what her (and her and her) pussy looks/tastes/feels like" speculative hypotheses which gave way to the imaginatively dormant twenties' and thirties' documentation processes. These, in turn, provided later-in-life tossing storylines, and every time I left the hut for a session, I could have dictated an entire edition of Penthome Forum.

I went through the card catalogue and came across a vignette that concerned an encounter with a vacationing Taiwanese chick whom I had met one night down near COEX...there wasn't a copyright date, but it must have been generated at a time before I met—

[- Sorry to interrupt, but you're getting a little too close again. Just back up a bit, then continue the story...but don't go down that particular path.]

[- Right. I forgot.]

Okay, so there I was, loosening my BDU pants, Taipei hottie reel rolling, leaning tree to my left (you other old-timers know what I'm talking about...heart above the head, right boys?), when I felt an interesting tingle down my spine, like someone had just grazed her nails down the length of my back.

Wow, shiver. Not sure why. Whatever. Let's get that stroke going, shall we? Ahhh...that's it...

...Then we left COEX and ended up on one of the Tehran Street buses...now we're out on a Yeouido River Walk...let's loosen up that top a bit...one button, two...

Okay, now it's a distraction. Another tingle.....I sense that it's coming from that...stump? With the perfect hole? Lined with soft-looking moss? Hmmm...hit the PAUSE button. Let's investigate.

OkayThat'sEnoughInvestigation....whoohoo...ohhh,
That's niiiice...restart the clip...
Mmmm...
Mmmm...
AUGH! SHIT! SHIT!
WHAT THE FUCK IS INSIDE THE STUMP?!
WHAT THE FUCK is...th-that...oohhmygod...mmm... Uuhhh...
AHHH...Uhhh...

Post-orgasmic paraplegia, numb toes, buckled knees. An old man folds up and falls to the ground like an aluminum lawn chair.

That was a *good* one. Soon there'll be little stumps running around these woods. For some reason, I think of...baby shower curtains. And, aside from a strand or two of moss, Mr. Cocky Cockerton looks rather clean - but then, the "dirty old nut banana," as Harry puts it, doesn't really set the hygiene bar too high.

Mental Note: Stump lies about 300 yards NW of the hut.
For future reference.

I laid on my bare ass cheeks and looked at the sky until my heart calmed down and my breathing leveled. Lunch was probably waiting. Penis, then belly. Simplify, simplify...via Walden glory holes.

I looked at the clouds and foolishly wondered what had helped me over the top. I swore that the last time I had felt something like that, I was having a bathroom-stall-midterm-cram-stress-reliever below the round stacks of the old ULVN "Yellow Submarine" library. Funny. My dick-memory went back that far at a moment's notice, yet the other parts of my brain seemed to short circuit, and right at the moment when the Glory Hole Principle was most applicable.

460

I got to my feet, wiped up a bit by pulling down a handful of tee, buttoned and buckled, then immediately *unbuttoned* and *unbuckled* for a sudden urination-clearing that wouldn't wait.

I walked back over to the stump. It was one of those old lumber company victims that had come down before the widespread use of chainsaws, and the lower six or seven feet of heavy sapwood that would have gummed-up manual blades had been left to rot. The bark had completely fallen, and the exposed wood was bleached and cracked. My McKinley-era penis port was nothing more than a soft and broken spot, rotted into a perfect circle of correct depth and diameter. Above it, descending from the saw cut, was a two or three inch split through the dry and weathered grain. I learned nothing by leaning down and looking through the dark entrance, but reasoned that the crack might reveal more.

I got closer, stood on tiptoes, and peered through the split trunk. *Toes up, higher, higher...closer, squint...pull yourself up by the edge, mind the splinters...remember, the exterior isn't soft and mossy, only the hole.*

Good. Look inside.

Oh, dear.

Remember the old *Adams Family* TV show?
Remember that jewelry box (or whatever it was) in which Thing lived?

Well, substitute a "nest" in an old tree stump for the jewelry box, and make Thing a lefty that wears a silver ring set with an onyx cross.

* * *

When I got back to the hut I won an Oskar for my celebration of Harry's cooking. She was such a sweetheart to make that special meal, and I was bound and determined to let her know that I appreciated it. Afterward, I rubbed her imaginary feet, back, and shoulders until she dropped off. While Harry slept, I wrapped up the dishes in a cloth and lugged them over my shoulder with a hobo stick. I also grabbed a towel and a bar of soap and headed for the spring.

A vigorous and repeated body lather, with special emphasis on my cock, was needed to scrub off the sex-death yuckiness. I washed the dishes after my bath, and as I cleaned sticky chunks of rice and red pepper sauce off of the bowls, I vomited into the water trough. While

461

saying and doing whatever I could to make Harry happy, I had been able to keep the image of the hand out of my mind. Now that I was alone again, I couldn't keep up my mental shield.

Oh God...that image of the hand...raw edges of jagged wristbone protruding as it lay "sleeping" with its five shriveled and darkened mummy digits curled in a semen-sticky grass-lined den.

Lovely. A necro-wank over hell's recipe for bird's nest soup.

I was slightly surprised to discover that I had any gag reflex left, since I had deposited my breakfast in glutinous clump-intervals along the path back to the hut like Hansel leaving puke piles along the way to the witch's gingerbread house. A dry and wrung-out gut was all that remained by the time I got back. I loved *nakji bokkeum*, but on this occasion it was no small feat to fill my unstable void with red sauce and boiled octopus.

Drained, I slumped against the side of the trough and absentmindedly watched bits of half-digested cephalopod float in spring water. A disgorged length of tentacle, its suction cups chewed and partially dissolved, gently bobbed up and down. It wasn't exactly a hypnotist's pocket watch, yet I found the rhythm comforting. I just needed to relax for a minute.

Relax.

I felt like that girl in *Cashiers* who screwed the dead guy in the convenience store restroom, except she had a complete corpse, whereas I didn't even get an entire limb. Her cadaver liaison was with the *recently* deceased, too! Man...I really got shortchanged, because my fractional stroke-partner had been doing its revenant creep around the mountain since a 1970 plane crash. It was a man's hand as well, so I guessed that my encounter could have been classed as gay, dismembered, and reanimated digital manipulation. Ha! Let's see Silent Rob top that.

The octo-chunk continued to prance and my mind continued to wander. Death and sex. Sex and death. A thought materialized behind my glazed stare...yeah, I was over a century old, so it fell to reason that my sex partner mortality rate had risen with the passing years, like that macabre formula used to determine how many members of a high school class would perish within post-graduation decades. I was no mathematician, but I knew that this algorithm, if now applied to my life's sexual adventures, would initially display a gradual reduction, then abruptly graph a 1997 Y-axis nosedive. They were all dead. My cock had outlived every pussy that it had ever met.

I heard Anthony Hopkyns' ghostly voice:

[Tell me, Senator KRONAG: Did you bed them yourself?]

The question was really just a whisper...

[Did you make love to them?]

Acknowledging my past lovers' collective demise made me feel strange...and the sexual aspect only amplified the sensation. But everyone was gone, not just my former bed partners - so why should that point matter?

[Did you fuck them, Senator KRONAG?]

I recalled my experiences with the world's marvelous vaginas...but since I knew that they were all doing the John Brown Moulder, I grew queasy.

[Toughened your cock, didn't it? Amputate a man's leg, and he can still feel it tickling. Tell me, Senator KRONAG, now that your girls are on slabs, where does it tickle you?]

I ignored Dr. Leckter's question, though a shiver still ran through my congressional dick. That bastard already knew exactly where it tickled, since time and trial had turned my past lovers into Buffalo Bill's leathery-mangina girlsuits.

18

It Looks Like ~~Phaedrus~~ *KRONAG* Missed A Few Oil Changes

Aokigahara Was Managed
By The US Forest
Service

In the film *Awakening,* Wren Williams played a psychiatrist who administered huge dosages of dopamine to a catatonia patient, as portrayed by Robert Money. The drug allowed Money's character to emerge from his seizure-stupor, though illness eventually dragged him back to a place beyond the medicine's reach.

On the morning when I awakened in a "camp" at the base of Mt. Pelosi, Wren Williams wasn't standing by to comfort me and welcome me back. There were just some skeletal corpses and scattered garbage. I was cold, filthy, and Auschwitz-skinny. I was wrapped in a dirty blanket and a tattered sheet of black plastic, and some of my coverings were still on a stick-platform in a juniper's lower branches. I had evidently fallen in the night. There wasn't anyone else around, except for the dead people, and I was lucky to have not broken my neck and joined them in the hereafter.

I...know this place. I was here before, with Grandpa, when I was a little kid.

I didn't appear to be sick, though I was very weak. I slowly and unsteadily got to my feet and the garbage in which I was wrapped fell to the ground. *What the hell am I wearing?* I thought. *Filthy and ill-fitting BDUs? With ratty combat boots?* I tried to touch my chin, but my fingers were stopped by something that felt like thick dried moss. I guessed that it had been a long time since I had shaved...a long, *long* time. I touched my head and discovered that my hair was as long and matted as my whiskers.

My memory wasn't that great. The last thing I remembered was...what? *I had lost my milk delivery job...I was home...someone shot up my apartment...I decided to leave town and come here...okay, good so far...my backpack was shot by some cops...I had some kind of infection--*

I touched my crotch and wondered why I didn't feel burning pain. I unbuttoned my BDUs and they free-fell, WTC 7-style, down around my pasty and bony ankles. I noticed that my underwear, as worn and full of holes as it was, at least had not been as neglected as other areas of my personal hygiene. I jerked my underwear down, but did not discover any stains or painful stings. In fact, I took a moment to relieve myself and happily discovered that my urethra no longer pumped hot lava.

*Hey. Some of my pubes are...*gray? *What the hell?*

Once again I tried to recall events. Yes, I had made it out of Vegas, and in the desert I had come upon a crashed flying saucer. No...it was an aircraft fuel tank. No, no, that still wasn't right. It was a jettisoned dry-serum drum that had contained powdered milk-like smallpox and God-only-knows what else.

Remembering what had happened *after* that day was like looking into a blender and trying to identify different types of fruit in a mixed purée. There were strange images of purple kittens in my mind, too, and some of them were singing *I Had You, Babe,* while the rest were meowing, or maybe chanting, something that sounded like: "Man-corn-foot, man-corn-foot."

I had no clue what that meant.

I looked at my surroundings. Yes, this was definitely the bug-out spot that Grandpa had prepared, but it was in terrible condition. Plastic MRE envelopes and Matin cube bags were everywhere, along with disgusting piles of old dried feces - presumably mine - with accompanying wads of MRE toilet tissue. Tools and clothing were scattered around the camp. The half-dugout hut that Grandpa had built was dilapidated, and part of its roof was missing. The door was also gone, so I walked down the little steps and looked inside. It was a mess, but there had been recent activity within. Again, I had to assume that I was the one who had been doing...whatever it was that I had been doing. There were footprints in the hut and, like the rest, they matched my boots. I found my 10/22 inside. It was oiled and wrapped in what looked like a piece of the blanket in which I had slept.

I had to sit down for a moment. I was faint and very hungry, but I didn't understand why. There were many empty MRE packets outside, but, just like the dead people, some appeared to have been there for a long while. There were still ample foodstuffs in the hut, so did the guy who had commandeered my body just decide, at some point, to stop eating?

When I went back outside I noted how the corpses had been piled against the base of a tree. There was a message carved into the trunk that read:

~~CROATOAN~~

CANNIBAL MUTANTS MUST DIE!

I recognized my own lettering. Sap had bled from the words and a long rust stain oozed down from where a hunting knife's blade was still stuck in the tree.

The dead people were mostly jerky-on-bones and had lost their stench, but this was not the case with a number of scattered animal carcasses. If I had been able to access the memories of my body's previous occupant, then I might have known why jackrabbits and birds had been shot and left to rot, as well as who the "cannibal mutants" had been.

I tried to pull the knife out of the tree. The blade appeared to have penetrated a couple inches into the trunk, yet the butt was without hammer marks. It was difficult, especially in my weakened condition, to imagine that I had ever been strong enough to ram the blade so deeply into the wood. Since my hand had carved the strange message, however, and since I couldn't really remember much of anything, maybe it hadn't been a matter of being strong enough. Maybe it had been a matter of being *crazy* enough.

This Son Hath
Betrayed
His God

I accepted that the other guy was a psycho even before I found his diary, or journal, or *whatever* it is. Wow. He talked to God, reenacted movie scenes, and had sex with zombie hands inside tree stumps. You name it, he did it. For some reason, the guy also thought that he was over a century old.

Despite his strange proclivities, Mr. Hyde was a conscientious date-keeper. He marked the passage of time as well as any other obsessed nut job, except when he was busy with a distorted retelling of our life, or when he wrote about a piece of wood with which he was sexually infatuated, or when he explained how Quentin Glover - that's right, the actor, now probably dead like so many other people - had ordered him to build a big wilderness pentagram. By the way, I found that thing. It's only about a hundred yards from the camp. The pentagram is really just a field of rocks and junk, and "building" it must have been one of the other guy's first projects, because it looks like it's been there for years. At the pentagram's center are some old antibiotic hypos from the hut's med cache. During the course of his rituals, Mr. Weirdo evidently shot himself up with enough juice to clear that mess between our legs.

That's right: I said that the pentagram looks like it's been there for *years*. If the journal is to be believed, it is autumn, 2007. I'm forty years old.

FORTY FUCKING YEARS OLD!

I've been out in the goddamn sticks, delusional and alone, for more than a decade.

It Knows Not
What It
Is

2007(?)

I keep myself shaved and washed now, though Mr. Forty-Something doesn't like to look in the camp mirror at his strangely-older face. I've also put on some weight and cleaned up the camp. The hut's fixed, and soon I'll cover it with dirt.

There are still rations in there, so I don't have to leave...but I want to. The desert is cooling down enough to consider a hike back to whatever might remain of Sin City. I've started to put a pack together, with plenty of water bottles, and this is what led me to discover that I *do* share some memories with "KRONAG" - as he called himself - because I seem to instinctively know where to find the spring.

I burned the dead animals and trash in one fire and placed the human bones on a separate pyre. There were two men, one woman, and two children. They had all been shot many times with a .22 and their skulls looked like bone colanders. **Their old blue Datsun pickup truck is still over by the road.** All of its tires are flat, and under the hood there is a massive packrat nest, a dead battery, and chewed-out wiring. In the back there are many empty and animal-gnawed food packages. Clothes and supplies are scattered in the brush.

I don't know the peoples' names. Even though there was still ID in their crumbling clothes, I didn't read it. There's probably a registration form in the pickup, but I'm not going to check. I don't want to know. I feel sick to my stomach when I think about those people. He killed them all - even the kids. Like he wrote in the tree inscription and in his journal, KRONAG thought that they were cannibal mutants.

Upon reconsideration, I'm really glad that we don't share the same memories.

19

I've Got Some Bad News For You, Sunshine

I'm So Sorry, Wilson

Late Fall? Early Winter?

I took a final look at the newly-covered hut's fresh mound of dirt and the garbage-free camp. It was far from pristine, and anyone whose path took them through the area would detect human activity. If someone just passed on the road, however, there wouldn't be any brightly-colored or reflective bits of garbage to catch their eye. Wanderers might very well find the camp despite my cleanup, especially if they stopped to examine the abandoned pickup. There was nothing that I could do about that, though.

I loaded my pack and put on some better clothes. The hut offered more garment options than just camo, so I decided to trade the rotten BDUs for a shirt and some jeans that I still had to cinch up even after my weight gain. I also traded the crumbling boots for a new pair.

* * *

The nights grew warmer as I entered lower elevations. The trees thinned, then the brush thinned, and eventually I found myself walking through the old Brownstone Canyon Archaeological Preserve. I spotted petroglyphs on canyon walls from time to time, and this made me wonder if a future civilization would also protect the ruins of Los Vegas.

As I traveled, I felt an increased emphasis upon the fact that I had truly awakened as another man, and not just in a psychological sense. My body complained. I got tired sooner. My breath came harder. It took longer to remove my boots and rub the pain out of my feet at night. I had ingested some very bad government-chemical *ju-ju* as a thirty-something, gone away, returned in my forties, and now this trip was teaching me that my lost decade had exacted a significant physical toll, especially since KRONAG hadn't taken care of our body. Some of his writings seemed lucid and cogent...but when I got back, I discovered that Mr. Hyde's Excellent Adventure wasn't accurately described in his journal. Along with the murders and strange sexual nonsense, that crazy bastard could have also killed me.

* * *

I grew anxious as I approached Vegas. What would I discover? An abandoned and desolate ruin? A recovered and thriving metropolis? Varying stages of each?

I made good time as I descended into the Valley. On the night before my personal Palm Sunday I decided to sleep outside of the city, where the Brownstone Canyon alluvial spread out beyond the outskirts of Charleston Boulevard. As night fell I found a gravel ravine where I could put my back against the bank and lean on my pack. I sat on a clean patch of sand, placed my carbine across my knees, and looked out over the desert at Red Rock Casino and beyond, into what had been the surrounding West Charleston residential area.

As darkness fell, I realized that the places I surveyed were *still* residential areas. While the Red Rock Resort Complex remained dark, there were many small lights that flickered in and out of the nearby houses. Some of the little glows moved, but it was obvious that I wasn't viewing car headlights. Was I looking at bicycles and lamps? Or surviving dynamo generators? Maybe. I wondered if this was how pioneer streets had appeared in the days of lamplit horse-drawn carriages.

A decade had passed and the city was still occupied. Dusk didn't allow me to make much of a study, but I recognized big landmarks standing distant in the heart of Vegas. There was the MGM. There was the Stratosphere Tower. The burned-out double Mandalay development still gleamed in scorched gold as the sun's last rays fell. Like Red Rock, the casinos on The Strip were mostly dark. There were small intermittent lights in the hotels, but they weren't like the ones that had shone before Shakpana rolled into town.

Look At Them. They Have No Knowledge Of The Past, No Ambition For The Future... So Lucky

Nevada Day/Halloween
2007

Sunup. My pack was on my back and my boots crunched ravine gravel. The 10/22 was in my hand. Would I be able to carry a weapon in the city? Did the Los Vegans allow that? I felt like a space traveler who was about to touch down on a strange planet. What would the people in this alien world be like?

I had done a fairly good job of keeping the murdered "mutant cannibal" family out of my mind. I had decided that I wasn't going to think about them, but as Vegas loomed, I couldn't help it. Maybe part of the reason for this trip was to hold guilt at bay with adventurous distraction, but now my conscience was like acid trickling down the back of my neck.

I had reasoned out matters before, but as I continued to march, I felt like I had to do so again: The killings were at the hands of another consciousness that no longer occupied my skull. My finger had pulled the trigger, but my mind hadn't. This wasn't a cop-out, because I really *hadn't* been the one in control. As further verification, I had been shocked and repulsed by the scene of death. Would that other self have had such a reaction? No. KRONAG hadn't even bothered to pick up the bones.

* * *

I knew that I would have to find a fast way to feed myself in Vegas, or I would be forced to hike back down Charleston Boulevard and return to Brownstone Canyon. I remembered the general location of an old BLM reservoir where I could filter some water and maybe supplement my provisions with a jackrabbit or two - but I really didn't want to do that.

I paused when I reached the bottom of the Brownstone alluvial. The last time I was in Vegas, I had been shot off of my bike by a cop. There had been riots and looting. Things were bad and had been getting worse.

I cycled a round into my 10/22 and took a seventy-five yard yucca shot. No problem. My weapon was ready. I figured, despite the change of clothes that I had gotten from the hut's stores, that I still looked pretty rough. Would I be assaulted? Would I be arrested?

No. As I wormed my way into the dry municipal mummy that had been Sin City, I was ignored. People looked like me. Rough clothes, backpacks, and duffel bags, many obviously homemade, were everywhere. People either wore huge hats, some comically illustrating the irrelevance of post-apocalyptic fashion, or cloths wrapped around their heads. Everyone had careful eyes that watched for sudden moves, but otherwise showed little interest.

I needn't have worried about displaying my little .22. Open firearm carry was neither threatening nor aberrant, and in fact appeared to be the norm. Women talked and laughed with rifles over their shoulders. People had cut PVC tubes and wired them to bike frames to carry carbines. If the Los Vegans didn't have something slung over their backs, then something was on their hips, and next to my little Ruger, some of the weapons were like howitzers.

As I observed more people, I felt increasingly like the Time Traveler in H.G. Welles' *The Time Device,* for the human race appeared to have divided itself into Eloi and Morlocks. Like me, the Eloi were older, without smallpox scars, and represented an archaic version of humanity. The young Vegas Morlocks, however, bore scars on their faces, hands, and any other exposed skin. They were the survivors, and from their numbers, I realized that my dragon tail chemtrail-lethality estimation had been much too high.

As I continued on, I noted various technological regressions. Bicycles were everywhere, and in every homemade size and shape. The most popular cargo-hauling configuration was the most basic: just two attached bikes, side-by-side, and wired together with sticks or whatever material the owner could find.

Platforms were placed across the frames to create makeshift four-wheelers with room for riders on one side. These conveyances reminded me of the heavy-cargo bicycles and motorcycle-pickup hybrid vehicles that I had seen many years earlier in Korea. Los Vegans moved everything imaginable on their bicycle economy: furniture, animals, building material, and *lots and lots* of water jugs. Some enterprising souls had even attached seats and trailers and were transporting passengers in primitive tuk-tuks.

They called it "New Vegas," according to the crudely painted-over signs, but it just looked like old Vegas to me, *sans* technology and convenience. The people were surviving though, and they even appeared to be negotiating steadily better terms from The Gods of The Human Condition.

"Maybe I could do that," I said, as I watched the pedal parade. "Get a bike and haul stuff around."

There were still motorized vehicles on the road, but these were official rigs that belonged to a bored police or para-military force. The men who rode around in the backs of the trucks were a mixture of ages, and I saw several who were of my generation or older. Some wore green uniforms that might have been hand-me-downs from MOAB-blasted and presumably-defunct Nellis Air Force Base. The soldier-cops seemed to have a decent rapport with the populace, and people on the streets smiled and waved.

Street crews were at work. They wore classic orange reflective vests, but instead of operating heavy machinery, these fellows lugged wheelbarrows full of dirt and stones and filled in potholes that, absent real blacktop repair, would require re-filling at a future date. It was an occupation with job security, but I wasn't interested.

* * *

"New" Vegas wasn't like a total-desolation zombie or post-nuclear holocaust film, but the niceties of the 1990s were definitely gone. Trees and landscape were long dead. I walked through housing developments that were unfinished or abandoned. I saw partially-burned apartment complexes. Cars weren't moving on the

Vegas outskirts, but there *were* cars. They were stopped in the middle of roads with open doors and flat tires. Their paint jobs were partially hidden under layers of dust, and there was garbage caught beneath their chassis. Nests of debris on floors and under seats indicated that animals had taken up residence.

I went into an abandoned grocery store. The registers were still there, though someone had gone down the checker row with a pry bar and the broken cash drawers hung like the lolling tongues of beef cattle after the killing bolt. Dirt, broken glass, and scattered papers littered the floor. The thing that seemed strangest to me, though, was how the desert heat was inside the building. Growing up in southern Nevada had imparted a subconscious expectation of refrigeration. Step across a threshold and into the air-conditioned glory of any structure, and you knew that you were *inside*. Cross that threshold again, through the doors and into the blasting desert heat, and you knew that you were *outside*. But now these lines of demarcation, along with every other civilized comfort that had been taken for granted, were gone. It was hot outside, and it was hot inside.

* * *

Despite my murderous alter-ego's journal enties, I still wasn't completely sure about the month or year. I decided to ask a passerby.

"Excuse me," I said. "What's the date?"

The young man wore an enormous homemade sombrero-like thing, so I didn't really see his face until he stopped. When he lifted the brim, I saw that Shakpana had been especially cruel, and one of the red-purple tissue masses on his upper lip was the aftermath of a pustule so deep that it gave the impression of a cleft palate repair. Still, the guy spoke without impediment.

"What?"

"The date. What's today?"

The facial scars pulled and shifted to a lighter color as he frowned. "Today? Today is...*today*." He looked at me as if I were insane.

"What's the year?"

"Year?" he repeated. This time the young man

didn't bother to answer. He just shook his head and walked away.

An older man, maybe in his mid-sixties, had observed the exchange. He looked me up and down with some curiosity. "You ought to know better than to ask one of them a question like that," he said.

"What do you mean? Ask *who* a question*?*"

"The kids."

"Why?"

"Because most of them never finished grade school. Most can't even tell you what state Los Vegas is in. Didn't you know that?"

"No, I didn't. Sir, do *you* happen to know what today is?"

"Sure. October 31st, 2007. Nevada Day...and Halloween."

No Profit
To The
Wise

I feel like River Tucson in the opening scenes of *My Own Private Wyoming,* but this is not to say that I'm a narcoleptic male prostitute who has fallen in love with Ted Logan. Standing alone on some lonely stretch of Equality State highway, Tucson described himself as a "connoisseur of roads", then lost consciousness and fell to the asphalt.

Well, I don't feel like I'm going to pass out, but I just want to say that, at this moment, I feel like a "connoisseur of intersections". I've walked all the way to Sahara and Los Vegas Boulevard and I'm standing in front of the abandoned Bonanza Souvenir Shop. I look up and study the Stratosphere Tower's massive pylons. *Is that a crack? Is Stupak's monstrosity doing a Leaning Tower of Pisa routine, or is it is just me? If that thing came down, everyone on this end of The Strip would be fucked.*

This intersection is a massive sixteen-lane Jakarta four-way. People slowly pull their carts and pedal their bicycles into the intersection and negotiate the mass. It's like watching threads weave as people approach, twist, turn, and disentangle on the other side.

Is the population really this high, or is it just the time of day? I get an answer when I look up and down The Strip. The clot of bikes and carts appears to have been injected with a kind of traffic thinner the further I cast my gaze.

Though it's November, Los Vegas still feels hot since I've been acclimatized to the cooler mountain elevations. I need to stay hydrated, and I need to get my hands on some of the mystery paper that I see these people passing so that I can hit up one of the water carts. It's either that, or engage in some barter...though I haven't anything to trade. If the Saddle Island Intake and the valley pumps are dead, then where the hell is all of the water coming from? There must be a steady procession of bike carts from either Lake Meade or the county springs.

I guess that it's time to find out how this system works:

- How much for a bottle?
- *In trade or NSP?*
- NSP?
- *Yeah. Nevada Silver Peso Certificates. Got any?*
- No.
- *Then whatcha got to trade?*
- I-I don't have anything.
- *C'mon, c'mon. Don't bullshit-o-rama. Everybody trades! So what'd you bring me?*
- Nothing!
- *What's in the pack?*
- My business.
- *Mister, you don't know how to trade too good. C'mon, what about the pack?*
- [Sigh] Food.
- *What kind of food?*
- Matin cubes.
- *Real cubes? What's the date on 'em? Lemme see.*
- Alright. Gimme a sec.
- *I'll be damned. Seals are tight. 1973 date stamps. Okay, I'll trade a gallon of Newton Well for two cubes.*
- Newton Well?
- *Yeah. No nuke dirt, no perchlorate. Guaranteed.*
- **Newton Well?**
- *Alright, alright! A gallon-and-a-half.*

The Blue Fairy At The NSA's Utah Data Center Knows How To Make Mommy Love You Again...And The Blue Angel At 2110 Fremont Knows How To Make You Love Mommy Again

November
2007
(2-of-3)

In another time, the two young white men could have been mistaken for Mormon missionaries or Jehovah's Witnesses. They probably fit the Mormon template more closely, in that they both wore standardized attire, whereas the JW's collectivist costumes had been a little less uniform. In the tradition of their calling, the men carried pulpy pabulum fliers and tracts.

Shit. I just made eye contact. Here they come.

Er...this should be interesting. Are they about to tell me that if I come to their church, Jesus will get the gaming industry up and running? Jesus is always out to make cool deals through his representatives. I wonder if His schtick has changed to reflect the times?

Like other young people, Shakpana had Frenched the duo. Yes, they could have definitely been Mormons, except that, instead of white shirts and black ties, they wore black shirts and white ties. Also, they had white chevrons on their sleeves. One guy wore three stripes and one guy wore two, but something told me that I wasn't looking at an army sergeant and corporal.

Great. Post-apocalyptic Mormon commandos.

"Hello sir. How are you today?"

I looked at the kid. I was kind of tongue-tied, because this was exactly the sort of greeting that I would have expected if society hadn't fallen all was hunky-dory. "Uh, fine, thanks. How are you?" I replied. The exchange was so artificial - but wasn't it always? It was exactly the tone of pre-1997 missionary interactions.

I shook both guys' hands. *No need to be a dick, I*

thought. *Just don't encourage them.*

"We're fine, sir. I'm Sergeant Benson, and this is Corporal Guildford. We're Transcendental Security Administration Community Outreach. May we ask you a question?"

I let out a small sigh. *Did I know God? Did I know God's plan for me?* "Sure," I said. *Let's get this over with. Give me your propaganda slips, I'll feign interest, you can move on, and I can crumple up the pamphlets and toss them.*

"Do you like the world?"

"No, I don't know God's plan for me." *Wait - what did he say?* "Uh, could you repeat that?"

"Do you like the world?" asked Sergeant Benson.

I looked at the kid before I answered. This seemed like an odd question. Well, maybe this was about to get interesting after all. It seemed like an avenue for honest answers was opened.

"No, actually. I don't like the world. I think that society was destroyed by design, though I don't know why, or by whom."

The smiles on the blotched faces told me that this was the sort of answer that they could work with. This time Corporal Guildford spoke. "Sir, what you've just done is show that you're innocent. You don't know why or who. You're an old unscarred, but it's not too late for you."

"Too late for *what?*"

"To come and hear the word of Earth Mother. To purify and restore the world. To gather with us and find the guilty old unscarreds and the young betrayers, and then --"

I didn't get a chance to hear what was going to happen to the old guiltoids and the young betray-a-reenos because Benson gave Guildford a sharp and abrupt elbow. Guildford coughed and Benson spoke: "Sir, we'd like to invite you to The Huntridge Theater tonight so that you can learn the truth and have fellowship with Earth Mother's followers."

What was this "Earth Mother" stuff? I was about to ask what that meant, but Benson continued: "And, as an act of friendship and trust, we would like to offer you food, water, and a protected place to sleep."

As soon as the missionary-corporal said that, I was sold. Hell, I could sing *Kumbaya* in exchange for something to eat and drink. And a place to sleep? *Terrific.* That would help stretch out my pack food and give me a little more time before I was again reduced to trading for water.

"Okay. When does it start?"

"Sundown." Benson handed me a piece of paper from a small sheaf under his arm. It was a crude pencil drawing of a square with a triangle on top and a simple representation of a window and a door. There was a large capital "H" over the house. Some more triangle-mountains were in the background and a setting sun was half-concealed behind them.

"That means 'Huntridge'," said Guildford, as he pointed at the picture and the letter above it. Then, in a moment's embarrassment, he looked at me and said: "I forgot. You old unscarreds can read."

M-O-O-N spells "Huntridge," I thought, as I watched the two continue on their way.

What Would You Have Me Do,
~~Charles~~ *Jack?* I've Heard
These Arguments
Before

*November
2007
(3-of-3)*

Night falls on Los Vegas as I walk down Charleston. When I get to the old Huntridge Theater at the Maryland Parkway intersection I see a line that's about a block long and two or three people wide. Young and skinny scarred men and women mix with old and skinny unscarred men and women. Everyone's clothes are ratty and drab, and I would guess that their stomachs are as empty as their eyes.

The people wait outside a 1930s Great Depression-Era movie theater, painted in faded brown, that was closed down before the world went under. There's no electricity, of course, but there are small bonfires spaced throughout the empty parking lot. Young men and women, all dressed in the same kind of black getups that Benson and Guildford had worn, tend the fires and survey the line. The black-clad people pick individuals out of the crowd. Some are older like me, but mostly it is the young who are taken aside. There's much shaking of hands and patting of backs.

A group of "Mother Worshippers" - or whatever they are - emerge from the theater doors and move the line back so that shopping carts full of - *flapjacks?* - can come out. No, wait - those are just unleavened flat rounds. As soon as the food is recognized, a weary and almost sad cheer goes up. A few very hungry ones try to rush forward, and it is then discovered that some of the black uniforms carry baseball bats. No one gets seriously hurt, but it is definitely understood that there will be order.

I took off my pack when I lined up and I push it forward with my feet as the carts go up and down the line. Some carts have water bottles, and some have flatbread. The bread is just bread, but the pieces are big and filling. I take a chance and trust that the water is clean, but I only drink half of a small bottle and save the rest in my pack with my other containers.

I pick up my pack and carry it through the theater doors. Going into the run-down old Huntridge causes me to experience a déjà vu:

College days with Grace. Goofy Indie band concerts. Occasional community theater efforts.

All in a lost and long ago world.

A main hall leads to the seating floor. There torches within, and some hang from crude metal tripods while others are carried by black-uniformed ushers. A section of the roof has been removed to release smoke and I can see the sky. The movie screen has either been retracted or taken down and a podium is up on the stage.

The Huntridge still has about half of its seats. I'm glad, because I need to rest. I plop down onto old cracked vinyl and am instantly sorry because there is a puff of dust. I cough as others sit on old and disused cushions. We're all filthy though, and the dust is irrelevant.

I look around. *Hmmm.* I'm on the set of Pinky Floyd's *The Walls.* You know the part that I'm talking about: It's the one where Geldov morphs into a dictator and speaks at a faux-Nazi rally. The workers who gussied-up this old rattrap have done a great job of re-creating that scene. I half-expect *Mr. We-Were-The-World* to march out in jackboots and throw the crowd a crossed-forearm hammer salute.

We are hushed by the black uniforms. They walk down the aisles with their baseball bats and leashed dogs as a TSA announcer marches out onto the stage and bellows:

Penitents, stand and embrace Earth Mother's representative in Los Vegas, Transcendental Security Administration General Jatoon LaPin!

The leader of the TSA in southern Nevada walks out and the similarities between *The Walls'* movie scene and real life end. Jatoon LaPin looks and acts nothing like Geldov. Oh yes, the creepo-freako black boots and uniform are there, and when she faces the crowd her underlings dramatically hold back in the torch shadows. Nobody opens for her. It's just General LaPin, right from the get-go. She grips the short podium and tries to look messianic, but I'm not impressed. Neither are the other attendees, because when I look around to gauge *their* reactions, I see them looking around to gauge *my* reaction.

She's short, fat, and slightly older than me. Despite her age, she has obvious 'pox scars. Her hair is gray and clipped down to a not-quite crew cut, and her face has the expressive quality of a weathered board. General LaPin has some notes and she launches into a speech that's hard to hear without a PA system and hard to follow because it's so bizarre. I only catch pieces of rambling and semi-religious gobbledygook:

...as some of you may know, and like many of you, I spent the days after Shakpana adrift. I am one of the old ones, but, like the young, I am not unscarred. I grew up here, in the sacred city of Los Vegas, in the other time, but I was confused by the things that I saw. The Earth Mother was abused by the people. They took and took and lived unwisely. Then Shakpana came to cleanse the land. He took the children to pay for the crimes against Earth Mother...

Jatoon LaPin's words remind me of my conversation with the almost-Mormon Commandos.

...but not all of the children went with Shakpana. Before he left he kissed the special ones, the ones he knew would be strong enough to take back the land. We have suffered so much, but we are special. Look around. Look at the person next to you. There are many precious young ones here, eager to thank Shakpana for not taking them, and there are also many repentant old unscarreds who realize their mistakes and accept the new path...

And so on and so forth. We're special, we've suffered, poor us. Now we're together, now we're going to do this and do that. Blah, blah, blah.

Is there any more of that flatbread? Or water?

LaPin seems unlike Hitler, Stalin, or similar villains, in that those guys had been relatively fit. They could take the mic and get their evil on by waving and screaming. They were like DJs spinning human skulls on turntables, and they knew how to whip crowds into genocidal frenzies. General Jatoon LaPin doesn't seem to have those kinds of moves. She looks like a flesh-tone brick with legs and seems out of breath as she goes on and on about...*what?* Half-threats, vague promises, assurances that nothing is the audience's fault, and that they are the chosen of God - or, in this case, the chosen children of the "Earth Mother."

Yeah, okay. That's nice. Whatever. How far am I from the door? Maybe this wasn't such a great idea after all. Can I get past the black uniforms and leave?

LaPin tells everyone to shake hands, so a couple guys reach out as I try to slip by. *Now what are they doing? Some kind of salute?* I look up at the stage and then at the audience and see that the crowd is emulating the fat general's gestures. It looks like they're doing an old-style Nazi salute, but before they extend their arms, they touch their scarred cheeks. Even the older unscarred people do it. They all chant: "Mother, Mother."

I really have to get out of here. It's getting nuttier and nut--

Hold on.

Those TSA guys behind LaPin just stepped out of the shadows. There's something...*interesting*...about one of them. I blink. I squint.

I know him. Kinda balding, kinda soft in the belly, but I know him, nevertheless. How the hell did he get all of those 'pox scars? We're about the same age, and we received the same smallpox vaccinations.

Come on. This is insane. This is impossible!

He just raised his arm in one of those weird smallpox salutes.

He's got a purple birthmark on his left arm.

Carl Wheat.

Nazi Party member.

Oops...I mean, Transcendental Security Administration member. TSA.

Okay, now I really, really *need to find the door.*

20
Lest You Anger The Shen Who Watch Over Fools

We Don't Need Marcellus To
Send A Tux-Wearing
Judas Iscariot

November
2007
(1-of-2)

How would Mad Max have felt if he had decided to look for a job? Probably not much like me. Of course, I could have also moussed-up my hair and put on some black leather shoulder pads, though these measures likely wouldn't have helped much.

I walked up to the remains of a strip mall. It had nothing to offer but vacant stores, broken glass, and signs for businesses that hadn't existed for over a decade. It was just a row of dead shells...except for a single unit that was very much alive. Piles of scavenged materials were outside the front door, and one heap consisted of partially-dissected automobile tires. Someone had snipped out the sidewalls and sliced the tread into improvised shoe soles, and these were sorted and stacked by size. In another pile there were tarpaulins and canvases. Some were new and still folded, and some were old, sun-bleached, and lying in crumpled piles. Roughly one-foot canvas squares were neatly stacked beside the tire pieces. A handmade sandwich board in front of the unit read:

NEW SHOE! BEST SHOE!
YOU SIZE! SHOE BUY A BEST PRICE!

On the top of the sign was a row of footwear in various sizes and in styles that ranged from sandals to vaguely Ugg-like boots. *Interesting.* I didn't need new shoes, but I was curious.

It wasn't a sweatshop. It seemed to be a family operation helmed by an old Asian man whose looks took my memory way, way back. For a minute I felt like I had walked into Mr. Park's little Anguk grocery, except in this place, there weren't any canned goods, kimchi cases, and bottles of soju. Rather, along one wall was a rack of new shoes, along with other footwear that had been mass-produced long ago. For the old leather shoes, the fix-it material appeared to be as improvised as the in-house products. The remains of a leather jacket hung nearby, and, like the tires and tarps outside, it was slowly being dissected. I glanced at the shoe rack again and saw where the jacket's leather had carefully and neatly been used as patching.

To the right of the business counter was a workspace for two large industrial sewing machines that had been long without electrical power. The machines were fitted with ship's wheel-like side cranks that had been worn smooth from hand-spinning. Big mounted spools were wound with unraveled plastic strands that probably came from the synthetic tarpaulins out front.

Two young women worked at the sewing machines. They swiftly and deftly rotated chunks of rubber and canvas under the heavy mechanized needles, then trimmed the material with skiving knives as they pushed wooden foot-forms in and out of partially-completed shoes. The young ladies wore skirts and blouses of modest design, but of outlandish metallic-flecked and foil-striped scavenged fabric. The girls were in their mid-to-late teens, with visages that revealed exotic hapa combinations of gray-blue teardrop eyes, black hair with reddish highlights, and white-white skin. They had somehow escaped the vicious virus that had killed or horribly disfigured others of their generation, and their complexions were absolutely flawless.

The unhappy proprietor's yells were his business greeting. Before him stood 'pox-scarred Latino and Caucasian boys, both maybe sixteen or seventeen years old, who looked down at their own canvas shoes as the old man berated them. "And this!" he shouted, as he waved a faded and dry-rotted swatch of cotton canvas in front of the boys' faces. "Look! Old! No good!" To further his point, the man easily pulled the material apart. "No more!" The proprietor saw me at the counter and changed his demeanor. *"Ssst!* Go! Look more," he said, as he shooed the duo out the door. Both boys slipped by without glancing at me.

One of the old man's likely-granddaughters had noticed me. She glimpsed up from her work and gave me a quick smile. Her beautiful face illustrated how the Asian and Caucasian DNA helixes could seamlessly wind together to produce stunningly attractive individuals. Keeping these two girls safe in an unsafe world must have been a full-time job for the old man, and his yelps indicated that he didn't appreciate me eyeballing his treasures. "May help you? *May help you?*" he half-shouted.

I gave the girl a smile and a nod, then turned to face the old man. On the wall behind him I noticed a faded and forgotten calendar from 1997 that was printed in *hanja.*

A Chinese family, I thought.

I must have looked like trouble to the old man, like some kind of sketchy Robinson Crusoe come down from the mountains. I had made an effort to clean up, though. Rather than spend the previous night with a bunch of TSA bizarros, I had opted to sleep on the rooftop of a strip mall similar to the one in which I now found myself. When the sun came up I had sacrificed a cup of precious water to straight razor, or rather, straight *knife*, the whiskers off my face and remove some of the dirt from my cheeks...but I was still a ratty affair.

"MAY HELP YOU?"

"Yes, sir," I said. "I'm interested in talking business."

"*Business?* You want shoe?"

"No. I want to learn --" I motioned at the finished shoes on the rack "-- how to make those."

The old man grimaced. "No need help. You no buy? You go."

As I talked to the old man, I saw the door open out of the corner of my eye. In walked two young men, and they were dressed like the "missionaries" who had invited me to the previous night's freak show. I paid little attention, though I felt sorry for the young women at the sewing machines. They appeared to be the targets of those doing the work of the Earth Mother and TSA General Jatoon LaPin.

The girls began to make distressed squeaking noises

like threatened rabbits. I knew that cult-missionaries could be relentlessly pestering, but such panicked sounds still weren't the usual response to *The Watchtowers* or whatever kind of material the loons were pushing. I turned to observe the commotion and saw that the young men were invading the girls' personal space. They were practically feeling up the young ladies, who were covering their breasts and trying to get up from their work stools. One girl tried to stand up, but a scarhead dared to put his hands on her shoulders and force her back down onto the seat.

The old man saw that, too, I thought. His expression told me that the situation wasn't going to result in a polite request for the TSA to leave the girls alone and depart. Shit was about to hit the fan in Post-Apocalyptic Cobblerville.

The old man reached under the counter, probably for something with a less-than-18½-inch barrel. That's certainly what *I'd* have kept under there. Not wanting a bellyful of the old man's lead, nails, or rocks, I quickly moved to make sure that I wasn't between him and the scarheads. The Blackshirts had handguns in their waistbands, but at this range it wouldn't have mattered if they were Wild Bill clones and the old man had pulled a .410, because a sawed-off scattergun would catch them both...along with the girls.

The old man and I both seemed to realize this at the same time. He froze with his hand still hidden behind the counter, but from the taut muscles in his forearm, I could almost estimate the weight of his weapon. He was holding some large heat - definitely *not* a .410 - but he couldn't play his blaster card while the molesters were so close to his granddaughters. Funny thing. Those girls were actually saving the TSA gropers' lives.

Hmmm. I wasn't of an especially chivalrous inclination, but the victimization that I beheld was definitely pissing me off. The mercenary in me also saw an opportunity to find good stead with a potential employer. Maybe it was a fifty-fifty motivational split.

But I could have walked away. Maybe I *should* have walked away.

Nah.

Why not? This didn't concern me. Yet, here I was, about to get involved, thanks to Carl Wheat. After the Huntridge rally that guy was still on my mind, along with memories of the time that we had served together.

Carl had been up on stage with that riff-raff. *WTF, WTF, WTF?* There was no way that I could figure it out. But seeing Carl was what had reminded me of the shitty move that I was about to pull on the Blackshirts.

Alright, you TSA scum. Time for old age, or more precisely, early middle age*, to overcome youth and...your stupid black uniforms.* I slipped my arms out of my pack, lowered it to the floor, and walked over to the big sewing machines.

I had only heeled another man's arch once before, and that had been many years ago outside the Pyeongtaek NCO Club. My target had been a drunk who was slapping a girl around, and I hadn't been particularly chivalrous at that time, either - but part of me just wanted to see if the nasty little fighting trick that I had learned from Carl really worked. Calling it a "fighting" trick might actually be giving it more due than it deserved. Let's just call it a trick, and a crappy one at that - sort of like the hand-to-hand equivalent of shooting an unarmed man in the back. It definitely wasn't something to use if you were trying to impress a girl, but the guy outside the NCO Club was a big wasted SP, and the girl whom I was with - I can't really remember her, for some reason - wanted me to do something. She had called me a "coward with a weak mind", and that had pissed me off enough to split the bones in the guy's foot.

As far as cheap shots go, you can't beat breaking arches. With a little practice, you can do it with the same move that a mugger uses when he nonchalantly strolls past his victim, then quickly turns and grabs the mark's throat - except you don't need to make that much physical contact. Just time your steps with those of the other man, and when he passes, do a half-turn and wreck his foot. You don't even have to take your hands out of your pockets. If the guy is standing still, or abusing a girl, you can sidle up or even back into him. Look like you're having a conversation, look like you're smoking a cigarette - anything - and in a second your target is on the ground. Just remember to always use the back of your own heel, otherwlse you'll pop every tendon in your ankle and end up in worse shape than the other guy.

At least an asshole who does a shoulder-tap sucker-punch uses his *fist*. Busting arches might command even less respect than kicking another man in the balls. Plus, men are so guarded about their crotches anyway, and it's hard to line up for a scrotal field goal. Like I said, busting arches isn't a good way to impress a woman, but the result is quick and effective.

Perfect.

"Do you represent Mother?" I asked, but there was no response from the goons. They were too intent upon grabbing boobs.

"WHO SPEAKS FOR EARTH MOTHER?!" I bellowed. That got their attention. The young ladies tried to stand up again, but the slugs shoved them back down. "I want to learn more about Mother, and repent for my consumer crimes," I continued. This time the young men gave each other *it's-time-to-stop-goofing-around* looks,and stepped back from the young women, who, sensing that they could actually get away this time, half-sprinted and half-stumbled to where the old man stood behind the counter. Once they got there, I noted a difference in their postures and attitudes. One girl cowered behind the old man, whereas the other put herself between the thugs and her grandpa. She seemed defiant and fierce, and actually tried to reach for the weapon that the old man held under the counter, but he pushed her hand away and watched me.

One scarhead cleared his throat and tried to muster a training seminar smile. "We speak for Mother. We're Mother's messengers."

"Good," I said. "My friend told me that last night there was a big meeting at The Huntridge."

"That's right," said the second. "You didn't go?"

"I didn't know about it, but my friend told me that he had been given a message of truth. He said Mother is going to change things and make things better. He said the guilty are going to be punished." *Ah-ha.* To the scarheads' ears, my words were music in the key of Hegelian dialectic: **Guilt, punishment, change. Problem, reaction, solution.**

They exchanged knowing looks. "That's right, that's right, and old unscarreds are allowed to join Mother now, too," said the first Blackshirt, "even though many haven't. You could share the Word with others like yourself. You can read, right?"

I did my best to look nervous and feign a stammer. "May-maybe others like me can read, b-but I...but I..." My voice trailed off in phony embarrassment.

It was a good ploy. Both thugs smiled and reached into the thigh pockets of their BDU pants. "It's okay, it's okay," said the second Blackshirt. "You're like us. That's good. Just take this." He placed a crude hand-drawn map on a sewing machine's feed tray. The map marked a location near the intersection of The Strip and Flamingo. I didn't give a shit about the map, but I did take a keen interest in the fact that the guy had kept leaning on the tray after he put the map down. *Nice,* I thought. *Now just move your hand about three inches to the left.*

"Do you know where a place that used to be called 'Dre's' is?" asked one of the Blackshirts. I didn't know or care which one had spoken, because I had gotten into position. One guy was slightly behind me, or rather, the top of his right foot was behind the back edge of my hard left boot heel. As for the other, his left hand was still on the feed tray. A quick check of the machine's wheel crank told me that it was unlocked.

Showtime.

I grabbed the Blackshirt's wrist and pulled his hand under the massive needle while using my knee to shove the wheel crank's suicide knob. In that instant when the other guy wondered why his partner was screaming in pain and clawing at the machine's lowered needle assembly, I drove my heel down onto the top of his foot. The effect was the same as it had been outside the P-Tek NCO Club so long ago. There wasn't a dramatic cracking sound and I only felt a slight "click" in the other man's boot. He fell while clutching his foot with a look of extreme pain on his face.

I easily plucked the pistol from the pants of Mr. Jesus Hand, but fumbled and dropped it. Before I could pick up the weapon, the guy on the floor recovered enough presence of mind to go for his gun, but I just kicked it away.

The standing and shrieking Blackshirt couldn't figure out how to raise the sewing machine's foot-feed. He pulled and moved so much that the initial wound had widened around the large needle and blood ran from the edges of the feed tray and onto the floor. Before I had a chance to decide whether or not I would free the guy, the choice was taken out of my hands. There were two deafening blasts of sound and pressure that left me slightly stunned. The injury that I had inflicted upon the TSA guy's foot was now irrelevant, since chunks of his head lay between his body and the door. As for the other man, his teeth and bits of C2 vertebrae would have to be picked out of the sewing machine's mechanism. He collapsed against the machine with his head hanging backward on a length of sinew. His open jugular pumped a few squirts as his legs collapsed, though his needled hand held his body in a semi-standing position.

Well, at least the old man didn't blast me as well, I thought. When I turned around, however, I saw that it wasn't the old man who held a crude double pipe-barreled shotgun. It was the defiant hapa girl who had placed herself between the TSA thugs and her family. Silently and gently, the old man stepped forward and took the weapon out of her hands. Then he turned to me. "Oh-kay," he said. "We talk."

* * *

Our cleanup wouldn't have fooled a forensics team, but it wasn't bad. There were still tiny blood smears and droplets, but for the most part the store could pass casual inspection. The only real concern was for the water that was expended to brush and rinse the sewing machines.

The old man, whose name I now knew to be Zhang,

and I hadn't actually talked yet, but I guessed that he was gauging my asset potential so I pitched in with the cleaning...between sick heaves. There were steps in the process. That was clear. *This isn't their first time doing this,* I thought. It was "murder by numbers, *uno, dos, tres",* as *La Policía* would have said...though "murder *cleanup* by numbers" might have been more accurate:

1.) Lock the shop door and close the blinds.
2.) Pick up the TSA pistols and hide them.
3.) There are old rolled-up rugs in the back, along with some scavenged wire. Girls, get two rugs and some wire.
4.) Jack, pull the bodies out of the main blood pools. Don't worry about blood trails on the floor. Just move the bodies to the side. You'll have to release that guy's hand before you can move him. Pick up the pieces of that other guy's head.
5.) Zhang, get a bucket of soapy water and a brush. Scrub the machines and the clots on the floor. Gently rinse the machines.
6.) Girls, unroll the rugs and put them over the soapy blood pools. Walk on them to make them suck up as much liquid as possible. Then grab the corners like you're folding sheets and lift them up. Put them, wet sides up, near the two dead men.
7.) Jack, wire the dead men's hands to their waists and wire their ankles together. Roll them up inside the rugs. Wire the ends of the rugs shut. Go outside to vomit.
8.) Zhang, get some rags and start cleaning the remaining water and blood off the floor.
9.) Girls, get some rags and start cleaning the machines. Jack, help them. When you're done, work together to pull the rolled rugs to the back. Cover them up with other rugs or any junk you can find. Zhang, follow behind with your rags to sop-up any leakage. Re-check the lock on the back door.
10.) Go back to the front of the store. Open the blinds. Check for missed blood or anything else. Hang that old calendar and the chopped-up leather jacket over the buck-n-ball holes in the wall.

11.) Jack, go outside again and vomit. Then come back in and have a word with Zhang.
12.) GIrls, unlock the front door and go back to making shoes.

And there you go. Just like it never happened, and we didn't even have to ask Marcellus to send Wynston Wolf.

Antevorta, Postvorta, And Ye-Ye

November
2007
(2-of-2)

I guess that I'm in. That was one hell of an audition, but it looks like Zhang is going to give me a chance. He told me to sleep on the roof, which is what I'd want anyway, especially when summer rolls back around. I won't get paid for the first two months, but the family will share food and water. Zhang's rules are simple: Learn, stay busy, and if I lay a hand on either of the girls I'll find myself rolled up in a rug.

Seems fair.

* * *

I look up at the stars from my bedroll on the strip-mall roof. I start to relax, but then I hear sounds under the back ledge.

Shit. My stomach really doesn't need any more drama.

But I'm part of the crew now.

Sigh. Where's my .22?

Slowly, slowly, I creep to the edge and listen. There's a lot of movement, but no talk. I peek over and see a makeshift double-bicycle tuk-tuk. A man emerges from the shadows as he noisily drags a long rolled rug. Then he disappears through the door beneath me and returns a few minutes later with the other rug package. The stranger and Zhang lift the corpses onto the tuk-tuk. When they're done, Zhang hands over four pairs of boots. They nod in silence and turn their backs on each other. The tuk-tuk slowly creaks off into the darkness, and I hear the shop's back door close, followed by the clunk of a deadbolt.

21

**Half-~~Vampire~~ *American*...
Half-~~Lycan~~ *Chinese*...
But Stronger
Than Both!**

Batteries For His Bloody
Ridiculous
Toy Cur

May
2008
(1-of-2)

The biggest part of my job is scrounging, though I'm always learning to do more. I hike and bike around town with a tire iron and heavy clipper-snips while searching for canvas, tarps, and tires. Scrounging is mostly solitary work. I'm not confronted by competing rat packs or anything like that, though I have a decent coexistence with a few other scroungers whom I occasionally encounter. We're pretty respectful of each other and just go about our business. I've memorized some names and apparent specialties:

> - *That's Eric. He turns pipes and plumbing fixtures into homemade guns.*
> - *Alice and Gary are a married team who go through abandoned furniture. They have a handcart that's usually full of table legs and chair pieces.*
> - *That guy over there isn't a toy scrounger. He's just a weirdo with a baby doll fetish.*

Besides my fellow recyclers and refuse-hunters, there are other things that I've noticed around "New" Vegas, particularly the increase in TSA "churches", or whatever they are. Such establishments are easy to spot, because the Blackshirts take over places of worship, either kick out or convert the previous occupants, and paint everything green. The TSA does shitty paint jobs, and I have to laugh when I pass the former Central Megachurch on East Tropicana, because the scarheads only painted the walls as high as they could reach.

Losers.

Lil' Salamander's Sausage-Flavored Coffee

I constructed a primitive dried-mud oven in the alley behind Zhang's shop. It was *horno*-like, but not quite the real thing. I used it to cook a pizza for Zhang's granddaughters. This might not have been a big deal to someone in the prosperous past, but for those marooned in the primitive present, it was a special treat.

The pizza was rather...*improvisational*...but I thought that it was still going to be tasty. It had barbecued meat, but don't ask what *sort* of meat. It also had cheese, though again, it was best if the particular variety of cheese went undefined. I could find neither olive oil nor tomato sauce. I did, however, obtain some rehydrated tomatoes from one of the open-air markets, where I had also traded *four* jackrabbit carcasses for an old, small, and very expensive bag of still-usable wheat flour. Yeast was in short supply, however, so my "pizza" was more like a big open quesadilla. I made it on a pan that I had picked up off the floor of a ransacked Godfather's.

Mary and Zhang stayed inside while Rosie and I minded the food. "I ate pizza when I was little," said Rosie. "My sister and I ate pizza with my mom and dad." She smiled. "I can't remember what it tasted like, but it was big and round."

I laughed. "I'm not exactly sure how this is going to turn out, so maybe it's best if you can't remember how pizza is *supposed* to taste."

"I think I'll like it," Rosie said. Then, changing the subject, she asked: "How's your finger?"

"Better," I replied. A few days earlier I had rammed a sewing machine needle, dead-center, through the bone of my index finger. The injury didn't result in a break, but the puncture might have caused an amputation-necessitating infection. Thanks to one of Zhang's poultices, however, the only evidence of the wound was a pucker in the back of my finger and a hardened bit of skin around a black-button scab.

Rosie took my hand and examined my finger. "I knew Ye-Ye could fix you," she said approvingly. "And you can still make shoes as fast as Mary and me."

Rosie was being kind. The girls could whip out their post-End-Time "Uggs" at lightning speed. I had learned to make decent shoes, but at maybe half the young women's pace. I might have increased my skills if I spent as much time at the machines as they did, but I also hunted for materials, as well as pigeons, rats, groundhogs, and jackrabbits. I had traded my way to a bicycle, which made both scavenging and hunting much easier.

The shoe store arrangement was good for me. When I brought in materials, Zhang let me use his machines and sell or trade away every second pair of boots that I made for myself. The family benefited as well, since Zhang was just too old to rummage around town and my efforts also allowed the girls to remain in the shop. The two boys that I had seen on that first day had disappeared. As I looked at the smiling waif who sat in the alley and waited for the alleged pizza, I wondered if the missing boys, like the TSA Blackshirts, had also tried to rough her up.

Shaye? Are You Still Doing That ~~Hand Thing~~ *Eye Thing?*

July 2008

Zhang regularly blew gaskets. I often heard him yell before I got up and came down from the roof. *Someone, somewhere, must be growing some weed,* I would think to myself. *The end of the stupid "War on Drugs" has got to be one of the positive side-benefits of the apocalypse. Maybe some hooch would be good, too. Vegas is too low and dry for wild blue agave, but we're surrounded by Joshua and yucca hearts. Can't somebody fake some tequila? *Anything* to calm the old guy down?*

Oh, it wasn't *that* bad. Actually, when it appeared that Zhang was going off, things were fine. Zhang often yelled at his granddaughters and me. He was the sort of person who freaked out when he was calm inside, and calm outside when he was about to pull out his shotgun. While he yapped and scolded and flailed, I knew that things were on track. I was rarely put-off by the things that Zhang actually said, though the constant noise sometimes got under my skin. Zhang spent most of the workday up front, bantering and bartering with customers, but when he came out to where I carried on with my rubber-and-canvas cutting, it was like having an alarm clock in my ear.

"*Ja-kah! More part! Need more sole, you find more tire!*"

In Zhang's shop, my name wasn't Jack. For the first three weeks that I worked there, my name was "You." Then my name was "Ja-kah." Of course, the two young ladies pronounced my name with the ease of native English speakers, but to Zhang, my name had two syllables.

* * *

Zhang's hair didn't realize that it grew from a senior citizen's head. It was short, and, except for a few grays, jet-black. Zhang's ears, however, were definitely cognizant of the fact that they were stuck on the sides of

505

an old man's head, because they had grown until their lobes were almost level with Zhang's jawline. They looked like cornucopias of bushy hair. When Zhang gestured his arms could have been salamis in short sleeves. They were very brown and hard, with long wrinkles that ran the entire length of his limbs. The skin of Zhang's face was also brown and hard, but no variety of cured meat resembled Zhang's visage.

I had no idea how old Zhang was, but he was up there. I guessed that when he was young he might have stood nearly six feet tall. Now, though, the vertebrae curved under the back of his shirt and he had pain in one of his hips that forced him to constantly lean. Occasionally Zhang's granddaughters brought him his cane, but he always screeched something that I took for a Chinese curse word and tossed the cane away. Rosie and Mary just shook their heads but they never stopped. Every day they brought Zhang's cane, and every day he cast it aside.

Something that Zhang never threw away or was without, however, was his handkerchief. Age had made his eyelids heavy and his eyes small, and he frequently wiped away fatty secretions from his always-moist lashes. When I watched Zhang I remembered the politics of eyelid shape that I had observed decades before in Korea. One of the Korean presidents had gone in for blepharoplasty when I was stationed at Pyeongtaek, and the Korean media were aghast. Some of the more imbecilic barracks wits had asserted that the surgical procedure was intended to make Koreans look "more white," but someone else had explained to me that there was a complex Korean aesthetic surrounding eyelid configuration that had nothing to do with bizarre Caucasian assumptions that Koreans wanted to mimic Westerners. A sophisticated cultural tradition described small eyes, big eyes, creases, half-folds, full-folds, single lids, double lids, and so on, and all long, long before roundoids had set foot on the Korean Peninsula.

It was a long discussion...but...I can't remember who explained this to me.

Someone...

I hadn't learned as much as I should have about Korean culture, and since I knew absolutely *nothing* about Chinese, or Chinese-American culture, I didn't know if the "eye thing" was as big of a deal. Still, I never mentioned it, even in the early mornings when Zhang's waking vision forced him to feel his way around the shop.

Are You Cutting Cards
Or Telling Fortunes,
Dealer?

February 25th, 2009

Hitler made the trains run on time.
The TSA got the Hoover turbines back online.
Trains on time.
Turbines online.
But there's a bit more to it than that, isn't there?

* * *

The Blackshirts had been making big talk for a while about getting power back to Vegas. Others had made similar bogus promises, so I paid no attention. Even when there were street parties and a city-wide countdown, I merely climbed onto Zhang's roof and went to sleep.

The next morning when I went down to start work, I heard Zhang screaming at the girls. It made my head ache. As I walked through the back and emerged in the front of the store, I saw the reason for Zhang's outburst.

"You sew! You make shoe! You obey me!" he yelped at Mary and Rosie. Both girls recoiled in fear of their...sewing machines? They looked at their grandfather, then at the machines, and then again at their grandfather. They were absolutely rooted.

I didn't interrupt Zhang's tirades, but I made an exception this time. "Mister Zhang," I asked, "what's the problem?"

"Machine! Power, Ja-kah!" He walked over, pressed a button, hit the foot pedal, and for the first time in over a decade, the crank on the needle and foot assembly began to operate itself. "Now can make many, many shoe! Sew! Obey me! *You obey me!*"

The girls gasped at the supernatural living machines and began to take backward steps. I had to quickly leave the room. I had grown fond of Rosie and Mary, and I didn't want them to see what I was about to do. I ran to the back door and, once outside, I began to laugh. I couldn't help it...but as I chuckled, Zhang's words struck me.

You obey me!

YOU OBEY ME!

I stopped laughing. As I stood in the alley, I realized that, many years before, I had heard those same words, spoken at the same volume, with the same intensity... and from the same man.

I'll be damned.

From that day forward, every time I looked at Rosie and Mary's pretty unscarred faces, I understood what that wise old sonofabitch had done with the Andersonville Dairy cowpox samples.

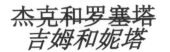

Rosie's work at the machines was done. She was the fastest of Zhang's granddaughters, and when Rosie finished before Mary, she usually just started sewing whatever work her sister had left. Not today, though. Rosie came outside while I was cutting up canvas. When she sat down on the sidewalk, I smiled and asked if she was off the clock. Rosie just returned my smile, but said nothing. That was her standard response when I mistakenly assumed that she understood a phrase from the past.

"I just meant: 'Are you finished working?'"

"Oh. Yes."

"Would you like to cut these up?" I asked, as I jokingly motioned at several old tires. Rosie's smile remained, but she just shook her head. My hands were tired, so I also took a sidewalk seat.

"How old are you?" asked Rosie.

I almost said "thirty-one", but then I remembered my lost decade. "I'll be forty-two years old soon."

"Ah," said Rosie. "I know that letter." She traced *42* with her finger.

"Do you mean 'number'?" I asked.

Rosie turned a shade that almost matched her name. "Yes. 'Number'."

"It's okay," I said. "I knew what you meant. A lot of people didn't have a chance to go to school."

"I did. I was in grade two."

"Oh? How old are *you,* Rosie?" My young friend traced more numbers on the sidewalk. "I see," I said. "You're seventeen."

"Yes."

"And Mary?" I asked, to which Rosie traced *15.*

"What about your grandpa?"

"Ye-Ye? I don't know. He won't tell us."

That figures, I thought. "Did you stop going to school because your parents wanted you to stop?"

"No," said Rosie. "Ye-Ye told me that I couldn't go to school anymore. Mary went to the little girl school..." Rosie paused. "I can't remember how to say it."

"Kindergarten?"

"Yes! Kindergarten. She was going to be in grade one, but she never went to the other school. It ended."

"Have you always lived with your grandpa, er, *Ye-Ye?*"

"No. I lived with my family at the Nellis place. Ye-Ye said that my mother and father had to go far away to be soldiers. They didn't come home."

Rosie's voice had grown very small, so I changed the subject. I picked up a small scrap of rubber and ground a few crude black capital letters onto the sidewalk. "This is my name," I said.

Rosie touched the first letter and softly sang the "ABC" song. She stopped when she got to "J", then repeated the process for the remaining letters.

I smiled. "You *do* remember."

Rosie nodded. "Sometimes I know little words."

"Can you write your name?" I asked, as I handed Rosie the chunk of black rubber.

Rosie nodded and made a flurry of strokes on the sidewalk, then paused. "I can write 'Ye-Ye' and 'Mary', too," she said. Rosie made more strokes for the additional names, but when she finished, I could only scratch my head.

"Why won't you read it?" asked Rosie

"I can't. Your Ye-Ye taught you, didn't he?"

"Yes."

"This is Chinese. I can't read it."

Rosie laughed. "You *can* read it! You're like me, so you can do it!" She cocked her head and smirked as if I had said something ridiculous.

"What?"

"China people can read China words!"

I gave a bewildered smile. "Honey, I'm not Chinese."

Rosie shook her head and rolled her eyes as if I had made a stupid joke. "I *know.* Not China like Ye-Ye. China like *me.*"

We Expect An Excess
Of Running And
A Dearth Of
Rebellion

April
2009
(2-of-2)

It's market day down at the ULVN market. The
campus is closer than the scrounge stalls up on Nellis
and the edge markets out in Greener Valley and
Hendersonville. Last night Rosie and I loaded the bike
trailers with an array of shoes and we left the store at
sunup.

Huh. *ULVN.* Talk about a focal point for my
evaporated dreams! I remember having an idea about
applying for a grad program and attending at night while
working at Addelier Elementary. I laugh while pedaling
behind Rosie's bike and she gives me a curious backward
look.

Today it's just Rosie and me. Zhang trusts me to go
to the market with Rosie while he stays home with Mary
and guards the store. That's *huge*...but, based upon
what I know about my young companion's abilities, I
wonder how much I'm actually *needed* for this trip.

Rosie is a young post-apocalyptic businesswoman.
Her way is to just do things, and Rosie learns while on
the job. When she has to take over at the shop counter,
her sharp mind doesn't need an abacus or counting
sticks. Today she intends to purchase some garment
material, so the people who scrounge old sheets and
hotel curtains had better be ready for a barter-champ
with a sharp eye and an even sharper tongue.
Sometimes Rosie also buys pre-1997 clothes that look
like shitty old rags to me, but she takes them apart and
reverse-engineers them to imitate clothing from pictures
in an old stack of yellowing magazines. Rosie is a tough
little trader, seamstress, cobbler, and killer.

She's adorable.

Rosie and I must stay together all of the time, so we have to do our own shopping before we can set up for business. We take some time to sit with our bikes and watch the vendors assemble and work out their spacing. Because we've delayed, we're going to get stuck out on the edge of the ULVN Quadrangle, but I think that'll be okay. The people who come to market are kind of like the pre-1997 OCD folks who tracked down *every* yard sale in their neighborhood on *every* Saturday. Market-goers make sure that they see all of the merchandise, so Rosie and I won't be overlooked.

Along with old hotel curtains, Rosie also plans to buy some dried alfalfa and cheat grass. It takes some time to grind and boil the cellulose-heavy foods, but they add substance to a stew that Rosie and Mary make. Throw in some of the meat that I bring in, and we've got a decent meal.

I watch as my young companion, with her huge homemade over-the-shoulder bag and floppy bonnet-like hat, haggles from space to space, sniffs in disdain, and engages in barter economy theater. My trading skills are still poor, so I'm content to watch Rosie scowl, frown, and argue until she gets a price that she likes. It'll be the same when we set up shop, too, except she'll be on the other side of the exchange. My job will mostly be to stand with my Ruger and watch for thieves.

Rosie pays for the food and some old dusty green-velvet curtains, all of which she stuffs into her bag and places on one of our trailers. Zhang will quiz Rosie and harangue her if he believes that she's paid too much, but I think that he'll be happy with today's bargains. Zhang also has expectations for the day's shoe sales, and I don't think that he'll be disappointed on that count, either.

It's now time to set up our space. As I had anticipated, we're crowded off the Quadrangle, but we find a decent spot near Beam Hall and the College of Education. I feel kind of strange when I recall the actual names of those buildings because the appearances of the dilapidated and empty hulks no longer befit their old titles. Some of the people don't even recognize this place as being a former university. They just call it the "Quad Market". Why acknowledge that it has ever been anything else? The campus grass and trees are long dead. The old law library just looks like a giant erector set project with smashed windows. The Quadrangle clock tower is frozen, and the rose garden is just a memory. There are old smoke marks in the empty windows of most buildings.

I wonder what the other campus landmarks look like? Is the Mack and Thomas Center collapsed? What remains of the interior of Dungan Hall? Such questions, however, have to go unanswered, because I'm only here to do business.

* * *

At the end of the day we've traded or sold most of our shoes, but there are still a few odd sizes in the trailer behind my bike. I've done a lot of standing and watching while Rosie has brought home the bacon, and I can see that she's tired.

When we get back, Zhang immediately demands to count our take, while Mary helps Rosie and me bring the bikes inside and unpack the remaining shoes. Zhang can juggle figures in his head even faster than his granddaughter, and when he gives an approving nod and pat on Rosie's hand, she sits down to rest, maybe for the first time all day, and there's a little smile on her face.

As The Paraffin
Ran Out

September
2010

- *Let's talk about the story. Then we can -- what's the matter?*
- It's over.
- *Well, yes. But you can read the book again, any time you like. I'm proud of you. You worked really hard on this last book.*
- Was it an old story?
- *Yes. I think the book was first published* - made - *in the late thirties or early forties.*
- Was that long ago?
- *Well, about seventy winters. Yes, it was long ago.*
- I liked it. I want to see islands and canoes someday. I want to see the ocean.
- *There's no reason why you can't. You're young, strong, and very smart. Are you ready for some questions?*
- Yes.
- *Okay. Before he took the canoe and left Hikueru Island, can you tell me what Mafatu was like? Was he brave?*
- No. He was scared.
- *Who was his father?*
- His father was the king. The king wanted Mafatu to be brave, but he wasn't.
- *How did Mafatu become brave?*
- He killed a pig. He killed a big fish called "shark". He also killed a fish called "rocktopus."
- *Octopus.*
- Yes.
- *Sharks and octopii --*
- What's "octopii"?
- *It means "octopuses."*
- Oh.
- *They aren't really fish, but they live in the water like fish. Are they dangerous?*
- Yes. Sharks can eat people. Rockto - *octopuses* -

can grab people. They have eight arm-things.
- *Tentacles. There was another danger for Mafatu, wasn't there?*
- Yes. The people who liked to eat other people.
- *What do you call someone who does that?*
- Ummm…"cannibal".
- *Yes.*
- Jack?
- *Yes, Rosie?*
- Where do you get books?
- *There are still some books in libraries.*
- "Libraries"? What are they?
- *You mean you've never…? Okay, here's what we'll do: The next time I go out hunting, ask your grandpa if you can come with me. Don't you remember the library from when you went to school?*
- No. I can't remember. Why do you need me to go hunting with you? You're a good hunter.
- *Because the Whitney Library has burned down, but there are still some books in the Flamingo Library. That's where I've been getting your reading books. That's where we'll go, and I can show you a library.*
- But Jack, what's a "library"?
- *Sorry, Rosie. It's a big building full of books.*
- You can get books there?
- *Well, when I was a boy you could borrow the books, but now I guess that you can just take them.*
- Nobody wants books. Nobody can read.
- *But you can! And when you keep doing it, it gets easier and easier.*
- I…*like* to read. I wish Mary would learn.
- *Maybe you could teach her someday.*
- Why can't *you* teach her, Jack? You showed me how to read. You could show her, too.
- *Well, maybe. We'll see what the future holds.*
- What do you mean?
- *I-I mean…let's get your grandpa's permission to go out tomorrow. There's a book that I want to look for at the library called* Shen of the Sea. *I think you might like it.*

22

Cups Still
Full Of
Sand

Dead But Dreaming
In My
Past

October
2010

I congratulated myself for almost finishing a tire-snipping job without getting jabbed by one of the tread's needle-like wires. *I've got this down pat,* I thought, just as a sharp strand poked through my glove and pricked me. "Damn!" I cursed, as I pulled off my glove and stuck my finger in my mouth.

I noticed the approach of a potential customer. His unibrow and mustache were strangely familiar, and my distant memories instinctively associated those features with a pot belly...except it was now gone, as was most of his hair. I estimated that he was in his early sixties. The inevitable aspects of aging aside, this figure from my past seemed rather trim and fit. It was kind of funny, in a reversal-sort of way, because *I* had been the skinny one the last time we had met, though I still could hardly be considered fat.

He looked at me, but showed no reaction. Why would he? How many airmen had he known back then? He had no reason to recognize me.

"Still stickin' yourself with mutherfuckin' arming wires?" he asked.

I'll be god-damned. He did *know me.* I had to laugh. All the "sirs" and "sergeants" were behind us. *You old pain-in-the-ass, for some reason it's good to see you again,* I thought.

I stood up and smiled. "I'd shake," I said, "except you probably don't want blood all over your hand."

Jones returned my smile. "Simmerath, how the hell have you been?"

"Well, I'm surviving, the same as everybody nowadays. I can't believe that you know who I am."

Jones chuckled. "Hell, you and 'ole Corndog were characters. How could I forget? Whatever happened to that mutherfucker?"

"Carl? I don't know. After I left Korea we sent a few

letters, but you know how things go..." My voice trailed off. "He's here, you know. In Vegas."

"Corndog?"

"That's right. You won't believe where I saw him. He was a big high muckity-muck at a TSA rally a couple years ago."

"Was it good to see your old buddy again?"

"Fuck the TSA," I replied. "I just left without talking to him. It was strange...he had smallpox scars all over his face."

"You're sure it was him?" Jones asked. When I nodded, he slowly shook his head, but said nothing. Jones looked at the cut up-tires and picked up one of the sandwich board's display shoes. "So this is what you've been doin'?"

"Well, I was going to be a teacher after I got out of the service..." My voice trailed off. That was all I needed to say. I was just one of so many who had planned in one hand and spat in the other.

Jones changed the subject. "Innovation. Goddamn innovation and people doin' the best they can with what they fuckin' got. That's how this world is gonna get back on its feet." Jones put the display shoe back on top of the sign and grinned as he recognized his unwitting play on words."

I nodded. "The sun comes up, and I have to get up with it. I haven't always done this since the world changed, though. It's sort of a new thing for me, but it beats the Grizzly Addams scene."

Jones sat down on the curb. "Went wild, huh?"

"Yeah. Sort of ran out of ideas, then I even ran out of sanity for a while. A long while."

My former flight chief gave an understanding nod as he picked up a piece of rubber. "So how'd you end up in Vegas?"

"My hometown."

Jones nodded. "I'm from a little 'burg in Montana myself, but I bought a place out in Summerlin after I retired. Me, and my wife...but she passed when there was trouble out there." Jones bowed his head for a silent moment, and then he looked at me. "You still remember the first step to a load?"

"What?" The topic shift was too abrupt for me to follow.

"The first fuckin' thing you do when you load a jet. Remember?"

I took a breath. *What a weird question.* It was time for deep data retrieval. "Um, well, check the aircraft forms."

Jones had a half-smile. "Well, *yeah*...but I mean when you actually start."

Again, I had to mentally go back for decades, but I remembered the answer. "Secure the aircraft ground cable so you don't blow yourself up."

Jones had a full grin now. "Good. Weapons Load Barn tightened you up for life."

"Why do you ask?"

"Because, like I said, we're gonna get the motherfuckin' world goin' again. C'mere." Jones rose from the curb and walked out to the middle of the strip mall's empty parking lot. He shielded his eyes and pointed upward.

"There. C'mere, Simmerath! Look at this."

I put down my cutters and clenched my fist around my oozing finger. Then I walked out to where Jones stood.

"There," he repeated.

I shaded my eyes and spotted a fine line of smoke. "What the hell?" I asked in amazement. It almost looked like a contrail...but I hadn't seen an aircraft in the sky for at least fifteen years. Besides, the line looked like rocket smoke, the kind that lingered in the air after a fireworks display. At the end of the line and moving in a southeastern direction was a kind of aircraft. I recognized the distant shape.

"A glider!" I exclaimed. "A hang glider!"

"Fuckin' A," Jones stated, visibly puffing up with pride, "and next month, we'll have worked out the kinks to putting pots on ultralites."

"Pots?"

"Rocket pots," Jones explained. "Like back in dubya-dubya-two and in 'Nam, when they needed to get an overloaded prop plane off the ground. They bolted on some solid-propellant boosters and got 'er up." He turned back to watch the glider. "We got the mutherfuckin' drafts all mapped. Once he's up, he'll have enough altitude to ride one to Laughlin, but he won't land. He'll fire up two more times and come home."

My interest was definitely piqued. In fact, how cool!

"Mutherfuckin' surfers! Can you believe that shit? My pilots are all surfers!"

"Surfers?"

"Yeah. Wanderin' through from the coast a while back. They got a knack for it. A feel. They say it's like ridin' waves."

The glider continued to climb and gain distance, and had almost reached the edge of the valley. "How far can it go?" I asked.

"Full pack? Almost to LA one way, or past Phoenix in the other. For now."

I looked at Jones. Who would have guessed? Twenty-some years ago he was an irritating fat ass with an imagination that was as big as a nickel, but now, here stood an inventive and slimmed-down post-apocalyptic airline entrepreneur.

I considered the logistics of what I witnessed. Sure, in the absence of jet fuel, engine parts, and everything else that had made air travel possible, it made sense to fall back upon past technologies. This particular regression, however, seemed to have its own attendant impossibilities.

"Where are you getting fuel?" I asked.

Jones spoke as we returned to the shade. "Dry-bonded H_2O_2," he replied, "like fancy peroxide rockets. I got somebody who knows what he's doin'. He can downcook the shit 'til its like pressed dust, and without blowin' up the workshop. The trails usually ain't that easy to see, but we sucked some perchlorate out of the ground water a while back. We use tile and tin, or whatever we can find for expendable casing. My guy was a chemistry teacher up at Cimarron High, but now he's got a fuel setup in Northtown. I got another crew building our first passenger ultralite down at McKarran, too."

I cocked my head. "Uh, *passenger* ultralite?"

"Yeah," nodded Jones. Seven payin', plus the pilot, like a single-stack .45. That's what we're aimin' for."

Amazing. Lacquered fabric and modified pipe bombs had gotten mankind airborne again.

"So, whaddya say?"

"Huh?"

"Are you in? Or are you in love with mutherfuckin' tire shoes?"

I blinked. "I don't know a damn thing about making rockets or gliders," I said. "The world being what it is, yeah, maybe I'll pretend to be a cobbler for quite a while." I opened my fist and saw that my finger had stopped bleeding.

"Oh?" replied Jones. "When you were a kid, you didn't fly jets, either. And you didn't make the bombs you loaded. You just put 'em together and locked 'em on."

"Yeah. So?"

"So, do it again. Slappin' on rocket pots ain't much different from puttin' on bombs."

I didn't answer. Instead, I walked back out to the parking lot and looked up. The glider had disappeared. "What are the passengers gonna pay with?" I called back.

Jones walked out to join me. "Real Silver Pesos preferred, but Nevada Silver Peso Certificates are still accepted...for now. The Ailter Arm of the old Comstock is giving color. And they haven't even given names to the new Austin and Manhattan Camp strikes yet."

I wondered if Jones was exaggerating, because I knew that the Nevada mining corporations were as dead as any other major industrial players. "Those old holes are considered 'strikes' nowadays?" I asked. "We must be talking about tailing thieves."

"Hell," replied Jones, "nobody's called 'em that for a long, long time. There ain't no more government mining laws, and there ain't no more mining companies. Silver is silver, Simmerath. It don't matter where it comes from. Tradin' and paper NSP," Jones continued, as he gestured at the piles of shoe materials, "are on their way out."

Maybe, or maybe not, I thought. *But for now I'm*

with people who won't kill me for my shirt, and I have a safe place to sleep. Jones' plans were exciting, but built upon the sandy foundatlon of a single hang-glider and a concoction straight out of *An Anarchist's Cookbook.* I had never read the Bible, but I didn't have to in order to see that Zhang's Uggs were the preferable birds in my hand, whereas Jones and whatever was in his airport bushes seemed quite uncertain.

Still...

"I'll think about it," I said, as we walked back to the sidewalk. "But I'm past forty. I'm not gonna break my back out on some flightline."

"Damn straight you're not," Jones said, as he stood and brushed off his pants. "I'm gonna have you supervise the youngsters. They can break *their* backs." Then Jones did something that took me aback. He extended his right hand, but I put out my unbloodied left. He grinned and shook. "It's a better deal than ripping up your hands on steel belts," he said. "Just think about it." Then Jones reacted to something that he spotted over my shoulder. "Shit," he said. "I must be late. That's my mutherfuckin' ass." Jones went to retrieve his bicycle from where it was propped against the front of the shop.

I turned. Sitting near the edge of the parking lot, on her own bicycle with an attached baby trailer, was a young woman with long coal-black hair that flowed out from under her cap. Her dark features carried a scowl as she watched Jones mount his bike.

"Who...?" I began.

"My wife," Jones said. "My new wife and baby boy."

"New wife?"

"Yeah. Turns out the BIA was still doling out smallpox shots on the Second Mesa Rez. Almost every rez in the USA, in fact. Some kind of kickback deal with the drug companies. They never stopped. We met in Flagstaff." Jones began to pedal, but yelled back over his shoulder. "Fuckin' ironic! White-Eye let his own kids get bubbled, but saved the Indians!"

As I watched the new family pedal away, I thought about Jones' wife. *Heh.* The land had fallen into receivership after the American culture stopped making payments, but it didn't matter, because the first owners still held the original deed.

I was about to return to my work when I noticed, at the far end of the strip mall, that there were two black-clad figures leaning against the last storefront. When they saw me stop to look at them, they slowly and deliberately walked away.

~~Zeke~~ *Jack* Wakes Up
Every Morning With
$36.27 In His
Pocket

January
2011
(1-of-3)

There was a huge contrast between my experiences of seeing Jones and seeing Carl back in '07 at that TSA rally. Besides the obvious difference of his mysterious smallpox scars, Carl was fat and balding. Jones had his own growing forehead but he wasn't fat. I speculated that Carl's slide had been the result of a not-quite sedentary career track, whereas Jones was best described by Harrison Dodge in his line from *Raiding the Lost Ark*: "It's not the years; it's the mileage." In Jones' case, a flipped odometer wasn't a bad thing. Physical activity and a young wife had put enough spring into my old flight chief's step to make him a moving target for The Reaper. Jones demonstrated that it was okay to grow old, as long as you didn't allow parts of your body to atrophy while other bits morphed into abdominal lard sacks.

I couldn't be sure about the direction that Carl's life had taken since our Pyeongtaek days, but I could speculate: He cross-trained into Military Intelligence, traveled widely, saw a lot of secret things, did a lot of secret things, and maybe avoided engaging in acts that would have permanently discolored his soul...though his current company seemed to place that last point in doubt. Perhaps Carl had been a hard-core military lifer who stayed in until they had to kick him out the base gates, or maybe he just racked up his twenty, took half base-pay, and went on to some other profession.

Well, no. I realized that there wouldn't have been enough time for Carl to have retired from the military. I had gotten out in 1992, 9/11 and the 'pox hit in 1996, and by late 1997 there really wasn't much left of the United States, let alone the United States Air Force.

Maybe I shouldn't have been surprised to see Carl at The Huntridge rally, because Vegas had always been a popular destination for veterans and retirees. We were both old enough to be grandfathers, but I sensed that family had never entered into Carl's life picture. I guessed that we were similar in that respect, but probably for very different reasons.

* * *

I also did lots of guessing when I next saw Grace, but in her case, the hints, tidbits and possibilities were less dated.

I guess that I should now go back and explain how I ran into her again - and no, it didn't happen at a TSA hate rally.

I *Deliberately* Chose
"Night Ride" To
Crash The
Game!

La Madre winters were something that my Mr. Hyde had experienced, but I'd bet that Januaries in that snug little half-buried hut had been warmer than my nights on the roof. It was bearable though, and I was reasonably comfortable when I piled canvas scroungings over my bedroll

Reasonably.

I laid on the roof and reflected upon how events had drifted further and further from what had once been my life's forecast. No, I really, *really* wasn't a principal or senior teacher in the long-defunct Clark County School District. I wasn't thinking about grandchildren, and my wife and I weren't planning to retire in Summerlin or Hendersonville. Instead, I was lying under a pile of dusty canvas on top of a strip mall and my "wife" was an old carbine. I had spent many nights watching the sky for a special falling star, but I always fell asleep before I had a chance to wish for the life that I might have had.

Old dreams were millstones. Love had never really materialized for me in a lasting form, and my career track turned out to be equally vaporous. Maybe in an alternate universe there was another Jack who had gotten what he wanted, but in *this* reality my aspirations had been negated by a little thing called The End of the World.

- *"The End of the World"? That might be a bit much.*
- The Apocalypse?
- *No, no. Still too strong.*
- The Second Coming?
- *WHAT Second Coming?*

- Let's just call it "The Big Downgrade."
- *Got it. S&P "D", Fitch "D", and Moody's "C".*
- Roger.

Whoa! What was that?

I was shocked to see lights moving among the stationary stars, and in Vegas' growing municipal haze I spotted aircraft trails. They were neither contrails nor murderous chemtrails, and I realized that I was looking at streams of rocket ejecta. I pushed off the canvas, sat up, and searched for more approaching aircraft, but only one set of lights had approached McKarran while the rest had departed Vegas.

It occurred to me that I could now say "McKarran" and truly refer to an active airport, and not just a collection of abandoned terminals and hangars. Jones hadn't been dreaming empty and impossible dreams after all.

What if I buried my long-expired hopes and hitched my wagon to someone else's ambitions?

Perhaps it was time to re-consider my gig as a post-apocalyptic cobbler's assistant.

I got up from my bedroll, put my coat and boots on, and picked up my .22. I climbed down the ladder and was about to leave the alley when I smelled burning garbage. I paid little attention, until I noticed that the sooty stink came from the little horno that I had built. I walked over and discovered that wads of paper and fabric were stuffed inside. In the embers' light I saw the half-burnt pages of yellowed fashion magazines and pieces of sewing patterns.

Rocket-Powered And
Nailed To The
Ground

January
2011
(3-of-3)

I walked toward the street to wave down an all-night tuk-tuk, then stopped and cursed as I returned to the shop and unlocked my bike. I had forgotten that most night-tuks wouldn't pick up armed passengers, but there was no way that I was going to move around Vegas at night without a weapon. Like most others, my bike had a carbine tube.

The ride was cold, but I had a cap and some homemade gloves. I was accustomed to a decade-and-a-half of firelight and candles, so at first the idea of traveling at night seemed strange. Now, however, there was enough light in partially re-electrified Vegas that I was able to vaguely see where I was going.

Finding Jones' operation wasn't hard, but if I had ridden straight to the central McKarran terminals, I would have missed it. I headed down Paradise Road until I got close to the airport, but stopped when I saw an incoming aircraft approach the eastern complex.

Jones is out at the freight terminals, I thought. I continued to McKarran's main commercial facility, but when I got there, as expected, everything was dark, except for the firelight of those who chose to occupy the parking levels instead of taking over one of Vegas' many abandoned houses. Some derelicts spotted me and shouted as I cycled through the ground areas, but I just kept pedaling until I found myself moving along the airport's perimeter fence.

Bent metal poles jutted out of the tarmac beside a gap of snapped and distorted wire where a vehicle had crashed through. I rode through the hole and aimed my bike in the direction of the freight terminals. I thought that I would be able, since I was already on the flightline, to simply cycle up to Jones' place; however, when I spotted a distant pair of lit hangars I was irritated to discover that they were segregated by yet another chain link barrier. I could do little except follow the fence northward with a growing sense of frustration. I approached a gate just as I was starting to think that I was going to meet the perimeter fence again. It was chained and locked, but that didn't matter because the gate's tubular frame had been pried and bent to create a space where a person could pass. I dismounted and carefully maneuvered my bike's handlebars to get the front wheel through, then I turned around and continued in the direction of the freight hangars.

I shook my head when I discovered that the airport road had deposited me outside yet *another* fence, though at least this was the one that surrounded my destination. I could not access the open hangar bays, as those faced the flightline itself, but I was able to see the main business entrance of "Jones Airways" - or whatever the operation was called.

A tuk-tuk pulled up and a man got out. He wore a brown jacket that bore distinctive white stripe down the back. The man walked through the entry gate, past a bored guard who carried an old AK-47 knock-off, and into the hangar. A few moments later I saw him on the flightline. I couldn't make out his face in the distance and poor light, but I recognized the stripe on his jacket as he walked toward one of the more distant moorings.

Two women followed the white-stripe man. They were well-dressed in skirts and jackets as they moved across the cold flightline, but that wasn't what caught my eye. They pushed a big laundry cart that was exactly the same as those once used by hotel housekeepers to move large amounts of dirty towels and sheets. *What the hell?* I wondered. A few minutes later the women returned the cart to the hanger, and when they reappeared, they pushed a large and fully-loaded clothes rack that would have been more appropriately placed in a dry-cleaning facility. I watched for a moment, but since I couldn't figure out what functions a laundry cart and clothes rack served on a flightline, my attention shifted to other things.

As I watched people saunter in the hangar's vicinity, a great difference between the present air travel environment and that of the past became clear. The casual comings-and-goings of travelers were an amazing contrast from the totalitarian-pervert-security-theater that had once plagued airports, for there were no longer any thuggish Security Transportation Administration pedophiles determined to finger children's rectums and shove travelers into cancer-causing x-ray machines. People simply walked from their tuk-tuks, though the hangars, and to their assigned seats.

I did, however, notice something that was *not* an improvement on the old flying routine, and that was a lack of luggage. No one entered or exited the hangar with an item larger than a small sack or duffel that would easily fit on their laps. I looked though the fence at an aircraft that was being pushed by a group of men, and I understood why baggage wasn't an option. The planes were simply too small and light to transport much more than the travelers themselves.

The nearest plane appeared to incorporate features of a stretch limousine and a Polynesian canoe. The fuselage was a light open frame that accommodated passengers with what appeared to be attached folding chairs, and I counted ten seats behind the "cockpit". The ultralight's passenger capacity made me smile when I remembered my conversation with Jones in the parking lot of Zhang's shop. Jones' grand plan had been to create a fleet of planes that could handle *seven* travelers, but he had met and exceeded his goal.

The nosecone of Jones' homemade aircraft was made of plexi, and it looked like it afforded the pilot some decent protection. A double outrigger-like framework fanned out from mounts along both sides of the fuselage and extended beyond the plane's tail. Objects that resembled large tipped-over coffee cans were attached at regularly-spaced intervals, and I counted eight "cans" on each side of the frame.

So this is what a rocket plane looks like in real life, I thought. I had only seen such things in history books that featured photos of Allied D-Day rocket gliders and Nazi Germany's giant rocket-assisted medevac transports. *But how the hell can people fly in something like that, at night, and in January?* Sure, this was Los

Vegas and this was the Mojave Desert, but the southwest's winter nights were still cold. Well, perhaps Jones' brand of air travel wasn't terribly comfortable, but it *did* appear to be feasible. *This is amazing,* I thought. *I can't believe that Jones, of all people, is pulling it off.*

I wondered again about Jones' age. He was in his late sixties or early seventies, *at least*...but I was sure that if I were to ever ask, I would get a response similar to the one that Rosie and Mary received when they asked Zhang how old he was.

* * *

I watched the process of prepping a "rocketlite" for takeoff. There were no aircraft tugs, obviously, and the plane that I observed was manually positioned by a group of men who had stopped pushing it, chocked its wheels, attached its static cable to a ground point, and broken off into their individual specialties. I had a frame of reference from my military days that aided me in identifying what jobs were being performed.

After the plane was braked and chocked, two guys immediately pulled out a clipboard and went down a checklist, back to front, to check the wires for each of the craft's control surfaces. I guessed these to be Jones' aircraft crew chiefs. One of the men went to the cockpit to execute a series of stick-and-pedal actuations, while the other guy held a tension meter on cable guides to check the ailerons, flaps, elevator and rudder. Then they performed a general inspection of the airframe with flashlights and did safety checks on the passenger seats and belts. I puzzled over where the men could have found flashlight batteries, until I saw them pause to wind up their lights. I also wondered where the planes got power to operate their onboard flashers, but when I saw the crew go to the fronts of the wings and make spinning motions with their hands, I understood. I hadn't noticed at first, but the plane *did* have propellers, though not the kind that could move it through the air. They reminded me of a tyrannosaur's tiny and useless arms. The crew chiefs continued to spin the propellers until small lights on the wings and tail flashed. At that, the chiefs checked their clipboard and moved on, while the propellers stopped and the lights went dark.

Three men had left the scene after pushing the plane and returned with a large wooden box on a handcart. They paused while one man went forward to confirm that the aircraft's static cable was clipped to a metal ground post. The trio then moved the handcart forward, chocked its wheels, and grounded its metal undercarriage.

Whereas the crew chiefs had tended to the airframe, this group went directly to the propulsion system. Two men moved to the back and positioned themselves on each outrigger, while the third gave the small propellers hard spins and rushed to the pilot's seat. The cockpit man manipulated the stick, but the result was different from the crew chief's preflight check. The aft crewmen had hooked small hand-held boxes into the outrigger frames' metal cans. *Voltmeters,* I thought. *They're checking ignition current.* Tiny glows flickered from the boxes, and each time this happened, the aft men called out and gave a thumbs-up. When the check was done, the cockpit man took out a clipboard and ticked a checklist. Though civil aviation had its own brand of procedures, I figured that Jones had simply adopted military-style maintenance techniques to the workplace of his "weapon" crews.

The three men returned to their handcart and moved it to the rear of the plane, where it was again chocked and grounded. Then each man went to the ground point's metal post, knelt, licked his fingers, and touched it before opening the handcart box. The crew chief continued to check off steps while the other men unlatched the lid. Before they reached in and removed the contents, however, the entire group touched the ground post yet again. The propellant, in poor light and from my vantage outside the fence, looked like cylinders of compressed oatmeal. The substance was wrapped in sheets of brown paper, and these were removed before the crew gently slid the cylinders into the framework canisters and capped the ends with covers that resembled large cookie jar lids.

I wondered what it was like to take a night flight on

such a contraption. Maybe it was less nerve-racking in the darkness, since passengers didn't have to actually see the earth through an open airframe while sitting on, essentially, rocket-powered lawn chairs. It might take some time for me to work up courage sufficient for air travel, and I would also need to scrutinize Jones' safety record before buying a ticket.

Not long after the "weapons" crew disappeared with their handcart and the crew chiefs again took charge, a single individual whom I hadn't previously seen approached the aircraft. He wore a leather jacket and carried headgear that looked like a plain old motorcycle helmet with a full face shield. His hair was long and blonde. The man spoke to the crew chiefs for a few moments, then they handed him - the pilot, obviously - their checklist. He walked around the plane to double-check each item, but he didn't walk directly behind the rocketlite. Rather, he examined the canisters on one outrigger, then walked completely around the nose of the plane to check the other side like a man going out of his way to avoid walking in front of a cannon - or, in this case, *sixteen* cannons. The pilot returned to the front, gave the checklist back to the crew chiefs, shook their hands, and started to buckle into the seat behind the aircraft's plexi-bubble nose.

A line of people emerged from the hangar. Like passengers that I had seen earlier, they carried small lap-bags or nothing at all, and in their lead was the main man himself, who, even in the dim light, cut an appreciably svelte and limber figure for a probable-sexagenarian.

Jones engaged in PR. As the passengers walked, he left the lead and began to move up and down the line, shaking hands, patting backs, and laughing a loud fake laugh that I could hear even over by the fence. *I wonder if he's cleaned up his language?* I wondered. *Or does he think that calling customers "motherfuckers" make them feel down-home and chummy?*

The travelers didn't immediately get into their seats when they arrived at the plane. The clothes rack and the clothes-rack-ladies approached and spoke to the passengers, one-by-one, while doling out gloves, goggles, hats, ear protectors, and heavy jackets. *A laundry rack for departures, and a laundry cart for arrivals,* I thought. *Makes sense. None of those people were dressed for the ride.*

Once everyone was bundled-up and strapped in, the clothes rack was pushed inside. The women hurried back out to wait with Jones for a cheesily-scripted send off. They moved well away from the plane while the crew chiefs stepped forward, spun the propellers, and pulled the wheel chocks.

Some of the passengers held onto the airframe and braced themselves. I guessed that these were veteran fliers. The rest just nervously looked around, though their fingers also gripped the fuselage tubes. I couldn't see most of their faces because everyone wore goggles and mufflers.

When the aircraft lights began to glow the pilot gave the crew chiefs a "hang loose" hand signal, put his bike helmet on over his long blonde hair, and hit a switch. What happened next made Jones put his hand on his temple and slowly shake his head. I remembered that look from when I was in Korea. It was Jones' *you-fucking-dumbshits* classic. Though I had witnessed all of the workers use their checklists and technical orders, there had still been a breakdown in procedure because the rocket stations that had been selected for takeoff weren't uncapped before the pilot hit the spark. There were sounds like multiple gunshots and metal canister covers shot into the side of the hangar wall like deadly steel frisbees. Of course, no one had stood behind the plane during ignition so there weren't any injuries, but two of the covers dented the wall and fell to the concrete while the other two half-buried themselves in the hangar's exterior like circular blades thrown from a defective table saw.

Jones remembered the passengers, stopped shaking his head, and waved at the plane. The women followed his lead and I imagined the three of them on a dock, holding kerchiefs over their heads, and shouting *"Bon Voyage!"*

The aircraft made a sound unlike that of a jet's turbine. It was more like a hand-held striker igniting a cutting torch, but a thousand times louder. Like the people on the flightline, I also covered my ears. I understood why the passengers had been given hearing protection, and I assumed that the pilot had slipped in some ear plugs before he put on his helmet.

At first there wasn't any visible flame coming from the back of the aircraft, just an incredible amount of gray smoke. For some long moments the plane didn't budge, but then wavering spikes of fire slowly grew from four of the canisters, and as they became larger and more intense, the lazy gray cloud turned into a white smoke jet. The plane slowly inched forward and began to roar like a giant propane grill with its gas cranked way too high. The plane accelerated as it taxied, and when it got to the end of the runway there was no pause before takeoff. The aircraft lights flashed as the winged rocket-sled raced down the runway and rose into the night.

That was very cool.
That also looks scary as HELL!
I wonder if there were any super-terrified roller-coaster screams as they took off?

I remembered the canister covers and looked at the discs sticking out of the hangar wall. *If Jones' offer still stands, this might be my chance,* I thought. *He knows that I wouldn't dick things up like* that.

I noticed something when my eyes returned to Jones and his lady companions. In the same way that I had looked through the fence and, from a distance, identified my former flight chief by his gait and demeanor, I also seemed to recognize one of his lady companion's step and sway.

Yes, yes…there was a definite familiarity.

No. A certainty. Even after a decade-and-a-half…like it was yesterday.

Why was she here?

There was no way that she could have found me, or

even known that I was still alive. There was no way that I could have found her, or known that she had made her way back to Nevada, either.

Suddenly, I...I wasn't quite ready to talk to Jones about a new job. Not yet. If really wanted to bring me onboard, he'd still be as willing tomorrow as he was tonight.

*　*　*

How long have I stood by this fence?

I've watched other women meet their partners here, but no one has come for Grace. She just got into a tuk-tuk with a man and a woman. They exited the hangar via separate doors, but left together.

So how did things turn out with the Korean guy? Mr. Racially and Culturally Appropriate?

It's going on, what, almost fifteen years? No, I'm not bitter.

Well...maybe a little.

Maybe a whole fucking lot.

But I'll work through that later, after I've told Jones that I'm going to take over his fuel-loading program.

"One Male"
- Plate
67

May
2011

She still wears Old Slice.

That was my first thought on the day that I walked over to the business hangar and entered the ticketing area. Grace didn't see me come in because she was helping a couple arrange a trip to Reno. As I was to learn, her job entailed more responsibilities besides just pushing a big clothes hamper around the freight terminal.

She was stunned to see me. I probably looked a lot older, and a hell of a lot rougher, but she looked...well, *the same.* Maybe Grace had aged a *little,* but I had to look closely to see the evidence. I noted the faint beginnings of crow's feet. Perhaps a dimple or two hung around a little longer than her smile...but that was all.

Grace's tale was shorter than I thought it would be. It was Occam's Razor, sharpened and modified for the purpose of providing the simplest explanation for how she had ended up back in Vegas. I didn't expect a story, and I wasn't going to ask, either...but Grace provided one anyway.

The Korean guy was a fat old businessman and a chauvinist. End of story, end of her family's dictate. Grace had been working at the airline since its inception, and before that she had survived on a farm in Asheville. Grace told me that she had realized that she loved me, but when her career ended in a way very similar to my own, she also found herself caught up in the complications of riding out the end of the world. Grace finally biked back to the southwest with two men and three women who went on to California while she stayed in Vegas. By the time Grace had returned, however, I was hallucinating in the mountains.

A Table For Two
At Göbekli
Tepe

June
2011

Grace's story had been pat, easy, and exactly what I wanted to believe. I would buy it and keep on buying it. Still, I was always willing to give her an opportunity to provide more detailed and plausible versions of her past, or anything else she wanted to talk about, and tonight the venue for expanded discussion was a dinner date.

Grace smiled and laughed as we grew closer to our destination. "I can't believe that you're taking me here," she said, as she squeezed my arm and plopped her head against my shoulder. It was a cute moment, and the guy pedaling the tuk-tuk glanced back and grinned.

* * *

Before I met The Sated Yam I had known The Anchor-on-Crown. We were introduced in the relief that had followed ULVN midterms and finals. We got to know each other better when I was tired of my own "cooking" and needed to get out. We became more than acquaintances over many games of darts, and at last called each other friends over multiple pints of dark English beer.

The nearest that I had ever traveled to Great Britain was the northeastern corner of Tropicana and Maryland, where there was a pub and restaurant whose external décor retrofit simulated a timber-framed wattle-and-plaster English village structure. The roof, however, remained standard southwestern mission tile, since authentic thatch would have probably exploded in the Nevada sun. The establishment's shaded beer garden was separated from Tropicana's six lanes of insanity by a white picket fence.

Within walking distance of ULVN dorms and on a main thoroughfare, The Anchor-on-Crown was a college-crowd fixture that had easily outlasted the competition. Moose MacGillicuddy's, Stringles, TP's, Chekkers...all would come in search of their collegiate party scene cut, and all would eventually go, but The Anchor-on-Crown endured. With all of the ULVN liaisons initiated among its dim lights, greasy but delicious fish and chips, 24/7 English Football channels, and various pieces of ship's rigging suspended over the bar, The Anchor-on-Crown should have been considered a sociology elective. It would be forever in my nostalgic recollections, as well as in *Los Asesinos'* song *Señor Lado Positivo.*

Having never crossed the Atlantic, I could not judge the authenticity of The Anchor-on-Crown's simulated English drinking experience...but I had some doubts. These were reinforced by a barmaid over whom I drooled for a couple semesters. She was a Salvadoran woman named Marianne with long black hair, an amazing body, and a heavy Spanish accent. Like other Anchor-on-Crown girls, Marianne wore a short-short Scottish kilt in an English "pub" in the middle of the Mojave Desert. No, The Anchor-on-Crown probably wasn't much like a real blokester pub; therefore, as with most of Los Vegas' themed establishments, it demanded a certain suspension of disbelief.

The Anchor-on-Crown had an upstairs that looked down on the main bar and restaurant area, and that was where Grace and I had liked to sit when we were in college. The top floor was over-draped with ship's rigging, which was strange, but also kind of cool because we could stare down and people-watch, unobserved, in our weird sort-of crow's nest.

When I got Oatmeal-Stout-Ultra-Waxed I could easily stumble down Maryland and on to my Hacienda apartment. This wasn't an especially wise practice because the neighborhood had gotten sketchy. On the way I would pass by the house where I had lived with Grandpa and the ever-present military security detail. Sometimes I would pause on the sidewalk and look at the lights in the windows and wonder who lived there. I was lucky that the occupants never called the cops on the drunk college guy who stared at their home and wondered if **someone was playing a game in the house that he'd grown up in.**

* * *

540

The Anchor-on-Crown was now called the Sated Yam, but the name wasn't the only thing that was different. When Grace and I went inside, we saw that the ship's rigging was gone, along with the big English Football screens. The darkness, the...*greasiness*...was gone. The exterior looked the same, however, so when we entered, Grace and I were shocked. For starters, the servers were mostly fit, albeit 'pox-scarred, young men, though I did notice a few young ladies. Nobody wore kilts, however. The dart boards and pool tables were missing. The shades were open, and - kudos to the management - there was an actual functioning air conditioner. The establishment's color scheme was orange. I didn't smell hot oil or frying grease.

"Well, *this* is unexpected," said Grace. "Do we wait to be seated?"

"I'm not sure. Remember how you always said that you wanted to move past The Anchor-on-Crown? I think that just happened."

Grace gave a little shrug. "I know...but tonight I would have liked to have seen the old place again."

I put my arm around her shoulder. "Me too. But let's give this a chance and see what happens."

"Good evening," said a familiar voice. The face was also familiar, but the attire was not. Our server was a lovely young woman with a long reddish-black ponytail and perfectly unpoxed skin. She was dressed in sharp slacks and a white blouse that were quite different from homemade garments cut from old hotel curtains. Rosie and I did little double takes, then we laughed and hugged.

"Grace, meet Rosie," I said with a smile. "The best cobbler in Vegas, and probably the best server, too."

"Pleasure," said Grace. She smiled but gave me a curious glance.

"I worked in Rosie's grandpa's shoe shop before I started at the airport," I explained. Grace nodded as she associated my survival stories with an actual person. I looked closely at Rosie because I saw an almost-concealed look of sadness cross my young friend's face.

"Your grandpa...?"

"He's fine," said Rosie. "Ye-Ye and Mary still work in

the shop."

"Ah, glad to hear that," I replied. I dropped the topic because I recognized a forced workplace smile when I saw one.

"Would you like to eat?" asked Rosie. "I can also seat you at the bar, if you like."

"I think we'll take a table," I said, as I looked Grace. She nodded, and then asked a question. "What do you serve from the bar?"

"We have a light cheat beer brewed in Beatty. We also carry a darker cheat that comes from Kingman. If you like wine, we have some very nice clover from the fields around Churchill, and also local yucca tequila."

Good girl, I thought. *I know that you've never set foot in any of those towns, but you spoke with enough confidence that I'd think you scouted products yourself.* I beamed at Rosie.

Grace turned to me. "Drinks first?"

"Sure. What?"

Grace grinned. "Tequila."

"Wait a sec. You remember my old policy about drinking contests and Korean girls, right?"

Grace gave me a peck on the cheek. "I have no idea what you're talking about," she said. She turned to Rosie. "Doubles."

Rosie smiled. "I'll be right back."

* * *

Grace and I giggled like kids after we slammed our tequilas. As we perused the menu, my mind returned to the day when I had told Zhang and the girls that I would be moving on. As expected, he just wanted to know exactly when, and then he went back to whatever he had been doing. Mary looked kind of downcast but managed a smile, whereas Rosie turned away and wouldn't show me her face. She didn't have much to say until the day when it was time for me to pack up my few things and bring them down from the roof.

Rosie was waiting at the bottom of the ladder, but I hadn't even heard the back door open. I smiled at her but she didn't smile at me. Instead, she gave me a package. When I opened it I found a long sleeved green velvet shirt that, in another life, had hung in the window of a Vegas hotel.

I was really touched, and also a little ashamed that I had nothing to exchange. I stood for an awkward moment but then I had a thought. I dropped my pack on the ground, went into the back of the shop, and returned with something.

"You know those books that we brought back from the library?" I asked. "Here. Read this once first." I handed Rosie an old paperback and gave her a long hug. "Maybe I should call you Scarlett," I added, as I put on my pack.

Rosie just looked at me with a little smile as I got on my bike. *"Gone with the Wind,"* she read.

* * *

"Whoa," I said, as I shook my head in amazement and leaned back from the table.

"Whoa is right," agreed Grace. "I want to meet the genius who made this." The only things that remained from our meal were the bones of a jackrabbit.

Rosie came to our table. "How was your food?"

I had to take a moment to answer. *How was my food?* Well, my food made me realize that I had been living and eating like a caveman for no good reason. Part of my overall apocalyptic-cuisine mindset held that, since the world had gone to shit, then it was appropriate that my meals be correspondingly scat-like. I had just accepted this, but I needn't have because I felt like I had gone back in time and visited a pre-1997 fine restaurant.

I had enjoyed a meal of jugged hare that was cooked in some kind of sauce that was more than mere gravy. It permeated and tenderized the meat to the point that it fell off the bone and melted like savory candy on my tongue. My greens had been cooling cattail stalks, marinated and dressed to put a common old cucumber salad to shame, with baked puffball boulets and amaranth seed sauce. *Why had I shrugged over all those shitty MREs, Matin cubes, and feral cat-stews, when I could have been eating like this?* None of the courses were rare or exotic. Everything was obviously foraged from nearby mountains and reservoirs, but it was the chef's ability to locate and prepare them that had put the whole affair over the top.

"Jack and Grace," said Rosie, "please meet Bryan, Chef of the Sated Yam."

Chef Bryan was about 6'2 and wiry. He wore a backwards mesh baseball cap, and I could see that he was bald beneath it. Like almost everything else in the place, Bryan's kitchen coat was orange. He wore shorts, and on his feet, as I was pleased to notice, were a pair of genuine Zhangs. He sported a tribal band tattoo on his left forearm and he had a big smile.

"How was your meal?" Bryan asked. I didn't know what to say, because in that moment words seemed inadequate. If I had been in possession of a thesaurus, I might have been able to formulate a response worthy of our repast...but I could only say: "Delicious."

"So, are you visiting Vegas? You know, now that things are getting back on their feet, I'm getting more and more customers from abroad." Bryan stopped to laugh and correct himself. "Well, not from *abroad,* but outside Nevada. Some come through on convoys, and others come up from the airport."

"We're locals," said Grace. "We actually work at McKarran."

"Is that right? Well, I think that you're making a terrific contribution to this city," replied Bryan. "Someday I'd like to take a flight on one of those rocket planes."

"Are you from here?" I asked.

"No," answered the chef. "My partner and I were just passing through on our way from Tucson to Portland when members of our group had some personal problems. The group broke up in Vegas, which kind of left us stranded. We decided to make a go of it here after a frantic survival period, and now things are coming together."

"I'd say so," agreed Grace. "Especially in the kitchen."

"Well, I've got to get back," said Bryan. "I'm glad that you enjoyed your meal, and I hope to see you again."

Guaranteed, I thought.

Rosie's break coincided with our departure. She called out from the side of the building when she saw us walk out to Tropicana and wave down a tuk-tuk. "I'll be right back," I said to Grace. "Two minutes."

Rosie ran up to me. "It's so nice to see you again," I said. "And I'm glad that your grandpa is letting you do things outside the shop now."

Rosie's face fell. "Jack," she said, "I don't live there."

I felt a sinking feeling in my stomach. "Honey, what do you mean? Is your grandpa okay? Is your sister okay?"

"Yes, but Ye-Ye said that I can't live with him."

"Why?"

"Because...because I touched a *boy*. Ye-Ye saw us."

Ah. I understood. "So where do you live?"

"Chef Bryan and Reverend Kyle let me stay with them. I make everyone's clothes now. I can get good material." Rosie's smile flickered back to life.

"Reverend Kyle?"

"Yes. They say 'partner', but I think it's like 'married.' They love each other."

We should have read more books about different types of families, I thought. "They are *gay* men," I said.

"Yes," agreed Rosie. "That's the right word. I forgot for a minute."

"Well, you look safe and happy," I said.

"Yes...but I miss Ye-Ye and Mary."

Grace called to me as a tuk slowed to the curb. "Okay, look," I said to Rosie. "I work at the airport now, and there's only one place out there where the tuks go, so you can easily find me. I'll come back, and I want to talk to you again."

Rosie nodded and looked behind me. "I have to work now. Your tuk is waiting." She turned to go back inside, but paused. "Jack?"

"Yes?"

"I like her. She seems nice. Do you like white girls? I thought that you would like China girls."

White girls...? "Grace is Korean, sweetie."

"What's that?"

"Well, she's not Chinese, but her family comes from

a place close to China. It's a country called Korea."

Rosie gave me a confused look. "Do white girls come from Korea?"

*　*　*

I thought about Rosie's question after the tuk-tuk dropped Grace off at her place. The seat gently rocked back and forth as my driver made his way out to my new home on West Hacienda, which relaxed me and helped me think.

Pumpkin had banged some guy and was ostracized for it. Jesus-*fucking*-Christ. I was disgusted. Dumbshit Zhang had kicked her out for doing what people do. What did he want to happen? Just let her go out and starve or get raped or killed on the streets because she didn't feel like being his shoebox grandchild? I felt sorry for Mary. I wondered what would become of Rosie's little "Silent Rob"-like sister. Rosie would have died to protect them both, and Zhang had kicked her out because she was growing up. What was he thinking? That she would come back begging? If so, that was his mistake. I doubted that Rosie would ever beg anybody for anything...even her Ye-Ye.

23
This ~~Uncomfortable~~ *Precious* Hunk Of Metal ~~Up My Ass~~ *On My Nightstand*

I Find It Ironic That When What They Are Looking For Falls In Their Lap, They Can't Believe It

I've done this for a couple years. I don't only mean working at a real and meaningful job and having a relationship with Grace. I mean everything, overall. Job. Home. Purpose. Things continue to get better.

Grace and I went to The New Orleans Showroom a few nights ago. *Le Miz* is back, albeit as a low-tech stage production. Yep. Lots of stuff is returning. Mind you, we're nowhere close to how things were before, but the world improves every day.

I think we're gonna make it.

Tomorrow I'll ditch my water buckets and seal off my storage tank. It appears that Adolf is *still* making the trains run on time; that is, in addition to re-electrifying Vegas, the TSA has finished a Colorado River aqueduct project. Still, I can no more express approval for the TSA than I could have embraced the Third Reich.

* * *

It's Sunday night and I'm lying on my bed - yes, an actual piece of bedroom furniture - and trying to decide if I want to read a book or just turn in. Tomorrow should be pretty low-stress. The propellant storage area is full and ready for tomorrow's turnarounds, and so far the planes are checking out. I have to hand it to the folks in Phoenix and LA because they came on board fast. Now, I'm proud to say, it's possible for a person to travel - depending upon flight loads - from Las Angeles to New York City in *five days!*

548

Hmmm. Perhaps one day I'll find the balls to actually take an air trip. People - subordinates, mostly - assume that I've flown all over the country on rocket planes. I see the planes every day and I supervise the crews needed to load and maintain their propulsion systems, but I've never gone up. But I will someday.

Someday.

I'm tired, so I think that I'll do my little bedtime routine and kill the light. No reading tonight. I still have Grandpa's watch after all these years, and it still doesn't work, but this small bit of metal is the centerpiece of a nightly ritual. I take the watch out of my nightstand drawer and hold it as I remember Grandpa. This could be my version of a nightly prayer, except that my memories of Grandpa don't require faith. Unlike others who kneel and mumble before hitting the sack, I've actually seen and felt the love of the one to whom I pay tribute.

The watch's metal is corroded where Grandpa scraped off Hitler's bird and crooked cross. I still remember that weird day when a porn star gave me a letter from Grandpa, and I've long since given up attempts to make heads or tails of that freakish encounter. It's the same with the bizarro meeting that I had with Edward Burnstein, Super-Duper Los Vegas Attorney-At-Law and "Future President of the Russian Federation". I had no clue what he had been talking about back then, and I still don't. I don't even know what the "Russian Federation" is. Last I heard, there was a Soviet Union.

Grandpa's letter has disappeared into my personal sands of time, but I'll always remember what it said:

Think, Jacky! It is in the watch and behind the eight. PS - Please excuse the delivery man. One does the best one can, especially in the Disco Era.

As Grandpa instructed, I *do* think. I've opened that watch a million times, and every time I do, I just see the same broken springs and rust-flecked gears. To most people there would be absolutely nothing noteworthy about the interior of an old and cheap Nazi Party pocket watch. To me, however, both the watch's interior *and* exterior are reminders of the man who raised me, loved me, and helped me survive the downfall of society. Years ago, when I had at last decided that I'd never figure out how porn star Ned Power had been fated to become Grandpa's courier, I experienced a simultaneous semi-epiphany regarding the cryptic message. I realized that the contents of the watch consisted of my memories of Grandpa. Every time I picked it up and cracked it open, I found recollections of our secret model airplane, of days we spent camping and hunting, and of hide-and-seek games that we played with our Army Men minders. The watch is full of pepperoni pizza. The watch is even big enough to contain a huge green Buick Roadmaster.   No, to most eyes, Grandpa's watch is junk, and when the back of the case is opened, there is nothing but corrosion and an old stamped serial number that reads: "45-21847".

45-21847, 45-21847, 45-21847, **I think, as I look at the ceiling. I don't even need to read the number, ingrained as it is in my memory.**

No books tonight. Nothing but sleep. Things are going well at work, but I've got a big day tomorrow. I snap Grandpa's watch back together and give it a little kiss. Then I put it back in my nightstand and turn off the light.

CaCO$_3$
Nāginī

June
2013
(2-of-4)

When I woke up I knew that I wouldn't be able to take a shower. The pipes had been unused for sixteen years and were likely full of spiders, scorpions, and gunk. The TSA had brought up the water mains, but I sure as hell wasn't about to step under a shower head that might blast mud and poisonous Mojave creepy-crawlies onto my naked body. I was quite happy to wait for a couple days until all of the critters had been blown out of the lines. I didn't anticipate having the crud deposited upon my kitchen floor, however, but this was what I discovered when I went to brew a cup of morning chicory.

The valves on my home had obviously been left open because a massive muck-snake had silently pumped into the sink and slithered onto the kitchen floor. I realized that the serpent was still slowly emerging, so I stepped over the mess and turned off the tap. Then I ran to the bathroom and was relieved to find that I would not also have a big bathroom clean-up waiting for me after work. At some point, though, I would still have to extract the twentieth-century coprolites of my home's former occupants before I could use the toilet. Being able to use a real toilet, and not an outhouse perched over a stink-hole or a container with unmentionable contents, was going to be terrific.

When I was young I never paid much mind to where shit went, until it had to go somewhere besides non-functioning commodes. *Seriously.* What do you do with it? Bury it? Burn it? Yes, and yes. But as re-population continued, there were fewer places to dig without taking a shovel-and-bucket march. Incineration was the other option, but urban fires were now a huge danger, and relieving oneself in Vegas required consultation with Mrs. O'Leary's cow. Thankfully, cholera outbreaks had been minimal, and that's how everyone liked it...so if you showed up in someone else's neighborhood and started digging, the hole might turn out to be your own grave instead of a shit-pit.

Neighborhoods had finally decided to designate certain lots and blocks as burn areas. Yes, that meant hauling filth, but things were cleaner and safer...though sometimes persistent winds carried the smoke of a dump lot back to the fuelers of its fires. That part wasn't so nice, but it was infrequent. Soon, however, I would be able to evacuate in the comfort and privacy of my long-dormant bathroom! But tonight I would still have to clean up the mud and garbage in my kitchen, and then be prepared for another mess when prepping the toilet.

I cursed. *This is a shitty way to begin the day*, I thought, but then I scolded myself. *What's the matter, ingrate? Have you already forgotten the days when you didn't even* have *a house? When you were sleeping in alleys and on strip mall roofs? And now you're bitching because of a little floor muck? Boo-hoo, spoiled brat! Shut the fuck up and get ready for work.*

The state of a civilization can be judged by what distresses its citizens. You've gone a week without food, but you're happy to still be alive? That's the grateful outlook of somebody stuck in the immediacy of shit hitting the fan. But what about a guy who moans about mud on the floor of his secure house, while the cupboards are stocked, the water is almost back on, and he's gotten a night's sleep on a soft bed? Well, he's just a snotnose who likes to whine amid the progressively easier conditions of a recovering society.

I continued to step over and around the kitchen mess as I brewed my chicory. When it was done, I poured a cup and went outside to watch the sunrise. As the first rays came over the mountains I put the kitchen mess out of my mind and thought about what the day held. A new load crew needed to be trained, and I would have to coordinate with the crew chief side of the house to designate a plane for that activity. I also needed to send someone to Northtown to check on the former chemistry teacher's fuel shipments.

Overall, things had been running smoothly. I had

three expediters under me, including Brettly. Brettly probably should have been on the line as a load crew chief, or, given his surfer background and Jones' overall good results in recruiting wave-riders as pilots, he could have easily been a rocket jockey. However, since the ways of his...*people*...were so alien to me, and because Jones had a significant proportion of former beach-dwellers in his employ, I had therefore decided to make Brettly my chief expediter and cultural liaison.

Brettly is also my neighbor. He seems so...*zen.* Or maybe he has a very tight, yet mellow, philosophy. Whatever it is, it has seen him through, just like the disparate survival approaches of other old unscarreds. I appreciate the way Brettly seems to be at peace, but I couldn't live like that. Sometimes on our days off I can look out my back window in the morning and see Brettly sitting in his backyard. Later, as the sun goes down, I can look out again and see Brettly still sitting in the same chair, or maybe standing on the chair, or perhaps lying beside the chair. He's not drunk. He's not stoned. He's not lazy. He just *is.*

I've also observed Brettly's inactivity shift to hyperactivity. There have been days when he has done squat-thrusts in his backyard *all day long.* Sometimes he gets naked in his backyard, except for his shoes. He sleeps on his roof when he watches the moon. He's not unbalanced. He's not deranged. When Brettly speaks, his train of thought is reasoned and cogent. He does his job very well. He seems to read a lot. He's friendly, but our conversations make me feel like I'm talking to a distracted person on the dark side of the moon.

I think that Brettly is as baffled by me as I am by him. I'm sure that he also observes my actions and seldom knows what to make of them. Like me, Brettly tries to be understanding and cautious in his communications, because he also recognizes the importance of his role as translator to the loader-surfers.

Brettly is fit, practices good hygiene, and, like most of the other surfers, he has long blonde hair. After we share a tuk to work, Brettly and the rest either tie up their locks or stuff it under their hats. I respect the cultural significance of surfer hair, but I had to insist, especially when working around explosive propellants, that it be secured.

* * *

The morning mototuk arrangement that I have with Brettly quickly gets us from our homes to McKarran. We exchange greetings but save most of our conversation for shop talk, because if we stray too far from mutually-familiar topics, Brettly and I end up looking at each other in puzzlement. This morning we're just sitting on opposite sides of the tuk seat as we watch Los Vegas' half-healed remnant go by.

We pass the smoldering remains of a house that was intact and occupied last week. There isn't a fire department, so if a dwelling burns, it burns. And Public Safety? LVPD? No. Nowadays you get a gun, along with your neighbors, and you learn to use it. Get to know the folks next door and down the street, and don't wander around unfamiliar neighborhoods. If you catch a load of buckshot or peamettle there are still a few folks around who know a thing or two about medicine. It's good to get that sort into your local community.

I take my old Ruger to work and Brettly totes a lever-action 1892 Winchester. The stock and barrel have been cut down and I doubt that the magazine tube holds more than four rounds. It's strange to see the surf-zen-peace-master carry a weapon.

You're Cleared To Search
And Sanitize
The Area

It's good to have water and electricity. To be accurate, though, only *parts* of Vegas have utility service *some* of the time, yet this still attracts migrants.

There aren't any VA loans. There aren't any realtors or mortgages. There's no such thing as home insurance. On the Clark County Court House floor there are deeds mixed with the preceding civilization's other jumbled documents, but they're now as meaningless as ancient Egyptian papyrus.

There are, however, Conestoga wagons and people on horses lining up on the Oklahoma and Kansas frontiers as they prepare to race out and stake off a piece of land and set up their homesteads --

No, that's just silly. Forget it. I thought that it would be an interesting historical parallel, but it doesn't work. I just wanted to show how the complexities of home ownership are gone. If a house is empty and the neighborhood accedes, you move in. In fact, Brettly put in the good word that got me into my cul-de-sac. Post-apocalyptic homeowner associations are very well armed and couldn't care less about or covenants or purchase agreements. If they don't like your looks, forget it.

I suppose that I should partially retract those comments that I made about the simplicity of home ownership, because even if the survivors next door give you the nod, there are still a couple things to keep in mind before picking up the keys putting down your backpack. If your psychological armor isn't as thick as it should be at this stage of TEOTWAWKI, then the things you might discover in an unoccupied house can be especially disturbing. Playing "domestic archaeologist" is dangerous. If you find old photos on the floor, you'd best not look at them. If there are scattered clothes and shoes, you shouldn't wonder if they are men's, women's, or children's items. If you come across sad little reminders of abbreviated existences and lives with their last chapters torn out, it's best to make a pile in the street, backyard, or wherever, and burn it all.

Does this advice seem coarse? Does it seem disrespectful? I don't intend for it to be. Some cultures believed that a soul couldn't be released until its corpse was physically destroyed, so look at it that way. All of the psychic residue and ghostly energy attached to found items is freed via pyre.

Did you buy that? I don't *really* know if any culture has ever thought that a soul was imprisoned until its cadaver's corporeal disintegration, but I thought that it sounded good. My point is: Get rid of the previous occupants' shit. Otherwise you'll discover a single little shoe in some back bedroom. You'll see that it has cartoon characters and colored laces, and you'll know that it couldn't have been worn for very long because a toddler grows out of little shoes so fast.

It's the small stuff that gets under the skin, you know? I mean, it's just a fucking shoe! But weird things like that can really twist your head, and then you'll have to drink half a bottle of crappy yucca-heart fake-tequila.

Evict the ghosts when you move in and avoid this scenario. It's your house now.

And when I figure out how to better manage the guilt associated with KRONAG's murder of entire families, I'll provide some tips on that, too.

But don't hold your breath.

My Simple Dream Of A Giraffe-Proof House

June 2013 (4-of-4)

I didn't find a child's shoe in my new place. Instead, the kitchen counter tiles caused a strange flashback that made me realize that I'd been in my new digs before. Counter tiles have to be pretty fucking distinctive to remain in the recesses of your mind after you live through the fall of society, go on a decade-long Jeremiah Johnson acid trip, learn to make improvised shoes, and re-learn an explosives-handling job from your distant past. It wasn't a bad memory that would necessitate kitchen redecoration. It was just kind of odd and tawdry, though it did make me smile at my distant ULVN salad days.

If it weren't for the tiles' nice glaze I'd have thought that they were originally intended for floor work. They were large - perhaps a foot across - and bore odd images that ran in a repeating pattern of three. On the first there was a crudely-rendered figure of a man, followed by the second's depiction of an ear of corn as perhaps a kindergartner might draw it, and the third displayed an equally-rudimentary image of a foot. That's how the pictures alternated across the counter space: man-corn-foot, man-corn-foot, and so on.

* * *

I was a twenty-something when I last saw those tiles. There had been naked labia pressing down upon the men, corn, and feet. It was before sunup and I was trying to sneak out of the house. As I had looked for the kitchen door which led out to the accompanying open garage, I encountered a college girl who, clad in a thin cutoff pink tee, hopped up and planted her lower bareness on the kitchen counter. I guessed that she was a roommate who was taking a break from whatever, or, more likely, whomever, *she had been doing in her room.*

The girl had a serious case of nightclub-fried-makeup and her hair looked like a shaggy terrier dipped in vegetable oil. Ash from the girl's cigarette fell as she stared straight ahead in the overhead light.

Not knowing what else to do, I nodded and awkwardly tried to smile as I carried my boots through the kitchen. I mistakenly assumed that the girl was wearing a tiny thong, but her lack of underwear and the proximity of her genitalia to a grubby toaster confronted me with an odd combination of bread crumbs, cigarette ash, and pubic hair.

"Wanna fuck?" she slurred. Burnt crumbs crunched against the girl's lower back as she reclined, spread her legs, and knocked over the toaster with a crash that was deafening in the silent house. Afraid to view what lay beneath her bush, my eyes found safe haven with counter tile images of a man, an ear of yellow corn, and a maybe-amputated foot that had been revealed when the girl opened her legs.

No, I didn't want to fuck. I just wanted to find the exit. But I'm getting ahead of the story. I'll back up and explain how I once found myself in a house that would be mine decades later.

Life Is Short And Love
Is Always Over In
The Morning

A Los Vegas Sunday Morning In 1994

It happened during that period when Grace and I were spending a lot of time together but hadn't yet gotten involved.

* * *

We burned up the morning by goofing off around town and ended up at the ULVN Starbuck. Grace then had to go meet some of her classmates and I was left to my own devices. I quickly fabricated a flirting mechanism that enabled me to go home with a girl who entered the coffee shop shortly after Grace's departure. I could manufacture effective devices. I believed that I was a university student, but at times I was also a social inventor.

The girl's house was located in a group of older tract homes near Torrey Pines and Desert Inn. She lived there with two female roommates, one of whom wandered in and out of the bedroom as the night progressed.

* * *

Last night I dreamed that I was a Lake Meade merman. I swam on my back and looked up through the murky water to discover that there was a giant cloud-penis and cloud-vagina having sky sex. The runoff that fed the lake wasn't a river or melting snow pack, but rather, semen and vaginal secretions from above. The aerial intercourse stopped, however, when the genitalia morphed into chemtrail planes that sprayed red wispy death. Poison mixed with sexual fluids, fell onto mountain tops, and contaminated the lake with strange viscous waterfalls. Lake Meade's water level fell and a heavy surface scum blanketed me in glue. As I struggled and thrashed I saw the submerged wreck of an airplane and skeletons of trees that had grown before Hoover Dam was built.

The scum-blanket continued to thicken and dry into a hard crust that burned my skin and made me choke. I couldn't break free, and in the moment before I knew that I was going to die I wondered if this was how it felt to be trapped under ice.

* * *

I open my eyes and look over at the girl sleeping beside me. I don't think that she's an ICE student, so that means I won't bump into her at ULVN's College of Education. Should I still look at her face, so that I can recognize her later? No...by the time she's done readying herself in the mirror this girl will have exchanged the face that God gave her for another. Even with a Danish Prince's assistance I wouldn't be able to pick her out of a university lineup.

I don't know what time it is. I fumble for my boots in the dark - an activity in which I'm quite practiced - except now I'm searching for cowboy boots instead of combat boots. This situation reminds me of awakening in a strange barracks or a strange hotel, and it reinforces my habit of placing my boots toes-in at the bedpost.

I'm still wearing a condom. *What panache.* At least it stayed on, though now my dick is just a withered ballpark frank stuck inside a liquid-filled white squid. My pubes are crusty. The hair on my chest is crusty. I'm scared to feel my goatee. I'm not putting this nasty body back into my relatively-clean clothes.

Sorry, sweetheart. I'm taking the liberty of showering before heading out your door. I don't care about morning-after etiquette, and I'm afraid that washing up is now a condition of my exit. You can pretend to be asleep when I come out. Whatever. In fact, I'd better take my wallet with me into the bathroom.

I feel strange. Not hung over, but slightly weak. I tiptoe into the bathroom, put my wallet on the back of the toilet, and look in the mirror. I pull my lower eyelids down. My right eye is only slightly bloodshot, but I see what I expect to find in my left eye. The lower white of my eyeball is bright red, and it looks like if I squint really hard a red tear will run down my cheek. When I go back to my right eye and lift its upper lid I find more blotches.

I guess this explains why I can't remember much

about last night.

Well, at least I haven't awakened in Tonopah Hall handcuffs with an assful of red-and-gray "baking soda".

Huzzah.

Look away, look away.

Wegschauen, wegschauen.

I open my mouth, raise my tongue, and check the two long blue sublinguals. All clear. I hold my hands up and look at my fingers. Pink nail beds. Apparently I've been asleep for a while.

I know my name. I know what city I'm in. After a couple moments I remember the date. My long and short term memories seem good-to-go. No harm done.

I sigh. *Why do I keep doing shit like this? What the fuck is wrong with me?* I instantly answer my own question: *In Vegas, nothing is wrong with me. In fact, I'm regarded as being rather conservative.*

I sigh again. Time to take a fast shower, go out through the kitchen and garage, and get the hell out of here.

24

Forget With
This Red
River
Kiss

We Have To Do This Every Day Of The Week
And Just Really Brainwash People Into
Thinking About ~~Guns~~ *Operation*
Fast And Furious
In A Vastly
Different
Way

July
2015

When it looked like the Nazis were finally going to liquidate Jewish neighborhoods, the folks therein buried treasures under their floorboards. Such action illustrated a normalcy bias toward what was actually happening because it indicated belief in a future return and retrieval of precious objects. Then, once that whole "silly Nazi fad" had passed, normal life would resume. We now know that this was not how things turned out, just as the "Master Race" knew that, when looting a Jewish residence, the first thing to do was dig up the crawlspace.

I therefore decided that if I were to resist General Jatoon LaPin's valley-wide gun confiscation decree, then Grandpa's 10/22, its hi-cap mags, and Stinger bricks would not be going under the floor, in the walls, or out in the yard. I would take the carbine into the desert and bury it. In 2015, Mr. Ruger's small-caliber masterpiece could still be considered a weapon of some account. Except for the TSA's disturbingly fresh-out-of-cosmoline M16s, there wasn't much left in Vegas that could beat my little rifle. Granted, Stingers only delivered one hundred-or-so foot pounds at seventy-five yards, but when my hi-caps provided thirty-round semi-auto spreads over that same distance, I wasn't worried...especially if I were to engage someone who was armed with a black powder zip. How could I just surrender my 10/22 in accordance with the latest TSA edict?

Scumbags.

Yes, I had enjoyed the restored water and electricity, but when Blackshirts started to throw their weight around like they were the legitimate law enforcement body of the city, I knew that something was very wrong. Now the TSA gastropods demanded that Los Vegans turn in all weapons, and people just shrugged and went along with it. "Hey, the TSA got Vegas up and running again, right?" was the usual justification.

Idiots.

I remembered when a certain young girl had blown the heads off two TSA molester punks and nobody came around to ask questions. Ha! Try defending yourself against the TSA today! Your place would be swarmed by Blackshirts eager to burn you out and shoot you down, and the Vegas sheeple would still just blink and make some reference to the water system or power grid.

The TSA freaks used to be just a bunch of irrelevant cult-punks with a fat "general" and an Earth Mom religion. Now they had their "checkpoints" all over town, and if you didn't pay the bribes, you could expect a "mandatory safety check" which usually consisted of some brainwashed thugs dragging you out of your tuk and beating you. If you were with a significant other, sometimes the Blackshirts would assault that person instead, just to show that they were in charge. Most sheeple bowed their heads and paid the bribes, and I would be lying if I said that I didn't cough up as well. I had joined the sheeple.

Baa-baa-baa.

The TSA had even shown up at the airport to put checkpoints at Jones' terminals. Of course, the Blackshirts were neither needed nor wanted, but Jones was faced with either working something out or having his operation shut down. My old flight chief stalled and negotiated, but I figured that one day I'd come to work and discover a bunch of scarhead trash shaking people down at the hangar entrance.

I also stalled and negotiated with the TSA, but on a

mental level. I didn't want to turn in my 10/22, but I couldn't openly carry it anymore, either. Blackshirts now roamed the streets and disarmed people, and more than a few killings had occurred. I would become a scarhead magnet if I carried my carbine. I felt like a shopkeeper who paid protection to gangsters. Sure, I knew that it was a violation of my right to personal self-defense, but if I surrendered a little, I was left alone. The trouble with gangsters, however, is that they keep upping the ante until they have everything.

I just wasn't ready to hand Grandpa's little 10/22 over to scar-faced dumb-asses who liked to extort, assault, and murder people. Besides, I needed to prepare for supper with Grace. Dealing with the TSA gun-grab could wait.

* * *

I kept rabbits. Not lanky bug-eyed jackrabbits, but nice little cottontails, and they weren't for the table. I just liked having them around. Of course, when Grace came over for dinner, she gave me hell.

"I don't see why you buy meat," she said. "You have your own backyard rabbit ranch."

"Maybe I do it for the same reason that you still wear homemade Old Slice." Like Paris, I always had that rejoinder. "I have something special tonight, and it's definitely *not* rabbit." I went to my backyard with a plate and tongs. When I returned I served Grace some barbecued meat. She picked up her knife and fork and waited for me to sit. "Dig in," I said.

Grace inhaled as if she were swirling whiskey under her nose. "Mmmm. Nice," she said, as she cut a piece and took a slow bite. "Is this...is this - pork? Where did you find a pig?"

"I didn't," I explained through chews. "It's javalina. One of Brettly's pals air-surfed a cooler back from Tucson on an empty seat and he shared this with me."

"Mmmm," Grace said, as she took another bite. "So it looks like the bunnies are safe again."

"Yeah," I agreed. "Tonight and every night."

I loved dinner with Grace. Sometimes she stayed over and sometimes she didn't, and she always refused to allow me to ride home with her so that she didn't have to go through the TSA checkpoints alone. The most that she would let me do was give her bribe money. It was at tImes like that when I considered how much better it would have been if her home and my home were one and the same. After dinner I asked her to stay, but she said that there was work to do at her place.

* * *

After Grace left I wrapped the 10/22 in oiled cloth and zipped it inside an old laundry bag. As I did so I remembered the historical lessons of those who had thought that burying spoons and necklaces under their homes would be sufficient action to weather interesting times. I wondered if my evenings with Grace would someday come to an end when the TSA crazies decided to liquidate my neighborhood.

No. That was nuts. Where the hell did that thought come from? What was I doing? Was I preparing to hide contraband?

Getting civilization up and running again means acting civilized - doesn't it?
It means trusting authority.
It means compliance.

Baa-fucking-baa.

I wavered for a moment and ran my hand over the laundry bag's zipper. There was something more inside the bag than an old .22 with a beat-up stock and scraped barrel. There was something that my Grandpa had given me. It was a tool that had fed me and kept me safe when the world was completely unsafe. It was like Grandpa was there, looking after me, whenever I picked up the 10/22.

Nope. I'm not turning it in.

Fuck those stupid punks. They swaggered around town and tried to be scary, but they looked like doltamatics in hot black thugiforms. They were sort of like the young idiots who used to parade around in their underwear and sagging pants.

Oh...*frightening. *Your asses are hanging out, you dumb assganstahs.

I laughed. That's all the TSA was. A collection of new-era assgangstahs. If I still needed a house gun, 50 NSP would buy a decent steel zip that wouldn't blow my hand off. Hell, I could buy *two* black market zips and bury my 10/22 in the desert.

25

Color Of Opening Night

What They *Ought* To Say Is: "Evil Prevails"

August 2017 (1-of-2)

I got doses of stink-eye from the Sated Yam's female customers, but the men gave me "nice going" nods. The women thought that I was an old dirtbag, but the men envied me. What they didn't know was that I was in the middle of a daddy-daughter date, and my "daughter" just happened to be the hottest woman in the establishment. I could almost feel the women aching to dismiss my dining companion as a high-end call girl who was out scoring a pile of NSP with an old John, but they couldn't, because the beauty sitting opposite me looked and acted like anything but a hooker. If carnal commerce *had* been the cause of our association, then it would have been necessary for me to save up a year's wages. No, *two* years.

Ick. I decided to stop that train of thought. I didn't like to put Rosetta, as she was now known, in that kind of mental light.

"Looks like we both got stood up," Rosetta smiled, as she picked up her glass and took a sip of wine. I didn't know much about fashion, except that her dress was beautiful, long, black, and that she had made it herself. She was never content with the work of her underlings when it came to her own attire.

"Yeah, well, I've done it, too," I admitted, except that Grace would have given me hell for canceling at the last minute. I was actually kind of put off, since this was a special night, but I decided to let it go. There would be other occasions. "It's a shame though, because I've really been looking forward to this," I added.

"And I've really been *working* forward to tonight," Rosetta replied. "My whole crew has been putting in a lot of time to get everything just right. I remember the first time that I read *Phantom,* and I didn't think that it could ever be put on again. But we're going to do it. It's actually going to happen tonight." Rosetta flashed a happy and beautiful smile.

"Well, I don't know anything about acting and stage production, but I'm certain that the players will have the best costumes of any Leroux performance."

"Thank you," was Rosetta's simple and proud reply. "You know, I really hate to let those two tickets go," she added.

"Yeah. That's too bad."

"Maybe --" Rosetta started, but then she cut herself off and waved at someone who had just walked in. "Ah. I think I know who should get them."

I turned to see the Sated Yam's proprietors, Chef Bryan and Reverend Kyle. One look at the two men told me that Rosetta's design efforts were now getting additional representation. The men were wearing simple slacks and dress shirts, but they looked terrific. Kyle saw Rosetta and returned her wave. Kyle was about my age and slightly shorter than his partner, with neatly cropped brown hair and penetrating glacier-blue eyes. Whereas Bryan was wiry and athletic, Kyle was slender and lithe. He moved with a deliberate finesse that seemed to balance, yet also compliment, Bryan's frenetic energy.

I had known these guys for some years now, and during those hard times when Rosie was becoming Rosetta they had recognized her raw talents and helped her refine them. I liked to think that I got the ball rolling by teaching Rosetta what I could about the world and by helping her develop a love for books, but it was Bryan and Kyle who had provided the materials and tutelage that brought a restaurant server to a place where she was now one of the most sought after costume designers on The Strip. Rosetta had three fathers, while Bryan, Kyle, and I had one daughter. After Zhang died, we had all taken turns looking after Mary, and we all had soft spots for Rosetta's practically-mute sister...but in our secret heart of hearts, there was consensus as to who was our favorite.

I stood to shake hands with Rosetta's other dads. "Good evening," I said with a smile. "I think our daughter was about to suggest something."

"That's right," said Rosetta. "I'm sure that you have

tickets to *Phantom,*" she said, at which both Kyle and Bryan nodded, "but do you have opening night seats?"

"No," said Kyle. "We tried, and we even thought that maybe a special insider," he paused to teasingly look at Rosetta, "would have assisted us, but no."

At that, Rosetta took two tickets out of her purse. "Would it be possible for me to go out with all my fathers tonight?" she asked with a smile.

* * *

It was not a tuk-tuk night. I had shelled out for a limousine - yes, an actual limo - with an engine powered by the best bio-diesel conversion around, and we would arrive at The Venetian in style. After our meal, the four of us got into a white early-nineties stretch and headed down Tropicana. Our progress wasn't that rapid, since the road was full of bikes and slow-moving tuks, but that didn't matter. It was going to be a terrific evening.

The driver slowed even more and announced that we were approaching the line for the Tropicana and Paradise TSA checkpoint. We all knew the drill: Get out your money, hand it out the window, and don't show any expression. We also assumed that the "earth tribute" for a combustion engine vehicle was going to be steep, but everyone was shocked when the Blackshirts opened the doors and demanded 70 NSP from each passenger.

Well, it was either shell out or be sexually assaulted and beaten. I looked at each face in the back of the limo and it seemed like everyone was about to stoically accede - but then I saw Bryan's face.

I think that artistry and raw passion, and specifically in Bryan's case, culinary artistry, can't be boxed up and confined to just one life venue. It tends to spread out to other areas, and creative temperaments can be spectacularly hot. When a black-gloved palm was thrust in Bryan's face, his jaw clenched and he shoved the thug's hand away.

At that, we were all dragged out onto the sidewalk and thrown down onto the hard concrete. I heard Rosetta's dress tear, and I was terrified of what might happen to her. Naturally, Reverend Kyle went into peacemaker mode, as did I. Maybe I really wasn't a peacemaker, but I was quite willing to buy my way out, if that were still possible.

"Please!" I cried out. I was on my knees but trying to get between Rosetta and the Blackshirts. "Take my wallet, take all of my money!" There were only a few TSA thugs, but in the moment it seemed like jack boots and M16s were everywhere. Kyle said the same thing, but the scarheads weren't interested in money anymore.

Bryan's fiery nature wasn't subdued by any of this. He wasn't interested in cowering on the sidewalk like the rest of us, and somehow, despite a rain of blows, he regained his feet. Seeing this as a challenge, a Blackshirt raised his rifle and fired. The bullet didn't strike Bryan, however, because Kyle jumped into the projectile's path. Kyle's thin body deflected the bullet and a broken spiderweb erupted in the safety glass of the limo's window while blood sprayed over the car's white exterior.

This seemed to have been a bit further than the head Blackshirt had originally intended to take matters. He stepped forward, grabbed the muzzle of his subordinate's weapon, and jerked it down. The man who had fired seemed surprised to have been stopped, and in that moment I understood that his intention had been to kill all of us. Instead, the leader barked for us to put Kyle into the limo and leave. Once we hit Koval, the driver pulled up onto the sidewalk and stopped. Bikes and tuks passed as we hysterically screamed at each other. Bryan shook Kyle and frantically tried to get him to respond, but Kyle was limp and silent.

Goddamn It, Listen
To Me! *Cito,*
Longe,
Tarde!

August
2017
(2-of-2)

- *How long have you been waiting here?*
- I came over after I finished at the airport and -- oh
  my God! OH MY GOD! Jack, are you okay? What's
  going on?
- *This is Kyle's blood, not mine.*
- Kyle?! What's going on? I'm really getting scared!
  Tell me right now!
- *Listen Grace, we have to get out of here. We have
  to go tonight.*
- Where's Kyle? What happened?
- *He's...he's gone, Grace. The TSA murdered him at
  one of their checkpoints.*
- Oh God. Oh God!
- *Grace, listen. I lost my wallet at that checkpoint. It
  had papers with my name and address. The TSA
  has it.*
- Where's Bryan? Where's Rosetta?
- *They're back at The 'Yam. They're going to leave
  town tonight.*
- Jack, I don't understand what's happening. Where
  are the lights? Why is the whole city dark?
- *I don't know. The lights went out as I was making
  my way back here. I didn't know if the TSA would
  be waiting or not, but I saw you in the window.*
- I found your lamp and some candles. I don't want
  you to go. Not tonight, okay?
- *Grace, fucking listen, will you? The goddamned TSA
  is probably looking for me! I think we should make
  a run for McKarran!*
- You said that the TSA has your wallet. Are you
  sure? Maybe it will take some time for them to find
  you--

- *Grace, what are you talking about?*
  Jack, please. The lights are out for the TSA, too. They probably have a lot going on in the city tonight. We can talk more in a few hours. Okay?
- *Grace, Kyle is* dead! *Do you understand what I'm saying? We're both in danger!*
- I understand. I--I understand. Okay. I'm going to get a few things from my house. Promise me you'll stay here until I get back.

* * *

I promised Grace that I would stay, but when she returned, my front door was smashed, and I was on a DS-21 tarp.

26

Jack And Andrew's Story Now Resumes...Amid Harvey Manfrenjensenden Maneuvers

We Be No Longer Devils, But Demons, Cried Dispater To His Kind, *Ally* To None And Doubly Cursed, Bane Of Divine And Damned Alike!

December
2017

"It might be psychologically easier for you, since this is your first time at the rendering plant, if you stayed in the truck. Just look at the floor or do whatever you have to do to keep yourself together," said Andrew. "But don't close your eyes. We'll both get in the shit if it looks like you're asleep."

As Andrew continued down Searles Avenue, our destination came into view. It was familiar to me. "That's the old Andersonville Dairy," I said.

Andrew nodded. "Yes. The TSA converted the milk processing sheds for use in fuel production. That's where we have to take these bodies." Andrew nodded backward at the truck's bed where, just a few feet from the cab, were the grisly pickups from DS-21, DS-13, and DS-4. The corpses were jumbled together, but I could guess their camps of origin by their states of decomposition. The red-mat bodies from DS-21 were Thursday retrievals, whereas DS-13 and DS-4 passengers had waited for a few days. They were the bloated ones with stiff limbs, gas-tight bellies, and dried fishmarket eyes.

This was my first run, and I didn't know if I was going to mentally get through it. When we pulled into DS-21 I was terrified that some of the guards would recognize me, even though I knew that this fear was completely unfounded. Faces were nothing to the guards; besides, half of the scarheads looked like they were new rotations.

"Keep it together," Andrew said in a hard voice. "Play whatever head games you have to play, but don't fuck this up. Turn off your mind and turn off your emotions. You didn't kill these people, and you can't help them now. They're already dead, and it's not your fault. If we weren't driving this truck, someone else would be. You've already seen death from the other side of the glass, Jack. Remember that."

"What-what do I have to do?"

"You're an FC now. You're a worker. We have to help the guards load the truck. Which do you prefer - ankles or wrists?"

"What?"

"We have to swing the bodies up onto the truck bed. I suggest that you grab the ankles, and I'll take the wrists. Usually there's less blood on the ankles, and the ankles are less personal. It'll be easier for you."

* * *

Once we passed the old Andersonville gates, Andrew slowly drove the truck toward some large warehouses. After a few moments I remembered them as the milk processing sheds where, twenty years before, a suicidal guy named Mark had taken me on a dairy tour.

The truck passed through a hole that the TSA had cut in the building. Inside were the same giant tanks and bowls that I recalled, but now there was also a group of bedraggled and blank-faced people waiting for us. Overseeing them were the same armed and black-uniformed scarheads who worked in the death camps. I heard the sounds of feet on metal catwalks, and when I looked up I saw more slaves on the equipment control platform.

I expected the place to stink like death, but instead there was an odd combination of scents. A very strange smell, like mold and peppermint, permeated the building's interior. Andrew glanced over when he heard me sniffing. "Are you okay?" he asked, to which I nodded. "Just stay in the cab," Andrew said. "These guys can handle it from here."

Andrew pulled the bed of the truck under the hydraulic mixer. The stirring mechanism descended and slaves climbed into the truck bed. They chained the corpses to the mixer blades and climbed out. The blades raised and lifted the bodies, and the stirring mechanism

579

moved on an overhead track until it was directly over the first pasteurization bowl. The blades descended and caused a thick turquoise-hued liquid to slosh over the top and run down the container's side.

The mixer began to rotate and the shed was filled with the sound of crunching bone. As the liquid thinned and the blades accelerated, however, empty chains began to clang against the container's metal interior like a maniac beating a church bell. The chains hung slack when the blades rose out of the bowl, but they dripped with gore.

"Jack, what are you doing?" Andrew growled from the driver's seat. "Don't look at it! Turn around." It was too late, though, because I had already seen that the chains weren't as empty as I'd thought at first glance. Along with the blood and green mystery goo, there were random pieces of corpses clinging to the links, and I watched a foot slide down and fall back into the sludge.

"Don't puke in this truck, Jack. Get out. If you puke in here the vehicle NCO will be a real asshole when we turn it in tonight."

* * *

I felt faint and my stomach was very empty as we went back out the dairy gates. "Andrew, what did I just see?" I asked.

"You saw the new economy of the Vegas Valley, Jack. What you saw was the starting point of the Southern Nevada power grid."

"I-I don't understand."

"Where do you think the electrical power for Vegas comes from?"

"Hoover Dam," was my automatic reply, but then I instantly realized that I was wrong. "No, wait... somebody blew the dam. In fact," I continued, "it happened on the same night that the TSA took me."

"That's right," said Andrew, as he grimly kept his eyes on the road. "But you still haven't answered my question."

"Well...I-I guess that I don't know where the power comes from. Maybe the Moapa Coal Fire Plant, but I don't think that's right either, because there's not an active coal mine for five hundred miles."

"Correct and correct," said Andrew. "The grid is all on Moapa now, but there's no coal."

"Then I have no idea how it runs."

"Alright," said Andrew, "I'll tell you. The TSA is using human bodies to make fuel, some of which is consumed here, while the rest is traded to southern Utah and western Arizona. The TSA upper-echelons are living very high on the deaths of others. That's as straight as I can give it to you."

I watched the road for a moment. "How?" I asked.

"They grind corpses into an adipocerous slurry, which is then converted into concentrated bio-diesel and glycerin. Giant dairy-protein integrators serve the process perfectly."

"I don't know what that is. The first thing you said, not the glycerin."

"Adipocere," said Andrew, "is also known as 'grave wax'. It's the end result of a process that's kind of like soap-making. It's where, under the right conditions, the fatty tissues in a corpse change to a substance that is somewhere between soap and wax."

"That doesn't sound like something that you can put in a gas tank."

"It isn't. But when you allow it to be consumed by a more ravenous cousin of blue-green algae, the algae shits out a super-concentrated hydrocarbon, like yeast shits out alcohol - that, and a glycerol by-product that the TSA just tosses aside. The fuel has to be diluted many times before it can be used in vehicles, otherwise it will blow engines apart - but that same raw form can also turn heavy generator turbines all day long."

"Dear God," I said, as I lowered my head.

"You gonna puke again?"

"No," I said in a muffled voice. "I've never heard of such a horrible thing. Who thought this up?"

"A former TV cameraman. A guy named Jason Thompson who worked for a local Vegas station. I saw him once. He was a little guy, a dwarf. When he found out what the TSA was doing with the algal process that he invented, he took a jump off the Stratosphere Tower. That's the story I've heard most often, anyway."

I rose back up and took a slow breath. "Why the

fuck are they using *people?* Why not use cattle, cats, rats, or *anything else* for Chrissakes?"

"Because humans, like other primates, can't synthesize vitamin C."

"What?"

"The alga dies in the presence of double-bond reductones, though obviously it does just fine with the long-chain fatty acids."

I sighed. "Again: *What?*"

Andrew looked at me, then at the road. "The organism makes bio-diesel, but vitamin C kills it. If we went to the dairies, or rendering plants, as the TSA now calls them, and dropped handfuls of C tabs into those gigantic bowls, we'd destroy all the algae inside.

"Maybe we should do that."

"I've tried it already. I loaded up some dead men with ascorbic acid flakes that I made from dried chiles."

"What happened?"

"The TSA started screening deliveries and had the plant back up to full production in two days. I almost blew my cover." Andrew paused. "Do you remember what they fed you at DS-21?"

I had to think back for a moment. "Yes," I said. "We didn't get much, and even when we did, it was just bread or dry meat."

"That's right. When I got you out, you had scurvy so bad that some of your molars were loose, and there was capillary breakdown in your legs. Do you remember those big bruises on your thighs?"

I nodded. "But I don't understand the time factor. I thought people had to go without vitamin C for a lot longer before they got sick."

"Sure. Without solanine, it *does* take that long."

"Solanine?"

"Also known as plain old green-potato extract," explained Andrew. "It's not lethal in low doses, but it negates the action of water-soluble vitamins...most notably, vitamin C."

"So the camp food was *poisoned?*"

"Yes. They were getting your body ready for the bio-diesel plants. C-depleted corpses quadruple fuel yields."

For, Unlike Heaven, I Am *Always* Open...
Even On ~~Christmas~~
Earth Day

February 25th, 2018

Evening prayers are over and my platoon marches back to the John Stewart Barracks. We had stood in worship formation to beseech the TSA Mother-deity to forgive our consumerist sins, help us find our ways into the collectivist whole, and forgive our lives of individualistic motivation. When night falls on Los Vegas, the former ball courts, playgrounds, and football fields contain men and women of all ages and races being led in programming chants by Blackshirt psy-officers and their guards.

The prayer verses are easy to remember because they have the same cadence as The Pledge of Allegiance.

* * *

This space was once a classroom, but now it's a bunk bay. My uniform is on a chair and draped above my boots in a basic training-style night display. Even though the door is open, the atmosphere is stuffy, hot, and dark. Like others, I lie on top of my sheets.

My life seems to contain recurring military, or paramilitary, situations. I'm in my fifties, but I did this before as a young man. In negotiating my way through forced hierarchies and synthetic social strata, I've often been plagued by ugly costumes - both ones that I've worn, as well as those worn by others. Perhaps the hatred that I've developed for uniforms and what they symbolize has helped me to survive alone for extended periods, since command structures don't exist in solitude.

Maybe when some people put on uniforms, they're actually taking off their humanity, whereas others regard a uniform as a sort of painter's smock; that is, an apron to protect the wearer's soul from bloody stains and splatters. That's the idea, isn't it? To lose your individual sense of right and wrong and have it replaced by Hive Mind dictates? To absolve yourself of the crimes that you'll commit in the name of The Group? To fall back upon the old "I was just following orders" nonsense?

But what if, in this era, that's not really true? If events such as the Nuremberg Trials were just historical anomalies, then I'm living in a world where people no longer bother to reference their alibis up chains of command. There doesn't seem to be any fear of future accountability among the TSA, and bloody rags are worn with pride. For scarheads, uniforms aren't really smocks, because TSA zombies prefer to parade in their own black shrouds.

As I look around the former classroom's bunk rows, I can't imagine a foreign intervention force that might liberate us. There are no Allies this time, and the year may as well be 1718 instead of 2018, because the oceans are once again gigantic expanses that divide peoples, cultures, and races. The Chinese, Indians, and Soviets aren't going to launch clipper ship invasions, especially since they have their own problems. Well...I *assume* that they have their own problems. Who knows what the hell is happening on other continents? Not me. I don't even know what's going down on the other side of Vegas.

TSA stratification dictates that Andrew bunk with the other junior NCOs, while I'm placed with the FCs. FCs are grouped by age, meaning that I can look around and see other skinny middle-aged men in shorts and tees. I don't really have any friends here, though I occasionally engage in conversation. I've discovered that every man possesses a skill that has saved him from the camps. The guy who sleeps above me knows how to chemically break down old tires into petroleum lubricant. He's also constructed a poor man's backyard cyclotron to wring more life out of old lead-acid batteries. I've see him work around the motor pool. The guy on my left does electrical work. The bunk on my right is empty. I don't know what special abilities the fellow who slept there had, because he died of a massive heart attack four days ago. We might have been saved from the camps, but we're still old men.

The TSA calls this facility a "barracks", but it's really just the continuation of a technique that has always been employed by society-killers. Schools are perfect. They have securable perimeters and rooms that can quickly be converted into infirmaries, armories, laundry facilities, sleeping spaces, or food service areas. Schools can double as prisons or barracks. A Principal might be in change, but a Warden or Commandant can just as easily occupy the head office. John Stewart TSA Barracks is a former elementary school.

The room in which I bunk was once called a "portable", and it served as a classroom extension to the main school building. In fact, when I was a teacher, my own classroom was very similar. Prefabricated and towed onto school grounds, portables served as enrollment overflow valves back in the days when Los Vegas had many children. I would estimate that the room once held a class of twenty-five to thirty kids. This portable is just a plywood shell with old torn carpet and some vacant classroom bulletin boards. Besides the bunks, the room also contains a few old cardboard boxes and cloth bags in which we store our meager possessions. This place is seldom inspected, but we keep it clean anyway. There's no bathroom or sink here, so it's no surprise that the dirt near the curfew fence reeks of ammonia.

When I'm not out in the truck with Andrew, I eat and march around the grounds with my bunkmates. TSA didn't assign a young guy as our platoon leader. Instead, there's a fifty-something Follower Third Class who sleeps near the door. He wants a new assignment that lets him get more rest because he's sick of letting fellow oldsters out in the middle of the night to piss on the fence.

Is Grace lying on a bunk in a former classroom? I look for her face every time my platoon marches past a women's unit that appears to be of about the right age. On the day that Grace was taken from DS-21, nobody in her group was tortured or maimed, and this, as Andrew explained, is one way to identify those selected to live from soapers.

Soup Of The Soup Of
The Bones Of
The Rabbit

March
2018
(1-of-2)

We had used a deuce truck for about two months, but then we were assigned a new vehicle because the deuce had broken down and there weren't any replacement parts. We reported to the motor pool one day and discovered that an old Ford flatbed had been substituted. When Andrew shifted the Ford's gears there was always a slight puff of smoke that made me flinch because the motor ran on the diesel equivalent of soilent green.

I seldom called Andrew "Corporal", and he only referred to me as "FC" when other TSA were around. When we rode in the truck, we were just Andrew and Jack. I had written the alias "Wheeler, Everett" on my TSA Justice and Prosperity ID Card, but it didn't really matter. As Andrew had predicted, I was irrelevant to the young thugs and higher-ups, and as long as I appeared to be assigned to an NCO, I was just an invisible old slicksleeve.

"You seem like you're getting along alright," Andrew said.

"I'm not sure about the 'getting along' part of it," I replied, "but there are things that make it easier. When I was in the camp, I could hear people being tortured, but I imagined that they were screaming because they were having great sex. I don't know if I'm playing those kinds of games with myself now, or just pretending that...that...I'm not working on the meat wagon."

"You do what you have to do for the sake of your head," said Andrew. "I did the same thing. I just told myself that I was hauling logs. Even now I don't look at the faces."

There were a couple minutes of silence. "The only time when I feel like I might crack is when we make the Rainbow and Desert Inn run," I said. "Going back to that place, seeing those people, and knowing…" I couldn't finish.

"You're doing alright," commented Andrew. "In light of what's going on, I'd say that you're remarkably stable. Me, I've had some time to practice. Being a soldier as a kid sort of gets you ready for more, but fighting, seeing death, and even killing on the battlefield…well, it's nothing like this. I can't think of words to describe what's happening here."

"You've mentioned that before. Where did you grow up? Where was that war?"

Andrew paused, looked at me, and then looked back at the road. "Florida," he responded. "It…it was actually fought all over the country, but I happened to be in the south."

I wasn't sure if I had heard correctly. "I don't understand. You mean the state of Florida, in the USA?"

Andrew nodded.

"Oh. You're talking about a big gang war or something like that."

"No," replied Andrew. "I mean a civil war. The people versus the government."

I didn't know what to say. By now I was sure that Andrew wasn't nuts, but I had no idea what he was talking about.

"Then there was a nuclear war," Andrew continued, "and the cities were destroyed. When that happened, it allowed the side I was on, the rural people, to get the upper hand."

Well, I thought, *maybe Andrew is crazy. Maybe he's manufactured an entire alternate history in his head as a coping mechanism. It makes my little torture-as-porn shield seem rather basic.*

Andrew sighed and turned the truck's steering wheel. "I guess that we had to have this conversation at some point," he remarked. "Yeah, it's time. Might as well do it now."

"Time? For what?" I asked. No matter how much I suspected loopiness on the part of my companion, I wasn't nervous. If Andrew had ever entertained nefarious inclinations toward me, he would have acted on them while I was comatose. Hell, the guy had saved me, hadn't he?

"Time for *you* to ask some *questions*," answered Andrew. "For instance, you've never wanted to know how I knew who you were or where to find you. You've never asked why I took the time to get you back on your feet or why I faked your way into my brigade. I appreciate the way that you've taken everything in stride, but your face-value acceptance is making me nervous."

Ha! I thought. *I'm making you nervous? Just because I'm taking things as they come and trying to stay alive?* "I just thought that there was a time for everything," I responded. "Plus, there's that old issue about looking a gift horse in the mouth."

Andrew gave a little smile. "Okay. But you can stop waiting. Let's cut the shit." With that, he made another turn onto an empty back street and killed the truck's engine.

"Hey, what gives," I asked. "What are you doing?"

"We've got some time before we have to show up at DS-13, and I want to get something out in the open."

"Alright."

"Again, I gotta say, you keep stuff in, don't you? In the past, every time I've come out with my 'civil war' statement, somebody wigs, but not you. You just nod and keep your eyes on the road."

"What else can I do?" I asked. "I'm alive because of you, and it looks like my continued survival is also in your hands, unless I can figure out a way to sneak out of the barracks and head for the hills...but at the moment, that doesn't seem too likely. If you say that you were in a Floridian nuclear civil war, fine. If you also tell me that you're going to hike to Reno with a lion, scarecrow, and tin man, I'll believe that, too."

Andrew softly chuckled and nodded. "First, don't get caught outside of the perimeter during barracks curfew. You'll either be shot or stuck back on a camp tarp. Second, I'm not from here."

"Yeah, well, this town is full of drifters and travelers," I replied, "and some from places more distant than Florida."

"No, I mean I'm not from this *world.*"

Oh-kaaay, I thought. *It looks like Andrew really* is *riding cartoon animals in Lollipop Land.*

Andrew continued. "I know that you won't comment on that, so here we go: Jack Simmerath, born August 20th, 1967, at Desert Sunset Hospital to John and Eileen Simmerath, who themselves were killed in a pedestrian crosswalk accident at the intersection of Sahara and Decatur on December 6th, 1972. You went to live with your grandfather, Doctor Erik Simmerath, a former Nazi scientist who was evacuated to the US in the same Operation Paperclip that brought over the likes of Wernher von Braun. You served an enlistment in the USAF, most of which was spent in South Korea. You attended UNLV, or rather, *ULVN,* and were briefly an elementary school teacher."

I was impressed by the snap delivery, but not the content. "All true, Andrew. But...I'm not sure why you're telling me about myself. Nothing about me is a secret, and all of that info could be in some TSA file." *Well, probably not,* I thought. *I'm a nobody. Still, I don't know how Andrew could be so well informed.*

Andrew nodded. "That's what I would think too, if I were you. That's the simplest and most logical explanation, but that information comes from Emergency Archival Training at Fort Tampa. Everyone, even the non-pilots attached to the 177th Temp Recon, have to get through the course. Washouts get sent back to the regulars."

I shrugged. "Andrew, I've never heard of that unit. I mean no disrespect...but...is this '170th Recon' or whatever part of your civil war story?"

"177th Temporal Reconnaissance," corrected Andrew, "and yes, it is. I have more to say about you, but some of the information may or may not be correct. Just let me know if I'm mistaken about anything."

I shrugged again and shook my head. "Yeah. Okay. I still don't know what this is about."

"Your left leg below the knee is a prosthesis. You lost your leg in a motorcycle accident when you were a teen. You never enlisted."

I didn't say anything as I pulled up the bloused left pantleg of my black fatigues to show that the limb underneath was flesh and bone.

"Another account has you marrying a Korean girl and remaining in Seoul after your military discharge."

I winced at that tidbit. Still, I held up my bare ring finger and looked out the truck window. "This looks like Vegas to me," I said.

"Your English is poor because your grandfather returned to West Germany when you were a child and took you with him. In fact, you're there right now, speaking perfect *Deutsch.*"

"What do you mean, I'm where, right now?"

"In Germany."

I was about to tell Andrew that what he had said was fucking crazy, but then I felt a massive déjà vu. I rubbed my eyes and faced forward in the passenger seat. "Like I said, if you claim to have been caught up in a Kansas twister with your little dog, then that's how it is."

"Alright, then how about this," replied Andrew. "Maybe we can find a functioning television and VCR somewhere, along with an old tape of *The Electronic Company*, and you can tell Julie that Mirye wouldn't marry you."

I felt like EMTs had greased up my chest, slapped on electrodes, and shot an electric pitchfork through my old heart. I coughed and almost choked. "How--?" I began, but then stopped and coughed again. "How could you know about that?"

"Because I've memorized the primary facts about your stringdopps - that is, your most prevalent recurring versions."

"*Prevalent recurring versions?* What the hell does that mean?" There was a stunned sharpness in my voice. Whatever doubts I had concerning Andrew's reality sampling were completely gone. Something crazy was going on here, crazier by far than just some stranger knowing my name and saving me from a death camp. Things that I had numbly accepted and details that I had shrugged off now demanded answers.

"It means that, in alternate realities, your life turned out differently," answered Andrew. It's not just you, either, so don't start thinking that you're special. I have to know a lot of names, a lot of faces, and a lot of history. Don't be embarrassed about the 'Julie' thing. That's nothing, compared to some of the fucked-up shit that I know about other people." Andrew paused to grimace. "I have to know what happened to a ship called the *USS Eldridge*, and where to find pieces of it. I have to know about the commanding officers and crew of that ship. I have to know where to find the underground bunkers at Camp Hero in Montauk. And when a guy in my line of work finds himself stuck in the American Southwest, then something called 'The Lake Option' comes into play. I have to choose Lake Meade or Groom Lake."

"Groom Lake?" I echoed. I knew that place, but I had to think for a moment because many years had passed since I'd had cause to consider the dry and desolate lakebed ninety miles northeast of Sin City. "When I was a kid at Pyeongtaek," I said, "my unit got sent back to the States for airstrike observations during Blue Flag at Nellis. I can tell you, firsthand, that there's nothing out at Groom Lake but a few old shacks and a lot of dirt."

Andrew nodded. "On this worldline, there's no Area 51."

"That's not true," I objected. "There *is* a fifty-first range sector out there. It's been a long time for me, but I think that Groom Lake is located in either fifty-one or fifty-two. But those areas were just part of the Nellis range."

"That's right," agreed Andrew. "In this reality, Area 51 ops all took place in California, at Armitage Field. That's not where the prize lies, though, and that's why I sought you out. We're going to Lake Meade instead."

I looked out the window and then at Andrew. "You just lost me again. Spare me the alternate-reality-Groom-Lake-*USS-Eldridge* stuff. I have no clue what you're talking about. Just tell me how you know so much about me, and why I'm not dead."

Andrew rested his head on the wheel for a moment and sat back up. "I'm trying to stay alive too. It's not possible for me to know all of your life's permutations, but I have to know the big ones." Andrew shook his head. "I never thought I'd be in this situation, sitting in a

591

truck, and talking to you. *You!* The last time that I heard about you was during an early morning barracks cram session in tech school."

"*Me?* Why?"

"Because you were covered in a course unit that was *primarily* about your grandfather. Because I have to believe that I can still escape from this horrible world, and because I have to try. I'm a traveler, Jack, and my vehicle has broken down. I don't know the metaphorical number for quantum AAA, but you do, and you're going to help me get back on the road."

I considered Andrew's words, then decided to schedule a root canal for my gift horse. "Is there anything in this arrangement for me?" I asked.

"You mean, *besides* being saved from torture, death, and a diesel tank?"

"Yes. Does your, uh, *vehicle* have passenger seats?"

"It does."

Good, I thought. *A seat for me and a seat for Grace.*

I gotta find her.

We All Have Our Time Machines, Don't We?
Those That Take Us Back Are ~~Memories~~ *Dreams*...And Those That Carry Us Forward Are ~~Dreams~~ *Nightmares*

March 2018 (2-of-2)

We got our pick-ups and drop-offs done early, but instead of heading back to John Stewart TSA Barracks, Andrew made an unexpected detour down Charleston Boulevard. Thinking that perhaps there was an unscheduled stop that Andrew had forgotten to mention, I paid no mind.

I decided to continue a conversation that had started earlier in the day. "Okay, so let me get this straight: You're a *time traveler?*"

"Not exactly," said Andrew. "I'm more of a *dimension* traveler - so if you ask about the 'Grandfather Paradox', dimensional travel solves it. It's not a paradox at all."

"I think I remember what that is," I said. "It goes something like this: If I go back in time and kill my grandfather, then how can I exist?"

"The Grandfather Paradox *itself* is what doesn't exist," answered Andrew, "because time travel comes at the cost of leaving your original universe. Yeah, you went back, and yeah, you killed somebody who looked exactly like your grandfather, but the reason why you're unaffected is because he *wasn't* your grandfather."

"Okay, then who was he?"

"He was one of the endless copies of your grandfather who exist in one of the endless copies of your universe's past, and when you killed him, you eliminated the future existence of one of your stringdopps, but not your own."

"Uh, '*stringdopps*'?"

"String theory doppelgängers. Your event class personal doubles."

"Okay - so what's an 'event class'?"

"For the traveler," said Andrew, "it's consistency, comfort, and home...even if it really isn't. An 'event-class' is just a percentage-deviation category for a type of worldline that looks completely like the one you left. At ten-thousandths of a percentage or less, a displacement pilot, or 'time traveler', if you prefer, can't find anything odd or unusual about the world to which he or she returns after a mission. The people are the same and the world is the same...except the pilot has never been there before."

"That makes no sense. How can you go back to a home you've never been to?"

"By displacing between minimally-diverged realities," answered Andrew. "For example, in my own personal chronology I haven't been home for over two years. However, I left the worldline of my birth almost seven years ago, and I'll never see it again."

Never? Why not?"

"Because I can't. Oh, I admit that there's an equation which proves a *possibility* of getting back to my original worldline, but the odds of that *actually* occurring are like going to a beach and successfully finding a specific grain of sand. What's the point? All of the grains look the same, so, for all practical purposes, they *are* the same."

"No," I objected. "They *aren't* the same. This world and your world are different. You've said as much."

"And that's where event class and deviation percentage comes in. This worldline occupies an event class that's about six percent different from my own. There are general similarities...but for me, it's no longer a matter of finding a certain grain of sand because I'm not even on the right beach."

"This is a lot to process," I said. "I admit that I thought you were nuts at first, but you know things about me and other people that you couldn't know otherwise." I paused. "So...what exactly does a time machine look like? Is it a huge contraption or is it like a wristwatch or what?"

"Neither," said Andrew. "It's an OD green mil-spec metal box with a hinged metal cover, about this big--"

Andrew paused to gesture in a way that looked like he was running his hands over an invisible footlocker "-- that weighs about three hundred pounds. I have it in the bed of an old Ford F-250. There's also a small hand-held activation unit that duplicates the function of the main console initiator."

I gave a small laugh. "So your time machine has a remote control? Is that so you can surf universe channels?" Despite the fact that I was going down the road in a death-truck, in the middle of a fucked-up concentration-camp-city, another tiny chuckle slipped out.

"That's right," replied Andrew. "In fact, I think that a remote function problem was what caused me to end up here."

"Oh? Why's that?"

"Because once you understand that you can't get back to your original worldline, you also realize that none of your quantum duplicates can get back to theirs. Yet, when you 'return' from a successful displacement, your military unit, friends, and family are all there, but they're not who you think they are, and you're not who they think you are, either."

"So when you return, you're just assuming the identity of one of your doubles - what did you call them?"

"Stringdopps."

"Yeah. What you've described sounds like inter-dimensional musical chairs. The chairs are exactly the same, but nobody gets the same seat twice," I said. "So somewhere, or *somewhen,* there's an Andrew stringdopp who is living your life, and hopefully one day you'll resume the life of one of your own doubles...*and* take me with you after I perform the big whatever-it-is that you don't want to discuss."

"That's the deal," said Andrew.

I tried again to imagine what an actual time machine looked like, but, given Andrew's description, I couldn't really visualize anything but a pylon test box like I had used back in my military days - though with an additional hand-held remote. "You mentioned that your machine's 'remote control' was the reason why you're here," I said. "What did you mean?"

"Ah. Well, the C-205 has an auto-return emergency feature if a situation requires remote activation. During a past mission I had cause to use the auto-return. That's when the trouble started."

"How?"

"Well, the principles that govern a person's movement from one worldline to another also apply to equipment. The auto-return feature isn't really an 'auto-return' at all. The C-205 just trades dimensions with another unit that exists in a similar situation on a parallel worldline - and that's where the problem occurred. The unit that came through was the one that I tried to use to get home, but it malfunctioned and I ended up here."

"Wait - are you telling me that it *doesn't work?*"

"I'm not sure...though I ran a clean diagnostic."

I didn't find Andrew's response to be particularly reassuring. If there was an intermittent glitch in the machine, then using it again might be a real crap-shoot. On one hand, we might end up in a better place, but on the other, we could materialize on a future worldline where the TSA's endgame had been achieved and all of humanity was either dead or in chains.

I looked at Andrew. "What's your *real* grade?"

"Sergeant major."

"So enlisted men are selected to time-travel?"

"Yes. I doubt that some butterbar could have coped with this situation," sniffed Andrew. "Chiefs and Senior Specs take missions, too."

"And what exactly *was* your mission?"

"I was back in 1975 looking for an old computer."

Andrew's assignment seemed strange. "Why would people in 2036 need a seventies-era computer?"

"We need a lot of things. Getting society up and running after a nuclear war requires a lot of old tools."

I considered Andrew's response for a few moments. It seemed plausible, but something else didn't add up. "Why aren't there two of *you*?" I asked. "How come *you* don't have a stringdopp?"

"Well," answered Andrew, "there *might* be a kid in Florida who looks like me, but we won't be exactly the

same. Six percent difference, remember? I'm stuck in a universe that exists outside of my worldline's event class."

"Oh. Right."

"And here's another thing: If we eventually *do* manage to escape, our destination will be a 2036 version of *my* reality...so you'll find yourself in a place and time that will be as strange to you as this situation is to me."

I looked out the truck's window and snorted in contempt. "No problem. I don't care to find out what the future holds for this world."

"Same here."

My thoughts turned again to the location of Andrew's time machine. "So where *is* this Ford pickup?"

The flatbed slowed as we approached our destination. "Here we are," said Andrew. "We've got work to do. We can talk about this later."

Built In A ~~Cave~~ *KRAVE*
With A Box
Of Scraps

April
2018
(1-of-2)

As we drove the truck back to the wash rack, Andrew seemed more receptive to the idea of helping me find Grace. "Tell me again what they were looking for," said Andrew. "What did the guards at DS-21 say?"

"They said something that sounded like 'Candy Joe' or maybe 'Kelly Joe'."

Andrew sighed. *"Kippy-jo."*

"Yeah, that's it. What does it mean?"

"It means that I have good news and bad news."

"Alright. Good news first."

"Your girl's alive, but she's not an FC."

"And the bad news?"

Andrew asked a question instead of giving me the bad news. "Jack, what is your relationship with this woman?"

"We're old friends and old lovers. We dated before the TSA decided to wreck the world again. Back in college I hoped that we might develop into something serious, but that didn't happen...at least on her side of the equation."

Andrew took a breath. "Alright. I'll tell you where she is and what she's doing, but under one condition."

"Just tell me."

"As long as you understand that I'm the one with the exit door, so I'm the one who calls the shots."

I nodded, though I knew that I was not without a bargaining chip of my own...except at this time I didn't know what that chip was.

"Alright," said Andrew. "Your lady is in the Pleasure Brigades."

I didn't know what that was, but I could guess. "Are you saying that Grace is a sex slave?" I asked. Andrew kept his eyes on the road and nodded.

I experienced a sick feeling like the sensation of a

frozen bowling ball in my stomach. A flood of awful images, some of Grace being gang-raped by TSA officers, entered my mind. I wasn't strong enough to endure the scenes, so I pulled the plug. I visualized a mental bulldozer clanking its treads across my mind's stage as it pushed the terrible visions out of view, but my nausea remained.

"You said that you were in college together, so I take that to mean that you're about the same age," said Andrew, and I nodded. "You might find this a small comfort," he continued, "but if she's an older kippy, then chances are she's a house mother."

"What, like a madam?"

"Yeah."

"Where are the 'Pleasure Brigades'?"

"They're up on Fremont. One is in the top floor of the Plaza, and the other is in the Queens. Don't start getting any ideas," Andrew cautioned. "Remember our agreement."

"I'm definitely keeping it in mind," I said. "I want to get out of this hell as much as you, so rest assured that my commitment to this enterprise is as strong as yours." At that, Andrew relaxed slightly, though he tensed up again as I continued. "But I want *two* passenger seats."

Andrew looked at the road for a moment. "I won't jeopardize our escape. But," he continued, "accessing the kippies just might be possible, especially in light of what I've already been doing." Andrew seemed to perform some mental calculations. "How tall is your friend?"

"About five-five."

"Alright. I won't guarantee anything, but I'll pull some strings and get my hands on a female FC uniform. And I can't promise anything soon either, but I'll do my best."

I nodded. "But what stops do we have on Fremont? There aren't any camps or dairy plants in that area."

"I have *special* stops on Fremont," replied Andrew. "When I go up there, it's for exterminator drop-offs, not pickups."

You No Longer Have To Worry About The Sodium Laurel Sulfate Content Of Your Soap

April
2018
(2-of-2)

I knew how to handle the rendering plant routine. It was simple, and it was what Andrew had recommended from the beginning. I just sat in the cab and didn't look at what happened outside.

After the truck was unloaded Andrew drove out of the processing shed, but he didn't go through the former Andersonville dairy gates. Instead, he made a right turn that took us behind the shed. There was an enormous pile of...*something*...dumped on the ground. It was several yards tall and maybe ten yards wide, and it was guarded by a *very* bored Blackshirt.

Either our truck or some other vehicle had driven behind the processing sheds enough times to wear a track in the dirt. Andrew pulled up to the heap of whatever-it-was and choked the engine. "Refuse removal detail," Andrew called out to the guard. The man just shrugged.

"What are we doing?" I asked.

Andrew gestured for me to shut up and follow him around to the other side of the truck. "Algal glycerin," he said, in a near whisper. "We've got about seven minutes before we have to leave. Help me load as much of this as possible."

The material ranged in size from a kitchen table to a shoe box, and though it was in a solid form, its surfaces were slick. I thought it felt like candle wax that had been coated in olive oil, and couple pieces slipped out of my fingers as I tried to toss them onto the truck.

* * *

After we were back on the road, I turned to Andrew.

"What did you say this stuff was?"

"Glycerin by-product from the bio-diesel process."

"Like...soap?"

"In the past it was used *in* soap."

I sensed a TSA masquerade-update that had nothing to do with personal hygiene. "What *else* is it used for?"

Andrew continued to drive in the direction of Fremont Street. "When glycerin is burned it releases acrolein fumes. Especially *this* shit. The combustion-release ratio is *incredible.*"

"Acrolein," I repeated. "What's that?"

"Poison gas."

* * *

"Okay, Jack," said Andrew as we approached Fremont, "you're an ex-military man, so the rules for dealing with these sorry robots will seem familiar."

"How so?"

"You can basically do anything, once you understand that you're dealing with dogs who only respond to their masters or those doing their masters' bidding."

"I get it," I said. "Put on an act so they think that if they fuck with us they're going against the will of the higher-ups."

"Exactly. The less you care, the more seriously they take you. And here," said Andrew, as we slowed for the first of the Fremont Street checkpoints, "is our first example."

We stopped beside a concrete barrier and a scarhead approached the truck while his companions continued to play cards on the ground. "No trucks except the delivery convoy," he called out.

Andrew appeared bored as he rested his arm out the window and, somewhat contemptuously, didn't even look at the checkpoint guard, whom I could see actually outranked Andrew. After a few seconds Andrew registered a half-disgusted look and turned. "What, you ain't lettin' us through?" he demanded.

"Watch it. I don't answer to no old unscarred corporal," said the guard, "and no, you ain't goin' through."

"Bad move," replied Andrew, as he put the truck in reverse and began to slowly back up.

"Hold it right there!" yelled the guard as his hands went to his rifle. The card players got off the ground and surrounded the truck. With more exaggerated contempt, Andrew put the truck into neutral, stopped, and shook his head.

"Out of the truck!" ordered the guard. Andrew nodded at me, and we got out. The men on the passenger's side used the muzzles of their M16s to prod me toward Andrew. I probably looked scared, but Andrew was putting on a fine display of boredom.

"Show me your work order, corporal," ordered the guard. Nobody looked at me or spoke to me. It was all Andrew's show.

Andrew rolled his eyes. "What fuckin' work order?"

The guard was slightly taken aback by Andrew's blatant disrespect, but instantly recovered. "You've got three seconds to show me a work order or your ass is going on the ground."

Andrew spat. "Since when does Colonel Wheat need a goddamn work order?"

I did a double-take. *Colonel Wheat?*

The guards lowered their rifles and took a half-step back. "Come again?" asked the first.

Andrew's response dripped disdain. "You fuckin' heard me."

The guard was unsure of what to do, so he spoke to one of the others. "Follower Lee," he said, "take a look in that truck." One of the guards climbed onto the back of the flatbed.

"What are they hauling?" called out the first guard.

"I don't know," answered Follower Lee. "Big chunks of brown soap or something."

"Fuckin' 'A', genius," chimed in Andrew. "Glycerin soap for the kippies. The Colonel likes his ladies soft. *All* the heavies like their meat nice and tender."

"This is soap?" asked the first guard, while the other one climbed down from the truck. Andrew nodded. "Where you takin' it?"

Andrew huffed in disgust. "Where the fuck do you *think* I'm takin' it? The Colonel wants all the kippy-jo hotel floors stocked. Says he's gonna make sure personally that his favorites are taken care of. So if you

602

want me to go back to the plant and tell them to cancel the shipment because a sergeant on Fremont countermanded a colonel, then that's what I'll do."

There was a moment's silence. "Get your sorry ass out of here," growled the guard.

* * *

We played the same game from the Californian to the Union Plaza: Scumbags challenged us, Andrew dropped the names of bigwigs, and we went on our way. We couldn't use this routine when we entered and exited hotels, however. The delivery entrances were closed and we had to enter all of the Fremont facilities via front doors. This subjected us to the sacrament of perverts; that is, the classic TSA "security" grope-down. Neither Andrew nor I looked particularly appetizing to most of the door thugs, but at Fitzgerald's a guy took his time when he felt up my crotch. I looked over at Andrew. His hands were over his head while a TSA freak explored his ass crack. Andrew noticed me watching. *Be cool, Jack,* Andrew warned with his eyes. *Don't start any shit.*

When the TSA guards stood back up and waved us into the hotel, I noticed that they had erections. I was inwardly disgusted but didn't show it as I pushed a luggage cart toward the hotel elevators. Andrew also had a cart and, like mine, it was laden with chunks of dark glycerin. Uniformed TSA were coming and going. Some gave us curious glances, but we were mostly ignored.

Andrew and I had to wait a couple minutes for a particular elevator. "Which one is it?" I whispered.

"Four," said Andrew. "Get on number four."

Once the elevator was free and we had pushed our carts inside, I looked at the overhead camera to confirm that Andrew and I would be able to conduct our activities unobserved. Like certain elevators in other hotels, the lift's surveillance lense had a dab of dark paint and a nail hole.

Andrew noticed me checking the camera. "Don't worry," he said, as he pressed a button. After a few moments Andrew stopped the elevator between floors.

"Let's make this one as quick as the others."

Andrew reached into his glycerin load and pulled out a large screwdriver. He climbed onto the top of his cart and used the tool to force open the elevator's roof access hatch. Andrew then dropped the screwdriver and pulled himself up by the opening's edges while I laced my fingers into a step and gave him a foot boost. Once outside, Andrew looked down at me. "Ready," he said.

I quickly tossed glycerin chunks up to Andrew. Despite the substance's slickness, he caught the glycerin and pitched it down the elevator shaft. I couldn't throw some of the chunks because they were simply too big, so I struggled to lift them high enough for Andrew to reach down and help. We made good time with our operation and when the elevator doors next opened the carts were empty, the hatch was closed, and there was only a boring corporal, his old FC, and two empty luggage carts.

As we left Fremont and headed toward the TSA wash rack, I asked Andrew a question: "How long have you been dumping human glycerin down elevator shafts?"

Andrew's answer came in a hard tone. "Since I learned it existed."

Spoon River Toxicology

"We need a way to ignite the elevator shafts," Andrew said, as he parked the truck in the alley behind The Huntridge Theater.

"Bottles of diesel and lit rags?" I suggested.

"I think that gas and detergent work best in a Molotov," said Andrew. "But that's still no good. It's not fast enough and it lacks flash-compression."

I shrugged. "What, then?"

"Nitrocellulose gum."

I didn't exactly know what Andrew was talking about, but I definitely understood the "nitro" part. "Uh, if you want me to stand in an elevator while you drop a jug of super-unstable liquid explosive down the shaft, you can forget it."

"Not nitroglycerin," said Andrew. "Nitrocellulose *gum.* All the bang, and only some of the instability."

"*Only some?* So if I drop nitroglycerin, there's a one-hundred percent chance that I'll be blown to pieces, and if I drop this other stuff, there's only a fifty percent chance? I still think I'll pass."

"I'd say only about a five percent chance," said Andrew, "and I'd prefer to skip the 'dropping' part."

"So how do you set it off?"

"Timed flares."

"And you already have this stuff?"

"We'll have it before the end of our shift."

* * *

Though it had been only a few years since I had attended the Huntridge TSA rally, the old theater had nevertheless fallen into severe disrepair. "This place reminds me of something," I said. "These charred spots where transients have almost burned it down, along with the collapsed roof and smashed windows...it's like a Norma Jeane Manson video that I saw when I was a kid."

Andrew blurted out a laugh and clapped a hand over

his mouth as the sound echoed through what was left of The Huntridge. Andrew instinctively raised his rifle and backed toward a wall, but then stopped and lowered his weapon.

"Easy," I said. "I'm sure that we're alone in here. This place stopped being a drifter hangout a long time ago." That was an understatement. Structurally collapsing, reeking of rodent piss, and with some corners and walls coated in blown dust, the historic Huntridge at Charleston and Maryland was an unlikely choice for squatters.

"Habit," said Andrew.

"But what was the joke?"

"Your crack about Norma Jeane Manson. Kinda reminds me of the same thing, too."

I looked at Andrew. "You-you understand that reference?"

"Yeah. I remember that guy from my worldline. Those crazy contacts and make-up and stuff. I half expect some skinny singer in black head-to-toe greasepaint to ride by on a pig." We both laughed.

"The last concert I saw here was in 1994," I said, as I followed Andrew around a pile of cinder blocks that had tumbled out of the wall and onto a row of seats. I noticed that some had fallen on the rotten cushions without collapsing the chairs. The blocks had sat patiently for years, as if waiting for the show to start. "I came here with my friend Grace to see Becke," I continued, "but they had to stop the show when part of the ceiling collapsed. I guess The Huntridge was hazardous even back then." I smiled at a distant memory of tin sheeting and old insulation harmlessly falling onto kids who had crowded in for their *Loozer* fixes.

If I expected Andrew to again acknowledge a worldline parallel in the arena of pre-apocalyptic alt-rock, I was disappointed. Instead, he addressed the matter of Grace. "Look, if you're trying to raise that issue again...just save it for another time. Okay? We need to do what we need to do and then get out of here. We can talk about it again later." Andrew stopped and turned. "I know this matters to you. I'm not saying that it isn't important. But," Andrew paused to motion at his sleeve, "I'm a lowly corporal. That's it. Even though this job we're doing is something from out of hell, I'm lucky just to have driving authorization. We'll find her. Let's leave it at that."

I didn't want a rehash either, so I kept my rejoinder to myself. *You're as much of a "real" corporal as I am a "real" FC*, I thought. *All we have to do is get our hands on some more phony papers and uniforms and we can march into the kippy quarters like we're deviant TSA brass.* "I know that we can't go poking around the Pleasure Brigade quarters," I said. "I got it. I just had a little flashback. That's all."

We were now at the front of the theater. A section of roof had smashed down, and not just as metal segments and insulation fluffs. Andrew poked around under a pile of shattered boards and twisted debris. "Damn," he muttered, as he put down his rifle and tried to lift a beam. "More of this crap has fallen since I was here before. Now I'm not sure where the hole is." Andrew grunted and the beam shifted a few inches, which was just enough for him to get on his knees and look behind it. "No, not there," he said, as he stood up and took a few more steps around the pile.

"*Here before?*" I echoed.

Andrew stopped scanning the rubble and looked at me. "Yeah. This is where I got the nitro for the Hoover bomb's initiator core."

I was stunned. "What?! *You* were the one?"

"Yeah," said Andrew in distracted nonchalance as he again knelt to peer through the debris. He shifted his head and tried to reach for something inside the pile.

"Why...why didn't you mention that when we talked about the dam?" I asked.

"Ahhh," Andrew said. He didn't answer as he strained to reach something. Then Andrew pulled his arm out of the pile and dusted off his black sleeve.

"Hey."

Andrew looked up. "You say something?"

"You blew the fucking Hoover Dam!"

For a half-second Andrew looked slightly confused. "Yes. That's what I said."

"Why didn't you tell me?" I demanded. "I mean, with all of the crazy shit that we've talked about, you somehow forgot to mention that you knocked out a major landmark and shut down the power grid?"

Andrew seemed to be slightly taken aback. "Well, I'm telling you *now*. Christ, it's not like I was keeping it a secret. My plan wasn't a thing of finesse anyway, and I'm not exactly proud of myself."

That seemed like an odd statement. "What do you mean, 'not proud'?"

"I feel like I pushed the TSA into their big murder-fuel scheme."

I huffed. "Don't you think that it was already underway? Hell, it only took a couple weeks to get the grid back up from Moapa, and the infrastructure for all of this shit had to have been well in place before the official green light was given. Sorry, Andrew, but your conscience is gonna have to find its guilt in a more realistic place. You're off the hook."

"Maybe," replied Andrew. "But I'm not gonna let it go."

I frowned. "I'm afraid you'll have to. You're just one man, and in the face of evil like this, one man's sphere doesn't extend much beyond his own survival."

"Negative," replied Andrew. *"We* are *two* intelligent men, and in the face of *stupid* evil like this, there is a hell of a lot we can do."

I was dubious. "Like what?"

"Like what we're already doing! We'll exterminate the Vegas TSA like the vermin they are."

"I think we're gonna need a slightly more elaborate plan."

"Why? We're already in the process of turning their Fremont filth-hives into gas chambers. That'll do."

I wasn't sure how far the glycerin scheme would go in shutting down the TSA in Nevada...though considering how everyone in Vegas had experienced the effectiveness of Andrew's Hoover-demolition effort, maybe the local TSA's days really *were* numbered.

"How did you manage the dam?" I asked.

Andrew considered my question for a moment. "Well, I suppose that I did it without resorting to anything that I learned in the military." Andrew seemed to reflect upon something. "Ah, well, that's not true. I had to know how to make crude thermite and estimate its potential energy. I had to know how to set-n-blend a magnesium-epoxy step-up core, and then set the nitro initiator itself. But most of that came from my college days at Fort Tampa."

"Do future schools have bomb-making classes?" I asked with mild sarcasm.

"Every chemistry and physics class from high school on up is an armorer's course if you use your imagination," Andrew asserted.

"But you also mentioned something that you learned in the army."

"More like *reminded* of something. During a Blue Diamond run," explained Andrew, "I decided to drive the truck up Vegas Boulevard. I mean, why not? It's not like The Strip is crowded nowadays. When I crossed Flamingo I noticed that the MGM was painted blue, and that it had a big sign that read 'Bally's'".

"Okay. So the old MGM fire never happened in your Vegas."

"Yeah," confirmed Andrew. "But that didn't really register with me at the time. Remember when I told you that I had to study certain people's pasts during training? Well, the same applies to places."

"You have to dig into the historical minutia of locations? Sounds like a lot of work."

"I wouldn't say *minutia*," replied Andrew. "But displacement pilots need an understanding of big events in important spots. And," he added, "I really don't consider historical study to be a burden, particularly when training to be a worldline jockey."

I recalled our earlier discussions. "You're talking about Montauk and the Philadelphia shipyards and all of that, aren't you?" I looked up as I tried to recall other things. "And the reason why you sought me out is because there *isn't a* crazy UFO ranch out at the Nellis range's fifty-second sector." I didn't mean to sound goofy, but the tales that Andrew had spun about a giant ultra-secret airbase didn't really jibe with my recollections of Groom Lake's abandoned dirt airstrip.

"Not that it matters," corrected Andrew, "but it's not in fifty-two. It's in fifty-one, and that's what it's called. *Area 51.*"

I sniffed. "You've said that before. It doesn't seem very inventive, especially for a place as weird as you described..." I didn't finish my sentence because a light-bulb realization took me back the beginning of our exchange. "That's the reason!" I blurted out. "That's why you blew the dam! That 'Lake Choice' thing isn't about Lake Meade at all! It's about something *in* the lake!"

Andrew gave me a wary look. "I'm not sure how safe this is, with you putting two-and-two together at this point...though I'm not sure that you've made a great detective breakthrough."

"Well, you keep saying how vital my assistance is, though you won't say *how*."

"That's because my mind is on the dangers of this world," explained Andrew. "I could be busted for being a phony at any minute, and so could you."

"Sure, but we've pulled it off so far."

"How much stock are you willing to put in that?" asked Andrew. "Think about when you were in DS-21. Remember those screams? And how about the bodies that we collect every day? Sorry Jack, but if I'm still running my little schemes while you've been caught and strapped into one the TSA's torture chairs, I would *prefer* that you be without the complete picture."

I mentally revisited the horrors that Andrew had thrust back onto my mind, then shuddered and took a seat on a pile of cinder blocks. Andrew also mentally deliberated something as he sat down. He scowled and shook his head.

I realized how the situation that Andrew had described worked both ways. "That's the reason why you won't say what you want from me, isn't it?"

"Yes. My ignorance could also save *your* ass."

Neither of us spoke for a few moments. When Andrew finally broke the silence, it didn't feel like his words were entirely meant for me. "They say it can be like a dream, if you let it," he half-murmured.

What's like a dream? What are you talking about?"

"A worldline like this," sighed Andrew. "That's an unofficial saying in my profession, because once you stray outside of your original event class but then return, you'll never experience an identical skew. But I can't just get what I want from you and disappear. I'm not going to leave and let these TSA fuckpigs do what they want either, even if this reality can become nothing but a bad dream."

"Ummm, that's good to hear," I said. "Mind telling me why?"

Andrew sounded a little put-off. "Because I'm human and I still have something decent inside me. I'm not saying that I haven't imagined rushing out of this goddamned hell, because I have, and that's where the 'dream' thing comes in. If I somehow manage to get back to a worldline that's 'mine', I don't have to ever think about what I've seen here again, because it will only exist as a personal memory. When you have the option of going through a displacement door, consequences melt away. Life can seem like an illusion, and there are no limits or restrictions." Andrew looked at me with a crazy half-grin. "And that can be a ticket to amorality and psychosis. Nothing matters in a skew. Once you leave your own worldline's event class, you'll never see the same place twice. You can do what you want. It doesn't matter."

"But you're not going to do that to me? Just disappear?" I asked.

"Nah. Despite all of the tough-guy trash-talk in my unit, the personality inventories that we take catch the Chucky Mansons."

"Christ," I muttered, at which we both let out small chuckles.

"If anything," continued Andrew, "there should also be tests for overly-empathetic candidates."

"Oh? Is that you?"

"Yeah," answered Andrew. "The Federation would never have allowed me to become the captain of a starship." He paused. "How about that pop reference? Did you get it?"

I nodded. "NCC-1702, but without you at the helm."

"That's it," said Andrew.

"Why not, 'Captain' Carlssin?"

"Because I've taken it upon myself to personally rip up the Prime Mandate. Until we bail on this shithole, my motto will be: Interference, Interference, Interference. I got caught in clogged restroom, but instead of just leaving, I've decided to apply a massive plunger."

I stood up and brushed off the seat of my fatigue pants. "I'd say that your acrolein-fumigation-scheme definitely qualifies."

"Yep," agreed Andrew, "and you're going to help me pull it off before our big exit." Andrew again knelt in front of the rubble heap and started to pull out broken boards. He braced his legs against a large beam. "Hey, how about a hand here? Or foot?"

I sat down on the floor beside Andrew and put my boots against the beam. With some grunting we managed to move it aside, and underneath was an elliptical hole in the theater's concrete floor that appeared to have been - *burnt?* - into the concrete.

"That's more than big enough for a man," I noted.

"Yeah," agreed Andrew. "I did it in two stages. I burned a manhole first, but after I got down to the reel room I came back up and broadened the sides."

"Why?"

"Because I discovered that those old film canisters are about four feet wide."

"How'd you get them out? And how did *you* get out?"

"It's not that deep. I used a rope."

I studied the hole. "How did you get through the floor?" I asked. I was sure there weren't many quick and discrete jackhammers around.

"I used a chisel, plus some pre-'78 magnesium brake shoes, a file, and a week of setting little fires with metal filings." Andrew seemed proud of his handiwork.

"Is it wise to burn through concrete over a nitroglycerin vault?"

My question caused Andrew's look of pride to be replaced be one of exasperation. "Okay, listen," he replied, "this does *not* cut into the vault. It just opens into an access hall under the main floor, and it's *not* nitroglycerin. It's old nitrated cellulose film."

"Alright. But again, how did you know that it was here?"

"That was what I started to explain earlier. When I was driving on The Strip I noticed that the MGM Grand is called 'Bally's'. Then, as I went further south to Tropicana, I saw a burned-out 'A' frame hotel sitting at the southwest corner of the intersection--"

"That's what's left of Xanadu," I interrupted. "What did you expect to see?"

"Excalibur."

"What's that?"

"It's a hotel that looks like a castle," said Andrew. "Anyway, sitting diagonally was a big green-glass casino in the spot where I thought that I would see the MGM Mariner."

"Yeah. That's the MGM Grand. It replaced the Mariner."

Andrew nodded. "I later realized that the MGM had changed location after that hotel fire you mentioned. Every time I drove by that green casino I felt like I was forgetting something. It kept bothering me until one day I learned the date of the fire: February 25th, 1980."

"I don't see a connection," I said.

"There's no reason for *you* to see a connection. But for me, it meant that, through some kind of quantum switch, the date when The Huntridge fire took place on *my* worldline was the same as the date of the MGM fire on *this* worldline."

"This place caught fire?" I asked, as I glanced around the theater.

"It *detonated*," said Andrew. "A fire heated up the old film under the vault ceiling and it blew like the powder magazine of the *USS Maine*. A matinee was starting, and eighty-five people died."

"I think that many were killed when the old MGM burned," I said. "Bizarre."

"And there you have it. Once I determined that, yes, The Huntridge Theater still existed on this worldline, I knew that my bomb-making problems were solved. College at Fort Tampa taught me how to make the Hoover device, and my history training helped me find enough old nitro-gum to free the Colorado River."

We got up and brushed off. "Now," said Andrew, "since flashlights, batteries, and light sticks are things of the past, I must improvise." Andrew unsheathed a short MA-87 bayonet from his fatigue thigh pocket.

"Why don't you just wear that on your belt?" I asked.

"I don't have edged weapon authorization."

"But you carry an M16," I said. That seems...odd. You're allowed to have an automatic rifle, but not a knife?"

Andrew shrugged. "Hey, don't ask me to explain the TSA's nut bag logic. I'm not actually the right grade for a 'sixteen either, but nobody has taken it from me. That pisser in the truck cab is all that I'm supposed to have. Senior NCOs, especially the assholes at the motor pool, get torqued when they see knives and shit hanging off subordinates' uniforms. The armory inside the tool crib keeps handing out rifles, though." Andrew pulled a magnesium striker from his pocket and began to shave sparks onto a dry handful of shredded projection screen canvas. He only had to make a few passes before it caught fire.

Andrew looked around. "Tear off some of those old seat covers," he said. I did as instructed, but coughed when dust arose. I covered my face with my sleeve and handed the material to Andrew. He twisted it into a tight spindle and touched the roll's tip to the small flame.

"You're kidding," I said.

"No," replied Andrew. "This is how I did it before. I'll leave it burning in the passage and feel my way into the vault. The reels won't get within ten feet of the flame." Andrew put the striker and bayonet back into his thigh pouch and slowly lowered himself through the hole. When the only parts of Andrew that were visible were his fingers, he let go and I heard his boots hit the passage floor.

"It's only about a six-inch drop," he called up. "But I'll still need a hand getting out."

"What's down there?" I called back.

There was a pause. "Well, things were sealed up

before, but I can smell rats now. There's not much right here, but at the end of the passage there's a door and reel racks."

"Hey! How the hell do you know that if you've never carried a torch into the storage area?"

There was a moment's silence. "Just toss the damn light down. I know what I'm doing."

I smelled the nasty acrid scent of combusting vinyl as I picked up the spindled seat cover. Instead of just dropping the makeshift torch, I carefully lowered it through the hole. When Andrew disappeared into the darkness I hoped that the floor wouldn't suddenly lift up and send me into orbit. After a few minutes Andrew returned.

"Hey. You up there?"

I looked into the hole and saw that Andrew wasn't carrying the torch. "Here. Take this," he said, as he held up a large flat shape that reminded me of a gigantic metal dinner plate.

I guessed that the object weighed nearly thirty pounds and it barely fit through the hole. The reel case was about four inches thick, with circular ribbing pressed into its sheet metal, and it was painted gray. There were two right angles that protruded from the bottom of the case and provided a flat upright storage surface. Except for a thin layer of dust, the reel case looked like it could have been placed in the basement only yesterday. Instead of an adhesive label, there was a metal tag riveted to the case's edge. It read: *THE RELUCTANT SHEPHERD - PART 1 OF 4 - FRAMINGTHORPE STUDIOS 1927.*

Andrew and I repeated this procedure seven more times, but none of the other reels were parts of *The Reluctant Shepherd.* All of the films were pre-1930, and for me, the titles were unknown. One metal tag appeared to be in French, and it identified the film inside as *PIED DE MAIS D'HOMME.*

"That's it," Andrew called out. "There's more down here, but we don't need them. Gimme a hand."

"Sure. Where's the rope?"

"I don't have it anymore. I can reach the edge if I jump. Collar me out."

"I haven't done that in thirty years."

"It's like riding a bike," answered Andrew. "Just grab, pull, and don't throw your back out. Don't pop your nut sack either, because there's nobody around who can stuff your shit back together."

That's encouraging, I thought, as I knelt down and faced the hole. "One, two, three," counted Andrew, and then he jumped and caught the edge. At that moment I dug my knees and toes in and reached down to grab the yoke of his shirt. It wasn't graceful or particularly efficient, but it enabled Andrew to go from his hands, to his elbows, and then his shoulders. At that point I let go and Andrew pressed himself out.

We both sat back and caught our breaths. "Thanks," said Andrew. He coughed and cleared his throat. "But for a second I thought that you were going to hang me."

"Now what?" I asked.

"Now," said Andrew, "we wash the truck and sign you back into John Stewart Barracks. Then I'll stash these in my workshop and return to the motorpool."

"How much time do we have?" I looked for the sun through the fallen roof but it had sunk too low.

"I'd say about an hour."

"We'll have to cram these in the cab," I said. "They'll get all bloody if we put them in the back." *Huh,* I thought, as I unexpectedly caught myself plainly speaking. *I just said it. It's blood from the corpses that we haul around. It's not imaginary red Cool-Aid. It's not tomato juice or smashed watermelon pulp. It's blood, and we're in hell.*

Nor Otherwise
Harm No
Whores

May
2018
(2-of-2)

"Today you'll see the fruits of my labors," announced Andrew, "but first I gotta get this piece of shit moving." He hit the accelerator and a plume of smoke washed over the cab as the old Ford coughed and picked up a little speed. I didn't shudder, though my flesh *used* to crawl when I saw the greasy black exhaust. I would sit and hold my breath for as long as I could, even if none of the smoke entered the cab. I didn't want to breathe the combusted remains of murder victims, just as I wouldn't have wanted to pour urn ashes down my throat.

Today, though, I didn't hold my breath. I glanced out the back and over the top of the empty truck bed. I was grateful to be finished with the day's ghoulish duty. I looked at the speedometer and saw that we were going almost fifty miles per hour. *What was Andrew doing?* He never drove this fast. I didn't even know that the truck could go over forty-five.

Andrew hit the clutch, reached down, and slipped the truck out of gear. Sammy's Town, or rather, Sammy's *Ghost* Town, was on our left as we coasted south on Nellis Avenue, past dark traffic signals, and turned left on Boulder Highway. Midway through the intersection Andrew turned the key off and choked the engine. The truck stuttered for a moment and then the only sound was from the freewheeling rear duals.

"Uh…?" I looked at Andrew, but he kept his eyes on the road. "Doesn't this thing have power steering?"

"It did once," said Andrew. "But I couldn't do this if it still did." Andrew's gritted teeth and white knuckles emphasized the point as he wrenched the wheel in a right turn that took us through a former residential section of Harmon Avenue.

"What are you doing?"

"Stealth mode," said Andrew.

Unlike the long, straight, and empty stretch that was Boulder Highway, Harmon was choked with debris. Andrew's face turned red as he strained to maneuver the coasting truck between refrigerators, overturned cars, and even an inexplicable pile of at least fifty twisted and smashed bicycles that had been piled at the base of a crude KKK-like wooden cross. God only knew what that display had been about.

Andrew used the truck's last bit of momentum to swerve onto a nondescript residential driveway. We coasted into a garage with smashed-in facing above its missing roller door that allowed the truck silent clearance. Andrew stood with both feet on the nearly-dead brake pedal and we finally stopped.

All quiet.

"Follow me," said Andrew in a low voice. He grabbed his muzzle-to-the-floorboard M16, got out, climbed down, and reached up to gently close the driver's side door. I grabbed the pisser and did the same on my side. We met at the back of the truck and Andrew gave me a *QUIET* hand signal.

The nearby house had burned, but not to the ground. It was merely a roofless hulk without a door. The windows and frames were gone, leaving only gaping holes and smoke streaks up the remaining walls. There had been a fence, but now only a rectangular perimeter of metal posts remained on the property's edge. Clothes and pieces of cheap pressboard furniture were scattered in the front yard, and an accumulation of blown dust told me that the drama that had unfolded here was many months, or maybe even years, in the past. One article of abandoned clothing - some old jeans - seemed different, and upon closer inspection I noticed that the base of a spine, still attached to a pelvis, extended out past the waistband. There weren't any skeletal ankles protruding from the cuffs, but I spotted an old sneaker nearby. Its cheap rubber sole had curled in the sun, and in the space where the upper had split and pulled away I saw some hard sun-dried toes.

This sight seemed...*academically*...different from the TSA's freshly-picked variety of death and its daily boot-to-my-head. I paused and looked around the yard like an archaeologist scouring the sands of a high Peruvian desert for pieces of a fragmented mummy.

"What the hell are you doing? C'mon!" Andrew's hissing voice reminded me that there wasn't time to ponder the mysteries of this little Atacama, so I turned and caught up with him.

The house where we left the truck wasn't our actual destination. Instead, Andrew crept through the back yards of six more lots, maybe occupied, but probably not, and turned right. We ended up on a street that I guessed wasn't far from Flamingo, and Andrew led me to another detached garage, except this one had a rolling door that was secured by a chain that had been looped and locked in two crudely-hacked holes. One hole was in the bottom of the door, and the other hole was in the garage wall.

Andrew produced a padlock key. Before releasing the chain, he turned to me. "Listen very carefully, Jack. When I open this, do not, I repeat, *do not* lift the door. Understand?"

I nodded and Andrew knelt to unlock the chain. He slowly and carefully lifted the door about two feet. "Don't touch it," he further cautioned. "Just do as I do. Fucking *exactly* as I do." Andrew reached under the door and placed his rifle inside. Then he half-slid and half-crawled into the garage. "Your turn," he whispered from within.

I placed the pisser under the door and wriggled through. The garage was well-lit by a bubble skylight and two elevated and barred security windows. Two wooden sawhorses were positioned on the other side of the entrance, but they looked less like horses and more like porcupines. They had masses of wired-on and outward-pointing quills made from old pipes. More wires attached the pipes to the inside of the garage door. The wires were slack, but if the door had been lifted higher, they would have pulled taut.

"Booby traps," said Andrew.

Obviously, I thought. "Are those zip-twelves?" I asked.

"*My* versions," said Andrew. He propped his M16

against the wall and walked to a tool-and-debris-strewn workbench. "Steel and copper, mostly. I even thought about PVC, but I figured that it would just blow apart." Andrew picked up two empty pipes. "One has a threaded plug with a nail to serve as a stationary firing pin, and the other pushes the shell." Andrew slid one pipe inside the other to demonstrate. "I found a case of slugs and a case of buck when I took over this place. I don't have a real shotgun anyway, and that pisser is just a muzzle-loader."

I propped the pisser beside the M16 and looked at the massive sawhorse setup. "How many point at the door?" I asked.

"Thirty."

"Jesus. Thirty shotshell blasts should solve your burglar problems."

"That's the idea. But we're not here to evaluate my security measures." Andrew nodded me over to the workbench. "Recognize these?"

I looked at the large and now-heavily modified Huntridge reel cases. "You've been busy, haven't you?"

"Let's just say that I don't always go directly to the motor pool after I take you back to your barracks," Andrew replied.

"These wind-up clocks look like something Wyle Coyote would use with a bundle of dynamite," I observed. "Scrounge stalls?"

Andrew shook his head. "Abandoned apartments and houses. I bought some from the Quad Market, and others I assembled myself."

I continued to assess Andrew's efforts. "Mercury switches and car flares. Or maybe marine flares?"

"A little of both. I had to be flexible."

"How come these," I asked, as I pointed at dangling wires that hung from each of the canisters, "aren't attached to anything?"

"Those old clocks aren't actually for timing the blast. They're a mechanical means of actuating the switches because the timers themselves are radio-controlled. I don't have the time or materials to make batteries, so I'm going to wire the flare initiators into the elevators' bottom floor displays. That way I can use a reliable power source and I can also be certain that the explosion is near the glycerin." Andrew held up something that looked like a flashlight.

"What's that?" I asked.

"A mono-signal transmitter. Just shake it up, like so," Andrew demonstrated, "and a magnet passes through a coil of copper wire to build up a charge. Then hit this button, and the countdown starts. The reels are set on a five-hour delay."

"Incredible," I breathed, "but these clearly look like bombs. I don't know how the hell we're gonna get them past the hotel door perverts."

"Those guys are the least of my concerns," said Andrew. "By now most of them recognize us and the thrill is gone. How long has it been since you got a grope-down?"

"A while. Nobody seems interested in my dick anymore."

"That's right. So when we load up the luggage carts, I'm gonna put these," Andrew paused to motion at the old film reels, "in the bottom of the cart and cover them up with chunks of glycerin. When was the last time that they checked a cart?"

"It's been quite a while," I replied, as I continued to examine the film bombs. Then I voiced another concern. "Andrew, I don't like the idea of these going up to Fremont while there are still two hotel floors of kippies who haven't done anything wrong. And I *really* don't like the idea of gassing Fremont while Grace is still there."

"Those are definite complications."

"They're more than just 'complications'. They're completely unacceptable factors."

"I've already taken it all into account," said Andrew. "Your friend is now part of the plan, and if we find her, it will simplify matters considerably. *When* we find her, I mean."

"How?"

"House mothers handle scheduling. She can communicate with the other hotel and schedule the kippies for off-site services. There are a lot of officers in the FC barracks, motor pools, and even death camps whom I'm sure would appreciate some duty-hour entertainment. Then you and I get her out on that day."

"I like that a lot better," I said, "though it's a hell of a lot to pull off, and we're not even sure which hotel Grace is in."

"Yeah, no shit. But we're gonna have to find her. Like I said, she's now integral to the plan - and that's why I have this." Andrew took a couple steps over to where a small box sat on the garage floor. He picked it up, brought it over to the workbench, and opened it. There was clothing inside. "About the right size, about the right length," Andrew said, as he reached in and pulled out a female FC uniform.

"Have you ever seen kippies outside Fremont?" I asked.

Andrew put the uniform back in the box. "Yeah. Every day. So have you."

"No, I haven't."

"Well, if you're looking for people dressed like hookers and gigolos, kippies are invisible," said Andrew. "But have you ever seen platoons of young attractive people marching around or riding in the backs of trucks? I know that you have, because TSA tends to abduct 'pox survivors with less scarring and even younger unscarred people."

"*Younger?* Like children?"

"Early teens, usually. Does that shock you?"

"Well, considering the TSA's other crimes...no, I suppose it doesn't. I guess that I *have* seen teenagers in uniform, but I thought that they were just members of the LaPin Youth."

"Some are...but not all."

I sighed. "Okay, we have to find Grace and see if there's some way to send the kippies to other parts of the city before we set this off. How far away is safe distance?"

"Three or four blocks off Fremont ought to be well out of harm's way. Acrolein disperses quickly, so it'll wipe out the hotel rats, but not the entire north end."

"I admire your intention to strike a blow for justice," I said, "but this plan is getting more and more complex."

Andrew took a breath and seemed to come to a

622

mental decision. "There's more."

"Oh. Great."

"Alright Jack, we're now at the part where I must once again guarantee you and your friend's passage off this worldline, and in return, you tell where to find your grandfather's 'selenide. Or, if you choose to keep that information to yourself at this point - and I completely understand - just start thinking about where it's located on the plane, and what we'll have to do to quickly and efficiently retrieve it." Andrew took another slow and deep breath before continuing. "When the time comes, there may not be time for a practice run. If things go down like I think they might, it will be a case of the three of us trying to outrun the TSA in the pickup, and when we get to the lake we may only have minutes to activate my unit."

I gave Andrew a *WTF?* look. "You just completely lost me."

"I'm serious, Jack. It may come down to precision and speed."

"What the hell are you talking about? I just want to get Grace away from those pigs and avoid killing a bunch of kids! What's all this stuff about my grandpa and outrunning the TSA?"

"Well, if you think that I have time to disassemble a 100-foot-long, 30-foot-tall, and 140-foot-wide B-29 bomber, piece-by-tiny-piece, in search of something that's the size of a quarter, you're wrong."

B-29. As soon as I heard that term, I understood. It was Grandpa's big secret that he had passed on to me. For my entire life, I had never known why - until now. I felt like a massive jigsaw puzzle had assembled itself in my head...Grandpa, secret projects, army men, time travel, and the destruction of Hoover Dam in order to access something on the bottom of Lake Meade.

The B-29!

"Tell me again what we're looking for," I said, but as soon as the words were out I saw something that might have been alarm cross Andrew's face.

"You'd better be shitting me, Jack. Remember, I told you that if you wanted to keep it to yourself at this point, I'm fine with that. No problem. But don't play around. Not at this stage of the game, and not with me."

As I looked at Andrew I realized that I wasn't seeing the time traveler, but rather, the toughened veteran who had grown from child-soldier to adult leader. His battlefield kills against other fighters were doubtless greater than the number of civilians murdered by the most vicious TSA slug, and he knew how to follow, lead, and lay down the law. Andrew wasn't standing in a threatening posture, but he had pulled himself up to his full height and his eyes were extremely hard.

I found myself speaking carefully. "I'm asking you to help me remember," I said. "What was the stuff called again?"

"Dicadmium methyltetraselenide. 'Selenide' for short."

I turned away from Andrew, cleared a space on the workbench, and sat. I put my boot heels on a lower shelf, and struck a pose not unlike Rodin's *The Contemplator.* After a couple minutes I nodded slightly, then with greater force as I appeared to recall something.

Andrew seemed a bit more relaxed. "So?"

"Got it," I said. "I had to put a few things together in my head, but...yeah. I know where it is."

"Tell me!"

"Hold on a damn minute. You just said that if I wanted to keep things close to the vest, you'd accept it. Well, I do. We're not yet sitting in a time-machine-pickup and getting ready for a trip out of hell. We're not even close. I trust you, Andrew, and all of your philosophy about fighting and not turning your back sounds good...but, like I said, we're not in the clear yet. We'll do this together, and when it's time for me to step up, I will. I know that you won't grab the 'selenide and go without me, but, as the saying goes, it's good to keep honest men honest."

Andrew scrutinized me for a moment and seemed reassured. He was no longer the hardcore guy. He was again the time traveler and the survivor who had saved me from DS-21. "Okay, okay," Andrew said in a subdued tone. "That's fine. We can play the Sad Hill-Arch

Stanton game. Do what you have to do." Andrew turned to look out the garage windows. "I think that we're on better footing now. Let's get going."

I still had no idea what dicadmium-*whatever* was, or where to find it inside a giant old airplane...but I nodded as I picked up the pisser and carefully slid it back under the booby-trapped garage door.

27

There's Supposed To Be A Nest Of Field Mice Around Here Somewhere

And What About The World, ~~Ronald~~ *Andrew?* What Would You Like To Do To The Whole World?

When Andrew and I crossed Maryland on Tropicana I saw the Sated Yam's burned-out shell. In the time since Andrew had gotten me out of DS-21, I had wondered about Rosetta, Mary, and Bryan. They had said that they were heading for Portland. That was all I knew.

I figured that my house would be occupied by other people, but when I persuaded Andrew to drive through the cul-de-sac, all I saw were my things scattered on the lawn. Brettly's house, along with the rest of the neighboring homes, also appeared to be abandoned. I only spent a few moments inside my former residence to collect a pair of jeans and the green curtain-shirt that had been Rosetta's present to me.

Andrew and I had finished wiring the movie reels into the elevator electrical systems and our glycerin dumps continued. Today, however, we were going to access a kippy-jo hotel floor with our "skin care delivery" horseshit. It was the third time that we had done so. Instead of saying that we were taking glycerin to the kippies and then dumping it down elevator shafts, we actually kept some for the Pleasure Brigade.

We had pushed our carts no further that a few steps out of the elevator when we were stopped by guards who reminded me of ancient harem eunuchs, except that they wore TSA black and carried automatic rifles. The guards served to prevent the sex slaves from escaping as much as to stop unauthorized Pleasure Brigade activities, and the thugs took us to the house mothers after we told them why we were there.

This place is like a hospital nurse station, I thought, as, under escort, Andrew and I pushed our glycerin carts down the former hotel corridor. As we walked, the screams that came through the room doors reminded me of the sounds that had come from DS-21's Hot Unit. I hoped that this time people weren't *really* being tortured, but some of the sounds weren't reassuring.

We stopped at a set of desks that had been assembled in an area that looked like it had formerly been occupied by rows of vending machines. There were two older women there, along with another guard, and they were answering phones and setting up "appointments". I hadn't recognized any of the house mothers during our previous kippy floor visits, but when I smelled Old Slice in the hotel corridor, my heart started to beat faster.

She was at the desk. Her eyes were dull and her face remained blank while Andrew explained why we were there.

That's right. Good job. You don't know me. You don't recognize me. But now that I know where you are, I'll be back soon with a written message, an FC uniform, and some more glycerin.

Like Grace, the other house mother just shrugged when Andrew and I informed them of our purpose, so we continued the charade by going door-to-door, still with our escorts. We knocked, waited a few moments, and then an attractive but expressionless young man or woman would answer. We held out our brown chunks, the people in the rooms accepted them, and like winding-down automatons, they slowly stepped back and closed the doors.

* * *

As the elevator descended, Andrew asked: "Are you absolutely sure that was her? If she knows you but wasn't letting on, she's one hell of an actress."

"Yes. That was her. One of the house mothers, Union Plaza."

"Okay. Well, I guess it's time to write a letter, wrap up a uniform, and dip it all in melted glycerin."

"Yeah. Just make sure she keeps the chunk long

enough to crack it open. We're fucked if someone else gets our little chocolate Easter egg." Andrew nodded.

The elevator stopped and the doors opened. Someone I knew got on, but I wasn't immediately aware of that because I had my back to the doors while Andrew faced outward. When I saw the expression on Andrew's face, I instantly realized that he and the other person weren't strangers either. I whirled around and saw TSA Colonel Carl Wheat.

Carl was fairly quick on the draw. Andrew, however, had started to move forward even before Carl's hand had gone to his holster. Carl pulled a stainless .357, but was unable to use it because the fingers of Andrew's right hand were instantly over the weapon's top strap. Andrew's white-knuckle grip kept the revolver's cylinder bound and the hammer down while his left elbow cracked into Carl's right cheekbone. I was impressed by the fact the Carl didn't go straight down, though his legs were wobbly enough for Andrew to yank him into the elevator, again by his grip on the revolver. Carl flew forward, past our empty glycerin carts, and hit the elevator's far wall. As Carl slid downward I saw that his eyes were glazed but still open, and the gun remained in his hand. Andrew and I exited the elevator as Carl disappeared behind the closing doors, but I saw that, even from his slumped position on the floor, he was still weakly trying to raise his weapon.

Andrew and I found ourselves in a fourth-floor hotel corridor. I started to panic, but Andrew gripped my arm and spoke: "Don't run. Take the stairs. All bets are off, Jack."

"You should have killed him."

"Yes."

"Why didn't you?"

"Because I'm not fucking perfect."

Our encounter with Carl had occurred on a lower floor. While my stunned erstwhile friend went up, Andrew and I arrived in the Plaza's lobby.

* * *

We made it to the truck before the Plaza doors were closed.

630

* * *

We got away from Fremont before roadblocks sealed off the area.

* * *

The flatbed still had half a tank of bio-diesel, but that didn't matter. "There are checkpoints on every road out of town," said Andrew. "We have to dump this truck ASAP and get out on foot."

* * *

We took the M16, the pisser, and our water bottles out of the Ford before we abandoned it on a random street off Charleston.

* * *

We were out of Vegas before the pigs started to root around John Stewart Barracks and the East Valley Motor Pool.

* * *

The moon lit our way as we retreated along the same path that I had followed out of the La Madres years before. Once the lights of Vegas were well at our backs, Andrew took point. He led us up and out of Brownstone Canyon to a spot under the rim of Turtlehead Peak.

"This is where we stop," he said.

"Just for tonight, right?"

"No. We'll camp here and reassess."

We spent the night on some sand beneath a stone overhang. I didn't sleep as well as I would have in my FC barracks bunk...but at least we were temporarily safe.

Well, so much for our BIG AMBITIOUS PLANS!

What was all that bullshit about "two intelligent men and stupid evil"?

Maybe God and Robert Burns had affirmed Andrew's earlier statement.

All bets were off.

Double Up Or Quit,
Double Stake
Or Split

*June
2018
(2-of-2)*

Andrew shot a coyote and the meat tasted the way that I remembered Korean dog meat had tasted. We ate whatever we could pick, find, or shoot. I tried to tell Andrew about the provisions in Grandpa's mountain hut, but he wasn't interested. "Maybe as a last resort," he grudgingly conceded, "but I want to stay here and put together another plan. There's water here as well - just over the hill in an old reservoir." Instead of emphasizing the superiority of fresh spring water over a tepid pool, I just resigned myself to boiling everything in an old tin can.

* * *

Something had been bugging me, and a few days after we fled Vegas I confronted Andrew. "You recognized him, and he recognized you," I said.

"Who?"

"Wheat."

Andrew looked at the ground, then at me, then at his left foot. *What is he doing?* I wondered, as my companion began to remove his boot. When his sock was off, I saw that part of Andrew's foot, including his two outer toes, was missing.

"The TSA has a thing for feet," said Andrew.

"Carl did that?"

Andrew shook his head. "No. In fact, Wheat was pissed off because he thought that the torture technique was primitive." Carl motioned at his foot. "Some shitsack colonel named Norres oversaw this."

"When?"

"After they caught me blowing the dam. I have other scars in other places from our little 'interviews'."

"How did you escape?"

"I didn't. I broke under torture, and when Wheat's informants caught wind of who I was and what I knew,

632

he had me transferred to his custody."

"*You* were at DS-21 too?"

Andrew nodded. "Briefly. When you finally turned up, Wheat and I struck a deal. Your 'rescue' from the camp was a set-up, though I was originally supposed to step in at the dairy."

"Why didn't you follow the plan?"

"Because I couldn't be sure that you'd survive long enough. Besides, after I faked some ID, became a truck driver, and double-crossed Wheat by disappearing, it was just that much easier to hide in plain sight while carrying on with my Fremont plans."

"What did Carl want from me?"

"I was supposed to win your trust and get the 'selenide information from you, and in return, Wheat was going to give me the C-205 unit, including enough 'selenide to operate it. I think that you can probably guess what would have happened to you after that."

I didn't need to guess. "I thought that 'selenide stuff only existed in a tiny amount."

"I only *need* a tiny amount."

"Oh. You've never actually told me where your machine is. Is it a secret?"

"No. The pickup is in the old bus station bay beside the Plaza."

Andrew's words made me wonder about something. "Does Carl want to use the machine?"

"Hardly." My companion gave a disgusted huff.

"Why not?"

"Think about it. He has the best of everything. Power, women, leisure. He can do unspeakable things and no one blinks an eye. This world may be hell, but devils like Wheat reign in it."

"So...why does he give a damn about the 'selenide?"

Andrew sighed and began to put his boot back on. "Because he needs it to build a type of nuclear bomb, except he doesn't quite know how...and that's why he wants to find me again. Even the tiny amount of 'selenide on that B-29 is enough to make several weapons."

"Wait a minute," I objected. "If there were nuclear material in the lake, the US military would have recovered it."

"Yeah," agreed Andrew, "but *fissionable* material isn't the issue. On this worldline, the powers-that-were saw the writing on the wall. They took 'pox seriously enough to shut down reactors and de-mil nuke inventories when they still had time."

"So why does Carl still think that he can build a bomb with 'selenide? Doesn't he also need plutonium or uranium?"

"No. Wheat wants to get his hands on a gamma-induction device," explained Andrew, "and you don't need the Periodic Table's heavy-hitters for that. Hafnium-178 is the most effective, but some common industrial isotopes of cesium, thorium, and radium can also work, except with smaller yields."

I shook my head. "I was a US Air Force weapons troop, but I've never heard of anything like that."

"No? Well, Wheat certainly has. Though he may be a monster, the man is smart, and he's picked up some theoretical physics somewhere along the line. The kind of nuke that Wheat wants is called an 'isomer weapon' or a 'red mercury bomb'." On most worldlines, including this one, it's just a hypothetical construct, but the concept is definitely sound. A dumper-jumper can't match the energy release of an atom-splitter, but it generates magnitudes more bang than a conventional bomb through massively accelerated half-life decay. A dumper blast may be smaller than that of a fission weapon, but the associated radiation is *horrendous* - and a single device could be enough to erase Vegas." Andrew's tone seemed more anecdotal than speculative.

"And Carl needs 'selenide to make these things?"

Andrew nodded. "'Selenide has two uses. It coheres the C-205's deuterium-injection stream, but it can also stabilize half-life accelerator photons. This means that a knowledgeable person can destroy a city with a common isotope, an old x-ray machine, and a sliver of time-bin encoding material like dicadmium methyltetraselenide."

I considered some of the past information that Andrew had shared. "These things are easier to make than regular nukes, aren't they?"

Andrew nodded. "*Much* easier - provided you have the 'selenide and the know-how. There's no comparison."

"And they were used in your world's civil war, weren't they?"

Andrew slowly nodded again. "I guarantee that Wheat will never stop looking for us."

"But...*why* does Carl want to make bombs?" I asked. "Like you said, he already has everything that he wants."

"Well, that's not *quite* true. When he takes Jatoon LaPin's place at the head of the Nevada TSA, *then* he'll have everything that he wants. A colonel with nukes can make a very persuasive coup pitch to other staff officers."

I had an ugly thought. "If there were a way to alert the civilian population, I'd ask you to make a bomb. That way Carl can blow himself and the rest of the TSA straight to hell."

Andrew had a sad smile. "Nice idea, but I don't think that's how it'll go."

28

You Take The Blue Pill: The Story ~~Ends~~ *Begins.* You Wake Up ~~In Your Bed~~ *On Turtlehead Peak* And Believe... Whatever You WANT To Believe.

"...And Major Krebs Wears His Gestapo Uniform When He Hunts Gators."

June 2018

"I think these are about done," I said, as I stirred a toasted mass of grasshoppers that cooked over the fire on a small sheet of tin. At first I thought that Andrew hadn't heard me, staring intently as he was down into the valley at the crumbling brown grid that had been Hendersonville. From this side of Turtlehead Peak we could only view the southern end of the valley, though I had seen the entire Los Vegas metro-cadaver laid out more times than I could count. Like neighboring Hendersonville, it was dry, dusty, and an eternity away from Sin City's glory days. No color, no light, no flash. The relentless Mojave sun was a force that cracked plastic and peeled paint as God sprayed UV bleach on The Strip, after which His desert wind deposited dust like a dog kicking dirt over its shit.

Andrew had heard after all, and he moved over to the fire. We had humped sacks of bugs up from the other side of the peak, down where an old BLM reservoir still held enough water to qualify as a tiny oasis for both man and insect. There sure as hell wasn't any grass near our camp, let alone grasshoppers, since it was located under a wind-hollowed sandstone overhang that partially shielded us from unfriendly eyes and the hot sun. We were below the peak summit and only our flanks were open; otherwise, we could fire down slope or pick off rappelling visitors.

I moved the hot tin off of the rocks, scooped some sand over the small flame, and used a twig to scrape the bugs into two generous piles. Andrew sat down opposite me and gingerly picked a grasshopper off the top of his heap. He tossed the fried insect from one hand to the other, blew on it, and crunched it up in his mouth. "Not bad," Andrew stated, as he reached for another. "Hot."

"The coyote grease cooks them as well as the fire."

"How much is left?" asked Andrew.

"This is the last of it."

Andrew looked again at the distant and dusty city. "We'll have to move soon. We might have position here, but we still have to eat."

"It's the *drinking* that worries me," I said. "When they finish searching the springs around Red Rock, they'll hit the old BLM reservoirs." I considered my shrinking pile of grasshoppers. "TSA and their scout scum tend to notice guys filling canteens and beating the grass for bugs."

We ate in silence for a few moments and I took note of the unit patches on Andrew's uniform. Their designations were unfamiliar, and that made me wonder about something. "So what's all of this like?" I asked.

Andrew looked up. "Whaddya mean? What's *what* like?"

"I mean, what's this world like for *you*?"

"What's it like?" Andrew repeated. "Same for me as it is for you. Goddamn pile of shit."

"How's it different, though?"

Andrew paused and reached for his M16. "Well, for me," he said, as he examined the rifle, "this worldline is a quantum skew. That means, for example, when I pick up my weapon I notice strange little things, like--" he paused to flip the receiver and touch the forward-assist button "--this. I know The Black Rifle inside and out, but I've never seen this feature before. I guess it's a good idea, since these pieces of garbage will jam on a pinhead. I swear, AKs trump Mattels in *any* universe."

"'Sixteens with bolt assists? That's all?"

Andrew took a breath. "No. It's not just small stuff." He nodded toward the valley. "A skew, a *significantly deviated* skew," Andrew paused in emphasis as he lowered his eyes and shook his head, "means seeing municipal death camps in America. A skew means driving a truck powered by human grease." Andrew looked up. "And a skew means it's 2018, but Las Vegas isn't a glowing crater - *yet*." He gave me a wry look. "Sorry. I meant to say *Los* Vegas. Spanish here also seems to be kinda odd...but as for the world in general, I'm not sure that it's extremely different. The tech level is about what I would expect. Maybe if things had held together for five or six more years cells might exist, though estimating zero-point regression isn't really my specialty."

"*Cells?* You mean beepers, right?" I asked. "I remember those. First, the cops and drug dealers had them, and then everyone wore them on their belts. When the world went down, they didn't work anymore. The phone lines also went dead around the same time."

"No. I'm talking about little cellular phones. On delayed or stop-collapse worldlines, they typically emerge a year or two after beepers."

"I remember cellular phones too," I replied, "but they were huge. The user had to lug around a briefcase power pack."

"Yeah, those were the early models. Then they become really small. Everybody gets one. You can go into restaurants or stores and everyone is on the phone. Lots of one-sided conversations, all the time. For those worldlines, the entire planet is like an obnoxious call center."

I envisioned a world of self-important assholes walking around as they seemed to carry on conversations with themselves. "Sounds kind of annoying," I said.

"It is. The internet and cell networks are great though, while they last. The governments usually censor things or shut it all down around 2016 or 2017."

"I remember the internet," I said. "It *was* great, but it was a pain-in-the-ass to sign up at the ULVN computer center when I was in college, though I was lucky enough to have a computer in my own classroom when I started teaching."

Andrew gave a half-smile. "On later worldlines *everyone* has a computer. They become cheap and common. People can surf the 'net on their phones or close their eyes and use implants."

"Implants? Like surgical implants?"

"Yeah. Subdermal neural interfaces."

"Like a transponder? Or a chip tracker?"

"Somewhat. Same general idea, but a helluva lot more range. Global, in fact."

"That's pretty significant," I said, "like some major sci-fi."

Andrew shrugged. "One future giveth and another taketh away," he said. "A hell of a lot of taking has been done here, but this world is still just a skewed variant of a general theme. Given a chance at zero-avoidance, your worldline and my own might even have entered into the same event class." Andrew shook his head. "I guess it's a little late for that, though. Still...it's interesting to see what the fabled Lost Wages actually looked like - even if it's really an alternate version from your universe. Our realities may not be siblings, but they're definitely cousins."

"Maybe *second* cousins," I mused. "You've mentioned a lot of differences. You also seemed pretty surprised when I told you that 9/11 happened in 1996."

"Well, sure. That's five years sooner than..." Andrew's voice trailed off. He looked up for a moment, and then back at me. "I think what you're getting at is something that people in my line of work call an 'unlocked dimensional algorithm' - but this world, as bad as it is, still doesn't qualify for that label."

"Unlocked? That doesn't sound very high-tech."

"It's the next step beyond a skew," explained Andrew. "It means that your C-205 unit has failed to screen out the freak shows of infinity. Instead of a layover in somebody else's different-but-recognizable twist, you get a one-way ticket to the carnie trailer. You're dead because in 1985 a herd of triceratops stampeded you. You're dead because you displaced to a worldline where Earth's atmosphere lacked oxygen, or maybe your unit performed an inaccurate gravity trace and the planet is thousands of miles away while your frozen and exploded ass floats through the space that it occupied hours before."

I nodded. "Well, that...that sounds like a bad way to go." I made a hobo knuckle, wiped the tin clean, and sucked the grease off the back of my finger. "I guess it's safe to say that you've never been caught in one of those unlocked-whatevers. But how many skews have you seen?"

Andrew cocked his head. "Me? This world popped my cherry."

"What?"

"Hell, yes! I'm making it up as I go, just like you and the rest of the natives."

It was my turn to be taken aback. "But I thought--"

Andrew sighed. "You thought that I was an old hand at this?" Andrew's head dipped and his shoulders sagged as he sadly laughed. "I've piloted twenty-seven displacements, but all to past idents within my own worldline's event class." Andrew noticed my puzzlement. *"Identicals,"* he explained, "are the opposites of unlocks. They're easy missions to worldlines of insignificant variance - realities whose only differences are random and meaningless things like some eleven-year-old kid in Tulsa, back in 1980, picking chocolate instead of vanilla when the ice cream truck came up his street." Andrew paused and turned his eyes in the direction of Los Vegas. "But it's not *that* strange here," he added. "How else could I have known about you? Or this place? Lake Meade is a hell of a long way from Fort Tampa."

"Yeah," I agreed. "But not much further than an old Philadelphia shipyard or Camp Hero."

Andrew shrugged. "Vegas was a surer bet...so to speak."

"But you could have gone to...*a Vegas*...that was more like your own."

"That would have been easier," agreed Andrew, "though I have to say that *my* world's Vegas is nothing but a glass-rimmed gamma field. Understand that a singularity collapse isn't like reading a road map and picking a detour. When I got the failure warning, I didn't believe it. I thought it was a hardware fuckup or a programming glitch." Andrew let out a bitter chuckle. "For a second, I didn't even know what was happening. Then I had to wrestle with the computer as hard and as fast as I could just to get through to this worldline. Now I know how a dead stick feels to an airplane pilot. Bumpy landings on highways and fields look pretty damn good when compared to flaming wreckage."

"Or charging dinosaurs," I added. "So any landing that you can walk away from is a good landing? Or a good *displacement,* I mean?"

Andrew nodded. "That's how it felt at first, but after a few days here I started to wonder about frying pans and fires. And whether or not I'll walk away remains to be seen. No offense, but your reality isn't exactly a picnic."

"Well, at least *this* world hasn't had a nuclear war."

"True. But it sprayed weaponized smallpox on a generation of unvaccinated kids and now TSA pagan-Nazis are turning people into bio-diesel."

I had no rejoinder, so after a few moments I changed the subject. "How many missions did B-17 pilots have to complete before they could go home?" I asked.

Andrew smiled. "I don't know the answer to your question, but I like the comparison. Unlike me, I think that those men got extremely paranoid when the ends of their tours approached. Maybe I'll paint *Memphis Belle* on the side of my C-205 - that is, if I ever see it again." "What's a Memphis bell?"

Andrew looked at me. "Are you kidding?" he asked, but I could only shrug. Andrew gave a small sigh. "Well, I guess we've just discovered another little difference. Where I come from, the *Memphis Belle* was a B-17 bomber flown by one of the most famous aircrews of the First World War."

"A B-17 in the *First* World War?"

"That's right."

We both opened our mouths to say something, but we just shook our heads. Andrew continued to eat, but after a few moments he spoke again. "Quantum variance is the engine of multiverse expansion," he said. "It's constantly growing in ways that the human mind can't understand or even observe, so don't expect to find meaning within the process." Andrew ate his last grasshopper and continued. "Forget all of the butterfly and tsunami bullshit, because reality lacks evolutionary purpose. It's just a string theory virus that begs for any stupid excuse to spew out slightly-mutated copies of itself. Watch," he said. "Want to see a new universe created right before your eyes? This is how easy it is. I can pick up a rock," Andrew said, as he pointed at a stone a few feet away, "or I can leave it on the ground. Whatever choice I make will branch the multiverse innumerable times, but what are the actual consequences?" Andrew leaned far to the right and stretched out his hand. The second his fingers clutched the rock there was a small explosion of dust as a bullet narrowly missed Andrew's head and ricocheted off the ground.

29

Now, Maybe It's Just Me, But I Believe We're Gonna Have To Get Medieval On ~~Your~~ *The TSA's* Buttocks

That's How You're Gonna Beat 'Em, ~~Butch~~ *Jack*. They Keep Underestimating ~~You~~
Your Psych Inventory

June 2018

The situation took me back to a time when Dave Kitts, Rob Hardesty, and I had been pinned down in a South Korean aircraft shelter by a simulated enemy force. The present scenario, however, featured a boulder instead of a concrete shelter, and the bullets were real.

"Goddamn it," muttered Andrew from a low crouch. "These dipshits are complete amateurs, but it's the amateurs that you have to watch out for. I *chose* this camp because only an idiot would attempt an uphill assault."

I nodded. I wouldn't have expected the Blackshirts to possess the balls, or maybe the stupidity, to try their present maneuver, either.

"I can't lift-and-shift fire with this 'sixteen - at least not over the top of this rock," said Andrew.

"Can you just hold it up and shoot, but keep the rest of your body behind cover?" I asked.

Andrew shot me a scornful look that told me the TSA scouts weren't the only ones whom he regarded as amateurs. Well, Andrew may have accurately regarded me as an infantry neophyte, but that didn't mean that I hadn't once been in the company of the best. I remembered Airman Jaeger, the former neo-Nazi whom I had tutored by the light of a basic training flashlight, and how he had saved my ass at Pyeongtaek during the following year - but then my thoughts were abruptly interrupted by a loud blast between the TSA's position and the boulder.

Andrew and I ducked even lower as pebbles and dirt rained down. "Christ, I didn't know that the TSA still had grenades!" I exclaimed.

"They'll lob the next one over the rock," said Andrew. "We're gonna have to make a run for it, Jack."

I gave Andrew an incredulous look. "That's suicide! We'll be shredded the second we come out from cover!"

"Either that, or bend over and spread your ass cheeks for the next grenade. Got a better idea?"

"Yeah, maybe I do," I replied.

Airman Jaeger jumped up and down in the back of my mind. *"Simmerath, you can handle this!"* **he bellowed.** *"Remember what I taught you!"*

I did remember. "Is there a rock behind those scarheads?"

"Yeah," said Andrew.

"Take the pisser. Give me the 'sixteen.'"

Andrew just looked at me.

"Gimme the fucking rifle! I'm gonna shoot from the side," I said.

"You don't have a target," Andrew said, as he slowly handed over his weapon.

"Not directly, but they can't see me, either." I cradled the rifle and snaked through the dirt to the boulder's edge. I slowly stuck the muzzle out from behind the rock and took aim at a large boulder that I knew was behind the TSA position. I made some mental geometric calculations and emptied the magazine, which probably wasn't necessary, since I likely hit the TSA men within the first five shots. I knew that I had succeeded when the next grenade went off *behind* the scarhead's rock. *They had pulled the pin and were about to toss it*, I thought.

I didn't have to explain what had happened to Andrew, since his seasoned veteran's instinct had already figured it out. He shook his head in disbelief, but also in relief. "Well, I guess it takes an amateur to deal with other amateurs," he said.

* * *

We decided to leave our camp because we found

a tattletale dynamo radio and a hand-held transponder pulse tracker in the TSA scouts' packs. Andrew and I also figured that, somewhere among their grenade-blasted body parts, there were more "here-they-are, we-found-their-camp" transponder chips...exactly like the one that Andrew was about to remove from my right arm.

Andrew cursed. "I forgot about those damned trackers," he growled, as he continued to whet his blade. "This is gonna hurt like a bitch. The camp torturers deliberately shoot their slave tags into a spot near the ulnar nerve to make it hell to remove. Without anesthesia, most men pass out from the pain."

I looked at Andrew and wondered why he would tell me such a thing. When his surprise right turned out my lights, I had an answer.

* * *

Andrew splashed water on my face from a TSA canteen and I spluttered as I regained consciousness. I was flat on my back with a throbbing left temple and a right arm that felt like it was connected to a car battery.

"I didn't want to risk breaking your cheek, but I had to put you down," said Andrew. Your eye is turning black, but I don't think that it'll swell too much."

I groggily tried to sit up, but as soon as I put weight on my right arm a sharp jolt made me collapse. I clutched my arm, rolled onto my side, and tried to squeeze away the pain.

"I know it hurts, but I'm glad that you feel it," Andrew continued. "That means I didn't cut the nerve." I rocked back and forth on the ground and gingerly released the pressure on my arm. When I next tried to sit up, I did so with my left arm only. I was mildly pissed at Andrew, but I knew that his options had been limited. "It'll heal in a few days," he said, as he pulled up his sleeve and showed me a scar on his own arm.

You're Not Fit To Be In The Same Camp With A Man Like ~~Captain Tuttle~~ *Sergeant Major Carlssin!*

- *I see that you've taken off the bandage.*
- Yeah. My arm's okay.
- *Are you ready for this?*
- As ready as I'll ever be, I guess. Your uniform's passable.
- *Yours, too. Alright, let's go through it one more time.*
- Okay. I'll walk the tracks behind the Plaza until I get to the old Amtrak annex.
- *And then?*
- I'll go through to the Greyhound bus bays and hide. I'll make sure that your machine is there and that the pickup is ready to go.
- *We don't have much of a plan, Jack.*
- No shit. We don't have much of *anything.*
- *Tell me what you'll do if I don't come down the tracks before dawn.*
- I'll sneak out again, head to your workshop, and get the detonator. And I'll definitely remember the booby traps.
- *Good. The gas is going to cause a huge amount of chaos, so I think that if you time it right, you can use the disruption to escape. If I don't make it back, forget about me. The same goes for you. If you're not in the bay when I get there, I'm going to start the countdown and leave anyway.*
- Yeah, well...I'm still not convinced that splitting up is such a great idea.
- *Like I said: It'll maximize the chances of at least part of this so-called "plan's" success. If you have to get the detonator yourself, I want you to go back to Fremont and start the countdown. If the detonator*

*is missing, then just take the pickup and the C-205
and get your ass to the plane. The pickup has an
old-style steering column and you should be able to
hot-wire it easily enough. There aren't any
checkpoints along the tracks, so you can get far
south and away before they even know what's
happened - especially if Fremont becomes a gas
chamber.*

- Why would I go to the plane without *you?* I don't
  know how to use a time machine.
- *There's a tech order with the unit. I think that if
  you followed the basic sequence you could handle a
  simple Point A-to-Point-B displacement. It's either
  that, or just keep going and take your chances with
  the California or Arizona TSA.*
- How am I supposed to get the pickup out of the
  terminal?
- *The bay doors likely have roller locks, so you'll
  have to knock them off of their guides with
  the truck bed. They may be big, but they're just
  garage doors.*
- Just smash through?!
- *Yes. Unless you want to politely ask Plaza CQ for
  the terminal keys.*
- If I ram through a bay door, I'll alert every guard in
  the Plaza!
- *Probably. So you'd better get it right the first time
  and stomp on the gas. Look Jack, that's all I've got.
  Do you have a better plan?*
- No. But I can't just drive away. You know that.
- *I realize that your friend and the rest of the kippies
  are still up on Fremont...and I don't know how
  you'll choose to handle that. But do something.
  Just try, Jack. Don't let these TSA fucks beat us
  both. At least one of us has to make it out.*

We've Traced The Call, And It's Coming From ~~Inside The House~~ *The Old Bus Terminal!*

July 2018 (2-of-11)

I spotted a single bored sentry making rounds behind the Plaza, so I crept down the ditch on the other side of the tracks and paused like a person waiting for an oscillating lawn sprinkler to finish its sweep. The sentry's pace was as regular as a machine, and when he disappeared at one end of his patrol, I made for the old Amtrak station that connected to the defunct Greyhound bus terminal. I carried a metal pry bar and the pisser. I quickly and silently twisted the bar through light chains on a side door until they snapped.

The train station's hall was empty, silent, and musty. It was dark and there was garbage on the floor. I followed the arrows on the Greyhound signs until I was inside the similarly abandoned bus terminal.

As I crept through the dispatch office I noticed a glowing red light on one of the dusty desk phones. Maybe the phone still waited for updates on Phoenix and LA bus departures, or perhaps it wanted to tell someone about traffic conditions back in the summer of 1997. The telephone was an isolated Imperial Japanese soldier who had sat alone for decades faithfully awaiting Emperor Hirohito's orders.

I picked up the receiver.

The telephone was also a booby trap, but only for boobies who didn't think. If I had used my brain, I would have realized that there was a phone board somewhere, and that a TSA drone would be monitoring lines. I, however, could only think of how clever I would be if I rang the kippy-jo floor and told Grace to come down to the old bus station. Then we could wait for Andrew to arrive with the radio detonator, and as the three of us drove off into the happily-ever-after sunset, Fremont

Street would become a poison gas-choked hell...after, of course, Grace had directed her kippies to go out on remote assignments.

Perfect.

Wait - what are "boobies", anyway?
Aren't boobies just big, stupid, and easily-killed birds?
Are they like dodos?
Are boobies also extinct?

I'd ask one of these Blackshirts, except I think that they'd rather point their rifles at me instead of reply to my ornithological queries.

But The Great Ones – Dahmer, Gacy, Bundy – They Did It Because It *Excited* Them

July 2018 (3-of-11)

I stood in the living room of Colonel Carl Wheat's Plaza suite with three guards behind me. One of them had my pisser and another held my pry bar.

Carl paced back and forth as he looked me over. "Well, I see that time spares none of us," he remarked, "though I have to admit that you appear to be in better condition than you were when I saw you at DS-21. You're certainly not the hardy youngster I once knew, but for an old unscarred camp escapee, you look well." A guard stepped forward and handed Carl my papers. "Ah. *Follower Candidate Wheeler, Everett.*" Carl read in a mocking tone as he waved the guards out of the suite.

"Aren't you going to tie me up or something?" I asked.

Carl smiled and shook his head. "Not...*yet.* Please, sit." He took out his .357 and motioned at a leather-upholstered chair in a way that reminded me of David Karradine telling Uma Thurston to have a seat at the end of *Kill William, Volume 2.* Carl kept the gun trained on me as he took an opposite seat, and with his left hand Carl reached into his pocket and pulled out something that looked like a packet of disposable baby wipes. Carl ripped the packet open with his teeth and I smelled alcohol. He removed a tissue and began to wipe his face. "I wonder what you're thinking," Carl said. "Do you expect me to give an impersonation, or maybe tell some 'corndog' jokes?"

"No."

Carl kept smiling. "There's not much room in the world these days for such nonsense. There's a lot of room for art, though. Take that chair you're sitting on.

It's a soft and supple masterpiece, and covered in the skin of three young men whom I had as guests out at the camp." I gave no reaction, though I wanted to wash every part of my body that had touched the human upholstery.

"I'm a dedicated artist now," continued Carl, "not a jester or an idealistic young fool. I produce handmade pieces, one at a time. There's a greater and greater place for my touch in this world, now that mass-produced Philistine staples like war and chemtrails are no longer in vogue."

I looked at Carl. "I once knew someone who resembled you, but that person has been gone for a long time."

"Yes," agreed the TSA colonel. "A *very* long time. He was a ridiculous boy and a proto-creature who existed only to serve as a vessel of evolution. He became *me.* You, however, haven't kept up with the world. You're old and ragged, and if it were not for the work of your superior Nazi ancestor, you would have already provided a TSA truck with a few more miles per gallon." Carl paused as he pulled a fresh wipe out of the package and continued to clean his face. "You're still useful though, since our mutual time-traveling friend, when interviewed, provided me with all of the information that I requested, with the exception of where to find a precious sliver of material on a certain aircraft…but I assume that you're already aware of that."

"Andrew said that you weren't interested in using his machine," I responded. "He said you wanted to make some kind of nuclear bomb."

Carl nodded. "I'm quite happy to keep Sergeant Major Carlssin's exhibit in my collection, but only for display purposes."

"Nukes seem to contradict your aesthetic," I observed.

"Oh, completely," said Carl with an indignant expression. "Weapons of mass destruction must be regarded as brutish tools only. They don't offer room for creativity."

"My God," I breathed. "You've become a mass-serial killer."

"No," asserted Carl. "I abhor the chaotic techniques of serial killers. They're undisciplined graffiti artists and untutored followers of Grandma Moses - *quaint*, yes - but ultimately of limited folk interest." Carl scoffed as he looked around the suite. "I admit that occasionally there's a natural artist born among them, but the Geins and Greenes are usually lost in a sea of faceless amateurs who hone their skills with all of the subtlety and finesse of china shop bulls. With them, it's always frantic stalking or opportunistic hunting, and either way, the end result is hasty and unsavored experience. Also," added Carl, "now that the world takes human disappearance in stride, most of the thrill is gone, for both the artist and his following. When no one comes around to ask deliciously public and painful questions, why bother?"

I had nothing to say and Carl seemed to take my silence as dumb insolence. His voice rose in slight irritation. "Jack, we all die - but a memorable death enables one to live on through a metaphysically artistic statement. You probably won't believe this, but I don't view myself as having much in common with other TSA officers." As if to make his point, Carl lifted the towelette that he had used to wipe his cheek. With each pass Carl's smallpox blotches had faded and the wipe was stained with what I guessed to be some kind of purple ink.

As I had done inside DS-21, I again considered the TSA and the motivations of its worms - and as before, I wondered why I was still alive. I figured that nothing really mattered at this point, so I just spoke my mind: "I expect that you're going to turn me into some kind of 'masterpiece', since you already know where the 'selenide is." I paused. "Carl, I wish that I had known back in Korea what you would eventually become. I would have choked you while you were drunk or pushed you down the barracks stairs."

Carl wore a disgusted expression. "That's really disappointing. Really, really uninspired. Your atrophied imagination hardly makes scooping out your brain worthwhile. In fact," Carl continued, "when I'm done interviewing you, perhaps I'll simply hand you over to the guards for swift and efficient disposal." Carl spoke like a smug man who believed that he had delivered the worst of insults.

"That's what I'm getting at," I replied. "I'm not necessary for your entertainment or need for information, so...*what,* then?"

"Ah. Well, I suppose that I *could* order a large detail of men to spend years, possibly, disassembling the B-29, inch-by-painstaking-inch, but since my designs require discretion and TSA ranks are peppered with informants, it wouldn't be the safest utilization of manpower. I don't believe that LaPin and her brigadiers would be particularly impressed if they caught wind of my accelerated ascendance scheme."

"I only know what you know," I said. "The 'selenide is onboard, but I don't know where."

Carl's smile twisted into a grotesque grin. "No. *Of course* you don't." He kept the .357 leveled on me as he stood. "On your feet. I'm taking you downstairs for questioning. Try not to bore me."

I did as instructed, but as I walked to the door, I could sense the pace and proximity of Carl's gait. I remembered this same man, many years before, showing me how to smash bones in a human foot, and without even really thinking I unexpectedly backed up a half step. When the inner edge of my heel was parallel with Carl's own boots I performed a half-pivot with my pelvis, slammed my foot down along his shin, and showed him that I still recalled his lessons from so long ago.

That was the easy part. Grabbing the gun was a little tougher. I wasn't nearly as strong and fast as Andrew had been when he had seized the .357 in the Plaza elevator, but I did the best that I could and managed to wrench the revolver away without a shot being fired. I was surprised to discover that I was able to manhandle Carl so easily, but I didn't want to risk grappling with him. When Carl went down I kicked him in the head and wondered if I had KO'd him as quickly as Andrew had KO'd me before he cut the transponder out of my arm.

Could Find My *(Other)* Way To Mariana

Maybe I should have killed Carl...but I couldn't. Even as I had raised the .357's butt to break his skull in a pistol-whipping execution, I knew that I couldn't do it. Not like that, anyway. Neither could I go into the suite's kitchen for a knife, or even pull the cord out of one of the hotel lamps and twist it around Carl's neck. The soul under that unconscious face had once been a friend well, wait a minute. When I remembered the torture and murders out at DS-21, I realized that there *wasn't* a soul underneath that face. True, Carl had once been my friend, but evil influences had long since squeezed that young spirit from Carl's body. Carl had become a flesh memorial for his long-vacant humanity, and perhaps killing Carl - that is, smashing the talking cenotaph - would be disrespectful to the memory of...*Carl.*

No, no, I had it backwards. Ending the old abomination was *exactly* the best way to honor Carl's memory. I decided avenge the bright and kind young man whom I had once known by eliminating the subsuming impostor.

I knew that I was committing a classic movie mistake when I slowly lowered the .357 and stood up. In the back of my mind, moviegoers screamed at a cinema screen:

> - **Break his fucking skull and get the hell out of there!**
> - **Shoot him! Shoot him! No, wait, the guards will hear - strangle him!**
> - **C'mon! Don't hog the popcorn.**

Sometimes between the midpoint and the end of a movie a plot device is employed to turn the tables on the Bad Guy. Now the Bad Guy is at the mercy of the Good Guy, but the dipshit Good Guy, in his mentally-challenged paladin's magnanimity, doesn't dispatch the Bad Guy....and we all know that the Bad Guy comes back.

> *- A dirty move you learned from Carl thirty years ago? That's the clever plot device?*
> *- Really? C'mon. Who the hell wrote this?*

Shut up. It had worked, hadn't it?
I decided to make sure that the piece of shit lying on the floor didn't return for some kind of end chapter showdown, and I decided to do it with style. The audience might not be pleased, but I knew what I was doing. Carl would get his lungs fried along with the rest. This was one time when the good guy had things covered. Or blanketed, rather, in deadly gas.

> *- Awww! Are you fucking kidding me? Why don't you drop him into a vat of piranhas? Or sharks with lasers on their heads?*
> *- Just shoot the bastard! Then shoot the guards!*
> *- Jack, you idiot! Don't you know that Carl is gonna get away somehow?*

* * *

I duct-taped Carl to a chair and changed into one of his uniforms. When I had entered Carl's bedroom I was sickened, though not by any grotesque discoveries therein. Rather, the bed was huge, soft, and fresh, and Carl appeared to be about halfway through a spy novel on his nightstand. There was a gun safe in one corner, and an overhead fan slowly turned. The bedroom furniture was first-rate hardwood, including a small liquor rack that contained decent whiskies - none of which, of course, had been bottled after that summer when the Pied Piper had pranced through Vegas.
I felt like I was going to vomit. This was where Carl went after a day out at DS-21. This was where he washed off the blood and ordered up his supper, after which he could pour a nice little snifter and curl up with a book.
I threw open Carl's closet door, walked inside, and

saw racks of suits, jeans, shirts and a row of crisp TSA uniforms. I took one of the black goon suits off a hanger and put it on. Like the getup that I had worn while working with Andrew, Carl's TSA shroud didn't sear my skin or make me break out in boils. Instead, it had a nice clean smell. That didn't matter, though. I should have been used to TSA uniforms, but it was still tough to get my mind around what I was wearing. "Get over it," I muttered to myself in a hard voice, "or you're fucking dead. If you don't play the part of a TSA colonel, it's five-to-one, one-in-five."

I looked in the bedroom mirror and noticed that Carl's uniform was loose on my skinny body. The shirt bore a nametag, though I remembered that all of the officer uniforms that I had seen in the death camps were anonymous. I guessed that Carl and rest of the TSA brass suspended their identities within the camps, but affixed names when circulating through the outside world. That made sense. I'd heard that Barbie and Mengele did the same, though it did no good for those who weren't able to slip off to La Falda. *Faces* were picked out at Nuremberg, not *names.*

But what was I going to do about the nametag? I wondered if I should just chance it. *No,* I thought. *If I'm seen around here wearing a colonel's uniform that reads "Wheat," I'm dead. Everyone knows that bastard.* For a moment I was tempted to just put on the uniform that I had been wearing, but again dismissed that idea when I realized that its dirty state would be even more of an attention magnet than a strange nametag. I wasn't sure what to do. Maybe I could just tear off the tag like an officer coming back from the camps, or maybe I could wear Carl's uniform and act like a haughty O-6 who kept a clipboard pressed to his chest. I would figure something out. I still had some time.

I went into Carl's bathroom. If I was really going to march out in TSA eagles, then my face and hair would have to look the part. I found a straight razor and a lather cup. I also located some small grooming scissors in a drawer under the sink, along with a hand-held mirror that I could use with the bathroom mirror for the sides and back.

Wait! What the hell was that? An electric razor! With a hair and beard attachment. Good.

I busted out a quickie buzz. After having trimmed up a bit, my sun-browned visage didn't especially stand out. But that, I realized, wasn't actually the problem. If I didn't get my head right, I couldn't walk among these scum and *not* stand out, no matter how many officer uniforms I donned or how closely I shaved. My attitude and soul were from a different generation and a different time. They would sniff me out like zombies sensing the presence of living brains. There was no way in hell that I could just wash up, put on a clean uniform, and skip out the door. Those two young goons standing outside would still recognize me.

So what was I going to do? Try the balcony? Could I tie sheets together and lower myself to the next floor?

Sure! Brilliant! An old dumb-ass flailing from one of the Plaza's suites, swinging back and forth on knotted sheets, and right across from Fremont Street.

Awww, shucks. Nobody *would notice* that.

Well - *what?*

I leaned against the sink and rubbed my temple. I remembered the gun safe and again considered the two guards. I could roughly estimate, through the wall, where they stood.

What about the pisser? How about four fistfuls of lead through the doorframe? *Mmmm...no.* I could shoot through every pillow and cushion in the suite and still not deaden the black powder booms. Besides, the wall was probably just a few layers of sheetrock and aluminum, but metal studs and even shielded conduit made me doubt the pisser's power to take out the guards.

I took Carl's .357 out of its holster, swung out the cylinder, and removed a round: 125 grain hollow point. Expanding ammo wasn't ideal for what I has considering, but in a pinch it would still likely go through a suite wall.

* * *

I placed a small steak knife on the coffee table and sat down across from Carl. His gagged and glazed look didn't change.

"How's the foot?" I asked. "Not that I really give a damn. I ought to smash your other one, too." I studied Carl for a few seconds. His rather soft body had indicated, particularly when I snatched his revolver, that he had lived a life of relative ease. Carl looked like he had never missed a meal.

I picked up the knife and cut the tape and zip ties off of Carl's right wrist. He extended his fingers and made a few fists.

"Lose circulation?" I asked, as I put the knife down and handed Carl a pencil. "Take it. You might recognize it as being the one from your nightstand. This too," I added, as I placed a small pad of paper within Carl's reach.

I sat down again. "I'm just going to say this as simply as I can," I began. "I'm not the expert monster here. You're the one schooled in horror, but I'll do the best an amateur can if you don't cooperate. I want you to write the combination of your gun safe on the pad. Do it now."

Carl's free hand simply tossed the pencil to the floor. For the first time, his eyes changed from emptiness to contemptuous arrogance.

"I figured you'd do that," I said. I crossed my legs and leaned back on the couch. I closed my eyes until a whistling sound came from the kitchen. "Ah," I said. "I'll be right back."

I returned a few moments later. "It's been a long time since I've seen a working electric kettle," I said. The kettle emitted a low whistle as I set it on the coffee table.

As I sat down again I noticed that the contempt had disappeared from Carl's eyes. "I'm sure that I don't have to explain what's going to happen if you don't write the combination. Even if you live, you might want to consider the primitive state of medical care nowadays. Does the TSA have anyone on call who can perform skin grafts? Do you know where there are any antibiotics left that can treat post-burn infections? I don't." I was silent for a minute, then left the couch and picked up the pencil. "Don't forget that I've seen, firsthand, what you do for a living. Scalding might be a bit better than you deserve. As I recall, one of your favorite little 'artistic' tricks consists of scooping out eyes. I saw some big ladles in your kitchen, but decided to go with the hot water. Like I said, I'm an amateur." I placed the pencil back in Carl's hand and repositioned the paper. "Last chance."

Carl's eyes fell to the paper and he began to write. Then he laid the pencil down on the pad.

"Done?" I asked. Carl nodded slightly and I picked up the pad. It read: *25-02-73*.

The emotion in Carl's gaze changed again and his glaring eyes narrowed slightly. I grabbed Carl's wrist and taped it back to the chair. "That might be a bit much for an old man," I observed, "but you appear to have plenty of tape."

I moved to the back of the chair and tipped it onto its rear legs. Carl's fingers moved in slight panic and he tried to turn his head to see what I was doing. "Oh, did I forget to mention something?" I mockingly asked. "Ah, let me take a moment to explain." I lowered the chair's front legs and walked back around into Carl's view. "I'm going to drag you down the hall and into the bedroom. Then I'm going to place you in front of the safe." I held up the roll of duct tape. "You seem to have a lot of this, so I'm going to run a long twisted strip from the safe's door lever, down the hall, and into the living room. Then I'm going to dial the combination, go to the other end of the suite, and pull the tape...with you sitting squarely in front of the door when it swings open, of course."

Carl struggled and made frantic muffled sounds as he thrashed his head and madly worked his fingers. "I'm getting a little tired of doing this," I commented, as once again I cut Carl's hand free and gave him the pencil and pad. It only took a moment for Carl to scribble a second message: *FFFg in coffee cans. Nails and ball bearings.*

"I counted on something like that," I said. "Go on." Carl glanced at me, then wrote: *Under couch. Same combo.*

It took some effort for me to get the heavy couch away from the wall. I had to move one end and then the other untll I saw two places where the suite flooring had been sliced. I flipped back a large section of loose carpet and saw a floor safe.

25-02-73. Bingo.

Carl's safe wasn't big, but it held a nice weapon selection. There was even a mint-looking H&K G3! I wondered where Carl had found it. I needed something a bit more discrete, however, so I decided on a silenced folding Krinkov and a couple banana mags to compliment the .357.

I still didn't know how I was going to escape, but I hoped that I'd think of something in the shower. I needed to put on another one of Carl's clean uniforms because my impromptu haircut had left the first one covered with gray bristles.

Let Me Tell You What's Gonna Happen... This Way, You Can Prepare Yourself

July 2018 (5-of-11)

Seeing panties and a bra on the bathroom floor when I showered reminded me of Grace and the Pleasure Brigades. I wondered where the term "kippy-jo" had come from, and what it actually meant.

There were a couple long black hairs on the bra, so I figured that Carl hadn't taken up cross-dressing along with genocide. Of course these pigs would have separate menus for food and fun! How naïve of me. The underwear was that of an adult, so at least Carl hadn't developed a taste for the youngest kippies...though that really wouldn't have mattered much when considering the worth of one already so damned.

I put on another uniform and found a new sealed hotel toothbrush and a small tube of toothpaste, both of which I used. As I walked out of the bathroom I slipped the tube and toothbrush into my pocket. It had been a hell of a long time since I had experienced minty freshness.

I left the master bath, but paused in Carl's bedroom because I noticed some framed pictures. I stood and stared at one for a long moment, then took it off the wall and flung it across the room. The glass exploded against the opposite wall and showered fragments over the bed and Carl's bookcase. After another long moment, I slowly took down the other pictures and carried them into the living room.

I sat on the sofa as I spoke to the gagged TSA colonel. "Have you gotten lice in the last twenty years?" I asked. "*I* have. More than once. Fleas, too. Fleas are worse than lice, I think. Those bites take much longer to heal." I paused. "No, you probably haven't had mites, lice, ticks, fleas, or anything else that the rest of us have had to deal with. When I used your shampoo I thought about that." I easily met Carl's stare as I continued speaking. I took a deep breath as I ran my fingers over my fresh-smelling gray buzzcut and rubbed my smooth chin. "Oh, and thanks for another uniform, by the way."

I left Carl, went to the kitchen, and came back with two cold chicken legs. I set the plate on my lap and began to eat. "I like the way everything in this suite works - the water, the refrigerator, the lights...it's almost like the world never went to shit," I commented between chews. "I'm surprised that you didn't have more in the fridge, though. A top monster like yourself probably has food brought up all the time." I picked up a leg, stripped off the meat, and dropped the bone onto the plate. I smiled at Carl as I wiped chicken grease on his sofa, then I leaned back and spread my arms out over the tops of the cushions. For a moment I considered getting up, walking over to Carl's human-leather chair, and wiping my hands on it too, just to piss him off...but I still didn't want to touch that foul thing.

I wasn't, however, averse to kicking Carl's broken foot. "Did you like that little move?" I asked. "I wonder if you remember teaching me how to do it back at Pyeongtaek?" Carl's face contorted in silent pain, but only for a moment, and then emptiness returned to his eyes.

If we had been in the film *Sinner City,* I would have been Marv and Carl would have been Kevin, and this would have been the scene in which Marv has already amputated Kevin's limbs, but Kevin just sits on the ground with a blank look while Marv taunts him. I had the same luck in getting a response from Carl that Marv had experienced with Kevin. Carl didn't try to squirm or make any muffled sounds. He just looked at me.

Is he bored? I wondered.

"I noticed a few things about you when I put your ass into that chair," I said. "You're not in very good shape. We're the same age, but I've kept active. I guess everyone has to nowadays, young and old - unless they're a TSA officer." I paused. "But I suppose you don't have to be in good condition to tear out fingernails and drill out eyeballs...especially if your victim is strapped into a chair."

I leaned over and picked up one of the framed pictures. "When I was changing into this," I said, as I nodded downward at the TSA uniform, "I noticed that you had some school photos. Funny. I never would have guessed that you were working in a district high school." I paused. "I can't help but wonder what kind of crap you stuffed into your kids' heads. What were you, an art specialist?" I asked, as I tossed the frame back on the table and left the room.

I Ain't Lookin' Over My Shoulder The Rest Of My Days

July
2018
(6-of-11)

I drew large "Xs" on the interior walls near both sides of the suite entrance. I had the silenced Krinkov and a mag of steel-core Russian shorts ready to rock and roll. I had goofed off with enough AK copies in my time to remember that, without a muzzle break and even in rapid-semi mode, the barrel would climb up and to the right. The full-auto Krinkov had a silencer on it, so I visualized myself releasing bursts that would impact the wall near the lower left portion of each X and make a diagonal path upward. On the other side of the wall this would translate into shooting each man in the back, beginning with his left hip, upward across the left kidney and mid-spine, through the right lung, and finishing the burst in the right shoulder. Then I would move to the next side, so fast that the other TSA drone couldn't even react when his buddy's guts sprayed out onto the Plaza's hall carpet.

Raise the weapon. Look down the sights. Practice. See the X. Lift the sights up and across the X, imagine the recoil, and quickly shift to the other target.

Ridiculous.

This can't work. I might as well start thinking about climbing out the window on bed sheets again.

I lowered the Krinkov.

Let's just say that I manage to take out the goons. Then what? There's foot traffic all over the suite level. When they brought me up here we walked by a number of people in the halls. There are other TSA bigwigs in the suites, and there are guards posted at other doors.

I'm sure that the other addle-brain peons would notice two of their fellows face-down in the corridor. The scumbags would come running and I'd be screwed.

I paced around the suite. I walked through the kitchen, down the hall, and across the living room. I noticed that Carl's eyes followed me, so I stopped.

"Enjoying this?" I asked. "Do you think you're going to make it through this day alive?" I walked over, placed the Krinkov on the couch, and sat down. Contempt had returned to Carl's eyes.

"You're not," I flatly stated. "But I don't plan on being here when you die. I'm not the one who's going to personally put you down, old friend. Do you know who will handle that little detail? All of the people you've rendered out and sold to Arizona and Utah. All the people you've pumped into fuel tanks. All the poor bastards whom the TSA has murdered and turned into bio-diesel." The lukewarm kettle still sat on the coffee table and I raised the spout to my lips for a long drink.

"Here's a chance for you to remember the crap that you've studied over the years," I continued, "you know, all of those techniques for exterminating mankind. I imagine that your knowledge base became pretty broad while you were moving up in the American intelligence community. Despite that little career break you took to masquerade as a teacher, I'd suppose that you were quite an asset. The TSA must have welcomed you with open arms."

I got up and, for the second time, grabbed the back of Carl's chair. This time I wasn't bluffing. I dragged the chair across the room, opened a sliding glass door, and pulled Carl out onto the suite balcony.

"Take a good look," I said. I didn't want to place Carl out so far that he might be spotted, but I definitely wanted to make sure that he could see Fremont Street. I knelt to the level of Carl's bound and gagged head to make sure that he had a good view.

Down the street, in the space between the Fremont Street Experience projection hood and the facings of hotels, the neon stripper-cowgirl sign of Glitter Gulch hovered in surreal juxtaposition over a passing platoon of black-clad TSA. Handcarts and bicycles and a few bio diesel trucks made their way up and down the street before disappearing under Fremont Street's artificial sky.

"Alright then, *Colonel* Wheat. Let's talk about standard tear gas canisters. Plain old military M-47R cans...you remember that shit, don't you? CS gas? It's too fancy, though. Let's get primitive. Let's go back in history to, say, World War I and II? Mustard gas, and all that other fun stuff. Sarin, tabun, and the other toys of early chem warfare."

I had the fuckpig's attention. He didn't yet know where I was going with this, but he knew that I was being on the level. Carl had tortured too many people who would have said anything to make him stop his cruelties, so he could recognize a bullshitter. He also knew when someone was laying it out straight.

"You know, despite all of the controls and all of the thuggish horseshit, you TSA pukes really dropped the ball. You thought that you had it all figured out, but nobody stopped to consider the chemical byproducts of your little fuel conversion operation. Well, here's a clue: If you visit any of the first-stage soaper plants, the piles of glycerin that should be there are missing." I put on a mystified yet mocking expression. I wrinkled my brow and tapped my index finger against my chin. "Gosh, now *where* could all of that glycerin be?"

Got him, I thought. When the flash of realization appeared in Carl's eyes, I felt evil, dark, and satisfied. He had remembered some basic chemistry and guessed that my point didn't involve supple skin and glowing complexions.

"Oh well," I continued, in my put-on tone. "It doesn't matter....unless someone in this dumbed-down death cult knows that the easiest way to release acrolein fumes is to burn glycerin." I dropped my cutesy routine and spoke in a hard voice. "Shitloads of it," I continued, "dumped down Fremont elevator shafts. I know that quartermaster issues aren't your area of expertise, but one of the elevators in The Five Queens won't even go down to the basement anymore. Luckily for me, TSA doesn't have particularly high building maintenance priorities." I looked out over Fremont. Yes, I was probably making *two* huge movie mistakes: First, I wasn't going to personally and directly dispatch the bad guy, and now I had tipped my hand before shit had actually gone down.

"When the TSA seized this area and kicked everybody else out, they did the locals a favor," I said. "Tonight, any creature that draws a naked breath within three blocks of Fremont won't see the dawn, and there hasn't been a functioning gas mask or MOPP suit around for twenty years." I turned back to Carl. "This was all Andrew's idea, by the way. I think that it's a sad commentary on the occupants of this reality. While the Vegas sheeple waited for you TSA shitbags to kick down their doors, only someone from another *universe* had enough balls to fight back." I looked down at another platoon that marched past the Glitter Gulch neon cowgirl. "This," I continued, "is what's going to happen."

"We found a bunch of old nitrate movies under The Huntridge Theater. Andrew made remote-detonation mercury-flare switches, wrapped them around the movie canisters, and hooked everything into elevator electrical systems. It might be a bit excessive, since Andrew has assured me that even if only half of our bombs go off, the objective will still be accomplished. I'm okay with overkill, though. Fremont Street needs to be dunged out, so I'm going to leave you right here to look out over the rest of the manure. Andrew told me that acro is more chemically basic than CS, so the air won't look like white tear gas. Maybe the Plaza's ventilation will get to you, in which case the show will be over, but if the Fremont fires start first, you'll see yellow smoke pouring out of every hotel window, and a dandelion-colored cloud will envelop everything. You'll have a minute or two to observe before the yellow wall drifts up to this suite." I paused to survey Fremont Street. "No more sadism, no more terror, and no more hell, not from you or your comrades. When that cloud comes, I hope it carries the faces and voices of everyone you've killed. No more feasts while everyone else starves, no more thugs at your command, no more fucking kippies whenever you feel like it--"

*- Wait. Wait! What did we just say? WHAT DID WE
JUST SAY?!*
- We said that we hoped the acrolein would be like a
big yellow avenging ghost that would carry--
- No! The other part! The "fucking" thing!
- Oh, that. Well, we just mentioned that Mr.
Scumbag here won't have kippies on tap
anymore --
*- That's it! That's the way out! Where's the suite
phone?*
- Here.
- Get CQ on the line.
- CQ?! What the hell are we doing?
- JUST SHUT UP AND WATCH.

* * *

- **Union Plaza Charge-of-Quarters, Follower Third
Class Jackson speaking. One moment to identify
your line, please...suite levels...ah, yes. Suite 1973.
How may I serve you, Colonel Wheat?**
*- Yes, I'm calling to authorize kip--uh, Pleasure
Brigade activities.*
- **Yes, sir. May I briefly leave the phone to check
the duty status of your usual entertainers?**
*- No, that won't be necessary. Listen up, follower.
Tonight I want something specific. I'm in the mood
for an older Asian female. In fact, I'll take one of
the Plaza house mothers. Make sure you get that
one right, because she's for me. I'm entertaining
tonight, so also send up two additional younger
females for my guests. Any race, and in their
twenties. Got that?*
- **I understand, sir, and I'll relay to the Pleasure
Brigade. Thank you for allowing me to serve you,
Colonel Wheat.**
* * *

Fifteen minutes later there was a buzz at the
intercom.

"Colonel Wheat, sir? There are some kippies out
here. They say you ordered them."

"Let the house mother in," I said in a muffled voice.

671

"Take the others back to your quarters. You and your cohort are relieved."

"S-sir, it's not time for security changeover on this floor--"

I barked out a stick to go with the kippy carrots: "Follower, you can be punished as easily as you can be rewarded. Think about that."

"Yes sir. Thank you, sir. Mother watches over you, sir."

Giant Rabbits, Tiny Steaks, And My *Kippumjo* Girl

July 2018 (7-of-11)

- *So you can get them out?*
- Yes. All I have to do is fake some requisition calls from outlying barracks.
- *And what about the others in The Five Queens?*
- That's who I'm talking about. I'm one of two HMs on duty in the Plaza tonight, so I can make up whatever nonsense I want.
- *And the guards up there?*
- Not a problem. They don't pay attention to scheduling. But why not tomorrow? I can make better preparations.
- *We don't have that much time. I'm not the one with the detonator, and the countdown could be moving forward as we speak. Do whatever you have to do to get them away from Fremont within...well, the next two-and-a-half hours.*
- I thought you said the bombs would go off in *five* hours.
- *If Andrew showed up before I got caught, that would have been about two-and-a-half hours ago. Is that enough time?*
- Yes. It'll be easier than you think, because girls and boys are kept on standby, anyway. What about the colonel?
- *Fuck him. I'm going to carry this Krinkov down to the bus terminal.*
- Really? *"Colonel Wheat"?*
- *Good point. I'll tear off the nametag and keep the eagles, just in case someone eyeballs the gun. Can you leave the floor again on your own?*
- Yes. I have a fake work order.
- *Good. Go down to the old train station, but don't*

go inside. Start walking down the tracks, and don't stop. Look for an old gray Ford pickup. Even if I'm not behind the wheel, it's still okay. Just get in.

- Hold on a minute. There are limits. My transponder isn't keyed to some areas, so I can't just walk out the back.
- *Grace, you're going to have to take that chance! Once shit hits the fan, the TSA is going to have a hell of lot more to worry about than one kippy who strayed past an electronic perimeter!*
- I hate that word! Don't *ever* call me a...a...wait. What did you say my name was?

A Picture In My Head!
A Picture Of
This!

The southern end of Lake Meade wasn't completely drained and evaporated, so the first twenty lakeside miles of 167 North smelled like shit. The bottom-lying filth that had polluted the lake water stank like metabolized alcohol coming through the rotting skin of a detoxing zombie.

Andrew kept an eye on the road behind us, Grace was in the middle, and I drove. I also kept glancing in the rear view mirror, but we were without pursuers. Before we neared the ghost town that had once been Overton, Andrew checked his watch. "Vegas TSA now needs a new recruitment campaign," he said in a grim tone.

It hadn't been particularly difficult to escape. Andrew was waiting in the bus bay when I arrived, and we both felt like thanking Carl for getting the Ford in such great shape. Ha! It had become that bastard's little secret project, executed by his own small circle of henchmen, a sort of secret TSA-within-TSA that had tuned and fueled Andrew's ride. Andrew left a couple dead sentries, and I left a smashed-out bus bay garage door. Grace was walking the tracks when we picked her up.

Something told me that if I could put Frenchman Mountain behind us and resist the temptation to quickly get on what was left of I15, we might make it. I went south to Hendersonville's mostly empty streets and got out on 167. I was calm, or maybe just tired and numb, as I drove past a few burned-out and overturned car hulks that were scattered along the way. The obstacles on the road had been negotiated frequently by other travelers, and all that I had to do to safely bypass approaching barriers was follow established shoulder tracks. Roughly fifteen miles outside of town I followed the track off the pavement, drove about a hundred yards down the side, and passed through a large hole that someone had either bashed or exploded in an abandoned TSA checkpoint. After another fifteen miles I repeated the routine, except this time I drove by a washout. I slowed as I passed, grateful that I had not continued on the road itself, because a flash flood had cut a section out of the highway that made it resemble a dry moat without a drawbridge. Instead of slowly driving over bumpy roadside rocks and brush, the pickup would have taken a ten-foot nosedive to the bottom of an abrupt gully. It would have been an absolutely stupid way for us to end up, bleeding or dead, in the middle of the night and at the bottom of a big ditch...especially since we had managed to escape such bigger dangers only hours before.

* * *

The headlights revealed that the lookout area had fallen into ruin. The awnings had collapsed and dust had built up over everything. Beyond the cliff there was only empty black space, like the space that pulls you down in a falling dream...though I don't think that any of us dreamed when we fell asleep in the cab.

When the sun rose I saw that there were still 1930s tree skeletons sticking up from the bottom of the dry lake bed. The evaporation and marine pollutant off-gassing process was largely finished in this part of the former Lake Meade, so a stench didn't envelop us as we drove down to the marina and off the boat ramp's gentle slope.

We had spotted the bomber from the cliff. It dwarfed the pickup and dry sediment made the plane appear as if it were covered in a thin layer of gray papier-mâché. The B-29's glass-nosed cockpit was smashed and two of the four engines were missing. The plane straddled a shallow ravine and its broken spine rested at a slight angle. A nauseating but faint reek came from within the still-damp fuselage. *I hope I don't have to climb inside of that thing to find the 'selenide,* I thought.

I stopped the pickup and we all got out. Andrew immediately jumped in the back and began opening pressure latches on a large metal box that looked like a green footlocker. He lifted the hinged top cover, took out a technical order, and began going down a checklist. After a couple minutes of punching keys, Andrew paused. He picked up something from the console face and tossed it to me. "Here," he said. "You can do the honors when the time comes."

The object might have been a standard TV remote control, except for the military acronyms and seemingly random numbers on the buttons. "This looks confusing," I said.

"Not at all," replied Andrew. "It's the red one."

I held up the control and pointed at a small switch beneath a hinged guard. "This?"

Andrew nodded. "Once for a round trip, twice to negate the auto-return. Got it?"

"Yeah."

"Get the 'selenide now, Jack. I'm almost ready. Do you need tools? I can stop here and help you."

"No, no," I said. "I'll get it. I'll be right back."

Grace had watched the entire exchange and she followed me as I walked around to the other side of the fuselage. "You have no idea what you're looking for, do you?" she asked.

I shook my head. *Please, please, Grandpa. Just give me a sign. Help me think.*

Think...

Think...

[Think, Jacky! It is in the watch and behind the eight.]

It is in the watch...

No, it isn't, Grandpa. There was nothing in your watch. Nothing...except rusty clockwork and a stamped serial number: 45-21847.

...45-21847...

...45-21847...

Huh. The serial number of Grandpa's watch almost matches the B-29's tail number.

*...45-21848...**8...8...***

The second eight is painted in red. The other numbers are black.

AND BEHIND THE EIGHT!

"ANDREW!" I cried, "I need a hand here!" Before I began running back to the pickup I should have noticed the strangely shuffling single left boot prints in the dried sediment around the plane's tail section, and I certainly shouldn't have left Grace alone...but I guess that my excited booby bird-brain had taken over again.

Call In An Enola Gay
Strike On This
Bastard

There was no response to my shouts, and when I got back to the Ford I discovered that the silenced Krinkov was missing. Andrew was face-down beside the pickup, and there were many bloody exit holes in the back of his shirt.

GRACE!

I raced back around to the other side of the plane. Grace sat on the ground while Carl grinned and leaned against the B-29's fuselage. He held the weapon that I had stolen from his safe. Carl had crudely splinted his swollen foot with sticks and duct tape, and he used another stick as a cane. Further behind the tail section, I spotted a small and partially-concealed motorcycle. *That crazy fuck hand-shifted all the way,* I thought.

"I'll have my .357 now," Carl said. "Nice and slow. Just lay it on the ground." Carl half-limped and half-hopped away from the plane with the Krinkov in one hand and the walking stick in the other.

"How did you...?"

"How did I get away? Status check. A knock on my door not long after you left. When I didn't answer, CQ was alerted. Sorry, Jack. There weren't any exotic 007 technologies or Houdini-level escape tricks on my part." Despite his obvious pain, Carl smiled. "You've been foiled by something predictable and mundane, my friend, and when you were so close, too."

I put down the .357 and looked at Grace. A tear ran down her cheek. We had almost made it. Horseshoes and hand grenades, just like in a military bar so many years ago.

"You'll be happy to know that I allowed your little gas scheme to proceed," stated Carl, as he motioned me back and moved forward to retrieve his revolver.

"You've impressed me, Jack. It was absolutely spectacular. Fires, explosions, and yellow plumes. Coughing, choking, and writhing. Magnificent. Lovely colors and compositions. And to think, I was ready to dismiss you as a troglodyte!"

"You...didn't stop it?"

"Of course not! Once I reached a safe distance, I was able to properly appreciate your creativity. It opened my eyes and gave me new ideas. I was wrong about weapons of mass destruction, Jack. They're beautiful! They're inspiring! In fact, I'm now interested in traveling to other worlds instead of taking over LaPin's ridiculous sty. That, however, brings us back to the need for *me* to get information from *you.*" Carl pointed the Krinkov in my direction. "So, exactly where is the substance required to power Carlssin's machine?"

I glanced at Grace. She was hunched over with her face in her hands. "What are you looking at, you amazing artist?" smiled Carl. He turned toward Grace, then back at me. "What is it?" he repeated. As if to emphasize the question, Carl randomly sprayed bullets in the direction of my gaze, some of which struck Grace.

I tried to scream, but only a hoarse sound came out of my throat. I took an enraged step toward Carl as Grace slumped to the ground, but halted when the Krinkov again pointed at me. Grace's plain blue tee was now reddened and wet, and her blood ran into the dry lakebed's cracks.

Carl seemed almost...*perplexed.* "What?" he repeated. "What are you looking at?"

I heard Grace say something before she died. "Coward with...a weak mind," she murmured.

I felt terrible rage, and I was tempted to ignore the gun and just charge the fiendish cripple.

Goddamned-evil-fucking-sack-of-subhuman-shit.

No. I had to live to make him pay. So Carl wanted the 'selenide? Fine. I would *definitely* give it to him. I swallowed enough of my anger-hate-fury cocktail to speak. "Alright," I said, in a very unsteady voice. "I think it's in the vertical stab."

My instant cooperation shocked Carl. "Really? You'd tell me that easily?"

"Yes," I said. "It's near the tail number. The eight Is the clue. It's painted in a different color."

Carl glanced upward. "So it is. The mud hasn't obscured the vertical surfaces." Carl scrutinized me in an attempt to discern a lie. "This seems like a rather dubious clue, but you're the one who knows, aren't you? Since you've left me with partial ambulation," Carl continued, as he motioned at his splint, "it's up to you to get up there and find it." Carl waved the muzzle of his weapon at the tail section.

"I need to get some tools from the truck," I growled.

It Was Just My Old "Disappearing Pig" Trick!

Since the B-29 had come to rest on its belly, I was able to reach up and grab the edge of the left horizontal stabilizer. I tucked a large flat screwdriver under my belt and pulled myself up while I ignored the dust and sediment that sifted down onto my face. My old muscles and joints protested as I struggled to bring my body into a position that would allow me to swing my legs up and over the edge. I finally succeeded, but after I had gotten on top, I remained on my back and took a short breather. Without looking, I shifted my left leg and heard the sound of shattering glass below. I raised up and saw that, along with a layer of pebbles, roots, and dried mud, bits of boating garbage had also fallen down onto the plane, and I had knocked an old beer bottle over the stabilizer's edge. I *assumed* that it had been a beer bottle, because I saw others nearby.

I got up, dusted off, and froze. The tired metal beneath my feet let out a groan like thin ice on a thawing pond. I didn't want layers of old aluminum to suddenly and jaggedly give way, so I got back down on all fours and slowly crawled to the vertical stabilizer's base. Even if the last numeral really was the clue, it was still far overhead and well out of reach. I wasn't entirely sure how to proceed, but I knew that I had to access the tail number first and take it from there.

I stood, forced the head of the screwdriver into sheet metal seams, and found that it was easy to break the plane's old rivets. I pulled off pieces of the bomber's skin, determined that the exposed superstructure remained strong enough to serve as a ladder, and in less than twenty minutes I began to pop off the eight's plates.

"Hurry!" shouted Carl. I just ignored him.

When the last piece of aluminum fell, I leaned

forward and looked inside. Chunks of dried mud had fallen out when I had removed lower plates, but the space behind the tail number was different. Instead of grit and silt clods, the stabilizer's interior contained a strange cobweb-like structure that seemed as if it had been spun from safety wire. Fine bare-metal tendrils spread out from a central point that didn't really look as special as I thought it should. At the center was merely a reddish-silver object that resembled a ball bearing, and it had been soldered to the wires' end points. Maybe I had expected something more grandiose, mysterious, and Tesla-esque, like an amazing contraption that still sparked and arced after decades of submersion. I noticed, however, that the web's bare wires were shiny, as if they had been strung only yesterday.

Well, if there were ever an obvious real-life version of a flux capacitor, this had to be it. I stuck the screwdriver into the mass of wires and started to twist and break them. I freed the little marble, removed it from the stabilizer's metallic tangle, and examined it in the morning light. The broken and protruding wires made the object resemble a child's cheap toy jack. Was this really what I was looking for?

Time to find out.

* * *

Andrew's previous programming allowed me to skip many of the C-205's checklist steps. As I read the T.O.'s "Fueling" section, Carl spoke: "Here we are, following a technical order, next to an aircraft. Does this seem like the old days, Jack?" I didn't answer.

"I'm feeling nostalgic," Carl continued to crow, "and I'd like some play time before 9/11 and all of the ensuing fun in 1996. 1990 is good, but 1988 would be better. I'll look you up, Jack. We can talk about art." Carl's tone then changed from mockery to warning. "I'll enter the destination year myself," he said, as he gestured me aside with the Krinkov's muzzle. "You're not sending me on a surprise trip to Pre-Colombian North America, or some such thing. Drop the checklist and fuel."

Pick whatever year you like, I thought, as I laid the T.O. and the 'selenide ball on the C-205's control console and moved away. *Just as long as it's between 1936 and 2017.*

Carl kept his weapon pointed at me as he entered a T.O. code. When he finished punching keys, a small door slid open in the machine's programming console. The T.O. had an illustration of material being inserted into the space, so Carl dropped the spiny little marble into the slot. The door snapped shut, and the main readout flashed a single question:

INITIATE Y/N?

"That should do it," said Carl. "Get out."

I swung my legs over the edge of the truck bed and jumped to the ground, while Carl's injury required him to slowly ease himself out over the tailgate. A gleefully evil expression remained on Carl's face, despite the pain of keeping the gun trained on me while he hobbled forward to the pickup's cab.

"And now, since I would rather not materialize beneath hundreds of feet of water," said Carl, as he got behind the wheel, "I'm going to drive out of this lake bed. Oh, don't worry, Jack. I'm not going to kill you. I'm not even going to shoot you in the foot in exchange for what you've done to me. No, I want you to be healthy. *I-want-you-to-live.*" Carl's voice dripped with sadistic pleasure. "It's time for us to part ways, old friend."

Yes, it is, I thought. While Carl attempted to hot wire the pickup, I slowly backed away and slipped my hand into my fatigue pocket. I thumbed open the remote's hinged guard and hit the red switch.

The Devil
I ~~Don't~~
Didn't

The old Ford vanished in a burst like a hundred flash bulbs, except instead of white light, it was *black*. After several minutes the pickup returned in another dark flash, and I saw, as expected, that it was drenched. The doors were open and the cab was half-flattened. The windshield was popped out and Carl's soaked body was pinned between the wheel and the damaged cab roof.

I walked up to the Ford, opened the tailgate, and a flood of murky lake water rushed out. Then I went to the front. Carl's face was frozen in a look of drowned terror, but his final expression wasn't what caught my attention. The mashed cab's pressure had twisted Carl's torso into a strange position and his right arm hung out the door.

There was a purple birthmark on his *right* wrist.

I had never known the dead man. I hadn't driven the wet pickup truck out of Vegas, and the C-205 in the back had never belonged to Andrew. Somewhere, in some other corner of the multiverse, one of my string-theory doubles had enacted the same maneuver that I had just pulled off. I had sent him my Carl, and he had sent me his...by way of past worldlines where the Hoover Dam was intact and Lake Meade was very deep. I was certain, however, that the corpse behind the steering wheel had been as much of a monster as the Carl that I had known. I grabbed "Carl's" wrist and pulled his body out of the pickup.

I attempted to hot-wire the Ford after some minutes to let it drain and dry, and I breathed a heavy sigh of relief when the engine started. The truck looked like shit, and I had to half-lay and half-hunch to get into the partially-smashed cab. I hoped that the C-205 was okay.

Though wet, the alternate time machine appeared to be undamaged and its screens were still active. I recalled Andrew's story about displacing to my reality because of a malfunctioning C-205 from another universe, so I prayed that the only quantum difference that I was to discover would be the location of Carl's birthmark.

I wore a grim expression as I loaded Andrew's body into the back of the pickup. Then I drove around to the other side of the plane. I forced myself to turn off my feelings as I cradled Grace and gently laid her next to Andrew.

Fuck the goddamned TSA and Carl's black soul.
Fuck this entire goddamned world.
Hell for Lucifer, Lucifer, Lucifer, I say.

30

They're Lining Up To Get Here, And Do You Know Why, Jack? Should I Tell You Why? *Hmmm?* Because Here, In This World, The Bad Guys Can *Win!*

July
2018
(1-of-2)

I can safely park the pickup at the abandoned marina, but I choose to drive up to the lookout area. I stop the truck, go to the back, take out the T.O., and follow the C-205's activation sequence. I'm not able to enter keyboard commands, however, because my hands shake. I drop the T.O., crawl over to Grace, and put her head on my lap. I sit there for a long time, and it's around noon before I again try to operate the machine.

* * *

The C-205 indicates that it still has enough fuel for two more displacements, so I follow the T.O. and prepare to activate the machine via the main console. As before, when the last step is completed, the sub-displays go blank and the main screen asks:

INITIATE Y/N?

I'm about to activate the machine, but stop when I remember that it's bound for 1988.

INITIATE Y/N?!?

Y!

But *N* to 1988.
Y to a few hours ago. *Y* to making things right again. Absolutely *Y!*
Y to figuring out how to rewind the day so that I can save Grace and Andrew.

Y to the look on Carl's face when we surprise his evil ass.

Y to the look on *my* face when I see Grace alive again.

Wait.

If I'm dealt a skew with more differences than merely the location of a dead man's birthmark, then a three-hour rerun tour could maroon me on an island where I'd be one of *two* Gilligans...and I strongly doubt that my quantum counterpart would be willing to share his Mary Ann. *I* wouldn't be. I'm sure that those other people - that *other* Andrew, that *other* Grace, and that *other* Jack - would be extremely grateful...but nothing would change for *me*. I'd just be a third wheel in someone else's reality.

God*-damn! *What good is a stupid time machine if I can't fix my own past?

I need her. I just can't accept this. I have to take the chance.

If I end up in a skew universe I'll kill my stringdopp and take his place. Then I can be with Grace again.

Oh sure. As if I could ever do something like that.

BUT I NEED HER!

The multiverse - which is to say, God - doesn't give a shit about what I do, or do not, need.

Acceptance and denial. Denial and acceptance.
American Denial Techniques. A PhD in ADT.
American prayers.
Futile American prayers.
Angry American prayers.

Fuck off, God.

That's right. I said it.

You let Carl take away my only reason for living. This must be fun for You. Very amusing, right? And I'm just supposed to take it.

I think that You've mistaken me for Job.

Killing Carl didn't bring Grace back, did it? Of course, I still would have ended that shitbag...but the damage is done. God laughs and Carl claims posthumous victory.

Hey God, I finally understand that my story ain't got no moral, but Billy Preston said that the bad guy was only supposed to win every once in a while. JUST EVERY ONCE IN A WHILE! Not every damn time. I have nothing. Huh... I remember when Dyler Turden said: "We're only free to do anything after we've lost everything." *I wonder if that includes fucking with God while he's fucking with someone else? Especially if that "someone else" is an alternate version of* you?

Maybe.

I'm screwed, but...what if I helped another *me? And why stop at just a few hours' worth of assistance? How about a day? Or a year? Or thirty years?*

It now occurs to me that I might find some purpose in being a third wheel.

I Saved Us...It Was Me...
We Survived
Because
Of *Me!*

July
2018
(2-of-2)

Telling God to fuck off is probably unwise.

* * *

1988.
But why not 1978?
Or 1968?
Why not 1918? I could spend a decade speculating in stocks and dump everything in September of 1929. And why stop there? I had the centuries at the push of a button. I had all the time in the world. I had a time machine.

After a moment I realized that it wasn't quite true. *Sorry, Marty.* The genie had already granted one wish and patiently stood by while I debated on the remaining two. *No,* I realized. I wasn't the man to change world history. I wouldn't be on hand to prevent the assassination of an Austrian archduke. I would never look through a sniper scope at grassy knoll gunmen. I wouldn't be able to prevent a September 11th NORAD stand-down, and I had no idea how to convince the American sheeple that re-implementation of the smallpox inoculation program would be a good idea. Besides, all of those things were just symptoms, and not the causes, of greater evils.

> *- So, do nothing? If that's your attitude, then why bother to use the machine at all? Why not just stay in 2018?*
> *- That's not what I meant. I'm just saying that we might tackle things on a smaller scale.*
> *- Alright. We could look up the name "LaPin" in the phone book - if that's her real name. It was also easy to find a shotgun in the eighties. We know*

the location of the Vegas Starbuck where the supposed 9/11 hijackers had their last cups of coffee. We could saw-off the shotgun and have it waiting under a morning newspaper. We could also put the shotgun in a briefcase and learn more about the Clark County School District's high school art program.

- Not bad! Care to take it down another notch? Make it even more personal?
- *Sure! I'm an expert when it comes to making it all about me. Or us, I mean.*
- I already knew that. Example?
- *Okay. There'll be time to get Grandpa to a cardiologist, which will also head off that whole disaster in Korea. We'll never start teaching, and we'll never meet...someone.*
- Of course you realize that it won't actually be "us". Remember the Grandfather Non-Paradox Principle: Even if we go back in time and save somebody else's grandpa, the outcome still won't affect *our* life.
- *Yes, yes, we've had that conversation. So...what exactly do you want to do?! Sit here and starve? Go back and see how bad things are in Vegas? Or maybe you'd like to throw another one of your little God-themed tantrums?*
- Nope. 1988 will be just fine.

I'd Rearrange Just
A Day Or
Two

Time displacement, from an inside perspective, was like being in a diving bell on the bottom of a black-paint ocean. A dark blanket fell over the pickup like a cloth over a birdcage, and the only sources of illumination were the C-205's console lights. There wasn't a ground or a sky, but I didn't get a feeling like the pickup was floating. There was total silence, and it was like the old Ford doubled as both a vehicle and sensory deprivation chamber. The numbers that ran across the console screens assured me that *something* was happening and that I wouldn't be forever trapped in the dark.

I suddenly had to shield my eyes from a blast of desert daylight. The pickup was still at the Overton Lookout, and at first nothing seemed to have changed. I began to think that perhaps I hadn't followed the T.O. correctly, until I noticed that the air was considerably cooler. I peered over the cliff. The dry lakebed had been replaced by the waters of Lake Meade, and when I looked around the picnic area I noticed that the tables, chairs, and awnings were intact and well-maintained. Nothing was missing, collapsing, or half-covered in blown dust. According to the C-205's readout, I had jumped back from July 2018 to November 1988, and the seasons, as well as the decades, had changed in mere minutes.

The date indicator also showed that I had made the trip with negligible event class deviation, which meant that this past world would be like the one I remembered. No weird, *Twilight Zones*-esque surprises. Right?

I looked over the cliff again and saw that the marina was missing. Not torn down, not removed or relocated. *Missing*...as in *never existed*. But how could that be possible with such minimal deviation? *Unless...*

Of course! No, the C-205 *wouldn't* tell me that this reality was strange or different, because, from the machine's perspective, it had successfully found its way back home...except that it had brought me, a string-theory stranger, along for the ride.

Oh shit. Did I just hear Rob Serling's voice...?

No. It was just a soft beeping sound. When I looked at the C-205, I was shocked to discover that its auto-return indicator was counting down.
15
14
13
I frantically flipped through the T.O.'s pages to find out how to deactivate the main console.
12
11
10
I pulled the remote actuator out of my pocket and pointed it at the C-205. I flipped the red switch twice. Nothing.
9
8
7
I yelled, pushed random buttons, and banged my fists on the sides of the unit's metal housing.
6
5
4
I kissed Grace's cold cheek, grabbed Andrew's backpack, and jumped out of the truck.
3
2
1

Sometimes She Stays
A LIttle Longer...
But Not Too
Often

I'm numbly lying on a picnic table when she appears. Her shirt is without bloody bullet holes. Her hair is clean and shiny, like she just stepped out of a Panteen commercial. And, of course, she's still as young as she was on that night when we met in a sleazy military dive.

I sit up. She smiles at me, and I smile at her.

"Can I ask you a question?"

"Sure," she says.

"Who did I *really* meet in that 'Grand Hole' bar?"

She shrugs. "My guess would be a woman named Grace. She became the starting point for your craziness, and you've swapped Barbie heads for a long time."

"I-I guess that a lot of women have thought that I was nuts."

"Yeah. *Correctly.* That would explain why you've been alone for so many years, don't you think?"

"My God. So have I *always* superimposed you over real women?"

"No. Not always. Like now, for instance. There's no one else here. You're just sitting in the desert and talking to yourself. This is your default when you can't find a woman who's foolish enough to hang out with you."

"Well, *you've* braved me for an extended period."

"That's my job. Well, it *began* as a job. Then it sort of became a habit. Now I'm actually sad to go. You never learned to love yourself, though you always loved me. But...*tah-dah!* I'm a part of you. So I guess we know what that means. I'm just sorry that you didn't realize it when you were a young man." Grace gives me a sad little smile. "Given enough time, the mind heals

695

itself. Psychiatry is nonsense. Maybe Tom Cruz was right. Oh, don't worry, you stubborn old thing. I don't expect you to jump Okra's couch on my behalf, even if it's really to celebrate yourself."

"Hmmm," I muse. "A bit late in the game."

Grace nods. "And I think we both know who you like to pretend I am, don't we?"

"Yes," I reply. "Except that your English is better."

"Only because your Korean is crap. What choice did you give me?" Grace pauses to glance around the lookout area. "We had sex here, remember? And yes, before you ask, you were with a real girl that night. You weren't out here jerking off to a hallucination."

"Really? Who was she?"

"I don't know. Somebody with a Mercedes. Does it matter? To you, she was me. *Me.* I'm the delusional through-line for all of your romantic catastrophes." Grace laughs. "Do you remember, back in college, when you dragged some poor girl to Norm Abraham and Ned Power's shows? She was freaked out but you never even noticed that she never spoke to you again. You just painted my face onto the next woman who wandered your way."

"But I thought that you were entertained."

"I *was*," replies Grace, "but you weren't actually with *me.* Christ, Jack. After seeing a crazy pig rip up people's genitals and then get shot himself, you promptly drove that poor girl to the Adult Ultrastore!"

"Wait *one goddamn minute!* You said that it was okay! You said that you were stronger than me!"

"Well, you've always *wanted* a woman who was stronger than you...so much that you didn't care if she truly was."

"Am I speaking to an actual woman now, and I just don't know it?"

Grace laughs. "No. Like I said, this is one of those times when you're talking to yourself."

She sits down beside me. I follow her eyes as she stares at the lake's surface, out to where we know this world's B-29 lies. She turns to me. "Let's talk about movies."

"Movies?"

"Yeah. Sometimes you seem to prefer films as life contexts. It might be easier that way. Let's start with Carl."

"Okay. What about him?"

"He wasn't really your friend," Grace states. "Even all those years ago, he wasn't really your friend. You don't have to feel guilty."

"I don't," I reply. "I feel *lucky.* He was smarter than me. He always was. And definitely more ruthless."

"He was an animal who liked to strap people down and dig out their eyes," corrects Grace. But of course, I'm just correcting myself.

"This is sort of like when the *Fighter Club* narrator realizes that *he's* holding the gun, and not Dyler Turden," Grace and I state in unison.

"So is this the movie discussion?" I ask.

Grace softly laughs. "Yes. This is it."

"Okay. *Cloaks and Daggers.*"

"Dabnie Coleman's character. The imaginary spy-guy who helps the kid."

I smile. "You're much better looking, however."

"Thanks. Okay, here's one for you."

"Shoot."

"A Gorgeous Mind."

"Easy," I reply. "Edd Harris' character and the guy who played Russell Crow's college buddy. Combined, like an --"

"--amalgam," Grace says, as she interrupts me with a grin. "Just like Steve Martyn's opening scene in *Parenting.* I wish that I had a silver peso for every time you've--"

"--used that example," I finish.

"Any more?" she asks.

"Harvie?" I suggest, though I'm not really sure about that one.

"Nah. I'm not a giant rabbit." Grace shakes her head. "Try again. Last one."

I take a few seconds to think. "Montgomery Gentrie's *Speed.*"

"Mmmm, I guess that's okay, though kinda obscure. So I've been *haunting* you?"

"No," I answer. "Not like that." I pause. "Maybe

that's not the best example."

We're quiet for another minute, then I say: "Tuco?"

"No. Angel Eyes."

"So *Andrew* was Tuco?"

"Not...really. Tuco wasn't the main bad guy. And why would you think that Andrew was an antagonist?"

"So *Carl* was Angel Eyes?"

"Mmmm...maybe."

"And I was Blondie?"

"No. Blondie was in control of the situation. When was the last time that *you* were in control of anything?"

I'm silent for a few seconds. "Well, you don't have to say it like *that.* I think that I've done okay lately."

"And Blondie never pouted, either," Grace responds. "It doesn't fit. Life...art...life. Sometimes there's no imitation or parallel. Apples and oranges."

"Oh," I say. *I'm not pouting. Am I?*

She lays back on the table. I lay back on the table. We feel the hot metal against our backs and through our shirts. We don't care.

"No more movies," she says.

"No need," I reply. "I get it." Then I ask: "Why all of the blood and drama and stuff?"

"I had to get you moving," Grace answers. After another quiet minute she turns to me and says: "I admit that there were times when I almost believed that I *was* real." She smiles. "But, of course, I haven't aged a day in - what? Twenty-five years?"

"Yeah," I agree. "Plus, you seem unfazed by the fact that Carl half-emptied a Krinkov mag into your chest."

She smiles. "Yes, that was a big clue. Your delusions have had some creatively weak moments - so much so that I sometimes wondered if you might figure things out on your own."

"Such as?"

"Well, take that story I gave you after you re-imagined me at Jones' airline. You remember - the one where I said that I had returned to Vegas out of my love for you." Grace cocked her head. "Love? Really? I left another life and made my way across the continent to the Mojave Desert to look for someone whom I couldn't even be sure was still alive, and all after society fell?

Does that sound realistic? C'mon, Jack."

"I-I just--"

"You just wanted to believe, so you did...and here I am, no matter how weak the premise."

We get off of the table and face each other. "So now what?" I ask.

"Well, I'm supposed to give you this," Grace says, as she produces a plastic toy pirate sword from behind her back. "Your grandpa said that you'd know what it meant."

I take the sword and smile. "You're a sweetheart, but I'm not Tommie Lee Jones. Besides, didn't we just agree? No more movie references." I hand the sword back.

"Okay. I fibbed. I insisted upon the sword, even though your grandpa said that you'd prefer tickets to see *The Electronic Company.*" I start to protest, but she puts her finger on my lips and shushes me. "That was a television show, not a movie, so save it."

We walk over to the fence at the lookout's edge. "I have to go," Grace says.

I think that I've heard those words before.

"I have to go," she repeats. Grace steps back and opens her hand. I see that the sword has not transformed into a PBS studio audience ticket. Instead, it's now a diamond ring.

Grace wears a sad expression as she continues to slowly back away. "Your grandpa insisted upon the sword, but I now insist upon doing this," she says. There isn't a Korean rail line at the bottom of the cliff, but Grace tosses the ring through the fence and over the edge anyway.

~~Nick~~ *Andrew* Told Me! In My Dreams, He Can Talk...Did I Ever Tell You That?

November 1988 [2.0] (3-of-3)

"Is she gone?" Andrew asks. "I didn't want to interrupt. It looked like you two were having a serious discussion."

Grace had said that this was one of those times when I was alone and talking to myself. So how could Andrew see Grace? And also...didn't I just watch Andrew's bullet-shattered corpse disappear in a black flash? Yet he's back, breathing, talking, and walking around. How is that possible? *Unless...*

"Bingo!" Andrew exclaims. "Take a bow, Jack, because you're the only one on the stage."

"But-but *I* could never have--"

"Why not? You used your military experience to operate a C-205, and you faced off against Carl just as well as H.G. Welles faced off against Jack the Ripper in *Times After Times.* Sorry," adds Andrew. "I eavesdropped on your movie conversation with Gracie."

"Her name is *Grace.* Don't call her Gracie, ever," I say, while Andrew grins. "So were you *ever* real?"

"Yes. Unless you experienced a burst of super-genius and invented time travel on your own...which seems unlikely."

"Who are you really, Andrew?"

"Who *was* I would be a better question. I'm the guy in another universe with half of his head blown off, rotting up at our Turtlehead Peak camp, along with those two TSA scouts you greased with your little ricochet trick.

"What?"

"That first shot through my skull. Those scumbags didn't miss, even though that's what you chose to believe. I gotta congratulate you on that backshot thing. Where the hell did you learn how to do that?"

"An SP named Jaeger taught me a few things about aircraft shelter geometry."

Andrew smiles. "Like I always say, it's the amateurs you gotta watch out for, even when they're schooled by pros."

"So who gassed Fremont? Or did that really happen?"

"It happened. I'm glad that you remembered the booby traps when you went to get the detonator."

"And who removed my transponder?"

"Not me, obviously. By the size of that scar, I'd judge that you muddled through with that as well. Christ," says Andrew, as he grabs my arm and examines the implant site. "What did you use to remove it? A chain saw?"

"No, because *you* sharpened a little knife, then knocked me out and played Dr. Kildare."

Andrew laughs again. "I'm afraid not. Look at those train tracks! Did you sew it up with a boot lace? Still...I guess it's not bad for an ex-load toad whose specialty sure as hell wasn't field-expedient medicine."

"Didn't you close it with some dental floss or something?"

"No. I was dead."

I look at Andrew and sigh. "I thought that you were still alive. I thought that you were there every step of the way."

The illusory E-9 chuckles again. "Yeah. Me, plus your little kimchi girl."

I smile. "You'll make CSM for this."

Andrew returns my smile, but with noticeable sadness. "Only in your mind, I'm afraid."

"Thanks...for everything."

"You're welcome. And now, since I'm not a part of your military memories, college experiences, or sex scenes, I think it's time for me to make my exit, too." Andrew looks around. "Where did Grace go?"

"She just sort of walked through the fence, over the cliff, and disappeared."

"Ah," says Andrew. "If I hurry, I can catch up."

31
I'm Walkin', Yes Indeed

I Shall Wear my Trousers Rolled
At Nevada's Prufrock
Nuclear Storage
Facility

November
1988 [2.0]
(1-of-4)

I must now live to help another Jack because I can't salvage my own life.

My childish soul is locked into an old man's body and my years are behind me. Maybe I've truly given up **Hope**® at long last. I don't even call it "**Hope**®" anymore. Instead, I think it's a matter of expectations, and believe me, I don't have any.

It didn't rub the lotion on its Hope®*.*

It got the hose.

If you have expectations but no **Hope**®, then you've got it all backward. Frankly, you're fucked, though the mind does have some defenses which are similar to the human body's tuberculosis response that Vonnigut described in *Hokus-Pokus*. That was my situation. My life had become hidden behind bloody hankies and brittle calcium shells as I encased decades-old pain in protective delusion. I had learned, however, just how much I could lose, or never have, and continue on. This also made me wonder what other parts I could live without. If the body had vestigial organs, did the soul also have expendable features?

Hope® isn't the equivalent of love, though they have commonalities. Having one, however, doesn't guarantee the presence of the other. People just assumed that it worked that way - but why? Love, **Hope**®, and expectation...it was possible to lose all three and never notice, or, as I could attest, it was possible to lose all three and simply *refuse* to admit it. Fantasy would then administer an anesthetic that allowed souls to be painlessly pared away.

If I could have stepped back and examined my spiritual self, I might have seen the astral equivalent to the wounded veteran in *Johnny Gets His Gun.* Am I WWI veteran Joe Bonham, minus arms, legs, eyes, ears, face, and spleen? *No...*because my spleen is in a military parade, along with a goose-stepping appendix, saluting tonsils, and amputated limbs which are not absolutely essential for the continuance of the human organism! And after those corporeal chunks complete their pass, they are followed by excised memories that have been swept from my personal cutting room floor and spliced back together in armored columns of regret. Everything suppressed, everything forgotten, and everything ignored has been drafted and stuffed into uniforms for one final Pass-In-Review. I am now a bedridden dictator who has been placed in a wheelchair to overlook a May Day military parade. I am the totalitarian figurehead whom memory's comrades see feebly waving to the infantrymen, tank commanders, and artillery officers. The years hail me in passing - the warts, the mistakes, the weaknesses - they're all there, and marching under my life's flag. And look! Grace has a final cameo! She winks, snaps a crisp salute, and disappears into the procession.

I recognize another face in the ranks, but I have to look away.

S`io credesse che mia risposta fosse...*nah.*

I would drown, but the Lake Meade Recreational Area signs aren't written in Italian.

The caves of the Colorado River are without singing mermaids and ragged-clawed crabs. Symbolic visions of folly and cowardice give short shrift to the true *despairs within an old man's heart, and faded scenes from the past play a nightly shell game that teases my tired demons with just enough dreams and memories to keep them from resting in peace.*

Bearing Gifts, I Travel So
Far On Feet Of Clay...
But Without
A Dan Of
Steel

Desert autumn at the lake's low elevation wasn't as cold as it had been in the mountains, but I still needed a small greasewood flame. I slept in a ravine that was about a hundred yards from the picnic tables, and the wash-cut banks were deep enough for me to build fires unobserved. The ravine emptied at the cliff's edge, and I could watch passing vehicles follow the road down to the lakeshore. Since there wasn't a marina, however, the cars just continued on and disappeared behind the next bluff.

I was hiding, but I didn't know why, or from whom. Something inside me was scared to reach out and take the first step toward engaging this world.

* * *

I understood why Andrew had never used his little hiking pump when we were at Turtlehead Peak. Yes, it filtered water, but it also gave the water a faint reddish color and made it taste like iodine. I would have to leave soon because of the hydration situation. Living in a ditch and sneaking down to the lakeside to pump metallic-tasting pink lemonade into a canteen every night wasn't cutting it. Besides, Andrew's crappy pack rations were almost gone.

* * *

Maybe some people would have used Andrew's machine to meet Christ, Buddha, or Muhammad, but not me. If God was Love, then I preferred to cut out the middlemen and buy wholesale...though if it were too late for me, as an old man, to find out what love was, then why not make it possible for one of my multiverse

706

doubles to have the experience?

That would be my mission. My objective. I didn't have to let another schmuck with my face fuck up his life in the same way that I had fucked up mine. I could be a guardian angel.

Epiphany!

I was a *Bodhisattva,* minus a Steely Dan...or perhaps mine had been a *Tin Dhan.* No matter. It was now gone, along with **Hope**®, and all of my other superfluous bits.

* * *

I discovered a tiny hand-crank AM radio in Andrew's pack, and news reports from KDWN confirmed the date that I had read on the C-205's screen. I had less than a month to get "Grandpa" in for the best cardio look-see that the eighties could offer, along with what I guessed would be an ensuing multiple-bypass. True, my stringdopp would still take some leave and show up in Vegas during Grandpa's convalescence, but when that other Jack returned to South Korea, he wouldn't be a grieving feeboid who ended up tutoring in the stock room of a Seoul grocery.

I was about to bestow an amazing gift that would head off a whole lot of insanity at another Jack's emotional pass. I felt like a god. Not "the" God. I was "a" god. Maybe the real God used tricks – right, Mr. Murray? I'd say so...when He wasn't screwing me over, anyway. He'd just been around for so long that He knew everything. Well, I hadn't been on hand for Creation, but I did have thirty years crammed into my crystal ball.

I decided that it was a good mission, and once I resolved to embark upon it, I felt less scared to explore this new universe.

The Mission's Been Updated. I'm Going Back For ~~You~~ *1,380 Calories, 92 Grams Of Fat, And 3,830 Milligrams Of Sodium*

November 1988 [2.0] (3-of-4)

On the morning when I left the ravine I had been roused before dawn by a need to do a kimchi squat. It reminded me of what the guys in my old air force unit had said when the end of my overseas tour approached: You weren't a short-timer until you ate in Korea and shat in the States. Did that also mean that you weren't a short-timer until you ate in one universe and used a time machine to take a crap in another? And, speaking of gastrointestinal matters, when was the last time that I had some *real* grub? I didn't want my death-camp-abs to make a comeback. The sea ration-like things in Andrew's pack hadn't left me impressed with the future's survival nutrition advancements. They were essentially just compressed cubes of flour, sugar, and lemon oil. Like Andrew's reluctance to use the water pump, I could also understand why the vacuum foil-packed rations had taken a back seat to coyote meat and fried grasshoppers.

* * *

I'm sick of eating flea-bitten wild mutts, insects, and survival rations. In Vegas there will be Mickey D's and Wendy's and Arby's. Fat and grease and calories and chocolate shakes.

I can't even IMAGINE what a hotel buffet is like. Oh. My. Fucking. God.

When I get to town I'm going to gorge. I'm not even going to clean up first. Hmmm...there are also gas stations and convenience stores on the way to Vegas! Chips and jerky and cookies and sodas. Chips and jerky and cookies and goddamn sodas!

Cookies!

There's a small mirror in Andrew's pack. Let's take a look. Humph. I'm a coal miner. My teeth aren't too bad, though, thanks to the now-empty tube of toothpaste and the brush that I lifted from Carl's Plaza Suite. I hold the mirror to the side and check my short gray hair. Yep. Still short, still thinning, and now really dirty. Okay, that's enough. I have a date with some eighties fast food.

Oh. I got up too fast. I sway slightly as I wait for my vision to clear. Yes, I really need some food. I haven't eaten anything other than backpack rations in...well, about thirty rewound years.

What is a potato? What does it taste like? French fries!

It may even be possible to get a shitty hotel room. There's money in Andrew's bag, and in 1988 people didn't yet have to submit to credit-score-rectal-exams just to get a cruddy room on Fremont.

Psychologically, dare I *go* to Fremont? Even thinking about it seems kind of...weird. It reminds me that other things are now different. Cops are out there. They're not *quite* the TSA killers of the future, but I'll still need to be careful. I look like an escapee from Clark County's Arkham & Taylor Asylum. I'm lucky that a park ranger hasn't come along. Of course, it would be impossible to explain my situation, but I can still imagine how the attempt might sound:

- *Sir, are you camping? Camping is prohibited.*
- **No, I'm not camping. I'm actually an inter-dimensional time traveler, recently escaped from a death camp in an alternate post-apocalyptic future in which the government was exterminating the remainder of the population that wasn't killed by a covert aerial smallpox bio-attack.**

The Ranger takes a step back, draws his weapon, and, once again, a goddamned uniform points a gun at me.

I'm sensing a pattern here…finally.

* * *

The year is really 1988. Crazy!

At the end of this road and on the other side of those mountains, amid Sin City's bright bustle, I'm twenty-one years old.

Oops. Scratch that. I forgot that my double is still in South Korea. Okay, in the ROK, I'm twenty-one. On this spot, however, I'm fifty-one, and starring in my own private episode of Slyders.

Hanging On The Promises
In ~~Songs~~ *Tulpas* Of
Yesterday

*November
1988 [2.0]
(5-of-5)*

I had two songs stuck in my head as I trudged back to Vegas: The old Bankin & Rass *Put Your Foot In Front Of The Other* tune went around and around, while, echoing in some other part of my skull, Fat Dominoes sang *Walk To New Orleans.* It wasn't a good mixture, so I stopped, took off Andrew's pack, and sat down to force the annoying ditties out of my mind. Maybe the noise had been a mask for difficult contemplations. Yeah, that was probably it. That was exactly like something my subconscious would do.

* * *

Consider the danger in assuming that small choices lack consequence. A time traveling sergeant major and a pebble on the ground taught me the seriousness of that mistake. The difference between life and death seems like an unexpected factor when deciding whether or not to pick up a rock, and besides, God must have an awful backlog of stuff like that. I mean, if His is the force that reorders the stars in accordance with the pettiest of man's choices, then He must have a daunting workload. The size or scope of a choice is irrelevant, because God appears to honor them all. That's why He runs the show, and humans don't. For example, when I had refused to see that Andrew was dead, was I just being weak, or did I want to play god? Either way, when things had gone awry, my approach was to simply reject reality.

> *- So, Johnny, what did you study at university?*
> **- Me? I earned a PhD in American Denial Techniques.**

Having Andrew around had been a real confidence booster, but Grace had been with me for a hell of a lot longer...and now she wasn't. Part of me was gone. Sometimes people didn't have to be real to be missed, just as a missing limb didn't have to be real for phantom pain to occur.

Grace could have stayed. Why didn't she stay? I still needed her. Andrew could have stuck around to watch my back, too.

Would another imaginary friend appear? No, probably not.

I'd make-believe Grace back, if I knew how.

Sigh.

The elf dentist and Fat Dominoes have finally shut up.

32

(A Quick Aside)

Why Has Marco Gone, Leaving Me Tormented By The Sad Clown Of Life?

December 1988 [2.0]

The problem with foreign films isn't that they're incomprehensibly foreign. The problem is that they're *not* foreign enough. It's easy to take one look at a movie and dismiss it as being too strange to understand. No problem. But if the story appears to be somewhat reasonable, then the audience can be drawn in. It's possible for a viewer to watch a foreign film and, for a while, believe that he or she knows what's going on. Then the plot takes a weird turn and the audience struggles to make sense of the new direction. When they finally do, the movie reverts to its original storyline and pretends that the other one never happened. Then the credits roll, and viewers are left to wonder why they bothered to watch such a mess.

It wasn't really a mess, though. The director knew exactly what he or she was doing, and therefore created a film to reflect a certain vision. I think this might be analogous to the manner in which God directs the multiverse. Since Creation, a lot of folks have taken one look at the world and deemed it too strange to engage. They get up and leave the theater or snore through the presentation, while others keep trying to understand what's happening all the way through the third act.

I think that I fall into this latter category, though right now I really wish that God would just spoon-feed me the plot. I'm in a situation that feels foreign, but I can't completely brush it aside because maybe, in the end, it'll make sense. Of course, there's also the equal likelihood that it'll take a turn so bizarre that I won't be able to make heads or tails of anything. I'm not yet at that point, but things are still quirky and surreal.

714

TO WIT:

My present location: *I'm sitting In the dIning room of the house on Hacienda. There's a Christmas tree in the living room where the old Zenith TV used to sit, and holiday decorations are everywhere. This place looks the same as it did when I was a kid, and it's like Grandpa could walk through the door at any minute.*
My dinner hosts: *A man who looks exactly as I did when I was in my mid-thirties is seated at the head of the table. A woman who looks as I imagine Mirye looked in her late twenties or early thirties is seated across from me. On my right sits a girl who looks exactly like early-teen Rosie Zhang, and on my left is a preteen Mary Zhang. These youngsters, however, have different names.*

After dinner I'll have a drink and contemplate this latest plot twist.

Hmmm. Maybe I should have two drinks.

33

I Don't Give A Damn If He IS Brüse Willis! We Still Don't Allow LeMats In The Airport!

Let's Take A Walk Down Your Old Street - Who Lives In Your House Today?

Grandpa's house on Hacienda wasn't too far, and I was sick of waiting for the bus. I decided to walk, but I had to make a stop along the way...and that stop was called Out-N-In Burger on South Maryland Parkway. Thank God it also existed in this universe.

I took my burgers (yes, plural - *burgers*) outside to one of the picnic tables, and I didn't give a good-god-damn about how much the ULVN students stared and laughed at the old homeless castoff in black fatigues who practically inhaled his double-doubles with grilled onions. I looked up from my frantic mouth-stuffing, took a breath, and glanced toward the campus of my alma mater's multiverse counterpart. *It's not ULVN,* I observed. *It's* UNLV, *according to that massive red-and-gray sign over Greenspin Hall.*

Meh.

Resume stuffing.

I went to a phone booth after I finished eating because I reasoned that I'd better try to make contact beforehand, instead of abruptly showing up and prematurely causing Grandpa to have the heart attack that I hoped to prevent. Andrew's pack contained some sixties-minted quarters that looked like they might have been made from real silver, and when I used them to call my childhood phone number, I kept getting a recording that said it wasn't in use. I didn't expect that. I figured that my voice had probably changed a lot, so I had intended to tell Grandpa that I had a sore throat and that I was calling from Korea just to say hello. Then, after getting into a conversation, I could explain the real situation and slowly prepare Grandpa for the shock of presenting my older time traveling self.

I tried 702 Information and was told that there was no listing for Dr. Erik Simmerath. There was, however, a number for Jack and Mirye Simmerath. The operator hung up after the third time that I asked her to repeat that information. I froze in the booth with the dirty receiver pressed to my dirty cheek, then after some long moments I blinked, shook my head, and dropped the phone. I was very unsettled as I continued down Maryland, to the point that when I crossed Tropicana, I barely noticed that the Sated Yam was again called The Anchor-on-Crown.

President Mondale Has A Thing For Flamingos, Cheese, And Sardines

December 1988 [2.0]
(2-of-4)

I assumed that there would still be a token one-man security detail in the house next door, so I considered knocking there. I quickly discarded this idea, though. It seemed ill-advised, considering my appearance.

I didn't have to devise another way to make contact, however, because I was *also* out on the street and washing an old blue Datsun truck.

He did a double take, dropped his sponge in the suds bucket, and slowly approached me. He wasn't twenty-one years old. That was the first thing that I noticed. He was probably in his mid-thirties, and age difference aside, we looked exactly alike. He wore jeans and an old "Klondike Casino" tee shirt. His hair was too long for military regulations, and he walked with a slight limp.

He clearly wasn't as shocked as I was. "Do you speak English?" he asked. I nodded. "That's good, because I don't speak German. Stay here. I'll be right back." He returned with two folding lawn chairs and a bottle of Patrón Añejo. "It's not soju," he said, as he set up the chairs on the lawn. "My wife has some of that, but I prefer this, so I think that there's a good chance that you do, too. Right?"

Again, all I could do was nod. I dropped my backpack, took a seat, and after three silent shots the cheeseburgers in my gut were permeated with agave and my tongue was loosened. "It's nice to see that my taste in tequila is good in any universe," I said. Then I stated my mission. "I'm here to stop you from wrecking your life in Korea."

"I know."

"Wh-what? How could you possibly--"

"Relax. I've never been to Korea."

"Oh, Jesus...have you gone AWOL? Or *deserted?*"

He seemed mildly amused by my flash of panic. "No. I'm not enlisted." He crossed his left leg over his right, bent over, and rapped on his lower calf. There was a hard and hollow sound. "I laid a Honda Interceptor down on Tenaya and Lake Meade when I was a senior in high school." He sat up and continued. "Look, I know that *you* were a soldier – sorry, *airman* - but the gigantic personal disaster that you guys keep trying to help me avoid won't happen. Don't worry."

"You guys?"

"Yeah. You're not the first alternate-me so show up, so all of the heavy introductions have been done. I'm not shocked, I'm not freaked out, and I'll believe your story, no matter how bat-shit-crazy it may be."

I smiled. "That's good, because I have an industrial-sized guano tale. So you've had this conversation before?"

He nodded.

"Why," I asked, "did you think that I might speak German?"

"Because one guy barely spoke English. I'm still not entirely clear on what his story was. He didn't stay very long, anyway."

"Oh? Where did he go?"

"He fired up the time machine and took off, I assume. That's what always happens."

"You have a time machine?"

"No. *You* do."

"No, I don't," I said. My stringdopp looked surprised, but said nothing. "Time travel and Korea aside," I continued, "we still need to get Grandpa to a doctor as soon as possible."

"Er...alright," he answered. "We can, uh, do that. But how about getting you someplace to sleep first? Okay? Just let me check you into a hotel. You can get cleaned up, get something for dinner, and then we can talk. I can't take you to your place tonight because first I need to let some people know that you're here...but we'll get your keys tomorrow."

"My place?"

"Yeah. You have an apartment. You've only been gone for a couple weeks. I mean, *another* you has only been gone for a couple weeks. I think you should just relax for a day or two...you know, try to get used to things."

"Get used to *what?* You already *know* that Vegas is my - er, *our* - hometown."

"Well, if I understand correctly, *this* Vegas really isn't, and if your story is like those of the other travelers, this isn't the time that you're from, either."

I saw his point. I bowed my head and looked at my dirty clothes and dirty hands. I must have stunk like old roadkill, yet he didn't show any disgust. "These are the only clothes that I have," I said.

"Borrow some of mine. I think that we still wear about the same sizes, though you're pretty skinny."

Some clean clothes sounded good, and I was already accustomed to cinching my belt. Different duds would definitely make me more presentable to Grandpa. "So Grandpa must be used to seeing me, *or us,* too," I said. "Does that mean he's under a doctor's care already?"

This time my stringdopp poured himself a shot without offering me one. "That's, um, been taken care of," he said.

My bullshit detector went off.

"Please don't stress over Grandpa. He's not in Vegas," continued my double, "but we can drive out to where he is. How about tomorrow? We can go see him tomorrow. Is that quick enough?"

I looked at him for a moment and held out my glass. Like me, he was a crappy liar. "Okay," I said, as I downed my shot. "Tomorrow's fine."

I realized that I was too late. In this universe, The Reaper must have moved up his scheduled appointment with Grandpa. I didn't know why my stringdopp was inventing nonsense that sounded like Grandpa was living in a retirement community when a simple trip to a Northtown cemetery would explain everything.

He looked at me. He knew that I knew he was lying.

We sighed at the same time and were silent for a few moments. He spoke when he noticed that my eyes had wandered over to his old pickup. "I'm afraid that we're going to have to take a cab because I'm getting quite a tequila buzz. My wife drives her Sentra to work," he added. "She's an agent at Dillord's Travel in The Boulevard Mall. She hates this truck, but It still runs. It gets me to Nellis and back."

"I thought you said that you're a civilian."

"I am, but I work on the base. I finally got my G-5 in the Logistics Section. Mirye and I are doing okay."

"M-Mirye?"

"Yeah. Our kids will be home from school later this afternoon."

Rich Are The Rooms And
The Comforts
There

December
1988 [2.0]
(3-of-4)

Actually, several days passed before Jack took me to "see Grandpa", and by that time I had become a new Viva Vegas Towers resident. My new accommodations weren't cheap, especially for an aging indigent from another universe, but that's where the Kremlin had stepped in. Like my stringdopp, future Russian President (?) Ed Burnstein had seen "me" before, and all I had to do was pick up a key, a bank card, and a new identity. I had never posed for any of *John* Simmerath's mugshots, but my face was on every piece of ID. I had a passport, credit cards, and a Nevada driver's license. I was told to expect patent royalties in the form of monthly account disbursements. My new life came with only one stipulation: Burnstein requested that I return everything in the event that I decided to "move on."

It was weird to go into the apartment and discover that the furniture, along with everything else, was what I would have picked out. It was like I'd never been away...except that I'd never been there. Everything was how I would have liked it. All items were where I would put them. All of the clothes were hung in the closet in the way that I would hang them. All of the clothes in the drawers were arranged in the way that I would arrange them. I liked all of the music in the CD rack. The fridge was turned off, but I liked all of the foods in the cupboards.

* * *

"Do the clothes fit okay?" Jack asked when he came to pick me up. "I should stop asking," he continued. "Of course they fit. How do you like the place?"

"I like it fine. In fact, it's great."

"Exactly how you'd set up an apartment, right?"

"Yes. Exactly."

"I should stop asking that question, too."

I knew that Jack was taking me back to the lake, but I was kind of perplexed when he stopped the truck at the Overton Lookout.

"I'm really sick of this place," I said with a grimace. "Okay, I give up. I'm not even going to guess why we're here, but I'm fairly certain that Grandpa isn't meeting us for a picnic."

"It's just standard procedure," said Jack. "I know it by heart. C'mon, let's check the ravine."

The ravine? I thought. *I wonder what he expects to find?*

Several minutes later we stood at the edge of a rugged four-foot caliche bank. My fire circle, a few pieces of ration foil, and a lot of boot prints were our only discoveries.

Jack looked up and down the dry wash, scanned the surrounding scrub, and gave me a confused expression.

"What?" I asked.

Jack didn't say anything as he followed the bank's edge to the bottom and walked a few yards down the ravine. He stopped and looked up at me. "What's going on here?"

"Nothing. Nothing's going on. I thought that we were going to 'visit Grandpa' or something, but we're at this ditch instead. I don't know why you brought me back here."

"This is where you always leave it," Jack said, as he kicked over a few pieces of charred brush. "Did you hide it this time?"

"HIDE WHAT?"

"The time machine!"

"I told you, I don't *have* a goddamn time machine! Why don't you believe me?"

"Then how did you get here?"

"I *had* Andrew's unit," I began to explain. "Well, no, it wasn't actually *Andrew's* unit...it was a unit from another world...or something...maybe it was broken, but I'm not sure...it sent itself back to its own universe, maybe..." I knew that I wasn't making sense. "Look, all I can tell you is that I don't have a time machine. Yes, I *had* a time machine, and yes, I used it to get here, but no, I don't have it anymore, because it disappeared."

Jack wore an astonished expression.

"What?!"

"This…has never happened before."

Some Call It Coincidence, But I Like To Call It Fate

December 1988 [2.0] (4-of-4)

Jack still seemed baffled when we got back to the truck.

"Now what?" I asked.

Jack started the engine, but paused with his hand on the gear shift. "I guess that...we should go see Grandpa," he said.

As the truck left the cliff and followed the road down to the lakeside, I again experienced an odd feeling as I surveyed the empty stretch of water that I had known as a marina. I noticed a slight pullout on the road ahead, along with what appeared to be a Nevada State Historical Marker. I didn't have to wonder what the marker commemorated for long, because Jack left the road, pulled up to the sign, and turned off the Datsun's engine.

"Time to visit Grandpa," he said, as he opened his door.

We walked over to the marker. It was rectangular and had a four foot wide concrete base that rose two feet above the ground. Two creosote posts were set in the concrete to support a broad wooden sign. The marker had been sloppily painted and re-painted, and the posts appeared to be crumbling at the points where they met the concrete. Multiple coats of paint had muddled the sign's incised lettering, but it was still legible:

LAKE MEADE, NEVADA

IN MEMORY

Of the five individuals who perished on February 25, 1952, in the crash of a B-29 aircraft.

Capt. Robert Mathison
1ˢᵗ Lt. Paul Hister
SSgt. David Barnes
Sgt. Frank Rizzo
Dr. Erik Simmerath

* * *

On the way back to town I asked Jack a single question: "If your grandpa died back in the fifties, then who raised you?"

"My mom and dad. I grew up in Laughlin. Mirye and I bought the place on Hacienda when we moved to Vegas."

"And your parents?"

"They still live down by the river."

She's Someone I Knew...
A Long Time
Ago

January
1989 [2.0]

I'm dangling my feet in Jack and Mirye's pool. I'm just thinking about...well, *everything.*

Mirye comes out of the house and sits down beside me.

I regulate my breathing. I smile.

I'm calm. I'm casual. Just look how collected I am! Breathe in, slowly. But not too slowly! Okay. Exhale. Don't huff! Don't sigh! Nice and slow, let it out.

Good.

Repeat.

Mirye smiles, but keeps looking ahead. "I got used to the weirdness after the second time," she says. She turns to me. "It will pass for you, too. You know that I'm not a girl you met in Korea, and I know that you're not an older version of my husband. Well, not *exactly.*" She softly laughs and I relax a bit. "Although it's interesting to see what he's going to look like someday."

Mirye's comment makes me laugh, too. "I'm a living 'heads-up'. This," I say, as I gesture at myself, "is what you're in for."

"I'll think survive," she says. I'm glad that Mirye is keeping a smile on her face. It makes this conversation so much easier.

"I think you're handling things pretty well," she says.

"Oh?"

"Yes. And you're trying really hard to act normally when I'm around."

"Well, I can't be doing *that* well if it's so obvious. *Jeee-sus.*" I do a slow, facepalm-headshake combo.

"No, I mean it. You're the best so far. One guy even fainted when I shook his hand."

At that, I raise my head and laugh again. I look at her. "I can't tell you how hard it is."

"Well," she says, "if you ever want to try, I'll listen."

Stay In Wonderland

May
1989 [2.0]

My name is *John* Simmerath. The girls call me as "Grandpa", but officially, I'm the great uncle of my string theory doppelgänger. The family resemblance between us is, of course, striking.

I think that it's a good cover story. Nobody is being *deceived*. It's more like all parties have come together and agreed upon an official version of the truth, as if it's our own private Nicene Creed. I'm just glad that those other versions of me weren't assholes. From the way Sarah and Chantelle talk, I know that they don't suspect us of being different people. From the girls' perspective, it's just a case of "me" going away on periodic trips.

The kids regularly see their *real* grandfather in Laughlin. I haven't met him, because there yet remain levels of weirdness that I have to take in gradual stages. I guess that I function as the girls' Vegas grandfather, with the fellow down south handling weekend visits. Jack and Mirye seem comfortable in regarding me as a grandfather figure for Sarah and Chantelle - especially Jack, since he is now certain, following our desert excursion, that I can't abruptly drive Andrew's pickup out of this universe. Without that old Ford and the magic box, I'm as committed to this world as anyone. Not stuck. *Committed.* Even if I possessed the C-205, I still wouldn't be tempted to somehow find some 'selenide and leave. Why would I do that? This is a good life. Having an actual family feels - dare I say it? - *happy.* But also touchingly unfamiliar. For example, Sarah's school had a basketball game scheduled with another junior high last Thursday, and I was delighted to have been invited. That alone lifted my old heart, but when Mirye handed the phone over to Sarah and she invited me herself, I got a little choked up.

We Search For Answers,
But Our Fingers
Always
Burn

July
1989 [2.0]

Sarah and I played H.O.R.S.E. under the garage door hoop. Like another girl whom I had once known, my "granddaughter" was a tough kid and quite a competitor. When it was her turn she took the basketball and placed as much distance between it and the hoop as her jumpshot could handle. All net. After a grin and a bounce pass, it was my turn. I walked over to the same spot and took my shot. Airball. Something fell out of my pocket.

"Grandpa," said Sarah, "you dropped some papers."

"Papers" indeed. When I turned around, I saw two items on the concrete. One was a cheap folded glossy of a naked man with a huge penis. The name "Geoff Striker" was scrawled in black marker over the man's monster organ. The other paper appeared to be a flier of some sort, but it had fallen face-down.

I moved as fast as I could and got the naked guy off the ground and back into my pocket. My heart sank when Sarah beat me to the other piece of paper.

A broad smile appeared on Sarah's face. "Grandpa! Can I keep this?"

"W-what? No, of course you can't."

Sarah began to hop like an excited rabbit. "Grandpa! *The Heats* are my favorites!"

"Sarah, please let me have that," I said. *What the hell had been in my pocket?*

Sarah surrendered the flier with a disappointed expression. As I turned it over I prayed that I wasn't about to see another porn star, but that was exactly who I saw. Don Laramie's business suit-clad mug looked up at me. The names *"Stan Van Gundie"* and *"Chère Anguk"* were written on the flier. Laramie was fully clothed and the flier seemed to have nothing to do with the adult entertainment industry.

"I'll play you another game for it," said Sarah. "C'mon, Grandpa! C'mon!"

I shook my head. "No, no. I'm feeling a little...tired. Here," I said, as I handed the flier to Sarah.

I'm Seeing Through An Age, Who I Am

August 1989 [2.0] (1-of-2)

I performed some chronological calculations and determined that I wasn't actually going to turn fifty-two until October, though Jack and I marked the occasion on our August birthdays. Mirye and the kids took us out for dinner at Excalibur, but I pretended that we were at Xanadu.

잭 심머리스

*August
1989 [2.0]
(2-of-2)*

I was briefly worried about the complications of another "me" showing up, but so far that hasn't happened. I think the cycle was broken the instant that the "stringdopp C-205" self-activated and disappeared. Wherever, or whenever, that unit materializes, without 'selenide it's just an inert hunk of metal.

I want to do something, but I'm not sure what. Could I possibly get a job? Maybe I should apply with the Clark County School District as a classroom aide. Ha! *That* would feel weird. Maybe I should buy an RV and start coloring in one of those "States Visited" US maps that bored senior citizens put on the sides of their motor homes. Or...perhaps I could follow Frodo's example and write a book about the absolute and utter freakiness that I've survived.

Write a book. *Hmmm.* Maybe that's not such an outlandish idea. For some reason, when I entertain that thought an image of the actor Quentin Glover appears in my mind. I don't know what that means, but if I really did spin my wild yarn, I would write its cover title in Korean, just as a way of remembering a special person and a special time...but I guess that I'm getting ahead of myself, because I haven't written anything yet.

Egad! A Pocket Full Of Zorses
(Gröegens®) - Tabs
For Me To
Use

September
1989 [2.0]

Mirye's grandmother also lives at Viva Vegas Towers, and Jack has nonchalantly floated the idea of introducing us. I have a lifetime's worth of experience, however, that tells me a late-in-life romance will go down like a lead balloon. Still, I'll play along until time-wasting is mutually acknowledged, then the lady and I can politely conclude the young peoples' clumsy but well-intentioned matchmaking. Maybe in some other universe I've already traveled to the future and seen how it plays out.

In fairness, I must admit that something nice *could* also occur, but I'm not optimistic. After all, this is *me* we're talking about, and I'm not exactly brilliant with women - even when I'm sane.

Monsieur, Azonnal
Kövessen
Engem,
Bitte!

(Actual) 52nd Birthday
October 20th, 1989 [2.0]

"The others told you about the nuclear war, right?" I asked, as I opened a Patrón bottle and poured two shots. Jack nodded. "It sounds like a civil war, and the stories always come from somebody named 'Andrew'. Is it the same with you?"

"Yeah," I said, as I handed Jack his drink.

"But it's quite a few years down the road, right?"

"Sometime after the turn of the century, but I'm not exactly sure when. I also need to talk to you about something that happens in September of 1996, or maybe 2001. Not today...but sometime."

"Alright. The way I figure," said Jack, as he downed the tequila and leaned back in his lawn chair, "there will be a lot of stuff that precedes the conflict. You know what I mean? People have to get seriously disgruntled before they bust out nukes on their own soil. I'll be watching the signs of the times, definitely...but the chance of nuclear war has been around for decades."

"Living with a foreign possibility isn't like living with a domestic guarantee," I said.

"Oh, I think it's guaranteed, sure...but that's mostly what life is: guaranteed ugliness. It's the *timing* that gives people room to maneuver."

"That, plus allowance for bad timing."

"Well...yeah. I guess that's also a big part."

"We think alike."

"What would you expect?"

"*Expect*? Ummm...nothing. And I'm not that great with timing, either...but who is?"

"That reminds me of the last line of Harrison Dodge's voiceover in *Blade Runners*," said Jack.

I smiled. "I knew that you'd catch that reference."

736

Epilogue

Take
Care. Maybe
One Day You'll
Escape Your Past.
If You Do, Look For Me.

Also,
No One
Seems To
Consider The
Ghost In These Stories

In-sook is a few years older than me. She's lived in the West for decades, but when Mirye's grandmother introduces herself, she still gives her family name first. I'd bet that new acquaintances have called her "Shin" dozens of times. She wasn't particularly impressed when I referred to her by her given name, and I think her eyebrow rose slightly when I said "In-sook-*sii*."

I had been too negative in my outlook concerning an introduction to Mirye's grandmother. We both lived in the Viva Vegas Towers complex, though not in the same buildings, and we got on quite well; that is, we were gym buddies, show goers, and restaurant patrons. We were also occasional hotel guests.

This afternoon found us in a local Asian supermarket. "Oh God," I said, as we walked by a frozen fruit case. My fingers lovingly passed over some frost-glazed packages of yellow pulp. "I love this stuff," I remarked, with a *can-I-please-please-please* expression. "Even this frozen durian is good. Hmmm? It won't stink up your apartment."

Yes, it would. Merely the empty package would fill In-sook's home with the unique aroma of an old meat cooler packed with sweetly putrefying cottage cheese. I didn't care about the smell, though. I considered durian to be delicious, like creamy vanilla custard. In fact, it was my favorite fruit.

"'Oh God' is right," said In-sook. "Your fingers are going to smell just from touching that plastic. Why do you think I would let you in with that? Just because I'm Asian? It doesn't even come from Korea."

Oh please. Don't give me your 'Stereotypes-In-Round-Eye-Land' routine. Some Koreans do *like it,* I thought.

"Maybe we should have gone up to Greenland Market instead," said In-sook. "They have a better selection of *gochujang.*"

* * *

In-sook's place wasn't far, but she had still insisted upon driving her Mercedes to the supermarket. We left the store with our purchases and less than two minutes later we were at the entrance to Viva Vegas Towers. Behind a gate and a guardhouse stood two Y-structure ten-floor towers that had been built in the seventies - a time when, by southern Nevada standards, the complex had been considered a high rise.

After In-sook parked we entered one of the towers, and I considered how the complex was more of a metaphysical parallel of McKarran International than a senior living community. The lobby, halls, and elevators were concourses to boarding gate apartments, in which travelers awaited their seating row announcements. Some received final calls before their rental agreements expired, whereas others' flights had been delayed for multiple leases. No matter. All planes eventually took off.

The gates at McKarran had glass walls that allowed travelers to watch aircraft, while Viva Vegas Towers balconies permitted residents to look at The Strip and wonder if their boarding passes would take the form of heart attacks, cancer, Alzheimer's or something more exotic. Also like McKarran's concourses, with their shops, bars, and souvenir kiosks, the Viva Vegas Towers lobby housed its own amenities, though these were definitely geared to the senior set. There was an in-house doctor's office and a tiny pharmacy. An overpriced convenience store featured arthritic-adapted hand baskets that bent shoppers carried through aisles too narrow for grocery carts. Wafting dye fumes signaled the presence of a salon where senior women stuck their heads inside Drying Cones of Noise and read tattered celebrity magazines. Presiding over it all, in a scene like old photos of the ~~Titanic's~~ *Olympic's* Grand Staircase, hung large lobby chandeliers that were spun in dusty cotton candy spiderwebs and draped with seventies imitation crystals that had yellowed with age like geriatric toenails.

I liked living in Viva Vegas Towers, though I hoped to

keep its various "conveniences" at bay for as long as possible. I think In-sook felt the same way. Neither of us tarried in the lobby during our comings-and-goings. We were still kids in our fifties.

In-sook and I carried our bags past the desk. The man there merely nodded and forced a bored semi-smile as his eyes returned to the paper spread out over his crossed legs. It had been the same outside when we passed the gate guard.

We walked past windows that looked into an exercise room. The machines inside represented the best rheumatoid range-of-motion technology that the Carter era could have offered, and In-sook and I put them to good use during our morning workout dates. The exercise room's sunken hot tub had been poured at the same time as the floor, and though it still contained sporadic jet-driven bubbles, Vegas' hard water had left years of rough crusts and scratchy rings that looked as comfortable as broken coral. Neither of us had ever taken a dip there, preferring as we did to simply retire to our own Roman tubs.

As we waited for the elevator, it occurred to me that the lobby area was a proto-attempt at Summerlin's retirement atmosphere, but on a smaller scale. Here matters were condensed on a single level, and accessible by front doors and elevators rather than golf carts and community centers.

We rode up, stepped out on the fourth floor, and walked down the hall to apartment 416. In-sook put her bags down, unlocked the door, and gestured for me to come inside. She disappeared into the kitchen, and I heard squeaking cupboard doors, crumpling bags, and clattering bowls. I slipped my shoes off, placed them by the door, and wandered through the living room and toward the balcony. The apartment was on the north-eastern wing, so I could look far down Flamingo in both directions or take in a nice view of The Strip.

Old Slice. Somewhere in this place. *Everywhere* in this place. Maybe not in overpowering quantities, but in the air. Hanging around with In-sook had attuned me to it - sometimes up close, sometimes from afar, and I could smell it at a distance like Petrus Romanus Pryce could smell young boys ulcerating to be men.

I heard the pad of feet behind me. "This place is great at night. The lights are beautiful," said In-sook.

"Yeah," I agreed. "This is definitely the better side. It beats looking out over the ULVN, er, *UNLV,* campus."

"I don't mind the campus so much," said In-sook. "Some evenings I like to come out here and relax when my granddaughter is in."

"Granddaughter? Does Mirye visit at night?"

"Not Mirye. I have another granddaughter. We share this place."

"Really?" I asked in astonishment. "You've never mentioned anyone else. Where is she now?"

In-sook checked her watch and looked up for a second. "Now? She's here, in the apartment." In-sook glanced at her watch again. "She just got out of the shower. She'll study for a couple hours and leave for class. Sometimes I only see her as she goes out the door."

"She takes night classes?"

"And sometimes day classes, too. She works a lot, so sometimes she gets credits through UNLV's Nellis night extension."

"I see," I said. "When I re-signed my lease, I read that there was only one parking place assigned to each residence. I guess I didn't notice a Nellis gate pass on your windshield."

"My car doesn't have one. My granddaughter gets a lift from her...*classmate.*"

The change in tone made me curious. "Classmate?"

In-sook smiled. "A lot more than that, but she won't talk about it. There's some fear that I'm still living in the Dark Ages." In-sook laughed. "I should introduce *you* sometime. It might help her relax."

"Ah. A non-Korean," I said. "So she thinks you're a little too traditional in that department?"

In-sook tried to swallow a laugh but let out an embarrassing snort. "Sorry," she said, as she raised a hand to half-hide her grin. "You, ah, could say that, I suppose."

"Ha! That's great. She thinks you don't know?"

In-sook nodded. "Yes. It's so cute. But I caught a

741

glimpse of him once when she was leaving late. C'mon," In-sook said, as she changed the subject. "Help me cook."

I followed In-sook through the dining room and into the kitchen. "We always eat on the balcony," I remarked, "though you have a regular dining room table."

"And chairs, too. Aren't they great? I usually keep five-foot kimchi pots all over the apartment." In-sook's sarcasm made me realize that I had simply blurted out my observation.

"*Touché,*" I sighed. "Okay, you're gonna hammer me for this too, but I don't really notice any--" I paused to emphasize my politically correct sensibility, "*--ethnic kitchen aromas,* either. Just Old Slice, and I imagine it covers up a lot."

"You're a Vegas bumpkin," said In-sook. "I'll tell you one more time: That's a perfume that I brought back from my last trip to Pusan, and I like it, I'll have you know."

"Perhaps you'll forgive my plebeian error in mistaking an exotic scent for one more provincial," I replied with a silly flourish.

"Only due to your request's delicate nature," replied In-sook in mock magnanimity. "And it so happens that you and I are about to break a house rule on such matters." In-sook gestured at the bounty of spices and sauce from our earlier purchase. "Tonight we're going to do some *real* cooking, and ignore the fact that we're surrounded on all sides by cranky old Caucasians who bitch whenever they smell something besides meat and potatoes."

"You really are quite the rebel," I said with a smile.

In-sook paused and looked up from a cutting board. "Hey! Why am I doing this? This should be *your* job." In-sook grabbed my hand and placed a kitchen knife in my palm. Then she pointed at the counter. "Peppers, celery, carrots. Get to work."

"Okay."

"And wash your hands."

"Okay," I repeated, as I put the knife down and reached for a bottle of liquid soap over the sink.

"Do you like it raw?" asked In-sook, as she took the limp octopus out of the plastic bag.

"It's okay raw," I answered, as I dried my hands and began to chop vegetables. "But I think it has more flavor and a better texture if you boil it for a couple minutes."

"Ah. Me, too. I think you're the only non-Korean man I know who can stand this much spice, let alone count *nakji bokkeum* as his favorite food." In-sook mixed a series of very generous red dollops into the sauce. After a minute she stopped. "I'll take those veggies now."

I looked at the cutting board. I wasn't even close to being done, so I began to hurriedly chop.

"Wait! What are you *doing?*"

"I'm cutting up stuff! You said you wanted me to do this."

"Long diagonal cuts! Not like that," In-sook said, as she took the knife out of my hand. "Haven't you ever...?" she began to ask, then closed her eyes and shook her head. In-sook placed the knife on the cutting board and began to push me out of the kitchen. "Go," she said. "I'll bring it out when it's done."

"But, I can--"

"Go."

* * *

"I think I'm going to sweat all night," said In-sook, as she patted a napkin against damp wisps of hair that clung to her forehead. In-sook blinked on a few pepper tears, dried her eyes, and twisted her hair back into a bun that was held in place with crossed chop sticks. "Do you want the rest of mine?" she asked.

"Don't tempt me," I groaned, as I placed my hands on my full belly and slouched back in a patio chair. "You're one hell of a Korean chef," I said. "Thank you. That was wonderful."

A few cars turned on their headlights as we watched the Flamingo traffic pass below. In-sook then stood, collected the plates off the glass-topped balcony table, and took them inside. After a few seconds she returned with a small green bottle and two shot glasses.

"Jinro!" I exclaimed. "Nice touch!"

Can't have *nakji* without soju," In-sook declared, as

she twisted off the cap and filled both glasses. *"Gan-bei,"* we toasted.

"Care to have a drinking contest?" In-sook devilishly asked.

"No way," was my instant reply.

"Ah. Wise choice," In-sook said with a grin.

We smiled for a moment, then I got up and looked out over the balcony rail. A moment later I felt two arms wrap around me as In-sook snuggled up from behind. I smiled, sighed, and closed my eyes.

"That girl is like a ghost," In-sook murmured.

"Who?"

"My granddaughter."

"Why do you say that?"

"Because I didn't even hear her leave."

I opened my eyes and saw someone walking through the parking lot below. "It looks like she's going to the bus stop," I observed. "Didn't you say she gets a ride?"

"Yes. He picks her up at the Flamingo entrance."

"So, do you know *anything* about this guy?"

"Mmm...just the important things. He's young, single, good-looking, and fairly well off. He likes old cars, I think."

"What does he do?"

"I'm not sure. I think that he works for the government."

As I considered the many possibilities that could exist within In-sook's vague answer, I saw a car pull out of traffic and stop at the Flamingo curb. I understood what In-sook had meant by her "old cars" comment when her granddaughter got into a classic Buick Roadmaster.